The Unseen Hand: Supernatural and Weird Fiction by Unknown Authors

The Unseen Hand: Supernatural and Weird Fiction by Unknown Authors

Including Two Novellas "Spring-Heeled Jack-The Terror of London", "Sweeney Todd, the Barber of Fleet Street", Three Novelettes "Man Abroad","The Mysterious Spaniard", "The Mysterious Stranger", and Eighteen Short Stories of the Strange and Unusual

Anonymous

LEONAUR

The Unseen Hand: Supernatural and Weird Fiction by Unknown Authors Including Two Novellas "Spring-Heeled Jack—The Terror of London", "Sweeney Todd, the Barber of Fleet Street", Three Novelettes "Man Abroad", "The Mysterious Spaniard", "The Mysterious Stranger", and Eighteen Short Stories of the Strange and Unusual

FIRST EDITION

Leonaur is an imprint
of Oakpast Ltd

Copyright in this form © 2014 Oakpast Ltd

ISBN: 978-1-78282-379-7 (hardcover)
ISBN: 978-1-78282-380-3 (softcover)

http://www.leonaur.com

Contents

The Weird Violin

The great Polish violinist, S——, was strolling aimlessly about the town, on a sunny, but cold afternoon, in November of a certain year. He was to play, at night, at one of the great concerts which made the town so musically famous, and, according to his usual custom he was observing passers-by, looking in shop windows, and thinking of anything rather than the approaching ordeal. Not that he was nervous, for none could be less so, but he came to his work all the fresher for an hour or two of idle forgetfulness, and astonished his audiences the more.

Turning out of the busiest street, he ambled into a comparatively quiet thoroughfare, and, throwing away an inch of cigar-end, produced a new Havana, lighting up with every sign of enjoyment. Now, it was part of his rule, when out on these refreshing excursions, to avoid music shops, and he had already passed half-a-dozen without doing more than barely recognise them. It is therefore very remarkable that, walking by a large music warehouse in this quiet thoroughfare, he should suddenly stop, and, after remaining in doubt for a few moments, go straight to the window and look in.

He had not seen anything when he first passed, and, indeed, he had merely ascertained, out of the corner of his eye, that one of the forbidden shops was near. Why, then, did he feel impelled to return?

The window was stocked, as all such windows are, with instruments, music, and such appurtenances as resin, bows, chin-rests, mutes, strings, bridges and pegs. An old Guanerius, valued at several hundred guineas, lay alongside a shilling set of bones, and a flageolet, an ocarina, and several mouth-organs were gracefully grouped upon a gilt-edged copy of *Elijah*.

Amongst the carefully-arranged violins was a curious old instrument the like of which the virtuoso had never seen before, and at this he now stared with all his eyes. It was an ugly, squat violin, of heavy pattern, and ancient appearance. The maker, whoever he had been, had displayed considerable eccentricity throughout its manufacture, but more especially in the scroll, which, owing to some freak, he had carved into the semblance of a hideous, grinning face. There was something horribly repulsive about this strange work of art, and yet it also possessed a subtle fascination. The violinist, keeping his eyes upon the face, which seemed to follow his movements with fiendish persistency, slowly edged to the door, and entered the shop.

The attendant came forward, and recognising the well-known performer, bowed low.

"That is a curious-looking fiddle in the window," began the artist, at once, with a wave of his hand in the direction of the fiend.

"Which one, sir?" inquired the attendant. "Oh, the one with the remarkable scroll, you mean. I'll get it for you." Drawing aside a little curtain, he dived into the window-bay, and produced the instrument, whose face seemed to be grinning more maliciously than ever.

"A fair tone, sir," added the man, "but nothing to suit you, I'm sure."

As soon as Herr S—— touched the neck of the violin he gripped it convulsively, and raised the instrument to his chin. Then, for a few moments, he stood, firm as a rock, his eyes fixed upon the awe-stricken attendant, evidently without seeing him.

"A bow," said the musician, at length, in a low voice. He stretched out his disengaged hand and took it, without moving his eyes. Then he stopped four strings with his long fingers, and drew the horse-hair smartly over them with one rapid sweep, producing a rich chord in a minor key.

A slight shiver passed over his frame as the notes were struck, and the look of concentration upon his face, changed to one of horror; but he did not cease. Slowly dropping his gaze, the performer met the gibing glance of the scroll-face, and though his own countenance blanched, and his lips tightened, as if to suppress a cry, the bow was raised again, and the violin spoke.

Did the demon whisper to those moving, nervous fingers? It almost seemed to be doing so; and surely such a melody as came from the instrument was born of no human mind. It was slow and measured, but no solemnity was suggested; it thrilled the frame, but with terror, not delight; it was a chain of sounds, which like a sick man's passing fancy, slipped out of the memory as soon as it was evolved, and

8

was incapable of being recalled.

Slowly, when the last strains were lost, the great violinist dropped both arms to his side, and stood for a few moments, grasping violin and bow, without speaking. There were drops of perspiration on his forehead, and he was pale and weary-looking; when he spoke, it was in a faint voice, and he seemed to address himself to something invisible.

"I cannot endure it now," he said. "I will play again tonight."

"Do you wish to play on the instrument at this evening's concert, sir?" inquired the dealer, not without some astonishment at the choice, much as the performance had affected him.

"Yes—yes, of course!" was the reply, given with some irritability, the speaker having apparently roused himself from his semi-stupor.

As the dealer took back the fiddle, he chanced to turn it back uppermost. It was a curiously marked piece of wood, a black patch spreading over a large portion, and throwing an ugly blur upon the otherwise exquisite purling.

"See!" gasped the artist, pointing a shaking finger at this blotch, and clutching at the shopkeeper's shoulder. "Blood!"

"Good gracious!" ejaculated the other, shrinking back in alarm. "Are you ill, sir?"

"Blood, blood!" repeated the half-demented musician, and he staggered out of the shop.

It was night, and the concert-room was crowded to excess. The performers upon the platform, accustomed as they were to such sights, could not but gaze with interest at the restless sea of eager, expectant faces which stretched before them.

That indescribable noise, a multitude of subdued murmurs, accompanied by the discordant scraping of strings, and blowing of reeds, was at its height; now and then a loud trombone would momentarily assert itself, or an oboe's plaintive notes would rise above the tumult; and, in short, the moment of intense excitement which immediately precedes the entrance of the conductor was at hand.

Suddenly, the long-continued confusion ceased, and, for an incalculably short space of time, silence reigned. Then a storm of deafening applause burst forth; necks were craned, and eyes strained in vain attempts to catch an early glimpse of the great violinist who was to open the concert by playing a difficult Concerto of Spohr.

It was noticed, that as the virtuoso followed the grey-haired conductor to the centre of the platform, he was unusually pale; and those who were seated at no great distance from the orchestra, observed also that he carried a curious violin, instead of the Stradivarius upon which he was wont to perform.

A tap on the conductor's desk, a short, breathless silence, and the sweet strains of the opening bars issued from the instruments of a hundred able musicians.

The soloist, with a sinking at the heart which he could scarcely account for, raised the violin to his shoulder, and saw, for the first time, that it had been re-strung. As he invariably left stringing and tuning to others, this would appear to have been a matter of no moment, and yet it had a strange effect upon him. Again that shudder passed through his body, and again he unwillingly met the glance of those diabolical eyes upon the scroll. Horror of horrors! was the face alive, or was he going mad?

The band, which had swelled out to a loud *forte*, now dropped to a *pianissimo*. The moment had arrived. Herr S—raised his bow, and commenced the lovely *adagio*.

What had come to him? Where were the concert room, the orchestra, the anxious crowd of people? What sounds were these? This was not Spohr, this sweet melody so like, and yet so unlike the weird music which he had played in the dealer's shop. What subtle magic had so acted upon those strains that their horror, their cruel mockery had entirely vanished, and sweet, pure harmony alone remained?

It seemed to the player that he stood within a small, but comfortably furnished room. Two figures were in the room, those of a beautiful young girl, and of a dark, handsome, foreign-looking man.

There was something in the face of the latter which vividly recalled the face upon the scroll, and, strange to say, a counterpart of the violin itself rested under the man's chin.

The girl was seated at a harpsichord, and, as she played, her companion accompanied her upon his strange instrument. From the costume of both, the dreamer concluded that they were phantoms of a hundred years ago.

"Ernestine," the man was saying, in a low voice, as he passed his bow over the strings, "tell me tonight that you have not dismissed me for ever. I can wait for your love."

"It is useless," replied the girl—"oh, it is quite useless! Why importune me further? I could never love you, even if I were not already promised to another."

A savage light gleamed in the man's eye, and more than ever he looked like the face on the violin; but he did not immediately reply and the music went on.

"You tell me it is useless," he said, at length, "and I tell you that it is useless. Useless for you to think of him. Do you hear?" he continued, lowering his violin, and leaning towards her. "You shall never marry him; I swear it by my soul."

The girl shrank from him, and the music ceased. Though he did not know it, the dreaming violinist had reached the conclusion of the *adagio* movement. He did not hear the deafening plaudits which greeted the fall of his bow; he knew nothing of the enthusiasm of the orchestra, or the praise of the conductor; he heard no more music.

Look! what is this? The girl has seated herself upon a couch, and her lover, his violin still in his left hand, is kneeling at her feet, passionately imploring her to listen. She expostulates for awhile, then repulses him and rises. A malignant fire darts from the furious foreigner's eyes; something bright gleams in his hand; he rushes forward, raises his arm to strike—

The presto movement had commenced, and an extraordinary circumstance soon made itself apparent to the audience. The violinist was running away with the band. Greatly to the horror of the conductor, the tempo had to be increased until a *prestissimo* was reached. Still the performer was not satisfied, there seemed no limit to his powers tonight; his fingers literally flew up and down the fingerboard; his bow shot to-and-fro with incredible swiftness; and yet the music grew quicker, quicker, until the unhappy conductor, who with difficulty pulled along the toiling band, felt that a *fiasco* was inevitable.

On, on rushed the fingers and the bow, faster, and faster still: a few of the bandsmen fell off from sheer exhaustion, and stared, horror-stricken, at the mad violinist. Some of the listeners rose in alarm, and many were only detained, by extreme anxiety, from bursting into loud and frantic applause.

Suddenly, with the loud snap of a string, the spell was broken. The orchestra, unable now to proceed, stopped in utter confusion, and a loud sigh of released suspense went up from thousands of throats. Then the whole mass rose in sudden horror, as the violinist dropped his instrument with a crash upon the platform, stared wildly around, clasped a hand to his side, and, with a strange cry, fell to the ground insensible.

For weeks the great violinist lay between life and death; then nature reasserted herself, and he recovered. But it was long, very long, ere he could again appear in public; whilst the weird and mysterious violin never again sent forth its strange and mysterious influence. It had been hopelessly shattered in that last night of its performance, which had well-nigh proved fatal to the world-famed player.

The Sutor of Selkirk

Once upon a time there lived in Selkirk a shoemaker, by name Rabbie Heckspeckle, who was celebrated both for dexterity in his trade and for some other qualifications of a less profitable nature.—In short, he was the Paul Pry of the town. Not an old wife in the parish could buy a new scarlet rokelay without Rabbie knowing within a groat of the cost; the doctor could not dine with the minister but Rabbie could tell whether sheep's-head or haggis formed the staple commodity of the repast; and it was even said that he was acquainted with the grunt of every sow, and the cackle of every individual hen in his neighborhood; but this wants confirmation."

From this curious beginning continues an "old wives' tale" from Selkirk, which I found published with no other author given in an old book from London called *The Evening Standard Second Book of Strange Stories,* which also has no copyright date. It seems that even though Rabbie's wife Bridget tried her best to restrain Rabbie's constant curiosity, her interference met with exactly that degree of attention which husbands usually bestow on the advice tendered by their better halves—that is to say, Rabbie informed her that she knew nothing of the matter, that her understanding required stretching, and finally, that if she presumed to meddle in his affairs, he would be under the disagreeable necessity of giving her a top-dressing." (I'm not entirely sure exactly what a "top-dressing" is, but as I suspect that Rabbie was of the sort who made himself "disagreeable" to anyone who interfered with him, I think this was likely to be a wife-beating threat, which in such an old tale was often treated as a matter for raucous comedy rather than as the serious thing we now think it to be.)

Because Rabbie had much work as a shoemaker to do in addition to his not-so-neighbourly "researches" into the lives of others, he usually rose early, "long before the dawn," and was one morning putting the final bits on a pair of shoes for the exciseman (tax collector), when a rather unusual customer came into his shop. The customer was "a tall figure, enveloped in a large black cloak, and with a broad-rimmed hat drawn over his brows." Rabbie was perplexed to have a customer so early, and moreover one who was a stranger in the town, and yet one he'd never had knowledge of. Rabbie tried his best to make leading conversation, but the figure ignored him, and instead picked up the exciseman's prospective shoe and tried it on, taking a turn around the room to make sure the shoe fit.

Though Rabbie was caught up in watching the mysterious figure, his other senses were working overtime as well:—

"'He smells awfully,' muttered Rabbie to himself; 'ane would be ready to swear he had just cam frae the ploughtail.'" But Rabbie had no time to think of this, because the stranger motioned for the other shoe, and pulled out a purse to pay for the pair. Once again, Rabbie noticed something odd: the purse was "spotted with a kind of earthy mould."

"'Gudesake,' thought Rabbie, 'this queer man maun hae howkit that purse out o' the ground. Some folks say there are bags o' siller buried near this town.'"

But imagine Rabbie's surprise when out of the open purse fell a toad, a beetle, and a large worm, which wound itself around the stranger's finger! Still, the tall figure in the black clothes held out a gold piece, and indicated in dumb show that he wished to buy the pair of shoes. But Rabbie, being a hard-minded, some would say eminently practical man, responded that—

"'It's a thing morally impossible,—hae as good as sworn to the exciseman to hae them ready by daylight,—and better, I tell you, to affront the king himself than the exciseman.'"

The stranger stamped his foot, shod in the new shoe, in anger, but Rabbie stuck to his point, nevertheless being conciliatory in his own terms by offering to make another pair for the strange visitor within a day's time, which finally the figure had to accept. So, he sat down on the three-legged measuring stool and held out his foot to the sutor, who measured it, all the while trying to find out something about his mysterious visitor through friendly conversation. But the figure was largely silent. When the measuring was done, Rabbie tried to insist on delivering the shoes himself, in order to find out something at least about where his visitor lived to satisfy his own curiosity, but the stranger replied, "'I will call for them myself before cock-crowing,'—

in a very uncommon and indescribable tone of voice."

"'Hout, sir,' quoth Rabbie, 'I canna let you hae the trouble o' coming for them yoursel'; it will just be a pleasure for me to call with them at your house.' 'I have my doubts of that,' replied the stranger, in the same peculiar manner; 'and at all events, my house would not hold us both.'"

Rabbie continued to try to insist on dropping in on his visitor at the latter's home, but the stranger instead gave Rabbie a kick in the seat of the pants that knocked him down, and walked out. Mystified but determined to be satisfied, Rabbie ran out the door behind the mysterious visitor in his red night-cap as a cock called for dawn, and reached the churchyard at the end of the street before he gave up, not finding his recent customer anywhere.

"'Weel,' he muttered, as he retraced his steps homewards, 'he has warred me this time, but sorrow take me if I'm not up wi' him in the morn.'"

With diligence which surprised his wife Bridget, Rabbie spent the whole of the day on his three-legged stool working on the pair of new shoes, and astonished all the neighbours by this as well, who all agreed "that it predicted some prodigy: but whether it was to take the shape of a comet, which would deluge them all with its fiery tail, or whether they were to be swallowed up by an earthquake, could by no means be settled" to their satisfaction. Moreover, Rabbie resisted every outside attempt to get him interested in local gossip, and instead worked steadily on the pair of new shoes.

Late at night, he had finished the shoes, and placed them beside his bed for the dawn. Suddenly, startling Rabbie with his presence, the stranger appeared, asking for his shoes.

"'Here, sir,'" said Rabbie, quite transported with joy; 'here they are, right and tight, and mickle joy may ye hae in wearing them, for it's better to wear shoon than sheets, as the auld saying gangs.' 'Perhaps I may wear both,' answered the stranger. 'Gude save us,' quoth Rabbie, 'do ye sleep in your shoon?'" Not answering, the stranger put gold on the table and took the shoes and left the house.

Not to be outdone by the visitor's reticence, Rabbie slipped out the door after him to follow and find where he went. Imagine his astonishment when the stranger went into the churchyard! Rabbie said to himself—

"'Odsake, where can he be gaun?'—'e's making to that grave in the corner; now he's standing still; now he's sitting down. Gudesake!

what's come o' him?'"

And though Rabbie looked all around him and rubbed his eyes, he couldn't see the stranger anywhere! This struck Rabbie as "uncanny," but his curiosity being still stronger than his fear, he thrust his awl into the grave so he could find the place again, marking it for further investigations.

By the time the sun went down that day, the news was all over town, and it was decided to go and open the grave "which was suspected as being suspicious." When the grave was opened and the lid forced from the coffin, a corpse was found, dressed in all its tomb clothing, but with a pair of perfectly new shoes on! With this, everyone else fled in all directions in horror, but Rabbie and a few braver souls stayed to "arrange" things more to their own satisfaction with the corpse. They agreed to nail the coffin and place it deeper in the earth, but Rabbie took the shoes back first, saying that the corpse had "no more need for them than a cart had for three wheels." After reburying the corpse as proposed, Rabbie and his friends went home, not at first thinking any more about the matter.

It's true, Rabbie did have some "qualms of conscience" about keeping the stranger's money and depriving him of the shoes he'd paid for, corpse or no corpse; but thinking that it would be a black mark against his family name to have made a pair of shoes for a corpse, and knowing that there was no court of appeal for the corpse, Rabbie soon put the matter out of his mind.

"Next morning, according to custom, he rose long before the day, and fell to his work, shouting the old songs of the 'Sutors of Selkirk' at the very top of his voice. A short time, however, before the dawn his wife, who was in bed in the back room, remarked that in the very middle of his favourite verse his voice fell into a quaver, then broke out into a yell of terror; and then she heard a noise, as of persons struggling; and then all was quiet as the grave."

When she went into the shop, the stool was all broken up, bristles all over the floor, and the door off its hinges. There was no Rabbie. There were, however, footprints, which she found to her horror led straight to the churchyard, to the grave of Rabbie's former customer! The ground was disturbed, and several locks of Rabbie's lank black hair were on the surface of the grass, whereupon Bridget ran to acquaint everyone in town with what she guessed.

The grave was re-opened, "the lid of the coffin was once more torn off; and there lay its ghastly tenant, with his shoes replaced on his feet, and Rabbie's red night-cap clutched in his right hand! The people, in consternation, fled from the churchyard; and nothing further has ever transpired to throw any additional light upon the melancholy fate of the Sutor of Selkirk."

I hope you've enjoyed this second Halloween post, a very old story from the British traditional *corpus* (or should I make a pun, and say "corpse"?); just remember, if an unearthly figure makes its appearance and requests your services, stick strictly by the letter of the law, and keep your curiosity in check, or you may wind up "Gude" knows where, like the Sutor of Selkirk.

Extracts from Gosschen's Diary

(The following striking narrative is translated from the *MS. Memoirs* of the late Rev. Dr Gottlieb Michael Gosschen, a Catholic clergyman of great eminence in the city of Ratisbonne. It was the custom of this divine to preserve, in the shape of a diary, a regular account of all the interesting particulars which fell in his way, during the exercise of his sacred profession. Two thick small quartos, filled with these strange materials, have been put into our hands by the kindness of Count Frederick von Lindénbäumenberg, to whom the worthy father bequeathed them. Many a dark story, well fitted to be the groundwork of a romance,—many a tale of guilty love and repentance,—many a fearful monument of remorse and horror, might we extract from this record of dungeons and confessionals. We shall from time to time do so, but sparingly, and what is still more necessary, with selection.) Original Editor.

******

Never had a murder so agitated the inhabitants of this city as that of Maria von Richterstein. No heart could be pacified till the murderer was condemned. But no sooner was his doom sealed, and the day fixed for his execution, than a great change took place in the public feeling. The evidence, though conclusive, had been wholly circumstantial. And people who, before his condemnation, were as assured of the murderer's guilt as if they had seen him with red hands, began now to conjure up the most contradictory and absurd reasons for believing in the possibility of his innocence. His own dark and sullen silence seemed to some, an indignant expression of that innocence which he was too proud to avow,—some thought they saw in his imperturbable demeanour, a resolution to court death, because his life was miserable, and his reputation blasted,—and others, the most numerous, without reason or reflection, felt such sympathy with the criminal, as almost amounted to a negation of his crime. The man under sentence of death was, in all the beauty of youth, distinguished above his fellows for graceful accomplishments, and the last of a noble family. He had lain a month in his dungeon, heavily laden with irons. Only the first week he had been visited by several religionists, but he then fiercely ordered the jailor to admit no more "men of God,"—and till the eve of his execution, he had lain in dark solitude, abandoned to his own soul.

It was near midnight when a message was sent to me by a magistrate, that the murderer was desirous of seeing me. I had been with many men in his unhappy situation, and in no case had I failed to calm the agonies of grief, and the fears of the world to come. But I had known this youth—had sat with him at his father's table—I knew also that there was in him a strange and fearful mixture of good and evil—I was aware that there were circumstances in the history of his progenitors not generally known—nay, in his own life—that made him an object of awful commiseration—and I went to his cell with an agitating sense of the enormity of his guilt, but a still more agitating one of the depth of his misery, and the wildness of his misfortunes.

I entered his cell, and the phantom struck me with terror. He stood erect in his irons, like a corpse that had risen from the grave. His face, once so beautiful, was pale as a shroud, and drawn into ghastly wrinkles. His black-matted hair hung over it with a terrible expression of wrathful and savage misery. And his large eyes, which once were black, glared with a light in which all colour was lost, and seemed to fill the whole dungeon with their flashings. I saw his guilt—I saw what was more terrible than his guilt—his insanity—not in emaciation only—not in that more than death-like whiteness of his face—but in all that stood before me—the figure, round which was gathered the agonies of so many long days and nights of remorse and phrenzy—and of a despair that had no fears of this world or its terrors, but that was plunged in the abyss of eternity.

For a while the figure said nothing. He then waved his arm, that made his irons clank, motioning me to sit down on the iron framework of his bed; and when I did so, the murderer took his place by my side.

A lamp burned on a table before us—and on that table there had been drawn by the maniac—for I must indeed so call him—a decapitated human body—the neck as if streaming with gore—and the face writhed into horrible convulsions, but bearing a resemblance not to be mistaken to that of him who had traced the horrid picture. He saw that my eyes rested on this fearful mockery—and, with a recklessness fighting with despair, he burst out into a broken peal of laughter, and said, "tomorrow will you see that picture drawn in blood!"

He then grasped me violently by the arm, and told me to listen to his confession,—and then to say what I thought of God and his eternal Providence.

"I have been assailed by idiots, fools, and drivellers, who could understand nothing of me nor of my crime,—men who came not here that I might confess before God, but reveal myself to them,—and I drove the tamperers with misery and guilt out of a cell sacred to insanity. But my hands have played in infancy, long before I was a murderer, with thy gray hairs, and now, even that I am a murderer, I can still touch them with love and with reverence. Therefore my lips, shut to all beside, shall be opened unto thee.

"I murdered her. Who else loved her so well as to shed her innocent blood? It was I that enjoyed her beauty—a beauty surpassing that of the daughters of men,—it was I that filled her soul with bliss, and with trouble,—it was I alone that was privileged to take her life. I brought her into sin—I kept her in sin—and when she would have left her sin, it was fitting that I, to whom her heart, her body, and her soul belonged, should suffer no divorcement of them from my bosom, as long as there was blood in her's,—and when I saw that the poor infatuated wretch was resolved—I slew her;—yes, with this blessed hand I stabbed her to the heart.

"Do you think there was no pleasure in murdering her? I grasped her by that radiant, that golden hair,—I bared those snow-white breasts—I dragged her sweet body towards me, and, as God is my witness, I stabbed, and stabbed her with this very dagger, ten, twenty, forty times, through and through her heart. She never so much as gave one shriek, for she was dead in a moment,—but she would not have shrieked had she endured pang after pang, for she saw my face of wrath turned upon her,—she knew that my wrath was just, and that I did right to murder her who would have forsaken her lover in his insanity.

"I laid her down upon a bank of flowers,—that were soon stained with her blood. I saw the dim blue eyes beneath the half-closed lids,—that face so changeful in its living beauty was now fixed as ice, and the balmy breath came from her sweet lips no more. My joy, my happiness, was perfect. I took her into my arms—madly as I did on that night when first I robbed her of what fools called her innocence—but her innocence has gone with her to heaven—and there I lay with her bleeding breasts prest to my heart, and many were the thousand kisses that I gave those breasts, cold and bloody as they were, which I had many million times kissed in all the warmth of their loving loveliness, and which none were ever to kiss again but the husband who had murdered her.

"I looked up to the sky. There shone the moon and all her stars. Tranquillity, order, harmony, and peace, glittered throughout the whole universe of God. 'Look up, Maria, your favourite star has risen.' I gazed upon her, and death had begun to change her into something that was most terrible. Her features were hardened and sharp,—her body stiff as a lump of frozen clay,—her fingers rigid and clenched,—and the blood that was once so beautiful in her thin blue veins was now hideously coagulated all over her corpse. I gazed on her one moment longer, and, all at once, I recollected that we were a family of madmen. Did not my father perish by his own hand? Blood had before been shed in our house. Did not that warrior ancestor of ours die raving in chains? Were not those eyes of mine always unlike those of other men? Wilder—at times fiercer—and oh! father, saw you never there a melancholy, too woeful for mortal man, a look sent up from the darkness of a soul that God never visited in his mercy?

"I knelt down beside my dead wife. But I knelt not down to pray. No: I cried unto God, if God there be—'Thou madest me a madman! Thou madest me a murderer! Thou foredoomedst me to sin and to hell! Thou, thou, the gracious God whom we mortals worship. There is the sacrifice! I have done thy will,—I have slain the most blissful of all thy creatures;—am I a holy and commissioned priest, or am I an accursed and *infidel* murderer?'

"Father, you start at such words! You are not familiar with a madman's thoughts. Did I make this blood to boil so? Did I form this brain? Did I put that poison into my veins which flowed a hundred years since in the heart of that lunatic, my heroic ancestor? Had I not my being imposed, forced upon me, with all its red-rolling sea of dreams; and will you, a right holy and pious man, curse me because my soul was carried away by them as a ship is driven through the raging darkness of a storm? A thousand times, even when she lay in resigned love in my bosom, something whispered to me, 'Murder her!' It may have been the voice of Satan—it may have been the voice of God. For who can tell the voice of heaven from that of hell? Look on this blood-crusted dagger—look on the hand that drove it to her heart, and then dare to judge of me and of my crimes, or comprehend God and all his terrible decrees!

"Look not away from me. Was I not once confined in a madhouse? Are these the first chains I ever wore? No. I remember things of old, that others may think I have forgotten. Dreams will disappear for a long, long time but they will return again. It may have been some one like me that I once saw sitting chained, in his black melancholy, in a madhouse. I may have been only a stranger passing through that wild world. I know not. The sound of chains brings with it a crowd of thoughts, that come rushing upon me from a dark and far-off world. But if it indeed be true, that in my boyhood I was not as other happy boys, and that even then the cloud of God's wrath hung around me,— that God may not suffer my soul everlastingly to perish.

"I started up. I covered the dead body with bloody leaves, and tufts of grass, and flowers. I washed my hands from blood—I went to sleep—I slept—yes, I slept—for there is no hell like the hell of sleep, and into that hell God delivered me. I did not give myself up to judgment. I wished to walk about with the secret curse of the murder in my soul. What could men do to me so cruel as to let me live? How could God curse me more in black and fiery hell than on this green and flowery earth? And what right had such men as those dull heavy-eyed burghers to sit in judgment upon me, in whose face they were afraid to look for a moment, lest one gleam of it should frighten them into idiocy? What right have they, who are not as I am, to load me with their chains, or to let their villain executioner spill my blood? If I deserve punishment—it must rise up in a blacker cloud under the hand of God in my soul.

"I will not kneel—a madman has no need of sacraments. I do not wish the forgiveness nor the mercy of God. All that I wish is the forgiveness of her I slew; and well I know that death cannot so change the heart that once had life, as to obliterate from *thine* the merciful love of me! Spirits may in heaven have beautiful bosoms no more; but thou, who art a spirit, wilt save him from eternal perdition, whom thou now knowest God created subject to a terrible disease. If there be mercy in heaven, it must be with thee. Thy path thither lay through blood: so will mine. Father! thinkst thou that we shall meet in heaven. Lay us at least in one grave on earth."

In a moment he was dead at my feet. The stroke of the dagger was like lightning, and. . . . . .

Horror: A True Tale

I was but nineteen years of age when the incident occurred which has thrown a shadow over my life; and, ah me! how many and many a weary year has dragged by since then! Young, happy, and beloved I was in those long-departed days. They said that I was beautiful. The mirror now reflects a haggard old woman, with ashen lips and face of deadly pallor. But do not fancy that you are listening to a mere puling lament. It is not the flight of years that has brought me to be this wreck of my former self: had it been so I could have borne the loss cheerfully, patiently, as the common lot of all; but it was no natural progress of decay which has robbed me of bloom, of youth, of the hopes and joys that belong to youth, snapped the link that bound my heart to another's, and doomed me to a lone old age. I try to be patient, but my cross has been heavy, and my heart is empty and weary, and I long for the death that comes so slowly to those who pray to die.

I will try and relate, exactly as it happened, the event which blighted my life. Though it occurred many years ago, there is no fear that I should have forgotten any of the minutest circumstances: they were stamped on my brain too clearly and burningly, like the brand of a red-hot iron. I see them written in the wrinkles of my brow, in the dead whiteness of my hair, which was a glossy brown once, and has known no gradual change from dark to gray, from gray to white, as with those happy ones who were the companions of my girlhood, and whose honoured age is soothed by the love of children and grandchildren. But I must not envy them. I only meant to say that the difficulty of my task has no connection with want of memory—I remember but too well. But as I take my pen my hand trembles, my head swims, the old rushing faintness and Horror comes over me again, and the well-remembered fear is upon me. Yet I will go on.

This, briefly, is my story: I was a great heiress, I believe, though I cared little for the fact; but so it was. My father had great possessions, and no son to inherit after him. His three daughters, of whom I was the youngest, were to share the broad acres among them. I have said, and truly, that I cared little for the circumstance; and, indeed, I was so rich then in health and youth and love that I felt myself quite indifferent to all else. The possession of all the treasures of earth could never have made up for what I then had—and lost, as I am about to relate. Of course, we girls knew that we were heiresses, but I do not think Lucy and Minnie were any the prouder or the happier on that account.

I know I was not. Reginald did not court me for my money. Of *that* I felt assured. He proved it, Heaven be praised! when he shrank from my side after the change. Yes, in all my lonely age, I can still be thankful that he did not keep his word, as some would have done— did not clasp at the altar a hand he had learned to loathe and shudder at, because it was full of gold—much gold! At least he spared me that. And I know that I was loved, and the knowledge has kept me from going mad through many a weary day and restless night, when my hot eyeballs had not a tear to shed, and even to weep was a luxury denied me.

Our house was an old Tudor mansion. My father was very particular in keeping the smallest peculiarities of his home unaltered. Thus the many peaks and gables, the numerous turrets, and the mullioned windows with their quaint lozenge panes set in lead, remained very nearly as they had been three centuries back. Over and above the quaint melancholy of our dwelling, with the deep woods of its park and the sullen waters of the mere, our neighbourhood was thinly peopled and primitive, and the people round us were ignorant, and tenacious of ancient ideas and traditions. Thus it was a superstitious atmosphere that we children were reared in, and we heard, from our infancy, countless tales of horror, some mere fables doubtless, others legends of dark deeds of the olden time, exaggerated by credulity and the love of the marvellous.

Our mother had died when we were young, and our other parent being, though a kind father, much absorbed in affairs of various kinds, as an active magistrate and landlord, there was no one to check the unwholesome stream of tradition with which our plastic minds were inundated in the company of nurses and servants. As years went on, however, the old ghostly tales partially lost their effects, and our undisciplined minds were turned more towards balls, dress, and partners, and other matters airy and trivial, more welcome to our riper age. It was at a county assembly that Reginald and I first met—met and loved. Yes, I am sure that he loved me with all his heart. It was not as deep a heart as some, I have thought in my grief and anger; but I never doubted its truth and honesty. Reginald's father and mine approved of our growing attachment; and as for myself, I know I was so happy then, that I look back upon those fleeting moments as on some delicious dream. I now come to the change. I have lingered on my childish reminiscences, my bright and happy youth, and now I must tell the rest—the blight and the sorrow.

It was Christmas, always a joyful and a hospitable time in the country, especially in such an old hall as our home, where quaint customs and frolics were much clung to, as part and parcel of the very dwelling itself. The hall was full of guests—so full, indeed, that there was great difficulty in providing sleeping accommodation for all. Several narrow and dark chambers in the turrets—mere pigeon-holes, as we irreverently called what had been thought good enough for the stately gentlemen of Elizabeth's reign—were now allotted to bachelor visitors, after having been empty for a century. All the spare rooms in the body and wings of the hall were occupied, of course; and the servants who had been brought down were lodged at the farm and at the keeper's, so great was the demand for space.

At last the unexpected arrival of an elderly relative, who had been asked months before, but scarcely expected, caused great commotion. My aunts went about wringing their hands distractedly. Lady Speldhurst was a personage of some consequence; she was a distant cousin, and had been for years on cool terms with us all, on account of some fancied affront or slight when she had paid her *last* visit, about the time of my christening. She was seventy years old; she was infirm, rich, and testy; moreover, she was my godmother, though I had forgotten the fact; but it seems that though I had formed no expectations of a legacy in my favor, my aunts had done so for me. Aunt Margaret was especially eloquent on the subject.

"There isn't a room left," she said; "was ever anything so unfortunate! We cannot put Lady Speldhurst into the turrets, and yet where *is* she to sleep? And Rosa's godmother, too! Poor, dear child, how dreadful! After all these years of estrangement, and with a hundred thousand in the funds, and no comfortable, warm room at her own unlimited disposal—and Christmas, of all times in the year!"

What *was* to be done? My aunts could not resign their own chambers to Lady Speldhurst, because they had already given them up to some of the married guests. My father was the most hospitable of men, but he was rheumatic, gouty, and methodical. His sisters-in-law dared not propose to shift his quarters; and, indeed, he would have far sooner dined on prison fare than have been translated to a strange bed. The matter ended in my giving up my room. I had a strange reluctance to making the offer, which surprised myself. Was it a boding of evil to come? I cannot say. We are strangely and wonderfully made. It *may* have been. At any rate, I do not think it was any selfish unwillingness to make an old and infirm lady comfortable by a trifling sacrifice. I was perfectly healthy and strong.

The weather was not cold for the time of the year. It was a dark, moist Yule—not a snowy one, though snow brooded overhead in the darkling clouds. I *did* make the offer, which became me, I said with a laugh, as the youngest. My sisters laughed too, and made a jest of my evident wish to propitiate my godmother. "She is a fairy godmother, Rosa," said Minnie; "and you know she was affronted at your christening, and went away muttering vengeance. Here she is coming back to see you; I hope she brings golden gifts with her."

I thought little of Lady Speldhurst and her possible golden gifts. I cared nothing for the wonderful fortune in the funds that my aunts whispered and nodded about so mysteriously. But since then I have wondered whether, had I then showed myself peevish or obstinate— had I refused to give up my room for the expected kinswoman—it would not have altered the whole of my life? But then Lucy or Minnie would have offered in my stead, and been sacrificed—what do I say?—better that the blow should have fallen as it did than on those dear ones.

The chamber to which I removed was a dim little triangular room in the western wing, and was only to be reached by traversing the picture-gallery, or by mounting a little flight of stone stairs which led directly upward from the low-browed arch of a door that opened into the garden. There was one more room on the same landing-place, and this was a mere receptacle for broken furniture, shattered toys, and all the lumber that *will* accumulate in a country-house. The room I was to inhabit for a few nights was a tapestry-hung apartment, with faded green curtains of some costly stuff, contrasting oddly with a new carpet and the bright, fresh hangings of the bed, which had been hurriedly erected. The furniture was half old, half new; and on the dressing-table stood a very quaint oval mirror, in a frame of black wood—unpolished ebony, I think. I can remember the very pattern of the carpet, the number of chairs, the situation of the bed, the figures on the tapestry. Nay, I can recollect not only the colour of the dress I wore on that fated evening, but the arrangement of every scrap of lace and ribbon, of every flower, every jewel, with a memory but too perfect.

Scarcely had my maid finished spreading out my various articles of attire for the evening (when there was to be a great dinner-party) when the rumble of a carriage announced that Lady Speldhurst had arrived. The short winter's day drew to a close, and a large number of guests were gathered together in the ample drawing-room, around the blaze of the wood-fire, after dinner. My father, I recollect, was not with us at first. There were some squires of the old, hard-riding, hard-drinking stamp still lingering over their port in the dining-room, and the host, of course, could not leave them. But the ladies and all the younger gentlemen—both those who slept under our roof, and those who would have a dozen miles of fog and mire to encounter on their road home—were all together.

Need I say that Reginald was there? He sat near me—my accepted lover, my plighted future husband. We were to be married in the spring. My sisters were not far off; they, too, had found eyes that sparkled and softened in meeting theirs, had found hearts that beat responsive to their own. And, in their cases, no rude frost nipped the blossom ere it became the fruit; there was no canker in their flowerets of young hope, no cloud in their sky. Innocent and loving, they were beloved by men worthy of their esteem.

The room—a large and lofty one, with an arched roof—had somewhat of a sombre character, from being wainscoted and ceiled with polished black oak of a great age. There were mirrors, and there were pictures on the walls, and handsome furniture, and marble chimney-pieces, and a gay Tournay carpet; but these merely appeared as bright spots on the dark background of the Elizabethan woodwork. Many lights were burning, but the blackness of the walls and roof seemed absolutely to swallow up their rays, like the mouth of a cavern. A hundred candles could not have given that apartment the cheerful lightness of a modern drawing room. But the gloomy richness of the panels matched well with the ruddy gleam from the enormous wood-fire, in which, crackling and glowing, now lay the mighty Yule log.

Quite a blood-red lustier poured forth from the fire, and quivered on the walls and the groined roof. We had gathered round the vast antique hearth in a wide circle. The quivering light of the fire and candles fell upon us all, but not equally, for some were in shadow. I remember still how tall and manly and handsome Reginald looked that night, taller by the head than any there, and full of high spirits and gayety. I, too, was in the highest spirits; never had my bosom felt lighter, and I believe it was my mirth that gradually gained the rest, for I recollect what a blithe, joyous company we seemed. All save one. Lady Speldhurst, dressed in gray silk and wearing a quaint head-dress, sat in her armchair, facing the fire, very silent, with her hands and her sharp chin propped on a sort of ivory-handled crutch that she walked with (for she was lame), peering at me with half-shut eyes. She was a little, spare old woman, with very keen, delicate features of the French type.

Her gray silk dress, her spotless lace, old-fashioned jewels, and prim neatness of array, were well suited to the intelligence of her face, with its thin lips, and eyes of a piercing black, undimmed by age. Those eyes made me uncomfortable, in spite of my gayety, as they followed my every movement with curious scrutiny. Still I was very merry and gay; my sisters even wondered at my ever-ready mirth, which was almost wild in its excess. I have heard since then of the Scottish belief that those doomed to some great calamity become fey, and are never so disposed for merriment and laughter as just before the blow falls. If ever mortal was fey, then I was so on that evening. Still, though I strove to shake it off, the pertinacious observation of old Lady Speldhurst's eyes *did* make an impression on me of a vaguely disagreeable nature. Others, too, noticed her scrutiny of me, but set it down as a mere eccentricity of a person always reputed whimsical, to say the least of it.

However, this disagreeable sensation lasted but a few moments. After a short pause my aunt took her part in the conversation, and we found ourselves listening to a weird legend, which the old lady told exceedingly well. One tale led to another. Everyone was called on in turn to contribute to the public entertainment, and story after story, always relating to demonology and witchcraft, succeeded. It was Christmas, the season for such tales; and the old room, with its dusky walls and pictures, and vaulted roof, drinking up the light so greedily, seemed just fitted to give effect to such legendary lore. The huge logs crackled and burned with glowing warmth; the blood-red glare of the Yule log flashed on the faces of the listeners and narrator, on the portraits, and the holly wreathed about their frames, and the upright old dame, in her antiquated dress and trinkets, like one of the originals of the pictures, stepped from the canvas to join our circle. It threw a shimmering lustre of an ominously ruddy hue upon the oaken panels.

No wonder that the ghost and goblin stories had a new zest. No wonder that the blood of the more timid grew chill and curdled, that their flesh crept, that their hearts beat irregularly, and the girls peeped fearfully over their shoulders, and huddled close together like frightened sheep, and half fancied they beheld some impish and malignant face gibbering at them from the darkling corners of the old room. By degrees my high spirits died out, and I felt the childish tremors, long latent, long forgotten, coming over me. I followed each story with painful interest; I did not ask myself if I believed the dismal tales. I listened, and fear grew upon me—the blind, irrational fear of our nursery days.

I am sure most of the other ladies present, young or middle-aged, were affected by the circumstances under which these traditions were heard, no less than by the wild and fantastic character of them. But with them the impression would die out next morning, when the bright sun should shine on the frosted boughs, and the rime on the grass, and the scarlet berries and green spikelets of the holly; and with me—but, ah! what was to happen ere another day dawn? Before we had made an end of this talk my father and the other squires came in, and we ceased our ghost stories, ashamed to speak of such matters before these newcomers—hard-headed, unimaginative men, who had no sympathy with idle legends. There was now a stir and bustle.

Servants were handing round tea and coffee, and other refreshments. Then there was a little music and singing. I sang a duet with Reginald, who had a fine voice and good musical skill. I remember that my singing was much praised, and indeed I was surprised at the power and pathos of my own voice, doubtless due to my excited nerves and mind. Then I heard someone say to another that I was by far the cleverest of the squire's daughters, as well as the prettiest. It did not make me vain.

I had no rivalry with Lucy and Minnie. But Reginald whispered some soft, fond words in my ear a little before he mounted his horse to set off homeward, which *did* make me happy and proud. And to think that the next time we met— but I forgave him long ago. Poor Reginald! And now shawls and cloaks were in request, and carriages rolled up to the porch, and the guests gradually departed. At last no one was left but those visitors staying in the house. Then my father, who had been called out to speak with the bailiff of the estate, came back with a look of annoyance on his face.

"A strange story I have just been told," said he; "here has been my bailiff to inform me of the loss of four of the choicest ewes out of that little flock of Southdowns I set such store by, and which arrived in the north but two months since. And the poor creatures have been destroyed in so strange a manner, for their carcasses are horribly mangled."

Most of us uttered some expression of pity or surprise, and some suggested that a vicious dog was probably the culprit.

"It would seem so," said my father; "it certainly seems the work of a dog; and yet all the men agree that no dog of such habits exists near us, where, indeed, dogs are scarce, excepting the shepherds' collies and the sporting dogs secured in yards. Yet the sheep are gnawed and bitten, for they show the marks of teeth. Something has done this, and has torn their bodies wolfishly; but apparently it has been only to suck the blood, for little or no flesh is gone."

"How strange!" cried several voices. Then some of the gentlemen remembered to have heard of cases when dogs addicted to sheep-killing had destroyed whole flocks, as if in sheer wantonness, scarcely deigning to taste a morsel of each slain wether.

My father shook his head. "I have heard of such cases, too," he said; "but in this instance I am tempted to think the malice of some unknown enemy has been at work. The teeth of a dog have been busy, no doubt, but the poor sheep have been mutilated in a fantastic manner, as strange as horrible; their hearts, in especial, have been torn out, and left at some paces off, half-gnawed. Also, the men persist that they found the print of a naked human foot in the soft mud of the ditch, and near it—this" And he held up what seemed a broken link of a rusted iron chain.

Many were the ejaculations of wonder and alarm, and many and shrewd the conjectures, but none seemed exactly to suit the bearings of the case. And when my father went on to say that two lambs of the same valuable breed had perished in the same singular manner three days previously, and that they also were found mangled and gore-stained, the amazement reached a higher pitch. Old Lady Speldhurst listened with calm, intelligent attention, but joined in none of our exclamations. At length she said to my father, "Try and recollect—have you no enemy among your neighbours?" My father started, and knit his brows. "Not one that I know of," he replied; and indeed he was a popular man and a kind landlord. "The more lucky you," said the old dame, with one of her grim smiles.

It was now late, and we retired to rest before long. One by one the guests dropped off. I was the member of the family selected to escort old Lady Speldhurst to her room—the room I had vacated in her favour. I did not much like the office. I felt a remarkable repugnance to my godmother, but my worthy aunts insisted so much that I should ingratiate myself with one who had so much to leave that I could not but comply. The visitor hobbled up the broad oaken stairs actively enough, propped on my arm and her ivory crutch. The room never had looked more genial and pretty, with its brisk fire, modern furniture, and the gay French paper on the walls. "A nice room, my dear, and I ought to be much obliged to you for it, since my maid tells me it is yours," said her ladyship; "but I am pretty sure you repent your generosity to me, after all those ghost stories, and tremble to think of a strange bed and chamber, eh?" I made some commonplace reply.

The old lady arched her eyebrows. "Where have they put you, child?" she asked; "in some cock-loft of the turrets, eh? or in a lumber-room—a regular ghost-trap? I can hear your heart beating with fear this moment. You are not fit to be alone." I tried to call up my pride, and laugh off the accusation against my courage, all the more, perhaps, because I felt its truth. "Do you want anything more that I can get you, Lady Speldhurst?" I asked, trying to feign a yawn of sleepiness.

The old dame's keen eyes were upon me. "I rather like you, my dear," she said, "and I liked your mamma well enough before she treated me so shamefully about the christening dinner. Now, I know you are frightened and fearful, and if an owl should but flap your window tonight, it might drive you into fits. There is a nice little sofa-bed in this dressing closet—call your maid to arrange it for you, and you can sleep there snugly, under the old witch's protection, and then no goblin dare harm you, and nobody will be a bit the wiser, or quiz you for being afraid." How little I knew what hung in the balance of my refusal or acceptance of that trivial proffer! Had the veil of the future been lifted for one instant! but that veil is impenetrable to our gaze.

I left her door. As I crossed the landing a bright gleam came from another room, whose door was left ajar; it (the light) fell like a bar of golden sheen across my path. As I approached the door opened and my sister Lucy, who had been watching for me, came out. She was already in a white cashmere wrapper, over which her loosened hair hung darkly and heavily, like tangles of silk. "Rosa, love," she whis-

31

pered, "Minnie and I can't bear the idea of your sleeping out there, all alone, in that solitary room—the very room too Nurse Sherrard used to talk about! So, as you know Minnie has given up her room, and come to sleep in mine, still we should so wish you to stop with us tonight at any rate, and I could make up a bed on the sofa for myself or you—and—"

I stopped Lucy's mouth with a kiss. I declined her offer. I would not listen to it. In fact, my pride was up in arms, and I felt I would rather pass the night in the churchyard itself than accept a proposal dictated, I felt sure, by the notion that my nerves were shaken by the ghostly lore we had been raking up, that I was a weak, superstitious creature, unable to pass a night in a strange chamber. So I would not listen to Lucy, but kissed her, bade her goodnight, and went on my way laughing, to show my light heart.

Yet, as I looked back in the dark corridor, and saw the friendly door still ajar, the yellow bar of light still crossing from wall to wall, the sweet, kind face still peering after me from amidst its clustering curls, I felt a thrill of sympathy, a wish to return, a yearning after human love and companionship. False shame was strongest, and conquered. I waved a gay *adieu*. I turned the corner, and peeping over my shoulder, I saw the door close; the bar of yellow light was there no longer in the darkness of the passage. I thought at that instant that I heard a heavy sigh. I looked sharply round. No one was there. No door was open, yet I fancied, and fancied with a wonderful vividness, that I did hear an actual sigh breathed not far off, and plainly distinguishable from the groan of the sycamore branches as the wind tossed them to and fro in the outer blackness.

If ever a mortal's good angel had cause to sigh for sorrow, not sin, mine had cause to mourn that night. But imagination plays us strange tricks and my nervous system was not over-composed or very fitted for judicial analysis. I had to go through the picture-gallery. I had never entered this apartment by candle-light before and I was struck by the gloomy array of the tall portraits, gazing moodily from the canvas on the lozenge-paned or painted windows, which rattled to the blast as it swept howling by. Many of the faces looked stern, and very different from their daylight expression. In others a furtive, flickering smile seemed to mock me as my candle illumined them; and in all, the eyes, as usual with artistic portraits, seemed to follow my motions with a scrutiny and an interest the more marked for the apathetic immovability of the other features.

I felt ill at ease under this stony gaze, though conscious how absurd were my apprehensions; and I called up a smile and an air of mirth, more as if acting a part under the eyes of human beings than of their mere shadows on the wall. I even laughed as I confronted them. No echo had my short-lived laughter but from the hollow armour and arching roof, and I continued on my way in silence.

By a sudden and not uncommon revulsion of feeling I shook off my aimless terrors, blushed at my weakness, and sought my chamber only too glad that I had been the only witness of my late tremors. As I entered my chamber I thought I heard something stir in the neglected lumber-room, which was the only neighbouring apartment. But I was determined to have no more panics, and resolutely shut my eyes to this slight and transient noise, which had nothing unnatural in it; for surely, between rats and wind, an old manor-house on a stormy night needs no sprites to disturb it. So I entered my room, and rang for my maid. As I did so I looked around me, and a most unaccountable repugnance to my temporary abode came over me, in spite of my efforts.

It was no more to be shaken off than a chill is to be shaken off when we enter some damp cave. And, rely upon it, the feeling of dislike and apprehension with which we regard, at first sight, certain places and people, was not implanted in us without some whole-some purpose. I grant it is irrational—mere animal instinct—but is not instinct God's gift, and is it for us to despise it? It is by instinct that children know their friends from their enemies—that they distinguish with such unerring accuracy between those who like them and those who only flatter and hate them. Dogs do the same; they will fawn on one person, they slink snarling from another. Show me a man whom children and dogs shrink from, and I will show you a false, bad man—lies on his lips, and murder at his heart.

No; let none despise the heaven-sent gift of innate antipathy, which makes the horse quail when the lion crouches in the thicket—which makes the cattle scent the shambles from afar, and low in terror and disgust as their nostrils snuff the blood-polluted air. I felt this antipathy strongly as I looked around me in my new sleeping-room, and yet I could find no reasonable pretext for my dislike. A very good room it was, after all, now that the green damask curtains were drawn, the fire burning bright and clear, candles burning on the mantel-piece, and the various familiar articles of toilet arranged as usual. The bed, too, looked peaceful and inviting—a pretty little white bed, not at all the gaunt funereal sort of couch which haunted apartments generally contain.

My maid entered, and assisted me to lay aside the dress and ornaments I had worn, and arranged my hair, as usual, prattling the while, in Abigail fashion. I seldom cared to converse with servants; but on that night a sort of dread of being left alone—a longing to keep some human being near me possessed me—and I encouraged the girl to gossip, so that her duties took her half an hour longer to get through than usual. At last, however, she had done all that could be done, and all my questions were answered, and my orders for the morrow reiterated and vowed obedience to, and the clock on the turret struck one. Then Mary, yawning a little, asked if I wanted anything more, and I was obliged to answer no, for very shame's sake; and she went. The shutting of the door, gently as it was closed, affected me unpleasantly. I took a dislike to the curtains, the tapestry, the dingy pictures— everything. I hated the room.

I felt a temptation to put on a cloak, run, half-dressed, to my sisters' chamber, and say I had changed my mind and come for shelter. But they must be asleep, I thought, and I could not be so unkind as to wake them. I said my prayers with unusual earnestness and a heavy heart. I extinguished the candles, and was just about to lay my head on my pillow, when the idea seized me that I would fasten the door. The candles were extinguished, but the firelight was amply sufficient to guide me. I gained the door. There was a lock, but it was rusty or hampered; my utmost strength could not turn the key. The bolt was broken and worthless. Balked of my intention, I consoled myself by remembering that I had never had need of fastenings yet, and returned to my bed. I lay awake for a good while, watching the red glow of the burning coals in the grate.

I was quiet now, and more composed. Even the light gossip of the maid, full of petty human cares and joys, had done me good—diverted my thoughts from brooding. I was on the point of dropping asleep, when I was twice disturbed. Once, by an owl, hooting in the ivy outside—no unaccustomed sound, but harsh and melancholy; once, by a long and mournful howling set up by the mastiff, chained in the yard beyond the wing I occupied. A long-drawn, lugubrious howling was this latter, and much such a note as the vulgar declare to herald a death in the family. This was a fancy I had never shared; but yet I could not help feeling that the dog's mournful moans were sad, and expressive of terror, not at all like his fierce, honest bark of anger, but rather as if something evil and unwonted were abroad. But soon I fell asleep.

How long I slept I never knew. I awoke at once with that abrupt start which we all know well, and which carries us in a second from utter unconsciousness to the full use of our faculties. The fire was still burning, but was very low, and half the room or more was in deep shadow. I knew, I felt, that some person or thing was in the room, although nothing unusual was to be seen by the feeble light. Yet it was a sense of danger that had aroused me from slumber. I experienced, while yet asleep, the chill and shock of sudden alarm, and I knew, even in the act of throwing off sleep like a mantle, *why* I awoke, and that some intruder was present. Yet, though I listened intently, no sound was audible, except the faint murmur of the fire—the dropping of a cinder from the bars— the loud, irregular beatings of my own heart.

Notwithstanding this silence, by some intuition I knew that I had not been deceived by a dream, and felt certain that I was not alone. I waited. My heart beat on; quicker, more sudden grew its pulsations, as a bird in a cage might flutter in presence of the hawk. And then I heard a sound, faint, but quite distinct, the clank of iron, the rattling of a chain! I ventured to lift my head from the pillow. Dim and uncertain as the light was, I saw the curtains of my bed shake, and caught a glimpse of something beyond, a darker spot in the darkness. This confirmation of my fears did not surprise me so much as it shocked me. I strove to cry aloud, but could not utter a word. The chain rattled again, and this time the noise was louder and clearer. But though I strained my eyes, they could not penetrate the obscurity that shrouded the other end of the chamber whence came the sullen clanking. In a moment several distinct trains of thought, like many-coloured strands of thread twining into one, became palpable to my mental vision. Was it a robber? Could it be a supernatural visitant?

Or was I the victim of a cruel trick, such as I had heard of, and which some thoughtless persons love to practice on the timid, reckless of its dangerous results? And then a new idea, with some ray of comfort in it, suggested itself. There was a fine young dog of the Newfoundland breed, a favourite of my father's, which was usually chained by night in an outhouse. Neptune might have broken loose, found his way to my room, and, finding the door imperfectly closed, have pushed it open and entered. I breathed more freely as this harmless interpretation of the noise forced itself upon me. It was—it must be— the dog, and I was distressing myself uselessly. I resolved to call to him; I strove to utter his name—"Neptune, Neptune," but a secret apprehension restrained me, and I was mute.

Then the chain clanked nearer and nearer to the bed, and presently I saw a dusky, shapeless mass appear between the curtains on the opposite side to where I was lying. How I longed to hear the whine of the poor animal that I hoped might be the cause of my alarm. But no; I heard no sound save the rustle of the curtains and the clash of the iron chains. Just then the dying flame of the fire leaped up, and with one sweeping, hurried glance I saw that the door was shut, and, horror! it is not the dog! it is the semblance of a human form that now throws itself heavily on the bed, outside the clothes, and lies there, huge and swart, in the red gleam that treacherously died away after showing so much to affright, and sinks into dull darkness.

There was now no light left, though the red cinders yet glowed with a ruddy gleam like the eyes of wild beasts. The chain rattled no more. I tried to speak, to scream wildly for help; my mouth was parched, my tongue refused to obey. I could not utter a cry, and, indeed, who could have heard me, alone as I was in that solitary chamber, with no living neighbour, and the picture-gallery between me and any aid that even the loudest, most piercing shriek could summon. And the storm that howled without would have drowned my voice, even if help had been at hand. To call aloud—to demand who was there—alas! how useless, how perilous! If the intruder were a robber, my outcries would but goad him to fury; but what robber would act thus? As for a trick, that seemed impossible.

And yet, *what* lay by my side, now wholly unseen? I strove to pray aloud as there rushed on my memory a flood of weird legends—the dreaded yet fascinating lore of my childhood. I had heard and read of the spirits of the wicked men forced to revisit the scenes of their earthly crimes—of demons that lurked in certain accursed spots—of the ghoul and vampire of the east, stealing amidst the graves they rifled for their ghostly banquets; and then I shuddered as I gazed on the blank darkness where I knew it lay. It stirred—it moaned hoarsely; and again I heard the chain clank close beside me—so close that it must almost have touched me. I drew myself from it, shrinking away in loathing and terror of the evil thing—what, I knew not, but felt that something malignant was near.

And yet, in the extremity of my fear, I dared not speak; I was strangely cautious to be silent, even in moving farther off; for I had a wild hope that it—the phantom, the creature, whichever it was—had not discovered my presence in the room. And then I remembered all the events of the night—Lady Speldhurst's ill-omened vaticinations, her half-warnings, her singular look as we parted, my sister's persuasions, my terror in the gallery, the remark that "this was the room nurse Sherrard used to talk of." And then memory, stimulated by fear, recalled the long-forgotten past, the ill-repute of this disused chamber, the sins it had witnessed, the blood spilled, the poison administered by unnatural hate within its walls, and the tradition which called it haunted. The green room—I remembered now how fearfully the servants avoided it—how it was mentioned rarely, and in whispers, when we were children, and how we had regarded it as a mysterious region, unfit for mortal habitation.

Was *it*—the dark form with the chain—a creature of this world, or a spectre? And again—more dreadful still—could it be that the corpses of wicked men were forced to rise and haunt in the body the places where they had wrought their evil deeds? And was such as these my grisly neighbour? The chain faintly rattled. My hair bristled; my eyeballs seemed starting from their sockets; the damps of a great anguish were on my brow. My heart laboured as if I were crushed beneath some vast weight. Sometimes it appeared to stop its frenzied beatings, sometimes its pulsations were fierce and hurried; my breath came short and with extreme difficulty, and I shivered as if with cold; yet I feared to stir. IT moved, it moaned, its fetters clanked dismally, the couch creaked and shook. This was no phantom, then—no air-drawn spectre. But its very solidity, its palpable presence, were a thousand times more terrible. I felt that I was in the very grasp of what could not only affright but harm; of something whose contact sickened the soul with deathly fear. I made a desperate resolve: I glided from the bed, I seized a warm wrapper, threw it around me, and tried to grope, with extended hands, my way to the door.

My heart beat high at the hope of escape. But I had scarcely taken one step before the moaning was renewed—it changed into a threatening growl that would have suited a wolf's throat, and a hand clutched at my sleeve. I stood motionless. The muttering growl sank to a moan again, the chain sounded no more, but still the hand held its gripe of my garment, and I feared to move. It knew of my presence, then. My brain reeled, the blood boiled in my ears, and my knees lost all strength, while my heart panted like that of a deer in the wolf's jaws. I sank back, and the benumbing influence of excessive terror reduced me to a state of stupor.

When my full consciousness returned I was sitting on the edge of the bed, shivering with cold, and barefooted. All was silent, but I felt that my sleeve was still clutched by my unearthly visitant. The silence lasted a long time. Then followed a chuckling laugh that froze my very marrow, and the gnashing of teeth as in demoniac frenzy; and then a wailing moan, and this was succeeded by silence. Hours may have passed—nay, though the tumult of my own heart prevented my hearing the clock strike, must have passed—but they seemed ages to me. And how were they passed? Hideous visions passed before the aching eyes that I dared not close, but which gazed ever into the dumb darkness where *it* lay—my dread companion through the watches of the night. I pictured *it* in every abhorrent form which an excited fancy could summon up: now as a skeleton; with hollow eye-holes and grinning, fleshless jaws; now as a vampire, with livid face and bloated form, and dripping mouth wet with blood.

Would it never be light! And yet, when day should dawn I should be forced to see It face to face. I had heard that spectre and fiend were compelled to fade as morning brightened, but this creature was too real, too foul a thing of earth, to vanish at cock-crow. No! I should see it—the Horror—face to face! And then the cold prevailed, and my teeth chattered, and shiverings ran through me, and yet there was the damp of agony on my bursting brow. Some instinct made me snatch at a shawl or cloak that lay on a chair within reach, and wrap it round me. The moan was renewed, and the chain just stirred. Then I sank into apathy, like an Indian at the stake, in the intervals of torture. Hours fled by, and I remained like a statue of ice, rigid and mute. I even slept, for I remember that I started to find the cold gray light of an early winter's day was on my face, and stealing around the room from between the heavy curtains of the window.

Shuddering, but urged by the impulse that rivets the gaze of the bird upon the snake, I turned to see the Horror of the night. Yes, it was no fevered dream, no hallucination of sickness, no airy phantom unable to face the dawn. In the sickly light I saw it lying on the bed, with its grim head on the pillow. A man? Or a corpse arisen from its unhallowed grave, and awaiting the demon that animated it? There it lay—a gaunt, gigantic form, wasted to a skeleton, half-clad, foul with dust and clotted gore, its huge limbs flung upon the couch as if at random, its shaggy hair streaming over the pillows like a lion's mane. His face was toward me. Oh, the wild hideousness of that face, even in sleep! In features it was human, even through its horrid mask of mud and half-dried bloody gouts, but the expression was brutish and savagely fierce; the white teeth were visible between the parted lips, in a malignant grin; the tangled hair and beard were mixed in leonine confusion, and there were scars disfiguring the brow.

Round the creature's waist was a ring of iron, to which was attached a heavy but broken chain—the chain I had heard clanking. With a second glance I noted that part of the chain was wrapped in straw to prevent its galling the wearer. The creature—I cannot call it a man—had the marks of fetters on its wrists, the bony arm that protruded through one tattered sleeve was scarred and bruised; the feet were bare, and lacerated by pebbles and briers, and one of them was wounded, and wrapped in a morsel of rag. And the lean hands, one of which held my sleeve, were armed with talons like an eagle's. In an instant the horrid truth flashed upon me—I was in the grasp of a madman. Better the phantom that scares the sight than the wild beast that rends and tears the quivering flesh—the pitiless human brute that has no heart to be softened, no reason at whose bar to plead, no compassion, naught of man save the form and the cunning. I gasped in terror. Ah! the mystery of those ensanguined fingers, those gory, wolfish jaws! that face, all besmeared with blackening blood, is revealed!

The slain sheep, so mangled and rent—the fantastic butchery—the print of the naked foot—all, all were explained; and the chain, the broken link of which was found near the slaughtered animals—it came from his broken chain—the chain he had snapped, doubtless, in his escape from the asylum where his raging frenzy had been fettered and bound, in vain! in vain! Ah me! how had this grisly Samson broken manacles and prison bars—how had he eluded guardian and keeper and a hostile world, and come hither on his wild way, hunted like a beast of prey, and snatching his hideous banquet like a beast of prey, too! Yes, through the tatters of his mean and ragged garb I could see the marks of the seventies, cruel and foolish, with which men in that time tried to tame the might of madness. The scourge—its marks were there; and the scars of the hard iron fetters, and many a cicatrice and welt, that told a dismal tale of hard usage. But now he was loose, free to play the brute—the baited, tortured brute that they had made him—now without the cage, and ready to gloat over the victims his strength should overpower.

Horror! horror! I was the prey—the victim— already in the tiger's clutch; and a deadly sickness came over me, and the iron entered into my soul, and I longed to scream, and was dumb! I died a thousand deaths as that morning wore on. I *dared not* faint. But words cannot paint what I suffered as I waited— waited till the moment when he

39

should open his eyes and be aware of my presence; for I was assured he knew it not. He had entered the chamber as a lair, when weary and gorged with his horrid orgy; and he had flung himself down to sleep without a suspicion that he was not alone. Even his grasping my sleeve was doubtless an act done betwixt sleeping and waking, like his unconscious moans and laughter, in some frightful dream.

Hours went on; then I trembled as I thought that soon the house would be astir, that my maid would come to call me as usual, and awake that ghastly sleeper. And might he not have time to tear me, as he tore the sheep, before any aid could arrive? At last what I dreaded came to pass—a light footstep on the landing—there is a tap at the door. A pause succeeds, and then the tapping is renewed, and this time more loudly. Then the madman stretched his limbs, and uttered his moaning cry, and his eyes slowly opened— very slowly opened and met mine. The girl waited a while ere she knocked for the third time. I trembled lest she should open the door unbidden—see that grim thing, and bring about the worst.

I saw the wondering surprise in his haggard, bloodshot eyes; I saw him stare at me half vacantly, then with a crafty yet wondering look; and then I saw the devil of murder begin to peep forth from those hideous eyes, and the lips to part as in a sneer, and the wolfish teeth to bare themselves. But I was not what I had been. Fear gave me a new and a desperate composure—a courage foreign to my nature. I had heard of the best method of managing the insane; I could but try; I *did* try. Calmly, wondering at my own feigned calm, I fronted the glare of those terrible eyes. Steady and undaunted was my gaze—motionless my attitude. I marvelled at myself, but in that agony of sickening terror I was *outwardly* firm. They sink, they quail, abashed, those dreadful eyes, before the gaze of a helpless girl; and the shame that is never absent from insanity bears down the pride of strength, the bloody cravings of the wild beast. The lunatic moaned and drooped his shaggy head between his gaunt, squalid hands.

I lost not an instant. I rose, and with one spring reached the door, tore it open, and, with a shriek, rushed through, caught the wondering girl by the arm, and crying to her to run for her life, rushed like the wind along the gallery, down the corridor, down the stairs. Mary's screams filled the house as she fled beside me. I heard a long-drawn, raging cry, the roar of a wild animal mocked of its prey, and I knew what was behind me. I never turned my head—I flew rather than ran. I was in the hall already; there was a rush of many feet, an outcry of many voices, a sound of scuffling feet, and brutal yells, and oaths, and heavy blows, and I fell to the ground crying, "Save me!" and lay in a swoon. I awoke from a delirious trance. Kind faces were around my bed, loving looks were bent on me by all, by my dear father and dear sisters; but I scarcely saw them before I swooned again.

When I recovered from that long illness, through which I had been nursed so tenderly, the pitying looks I met made me tremble. I asked for a looking-glass. It was long denied me, but my importunity prevailed at last—a mirror was brought. My youth was gone at one fell swoop. The glass showed me a livid and haggard face, blanched and bloodless as of one who sees a specter; and in the ashen lips, and wrinkled brow, and dim eyes, I could trace nothing of my old self. The hair, too, jetty and rich before, was now as white as snow; and in one night the ravages of half a century had passed over my face. Nor have my nerves ever recovered their tone after that dire shock. Can you wonder that my life was blighted, that my lover shrank from me, so sad a wreck was I?

I am old now—old and alone. My sisters would have had me to live with them, but I chose not to sadden their genial homes with my phantom face and dead eyes. Reginald married another. He has been dead many years. I never ceased to pray for him, though he left me when I was bereft of all. The sad weird is nearly over now. I am old, and near the end, and wishful for it. I have not been bitter or hard, but I cannot bear to see many people, and am best alone. I try to do what good I can with the worthless wealth Lady Speldhurst left me, for, at my wish, my portion was shared between my sisters. What need had I of inheritance?—I, the shattered wreck made by that one night of horror!

In a Fog

A few minutes before one o'clock on the morning of Sunday, the 8th of February, 1857, Policeman Smithers, of the Third District, was meditatively pursuing his path of duty through the quietest streets of Ward Five, beguiling, as usual, the weariness of his watch by reminiscent Aethiopianisms, mellifluous in design, though not severely artistic in execution. Passing from the turbulent precincts of Portland and Causeway Streets, he had entered upon the solitudes of Green Street, along which he now dragged himself dreamily enough, ever extracting consolations from lugubrious cadences mournfully intoned. Very silent was the neighbourhood. Very dismal the night. Very dreary and damp was Mr. Smithers; for a vile fog wrapped itself around him, filling his body with moist misery, and his mind with anticipated rheumatic horrors. Still he surged heavily along, tired Nature with tuneful charms sweetly restoring.

As he wound off a tender tribute to the virtues of the Ancient Tray, and was about sounding the opening notes of a requiem over the memory of the lost African Lily, surnamed Dale, one o'clock was announced by the bell of the Lynde-Street Church. Mr. Smithers's heart warmed a little at the thought of speedy respite from his midnight toil, and with hastening step he approached Chambers Street, and came within range of his relief post. He paused a moment upon the corner, and gazed around. It is the peculiar instinct of a policeman to become suspicious at every corner.

Nothing stirring. Silence everywhere. He listens acutely. No sound. He strains his eyes to penetrate the misty atmosphere. He is satisfied that order reigns. He prepares to resume his march, and the measure of his melancholy chant.

Three seconds more, and Policeman Smithers is another being. Now his hand convulsively grasps his staff; his foot falls lightly on the pavement; his carol is changed to a quick, sharp inhalation of the breath; for directly before him, just visible through the fog, a figure, lightly clad, leans from a window close upon the street, then clambers noiselessly upon the sill, leaps over, and dashes swiftly down Chambers Street, disappearing in the darkness.

Gathering himself well together, in an instant, Mr. Smithers is off and away in pursuit. His heavy rubber-boots spatter over the bricks with an echo that startles the sober residents from their slumbers. Strong of limb, and not wholly unaccustomed to such exercise, he rapidly gains upon the fugitive, who, finding himself so hotly followed, utters a faint cry, as if unable to control his terror, and suddenly darts into one of the numerous narrow passages which connect Chambers and Leverett Streets.

Not prepared for this sharp dodge, Mr. Smithers is for a moment unable to check his headlong plunges, and shoots past the opening a yard or two before the wet sidewalk affords him a foothold.

In great wrath, he turns about, and gropes his way cautiously through the lane in the narrow labyrinth of which the fugitive has disappeared,—always cautiously, for there are precipitous descents in Hammond Avenue, and deep arched door-ways, from which a sudden onslaught might be dangerous. But he meets no interruption here. Emerging into Leverett Street, he with difficulty descries a white garment distantly fluttering in the feeble light of a street-lamp. Any other colour would have eluded him, but the way is clear now, and it is a mere question of strength and speed. He sets his teeth together, takes a full breath, and gives chase again.

Mr. Smithers has now passed the limits of his own beat, and he fears his adventure may be shared by some of his associates. For the world he would not have this happen. Nothing could tempt him at this moment to swing his rattle. His blood is roused, and he will make this capture himself, alone and without aid.

He rapidly reconsiders the chances.

"This fellow does not know the turns," he thinks, "or he would have taken Cushman Avenue, and then I should have lost him."

This is in his favour. On the other hand, Mr. Smithers's action is impeded by his heavy overcoat and rubber boots, and he knows that the pursued is un-encumbered in all his movements.

It is a fierce, desperate struggle, that mad race down Leverett Street, at one o'clock on Sunday morning.

At each corner, the street lamps throw a dull red haze around, revealing the fugitive's slender form as he rushes wildly through. Another moment, and the friendly fog shelters and conceals him from view.

Breathless, panting, sobbing, he ere long is forced to relax his speed. The policemen, who has held his best energies in reserve, now puts forth his utmost strength.

Presently he gains upon the runaway so that he can detect the white feet pattering along the red bricks, rising and falling quite noiselessly. He ejects imprecations about his own stout boots, which not only fail to fasten themselves firmly to the slippery pavements, but continually betray by their noisy splashing his exact position.

As they pass the next lamp, Mr. Smithers sees plainly enough that the end is near. The fugitive touches the ground with only the balls of his feet, as if each step were torture, and expels his breath with unceasing violence. He does not gasp or pant,—he groans.

Just at the bend in Leverett Street, leading to the bridge, there is a dark and half-hidden aperture among the ill-assorted houses. Into this, as a forlorn hope, the fugitive endeavours to fling himself. But the game is up. Here, at last, he is overhauled by Mr. Smithers, who, dropping a heavy hand upon his shoulder, whirls him violently to the ground. Having accomplished this exploit with rare dexterity, he forthwith proceeds to set the captive on his feet again, and to shake him about with sprightly vigour, according to established usage.

Mr. Smithers next makes a rapid but close examination of his prize, who, bewildered by the fall, stares vacantly around, and speaks no word. He was a young man, apparently about twenty years old, with nothing peculiar in appearance except an unseasonable deficiency in clothing. Coat, waistcoat, trousers, boots, hat, had he none; shirt, drawers, and stockings made up his scant raiment. Mr. Smithers set aside the suspicion of burglary, which he had originally entertained, in favour of domestic disorder. The symptoms did not, to his mind, point towards delirium tremens.

Suddenly recovering consciousness, the youth was seized with a fit of trembling so violent that he with difficulty stood upright, and cried out in piteous tones,—

"For God's sake, let me go! let me go!"

Mr. Smithers answered by gruffly ordering the prisoner to move along with him.

By some species of inspiration—for, as the era of police uniforms had not then dawned, it could have been nothing else—the young man conceived the correct idea of the function of his custodian, and, after verifying his belief, expressed himself enraptured.

All his perturbation seemed to vanish at the moment.

The affair was getting too deep for Mr. Smithers, who could not fathom the idea of a midnight malefactor becoming jubilant over his arrest. So he gave no ear to the torrent of excited explanations that burst upon him, but silently took the direct route to the station.

Here he resigned his charge to Captain Morrill's care, and, after narrating the circumstances, went forth again, attended by two choice spirits, to continue investigations. On reaching Chambers Street, he became confused and dubious. A row of houses, all precisely alike excepting in colour, stood not far from the corner of Green Street. From a lower window of one of these he believed that the apparition had sprung; but, in his agitation, he had neglected to mark with sufficient care the precise spot. Now, no open window nor any other trace of the event could be discovered.

The three policemen, having arrived at the end of their wits, went back to the station for an extension.

There they found Captain Morrill listening to a strange and startling story, the incidents of which can here be more coherently recapitulated than they were on that occasion by the half-distracted sufferer.

On the morning of Saturday, February the 7th, this young man, whose name was Richard Lorrimer, and who was a clerk in a New-York mercantile house, started from that city in the early train for Boston, whither he had been despatched to arrange some business matters that needed the presence of a representative of the firm. It chanced to be his first journey of any extent; but the day was cheerless and gloomy, and the novelty of travel, which would otherwise have been attractive, was not especially agreeable. After exhausting the enlivening resources of a package of morning papers, which at that time overflowed with records of every variety of crime, from the daily murder to the hourly garrotte, he dozed. At Springfield he dined.

Here, also, he fortified himself against returning *ennui* with a supply of the day's journals from Boston. Singularly enough, five minutes after resuming his place, he was once more peacefully slumbering. The pause at Worcester scarcely roused him; but near Framingham a sharp shriek from the locomotive, and the rapid working of the brakes, banished his dreams, and put an end to his drowsy humour for the remainder of the journey. It was soon made known that the engine was suffering from internal disarrangement, and that a delay of an hour or more might be expected. The red flag was despatched to the rear, the lamps were lighted, and the passengers composed themselves, each as patiently and as comfortably as he could.

Lorrimer felt no inclination for further repose. He was much disturbed at the prospect of long detention, having received directions to execute a part of his commission that evening. Comforting himself with the profound reflection that the fault was not his, he turned wearily to his newspaper-files.

A middle-aged man with a keen nose and a snapping eye asked permission to share the benefit of his treasures of journalism. As the middle-aged man glanced over the New York dailies, he ventured an anathema upon the abominations of Gotham.

The patriotic pride of a genuine New-Yorker never deserts him. Lorrimer discovered that the maligner of his city was a Bostonian, and a stormy debate ensued.

As between cat and dog, so is the hostility which divides the residents of these two towns. So the conversation became at once spirited, and eventually spiteful.

Boston pointed with sarcastic finger to the close columns heavily laden with iniquitous recitals, the result of a reporter's experience of one day in the metropolis.

New York, with icy imperturbability, rehearsed from memory the recent revelations of matrimonial and clerical delinquencies which had given the City of Notions an unpleasant notoriety.

Boston burst out in eloquent denunciation of the Bowery assassin's knife.

New York was placidly pleased to revert to a tale of bloodshed in the abiding-place of Massachusetts authority, the State Prison.

Boston fell back upon the garrotte,—"the meanest and most diabolical invention of Five-Point villainy,—a thing unknown, Sir, and never to be known with us, while our police system lasts!"

New York quietly folded together a paper so as to reveal one particular paragraph, which appeared in smallest type, as seeking to avoid recognition. Boston read as follows:—

"The garrotting system of highway robbery, which has been so fashionable for some time past in New York, and which has so much alarmed the people of that city, has been introduced in Boston, and was practised on Thomas W. Steamburg, barber, on Thursday night. While crossing the Common to his home, he was attacked by three men; one seized him by the throat and half strangled him, another sealed his mouth with a gloved hand, and the third abstracted his wallet, which contained about seventy-five dollars in money."

This was from the *Courier* of that morning. New York had triumphed, and Boston, with eyes snapping virulently, sought another portion of the car, perhaps to hunt up his temper, which had been for some time on the point of departure, and had now left him altogether.

Lorrimer took to himself great satisfaction, in a mild way, and laughed inwardly at his opponent's discomfiture.

Presently, the vitalities of the locomotive having been restored, the train rolled on, and Lorrimer took to calculating the chances of fulfilling his appointment that evening. He at length abandoned the hope, and resigned himself to the afflicting prospect of a solitary Sunday in a strange place.

At eight o'clock, p. m., the Boston station was achieved. Then followed, for Mr. Lorrimer, the hotel, the supper, the vain search for Saturday-evening amusements, and a discontented stroll in a wilderness of unfamiliar streets, with spirits dampened by the dismal foggy weather.

He found the Common, and secretly admired, but longed for an opportunity to vilify it to some ardent native. His point of attack would be, that it furnished dangerous opportunities for crime, as illustrated in the case he had recently been discussing. He looked around for some one to accost, and felt aggrieved at finding no available victim. Finally, in great depth of spirits, and anxious for a temporary shelter from the all-penetrating moisture, he wandered into a saloon of inviting appearance, and sought the national consolation,—Oysters.

While he was accumulating his appetite, a stranger entered the same stall, and dropped, with a smile and a nod, upon the opposite seat. "I wouldn't intrude, Sir," he said, "but every other place is filled. It's wonderful how Boston gives itself up to oysters on Saturday nights,— all other sorts of rational enjoyment being legally prohibited."

Lorrimer welcomed the stranger, and, delighted at the opportunity of a bit of discussion, and still cherishing the malignant desire to injure somebody's feelings in the matter of the Common, opened a conversation by asking if Boston were really much given to *bivalvular* excesses.

The stranger, who was a strongly built and rough-visaged man, with nothing specially attractive about him, except a humorous and fascinating eye-twinkle, straightened himself, and delivered a short oration.

"Bless me, Sir!" said he, "are you a foreigner? Why, oysters are the universal bond of brotherhood, not only in Boston, but throughout this land. They harmonize with our sharp, wide-awake spirit. They are an element in our politics. Our statesmen, legislators, and high-placed men, generally, are weaned on them. Why, dear me! oysters are a fundamental idea in our social system. The best society circles around 'fried' and 'stewed.' Our 'festive scenes,' you know, depend on them in no small degree for their zest. That isn't all, either. A full third of our population is over 'oysters' every morning at eleven o'clock. Young Smith, on his way down town after breakfast, drops into the first saloon and absorbs some oysters. At precisely eleven o'clock he is overcome with hunger and takes a few on the 'half-shell.' In the course of an hour appetite clamours, and he 'oysters' again. So on till dinner-time, and, after dinner, oysters at short intervals until bed-time."

And the stalwart stranger leaned back and laughed lustily for a few seconds, until, abruptly checking his mirth, he, in solemn tones, directed the waiter to introduce ale.

Then occurred an interesting exchange of courtesies. Social enlightenment was vividly illustrated. The sparkling ale was set upon the table. In silent contemplation, the two gentlemen awaited the subsidence of the head. Then, smiling intensely, they cordially grasped the flowing mugs; they made the edges click; they paused.

"Sir," said one, with genial blandness.

"Sir," responded the other, in like manner.

Contemporaneously they partook of the cheering fluid. Gradually each gentleman's nose was eclipsed by the aspiring orb of pottery. The mugs assumed a lofty elevation, then fell, to rise no more. The two gentlemen beamed with amity. Each respected the other, and the acquaintance was formed.

Lorrimer was charmed to meet an intelligent being who would talk and be talked to. He flattered himself he had exploited a "character," and was determined not to allow him to slip away. He cautiously broke to his new companion the fact that he was a native of New York, and was a little surprised to see the announcement followed by no manifestation of awe, but only a lively wink. He reserved his defamatory intentions respecting the Common, and endeavoured to draw the stranger out, who, in return, shot forth eccentricities as profusely as the emery wheel of the street grinder emits sparks when assailed by a scissors-blade.

Lorrimer learned that this delightful fellow's name was Glover, and rejoiced greatly in so much knowledge.

Mr. Glover ordered in ale, and Mr. Lorrimer ordered in oysters,—and from oysters to ale they pleasantly alternated for the space of two hours.

Cloud-compelling cigars varied at intervals the monotony of the proceedings.

At length the young gentleman from New York vanquished his last "fried in crumb," and victory perched upon his knife. Just then the gas-burners began to meander queerly before his eyes. Around and above him he beheld showers of glittering sparks,—snaky threads of light,—fantastic figures of fire,—jets of liquid lustre. He communicated, in confidence, to Mr. Glover, that his seat seemed to him of the nature of a rocking-chair operating viciously upon a steep slated roof. Mr. Glover laughed, and proposed an adjournment.

As they settled their little bills, Lorrimer thoughtlessly displayed a plethoric pile of banknotes. He saw, or fancied he saw, his companion gaze at them in a manner which made him restless; but the circumstances soon passed from his mind, until later events enforced the recollection.

When they walked into the open air, Mr. Lorrimer first became intimate with a lamp-post, which he was loath to leave, and then bitterly bewailed his ignorance of localities. Glover good-naturedly suggested that his young friend would do well to take up quarters with him, that night, and promised to conduct him wherever he desired to go, the next morning. His young friend was not in the humour for hesitation, and, distrusting his own perambulatory powers, gave himself up, without reserve, to Glover's guidance. Linked together by their arms, they sailed along, like an energetic little steam-tug, puffing, plunging, sputtering, under the shadow of a serene and stately India-man.

The fog had now gathered solidity, and hung chillingly over the city's heart. How desolate were the thoroughfares! The street-lamps gleamed luridly from their stands, serving only to make the dreary darkness visible. Lorrimer's late merry fancies were all extinguished as suddenly as they had blazed forth. Even his sturdy guide showed a depression and constraint that strangely contrasted with his former gayety. He vainly drew upon his mirth-account; there was no issue. "Beastly fog!" said he, "we might drill holes in it, and blast it with gunpowder!" They approached the Common, and the hideous structure opposite West Street glared on them like a fiery monster, and seemed exactly the reverse of the gate to a forty-acre Paradise. Sheltering their faces from the wind, which now added its inconveniences to the saturating atmosphere, they struck the broad avenue, and pushed across towards the West End.

The wind sang most doleful strains, and the bending branches of the trees sighed sadly over them. Lorrimer was filled with an anxious tribulation, as he remembered the story of the villainy that, two nights before, near the spot where they now walked, and perhaps at the same hour, had been perpetrated. An impulse, which he could not restrain, caused him to whisper his fears to his companion. Glover laughed, a little uneasily, he thought, but made no answer.

Soon they reached the opposite boundary of the Common, and continued through Hancock Street, ascending and descending the hill. While passing the reservoir in that dull gray darkness, Lorrimer felt as if under the shadow of some giant tomb. Hastening forward, for it was growing late, they threaded a number of the short avenues of Ward Three, and at length, when young New York's endurance was nearly exhausted, reached their destination in Chambers Street. It must have been the fatigue which, as they crossed the threshold, propelled Mr. Lorrimer against the door, causing him to stain himself unbecomingly with new paint.

They mounted the stairs, and entered a comfortable apartment, in which a fresh fire was diffusing a most welcome glow, and a spacious bed luxuriously invited occupancy. Lorrimer had but one grief, which he freely communicated to his host,—his fingers were liberally decorated with dark daubs, to which he pointed with unsteady anguish.

"It's a filthy shame!" said he, with more energy of manner than certainty of utterance.

A section of the chamber was separated from the rest by a screen. Into this retreat Glover disappeared, and immediately returned with a bottle, from which he poured an acid that effaced the spots. "It will wash away anything," said he, laughing.

Lorrimer was superabundantly profuse in thanks, and announced that his mind was now at ease. By some mysterious process, not clearly explicable to himself, he contrived to lay aside a portion of his dress, and to dispose himself within the folds of balmy bedclothes that awaited him. In forty seconds he was dreaming.

Nearly an hour had elapsed when he half woke from an uneasy slumber, and strove to collect his drowsy faculties. His sleep had been disturbed by frightful visions. He had passed through a scene of violence on the Common; he had been engaged in a life-and-death struggle with his new acquaintance; he had been seized by unseen hands, and thrown into a vast vault. His brain throbbed and his heart ached, as he endeavoured to disentangle the bewildering fancies of his sleep from wakeful reality.

He lay with his face to the wall, and the grotesque decorations of the paper assumed ghostly forms, and moved menacingly before his eyes, thrilling him through and through.

In a few moments the murmur of voices close at hand aroused him more effectually. He then recollected the incidents of the night, and reproached himself for his wild excesses, and his reckless and imprudent confidence in a stranger. He dreaded to think what the consequences might be, and again became confused with the memories of his distressing dreams.

Three facts, however, were fastened upon his mind. He could not forget Glover's singular glance at his roll of bank-notes,—the hesitation to converse about the garrotte,—nor the bottle of acid which would "wash away anything." Would it wash away stains of blood?

The sounds of subdued conversation again arrested his attention. He listened earnestly, but without changing his position.

"Speak softly," said a voice which he recognized as Glover's,— "speak softly; you will wake my guest."

Then the words failed to reach him for a few moments. He strained his ears, and hardly breathed, for fear of interrupting a syllable. Presently he was able to distinguish a few sentences.

"Do you call this a profitable job?" said a strange voice.

"Oh, very fair,—worth about fifty dollars, I should guess. I wouldn't undertake such a piece of work at a smaller chance," said Glover.

"Shall you cut the face?" said the other, after a minute's pause.

"Of course," was the answer; "it's the only way to do it handsomely."

"Hum!—what do you use? steel?"

"Steel, by all means."

"I shouldn't."

"I like it better; and I have a nice bit that has done service in this way before."

From Lorrimer's brow exuded a deadly sudor. His heart ceased to palpitate. His muscles became rigid; his eyes fixed. His terror was almost too great for him to bear. With difficulty he controlled himself,

51

and listened again.

"Can it be done here?" asked the strange voice;—"will not the features be recognised?"

"There is nothing deeply marked, except the eyes," said Glover, "and I can easily remove them, you know."

"You can try the acid."

"The other way is best."

"I suppose it must be done quickly."

"So quickly that there will be no chance for any proof."

Lorrimer gasped feebly, and clutched the bedclothes with a nervous, convulsive movement. He had no power to reflect upon his situation; but he felt that he was lost. Alone and unaided, he could not hope to combat the evil designs of two men, a single one of whom he knew was vastly his superior in strength. His blood seemed to cease flowing in his veins. He thought for an instant of springing from the bed, and imploring mercy; but the nature of their conversation, with its *minutiae* of cruelty, forbade all hope in that direction. His brain whirled, and he thought that reason was about to forsake him. But a movement in the room restored him to a sense of his peril.

He saw the shadows changing their places, and knew that the light was moving. He heard faint footsteps. Hope deserted him, and he closed his eyes, quite despairing. When he opened them a minute later, he was in darkness.

Then hope returned. There might yet be a means of escape. They had left him,—for how long he could not conjecture; but now, at least, he was alone. What a flood of joy came over him then!

Swiftly and softly he threw off the bedclothes, and by the uncertain light of the fire, which was still glimmering, found his way noiselessly to the floor.

His trembling limbs at first refused to sustain him, but the thought of his impending fate, should he remain, invested him with an unexpected courage. Passing around the foot of the bed, he approached the door of the chamber.

As he moved, his shadow, dimly cast by the flickering embers, fell across the mouth of the enclosure whence Glover had brought the acid. He shuddered to think what might be hidden by that screen. He burned with curiosity, even in that moment of danger. For a moment he even rashly thought of seeking to penetrate the mystery.

Treading lightly, and partially supporting himself by the wall, lest his feet should press too heavily upon some loose board and cause it to rattle beneath him, he reached the door. It was not wholly closed, and with utmost gentleness he essayed to pull it open. With all his care he could not prevent it from creaking sharply. His nerves were again shaken, and a new tremor assailed him. Tears filled his eyes. His heart was like ice, only heavier, within him.

He stood for a minute motionless and half-unconscious. Then recovering himself by a powerful effort, he advanced once more. Without venturing to open the door wider, he worked through the narrow aperture, inch by inch, stopping every few seconds for fear that the rustle of his shirt against the jamb might be overheard. At length, by almost imperceptible movements, he succeeded in gaining the head of the staircase.

Then he believed that his deliverance was near at hand. He had thus far eluded detection, and it only remained for him to descend, and depart by the outer door.

Bending forward at every step to catch the slightest echo of alarm, he felt his way down through the darkness. The difficulty at this point was great. As one recovered from a long illness finds his knees yield under him at the first attempt to descend a staircase, just so it was with Lorrimer. At one time a faintness came over him, and he was obliged to sit down and rest. A movement above aroused him, and, starting up, he hurriedly groped his way to the street-door.

The darkness was absolute. He could discern nothing, but, after a short search, he caught hold of the handle and turned it slowly. The door remained immovable. By another exploration he discovered a large key suspended from a nail near the centre of the door. This he inserted in the lock, and turned with all the caution he could command. It was not enough, for it snapped loudly.

A voice from the head of the stairs cried out, "Who is there?"

Lorrimer was appalled. He shook the door, but it remained fast. Like lightning he passed his hand up and down the crevice in search of a hidden bolt. He found nothing, and felt that he was in the hands of the murderers;—for he could entertain no doubt of their design. In the agony of desperation he flung out his arms, and a door beside him flew open. He entered, and rushed to a window, which was easily lifted, and out of which he threw himself at the moment that a light streamed into the apartment behind him.

When Mr. Lorrimer had finished relating to Captain Morrill, with all the energy of truth, the more important of the above circumstances, that officer arose, and, calling to his assistance a couple of his force, started out in great haste in the direction of Chambers Street. Lorrimer, who had been provided with shoes, hat, and coat, went with them. After a little search, a row of houses with windows close upon the street was found. More diligent examination showed that the door of one of these was freshly painted. A vigorous assault upon the panels brought down the household. Mr. Glover, and another person whose voice was identified by Lorrimer, were marched off with few words to the station. Mr. Lorrimer's clothes were rescued, and an officer was left to look after the premises.

Mr. Glover, on arriving at the station, expressed great indignation, and employed uncivil terms in speaking of his late guest. Under the subduing influences of Captain Morrill's treatment, he soon became tranquil, and subsequently manifested an excess of hilarity, which the guardians of the night strove in vain to check. But he answered unreservedly all the questions which Captain Morrill put to him. His statement ran somewhat thus:—

"I met this young man, for the first time, a few hours ago, at an oyster-saloon on Washington Street. We drank a good deal of ale, and he lost his balance. I kept mine. I saw he had a pretty large amount of money, and doubted his ability to keep as good a watch over it as he ought to. So I took him home with me. On the way he would talk uneasily about garrotte robberies, but I refused to encourage him.

"You want to know about that alarming conversation? Well,"— (here Mr. Glover was so overcome with merriment, that, after a proper time, the interposition of official authority became necessary,)—"well, I am an engraver. My business is mainly to cut heads. Sometimes I use steel, sometimes copper. My brother, who is also an engraver, and I were discussing a new commission. I told him I should make use of a good bit of steel, which had already been engraved upon, but not so deeply but that the lines could be easily removed, excepting the eyes, which would have to be scraped away. My allusion to proof is easily explained: it is common for engravers to have a proof-impression taken of their work after it is finished, by which they are enabled to detect any imperfections, and remedy them.

"I am very sorry that my young friend should have considered me so much of a bloodthirsty ruffian. But the ale of Boston is no doubt strange to him, and his confusion at finding himself in a large city is quite natural. Besides, his suspicions were in some degree reciprocated. When I saw him flying out of the window, I was convinced that he must be an ingenious burglar, and instantly ran back to examine my tools. I am glad to find that I was wrong. If he will return now with me, he shall be welcome to his share of the bed."

Mr. Lorrimer politely, but positively, declined.

Captain Morrill urbanely apologised to Mr. Glover, and engaged himself to make it right in the morning; whereupon Mr. Glover withdrew in cachinnatory convulsions. Mr. Lorrimer was instructed to resume his proper garments, and was then conveyed safely to his hotel, where he remained in deep abstraction until Monday, when, after transacting his business, he took the afternoon return-train for New York.

The case was not entered upon the records of the Third District Police.

Man Abroad

Chapter 1: Reform is Necessary

"John," said the President of the United States to his private secretary, "did you send those nominations over to the Senate?"

"I did, sir."

"Were any confirmed?"

"Yes; the Ministers to Venus, Jupiter, Saturn and Uranus, and the postmasters at London, Paris, Rome, Berlin and Dublin. The asteroid consulships were laid over, and so were most of the nominations for the home offices, the post offices in South America, and the District Attorneyships of Asia and Africa."

"Well, drop a line to the State Department, telling the Secretary to telegraph to Mercury, Venus, Jupiter and Saturn, asking the representatives of the late Administration for their resignations. By the way, the man in Mars is to be retained—don't make any mistake. He is a good business man, represents us well, and I don't care if he is an oppositionist-he's good till he does something to be bounced for."

The private secretary withdrew. The president sat down at a walnut desk and opened a map of the moon, on which the volume and value of that satellite's principal products were illustrated in a coloured chart, while on the representation of the moon's surface itself corresponding colours indicated the regions producing the staples mentioned in the chart. The moon had just applied for a commercial treaty with the United States, and the question demanded of the president the gravest consideration, in the light of the productive capacity of the territories under American control.

At this point a messenger of Australian extraction entered, with a card.

"Show him in," said the president.

A minute later the Secretary of the Treasury appeared.

"I have just heard from the Secretary of State," said he. "The importers of the Transvaal will be anxious for this treaty, but there will be bitter opposition in Brazil."

"Well, they will have a chance to talk when the treaty goes before the Senate for ratification. Curious, isn't it, that after all the bitter fight which the House made at the end of the nineteenth century against the infringement of its prerogatives regarding revenue legislation, it should have come to yield so completely to the Senate in everything, as it does now?"

"Yes; did you notice how many bills were introduced in the Senate yesterday? two thousand three hundred and sixty."

"How many in the House?" asked the president.

"Fourteen. Speaker Smith told me last night that the members of the House didn't think it worthwhile to introduce bills any more; the Senate would kill them regardless of party, unless they favoured the millionaires, and bills of the latter kind always get introduced into the Senate first."

"By the way, how is Smith's senatorship fight coming on?"

"Oh! between ourselves, he has no show, and he knows it. Why, old man Pluterson, of Calcutta, is running against him, and they say he has bought up the whole East India Legislature."

"A blamed shame!" said the president; "but let's get to business. Who's a good man to negotiate this Moonish treaty?"

"Much Tin, of Pekin."

"Why?"

"Because he is rich enough to be beyond temptation, and honest enough to be a decent sort of a fellow when he isn't tempted."

"Let's see—isn't he vice-president of the Earth and Mars Ether Fast Line?"

"Yes."

"Then I guess he's rich enough for us. I think his grandfather held a controlling interest in that solid concern when it started."

"He's out inspecting the line somewhere, now."

"Any idea where?"

"I think he will be in Mars tonight."

"Telegraph and ask him how soon he can be in Washington."

"I don't think I can get off a despatch before tomorrow-a comet has interrupted the electric current for twelve hours, and is only half-way across its path."

"Oh! then the mail will reach him in time. I'll get Jack to write to him, so that the letter will catch him as he stops in the Moon on his way back."

The president pressed a knob twice, and Jack reappeared.

"Jack, write to the Hon. Much Tin, care American Minister to the Moon, asking him to wait there for a special commission from me, and for further instructions."

Jack retired. Half an hour later the Secretary of the Treasury also went home.

The Australian messenger brought in another card. It read "Weber Lockmore."

"Show him in!" again said the president. "Well, young man," said he, to the new arrival, "I have just half an hour to give you today. What can I do for you?"

"You have now been in office long enough to know your ground pretty thoroughly, and I want an interview."

"I supposed so." They seated themselves on opposite sides of a desk and the Washington correspondent immediately opened fire with questions.

"First, Mr. President, tell me the civil service reform outlook."

"Civil service reform," said the president, "has abolished one ancient maxim: 'To the victors belong the spoils.' It must yet abolish another; namely: 'To the Senate belong the spoils.'"

"Wait a moment, Mr. President. Do you regard the first maxim as entirely abolished?"

"I do, so far as its power for evil is concerned. It has, however, a power for good which must be recognized. In fact, there are very few, if any, doctrines to be found anywhere in the history of the world of thought, which have not a germ of truth at the heart of them. When, therefore, we speak of abolition, we cannot mean total abolition, and at the same time be rational. We can only abolish certain aspects or acceptations of a doctrine. The truth in it will live in spite of us, even if it has to take an entirely new shape to do it. Every doctrine or maxim represents some tendency, some craving of human nature, and in one sense is true. It may be but partially true in that it ignores some opposing but equally essential demand of human nature, and must be translated into some other mode of thought, as into a language, before it can be brought into consistency with that other demand; but that is the fault of mental language, not of the truth expressed by it."

"What, then, is the truth at the bottom of the old spoils doctrine?"

"Why, the truth that your newspapers are continually holding up to your readers, in your efforts to get good men to run for office: the truth that it is an honourable thing to serve one's fellow-men; that it is worth striving after; that the strivers should be rewarded in proportion to their merit in the strife. Now that we have got our principles clear, is it not becoming as clear that the abuse of those principles, and not their right use in harmony with the necessity of pure and effective service, is at the root of all the need of civil service reform?"

"I see, Mr. President. Now, tell me how far the maxim, 'To the victors belong the spoils' can, in your judgment, safely be applied to the public service as a permanent principle."

"It must be applied so far as to keep up the organization of opposing parties, and to stimulate public interest in the affairs of the government. To understand me, you must imagine the offices of the government divided into an upper and a lower stratum. Now, the best interest of the public service demands that that lower stratum shall be filled by persons who hold their positions during good behaviour, regardless of their politics; in other words, a permanent office-holding class. The original spoils doctrine, you will remember, made all these lower offices the prey of professional politicians. When the notion of civil service reform began to obtain, the spirit of the law would have protected the lower *stratum* of office-holders but for a term that was introduced into our political vocabulary to suit the occasion. This term was: 'offensive partisanship.' It was extremely elastic, and when executive supremacy passed from one party to another, the members of the defeated party who occupied the lower stratum were removed from their positions by the victorious members of the other party who had entered the upper stratum, on what were, in many cases, inadequate pretexts.

"An official might have conducted his office to the utmost satisfaction of all reasonable persons, but if he had exercised his right of free speech, or free press, to utter his partisan views in public, he was convicted of 'offensive partisanship' by superior officers, who united in their own persons the capacities of judge, prosecutor and jury. The subordinate official was beheaded, and his place was given to some even more 'offensive partisan,' in every rational sense of those two words, who belonged to the other party.

"But that application of the term was too absurdly unjust to last. It began to dawn on men's minds that a citizen did not forfeit his rights of citizenship—the rights to speak, to participate in campaigns, to manage them and to contribute to campaign funds-when he entered the public service. It was hard to root the idea out, because the vicious rotation principle held it in. One party would say: They turned us out when they had the power; now that we have the power, we will turn them out;' and thus history repeated itself with each party change, until it gradually began to be recognized that the interests of the public service were still suffering. Then a new principle was enunciated; namely, that a subordinate official who did not neglect his public duties, or abuse them for partisan purposes, was valuable in direct proportion to his participation in the duties of private citizenship, regardless of the party in behalf of which he performed the latter duties. At first, close watching was required, but gradually an unwritten law enacted itself-that official privileges must not be abused for party purposes, and official duties must not be neglected for party duties, any more than for any other cause."

"Are you hopeful, Mr. President, that this unwritten law will be universally respected in time?"

"I am."

"Why, then, may I ask, do you insist on making the upper stratum of public offices the permanent goal of party strifes? Why not make that stratum, as well as the lower one, exemplify civil service reform?"

"Because, my dear fellow, the upper stratum already exemplifies civil service reform. I have not yet told you where I would draw the line between the upper and the lower strata. It is a variable line, because parties and their principles vary. It is simply the line separating the offices in which party policy is carried out from those which have nothing to do with it."

"How, then, can you protect the office holders in the lower stratum by law?"

"I do not want any law. I want to do it by the pressure of enlightened public opinion, by unwritten law, by the right of the public to the best service that their officers can give them. Now, can't you see that when the people think a certain party's policy is demanded by the situation, the interests of the public require that the public service should be modified so far as to include men who will enforce that policy?"

"That is clear."

"Now, is it not equally clear that an office-holding aristocracy can be avoided by making the office-holders of the lower stratum feel that the office-holders of the upper stratum can turn them out if they neglect their duties or abuse their powers; that the offices do not belong to them, but to the public, and that their superiors, (who may, after any election, be new men with new ideas fresh from the people) have a motive to turn them out, if there is an excuse for doing so?"

"Mr. President, I think I understand you now."

"You can now see that civil service reform is not a question of laws, so much as one of the high or low tone of public opinion, and that it depends on the people themselves. The civil masters, and not the civil servants, make or mar governments."

"Now, Mr. President, tell me what you mean by the maxim: 'to the Senate belong the spoils.'"

"Simply this: that the president, no matter how desirous he may be of appointing good men to positions which are subject to confirmation by the Senate, must appoint only such men as the Senate is willing to confirm. Responsibility is divided between the President and the Senate, and each blames the other when things go wrong. I wish the Senate could be induced to surrender its Constitutional privilege of confirmation, but of course it will not. Civil service reform will never be accomplished until it does."

"What remedy can you suggest, Mr. President?"

"First, last, and all the time, the education of public opinion up to a plane at which good, honest, capable and independent men will always be elected to the Senate, and to the House. I say the House, because the president is forced to depend largely on members of the House for his knowledge of the character of those whom he appoints. Our territory now embraces the whole world, and may in time include other worlds, so the difficulty of one man doing more than acting on the recommendations of other men is likely to increase indefinitely. Secondly, the civil service must be reduced in depth, as it, by reason of continual territorial expansion, increases in extent. By this I mean that as many duties as possible must be continually referred back to the States.

"The States, in time, can distribute their duties among the country or other local district authorities, and the general principle must be pushed and urged everywhere, that individual and unofficial forces should do as much as possible of all that needs to be done, without the aid of any public authority or governmental machinery whatever. This principle must be the ultimate hope of every great country."

At this point the half hour which the president had at the correspondent's disposal expired, and another visitor arrived, evidently by previous engagement. The correspondent, of whom the reader will learn more hereafter, withdrew.

CHAPTER 2: GHOSTS GOSSIPING.

A bevy of ghosts sat gloomily around the edges of an extinct volcano's crater, on an undiscovered asteroid. One of them, an old man in form, with long white beard and a bald head that shone like a will-o'-the-wisp, sadly shook the will-o'-the-wisp from side to side and grumbled thus:

"I wish I could die a real death instead of a ghost of one. Soon there will be no place for us to go to. Hardly a day passes but an aerial and ethereal car lights on one of these asteroids and colonizes it with human beings. Look how they have settled and developed Jupiter, Mars, Venus, Saturn and the Moon. When I was alive on Earth, they used to tell me that a man couldn't live in the Moon or on any other planet; but he is doing so, all the same. He accommodates himself to his environment, just as the oysters and monkeys did before him. He is fruitful, and multiplies, and he is gradually taking possession of the solar system."

"When did he first extend his operations beyond his original planet?" asked another lazy old ghost, rubbing his eyes, and wondering in what century he was, anyhow.

"I think it was done just after the Americans conquered the rest of the world that was worth conquering," said the first ghost. "Nobody else would have thought of it. Do you remember when the Great Comet struck an asteroid out between here and Mars, and carried it toward the Earth?"

"Yes."

"Well, when it passed close to the Earth, some American explorers were wandering about the summits of the Himalayas, experimenting with telegraphy by means of upper air currents. As I understand the story, the solid nucleus of the comet struck the side of a peak on which twenty or thirty of them were holding a picnic, and broke it off, carrying it along in the air until it was farther from the Earth's surface than from that of the nucleus. Then it gravitated to the surface of the latter, and the picnic party were borne along the comet's path. The fog was so thick that they didn't know where they were for forty-eight hours. Two or three chemists in the party analyzed the soil, and found in it all the constituents needed to sustain life, animal and vegetable. They had some canned vegetables among their provisions, and they planted the seeds of these in the soil of the comet.

"The electricity with which the nucleus was charged caused a much more rapid growth of vegetation than takes place in the Earth-you remember how feeble the electricity is there-and they had a truck patch in full productiveness before they got into the neighbourhood of the Moon. The comet struck the Moon more directly than it struck the Earth, and stopped there. The party was shaken off and lodged on the Moon's surface, which they at once began to explore. They had provided themselves, for their mountain explorations, with instruments very sensitive to electric currents, and with the aid of these they soon detected a current flowing in the direction of the Earth. Then they determined to try to communicate with the Earth by intercepting the current. They repeated the following message a number of times:

"'We are in the moon; do you understand us? We are in the moon; do you understand us?'

"The current reached a wire on the plains of Russia, and the operators at the lonely country station thought some one of their number insane. They tried to find out who the insane operator was, but they could not trace the message to any terrestrial telegraph office. Then they agreed to telegraph: 'Hello, moon!' simultaneously from a hundred or so offices. Thirty or forty concurred so exactly as to affect the moon-bound current, and a conversation was opened. The scientists were told that animal life was not impossible, after all, outside of the Earth's atmosphere, for the electricity was so strong that it could be brought into play upon the moon's surface to make oxygen, nitrogen and carbonic acid gas, by developing, in proper proportions, the rapid cultivation of plants and herbs that give off these gases.

"An American inventor soon improved the ordinary electric air-car, so as to admit of its being steered outside of the Earth's atmosphere, and in a few months the overcrowded plains of Earth were losing population by thousands. The moon was rapidly settled up, then Venus, then Mars, then Jupiter, then Saturn, and now the asteroids. I don't think they have discovered this one yet, but there's no telling when they will."

A weary groan ran through the conclave of ghosts at the growing spirit of irreverence for old objects of awe.

"Why, when I was a man," said one who wore the aspect of a priest of the middle ages, "they were afraid of the planets-thought they af-

63

fected the fortune of men. One man was born under a lucky star, another under a malign star, etc."

"What worries me is the question what we are going to do about it," growled a lank ghost who had been silent heretofore.

"How many years have you old chaps been sitting here?" chirped a frisky young ghost, who suddenly made his appearance in the midst of the group, without asking anybody's—beg pardon, any ghost's—leave.

"What else are we to do," asked the ghost of the middle ages.

"Do? why, do as I did; hang around and watch your chances to occupy the bodies of newborn babies."

"Merciful heavens!" said the long-bearded ghost, jumping up. "I never thought of that."

"The more fool you," said the irreverent young ghost. "Why, I am only off on a midnight call. My temple is asleep in Saturn yonder. I have lots of time yet, before morning."

The young ghost's suggestion made a profound impression, and the ghosts' convention adjourned, soon to try the experiment. One ghost took possession of a new born babe that was murdered in ten minutes by its unwedded mother. It found the ten minutes of life so pleasant, that, being of a benevolent disposition, it stationed itself at the gate of the largest cemetery in the United States, and advised every ghost that came out, after bidding farewell to its dead home, to go and get a new one. A few other benevolent ghosts did this elsewhere. Ghosts whose second bodies died early, found their third bodies sometimes more and sometimes less agreeable. Information of general interest spread rapidly among ghosts, and in the course of time every crowd of ghosts instinctively sought bodies of that constitution best suited to its members. For ghosts of a feather flock together.

CHAPTER 3: THE JINGOES OF JUPITER.

"I rise to ask the Administration," said a representative from the First Moon, in the Parliament of Jupiter, "whether it has any information on the subject of a proposed commercial treaty, now being negotiated between the United States of America and the inhabitants of the Moon that accompanies the planet controlled by that nation."

The buzz that followed the remark, from members from the First Moon of Jupiter, showed, that, whether the Administration had any information on the subject or not, the report was news to a great majority of the members. Many faces were turned in the direction of an old man, who wore side-whiskers, and sat on a front bench with his hat pulled down over his eyes. The hat well concealed a settled frown, which evidently became deeper when the inquiry was heard. At length the old man slowly rested his hands on the edge of the bench beside his thigh, and lifted himself to his feet. Then he cleared his throat, and coughed, and cleared his throat again. Then he began to speak, in a drawling, halting and unmusical fashion.

"The Administration—ahem! is not prepared to make public the information which it may—ahem!—happen to—possess on the subject of—of negotiations in progress. There are—ahem! usually—circumstances which render it inadvisable to be premature in announcing—the—ah! the progress of-ahem! well, I may say, incomplete arrangements-which may, when completed, affect the interests of this government."

After uttering these words, apparently with great difficulty, the old gentleman dropped down into his seat again, with the air of having silenced an impertinent obstructionist. But long before he was comfortably seated again, the impertinent obstructionist was on his feet. His delivery was brisk and decisive, and he resumed possession of the floor with an air of triumph.

"Is the House to understand the prime minister to say that he is in possession of the information for which I was so presumptuous as to ask?"

With an annoyed expression, the premier again went through the arising act, which, in his case, seemed to consist principally of unbending his legs. He said:

"I will simply state, that—the—ahem! the government positively declines to admit—"

The pauses were so long that there was time enough at each one for a member with a rapid delivery to interject a complete sentence, if he chose to do so. What the first speaker chose to interject was:

"To admit that it knows anything about the negotiations referred to."

"To admit—the gentleman from the First Moon—into its confidence." And he sat down again, this time with the air of saying: "I shan't get up again." The first speaker was on his feet in a second.

"I trust," said he, sarcastically, "it will please the distinguished gentleman to know that, personally, I am entirely satisfied with his reply—or, rather, with his refusal to reply-to a perfectly courteous and pertinent inquiry. The honourable gentleman has succeeded in impaling himself upon both horns of a particularly uncomfortable dilemma. For, if the Ministry has not been shamefully neglectful of its duty to protect Jupitern interests—which, of course, none of us of the Opposition would presume to insinuate—it must possess no inconsiderable amount of information on the subject referred to. But this House has the undoubted right to that information-at any rate this right should be undoubted. The entire Opposition, and apparently not a few ignored supporters of the Administration—to judge from the whispered inquiries I hear upon my left—are anxious to know whether the Administration itself prefers to be in the position of neglecting to observe and inform itself about negotiations between other nations which may involve Jupiter's interests, or to take the responsibility of refusing to trust the people, or the people's representatives, with the truth concerning those negotiations. Either horn is sharp enough to be exceedingly disagreeable to the Administration, but the latter horn is the one upon which the Administration may be tossed so high that its fall will be final."

The cries of "Hear, hear," and the other expressions of applause, created such a hubbub that it was several minutes before any individual speaker could make himself heard without the lungs of a stentor. The lungs of the premier were not of that variety, but the enthusiasm of the Opposition over the point that their leader had made, and the anxiety of the Administration party about the consequences of the debate, alike contributed to the general curiosity to hear what the premier had to say, and the noise ebbed gradually. In the same halting manner as before, he said:

"If the honourable member from the First Moon does not know that there are matters at stake which are of far more concern to the Jupitern nation than commercial negotiations between the United States of America and its moon, it is high time that he undertook to inform himself better. He has seen fit to impeach the sufficiency of the Ministry's sense of responsibility to the people, because the Ministry refused to admit its responsibility to him. This is a trick which the gentleman, when he is older, will find to be older still than he is. Such tricks are not necessary, however, to bring the Ministry to a sense of what it owes the people. It may be a surprise to the gentleman from the First Moon, but it is nevertheless a fact, that a much more respectful mode of inquiry on his part would have been an equally effectual, and a much more prompt, means of securing the information which, I perceive, many members of this House desire, as he does, to obtain.

The Ministry deems it proper to give that information in a general way, and to withhold the details.

"The Ministry freely makes known to the House the fact that negotiations are in progress between the United States and its Moon, with a view to a commercial treaty; that their progress has been closely watched by this government from the beginning; that, so far, nothing has occurred to indicate a disposition on the part of either party to encroach on Jupitern rights, and that, consequently, this government has, so far, had no cause to interfere. The Ministry has the utmost confidence in the people, and is candid enough to make public such information as the people's best interests call for. It assumes, however, that the confidence is not all on one side; that the people, in their turn, have confidence in the Ministry; that they have, in expression of that confidence, entrusted it with the conduct of the details of management; and that they do not desire to burden themselves with these details, or to burden their servants with the added responsibility of continually explaining these details to partisan obstructionists. This is the position of the Ministry, and it is willing to stand or fall, according to the results of this policy."

It was evident, from the applause that broke out as the premier sat down, and from the nods which his supporters gave each other, that his reply was satisfactory, not only to the fair-minded of both parties in matter, but also to the sticklers for the maintenance of dignity in manner. The member from the First Moon was too shrewd a politician not to recognize the favourable impression which the reply made on most of those around him, so he at once reflected that degree of satisfaction in his own person. When he arose to speak again, his manner was so mollified as to be positively sugary, if not reverential.

"Nothing is farther from my thoughts, because nothing is less desired by my constituency, than the embarrassment of the Ministry by inquiries which cannot properly be answered. For myself, I am free to confess that I am satisfied with the courteous explanation which the venerable Premier has given the House, but, in the interests of those who are more radical than myself, and for whom I am reluctantly obliged to speak on this occasion, I would inquire if there are not grounds to suspect an intention on the part of the United States Government to annex the Moon, and whether the evidences of a desire to exceed the bounds of the planet to which that government is now confined are not to be regarded as dangerous to Jupitern interests."

The interest excited by this question showed itself in the profound silence with which the reply of the premier was awaited. But he only said:

"This government has received no evidence of any such intention on the part of the United States Government."

In a voice tremulous with the perception of an opportunity, the inquiring member said:

"The Opposition has such evidence." (Sensation.) "I have in my pocket a dispatch from a personal friend, now visiting Washington, the Capitol of the United States of America, stating that he knows of a formidable secret organization, the object of which is the extension of American power to the Satellite of that planet."

Immediately, a young and sharp-faced Administration member popped up, and said:

"A secret organisation of private citizens is not the government."

"But it is large enough to make its influence felt with the government; it includes a majority of the United States Senate, and it is only a question of time when it will include a majority of the House also, by those methods of purchase with which students of American institutions are familiar."

"I would like to ask the honourable member from the First Moon a question," remarked the sharp-faced orator.

"Ask it."

"If it was right for the people of Jupiter to conquer the Moons of Jupiter, to one of which the honourable member is accredited, is it wrong for the people of the United States to conquer and annex the solitary moon attached to that planet?"

"I am very glad," said the Opposition leader, "that the gentleman asked me that question. As I interpret the unwritten code of the rights of national extension, it is right, from an American standpoint, for that country to extend its domain. True patriotism should inspire every American to join the secret order referred to, to demand legislation favourable to its purposes, and to fight for them. But exactly the same rule of patriotism requires us to resist those purposes as calculated to interfere with our own similar purposes of gradual and indefinite extension. It is our duty not to wait till America starts out for a conquest of the moon, but to interfere at the earliest symptoms of close commercial relations. For the great nation that establishes such relations with a small nation will sooner or later absorb it politically, if given a chance."

The premier here arose, and interrupted him with: "It is our duty to respect the rights of these small nations to independence and self-government. The people of the Moon have as much right to govern themselves as we have to govern ourselves, and far more than we have to govern them."

The Opposition leader resumed: "I am again glad to have been interrupted. I hold, Mr. Speaker, that the right of self-government, as to personal liberty and property, is separable from the right of self-government in the choice of national allegiance. I hold that, when we subdue a world, respecting the private rights of its citizens, and giving them the benefits of Jupitern associations, Jupitern influence, Jupitern civilization, and Jupitern institutions generally, we are doing them a kindness in saving them from themselves, so far as they themselves would choose a different and inferior object of national allegiance. Do we not give them a Provincial Parliament for the conduct of their local affairs? Are they not as well off in that respect as they were before we subdued them? Are they not immeasurably better off in every other respect? Why, sir, it seems to me that the blindness of those who ignore the advantages of such a policy is insane! Their ignorance incapacitates them from the proper performance of governmental duties. That is the charitable side of it. A more uncharitable man than myself, Mr. Speaker, would call such a policy unpatriotic to the point of treason."

These words, impressively delivered, stirred up a tempest of applause. In fact, there was something in the manner of the orator which commanded a hearing, and smoothed the way for assent to the thing heard. He paused and looked all around him, and saw members clambering on benches, and on each other's shoulders, and waving their hats and handkerchiefs as they cheered. It was another opportunity, and he utilized it. He raised his voice, and its seductive and penetrating tones were heard ringing out above the buzz and roar of the assemblage.

"The time has come to arraign this Administration for its failure to guard Jupitern interests in other worlds, its miserable neglect of the means of information as to what is going on in those worlds that may imperil Jupitern interests, and its stubborn refusal to recognize the principles that should direct its conduct in any event."

The tempest of cheers broke out again, and yells of "Resign! Resign!" were dinned into the ears of the premier. He sat perfectly still, with bowed head, with hat over his eyes, as before, and with his frown deepened till the lines extended around the sides of his face. An anxious adherent took him by the arm and shook him, shouting in his ear, in a stage whisper: "Reply! Reply!"

The Opposition orator, still on his feet, looked eagerly in the direction of the premier, and said nothing. As his pause was prolonged, others looked. Many members had arisen from their seats, and were crowding around the premier with anxious faces. At length one of them motioned the rest back, and the confused buzz grew louder.

Five minutes later the premier's body was borne out amid an awed hush. The old man was deaf to applause, hisses and other Jupitern expressions of opinion forevermore. Five weeks later a fleet of electric ethereal ships bore an army of one hundred thousand Jupiterns in the direction of the moon, and Parliament was engaged in fitting out another army to follow it.

Chapter 4: Venus Seeks Revenge.

No sooner had the Venusian Minister to Jupiter notified the Emperor of Venus that an army of Jupiterns had started to invade the moon, than that potentate summoned a meeting of his advisers. Handing the telegram to each one in turn, he asked if the welfare of the Empire seemed to demand any action.

"It occurs to me," said the Minister of War, "that now is the time for revenge."

"On whom?"

"America."

"What reason have we to seek revenge on America?" asked the Minister of Finance, who was conservatively disposed.

"If there is any one here," said the Minister of War, "who does not intuitively feel that America is our enemy, it is useless to reason with him. Did not America drive us out of the world?"

"A few of us, but not many."

"Does not every patriotic Venusian feel, in his heart, that the few who were actually driven out by America represent the great bulk of our younger generation, in their wish that justice be done to them? Have we not an indefinable sense of wrong, received at the hands of America, as though the spirits of some who have suffered much from those avaricious aggressors had passed into our bodies at birth?"

"Come! come!" said the emperor, "let this wrangling cease. What does the Minister of War wish?"

That official, being directly appealed to, proceeded to justify his desire for a policy that would enable him to magnify his office. "I wish," said he, "to give counsel that will be to the national advantage, when I say that this is an excellent opportunity to feed fat the ancient grudge which many of us bear America. We cannot conquer America alone. Mars has tried it, Saturn has tried it, Neptune has tried it, and with what result? All have failed. But now that Jupiter is engaging America in a war, we can attack the same nation, divide its energies, perhaps conquer it, and control a Hemisphere, leaving Jupiter in possession of the other. Thus we will be revenged."

"There is another consideration," remarked the Minister of Public Morals, "which is of great weight with me just here. Should we succeed, as is probable under the circumstances, we can capture enough American women to make good the growing deficiency in our female population. Has your Imperial Majesty read the new census statistics? There are now only half as many women in Venus as there are men. There are four hundred thousand women in Venus who have five husbands, one million who have four, two million who have three, and four million, eight hundred thousand who have two. I am convinced that our polygamy system is evil, and that one husband for each wife is the proper proportion. I have refrained from expressing this opinion heretofore, because of the impracticability of remedying the present state of affairs.

"But this war between America and Jupiter offers us the opportunity we want. It is the only war between two other planets which has offered us a prospect of successful interference. The result of America's wars with Saturn, with Mars, with Neptune, could be foreseen by impartial powers. We foresaw it. The result of the war just declared cannot be foreseen. The two nations are so nearly equal in power that, without the interference of a third party, a long and bloody struggle is inevitable; with it, the fighting will be brief and decisive. If the peace party here can rise above country in this crisis, they will see an opportunity for the establishment of universal peace at the cost of a little self-sacrifice on our part. We fight, we win, we divide the American world with Jupiter. We make a Peace League with Jupiter, and the two strongest nations in the Solar System can influence the rest to join them."

"That is well said," remarked the emperor, while the Minister of Finance frowned; for, peace man as he was, he would have felt just a little delight in being able to report such a deficit in the treasury as precluded the idea of war. Unfortunately, there was no such deficit, and he could not dissuade his colleagues.

71

That quick, impulsive temperament, for which the Venusians are noted, is of great value in making preparations for war. The sudden recall of the American Minister from the Venusian Capitol to assume the Secretaryship of War was converted into a pretext, by an artificial construction, as an insult. An apology was demanded of the United States, but the president took no notice of the demand, and, in his haste to fill the vacancy before giving his attention to the war details that might make him forget it, appointed a citizen of German descent. The Venusians were furious, and the emperor had no difficulty in raising a large volunteer army to man the electric transports. No time was lost in concluding terms of alliance with Jupiter, contemplating the equal division of whatever territory should be conquered. The Jupitern authorities, however, knew that this arrangement would not be agreeable to either the voters at home nor the soldiers abroad, so they aimed to keep it secret till the close of the war. No officer below the rank of general was permitted to know it.

But a war correspondent of one of the New York daily papers got hold of it. His private electric car happened to cross a current, over which the general commanding the Jupitern Army was sending a message to the premier. An apparatus in his car registered it, and he halted long enough to turn aside into the current itself, and travel far enough in it to read the completion of the message.

It was a stroke of luck, but it was the making of him. He became famous from New York to Rome. At the first great battle, in the neighbourhood of the moon, the Jupiterns captured a brigade of Americans, with several thousand copies of the article containing the message, and the Jupitern soldiers read it eagerly.

CHAPTER 5: VENUS BECOMES A REPUBLIC.

Among the captured Americans were a few special agents of the War Department, chiefly detailed for spy duty. The Secretary of War, desiring to ascertain as much about the enemy's purposes as possible, had assigned some of these agents to regiments from sundry doubtful States. The political complexion of these regiments had been carefully canvassed, and the general of the army had been privately instructed to order them to the post of honourable danger, whenever there was a chance of reducing an adverse majority, or a dangerous minority, of the other party's votes, so as to ensure the endorsement of the Administration by the State in question at the next election.

The spies assigned to these regiments were generally men who were not in robust health, and therefore more likely to be exchanged, if taken prisoners of war. They were informed of the destination of their regiments, and were under instructions to surrender, individually, when the fight became lively; find out all they could, while prisoners, and then press their claims for an exchange, or use their discretion if they thought of any plan for misleading the enemy.

Some of these fell into the hands of the Jupiterns, and some were captured by the Venusians. One of the former heard his guards indignantly denouncing the secret agreement that the conquered territory should be divided equally between Venus and Jupiter. He immediately began to talk about his immense stock farm in one of the Asteroids, and what a fine country it was, though thinly settled.

The Jupitern soldiers seemed to take an interest in the Asteroid business, and the guards and others listened to the spy in eager silence. The mutinously inclined inquired if there was any political organization in his Asteroid.

"None," he answered.

"They are not American dependencies?"

"Some few are, but this is not, and others equally fine are as independent."

"Would you like to go back to your stock farm?"

"Very much."

The next day the spy was told that it had been decided to transport certain American prisoners to the Asteroids, and that he was among the number. The mutineers, however, had secretly decided upon this, and not the commanders of the army. The spy's glowing accounts of several Asteroids had suggested a scheme of wholesale desertion to the disaffected. A few hours sufficed for the arrangements. At a given signal, the objectors to the policy of equal division with Venus were to seize the electric transports, or as many of them as they could control, and start immediately to the thinly settled Asteroids, where they would set up an independent government, and fight for it if necessary.

Several of the spies captured by the Venusian wing of the enemy's forces no sooner learned the urgent need of Venus for a reinforcement of the female population, than they began to remember the time when they were attaches of the American Minister to Jupiter. The beauty of the Jupitern women was praised in unmeasured terms, and it was asserted, in the most emphatic manner, that there were many more women in Jupiter than men.

The Venusian wing of the army had been severely handled, and the soldiers were sufficiently discouraged to listen, with unusual interest, to anything that proposed an abandonment of the American invasion. When the news of a vast mutiny in the Jupitern army arrived, the Venusian generals held a council of war. The desertion of two-thirds of the Jupitern army did not look promising, so far as prospects of the conquest of American territory were concerned.

"I have it!" said one little marshal, impatiently. "Let us invade Jupiter, and capture the women we want there."

Doubts were expressed as to whether there were not enough men in Jupiter to repel an invasion. A copy of the last Jupitern census was consulted, and elaborate estimates made as to the number of able-bodied citizens who were likely to leave for the Asteroids as soon as they heard of the mutiny, in order to suppress it.

So momentous a question could not, of course, be decided without communicating with the emperor. He again summoned his advisers, and laid the situation before them. A majority favoured an invasion, while a minority stood with the emperor for the abandonment of the entire expedition.

The incendiary Republican press broke out the next day into appeals for revolution; for the overthrow of the Empire, and the instalment of a government that would represent the people, and aim to supply their wants.

By noon a howling mob surrounded the Imperial palace, and the emperor, after a few unsuccessful attempts to force the populace from behind their barricades, was forced to resign, and consent to the formation of a Constitutional Republic, of which the Minister of War was to be president. Another appeal was made for volunteers, this time for the Jupitern expedition. The people responded with great enthusiasm, and the army in the vicinity of the moon received orders to move in the direction of Jupiter, assured that reinforcements would follow at the earliest possible date.

CHAPTER 6: DIPLOMATIC CORRESPONDENCE WITH MERCURY.

Having defeated Jupiter and Venus in war, and got them into war with each other, there sprung up a variety of opinions at Washington as to what the United States ought to do next. There was a certain portion of the young and warlike element who made no secret of their desire to have a war with Mercury. It was the only important planet which the United States had not thrashed, and as it is not a very big planet, there was no question in their minds that the United States could thrash it. But just at this time there was no occasion whatever to pick a quarrel with Mercury.

Comparatively little was known at Washington about the people of Mercury. Commerce was restricted, and the king of that planet did not encourage the American Minister to his Court to make any researches with a view to increasing it. The Mercurians occasionally increased their wealth by sending out purely national expeditions, but they aimed rather to colonise desirable localities, than to bind themselves closer to other nations. The chief reason for this conservative policy was the fact that the people of Mercury were enormously rich, already. The humblest citizen was wealthy enough to be a member of the United States Senate. But the desire for wealth increases with the possession of it, and hence it happened that the King of Mercury, on learning that the able-bodied populace of Venus had chiefly gone off in several armies to fight Jupiter, decided to send an army of occupation to Venus.

The American Minister promptly notified the President, at Washington, of the appearance of the Mercurian Army of Occupation, ready to start for Venus. The Secretary of State lost no time in communicating with the king, by ethereal telegraphic currents, to the following effect:

Reported to this government that you intend to occupy Venus, in absence of Venusian armies. This government, having defeated Venus in war, claims first right to occupy territory, and will consider such action on your part as unfriendly to the United States.

The reply was as follows:

The King of Mercury declines to recognize your right to prevent others from occupying Venus, if you do not choose to occupy that planet yourself.

The Secretary of State at once sent, as a rejoinder:

The United States will take immediate measures to enforce its rights.

The next day the American Minister to Mercury was recalled.

CHAPTER 7: SENATOCRACY AT WASHINGTON.

One of the lower classes of Mercury's citizens sat in front of his cottage reading an evening paper. On the ground at his feet sat his four-year-old son, a youth of an inquiring mind, playing with several gold marbles. Occasionally he would look up at his father's face, and seeing the parent too much absorbed to notice him, resume consideration of the marbles. The child, however, soon wearied of his toys, and hurled the gold marbles into the street, taking advantage of the passing of a foraging cat to throw one so as to strike the animal in the side, the cat sniffed at the marble, and turned up his nose whiskers in disgust.

"Father," said the child, "what are you reading?"

"The war news, my son."

"What is the war news?"

"The army is coming home, my son."

"What is the army coming home for?"

"To keep the American army from invading Mercury."

"Where is our army now, father?"

"In Venus."

"What is the army there for, father?"

"To take possession of the planet, my son."

"What is the American army coming here for?"

"To take possession of this planet."

"Well, if it's right for us to take possession of Venus, isn't it right for them to take possession of us?"

"No, my son."

'Why not?'

"Run into the house and talk to your mother, my son."

The boy was silent for several minutes; then, as if a thought had struck him, he suddenly looked up again.

"Father, does Venus belong to us?"

"No, my son."

"Will it belong to us, if we get it?"

"I am afraid we won't get it, my son."

"Will it belong to the United States?"

"No!"

"Not even if they get it?"

"No."

"Why not?"

"Because it belongs to the people of Venus."

"Then it won't belong to us either, even if we get it?"

"No."

"Then we will be stealing, won't we?"

76

"You will understand these things better when you are older, my son. Now run away and play."

"I don't want to play. I want to hear about Venus."

"Good gracious!"

"What's the matter, father?"

The matter was that the father had read a later dispatch than anything else in the paper, announcing the sudden withdrawal of the American army from the atmosphere of Mercury.

"That is very strange," said the Mercurian.

"What is very strange?"

"I wonder if they can mean to back out in as disgraceful a manner as that?" mused the Mercurian, rather to himself, than as if taking any notice of the child.

"Who back out, father?"

"The Americans."

"Are the Americans going to back out?"

"It looks like it."

The dispatch which had excited the surprise of the Mercurian father was as follows:

It is reported that the President of the United States, in obedience to strong pressure exerted by the Senate, has ordered the withdrawal of the entire American army from the vicinity of Mercury.

That the Senate should have so much power will surprise foreigners, whose knowledge of American government is restricted to simple acquaintance with the Constitutional machinery of that planet. The original theory of American government was that the legislative, the executive and the judicial branches should be coequal. The Senate, which is the wealthy and aristocratic branch of the legislative third of the government, has virtually become the supreme power.

The president is generally under obligations to Senators for campaign funds, the Supreme Court is a sort of shelf for retired senators, and the House of Representatives bows to the expressed or implied will of the Senate in everything. This subserviency has been brought about by the judicious encouragement of the idea that one term in the House is enough for one man, and that he should stand aside and give somebody else a chance.

Thus nobody is a member of the House long enough to acquire experience that will raise him above mediocrity, and every ex-representative is sent to the State Legislature by one of the senators from his State, to whom he is supposed to be eternally grateful, when the time for a Senatorial election comes round. Thus senators remain in the Senate as long as they choose to stay there, and then retire themselves as Judges.

As the Senate confirms the president's appointments, he can do nothing without their consent; and as they ratify commercial treaties, by which the tariff, the source of all revenue, is regulated, they have usurped legislative, executive, and, indirectly, judicial powers, and the other branches of the government are but figure-heads.

In short, the senators are the bosses of the American planet.

Chapter 8: Weber Lockmore's Journal.

I had been appointed Minister to Mercury, in recognition of my services in discovering the secret agreement of the Jupiterns and Venusians to divide equally such American territory as they should conquer, and publishing it in the newspaper which I represented as war correspondent. When I was recalled, on the prospect of war between America and Mercury, I was engaged in an investigation which I very much desired to complete before returning home. I had therefore postponed my departure, and was just ready to start, when the news came that, through the influence of the Senate, the American Army had been ordered away from Mercury.

Just after my arrival, I had bought and paid for a large block of stock in a company that had been formed for the mining and preparation of Mercurian gold for the American market. Extensive new deposits had been discovered, far too large for the needs of the Mercurian market, which was already greatly overstocked.

The king and his ministers were likewise stockholders in this company, and one day they called a secret meeting of the Board of Directors, and, without taking a stock vote, ordered the issue of 100,000 new shares.

I inquired why this had been done, and what disposition was to be made of the money which I naturally supposed would be received for this new stock, but could get no satisfaction. All the large stockholders seemed to regard me with suspicion. Finally I hunted up the janitor of the king's council chamber, and by promising to send him certain American curiosities which he was ambitious to possess, but unwilling to pay for out of his hoardings, induced him to search with me in the heaps of paper removed from the king's waste basket, for memoranda regarding the meeting.

I was fortunate enough to find a memorandum containing a list of names, opposite each of which was a number. The sum of the numbers was the amount of new stock secretly issued. The names I recognized as those of most of the members of the United States Senate.

I immediately suspected that the stock was issued to the members of the United States Senate as a bribe, or rather in consequence of an agreement, in fulfilment of which they had forced the withdrawal of the American army and disgraced the United States in the eyes of the whole solar system. To satisfy myself, however, I visited the company's office and demanded the book containing the stubs of the receipts given when stockholders paid for their stock. As a stockholder, I had a right to see it. The treasurer, however, on the pretext of difficulty in finding it, delayed handing it to me, and I heard him tear something out.

I pretended not to notice this, made a routine examination of the book, and returned it, apparently satisfied. The stubs showed that the receipts for the new stock had been torn out, and the hurried manner in which this was done was registered by the adhesion of several corners of the receipts themselves to the stubs. I had to see another janitor, but the next morning I had those crumpled receipts. They contained no names, but were simply endorsed "U.S.S." I put them carefully away, and in a few hours completed my preparations for returning to America, paid my parting respects to the king, and left in a special electric dummy car for the Earth.

The discovery that the members of the Senate had betrayed the nation's honour filled me with shame, and I sat for some hours in my luxurious travelling apartment, meditating on the disgrace to which I would have to bear testimony, and wondering whether the State Department would publish such a scandal to the world. As for myself, I was resolved on my own course.

I would communicate my discovery to the Secretary of State, and if he feared to publish the facts, I would, with the proceeds of the sale of my own stock (which would make me as rich as any man on Earth, and nearly as rich as a Mercurian nobleman), buy up one or more influential newspapers, publish the whole story, and demand the abolition of the United States Senate by Constitutional amendment, and the election of Representatives in Congress on the merits of the candidates. I anticipated a bitter fight from the rich men of the Senate, but now that I was as rich as any of them, I determined to appeal to the "common sense of most" for the concentration of the appointing power in the President, and the legislative power in the House of Representatives.

My ethereal journey proceeded several weeks without interruption or event. But one day while I was asleep and dreaming of the power I should wield when I controlled several great daily newspapers, a sudden shock awoke me, and with a nightmarish fear that the car was tumbling through space, I arose and hastened to investigate.

CHAPTER 9: HENRYGEORGIA.

A small break in the machinery of the electric car had compelled a stoppage; fortunately we were in the vicinity of a stray asteroid, which, in the remote past, had cut loose from its fellows between Mars and Jupiter, and, drawn by some temporary source of attraction, had located its orbit between the Earth and Venus. The Ethereal Fast Line, on which I was travelling, had located a flag station upon it, but it was little used, although the company ran its cars so as to cross the asteroid's orbit at a point at which that body itself was due at the time of crossing.

A peculiar people inhabited this asteroid. There was but little communication between them and the United States, and the Jupiterns and Venusians had even less to do with them, while the inhabitants of Mercury and Mars ignored them entirely. The prevailing notion was that the population of this asteroid consisted of Socialists. The asteroid itself is known as Henrygeorgia.

While awaiting the completion of the repairs needed by the car, I strolled about the neighbourhood of the station, in the hope of meeting some of the inhabitants. I was not disappointed. I encountered an intelligent farmer, whose Yankee ancestry was evident from his fondness for asking questions and his sincere desire to hear the answers. Having given him all the information consistent with prudence concerning my past, my present, and my intentions for the future, I shut down the answer factory and opened upon him with an overproduction of questions.

"Your countrymen, I infer, are followers of Henry George, the prophet of San Francisco."

"Yes; we owe much of our prosperity and happiness to Henry George."

"You are Socialists, I suppose?"

"Socialists? By no means. We are Individualists of the most pronounced type. Why should we be Socialists?"

"I had supposed that land nationalization was practicable only through a system of taxation which would raise an enormous surplus revenue, unless the State cultivated and used the land as well as owned it. Either alternative would be Socialism, for the necessity of finding ways to spend the surplus revenue would develop a variety of governmental functions that would ultimately amount to the same thing."

"You are mistaken. David Dudley Field's celebrated objection to Henry George's theory has been obviated. We have no surplus revenue and no undue extension of the powers of government at the expense of Individualism."

"Pray, how was this accomplished, consistently with the realization of Henry George's ideas?"

"His idea was the concentration of taxation upon land, so that the natural opportunities for labour should not be limited, while the demand for those opportunities was unlimited in growth. The subordinate idea that everybody should pay rent to the government is by no means essential to the main principle.

"Our ancestors, as you have probably heard, colonized this asteroid on a Henry George platform, following him blindly, not only where he was right, but where he was wrong; ignoring the objections which he ignored, for the sake of the Utopia which he thought not inconsistent with a large surplus revenue. Socialism came, and Individualism went. Every foot of land was taxed, and corruption reigned supreme, as a result of the necessity of spending or stealing the contents of a plethoric public treasury. Our intellectual and moral development was checked, halted, and ultimately reversed. Wealth accumulated and men decayed. At length it occurred to our thinkers, in a lucid interval, that we should do less for man and more for men, and they took a new departure. It proved a success, and we have departed farther and farther from that era of blighting corruption ever since.

"This new departure was in the direction of economy—a revenue limited to the actual need of a government whose functions were restricted by the rule that governmental powers should not be given the benefit of any doubt whatsoever; the presumption being that the government had no right to do anything that could possibly be done without its aid."

"That is radical," said I. "I should imagine that with such a principle once adopted there would ultimately be very little use for a government after all."

"That is true—we have very little use for any power of government whatsoever. Our government's principal duty is to represent us in our external relations, and as we have very few external relations, we require very few officials. Our laws are so respected that they administer themselves, so far as we are concerned."

"Pray tell me how this doubtless admirable state of affairs was brought about. What was the new departure which you spoke of?"

"We found that a one-sided application of Henry George's theories sacrificed the moral benefit that comes from the sense of independence stimulated by land holding in the mind of the holder. The first question was, how to re-establish that sense of independence and encourage it, without sacrificing the benefits of a reasonable theory which prevented land monopolization.

"The answer was, the fixing by law of a certain area of land as the minimum taxable. As soon as it became understood that the holder of, say, less than ten acres was exempt from taxation, land broke up into holdings of less than ten acres as if by magic. Books on small farms had a boom, and the surplus revenue fell off at a rate that indicated that the solution of the difficulty was in sight.

"The next step was to tax unimproved land, rather than improved. The ten-acre minimum was repealed so far as absolutely idle land was concerned, and five acres was fixed as the minimum taxable area of pasture land."

"What are your laws regarding timber lands?"

"They are elastic. Local officials are authorized to regulate taxation on timber lands according to the demand and supply of timber, and to encourage timber culture by low tax rates, when necessary, upon land on which a crop of timber is planted. A discrimination is made in favour of the timber land holder who sells off a certain amount of timber a year, while the man who locks up timber land is taxed severely. The principle underlying our application of Henry George's doctrines is that the taxes should vary according to the area of a holding. In this district, for instance, ten acres is the minimum taxable, and between ten and twenty acres there is a uniform tax rate. Above twenty acres, however, the tax rate increases abreast of the area of the holding. The tax rate on a farm of thirty acres is fifty per cent heavier than it is on twenty acres or less."

"Whew! I guess you have no land monopolists in this asteroid."

"None, sir, and we don't want any."

"How do you arrange your taxation of building lots? Are they taxed in any special way?"

"They are assessed every year in accordance with the demand for land for building purposes in the vicinity, and when their assessed value reaches a certain sum per foot, they are taxed as building lots. An unimproved lot is then taxed more than an improved lot, and a badly improved lot more than a well improved lot. Sewer rents, water rents and gas rents are assessed on the lot holders who do not use sewer connections, city water or city gas, instead of those who do. A house of more than a certain number of rooms, with all sanitary improvements, and set back a minimum distance from the street, is exempt from taxation, provided its owner resides in it himself. If he owns two houses, he has to pay a tax on the one he does not occupy, and if he owns three, his tax rate is doubled; if four, it is tripled; if five, quadrupled, and so on. If he tries to evade the law by owning property in other folks' names, the law refuses to aid him in collecting rents, or to protect him against fraud on the part of his representatives in ownership.

"The effect of such a system, you see, is to discourage landlordism, squatterism, shantyism and bad sanitary conditions, for sewer and water and gas connections are furnished at low rates–in some cities for nothing. Individualism, independence, a respect for one's own rights, as well as the rights of others, and a wholesome jealousy of the powers of the government—all are encouraged by these laws. Our people read, and think, and vote intelligently, in the highest sense of the word, for their moral perceptions are cultivated to a degree of refinement commensurate with their superior importance."

"It seems to me," said I, "that you have drifted far away from Henry George, after all. Why should you call your world Henrygeorgia?"

"Because, although we seem to have improved upon Henry George, we have done so largely by applying one of his incidental suggestions to the evils otherwise inevitable as the result of his chief doctrine. He pointed out, more than once, that the old-fashioned way of taxing real property in a direct ratio to the degree of its improvement tended to discourage the spirit of improvement. On the other hand, taxation on the opposite principle encouraged improvement, and the more improvements the fewer the taxes. Thus it is always easy to keep down the surplus revenue. Henry George poisoned us unwittingly, but he gave us the antidote unwittingly."

"But, after all," said I, "what is the use of applying an anti-monopoly principle to land, when we have access to the entire Solar System? It was all very well for Henry George to write when men were still confined to the Earth, but surely there is more land available now than can ever be monopolised?"

"Certainly there is more land than can be monopoliaed, if Henry George's principles were applied everywhere. But they are not. A syndicate of your United States Senators can go and lock up a continent in Neptune any day. Every member of your Senate owns an asteroid now, and when your States multiply so that the number of your Senators increases still further, they may yet lock up the whole Solar System against the poor man who emigrates from Earth, and the squatter on a planet may be told to move on into the depths of space, and not to trespass on private property."

The flashing of a signal of electric light from the station where my car had halted for repairs warned me at this point that our interview was at an end. I bid the Henrygeorgian farewell, and in a few minutes was again whizzing through space.

CHAPTER 10: A POLITICAL REVOLUTION

I lost no time, on arriving in my native planet, in carrying into execution a plan on the attractions of which I had often dwelt in the early days of my journalistic experience, and which I had scarcely dared hope ever to realize. In fact, after I had attained a very fair standing in the profession, I had relegated this scheme to a place among the air-castles of my youth; satisfied with the realization of a more moderate ambition, which sought to teach the public, day by day, in plain but independent terms, the dangers and the duties of the hour, through the columns of a daily journal. When I found myself in a position to do this, I cared not that others who shared this opportunity with me failed to appreciate it.

I reflected that their indifference was no affair of mine, and that the thing of importance, to me, at least, was to make the best use of my time. I envied not the popular preacher who addressed a thousand or two of people once or twice a week, for I addressed tens of thousands of readers daily. Nor did I envy the author whose book is read by thousands, and who writes perhaps one book a year. But when I found that so long as I was only a salaried employee, I was, after all, not independent, but the slave of a proprietor, I also discovered that I was writing his opinions and not my own. It was all very well so long as his opinions and mine agreed, but when they were not in harmony, mine were not expressed and his were. So I longed again to realize the wild project of my youth to which I have referred.

This project, of course, was one requiring wealth for its fruition, but that quality never stops youthful projections. It was, in fact, the harmonious management of a chain of daily newspapers extending around the world. Now, by an unexpected result of my temporary engagement as a war correspondent, I found myself the possessor of a fortune that enabled me to accomplish this design.

I found intelligent people all over the world in a state of indignation at the as yet unexplained conduct of the Senate. No time was to be lost. By the free use of the cable and telegraph I obtained, within forty-eight hours, a controlling interest in one daily morning newspaper in each of the following cities: New York, Chicago, New Orleans, San Francisco, Pekin, Canton, Calcutta, Melbourne, Cape Town, Cairo, Constantinople, Rome, Berlin, St. Petersburg, Paris and London; and immediately assumed direction of the editorial policy of these sixteen journals.

I then sat down and wrote an exhaustive account of my discovery that the majority of the United States Senate had been bribed by the issue of stock to them without consideration, to force a disgraceful termination of the war with Mercury. I telegraphed this to each one of my sixteen newspapers, and gave a condensation of it to the Associated Press, Reuter's and other news agencies. I next prepared a leading article denouncing the United States Senate and demanding the amendment of the Constitution so as to abolish it and concentrate all executive power in the President, and all legislative power in the House of Representatives, holding each directly responsible to the people for the proper discharge of the duties assigned it.

This was put in type in the office of the New York Universe, and fifteen revises of it, or clean proofs, were taken. Each one of these was given to a member of the Universe staff, with instructions to each man to put the ideas into different language as far as possible without bad style. The fifteen approximations thus obtained were sent to the fifteen newspapers in other cities, to be used as the leading editorial article on the great sensation which they were all to contain.

It was in the midst of a fall campaign in which members of the House of Representatives and of the State Legislatures were to be elected. The existing Congress had been in extra session all the summer, and an investigation of the conduct of the Senate was in progress, bidding fair to produce the usual whitewashing result. Nobody seemed to know anything. The news from Mercury, however, told the story, and popular indignation at once reached a white heat. An angry crowd, composed not of lawless vagrants and adventurers, but of reputable and scandalized citizens, collected around the Senate wing of the Capitol at Washington, long before the hour of assembling, on the day of publication. A lawyer who had prepared a draft of the Constitutional amendments suggested, read them to the crowd and then thrust them into the hands of a scared senator who was trying to make his way to the Chamber. Mr. Senator had to promise to introduce, speak and vote for the amendments.

An army of messenger boys flew as fast as the crowd would let them, for the electric flying machines dotted the air in every quarter. Telegrams from all over the globe came in, advising the introduction of the amendments, and their adoption by Congress, and submission to the State Legislatures for ratification. The Senate was disposed to be stubborn at first, but the President, who expected to be re-elected and who had no objection to monopolizing the appointing power, told the senators individually in turn that he thought it inadvisable to tempt the populace to mob violence. At the mere hint of mob violence, the Senate of cowards agreed to the amendments. The House, of course, did what the Senate did, as it had done for many years.

From that day the campaign became a tidal wave movement all over the world. I devoted myself chiefly to the New York Universe, the London Fact, and the Calcutta Will of the People. I kept myself in constant communication with the other thirteen newspapers in my control, and all sixteen were daily engaged in stirring up the people to elect legislators that would ratify the amendments. For fear the rich senators would prevent their ratification by corruption, the sixteen newspapers urged the appointment of committees in every State to watch for evidences of corrupt methods, expose them, and prevent their success by appealing to public opinion and using money in every legitimate manner known to thorough political organizers.

The following are specimens of the editorial and campaign literature published from time to time during the autumn:

> The Senate ought to go. It has become the favourite resort of plutocrats. It has usurped the appointing power of the President, who, no matter how wise and good he may be, must nominate only such men as the Senate is willing to confirm. Every city has given its mayor, and every State its governor,

the power of appointment, with absolute independence of the body that formerly confirmed local nominations. The national government alone has adhered to the old worn-out plan of dividing responsibility.

As the power of appointment should be concentrated in the Presidential office, so the power of legislation should be concentrated in the popular body of Representatives. If they are not to be trusted without a check on their action, then the people themselves are not to be trusted.

But even if a check be needed now, it will not always be needed if the House is taught to do without it and take all the responsibility. When it is reduced to a question of fitness for trust, we are obliged to ask, 'Is the Senate to be trusted?' Not one man in the world can give but one answer to this question. If we are asked whether we will hereafter trust the Senate or the people, let us all answer, 'The People!'

Long before election day, it became so plain that every legislature would be favourable to the Constitutional amendments that many members of the Senate resigned in advance of the result. Nobody, as a rule, could be found to fill the vacancies.

The Constitutional amendments were ratified by three-fourths of the Legislatures within three months after the election. The King of Mercury, expecting a vigorous prosecution of the war from this result, made overtures for peace, offering an enormous sum of money as indemnity. Enough was accepted to pay off the national debt, and the rest was returned, with a message informing His Majesty that honest dealing by intelligent methods would thereafter suffice to secure the good will of the American people, and that venality was not our national failing.

CHAPTER 11: A HOUSE UNITED AGAINST ITSELF.

The Constitutional amendment abolishing the United States Senate proved highly beneficial to the public service. The President was the kind of man to appreciate his increased responsibility for the moral tone and business efficiency of the Executive departments, and his freedom from Senatorial dictation concentrated upon him the potential criticism of watchful public opinion. But before the first new Congress had been in session many weeks it became evident that the House of Representatives felt its vote. The aggressiveness of a party caucus when it finds itself in the majority for the first time for many years was feeble compared to the evident purpose of the House, when it discovered its power to exercise that power without restraint.

Desiring to get as strong a grip on patronage as possible, the representatives tried to establish an unwritten law compelling the president not only to consult them, but to defer entirely to them regarding appointments. The power of confirmation or rejection had, of course, been abolished with the Senate, but the Representatives depended on threats of the withdrawal of moral support, the passage of embarrassing statutes, and the refusal of legislation anxiously urged by the president, to bring him to terms, and every effort was made to deceive him regarding the character of persons recommended for appointment, in order to bring him into bad odour if he continued firm. The moral and intellectual tone of representatives elected in the era of Senatorial dictation had been so low that there was room for a great deal of reform in the character of the average congressman, and this reform had barely begun.

The president was kept much busier than usual writing veto messages. The old notion that anything could be done by Act of Congress seemed to be revived, and all sorts of foolish bills were pushed through on the log rolling plan. Never was the same lack of principle in recommending applicants for office, even when there was no desire to embarrass the Administration. A congressman would recommend a bad man for office just as readily as he would vote for a bad candidate on his own ticket, which is saying a good deal; and he would recommend two or more men for the same appointment without dreaming, or if he dreamed, caring, that his conduct was as heinous in morals as repeating at the ballot box.

The majority of the House of Representatives belonged to the Demagogue party, and were supposed, therefore, to be in full sympathy with the Administration. The Reprobates were without a leader, the Senate having been their stronghold. It was one of the emergencies in which the demand for a leader who is a leader indeed ignores all the minor aspirants, and seeks the man who has been ripening for years and biding his time. The Presidential campaign was approaching, and the Demagogues, president as the only hope of their continuance in power. Circumstances had required him to be so conservative that he had had no time to be aggressive, and his wise and conservative exercise of the veto power had rallied the Independent element of votes around him everywhere, so that his renomination was a foregone conclusion. The Reprobates had no issue at hand which the president did not represent better than any possible candidate of theirs. The result was that they had to make an issue or make no fight.

Their party leaders, all over the world, stood aghast, each one waiting for somebody else to speak and define the issue. Suggestions, large or small, were thankfully received, but for a time none came worth discussing.

At length, early in January of the Presidential election year, the issue appeared, and the man who made it appear was dragged out of what they called his obscurity by the leading politicians of the Reprobate party. As a matter of fact, however, he was eminent in the world of science. He was Alexander Beetlebrow, A.M., Professor of Biology in the University of Everest.

Professor Beetlebrow, in a lecture to his classes, had taken occasion to air his views on heredity. In the course of one of these talks he had remarked, incidentally, that the hereditary principle was better understood now than ever before, and that instead of abolishing hereditary Upper Houses (the Jupitern Parliament was beginning to discuss something of the sort) the time was coming when they could be better based on that principle than formerly. He further remarked that Congress needed the re-establishment of the Senate, and that a hereditary Senate, to be created by awarding Senatorships to distinguished and honourable citizens, and to be maintained (in possible default of the supply of distinguished and honourable citizens) by transmission from father to son, no further than the third generation, would not be a bad idea. One of the students was the son of the chairman of the Reprobate State Committee of Ceylon, a shrewd politician who stood high in the councils of the party. Writing to his father on the same day, he quoted from the professor's remarks, taking the occasion to ridicule his venerable preceptor as an ass and a crank.

His father, however, saw the matter in a different light. Here was an issue-the re-establishment of the Senate on approved principles of the most modern of sciences. Here embodying the issue was a candidate whose fame was co-extensive with the Solar System, and whose private character, as described a hundred times by newspaper correspondents of every possible bias, was irreproachable. The chairman of the Ceylon Reprobate State Central Committee said *"Eureka!"* and called a conference of leading politicians to meet him in the Siberian National Park, the following week. The result of that conference was the appointment of a committee to wait upon Professor Beetlebrow and ask permission to use his name as a candidate before the National

CHAPTER 12: A CANDIDATE DEFINES AN ISSUE.

Gentlemen:—In accepting the nomination for the Presidency of United States, tendered me with such marked unanimity by the National Convention of the Reprobate party, it devolves upon me to define, to some extent, the issue upon which that party has decided to base its campaign, and which I have the honour to represent. That issue is, in brief, the need of legislative reform by the restoration of Upper House of Congress, lately abolished.

The need of a select and conservative branch of the national legislature to act as a wholesome check upon a discordant popular branch has become painfully evident to every good citizen in the past few months. The people of the United States are not yet prepared to submit to mob rule under sanction of law, and while the Constitution arms the President with the *veto* power, his supreme and constantly increasing responsibility for the efficiency of the administrative branch of the government renders it physically impossible for him to give that attention to the legislation brought before him which is demanded for the due consideration thereof. Hence the need of a distinct and independent system of legislative checks and balances.

The excellent platform put forth by your convention embodies the issue far better than my words can do. It is not proposed to confer upon the restored Senate the power of acting upon the nominations made by the President of the United States. The appointing power is to remain concentrated in him, while upon the restored Senate will devolve the duty of vetoing improper measures passed by the House of Representatives. The simplicity and directness of this arrangement cannot be excelled. It is my confident belief that it cannot fail to commend itself to every thoughtful citizen, for the important reason that no President, however well fitted he may be for the performance of his duties as at present defined, or earnest in his intention to serve his country faithfully, can prove equal to the herculean task now imposed upon the Executive. I would not under any circumstances accept a nomination or an election to the Presidency, if called upon to discharge the duties now pertaining to that office.

I do not see how anyone can question the necessity of re-establishing the Senate, and confident that our views are in harmony on this point, I will now pass on to a consideration of the method of accomplishing this object, with which I have the honour to be specially identified.

The method in question is an application of one of the most obvious principles of the growing science of heredity to the problem of government. When the fundamental data of a science suffice to warrant the induction of a single principle, this principle may be wisely employed in a spirit of opportunism as the basis of experiment and invention. The urgent necessity for legislative reform in this instance removes our proposed experiment from the field of voluntary research, and imposes upon us the duty of realizing it as the nation's only avenue of escape from anarchy seated supreme in the citadel of power.

Until that period of the remote future when the popular branch of a nation's legislative body becomes practically infallible, the existence of a select branch will be useful, even if the members of the latter have no higher motive than to magnify the importance of the body to which they belong. The former United States Senate and the ancient British House of Lords both did good service from time to time, although the former was constituted on an arbitrary basis of States of almost every possible territorial extent, and the latter was governed far more by the individual interests of its members than by proper considerations of public welfare.

It is true that the old British House of Peers embodied the hereditary principle, but no one will pretend that that principle was ever afforded a fair test thereby. The institution was the outgrowth of feudal conditions which made a general spirit of selfish conservatism the ruling influence, while the principles of heredity and of other ancient or modern sciences counted for nothing at all.

Let us examine the teachings of heredity, with a view to ascertaining if it is not possible to base thereon a limited aristocracy in which the public interest shall be represented simultaneously with the best results of contemporary culture. The public is certainly very deeply interested in concentrating its best and most matured thought upon the problems presented from time to time in the administration of its affairs. The age is ripe for the creation of a Senate of brains, and if breeding can produce highly organized beasts, a similar result should be attainable with men, by substituting for compulsory union with select specimens of the opposite sex, the designation of men who are capable of making a wise choice when contemplating matrimony, just as they act wisely in deciding upon other matters of deep interest to themselves and to their race. Thousands have paid tribute to heredity by repeating the maxim, "*blood will tell*," but blood cannot be expected to tell for an indefinite period under haphazard conditions, either in man or in the lower animals.

When no special effort is made to preserve a breed by judicious combination, it will deteriorate gradually to the common level. When efforts for the preservation of a stock are circumscribed by the political necessity of marrying within a narrow range of families already more or less related by blood, like the sovereigns and nobility of ancient Europe, hereditary characteristics became intensified, no new and positive traits being introduced to counteract the tendency to predominance. Balance of temperament was destroyed, while the power to do evil remained, until the excesses indulged in completed the process of degeneration. Thus what was once known as hereditary aristocracy developed vicious representatives who brought it into bad odour, and we may see the same tendency today in remote planets settled by emigration from our own, and imitating the institutions of extinct races. Good blood requires occasional reinforcement from sources not related to it by consanguinity.

It is of the first importance, then, to ascertain at what point the introduction of new elements becomes desirable, not that we may formulate a plan for securing that introduction, but in order to learn how far it is safe, in creating a hereditary Senatorship, to depend upon the voluntary exercise of the prudence likely to be possessed by the head of the line and his immediate descendants, in the choice of consorts. If it can be discovered how many generations may elapse before a family stock will need the advantage of an exceptionally favorable union with another family stock, to preserve its distinctive value, the reasonable limit of a hereditary peerage may be provisionally and approximately indicated.

If a Senatorial family produces an exceptionally meritorious scion beyond this limit, the principle upon which original appointments to the Senate will be made will give the nation the opportunity of securing anew, and for another stated series of generations, the benefit of such highly organized products of the general policy of encouraging good blood in men. For the plan in question is that of appointing to the Senate any citizen of signal ability and character, for whose promotion there may be a popular demand, and offering to him the inducement of honor for his immediate descendants, with a view to encouraging him to marry well.

The fourth generation has been indicated more frequently than any preceding or succeeding one, as the point beyond which heredi-tary attributes, unless of extraordinary strength, become inappreciable through dilution with the characteristics of commonplace consorts. The law of Moses visits the sins of the fathers upon the children unto the third and fourth generation, and admits the descendants of Ed-omite and Egyptian parents to the Commonwealth of Israel only in and after the third generation of their removal from alien influences. The prophet's promise to Jehu, as a reward for his eminent services to the nation, that his children shall reign to the fourth generation, by which time the seer apparently expected that the vigorous traits of character which distinguished the hero would disappear.

Ancient Israel evidently had a firm belief in hereditary transmis-sion to the fourth generation, and what nation so likely to observe the phenomena of degeneracy so closely as the one in which, of all the races in history, race characteristics are so strongly marked and so resolutely maintained? Doubtless the fact that the progenitor of a line, if he lives to a good old age, will have the opportunity of exerting his personal influence upon his descendants as far as the fourth gen-eration, must, in all candour, be taken into account in distinguishing the influences due and not due to hereditary transmission, but this coincidence rather strengthens than weakens the position we take in favour of fixing the fourth generation as the extreme limit of a pos-sible hereditary senatorship.

To recapitulate, we are in favour of reviving the United States Sen-ate by a Constitutional amendment providing for the creation of one hundred senators by appointment by the President, said senators to be selected from among citizens distinguished in the spheres of states-manship, literature, art, science, philanthrophy, or any other field of human action in which individual services may command general recognition as deserving reward; said senatorship, on the death of a senator, to be conferred upon his oldest surviving son, and on the latter's death, upon his oldest surviving son, with whose death the Senatorship shall again pass into the hands of the President for be-stowal as he may think proper. Should the original appointee or his son die without issue, the senatorship is in like manner to escheat to the Republic for re-award. The fourth generation thus constitutes a limit which will never be reached, the safer policy being to make the third generation the extreme actual limit.

I see no reason why this plan should not be realized to the glory of the Republic and the advancement of every legitimate interest of mankind, and I pledge myself, if elected and charged with the duty of executing the Constitutional amendment which we are pledged to carry through, to exercise the appointing power, in this, as in other respects, with an eye single to the best interests of the world. With renewed gratitude for the honor conferred upon me, I am, etc.

Alexander Beetlebrow, A. M., PH.D.

Chapter 13: The President Accepts Renomination.

Gentlemen:—It is with feelings of pleasure and gratification that I accept the renomination for the office of President of the United States, tendered me by your committee on behalf of the great convention which you represent. I regard this renewed honour as a mark of the confidence of a great nation, and one that cannot be too highly esteemed. I congratulate you on the prospects of success which await you, and beg leave to renew my former pledges to administer the executive branch of the government with an eye single to the best interests of the whole people.

I trust that it will not be regarded as egotistical if I say that no doubt of the result ought to exist. Our opponents have taken the field with a platform which can hardly represent the honest belief of any well balanced citizen of the world today, and a candidate who, although personally entitled to our utmost respect, represents nothing in particular except his platform.

They deliberately propose to restore the United States Senate and to organize it on the hereditary principle. It is astounding that any one could hope for a following in the American nation, while advocating such a theory as that, and it can only be accounted for by calling to mind the fact that the unrestricted freedom of our institutions affords room for every possible form of absurd suggestion and discussion, on the theory that what is wise and politic can afford to concede every facility for the consideration of what is foolish and impolitic on its own merits.

That the leading promulgator of the idea of a hereditary Senate, limited in transmission of membership to three generations, should be able to acquire sufficient following for an organization, illustrates the fact, occasionally observed by clear headed members, that blind partisanship still rules no inconsiderable number of men. No one pretends that the mass of voters belonging to the Reprobate party believes in this theory. It has not had time to become a matter of general intelligence with them.

They have merely accepted it as an issue, in default of a better one, in obedience to the leaders who seized upon it as a forlorn hope. It is expected by them that the dissatisfaction with the course of Congress since that body began to consist of a single house will result in the concentration of the dissatisfied about any plan for the restoration of the Senate, just as the dissatisfaction of the Reprobate leaders with the issues which presented themselves led them to rally around an issue which had not been proved by experience to be worthless-the only such issue available.

As a matter of fact, however, the hereditary Senate issue is more absurd than the others upon which the Reprobate party has failed before the people, for most of the others were crystallized into laws, tried, and found wanting before they could be truthfully pronounced dead. Very little argument is needed to convince intelligent citizens of any party that a hereditary Senate would be useless to this country.

I will first grant, for the sake of argument, that which I propose subsequently to disprove; namely, that a Senate is necessary as a check upon the tendency of the House of Representatives to unwise legislation, and will endeavour to show that, even were this true, a hereditary Senate is not the sort of body needed, and that the hereditary feature would be a positive drawback to its usefulness.

Few words are necessary to show this. Hereditary senators, by which I mean more particularly the descendants of appointed or selected senators, would naturally take pride in the achievements and opinions of their ancestors. Their veneration for traditional doctrines would tend to close their eyes to the progressive views which other citizens would recognize as suggested by the altered and continually altering conditions of our national life. There is not, and apparently there never will be, until the constitution of human nature undergoes a miraculous change, any reason to anticipate that a hereditary legislative body, no matter how constituted in reference to minor details, can be anything else than a hindrance to progressive legislation or to progress without legislation.

The avowed purpose of the advocates of a hereditary Senate is to make directly available for the public interest the benefits to be derived from applying to mankind the theory of breeding. The only difference between the proposed application of this theory and its application to the multiplication of live stock, is that the human type is to pick out a worthy mate for himself, while the stock raiser picks out the mate for his blooded stock; it being argued that if a man has sense enough to choose in the one case for the lower animals, he will have sense enough to choose in the other for himself. It will not be disputed that there is ample material for the choice of new senators without resorting to any device of hereditary distinction; nor can it be denied that in this age of universal intellectual progress and development, the chances favour the selection of a better man from the list of worthy and eminent citizens by any plan which leaves to the designating power the largest freedom of action in the recognition of merit, than any hereditary senator would be likely to be.

Hereditary senators, on the date of accession to their honours, would average comparatively few years of age; their preparation for public duties, no matter how carefully looked after, would often be inadequate, and the assurance of well-paid positions, the tenure of which was independent of effort or merit, would encourage the processes of degeneration, rather than improvement, after they had attained the honour for which they were waiting. The lessons of history on this subject are based on permanent natural laws. History also proves to us that self-made men are of more value to a nation than those whose position is conferred upon them without proportionate effort of their own, and that civic honours derive no inconsiderable additional value from the fact that they are open to all citizens who shall deserve them, without regard to birth.

The importance of this feature of our institutions as an incentive to worthy ambition in all citizens is too great to admit of its sacrifice. I cannot believe that these reasonable and obvious considerations can fail to impress themselves upon all intelligent citizens, or that they require further elucidation from your candidate. I will therefore proceed to consider whether it is necessary to restore the United States Senate in any form whatever.

The cry for restoration is suggested by the mass of bad legislation passed by the House of Representatives at its last session, which tends to show the need of a more effectual check than the veto power of an Executive Department, controlled by one man. It is a physical impossibility for the President of the United States to give to each measure sent to him for his approval, that consideration which is demanded of him, entirely apart from the legal merits of the question, concerning which he must, of course, depend upon the Attorney General. A great pressure of legislation tends to distract the Executive from the duties of administration, and one or the other of the President's functions must inevitably suffer if the present tendency to an indefinite increase of national legislation, and a corresponding increase in the official machinery needed for effective administration, is allowed to continue. In my judgment, the time has come for a tendency to react from this indefinite growth, by mutual stimulation, of the volume of legislative and executive business. How this reaction may be brought about, I will now try to suggest.

It was formerly supposed that it was proper for Congress to legislate on whatsoever subjects of legislation were of general rather than local interest; but our recent history has shown that the question of Constitutional right of legislation is unimportant, whether compared with the demands of circumstances in which the immediate defence of the nation is involved, or with the question of efficiency in administration; to my mind the last-named question is the most important of all.

Whether such and such a law is enacted by the States in turn, or whether it is enacted by Congress, is a matter of small moment, except as concerns certain antiquated theories of Constitutional construction. The real point is to determine what legislative authority is best adapted for this duty, by virtue of its relations to the most desirable conditions of administration and enforcement. All other considerations are dwarfed by this. The non-enforcement and half-enforcement of existing laws is largely responsible for the continual pressure for further legislation. Better enforcement means less legislation, and better legislation.

It is evident that the elastic nature of the theory that Congress can provide for the general welfare has led us into a state of affairs in which the machinery of national administration is too vast and complicated to be properly conducted under one central head. As our national machinery is near the people all the time, why not have it more directly responsible to the people? Its present condition reminds me of a fruit tree in the centre of a field, the owner of which should undertake, by grafting again and again, on each branch, to have the entire field covered thereby. How much simpler it would be to cut off all branches that were unproductive, and shorten all that were so long as to trail on the ground unless propped up, and then to plant other trees elsewhere in the field. No one can doubt that the yield of fruit would be larger with many trees than with one. Is it statesmanship to do in a government what we would call insanity in an orchard?

The centres of administration, to command the respect necessary to proper enforcement of laws, should be directly responsible to limited constituencies. Then the limited constituencies would also feel responsibility, and take local pride in their success. Issues would not be so numerous as to conflict, as is always the case in enforcing the responsibility of the national government by rebuke at the polls. A constituency needs to be small enough, for administrative purposes as well as legislative, to admit of its electoral voice expressing an opinion as the opinion of one man—not as a confused mass of opinions, each man of the many millions expressing several opinions in one vote.

Before the days of prompt communication between all parts of the world, there was a time when local jealousies and difficulties of administration, variations of temperament, and other more or less impalpable, but powerful, obstacles, tended to prevent expectations of obtaining uniform laws from any source beside a common law making body. But the growth of the press, the emancipation of law courts from the rule of technicality, and the gradual assertion of that of equity, proper intent and natural construction, render it unnecessary to insist upon any such source of uniform legislation today. We are now one people, instead of an agglomeration of hundreds of peoples. What is recognized by wise men in one part of the world is very soon admitted by the wise men of all the other parts, for reasons and their exhaustive discussions travel around the world with lightning speed. We are, therefore, at liberty to seek that method of obtaining uniform legislation which is most in harmony with the principles of good administration, and the most direct means of obtaining it.

When the United States was confined to that portion of the North American continent which is bounded on the north by the present States of Quebec, Ontario, Manitoba and Victoria, and on the south by Mexico and the sea, there was a national convention, for the purpose of obtaining a uniform law of marriage and divorce, the foundation of which was due to the process which I now wish to recommend for endorsement by the State conventions of the party which you and I have the honour to represent. An association of citizens, founded for the purpose of investigating social problems, issued a call for a national divorce reform convention, and requested the governor of each State to recommend to the legislature thereof the appropriation of a small amount of money to pay the expenses of two delegates to said convention; at least one delegate to be a jurist learned in the law of his State.

The convention was to prepare a draft of an act to regulate marriages and divorces, and this was to be introduced into each legislature for enactment. This plan succeeded admirably. Most of the governors took up the idea at once, and others followed when they saw what the majority were doing. Acts constituting a commission from each State were passed by the legislatures, authorizing the governor to appoint the commissioners; the convention met, and harmoniously adopted an admirable measure, which, thus endorsed, was recommended by every governor and enacted by every legislature. To it the old United States owes its high plane of morality today. The success of the plan was largely due to the dangerous results of variation in State laws regarding marriage and divorce, and to the strong and conservative opposition which was excited against a plan for a National Divorce Act of Congress.

But there is no reason why the idea should not be indefinitely applied. In my opinion, each State ought to have one or more permanent law commissioners, and the Uniform State Law Convention, composed of these commissioners, should be in session several months of each year. There is no subject short of the relations of this planet to some other planet that such a body of approved jurists and intelligent citizens would not be competent to discuss and legislate upon. The results of their work would have no binding force upon any State. This would leave those results to stand or fall upon their merits, and if they did not appear to the general common sense as being worthy of enactment, they would never be enacted. Coming, however, before the public as they would if so presented, every merit in them would be promptly recognized, and their general enactment (if worthy) and harmonious enforcement would be only a question of time.

It is impossible to foresee the extent to which such an institution would be likely to encroach upon the traditional and acquired domain of Congress. This fact strongly recommends it to my mind as a safe and reasonably sure protection against the indefinite increase of Congressional legislation and of the machinery necessary to execute it. Congress would continually be freer to consider subjects that admittedly require its attention, and the executive would be able to devote time now spent on the details of local administration to the study of methods of improving the necessary machinery of national supremacy.

Congress cannot reasonably be expected to abdicate its present powers, in part, by taking the initiative in a process for their acquisition by State Legislatures; it remains for the States themselves to do this. Let the State organizations of our party endorse this plan, and the members of our party who are elected to the legislatures will feel honourably committed to it. In the event of that national triumph which we have every reason to anticipate, we will control the legislatures of most States in its interest, and the intrinsic wisdom of the plan itself will commend it to the minority party, which, under the discipline of defeat, will be likely to turn from hair-brained theories to practicable ideas that command the approval of advanced political philosophers.

This, then, is our substitute for the plan of checking bad legislation which our antagonists have proposed. The problem which it seems to solve is the issue of the campaign. On other issues, it is needless that I should address you now. The ideas expressed in my former letter of acceptance, and carried out, as far as possible, in my administration, have been kindly approved by you, and it has been the general sense of the party that I should define the position to be taken before the people. I have done so. It only remains for me to express again my appreciation of the honour which I have twice received at your hands, and to promise to endeavour to deserve it. I have the honour to be your obedient servant,

A. Mugwump.

Chapter 14: The Solar System at Peace.

Of course, the Reprobate move to re-establish the Senate on a hereditary basis proved a failure. With very few exceptions, the candidates in favour of the proposed Constitutional amendment were snowed under by the large majorities which the Demagogues polled everywhere. The largest majorities were those of candidates for the Legislature, defeating the Reprobates' nominated to propose the amendment. A distinctly anti-amendment Congress was also elected, which was natural, as the Representative who would favour the re-establishment of a check on the action of the body to which he belonged would lose his popularity with his fellow members, and his Presidential prospects would be seriously impaired thereby. Thus even the few Reprobate candidates for Congress who were members of the sitting Congress concealed their real views as much as was consistent with party fidelity to the head of the ticket.

The president's scheme for an inter-State convention for uniform State legislation took well, and Demagogue candidates for Governorships and for State Legislatorships came out in favour of immediate action on his suggestions. His triumphant re-election was generally construed as a popular endorsement of his suggestion, as much as a repudiation of the hereditary Senate idea. Candidates of Congress were less ardently in favour of it, but were afraid to oppose it after seeing how strongly and generally it was endorsed by the newspapers. Weber Lockmore's world girdle of newspapers advocated it with great vigour, and other leading journals favoured it, partly from a wish to be consistent, as they had generally committed themselves to a strong condemnation of Congress, and to the idea that its functions could advantageously be abridged.

Meanwhile, important events were occurring in other parts of the Solar System. The war between Jupiter and Venus had grown bitter, but the home feeling in either planet was still more bitter. The immense expense of fitting out aerial expeditions with all the artificial appliances for supplying soldiers with tolerable atmosphere until they should be acclimated, made it necessary to increase the taxes continually. Only by the most frantic appeals to patriotism could the Jupitern Premier keep his Parliamentary majority in line. He was reinforced from time to time by seceding members of the other party, but disgusted members of his own not only seceded, but talked openly of forcing open revolt, or an appeal to the planet. The premier privately conceded the necessity of resigning if he should again lose his majority. The House had gone against him several times, earlier in the war, and he had resigned, but had been again sent for to form a ministry, when the Parliamentary elections gave him a narrow majority of supporters. The majority was further reduced at each election, and the rate of reduction left little room for doubt that the tide of Jupitern sentiment was gradually turning against the long drawn-out war.

As for the Venusians, they had again become riotous. Of course, some of the citizens wanted to change the form of government once more, and processions of revolutionists paraded the streets to the music of the national anthem. The Republicans seemed about to be forced to take a position in favour of asking to be admitted to the United States. As this idea was supposed to be antagonistic to national independence, it excited bitter opposition within the party, and desertions strengthened the ranks of the Imperialists and improved the prospects of a revolution.

The idea of asking for admission to the Union of American States was suggested to the Venusian Republicans by the conduct of the little Republic of Henrygeorgia. The prejudice of both the Jupiterns and the Venusians against the peculiar institutions of this Asteroid had made the armies of both planets forage and fight on it without scruple, but rather with the zest of hatred. Its rich agricultural interests were robbed, to sustain the troops, and its manufacturing establishments were seized and converted to the use of contractors who were manufacturing artificial necessities of war. The Government of Henrygeorgia prudently avoided giving unnecessary offense to either combatant, but managed, nevertheless, to exist with the entire respect of its citizens. The National Assembly had temporarily modified its rules of procedure, so as to sit in secret, and quietly adopted and forwarded to Washington, by special messenger, an application for the admission of Henrygeorgia as a State. This was sought as the best way to escape the aggressions of Jupiter and Venus.

The Republicans of Venus, who were profoundly impressed by their continued defeat in the war with Jupiter, foresaw an ultimate surrender to that planet, unless they could secure the intercession of the only nation that had proved itself still more powerful. They thought they were sure of this, if they cultivated the American good will by seeking the admission of Venus as a State.

The Opposition in Jupiter also had a scheme for admission to the Union, but, of course, not as a single State. The old idea of the size of a State had gradually expanded with the admission of rival nations to the American federation, and even the proposition that the entire landed area of the planet Venus should constitute a single State struck no one as extraordinary; but the Jupiterns naturally thought their enormous and populous planet entitled to recognition in the shape of a whole league of States, each province being designated as one. The Opposition had such a proposal ready for transmission to Washington as soon as the government should fall, and the new Administration effect an organisation.

This was the condition of affairs abroad when the First Inter-State Convention for the Consideration of Uniform State Legislation assembled at Melbourne, Australia.

The Convention had hardly effected an organization, when a bombshell was thrown in by the announcement that commissioners from the "State of Henrygeorgia" had presented their credentials, and asked to be admitted to seats in the Convention.

"This a convention of purely American States," said a commissioner from Russia, "and I have not heard of the admission of Henrygeorgia to the Union." The Sergeant-at-Arms retired to consult the applicants, and returned to announce that they confidently expected to be admitted as a State before this Convention ceased its deliberations. This statement was greeted with a storm of laughter and hisses. A dozen motions were heard, to the effect that the application for the admission of Henrygeorgian delegates be laid on the table, but Weber Lockmore, who was present as a commissioner from New York, caught the President's eye, and moved that the petition be referred to a select committee of three, with authority to report at such time as should seem, to its members, advisable.

The Convention was evidently puzzled by Lockmore's motion. He was known to lean to Henrygeorgian views, but the President was believed to be a conservative man, who, if he appointed Lockmore chairman of the committee of three, could be depended on to see that the other two members were conservative.

The great bulk of the Convention, however, thinking it possible that Congress might admit Henrygeorgia before the Convention adjourned, and that it would then be necessary to admit the new State's commissioners, regardless of prejudice against Henrygeorgian institutions, saw in the motion only an easy way of disposing of the question for the present, without doing harm to any interest. Consequently, the motion was adopted by acclamation.

Lockmore's private purpose was to secure the admission of the delegates from Henrygeorgia without regard to the admission of that Asteroid as a State. He called a meeting of the committee on the third night after its appointment, and then wrote a personal note to each member, requesting a private interview on the first and second nights, respectively.

The interview on the first night was with a commissioner from Russia—the one who had made the first remark against the recognition of the Henrygeorgian commissioners. He was, of course, strongly prejudiced against Henrygeorgian institutions. Lockmore furnished him with a list of certain members of Congress, and requested him to communicate with each of them by cipher cable at his (Lockmore's) expense, regarding the prospects of Henrygeorgia's admission as a State. The list consisted largely of Congressmen known to Lockmore to be secret admirers of Henrygeorgian ideas, with a minority of opponents, whose replies would be likely to make the Russian believe in the representativeness of the list.

The other member of the committee, a quiet and languid Brazilian, entertained Henrygeorgian views. To him Lockmore also gave a list of certain Congressmen to be consulted by cable. It included all the most bitter opponents of the Henrygeorgian issue in the House, with a few advocates of the doctrines practiced in Henrygeorgia. The Henrygeorgianists, however, would have been found in the majority in a list formed by combining these two.

But little remains to be told. The anti-Henrygeorgianists in Congress pointed out to wavering members the danger of establishing a precedent for the admission of any other planet than the Earth, or any part of any other, to the Union. It would lead to endless complications. There could be, if Henrygeorgia was admitted, no good reason for refusing to admit other Asteroids, or Venus, or a whole union of States in Jupiter.

Lockmore knew that the Russian would waive his own views, if convinced that intelligent public opinion led in a different direction, and felt sure of the Brazilian. Every adverse response from Washington, he was convinced, would only reinforce him in his purpose to vote for a favourable report on the application.

The committee reported favourably on the fourth day, by a unanimous vote; Lockmore, in presenting the report, read the names of the Congressmen consulted, in alphabetical order. The list included all the leaders of both parties, and convinced the Convention that the committee had, in the frankest manner, sought and obtained the views of the most representative members of Congress, as to the probability that Henrygeorgia would be admitted as a State. The chances seemed to favour admission, for, as Lockmore well knew, the worst enemies of Henrygeorgianism proposed to admit the Asteroid first, and force the reconstruction of its Constitution afterward.

Not until it was announced at Washington that the commissioners from the would-be State of Henrygeorgia had been admitted to the Melbourne Convention, did the anti-Henrygeorgian members of Congress realize how they had been used. When they did, they determined to prevent the admission of Henrygeorgia, at all hazards.

A strong conservative sentiment was artificially created, in favour of the limitation of the American national authority to the American planet, and the offer of commercial treaties and international arbitration facilities to all remote bodies. But while matters were shaping themselves at Washington for the refusal of Statehood to Henrygeorgia, Lockmore took care to see that a Henrygeorgian amendment to State Constitutions was introduced, exhaustively debated, and amended into a very fair shape for experimental operation, by the Convention at Melbourne.

On the day of the defeat of the bill to admit Henrygeorgia to the Union as a State, Lockmore pressed the Henrygeorgian amendment for State Constitutions to a vote. He meanwhile blockaded all the cables by sending correspondence to his newspapers. The vote in Congress did not reach Melbourne until after the Convention had formally adopted the Henrygeorgian amendment by a substantial majority.

Other measures adopted were drafts of uniform laws for marriage and divorce, the regulation of primary and general elections, the prohibition of payment of public officials by fees, the regulation of corporations, the regulation of bankruptcy and forms of charters for cities according to population. All these forms were ultimately adopted by a number of States, and the benefits of this system of uniformity of legislation were extended to other planets, for when the Second Uniform Legislation Convention met, the Henrygeorgian precedent became the means of securing the admission of all *bona fide* applicants, and subsequent Conventions represented all parts of the Solar System.

Pichon & Sons, of the Croix Rousse

Giraudier, *pharmacien, première classe*, is the legend, recorded in huge, ill-proportioned letters, which directs the attention of the stranger to the most prosperous-looking shop in the grand *place* of La Croix Rousse, a well-known suburb of the beautiful city of Lyons, which has its share of the shabby gentility and poor pretence common to the suburban commerce of great towns.

Giraudier is not only *pharmacien* but *propriétaire*, though not by inheritance; his possession of one of the prettiest and most prolific of the small vineyards in the beautiful suburb, and a charming inconvenient house, with low ceilings, Lilliputian bedrooms, and a profusion of *persiennes, jalousies*, and *contrevents*, comes by purchase. This enviable little *terre* was sold by the nation, when that terrible abstraction transacted the public business of France; and it was bought very cheaply by the strong-minded father of the Giraudier of the present, who was not disturbed by the evil reputation which the place had gained, at a time the peasants of France, having been bullied into a renunciation of religion, eagerly cherished superstition.

The Giraudier of the present cherishes the particular superstition in question affectionately; it reminds him of an uncommonly good bargain made in his favour, which is always a pleasant association of ideas, especially to a Frenchman, still more especially to a Lyonnais; and it attracts strangers to his *pharmacie*, and leads to transactions in *Grand Chartreuse* and *Crème de Roses*, ensuing naturally on the narration of the history of Pichon & Sons. Giraudier is not of aristocratic principles and sympathies; on the contrary, he has decided republican leanings, and considers *Le Progrès* a masterpiece of journalistic literature; but, as he says simply and strongly, "it is not because a man is a *marquis* that one is not to keep faith with him; a bad action is not good because it harms a good-for-nothing of a noble; the more when that good-for-nothing is no longer a noble, but *pour rire.*" At the easy price of acquiescence in these sentiments, the stranger hears one of the most authentic, best-remembered, most popular of the many traditions of the bad old times "before General Bonaparte," as Giraudier, who has no sympathy with any later designation of *le grand homme,* calls the emperor, whose statue one can perceive—a speck in the distance—from the threshold of the *pharmacie.*

The Marquis de Sénanges, in the days of the triumph of the great Revolution, was fortunate enough to be out of France, and wise enough to remain away from that country, though he persisted, long after the old *regime* was as dead as the Ptolemies, in believing it merely suspended, and the Revolution a lamentable accident of vulgar complexion, but happily temporary duration. The Marquis de Sénanges, who affected the *style régence,* and was the politest of *infidels* and the most refined of voluptuaries, got on indifferently in unappreciative foreign parts; but the members of his family—his brother and sisters, two of whom were guillotined, while the third escaped to Savoy and found refuge there in a convent of her order—got on exceedingly ill in France.

If the *ci-devant marquis* had had plenty of money to expend in such feeble imitations of his accustomed pleasures as were to be had out of Paris, he would not have been much affected by the fate of his relatives. But money became exceedingly scarce; the *marquis* had actually beheld many of his peers reduced to the necessity of earning the despicable but indispensable article after many ludicrous fashions. And the duration of this absurd upsetting of law, order, privilege, and property began to assume unexpected and very unpleasant proportions.

The Château de Sénanges, with its surrounding lands, was confiscated to the Nation, during the third year of the "emigration" of the Marquis de Sénanges; and the greater part of the estate was purchased by a thrifty, industrious, and rich *avocat,* named Prosper Alix, a widower with an only daughter. Prosper Alix enjoyed the esteem of the entire neighbourhood. First, he was rich; secondly, he was of a taciturn disposition, and of a neutral tint in politics. He had done well under the old *regime* and, he was doing well under the new—thank God, or the Supreme Being, or the First Cause, or the goddess Reason herself, for all;—he would have invoked Dagon, Moloch, or Kali, quite as readily as the Saints and the Madonna, who has gone so utterly out of fashion of late. Nobody was afraid to speak out before Prosper Alix; he was not a spy; and though a cold-hearted man, except in the instance of his only daughter, he never harmed anybody.

Very likely it was because he was the last person in the vicinity whom anybody would have suspected of being applied to by the dispossessed family, that the son of the *marquis'* brother, a young man of promise, of courage, of intellect, and of morals of decidedly a higher calibre than those actually and traditionally imputed to the family, sought the aid of the new possessor of the Château de Sénanges, which had changed its old title for that of the Maison Alix. The father of M. Paul de Sénanges had perished in the September massacres; his mother had been guillotined at Lyons; and he—who had been saved by the interposition of a young comrade, whose father had, in the wonderful rotations of the wheel of Fate, acquired authority in the place where he had once esteemed the notice of the nephew of the *marquis* a crowning honour for his son—had passed through the common vicissitudes of that dreadful time, which would take a volume for their recital in each individual instance.

Paul de Sénanges was a handsome young fellow, frank, high-spirited, and of a brisk and happy temperament; which, however, modified by the many misfortunes he had undergone, was not permanently changed. He had plenty of capacity for enjoyment in him still; and as his position was very isolated, and his mind had become enlightened on social and political matters to an extent in which the men of his family would have discovered utter degradation and the women diabolical possession, he would not have been very unhappy if, under the new condition of things, he could have lived in his native country and gained an honest livelihood. But he could not do that, he was too thoroughly "suspect;" the antecedents of his family were too powerful against him: his only chance would have been to have gone into the popular camp as an extreme, violent partisan, to have out-Heroded the revolutionary Herods; and that Paul de Sénanges was too honest to do. So he was reduced to being thankful that he had escaped with his life, and to watching for an opportunity of leaving France and gaining some country where the reign of liberty, fraternity, and equality was not quite so oppressive.

The long-looked-for opportunity at length offered itself, and Paul de Sénanges was instructed by his uncle the *marquis* that he must contrive to reach Marseilles, whence he should be transported to Spain—in which country the illustrious emigrant was then residing—by a certain named date. His uncle's communication arrived safely, and the plan proposed seemed a secure and eligible one. Only in two respects was it calculated to make Paul de Sénanges thoughtful. The first was, that his uncle should take any interest in the matter of his safety; the second, what could be the nature of a certain deposit which the *marquis*'s letter directed him to procure, if possible, from the Château de Sénanges.

The fact of this injunction explained, in some measure, the first of the two difficulties. It was plain that whatever were the contents of this packet which he was to seek for, according to the indications marked on a ground-plan drawn by his uncle and enclosed in the letter, the *marquis* wanted them, and could not procure them except by the agency of his nephew. That the *marquis* should venture to direct Paul de Sénanges to put himself in communication with Prosper Alix, would have been surprising to any one acquainted only with the external and generally understood features of the character of the new proprietor of the Château de Sénanges. But a few people knew Prosper Alix thoroughly, and the *marquis* was one of the number; he was keen enough to know in theory that, in the case of a man with only one weakness, that is likely to be a very weak weakness indeed, and to apply the theory to the *avocat*.

The beautiful, pious, and aristocratic mother of Paul de Sénanges—a lady to whose superiority the *marquis* had rendered the distinguished testimony of his dislike, not hesitating to avow that she was "much too good for *his* taste"—had been very fond of, and very kind to, the motherless daughter of Prosper Alix, and he held her memory in reverence which he accorded to nothing beside, human or divine, and taught his daughter the matchless worth of the friend she had lost. The *marquis* knew this, and though he had little sympathy with the sentiment, he believed he might use it in the present instance to his own profit, with safety. The event proved that he was right.

Private negotiations, with the manner of whose transaction we are not concerned, passed between the *avocet* and the *ci-devant marquis*; and the young man, then leading a life in which skulking had a large share, in the vicinity of Dijon, was instructed to present himself at the Maison Alix, under the designation of Henri Glaire, and in the character of an artist in house-decoration. The circumstances of his life in childhood and boyhood had led to his being almost safe from recognition as a man at Lyons; and, indeed, all the people on the *ci-devant* visiting-list of the *château* had been pretty nearly killed off, in the noble and patriotic ardour of the revolutionary times.

The ancient Château de Sénanges was proudly placed near the

summit of the "Holy Hill," and had suffered terrible depredations when the church at Fourvières was sacked, and the shrine desecrated with that ingenious impiety which is characteristic of the French; but it still retained somewhat of its former heavy grandeur. The château was much too large for the needs, tastes, or ambition of its present owner, who was too wise, if even he had been of an ostentatious disposition, not to have sedulously resisted its promptings. The jealousy of the nation of brothers was easily excited, and departure from simplicity and frugality was apt to be commented upon by domiciliary visits, and the eager imposition of fanciful fines.

That portion of the vast building occupied by Prosper Alix and the *citoyenne* Berthe, his daughter, presented an appearance of well-to-do comfort and modest ease, which contrasted with the grandiose proportions and the elaborate decorations of the wide corridors, huge flat staircases, and lofty panelled apartments. The *avocet* and his daughter lived quietly in the old place, hoping, after a general fashion, for better times, but not finding the present very bad; the father becoming day by day more pleasant with his bargain, the daughter growing fonder of the great house, and the noble *bocages*, of the scrappy little vineyards, struggling for existence on the sunny hill-side, and the place where the famous shrine had been.

They had done it much damage; they had parted its riches among them; the once ever-open doors were shut, and the worn flags were untrodden; but nothing could degrade it, nothing could destroy what had been, in the mind of Berthe Alix, who was as devout as her father was unconcernedly unbelieving. Berthe was wonderfully well educated for a Frenchwoman of that period, and surprisingly handsome for a Frenchwoman of any. Not too tall to offend the taste of her compatriots, and not too short to be dignified and graceful, she had a symmetrical figure, and a small, well-poised head, whose profuse, shining, silken dark-brown hair she wore as nature intended, in a shower of curls, never touched by the hand of the coiffeur,—curls which clustered over her brow, and fell far down on her shapely neck.

Her features were fine; the eyes very dark, and the mouth very red; the complexion clear and rather pale, and the style of the face and its expression lofty. When Berthe Alix was a child, people were accustomed to say she was pretty and refined enough to belong to the aristocracy; nobody would have dared to say so now, prettiness and refinement, together with all the other virtues admitted to a place on the patriotic roll, having become national property.

Berthe loved her father dearly. She was deeply impressed with the sense of her supreme importance to him, and fully comprehended that he would be influenced by and through her when all other persuasion or argument would be unavailing. When Prosper Alix wished and intended to do anything rather mean or selfish, he did it without letting Berthe know; and when he wished to leave undone something which he knew his daughter would decide ought to be done, he carefully concealed from her the existence of the dilemma. Nevertheless, this system did not prevent the father and daughter being very good and even confidential friends.

Prosper Alix loved his daughter immeasurably, and respected her more than he respected any one in the world. With regard to her persevering religiousness, when such things were not only out of fashion and date, but illegal as well, he was very tolerant. Of course it was weak, and an absurdity; but every woman, even his beautiful, incomparable Berthe, was weak and absurd on some point or other; and, after all, he had come to the conclusion that the safest weakness with which a woman can be afflicted is that romantic and ridiculous *faiblesse* called piety. So these two lived a happy life together, Berthe's share of it being very secluded, and were wonderfully little troubled by the turbulence with which society was making its tumultuous way to the virtuous serenity of republican perfection.

The communication announcing the project of the *ci-devant marquis* for the secure exportation of his nephew, and containing the skilful appeal before mentioned, grievously disturbed the tranquillity of Prosper, and was precisely one of those incidents which he would especially have liked to conceal from his daughter. But he could not do so; the appeal was too cleverly made; and utter indifference to it, utter neglect of the letter, which naturally suggested itself as the easiest means of getting rid of a difficulty, would have involved an act of direct and uncompromising dishonesty to which Prosper, though of sufficiently elastic conscience within the limit of professional gains, could not contemplate.

The Château de Sénanges was indeed his own lawful property; his without prejudice to the former owners, dispossessed by no act of his. But the *ci-devant marquis*—confiding in him to an extent which was quite astonishing, except on the *pis-aller* theory, which is so unflattering as to be seldom accepted—announced to him the existence of a certain packet, hidden in the *château*, acknowledging its value, and urging the need of its safe transmission. This was not his property. He heartily wished he had never learned its existence, but wishing that was clearly of no use; then he wished the nephew of the *ci-devant* might come soon, and take himself and the hidden wealth away with all possible speed.

This latter was a more realisable desire, and Prosper settled his mind with it, communicated the interesting but decidedly dangerous secret to Berthe, received her warm sanction, and transmitted to the *marquis*, by the appointed means, an assurance that his wishes should be punctually carried out. The absence of an interdiction of his visit before a certain date was to be the signal to M. Paul de Sénanges that he was to proceed to act upon his uncle's instructions; he waited the proper time, the reassuring silence was maintained unbroken, and he ultimately set forth on his journey, and accomplished it in safety.

Preparations had been made at the Maison Alix for the reception of M. Glaire, and his supposed occupation had been announced. The apartments were decorated in a heavy, gloomy style, and those of the *citoyenne* in particular (they had been occupied by a lady who had once been designated as *feue Madame la Marquise*, but who was referred to now as *la mère du ci-devant*) were much in need of renovation. The alcove, for instance, was all that was least gay and most far from simple. The *citoyenne* would have all that changed. On the morning of the day of the expected arrival, Berthe said to her father:

"It would seem as if the *marquis* did not know the exact spot in which the packet is deposited. M. Paul's assumed character implies the necessity for a search."

M. Henri Glaire arrived at the Maison Alix, was fraternally received, and made acquainted with the sphere of his operations. The young man had a good deal of both ability and taste in the line he had assumed, and the part was not difficult to play. Some days were judiciously allowed to pass before the real object of the masquerade was pursued, and during that time cordial relations established themselves between the *avocet* and his guest. The young man was handsome, elegant, engaging, with all the external advantages, and devoid of the vices, errors, and hopeless infatuated unscrupulousness, of his class; he had naturally quick intelligence, and some real knowledge and comprehension of life had been knocked into him by the hard-hitting blows of Fate.

His face was like his mother's, Prosper Alix thought, and his mind and tastes were of the very pattern which, in theory, Berthe approved. Berthe, a very unconventional French girl—who thought the new era of purity, love, virtue, and disinterestedness ought to do away with marriage by barter as one of its most notable reforms, and had been disenchanted by discovering that the abolition of marriage altogether suited the taste of the incorruptible Republic better—might like, might even love, this young man. She saw so few men, and had no fancy for patriots; she would certainly be obstinate about it if she did chance to love him. This would be a nice state of affairs. This would be a pleasant consequence of the confiding request of the *ci-devant*. Prosper wished with all his heart for the arrival of the concerted signal, which should tell Henri Glaire that he might fulfil the purpose of his sojourn at the Maison Alix, and set forth for Marseilles.

But the signal did not come, and the days—long, beautiful, sunny, soothing summer-days—went on. The painting of the panels of the *citoyenne's* apartment, which she vacated for that purpose, progressed slowly; and M. Paul de Sénanges, guided by the ground-plan, and aided by Berthe, had discovered the spot in which the jewels of price, almost the last remnants of the princely wealth of the Sénanges, had been hidden by the *femme-de-chambre* who had perished with her mistress, having confided a general statement of the fact to a priest, for transmission to the *marquis*. This spot had been ingeniously chosen. The sleeping-apartment of the late *marquis* was extensive, lofty, and provided with an alcove of sufficiently large dimensions to have formed in itself a handsome room. This space, containing a splendid but gloomy bed, on an *estrade*, and hung with rich faded brocade, was divided from the general extent of the apartment by a low railing of black oak, elaborately carved, opening in the centre, and with a flat wide bar along the top, covered with crimson velvet.

The curtains were contrived to hang from the ceiling, and, when let down inside the screen of railing, they matched the draperies which closed before the great stone balcony at the opposite end of the room. Since the *avocat's* daughter had occupied this palatial chamber, the curtains of the alcove had never been drawn, and she had substituted for them a high folding screen of black-and-gold Japanese pattern, also a relic of the grand old times, which stood about six feet on the outside of the rails that shut in her bed. The floor was of shining oak, testifying to the conscientious and successful labours of successive generations of *frotteurs*; and on the spot where the railing of the alcove opened by a pretty quaint device sundering the intertwined arms of a pair of very chubby cherubs, a square space in the floor was also richly carved.

The seekers soon reached the end of their search. A little effort removed the square of carved oak, and underneath they found a casket, evidently of old workmanship, richly wrought in silver, much tarnished but quite intact. It was agreed that this precious deposit should be replaced, and the carved square laid down over it, until the signal for his departure should reach Paul. The little baggage which under any circumstances he could have ventured to allow himself in the dangerous journey he was to undertake, must be reduced, so as to admit of his carrying the casket without exciting suspicion.

The finding of the hidden treasure was not the first joint discovery made by the daughter of the *avocet* and the son of the *ci-devant*. The cogitations of Prosper Alix were very wise, very reasonable; but they were a little tardy. Before he had admitted the possibility of mischief, the mischief was done. Each had found out that the love of the other was indispensable to the happiness of life; and they had exchanged confidences, assurances, protestations, and promises, as freely, as fervently, and as hopefully, as if no such thing as a Republic, one and indivisible, with a keen scent and an unappeasable thirst for the blood of aristocrats, existed.

They forgot all about "Liberty, Fraternity, and Equality"—these egotistical, narrow-minded young people;—they also forgot the characteristic alternative to those unparalleled blessings—"Death." But Prosper Alix did not forget any of these things; and his consternation, his provision of suffering for his beloved daughter, were terrible, when she told him, with a simple noble frankness which the *grandes dames* of the dead-and-gone time of great ladies had rarely had a chance of exhibiting, that she loved M. Paul de Sénanges, and intended to marry him when the better times should come. Perhaps she meant when that alternative of *death* should be struck off the sacred formula;—of course she meant to marry him with the sanction of her father, which she made no doubt she should receive.

Prosper Alix was in pitiable perplexity. He could not bear to terrify his daughter by a full explanation of the danger she was incurring; he could not bear to delude her with false hope. If this young man could be got away at once safely, there was not much likelihood that he would ever be able to return to France. Would Berthe pine for him, or would she forget him, and make a rational, sensible, rich, republican marriage, which would not imperil either her reputation for pure patriotism or her father's? The latter would be the very best thing that could possibly happen, and therefore it was decidedly unwise to calculate upon it; but, after all, it was possible; and Prosper had not the courage, in such a strait, to resist the hopeful promptings of a possibility. How ardently he regretted that he had complied with the prayer of the *ci-devant*! When would the signal for Mr. Paul's departure come?

Prosper Alix had made many sacrifices, had exercised much self-control for his daughter's sake; but he had never sustained a more severe trial than this, never suffered more than he did now, under the strong necessity for hiding from her his absolute conviction of the impossibility of a happy result for this attachment, in that future to which the lovers looked so fearlessly. He could not even make his anxiety and apprehension known to Paul de Sénanges; for he did not believe the young man had sufficient strength of will to conceal anything so important from the keen and determined observation of Berthe.

The expected signal was not given, and the lovers were incautious. The seclusion of the Maison Alix had all the danger, as well as all the delight, of solitude, and Paul dropped his disguise too much and too often. The servants, few in number, were of the truest patriotic principles, and to some of them the denunciation of the *citoyen*, whom they condescended to serve because the sacred Revolution had not yet made them as rich as he, would have been a delightful duty, a sweet-smelling sacrifice to be laid on the altar of the country. They heard certain names and places mentioned; they perceived many things which led them to believe that Henri Glaire was not an industrial artist and pure patriot, worthy of respect, but a wretched *ci-devant*, resorting to the dignity of labour to make up for the righteous destruction of every other kind of dignity.

One day a gardener, of less stoical virtue than his fellows, gave Prosper Alix a warning that the presence of a *ci-devant* upon his premises was suspected, and that he might be certain a domiciliary visit, attended with dangerous results to himself, would soon take place. Of course the *avocet* did not commit himself by any avowal to this lukewarm patriot; but he casually mentioned that Henri Glaire was about to take his leave. What was to be done? He must not leave the neighbourhood without receiving the instructions he was awaiting; but he must leave the house, and be supposed to have gone quite away. Without any delay or hesitation, Prosper explained the facts to Berthe and her lover, and insisted on the necessity for an instant parting. Then the courage and the readiness of the girl told. There was no crying, and very little trembling; she was strong and helpful.

"He must go to Pichon's, father," she said, "and remain there until the signal is given.—Pichon is a master-mason, Paul," she continued, turning to her lover, "and his wife was my nurse. They are avaricious people; but they are fond of me in their way, and they will shelter you faithfully enough, when they know that my father will pay them handsomely. You must go at once, unseen by the servants; they are at supper. Fetch your valise, and bring it to my room. We will put the casket in it, and such of your things as you must take out to make room for it, we can hide under the plank. My father will go with you to Pichon's, and we will communicate with you there as soon as it is safe."

Paul followed her to the large gloomy room where the treasure lay, and they took the casket from its hiding-place. It was heavy, though not large, and an awkward thing to pack away among linen in a small valise. They managed it, however, and, the brief preparation completed, the moment of parting arrived. Firmly and eloquently, though in haste, Berthe assured Paul of her changeless love and faith, and promised him to wait for him for any length of time in France, if better days should be slow of coming, or to join him in some foreign land, if they were never to come. Her father was present, full of compassion and misgiving. At length he said:

"Come, Paul, you must leave her; every moment is of importance."

The young man and his betrothed were standing on the spot whence they had taken the casket; the carved rail with the heavy curtains might have been the outer sanctuary of an altar, and they bride and bridegroom before it, with earnest, loving faces, and clasped hands.

"Farewell, Paul," said Berthe; "promise me once more, in this the moment of our parting, that you will come to me again, if you are alive, when the danger is past."

"Whether I am living or dead, Berthe," said Paul de Sénanges, strongly moved by some sudden inexplicable instinct, "I will come to you again."

In a few more minutes, Prosper Alix and his guest, who carried, not without difficulty, the small but heavy leather valise, had disappeared in the distance, and Berthe was on her knees before the *prie-dieu* of the *ci-devant marquise*, her face turned toward the "Holy Hill" of Fourvières.

Pichon, *mâitre*, and his sons, *garçons-maçons*, were well-to-do people, rather morose, exceedingly avaricious, and of taciturn dispositions; but they were not ill spoken of by their neighbours. They had amassed a good deal of money in their time, and were just then engaged on a very lucrative job. This was the construction of several of the steep descents, by means of stairs, straight and winding, cut in the face of the *côteaux*, by which pedestrians are enabled to descend into the town. Pichon *père* was a *propriétaire* as well; his property was that which is now in the possession of Giraudier, *pharmacien, première classe*, and which was destined to attain a sinister celebrity during his proprietorship. One of the straightest and steepest of the stairways had been cut close to the *terre* which the mason owned, and a massive wall, destined to bound the high-road at the foot of the declivity, was in course of construction.

When Prosper Alix and Paul de Sénanges reached the abode of Pichon, the master-mason, with his sons and workmen, had just completed their day's work, and were preparing to eat the supper served by the wife and mother, a tall, gaunt woman, who looked as if a more liberal scale of housekeeping would have done her good, but on whose features the stamp of that devouring and degrading avarice which is the commonest vice of the French peasantry, was set as plainly as on the hard faces of her husband and her sons. The *avocet* explained his business and introduced his companion briefly, and awaited the reply of Pichon *père* without any appearance of inquietude.

"You don't run any risk," he said; "at least, you don't run any risk which I cannot make it worth your while to incur. It is not the first time you have received a temporary guest on my recommendation. You know nothing about the citizen Glaire, except that he is recommended to you by me. I am responsible; you can, on occasion, make me so. The citizen may remain with you a short time; can hardly remain long. Say, citizen, is it agreed? I have no time to spare."

It was agreed, and Prosper Alix departed, leaving M. Paul de Sénanges, convinced that the right, indeed the only, thing had been done, and yet much troubled and depressed.

Pichon *père* was a short, squat, powerfully built man, verging on sixty, whose thick, dark grizzled hair, sturdy limbs, and hard hands, on which the muscles showed like cords, spoke of endurance and strength; he was, indeed, noted in the neighbourhood for those qualities. His sons resembled him slightly, and each other closely, as was natural, for they were twins. They were heavy, lumpish fellows, and they made but an ungracious return to the attempted civilities of the stranger, to whom the offer of their mother to show him his room was a decided relief. As he rose to follow the woman, Paul de Sénanges lifted his small valise with difficulty from the floor, on which he had placed it on entering the house, and carried it out of the room in both his arms. The brothers followed these movements with curiosity, and, when the door closed behind their mother and the stranger, their eyes met.

★★★★★★

Twenty-four hours had passed away, and nothing new had occurred at the Maison Alix. The servants had not expressed any curiosity respecting the departure of the citizen Glaire, no domiciliary visit had taken place, and Berthe and her father were discussing the propriety of Prosper's venturing, on the pretext of an excursion in another direction, a visit to the isolated and quiet dwelling of the master-mason. No signal had yet arrived. It was agreed that after the lapse of another day, if their tranquillity remained undisturbed, Prosper Alix should visit Paul de Sénanges. Berthe, who was silent and preoccupied, retired to her own room early, and her father, who was uneasy and apprehensive, desperately anxious for the promised communication from the *marquis*, was relieved by her absence.

The moon was high in the dark sky, and her beams were flung across the polished oak floor of Berthe's bedroom, through the great window with the stone balcony, when the girl, who had gone to sleep with her lover's name upon her lips in prayer, awoke with a sudden start, and sat up in her bed. An unbearable dread was upon her; and yet she was unable to utter a cry, she was unable to make another movement. Had she heard a voice? No, no one had spoken, nor did she fancy that she heard any sound. But within her, somewhere inside her heaving bosom, something said, "Berthe!"

And she listened, and knew what it was. And it spoke, and said:

"I promised you that, living or dead, I would come to you again. And I have come to you; but not living."

She was quite awake. Even in the agony of her fear she looked around, and tried to move her hands, to feel her dress and the bedclothes, and to fix her eyes on some familiar object, that she might satisfy herself, before this racing and beating, this whirling and yet icy chilliness of her blood should kill her outright, that she was really awake.

"I have come to you; but not living."

What an awful thing that voice speaking within her was! She tried to raise her head and to look toward the place where the moonbeams marked bright lines upon the polished floor, which lost themselves at the foot of the Japanese screen. She forced herself to this effort, and lifted her eyes, wild and haggard with fear, and there, the moonbeams at his feet, the tall black screen behind him, she saw Paul de Sénanges. She saw him; she looked at him quite steadily; she rose, slowly, with a mechanical movement, and stood upright beside her bed, clasping her forehead with her hands, and gazing at him. He stood motionless, in the dress he had worn when he took leave of her, the light-coloured riding-coat of the period, with a short cape, and a large white cravat tucked into the double breast. The white muslin was flecked, and the front of the riding-coat was deeply stained, with blood. He looked at her, and she took a step forward—another—then, with a desperate effort, she dashed open the railing and flung herself on her knees before him, with her arms stretched out as if to clasp him. But he was no longer there; the moonbeams fell clear and cold upon the polished floor, and lost themselves where Berthe lay, at the foot of the screen, her head upon the ground, and every sign of life gone from her.

★★★★★★

"Where is the citizen Glaire?" asked Prosper Alix of the *citoyenne* Pichon, entering the house of the master-mason abruptly, and with a stern and threatening countenance. "I have a message for him; I must see him."

"I know nothing about him," replied the *citoyenne*, without turning in his direction, or relaxing her culinary labours. "He went away from here the next morning, and I did not trouble myself to ask where; that is his affair."

"He went away? Without letting me know! Be careful, *citoyenne*; this is a serious matter."

"So they tell me," said the woman with a grin, which was not altogether free from pain and fear; "for you! A serious thing to have a *suspect* in your house, and palm him off on honest people. However, he went away peaceably enough when he knew we had found him out, and that we had no desire to go to prison, or worse, on his account, or yours."

She was strangely insolent, this woman, and the listener felt his helplessness; he had brought the young man there with such secrecy, he had so carefully provided for the success of concealment.

"Who carried his valise?" Prosper Alix asked her suddenly.

"How should I know?" she replied; but her hands lost their steadiness, and she upset a stew-pan; "he carried it here, didn't he? and I suppose he carried it away again."

Prosper Alix looked at her steadily—she shunned his gaze, but she

119

showed no other sign of confusion; then horror and disgust of the woman came over him.

"I must see Pichon," he said; "where is he?"

"Where should he be but at the wall? he and the boys are working there, as always. The citizen can see them; but he will remember not to detain them; in a little quarter of an hour the soup will be ready."

The citizen did see the master-mason and his sons, and after an interview of some duration he left the place in a state of violent agitation and complete discomfiture. The master-mason had addressed to him these words at parting:

"I assert that the man went away at his own free will; but if you do not keep very quiet, I shall deny that he came here at all—you cannot prove he did—and I will denounce you for harbouring a *suspect* and *ci-devant* under a false name. I know a De Sénanges when I see him as well as you, Citizen Alix; and, wishing M. Paul a good journey, I hope you will consider about this matter, for truly, my friend, I think you will sneeze in the sack before I shall."

✶✶✶✶✶✶

"We must bear it, Berthe, my child," said Prosper Alix to his daughter many weeks later, when the fever had left her, and she was able to talk with her father of the mysterious and frightful events which had occurred. "We are utterly helpless. There is no proof, only the word of these wretches against mine, and certain destruction to me if I speak. We will go to Spain, and tell the *marquis* all the truth, and never return, if you would rather not. But, for the rest, we must bear it."

"Yes, my father," said Berthe submissively, "I know we must; but God need not, and I don't believe He will."

The father and the daughter left France unmolested, and Berthe "bore it" as well as she could. When better times come they returned, Prosper Alix an old man, and Berthe a stern, silent, handsome woman, with whom no one associated any notions of love or marriage. But long before their return the traditions of the *Croix Rousse* were enriched by circumstances which led to that before-mentioned capital bargain made by the father of the Giraudier of the present. These circumstances were the violent death of Pichon and his two sons, who were killed by the fall of a portion of the great boundary-wall on the very day of its completion, and the discovery, close to its foundation, at the extremity of Pichon's *terre*, of the corpse of a young man attired in a light-coloured riding-coat, who had been stabbed through the heart.

Berthe Alix lived alone in the Château de Sénanges, under its restored name, until she was a very old woman. She lived long enough to see the golden figure on the summit of the "Holy Hill," long enough to forget the bad old times, but not long enough to forget or cease to mourn the lover who had kept his promise, and come back to her; the lover who rested in the earth which once covered the bones of the martyrs, and who kept a place for her by his side. She has filled that place for many years. You may see it, when you look down from the second gallery of the bell-tower at Fourvières, following the bend of the outstretched golden arm of Notre Dame.

The *château* was pulled down some years ago, and there is no trace of its former existence among the vines.

Good times, and bad times, and again good times have come for the *Croix Rousse*, for Lyons, and for France, since then; but the remembrance of the treachery of Pichon & Sons, and of the retribution which at once exposed and punished their crime, outlives all changes. And once, every year, on a certain summer night, three ghostly figures are seen, by any who have courage and patience to watch for them, gliding along by the foot of the boundary-wall, two of them carrying a dangling corpse, and the other, implements for mason's work and a small leather valise. Giraudier, *pharmacien*, has never seen these ghostly figures, but he describes them with much minuteness; and only the *esprits forts* of the *Croix Rousse* deny that the ghosts of Pichon & Sons are not yet laid.

Spring-Heeled Jack—The Terror of London

Out of the enormous army of highwaymen, footpads, and house-breakers, who have made themselves famous or infamous in the annals of English crime, probably not one ever succeeded in gaining such a large amount of notoriety in so short a space of time as the subject of our present sketch, Spring-Heeled Jack.

This quickly acquired reputation was the result, probably, of the veil of mystery which shrouded the identity of the man who was known on all hands as the Terror of London.

It was at one time generally believed that Spring-Heeled Jack was no less a personage than the then Marquis of Waterford.

This, however, was distinctly proved not to be the case, although the manner of proving it does not redound to the noble *marquis's* credit.

That the Marquis of Waterford and Jack could not be identical is proved conclusively by the fact that the terrible apparition showed itself to many persons on the 4th, 5th, and 6th, of April, 1837.

At this time we find from an indictment which was tried at the Derby assizes on Aug. 31st, 1837, that the Marquis of Waterford, Sir F. Johnstone, Bart., the Hon. A. C. H. Villiers, and E. H. Reynard, Esq., were charged with having committed an assault on April 5th, 1837.

On that day it was proved that the defendants were at the Croxton Park Races, about five miles from Melton Mowbray.

The whole of the four had been dining out at Melton on the evening of that day, and about two in the morning of the following day the watchmen on duty, hearing a noise, proceeded to the market place, and near Lord Rosebery's place saw several gentlemen attempting to overturn a caravan, a man being inside at the time.

The watchmen eventually succeeded in preventing this.

The *marquis* immediately challenged one of them to fight.

That worthy, however, having heard something about the nobleman's proficiency in the "noble art," at once declined.

On this the four swells took their departure.

Subsequently the same watchmen heard a noise in the direction of the toll bar.

They proceeded there at once, when they found that the gate-keeper had been screwed up in his house, and had been for some time calling out—

"Murder! come and release me."

The watchmen released the toll-keeper and started in pursuit of the roysterers.

When the "Charlies," as the guardians of the peace were called in those days, came up with the *marquis's* party for the second time, the watchman who had declined the challenge to fight observed that one of the swells carried a pot of red paint while the other carried a paint brush.

The man who had by this time grown a little more valorous, managed to wrest the paint brush from the hand of the person who held it.

But his triumph was of short duration, the four swells surrounded him, threw him on his back, stripped him, and ten minutes later the unfortunate man was painted a bright red from head to foot.

They then continued their "lark," painting the doors and windows of different houses red.

Some time later or rather earlier, Mr. Reynard was captured and put in the lock up.

The *marquis* and his two remaining companions succeeded in making an entrance to the constable's room.

Once there they had little difficulty in forcing him to give up his keys.

Once having obtained possession of these they had little difficulty in releasing the prisoner.

This done they bore their living trophy back to their lodgings in state, and the little town resumed its normal condition of quiet repose.

The jury found the defendants (who were all identified as having taken part in the affray) guilty of a common assault, and they were sentenced to pay a fine of £100 each, and to be imprisoned until such fine was paid.

It is hardly necessary to add that the money was at once forthcoming.

So our readers will see that this disgraceful affair proves conclusively that the Marquis of Waterford and Spring-Heeled Jack had a separate existence, unless the *marquis* was gifted with the power of being in two places at once.

In the *Annual Register*, Feb. 20th, 1837, we find the following—

Outrage on a Young Lady.—Frequent representations have of late been made to the Lord Mayor, of the alarm excited by a miscreant, who haunted the lanes and lonely places in the neighbourhood of the metropolis for the purpose of terrifying women and children.

For some time these statements were supposed to be greatly exaggerated.

However, the matter was put beyond a doubt by the following circumstance:—

A Mr. Alsop, who resided in Bearbind-lane, a lonely spot between the villages of Bow and Old Ford, attended at Lambeth-street Office, with his three daughters, to state the particulars of an outrageous assault upon one of his daughters, by a fellow who goes by the name of the suburban ghost, or 'Spring-Heeled Jack.'

Miss Jane Alsop, one of the young ladies, gave the following evidence:—

About a quarter to nine o'clock on the preceding night she heard a violent ringing at the gate in front of the house; and on going to the door to see what was the matter, she saw a man standing outside, of whom she inquired what was the matter.

The person instantly replied that he was a policeman, and said, 'For Heaven's sake bring me a light, for we have caught Spring-Heeled Jack here in the lane.'

She returned into the house and brought a candle and handed it to the person, who appeared enveloped in a large cloak.

The instant she had done so, however, he threw off his outer garment, and applying the lighted candle to his breast, presented a most hideous and frightful appearance, and vomited forth a quantity of blue and white flame from his mouth, and his eyes resembled red balls of fire.

From the hasty glance which her fright enabled her to get at his person, she observed that he wore a large helmet, and his dress, which appeared to fit him very tight, seemed to her to resemble white oilskin.

Without uttering a sentence he darted at her, and catching her partly by her dress and the back part of her neck, placed her head under one of his arms, and commenced bearing her down with his claws, which she was certain were of some metallic substance.

She screamed out as loud as she could for assistance, and by considerable exertion got away from him, and ran towards the house to get in.

Her assailant, however, followed her, and caught her on the steps leading to the hall door, when he again used considerable violence, tore her neck and arms with his claws, as well as a quantity of hair from her head; but she was at length rescued from his grasp by one of her sisters.

Miss Alsop added that she had suffered considerably all night from the shock she had sustained, and was then in extreme pain, both from the injury done to her arm, and the wounds and scratches inflicted by the miscreant on her shoulders and neck, with his claws or hands.

This story was fully confirmed by Mr. Alsop, and his other daughter said that the fellow kept knocking and ringing at the gate after she had dragged her sister away from him, but scampered off when she shouted from an upper window for a policeman.

He left his cloak behind him, which someone else picked up, and ran off with.

And again on Feb. 26th, of the same year, we find the following:—

'The Ghost, *alias* 'Spring-Heeled Jack' Again.—At Lambeth-street office, Mr. Scales, a respectable butcher, residing in Narrow-street, Limehouse, accompanied by his sister, a young woman eighteen years of age, made the following statement relative to the further gambols of Spring-Heeled Jack:—
Miss Scales stated that on the evening of Wednesday last, at about half-past eight o'clock, as she and her sister were returning from the house of their brother, and while passing along

Green Dragon-alley, they observed some, person standing in an angle in the passage.

She was in advance of her sister at the time, and just as she came up to the person, who was enveloped in a large cloak, he spurted a quantity of blue flame right in her face, which deprived her of her sight, and so alarmed her, that she instantly dropped to the ground, and was seized with violent fits, which continued for several hours.

Mr. Scales said that on the evening in question, in a few minutes after his sisters had left the house, he heard the loud screams of one of them, and on running up Green Dragon Alley he found his sister Lucy, who had just given her statement, on the ground in a fit, and his other sister endeavouring to hold and support her.

She was removed home, and he then learned from his other sister what had happened.

She described the person to be of tall, thin, and gentlemanly appearance, enveloped in a large cloak, and carried in front of his person a small lamp, or bull's eye, similar to those in possession of the police.

The individual did not utter a word, nor did he attempt to lay hands on them, but walked away in an instant.

Every effort was subsequently made by the police to discover the author of these and similar outrages, and several persons were taken up and underwent lengthened examinations, but were finally set at liberty, nothing being elicited to fix the offence upon them.

Articles and paragraphs of this nature were of almost daily occurrence at this period, and the public excitement rose to such a pitch that "Vigilance Committees" were formed in various parts of London to try and put a stop to the Terror's pranks and depredations, even if they could not succeed in securing his apprehension. There could be no possible doubt that there was very little exaggeration in the extraordinary statements as to Spring-Heeled Jack's antics.

A bet of two hundred pounds, which became the talk of the clubs and coffee-houses, did more to add to Jack's reputation for supernatural powers than all the talk of mail-coach guards, market people, and servant girls.

A party of gentlemen were travelling by the then newly-opened

London and North-Western Railway.

As they neared the northern end of the Primrose Hill tunnel they observed the figure of Jack sitting on a post, looking exactly as his Satanic Majesty is usually represented in picture books or on the stage.

"By Jove! there's Spring-Heeled Jack," cried Colonel Fortescue, one of the travellers.

"Yes," cried Major Howard, one of his companions, "and I'll bet you two hundred pounds even that he's at the other end of the tunnel when we arrive there."

"Done!" cried the colonel.

And sure enough as the train emerged once more into the open air there was Spring-Heeled Jack at the side of the line, his long moustaches twirled up the sides of his prominent nose, and stream of sulphurous flame seeming to pour out from between his lips.

Another instant and he had disappeared.

The whole party in the train were almost paralysed for a time, although most of them had "set their squadron in the field," and hardly knew what fear meant.

Colonel Fortescue handed the major the two hundred pounds, and the affair became a nine-days' wonder.

The solution was, no doubt, simple enough.

Spring-Heeled Jack had sprung on to the moving train at the rear, and during its passage through the tunnel had made his way to the front, and then, with a bound, had made his appearance in front of the advancing train.

Be this as it may, the unimpeachable evidence of men of position, like the gallant officers, backed up, as it was, by the payment and receipt of the two hundred pounds, brought Jack with a bound, like one from his own spring heels, to the utmost pinnacle of notorious fame.

We have no particulars of the exact mechanism that enabled Spring-heeled Jack to make such extraordinary bounds.

To jump clear over a stagecoach, with its usual complement of passengers on top, was as easy to him as stepping across a gutter would be to any ordinary man.

The secret of these boots had died with the inventor, and perhaps it is as well.

We have no doubt that if those boots were purchasable articles many of our readers would be tempted to leave off taking in the Boy's *Standard*, so as to be able to save up more pennies towards the purchase of a pair.

Fancy, if you can, what would be the consequence of a small army of Spring-heels in every district.

To return, however, to our hero.

His dress was most striking.

It consisted of a tight-fitting garment, which covered him from his neck to his feet.

This garment was of a blood-red colour.

One foot was encased in a high-heeled, pointed shoe, while the other was hidden in a peculiar affair, something like a cow's hoof, in imitation, no doubt, of the "cloven hoof" of Satan. It was generally supposed that the "springing" mechanism was contained in that hoof.

He wore a very small black cap on his head, in which was fastened one bright crimson feather.

The upper part of his face was covered with black domino.

When not in action the whole was concealed by an enormous black cloak, with one hood, and which literally covered him from head to foot.

He did not always confine himself to this dress though, for sometimes he would place the head of an animal, constructed out of paper and plaster, over his own, and make changes in his attire.

Still, the above was his favourite costume, and our readers may imagine it was a most effective one for Jack's purpose.

These are almost all the published facts about this extraordinary man.

But we have been favoured by the descendants of Spring-Heeled Jack with the perusal of his "*Journal*" or "*Confessions*," call it which you will.

The only condition imposed upon us in return for this very great favour is that we shall conceal the real name of the hero of this truly extraordinary story.

The reason for this secrecy is obvious.

The descendants of Spring-Heeled Jack are at the present time large landed proprietors in South of England, and although had it not been for our hero's exploits they would not at the present time be occupying that position, still one can hardly wonder at their not wishing the real name of Spring-Heeled Jack to become known.

As it will, however, be necessary for the proper unravelling of our story that some name should be used we will bestow upon our hero the name of Dacre.

Jack Dacre was the son of a baronet whose creation went back as far back as 1619.

Jack's father had been a younger son, and, as was frequently the case in those days, he had been sent out to India to see what he could do for himself.

This was rendered necessary by the fact that I although the Dacres possessed a considerable amount of land the whole of it was strictly entailed.

This fact was added to the perhaps more important one that each individual Dacre in possession of the title and estates seemed to consider that it was his duty to live close up to his income, and to give his younger sons nothing to start in life with, save a good education.

That is to say, the younger sons had the run of the house.

They were taught to shoot by the keepers; to ride by the grooms; to throw a fly, perhaps, by the gardener; and to pick up what little "book-learning" they could.

Not altogether a bad education, perhaps, in those days when fortunes could be made in India by any who had fair connections, plenty of pluck, and plenty of industry.

Jack's father was early told that he could expect no money out of the estate, and he was also informed that he could choose his own path in life.

This did not take him long.

Sidney Dacre was a plucky young fellow, and thought that India would afford the widest scope for his talents, which were not of the most brilliant order, as may be expected from his early training.

To India he therefore went, and managed to shake the "pagoda tree" to a pretty fair extent.

In 1837 he thought he was justified in taking to himself a wife, and of this union Jack, who was born in the year of Waterloo, was the only result.

Fifteen years later Sidney Dacre received the intelligence that his father and his two brothers had perished in a storm near Bantry Bay, where they had gone to assist as volunteers in repelling a supposed French invading party which it was anticipated would attempt to effect a landing there.

This untimely death of his three relatives left Sidney Dacre the heir to the baronetcy and estates; and although he had plantation after plantation in the Presidencies, he made up his mind that he would at once return to the old country.

He therefore placed his Indian plantations in the hands of one Alfred Morgan, a clerk, in whom he had always placed implicit confidence.

This man, by the way, had been the sole witness to his marriage with Jack's mother.

A month later, and Sir Sidney and Lady Dacre, with their son, set sail in the good ship *Hydaspes* on their way to England.

Nothing of any importance occurred on the voyage, and the *Hydaspes* was within sight of the white cliffs of old Albion when a storm came on, and almost within gunshot of home the brave old ship which had weathered many a storm went to pieces.

All that were saved out of passengers and crew were two souls.

One, our hero Jack Dacre, afterwards to become the notorious Spring-Heeled Jack; the other, a common sailor, Ned Chump, a man who is destined to play a not unimportant part in this history, even if the part he had already played did not entitle him to mention in our columns.

And when we tell our readers that had it not been for the friendly office of Ned Chump our hero must inevitably have perished with the rest, we think they will agree that they owe the jolly sailor a certain amount of gratitude.

Ned Chump had taken very great interest in our hero on the voyage home.

Jack was such a handsome, bright-looking lad, that everyone seemed to take to him at first sight.

Ned's devotion to him more resembled that of a faithful mastiff to his master than any other simile that we can call to mind.

When Ned saw that the fate of the *Hydaspes* was inevitable he made up his mind that Master Jack and he should be saved if there was any possibility of such a thing.

The jolly tar bound Jack Dacre fast to a hen coop, and then attached his belt to it with a leather thong.

This done Ned threw the lad, the coop, and himself into the sea, and beating out bravely managed to get clear of the ship as she went down head first.

Had he not have done this they must inevitably have been drawn into the vortex caused by the sinking ship.

Fortunately for both of them Jack had become unconscious, or it is not likely that he would have deserted his father and mother, even at this critical juncture.

However, the *Hydaspes* and all on board, including Sir Sidney and Lady Dacre, had gone to the bottom of the sea ere Jack recovered consciousness and found himself on the shore of Kent, with his faithful companion in adversity bending over him with loving care.

As soon as Jack Dacre was sufficiently recovered, Ned proceeded to "take his bearings" as he expressed it, and knowing that Jack's ancestral home was somewhere in the county of Sussex, he suggested that they should move in a westerly direction until they should find some native of the soil who could inform them of the locality they were in.

They found upon inquiry that they had been cast ashore at a little village called Worth, in the neighbourhood of Sandwich, and that the good ship *Hydaspes* had fallen a victim to the insatiable voracity of the Goodwin Sands.

Shipwrecked mariners are always well treated in England, the old stories of wreckers and their doings notwithstanding, and Jack Dacre and the trusty Ned Chump had little difficulty in making their way to Dacre Hall in Sussex, though neither had sixpence in his pocket, so sudden had their departure from the wrecked ship been.

When Jack arrived at the home of his forefathers he found one Michael Dacre, who informed our hero that he was his father's first cousin, in possession.

"Yes, my lad," went on Michael Dacre, in a particularly unpleasant manner, "Sir Sidney's cousin; and failing his lawful issue I am the heir to Dacre Hall and the baronetcy."

"Failing his lawful issue!" cried Jack, with all the impetuosity of youth. "Am I not my father's only son, and therefore heir to the family honours and estates?"

"Softly, young man—softly," cringed Michael, "I do not want to anger you. Of course you have the proof with you that your father and mother were married, and that you are the issue of that union?"

"Proof!" cried Jack, fairly losing his temper. "Do you think one swims ashore from a doomed ship with his family archives tied round his waist?"

"There—there, my boy," said the wily Michael, "don't lose your temper; for you must see that it would have been better for you if you had have taken the precaution to have brought the papers with you."

"But," said Jack, quite nonplussed by his cousin's coolness, "Ned Chump, here, knows who I am, and that everything is straight and above board."

"Yes, yes, my boy," replied Michael; "and pray how long has Mr.

131

Chump, as I think you call him, known you? Was he present at your father's marriage? I do not suppose he was present at your birth," and Michael Dacre concluded his speech with a quiet but diabolical chuckle.

"I have known him ever since the day we left India—" began the lad.

But Michael interrupted him by saying, in a somewhat harsher tone than he had used before—

"That is equal to not knowing you at all. I am an acknowledged Dacre, and until you can prove your right to that name I shall remain in possession of Dacre Hall; for the honour of my family I could not do otherwise."

"But what am I? Where am I to go? What am I to do?" stammered Jack.

Meanwhile, Ned Chump looked on with kindling eyes, and a fierce light in his face that boded ill for Michael Dacre should it come to blows between them.

Michael caught the look, and felt that perhaps it would be better to temporise, he therefore said—

"Oh! Dacre Hall is large enough for us all. While I am making the necessary enquiries in India, you and this common sailor here can knock about the place. It will, perhaps, be quite as well that I have you under my eye, so that if you turn out to be an impostor you may be punished as you deserve."

After a short consultation, Jack and Ned Chump made up their mind that it would be best to accept the churlish offer.

"After all," said Ned, "you know that you are the rightful heir. And when the proofs come over from India you will easily be able to claim your own."

"Yes, Ned, I suppose we had better remain on the spot."

"Of course we had," said Ned. "There is only one thing against it, and that is that if I ever saw murder in anyone's eye it was in your cousin's just now. But never mind, lad, we'll stick together, and we shall circumvent the old villain, never you fear."

So it was arranged, and Ned Chump and Jack Dacre soon seemed to have become part and parcel of the establishment at Dacre Hall.

The sailor's ready ingenuity and willingness to oblige made him rapidly a great favourite among the servants and *employés* generally, while Jack's sunny face, and flow of anecdote about the strange places he had been in and the strange sights he had seen, rendered him a decided acquisition to what was, under the circumstances, a somewhat sombre household.

So time passed on, and the first reply was received from India.

This reply came from Alfred Morgan, the late Sir Sidney's trusted representative.

This letter destroyed in an instant any hope, if such ever existed, in Michael Dacre's breast that Jack might be an impostor.

But there was one gleam of hope in the cautiously-worded postscript to the letter.

"Do not mention this to anyone. I am on my way to England, and I may identify the boy and produce the necessary papers—or I may not. It will depend a great deal upon the first interview I have with you; and that interview must take place before I see the boy."

"What did this mean?" thought Michael Dacre. "Did it mean that here was a tool ready to his hand, who would swear away his cousin's birthright?"

Time alone would show.

Then again the improbability of such a thing occurring would sweep over him with tenfold force, and he decided to take time by the forelock and remove Jack from his path.

Michael Dacre had not the pluck to do this fell deed himself, but he had more than one tool at hand who would fulfil his foul bidding for a price.

The man he chose on this occasion was one Black Ralph, a ruffian who had been everything by turns, but nothing long.

He was strongly suspected of obtaining his living at the time of which we are writing by poaching, but nothing had ever been proved against him.

In the days when Jack's grandfather had been alive, Michael Dacre, who acted as steward and agent on the estate, always pooh-poohed any suggestion of the kind, and sent the complaining gamekeepers away, literally "with a flea in their ears."

The arrangement was soon made between Michael Dacre and Black Ralph.

The former was to admit the latter to the house, and he was to ransack the plate pantry, taking sufficient to repay him for his trouble.

He was then to pass to Jack's bedroom, which Michael pointed out, and to settle him at once.

He was then to proceed to Newhaven, where a lugger was to be in waiting, and so make his way with his booty over to France.

This the cousin thought would make all secure.

But he had reckoned without his host.

Or shall we say his guest, as it was in that light that he regarded the real Sir John Dacre?

The lad was a light sleeper, and on the night planned for the attack he became aware of the presence of Black Ralph in his chamber almost as soon as the would-be assassin had entered it.

Brave though Jack was, he felt a thrill of terror run through him as he thought of his utterly helpless condition, for Ned Chump had been sent on some cunningly-contrived errand to keep him out of the way, and he had not yet returned.

That murder was the object of the midnight intruder Jack Dacre never doubted.

There was but one way out of it, and that was to rush up into the bell tower which communicated with a staircase abutting on his chamber.

Once here he could ring the bell, if he could only keep his assailant at bay.

At the worst, he could but jump into the moat below, and stand a chance of saving his life.

In an instant he had left his bed, and dashed for the door.

But the assassin was upon him.

Jack just managed to bound up the stairs, and enter the tower.

Ere he could seize the bell-rope he felt Black Ralph's hot breath upon his neck. In an instant the lad had sprang upon the parapet. Then an instant later he was speeding on his way to the moat below, having made the terrible leap with a grace and daring which he never afterwards eclipsed, even when assisted by the mechanical appliances which he used in the adventures we are about to describe in his assumed character of Spring-Heeled Jack.

Our hero suffered nothing from his perilous jump worse than a ducking.

And it is very probable that this did him more good than harm, as it served to restore his somewhat scattered thoughts.

By the time Jack Dacre had managed to clamber out of the moat, Black Ralph had put a considerable distance between himself and Dacre Hall.

He had got his share of the booty, and whether Master Jack survived the fall or not mattered little to him.

He could rely upon Michael Dacre's promise that the lugger should be waiting for him at Newhaven, and once in France he could soon find a melting-pot for his treasure, and live, for a time at least, a life of riotous extravagance.

When Jack reached the house he found the hall door open, and without fear he entered; bent upon going straight to his cousin's room and informing him of what had happened.

Before he could reach the corridor which contained the state bedroom in which Michael Dacre had ensconced himself, Jack heard a low—

"Hist!"

He turned round and saw Ned Chump beckoning to him and pointing to the flight of stairs that led to their common chamber, and from thence to the bell tower.

Our hero having perfect confidence in his sailor friend obeyed the signal.

When the two were safely seated in their bedroom, Ned said, eagerly—

"Tell me, boy, what has happened?"

In a very few words Jack told him.

"My eye!" ejaculated Ned with a low whistle, "that was a jump indeed."

Then he continued—

"But who was your assailant? Could you not see his face?"

"No; it was too dark," replied Jack; "but there was a something about his figure that seemed familiar to me."

"Yes, lad, there was," said honest Ned Chump. "I met the ruffian but now, making the best of his way to Newhaven, no doubt."

"Who was it?" asked the lad.

"Why that poaching scoundrel, Black Ralph," answered Ned; "and you may depend upon it that your worthy cousin has laid this plant to kill you, and so prevent any chance of a bother about the property."

"What had I better do?" asked Jack. "I will act entirely under your advice."

"Well, my boy," said Ned, "take no notice; let matters take their course. We are sure to find out something or other in the morning."

And the two firm friends carefully fastened their door and turned in to rest.

In the morning the alarm of the robbery was given, but neither Jack nor Ned uttered one word to indicate that they knew aught about it.

"How did you get in?" asked Michael Dacre, roughly, as he turned towards Chump.

The would-be baronet's rage at the appearance of Jack Dacre unharmed, although his plate-chest (as he chose to consider it) had been ransacked, knew no bounds.

But Ned had his answer ready.

"I thought the door was left open for me, sir," he said, "so I simply entered and bolted the door behind me, and made my way up to bed."

"This is indeed a mysterious affair," said Michael Dacre, "but I have reasons of my own for not letting the officers of justice know about this affair. I have my suspicions as to who the guilty party is, and I think, if all is kept quiet, I can see my way to recovering my lost plate."

"Your lost plate!" said Jack, contemptuously. "Say, rather, my lost plate."

"I thought that subject was to be tabooed between us until Mr. Morgan arrives with the proofs of your identity, or imposture, as the case may be."

"Very well, sir," replied Jack; "so be it. But I cannot help thinking that Mr. Morgan ought to have arrived long before this."

However, in due course the long-looked for one arrived.

But instead of coming straight on to Dacre Hall, as one would have expected a trustworthy agent to have done, he took up his quarters at the Dacre Arms, and sent word to Michael Dacre that Mr. Alfred wanted to see hint on important business.

The message, of course, was a written one, as the people belonging to the inn would have thought it strange had an unknown man sent such a message to one so powerful as Michael Dacre was now making himself out to be.

In an hour's time the two men were seated over a bottle of brandy, discussing the position of affairs.

"And if I prove to the law's satisfaction—never mind about yours, for you know the truth—that the boy is illegitimate, what is to be my share?"

"A thousand pounds," said Michael.

"A thousand fiddlesticks," replied Morgan, grinding his teeth. "Without my aid you are a penniless beggar, kicked out of Dacre Hall; and with no profession to turn your hands to. Make it worth my while, and what are you? Why Sir Michael Dacre, the owner of this fine estate, and one of the most powerful landowners in this part of the county of Sussex. A thousand pounds—bah!"

The would-be owner of Dacre Hall looked aghast at Morgan's vehemence, and with an imploring gesture he placed his finger on his lip and pointed at the door.

Then under his breath he muttered—

"Five thousand, then?"

"No, not five thousand, nor yet ten thousand," said Morgan.

"Now look you here, Mr. Michael Dacre," he went on with a strong emphasis upon the prefix.

"Now look here—my only terms are these: You to take the Dacre estates in England, and I to have the Indian plantations. That's my ultimatum. Answer, 'yes' or 'no.'"

For an instant Michael Dacre hesitated, but he saw no hope in the cold grey eye of Alfred Morgan, and at last consented.

The two now separated, but met again the following day, when the necessary agreements were signed, and Mr. Alfred retired to Brighton to make his appearance two days later as Mr. Alfred Morgan, the Indian representative of the late Sir Sidney Dacre.

"My poor boy," he said, sympathetically, when he first met our hero. "My poor boy, this is a terrible blow for you."

"What do you mean?" asked Jack; "it was a terrible blow to me when my father and my mother went down in the *Hydaspes*—but Time, the great Healer, has softened that blow so that I should hardly feel it now, were it not for the doubts that my cousin here has cast upon my identity."

"Ah! of your identity there can be no doubt, poor boy," sighed Alfred Morgan; "and that's where lies the pity of it."

"How do you mean?" cried Jack, an angry flush mantling his handsome features.

"How do mean, poor boy?" went on the merciless scoundrel. "Why, the pity of it is that, although I know so well that you are the son of your father and mother, the law refuses to recognise you as such."

"And why?" yelled Jack, with a sudden and overwhelming outburst of fury.

"Because," meekly replied the villain, "your father and mother were never married."

"But," cried Jack, thoroughly taken aback by this assertion, "you were the witness to the marriage. I have heard my father say so scores of times."

"Aye, my poor lad; but your mother had a husband living at the time," and Mr. Alfred handed a bundle of papers to the family solicitor, who had not yet spoken, the whole conversation having taken place between Jack and Mr. Alfred Morgan.

A silence like that of the tomb fell upon the fell upon the occupants of the room as the lawyer examined the papers.

Ten minutes or a quarter of an hour passed, then, with a sigh, the kind-hearted solicitor turned to Jack and said, with tears in his—

"Alas, my lad; it is too true; you have no right to the name of Dacre."

Without a word Jack caught hold of Ned's hand, and, turning to his cousin, said, in a voice of thunder—

"There is some villainy here, which, please Heaven, I will yet unravel. Once already you have tried to murder my body, now you are trying to murder my mother's reputation; but as I escaped from the first plot by a clean pair of heels and a good spring from the bell tower, so on occasion I feel that I shall eventually conquer. Come, Ned, we will leave this, and make our plans for the future."

"Aye, Master Spring-Heels, make yourself scarce, or I will have you lashed and kicked from the door, you wretched impostor!"

"Yes, cousin, I will go," answered Jack, impressively; "and I will accept the name you have given me, as you say I have no right to any other. But, beware! false Sir Michael Dacre, the time will come, and that ere long, when the tortures of the damned shall be implanted in your heart by me—the wretched, despised outcast whom you have christened Spring-Heeled-Jack!"

As our hero uttered these words Michael Dacre's cheek paled visibly.

And indeed there was good cause for his apparent fear.

Jack Dacre had thrown such an amount of expression into his words and gestures as seemed to render them truly prophetic.

At this moment Mr. Reece, the solicitor, advanced towards Jack and, holding out a well filled purse to him, said—

"Take this, my lad; it shall never be said that Sam Reece allowed the son of his old playmate, Sid Dacre, to be turned out of house and home without a penny in his pocket, legitimate or not."

Jack, responding to a nudge from Ned Chump, took the purse and said—

"Thank you, sir, for your kindness. That there is some villainy afloat I am convinced, but whether I eventually succeed in proving my claim or not this money shall be faithfully returned. Once more, thank you, sir, and goodbye."

With this Jack and Ned left the room. As soon as they had taken their departure the "baronet," as we must style him for a time, recovered his self-possession to a certain extent.

Turning to the solicitor, he said—

"How much was there in that purse, Mr. Reece? Of course I cannot allow you to lose your money over the unfortunate whelp."

The lawyer, who, although the documentary evidence was so plain, could not help thinking with Jack Dacre that some villainy was afloat, answered the baronet very shortly.

"What I gave the lad, I gave him out of pure good feeling, I want no repayment from anyone. And, mark my words, Sir Michael Dacre, that boy will return my loan sooner or later, and if there is anything wrong about these papers I feel assured that he will carry out his threat with regard to yourself."

"What do you mean, insolent—" cried the baronet.

But ere he could finish the sentence, Mr. Reece calmly said—

"You do not suppose that the matter will drop here? The poor lad has no friends, and I was stupid in not having detained him when he proposed to leave this house. However, I missed that opportunity of questioning him as to his life in India, and the relations that existed between his father and his mother. One thing is certain, however, and that is he will appear here again."

"Well, and if he does!" asked the angry baronet.

"Well, and if he does he will find a firm friend in Sam Reece," answered the lawyer. "I shall retain these papers—not by virtue of any legal right that I can claim to possess. So, if you want them, you have only to apply to the courts of law to recover possession of them."

"Then you shall do no more business for me," cried Michael Dacre.

"I should have thought," replied the solicitor, "that my few words had effectually severed all business relations between us. As it appears that you do not take this view, allow me to say that all the gold in the Indies would not tempt me to act as your legal adviser for another hour. A man who can behave to an unfortunate boy-cousin in the manner you have behaved to Jack Dacre, legitimate or not, can hold no business communications with Sam Reece."

"But how about my papers?" quoth the now half-frightened baronet.

"I will send you your bill, and on receipt of a cheque for my costs I will return you all the papers of yours that I hold—save and except, mark you, those relating to the marriage of the late baronet and the birth and baptism of his son."

The new baronet looked at his ally, Mr. Alfred Morgan, but saw very little that was consoling in that worthy man's face.

He therefore accepted the position, and with as haughty a bow as he could possibly make under the circumstances, he allowed Mr. Reece to take his departure.

By this time Jack Dacre and Ned Chump were more than a mile away from the hall.

Ned, although far more experienced in the ways of the world than Jack Dacre, tacitly allowed the latter to take the lead of the "expedition," if such a word may be used.

Jack, boy as he was, was in no way deficient in common sense, so perhaps Ned was justified in accepting the youngster as his leader.

For some miles not a word escaped Jack Dacre's lips.

At last they arrived at the old-fashioned town of Arundel, and here Jack suddenly turned to his companion, and said—

"We'll stop here and rest, and think over what will be our best course to pursue."

"All serene, skipper," answered Ned, "I am quite content."

Jack gave a melancholy smile as he replied to the sailor's salutation—

"Oh! then you don't object to calling me your skipper, although you have heard that I am base born, and have no right to bear any name at all."

"Never fear, Master Jack—or Sir John, perhaps, I ought to say—there is some rascality at work, and I believe that that Mr. Alfred Morgan is at the bottom of it. But we shall circumvent the villains, I am sure, never fear."

"Yes," replied Jack, "I think we shall."

"Ah!" said Ned, "but how?"

"I have not been idle during our long walk," said Jack, as the two entered the hospitable portals of the Bridge House Hotel.

"I have not been idle, and if we can get a private room we will talk the matter over, and see how much money the good lawyer was kind enough to give us."

"To give you, you mean," said Chump, with a chuckle. "It's precious little he'd have given me, I reckon."

They managed to obtain a private room, and over a plain but substantial repast they counted the contents of the lawyer's purse.

To the intense surprise of both, and to the extreme delight of Ned Chump, it was found to contain very little short of fifty guineas.

The sailor had never in the whole of his life had a chance of sharing in such a prize as this.

With Jack, of course, the thing was different.

In India he had been accustomed to see money thrown about by lavish hands.

Between the ideas of Ned Chump, the common sailor, and those of the son of the rich planter, there could hardly be anything in common as far as regarded the appreciation of wealth.

But, nevertheless, the friendship that had sprung up between them in so short a time, never faded until death, the great divider, stepped in and made all human friendship impossible.

As soon as Jack had satisfied himself as to the actual strength of their available capital, he turned to Ned Chump and said—

"This money will not last long, and I do not see how I can do anything in the way of working for a living, if I am ever to hope to prove my title to the Dacre baronetcy and estates."

"That's as it may be, skipper," said Ned, "but I don't quite see how we are to live without work when this here fifty pounds has gone."

"That's just the point I have been thinking over," said Jack. "I am not yet sixteen, but, thanks to my Oriental birth, I look more like twenty."

"That you do, skipper," chimed in Ned.

"Well, then, I'll tell you what I intend to do."

"Go on, sir," cried the anxious sailor.

"Some year or two ago I had for a tutor an old *moonshee*, who had formerly been connected with a troop of conjurors—and you must have heard how clever the Indian conjurors are."

"Yes," replied Ned, "and I have seen for myself as well."

"Then," said Jack, "you will not be surprised at what I am going to tell you."

"Perhaps not, skipper—fire away," said Ned.

"Well, this *moonshee* taught me the mechanism of a boot which one member of his band had constructed, and which boot enabled him to spring fifteen or twenty feet up in the air, and from thirty to forty feet in a horizontal direction."

"Lor!" was the only exclamation that the open-mouthed and

open-eared sailor could make use of.

"Yes," continued our hero, "and I intend to invest a portion of this money in making a boot like it."

"Yes; but," stammered the half-bewildered sailor—"but when you have made it, of what use will it be to us, or, rather, how will it enable you to regain your rights?"

"I have formed my plan," answered Jack, "and it is this. I'll make the boot, and then startle the world with a novel highwayman. My cousin twitted me about my spring into the moat and my nimble heels. I'll hunt him down and keep him in a perpetual state of deadly torment, under the style and title of Spring-Heeled Jack."

"But," asked the sailor, "you will not turn thief?"

"I shall not call myself a thief," said Jack, proudly. "The world may dub me so if it likes. I shall take little but what belongs to me, I shall confine my depredations as much as possible to assisting my cousin in collecting my rents."

"Oh! I see," said Ned, only half-convinced.

The faithful tar had the sailor's natural respect for honesty, and did not quite like his "skipper's" plan for securing a livelihood.

But Jack, who had been brought up under the shadow of the East India Company, had not many scruples as to the course of life he had resolved to adopt.

To him pillage and robbery seemed to be the right of the well-born.

He had seen so much of this sort of thing amongst his father's friends and acquaintances that his moral sense was entirely warped.

So speciously did he put forth his arguments that Ned at last yielded.

The sailor simply stipulated that he should take no active part in any robbery.

For the faithful salt could find no other term for the operation.

To this Jack readily consented, and a compact was entered into between them as to what each was expected to do.

Ned promised faithfully to do all he could to assist his master in escaping, should he at any time be in danger of arrest.

Jack, on his part, promising Ned Chump a fair share of the plunder gained by Spring-Heeled Jack.

This arrangement entered into, the next thing was to make the spring boot.

Jack, who was possessed with an intelligence as well as physique far beyond his years, suggested that they should make their way to Southampton.

There, he argued, they could procure all they wanted without exciting suspicion.

Ned, of course, had no hesitation in falling in with this proposal.

A fortnight later and the boot was completed.

Completed, that is, so far as the actual manufacture was concerned.

Whether it would act or not remained to be seen.

To have tried its power in any ordinary house would have been absurdly ridiculous.

There was no place where it would be safe to make the trial spring save in the open air.

Jack had manufactured the boot strictly according to the old *moonshee's* directions, but he could not tell to what length the mechanism might hurl him, and he was a great deal too sensible to attempt to ascertain the extent of its power in any enclosed space.

So one morning, Ned and Jack started off from the inn where they were staying, for a ramble in the country, taking the magic boot with them.

Ned had by this time managed to allay his scruples and went into the affair with as much spirit as did Jack himself.

In due course they reached a spot which Jack pronounced to be a suitable one for the important trial.

The spot was an old quarry, or rather chalk pit, where at one spot the soil had only been removed for a depth of about twelve feet.

Descending this pit Jack placed the boot on his foot.

Ned looked on in the utmost wonderment.

He could hardly conceive that it was possible such a simple contrivance should possess such magical attributes.

To his astonishment, however, he saw his young master, for as such Ned regarded Jack Dacre, suddenly rise in the air and settle down quietly on the upper land some twelve or fourteen feet above.

Ned, who, although a Protestant, if anything, had lived long enough amongst Catholics on board ship and elsewhere to have imbibed some of their customs, made the sign of the cross and ejaculated something that was meant for a prayer.

To his untutored mind the whole thing savoured strongly of sorcery.

An instant later and Jack Dacre, who had thus easily earned the right to be called Spring-Heeled Jack, had sprung down into the quarry again, and stood by the side of his faithful henchman.

"Well, skipper," cried Ned, "I've heard of mermaids and sea-serpents, and whales that have swallowed men without killing them, but this boot of yours bangs anything I have ever heard of, though you must know, it isn't all gospel that is preached in the forecastle."

"It's all right, Ned," said Jack, "and with this simple contrivance you will see that I shall spring myself into what I feel convinced is my lawful inheritance."

"I'm with you," said Ned, as keen in the affair now as Jack Dacre himself.

"I'm with you, and where shall we go now."

"Well, old friend, I must purchase one or two articles of disguise, and then I think we will make our way towards Dorking."

"To Dorking?" queried Ned. "I thought you would have made your way towards Dacre Hall, especially as you said you wished to assist your cousin to collect his rents. Ha! ha! ha!" and the jolly tar finished his sentence by bursting into an uncontrollable fit of laughter.

"Well, you see," replied Jack, "that's just where it is. Although my poor father never dreamed that he would inherit the family estates, he had sufficient pride of birth to keep me, his own son, in spite of all that they say, well posted in the geography of the entailed estates of the Dacres. I consequently know that more than one goodly farm in the neighbourhood of Dorking belongs to me by right; and, therefore, to that place I mean to start to make my first rent collection, as I am determined to call my operations; for the terms robbery and thief are quite as repugnant to me as they are to you, Ned Chump."

"But, skipper, I never thought of you as a real thief," said Ned, "it was merely because I could not see how you could take that which belonged other people without robbery, that made me speak as I did. But if you are really only going to collect that which is your own, why there can be no harm in it, I am sure."

"That's right, Ned, and if I ever I do kick over the traces and make mistake, you may depend I'll do more good than harm with the money I capture, even if it should not be legally my own."

Four days later the two had arrived at Dorking.

Jack had provided himself with a most efficient disguise.

His tall and well-developed, although youthful, figure suited the tight-fitting garb of the theatrical Mephistopheles to a nicety.

Ned was perfectly enraptured at his appearance, and declared that

144

he could not possibly fail to strike terror into the guilty breast of his cousin, the false baronet, should they ever meet again.

Jack merely laughed, and said that that was an event which would assuredly come to pass sooner or later.

It was an easy task, in a place like Dorking, to ascertain which were the lands that belonged to the Dacres.

The first farm that Jack chose as the one for his maiden rent collection was at a small place called Newdigate.

Jack chose this for his first attempt, partly because of the isolated situation of the farm, and partly because the tenant bore a very evil reputation in the neighbourhood.

Our hero, it must be remembered, was at that romantic period of life when youth is apt to consider it is its duty to become as far as possible the protector of virtue and the avenger of injustice.

It was currently reported that the tenant in question, whom we will call Farmer Brown (all names in this veracious chronicle it must be understood are assumed) had possessed himself of the lease in an unlawful manner.

It was also said that his niece, Selina Brown, who was the rightful owner of the farm, was kept a prisoner somewhere within the walls of the solitary farmhouse.

Rumour also added that she was a maniac.

To one of Jack's ardent and romantic temperament this story was, as our readers may easily conjecture, a great inducement for him to make his first venture a call at Brown's farm.

Ned received strict injunctions to remain at the inn where they had taken up their abode, and to be ready to admit our hero without a moment's delay upon his return.

The night was a truly splendid one.

As Jack set out on his errand, an errand which might as a result land him in goal, he felt not one tittle of fear.

"Thrice armed is he who has hit cause aright," runs the old saying, and Jack certainly believed that he was perfectly justified in the course he was pursuing.

Modern moralists would doubtless differ; but we must remember what his early training had been, and make excuses accordingly.

He arrived at Brown's Farm, Newdigate, in due course.

Now came the most critical point in the career of Spring-Heeled Jack.

This was his first venture.

Failure meant ruin—ruin pure and simple.

If his wonderful contrivance refused to act in the manner in which it had acted at the rehearsal, what would be the result?

There could be but one answer to that question.

Capture, ruin to all his plans, and the infinite shame of a public trial.

But our hero had well weighed the odds and was quite prepared to face them.

Arrived at the farm he had no difficulty in finding out the window of the room in which Mr. Brown usually slept.

This window had been so clearly described to him by the Dorking people that there was no fear of Jack making a mistake.

With one spring he alighted on the broad, old-fashioned window-sill, and an instant later he had opened the casement.

The farmer was seated in a comfortable armchair in front of a large old-fashioned bureau.

He had evidently been counting his money and appropriating it in special portions for the payment perhaps of his landlord, his seed merchant, and so on.

The noise that Jack made as he opened the window caused the farmer to turn swiftly round.

Judge, if you can, his dismay when he found what kind of a visitor had made a call upon him.

On this, his first adventure in the garb of Spring-Heeled Jack, our hero had not called the aid of phosphorus into requisition.

His appearance, however, was well calculated to strike terror into the breast of any one.

Still more so, therefore, into the heart of one, who, like the farmer, was depriving his orphan niece of her legal rights, as well as of her liberty.

With a yell like that of a man in an epileptic fit, Farmer Brown sprang to his feet.

In another instant, however, he had sunk back again into his chair-rendered for the time hopelessly insane.

Jack, without any consideration of the amount which might or might not be due to the owner of the Dacre estates, calmly took possession of all the cash that he could find in the bureau, and then thought it was time to turn his attention to the alleged prisoner, Selina Brown.

Satisfying himself that the bureau contained no money save that which he had already secured, Jack was overjoyed at finding a document, hidden away in a corner of a pigeon hole.

This document bore upon it the superscription—"The last will and testament of Richard Brown, farmer."

In an instant our hero pieced together the story he had heard in Dorking, and arrived at the conclusion that the present Farmer Brown, although he had usurped his niece's position and concealed his brother's will, had at the same time, actuated by some strange fear, such as does occasionally possess criminals, dared not destroy the important document.

And here it was in Jack's hands.

There seemed no chance of immediate recovery by the farmer of his lost senses, so our hero coolly opened the document and read it through.

"As I thought," he muttered to himself.

"As I thought, the whole farm belongs to this girl, and this rascally uncle, one of the same kidney as my precious cousin, has simply swindled her out of her inheritance."

"However, I will see if I cannot manage to find her, and if I do, I think it will go hard if she does not recover her own again."

Then, taking up a pen, he selected a sheet of paper, and wrote upon it in bold characters—

Received of the tenant of Brown's Farm, Surrey, the sum of £120. And I hereby acknowledge that the above sum has been so received by me in payment of any rent now due for the said farm, or which may afterwards accrue until such sum is exhausted.

(Signed)   Spring-Heeled Jack.

N. B.—If this receipt is shown to Sir Michael Dacre, as he calls himself, its validity will be accepted without question, otherwise let him beware.

With a quiet chuckle Jack read this over to himself, then he laid it down in front of the jabbering lunatic, Farmer Brown.

"Now for the girl." Jack said, as he carefully put the will in one of the pockets of his capacious cloak.

The search for the girl did not take long.

The farmhouse was not a large one, and our hero's ears soon discovered a low moaning sound that evidently came from a garret which could only be approached by a rickety ladder.

In an instant Jack was at the top of the frail structure.

There, right in front of him, lay the object of his search.

She was a young and lovely girl about his own age.

Jack's heart gave one bound as he looked at her, then with a grateful sigh he said, fervently—

"Thank Heaven! I have come here. I take this as an augury that even if there is any wrong in the life I have chosen, I shall gain absolution for the evil by the good that will come out of it."

This philosophy was undoubtedly rather Jesuitical, but allowance must be made for the manner and place in which he had been brought up.

The girl seemed perfectly dazed when she saw Jack, but she betrayed not the slightest sign of fear.

She advanced towards our hero as far as a chain which was passed round her waist and fastened with a staple to the floor, would allow her, and with a child-like innocence, said—

"Ah! I know you, but I am not frightened at you. You have come to take me away from this. I do so long to see the green fields again. Take me away. I am not afraid of you."

For an instant and an instant only Jack hesitated.

His hesitation was only caused by his self inquiry as to what course he had better pursue under the circumstances.

He soon made up his mind, however.

With Jack to think was to act.

He had heard that one Squire Popham, a local justice of the peace, had expressed strong doubts as to the right of the present Farmer Brown to hold the farm.

To this worthy man's house our hero determined to convey the lovely child whom we have called by the unromantic name of Selina Brown.

To remove the chain from the girl's waist was work of no little difficulty, but perseverance, as it usually does, conquered in the end, and half an hour later Jack had carried the girl to Squire Popham's house, where, with a furious ring at the bell, he had left her, having first chalked on the door of the mansion the following words—

"This girl is the daughter of the late Farmer Brown, of Newdigate."

"Her father's will is in her pocket."

"Her wretched uncle is a jabbering idiot at the farm."

"See that the girl enjoys her rights, or dread the vengeance of

'Spring-Heeled Jack.'"

In another instant, and before the hall-door had opened to admit the half-unconscious girl, Jack gave one bound and disappeared from sight, and so for the time ended the first adventure of Spring-Heeled Jack.

Before we follow our hero any further on his extraordinary career we may as well finish the story of Farmer Brown and his niece.

When Squire Popham's footman opened the hall door he at first failed to see the girl so strangely rescued by Spring-Heeled Jack.

He, however, saw the chalk marks on the door, but was unable to read them—no extraordinary circumstance with a man of his class in the early part of the present century.

Then, turning round, he saw the poor girl.

There was a vacant look on her face that told the footman, un-tutored as he was, that she was "a button short," as he expressed it to himself.

The mysterious chalk marks and the "daft" girl were a little too much for the footman, and he hastened to call the butler.

This worthy could read, and as soon as he made his appearance, and had deciphered Jack's message, he directed his subordinate to call the squire.

When Mr. Popham, a typical country gentleman of the period, made his appearance, and read the inscription and saw the girl, his sympathies were immediately enlisted on her behalf.

"Confound Mr. Spring-Heeled Jack, whoever he may be, and his impudence, too!" cried the irate squire.

"Does he think that it requires threats to make an English magis-trate see justice done?"

Then bidding the butler to call all the men servants together, he instructed the housekeeper to see after the welfare of the poor girl.

As soon as the men had assembled Mr. Popham read Spring-Heeled Jack's message to them, and then for the first time recollected that he had not secured the will.

He told one of the men to go to the housekeeper's room, and ask for the document which was in the girl's pocket.

During the man's brief absence the squire told the men what he intended doing, and that was to go over to Brown's farm, and, of the wording of the will proved Jack's tale was correct, to seize the unwor-thy uncle there and then, and clap him in the Dorking watch-house.

A hasty glance at the will soon informed Mr. Popham that Jack had not exaggerated the facts of the case.

"Now, my men," he said, "we will get over to Newgate at once. It is as I suspected. The present holder of Brown's farm has no more title to it than I have. Let us go and seize him at once. You have all been sworn in as constables, so we have the law entirely on our side."

We may inform our readers that this was commonly the case in those days, when the guardians of the peace we few and far between, and immeasurably inferior to our present police, both in intelligence and physique.

The journey took some three-quarters of an hour—a much longer time than had been occupied by our hero, in spite of the burden which he had to bear.

The squire ordered the butler to knock loudly at the door, and his commands were instantly obeyed.

After a brief interval—so short, in fact, that it proved that the inmates of the house were up and dressed in spite of the lateness of the hour—the door was opened by a frightened-looking old woman.

"Who is it! What do you want?" she asked.

"I am James Popham, one of His Majesty's justices of the peace, and I want to see your master. Where is he?"

"Please, sir, he is in his bedroom," answered the old woman. "He has had a fit, and has only just recovered. Hadn't you better wait till the morning?"

"What ho!" thundered the angry squire. "We come in the name of the law. Lead us to your master's chamber at once."

At this juncture a querulous voice somewhere in the distance was heard to ask what was the matter.

Mr. Popham answered the query in person, for, pushing the woman on one side, he hastily ascended the stairs, two steps at a time, until he came to the door of the room from which the voice had apparently come.

Throwing open the door, Mr. Popham strode into the room, followed by his men servants.

"Mr. Brown," said the squire, "I arrest you in the name of the king, for suppressing your brother's will, and keeping his daughter, your own niece, in captivity since that brother's death."

Farmer Brown literally shook with fear.

Jack's sudden appearance had temporarily turned his brain, and he had hardly recovered his senses when this new and terrible surprise awaited him.

"It is false," he faltered. "My brother left the farm to me."

"Then what about the girl!" asked the squire. "Even if your brother did leave the farm to you where is his daughter now? Produce her at once, or you may be put upon your trial for murder instead of the lighter offence with which I have charged you."

Mumbling a few indistinct words, and still trembling violently, the farmer led the way to the foot of the ladder leading to the room where his niece had been for so long a time imprisoned.

Here he paused, as if he did not care to go up the ladder himself.

"Go on," said the squire, sternly, "and bring the girl down without any further delay."

Very unwillingly, but compelled by the force of circumstances, the farmer made the ascent.

As he entered the room a loud yell of terror and astonishment burst from his lips.

"She's gone!" he cried; "that must have been the foul fiend himself who called on me tonight, and he has spirited the girl away with him."

"What do you mean?" asked the squire.

In a few words the thoroughly cowed and frightened farmer explained the occurrences of the night to the squire, winding up by giving a description of Spring-Heeled Jack's personal appearance.

"This is indeed strange," said Mr. Popham. "But if it will be any satisfaction to you I may tell you that your poor niece is safe at my house, and I have her father's will in my pocket. You are my prisoner, and my men will at once take you to the lock-up at Dorking."

The crest-fallen farmer could not frame an inquiry as to how his crimes had been brought to light, and in silence he allowed himself to be carried off to the watch house.

Farmer Brown was tried at the next assizes, found guilty, and sentenced to fourteen years' transportation, from which he never returned.

His niece through kind treatment eventually recovered her senses, and subsequently married and became the mother of a large family of children in the very farm-house where she had been imprisoned in solitude until the light of reason had fled.

When Sir Michael Dacre's agent called at the farm when the rent became due, he found Squire Popham's people in possession, for that worthy man was not one to do things by halves, and he had made up his mind that his own farm bailiff should look after the interests of the poor girl until such time as she might recover her reason.

The agent was shown the receipt that Jack had given for the money.

That worthy was immensely puzzled, but seeing that there was nothing to be done save to take a copy of the receipt and return with it to Dacre Hall for further instructions, at once adopted that course.

When the baronet saw the receipt, and heard his agent's description of our hero—somewhat exaggerated as such things are apt to be by passing from mouth to mouth—his rage knew no bounds.

Of course he instantly recognised in the hero of the adventure his cousin, Jack Dacre.

Instantly summoning Mr. Morgan to his presence, for the unctuous agent had not yet returned to India, the two fellow-conspirators had a consultation as to what had better be done under the circumstances.

"My opinion," said Alfred Morgan, "is that you must grin and bear it. If you take any steps to secure the lad's apprehension and he is brought to trial, there is likely to be such a stir made over it as may bring witnesses over from the East, who may—mind you I do not say they will—but who may oust you from Dacre Hall, the title, and the other property which you possess.

"You must recollect that your late cousin was immensely popular in India, and his son would find a host of friends there to take up his cause."

The baronet had made many hasty exclamations during the delivery of this speech, but Mr. Morgan would not allow himself to be interrupted, and calmly continued to the end.

When he had finished, the baronet broke out rapidly—

"What do you intend to do, then? If the case is as you state, how do you intend to obtain possession of the plantations?"

"Oh! that's all right," coolly replied Morgan. "I care nothing for the barren honour of being called the owner of the Dacre plantations. I shall go back to India just as if I was acting for the rightful owner of the property—but with this important difference, that the rents and profits of the plantations will go into the pockets of Mr. Alfred Morgan."

"Then you won't help me to get rid of this spawn?"

"What time I am in England is entirely at your disposal," said Morgan; "but you must remember that my employer's interests require that I should return to India as soon as possible to look after his plantations."

And the wily villain concluded with a horrible chuckle.

"What course would you propose, then?" asked Sir Michael.

"Well, I think if I were in your place I would call on each tenant and warn him that someone is collecting your rents in a peculiar and perfectly unauthorised manner. Tell them the story of Spring-Heeled Jack at Brown's farm, but without disclosing your suspicions as to the identity of the depredator."

"Suspicions! Certainty, man," cried Sir Michael.

"Well, certainty, then," went on Morgan. "This will put them on their guard, and in the meantime you must wait and hope. If the boy continues this career much longer he is tolerably certain to get a stray bullet through his brains one of these days."

"I will start tomorrow," the baronet promptly said.

"And I will accompany you," said Alfred Morgan, with equal promptitude.

"Thank you, Morgan," replied Sir Michael. "I'll tell my man to go over to Arundel at once, and book two seats to London. We will go there first, as I have considerable property in the neighbourhood of Hammersmith."

"Have you?" sneered Morgan, with special emphasis on the pronoun.

The baronet coloured and bit his lip; but he dared not reply.

This was not the first time by many that his chains had galled him, and he heartily wished that Morgan were back again in India, although he knew that he should feel awfully lonely when the agent went away.

To return to our hero, whom we left as he was hurrying away from Squire Popham's house on the night of the rescue of Selina Brown.

Jack reached home in safety, and found the faithful Ned Chump waiting up for him.

The sailor's astonishment was as unbounded as his admiration when Jack gave him the history of the evening's adventures and showed him the money.

"£120!" said Ned. "My stars! and you haven't been away three hours altogether. Why, we shall make our fortunes fast!"

"Ah! Ned, Ned, where are your conscientious scruples now? But, never fear, I do not want to get rich in this fashion. I merely want to obtain my own—and this, my maiden adventure, has been so successful that I feel certain I shall do so."

Ned, recollecting what he had said to our hero regarding the morality of their proposed course of life, looked rather sheepish, but he made no reply, and a little while later the two separated, and made their way to their respective couches.

In the morning Ned asked Jack what their next step was to be.

"I think we will go back to Arundel, and take up our quarters there for the present. From that place I shall be able to reconnoitre and find out what my precious cousin is about. And the very first opportunity that offers I will show him a sight that will raise the hair on his head."

"All right, sir," cheerfully replied the sailor.

In the comparatively short time that the two had been together, Ned Chump had had ample opportunity of finding out that he had enlisted under a captain who was pretty well sure to lead him ultimately to victory, and the tar had therefore fully made up his mind that under no circumstances would he attempt to question Jack's plans or schemes.

Arrived at Arundel, they took up their quarters at the Bridge House Hotel, and passed some time in comparative quietude.

Jack managed to keep himself well posted up in all relating to Dacre Hall and its usurping tenant.

This he was enabled to do by reason of a disguise which he had assumed.

No one would have recognised in the dashing young buck, apparently four or five and twenty years of age, the lad who had so lately been turned out of Dacre Hall as an illegitimate scion of the ancient house.

Ned had contrived to give himself something of the appearance of a gentleman's body servant or valet, and the two represented themselves to be a Mr. Turnbull, a young gentleman who had recently come into a fine property, and his servant, who had come down into Sussex to rest after a course of dissipation into which Mr. Turnbull had plunged on having come into his inheritance.

Jack, however, did not find out anything of importance for some days, and then, quite by accident, he made a discovery which promised to make an interview between Spring-Heeled Jack and Sir Michael Dacre a very easy matter.

This discovery was made under the following circumstances.

Our hero was standing one evening in the entrance hall of the hotel, passing an occasional remark to the farmers and others who passed in and out, when he saw one of the gigs from the Hall drive up.

Jack was on the alert in a moment.

The man who had driven the gig was one of servants at Dacre Hall, who had shown a special liking for our hero, and this accidental encounter would give Jack an excellent opportunity of proving the strength or weakness of his disguise, even if nothing else came of it.

As the man descended from the gig and threw the reins to an attendant ostler, Jack advanced to the door of the hotel and met the servant from the Hall face to face.

The man looked at him full in the face, but not the slightest sign of recognition passed over his features.

Jack gave a quiet chuckle.

If this man who had shown him so many tokens of friendly feeling during his short sojourn at Dacre Hall failed to recognize him, surely he was perfectly safe from detection!

Not that Jack had anything to fear even if he was identified, but he felt that with such an adversary as he had in the person of Sir Michael Dacre, his only chance of success was to meet his cousin with his own weapons, and so long as he could preserve his *incognito* the chances were greatly in his favour.

But this chance encounter led to much greater results than the mere testing of the strength of his disguise.

As the man entered the hotel Jack turned round and followed him to the bar.

"I want to book two seats to London by tomorrow's coach," said the man.

"All right," was the reply; "inside or out, the box seat is already taken."

"Oh, inside," replied the servant. "Sir Michael does not care about outside travelling at this time of the year."

"Oh, then, Sir Michael is going up to town, is he?" asked the attendant.

"Yes," was the answer, "and the gentleman from India is going with him."

"Rather a strange time for him to go to town, isn't it?" asked the hotel official, with the usual curiosity of his class.

"Well, yes, it is; but I fancy there is something wrong with his rent collector, and I think he is going up to take his London rents himself."

"Oh! I see," said the attendant as he handed over the receipt; "I suppose you'll take your usual pint of October?"

The man smacked his lips with an affirmative gesture, and the liquor having been drawn and consumed, remounted his gig and took his departure. As soon as the gig had been driven off Jack turned to the barman and said—

"If my man comes in, tell him I have gone along the river towards Pulborough, and ask him to follow me as I want him particularly."

"Yes, sir," said the obsequious attendant, and Jack strolled out of the hotel.

As soon as he had left the inn he turned into the park, and made his way to a secluded nook.

This was a spot which had been chosen as a meeting place for Ned Chump and our hero.

They were precluded from intercourse at the hotel, as it would have seemed singular for a gentleman and his servant—no matter how confidential the latter might be—to have held much private converse at a place like the Bridge House Hotel.

This spot had therefore been chosen, and it had been arranged that when Jack left word that he had gone towards Pulborough, Ned was to make the best of his way to the cosy corner of the park, where our hero awaited his advent.

When Ned made his appearance Jack plunged into the middle of the question at once.

"Which way does the London coach go?"

"Through Brighton, sir," said that worthy, "and then straight along the London-road."

"If we went post from here after she had started could we get to London before she did!"

"Lor, yes," said Ned; "why, we could give her three hours' good start, and then get to London first."

"That's what we'll do, Ned," went on Jack; "but say nothing about this until the coach has started. There will be plenty of time then to order the post-chaise, and there are some people going by the coach who might be suspicious if they heard of an intended trip to town."

"Yes, sir," replied Ned.

"Why, Ned, old fellow, have you no curiosity? I should have thought you would have been in a burning fever to know the meaning of this sudden change in my plans."

"So I am, sir."

"Then why not have asked? Surely you know I have every confidence in you?"

"Yes. I know that, skipper; and that's the very reason why I did not ask. I knew you would tell me all in good time."

"All right, Ned," said our hero.

And he proceeded to inform the sailor of what he had overheard in the bar of the hotel.

"So," he went on, "we'll get to London first, track them from the coach to whatever hotel or house they may put up at, then we will dodge their movements well."

"But what good will this do?" asked Ned, who did not quite see how his young master was to benefit by this.

"Why, don't you see? As soon as my unworthy cousin has collected the rents he is bound to take coach again, either for Arundel or to some other place where my property lies."

"Yes, sir?" queried Ned.

"Well, I intend to stop that coach, and make my rascally cousin hand over to me the proceeds of his rent audit, and I think that will prove a very good haul."

Ned, now thoroughly enlightened, grinned and wished our hero good luck in his enterprise.

The two now parted, and did not meet again until nightfall.

In the morning Sir Michael and Morgan made their appearance in due course, and Jack surveyed the departure of the coach from an upper window.

He met his cousin's eye more than once, but the latter utterly failed to recognise in the dashing young man about town the lad he had virtually kicked out of his ancestral hall.

Alfred Morgan, however, favoured Jack with a prolonged stare, and our hero more than once fancied he was recognised, but whatever suspicion might have existed in his mind was allayed when he asked the guard—

"Who is that young spark at yonder window?"

"He's a young fellow just come in for a lot of money, and mighty free he is with it too, sir, I can tell you," replied the guard.

"What's his name?" asked Morgan.

"Mr. Turnbull, sir," said the guard, as he proceeded to adjust his horn for the final blast.

This answer, so coolly given, speedily quenched any latent spark of suspicion that might have existed in the agent's subtle brain.

The coach started on her journey.

Two hours and a-half later Jack and his faithful henchman were bowling along at a rapid pace in the direction of London.

Arrived at Croydon, they inquired whether the Arundel coach had passed, and were informed that it had not.

The last stage of their journey was therefore performed at a slightly reduced pace, and the post-chaise arrived at the coaching-house fully half-an-hour before the arrival of Sir Michael and Morgan.

This enabled Jack to order a private room, which he desired might look out into the yard into which the coach would be driven.

The two were shown to a room which most admirably suited the purpose of our hero.

When the coach arrived there was Jack, snugly ensconced within a dozen feet of the top of the coach, but perfectly invisible to anyone outside, while himself able to see and hear everything. The coach arrived.

Jack had no difficulty in ascertaining his cousin's destination in London; for, in an imperious voice, Sir Michael shouted—

"Get me a private coach at once, and tell the coachman to drive me to the Hummum's, Covent Garden, and look sharp about it."

This was his first visit to London since he had usurped the title, and he meant to make the most of his importance.

Bidding Ned follow, Jack swiftly descended the stairs, paid the score, and passed out into the streets.

Here he hailed a passing hackney coach, and arrived at the Hummum's some time before Sir Michael.

Jack engaged a couple of rooms, and then proceeded to make some slight changes in his disguise, so that Morgan might not recognise him as the man who had watched the departure of the Arundel coach that morning.

For the best part of a week Jack tracked his cousin with the persistency of a sleuth hound, until he felt convinced that the last batch of London rents was collected.

It was during this period that the supposed unearthly visitant first made his appearance in Hammersmith.

Although the newspapers of the time inform us that Jack committed many robberies, there is no doubt that this is incorrect.

All that he did was to visit each successive tenant after his cousin's departure, and ascertain from the terrified people how much money they had paid to the landlord.

There is no doubt that Jack caused an immense amount of harm by frightening servant-girls and children, and even people who ought to have known better; but we are not writing to justify Jack's conduct, but merely to extract as much from the diary or confession of Spring-Heeled Jack as will enable our readers to form some idea of what manner of man our hero was.

By these nocturnal visits on the Dacre tenants Jack soon found out how much money his cousin was likely to be taking home with him.

This sum was approximately £250.

A nice little haul for our hero if he could only land it.

During Jack's nightly absences the faithful Ned kept watch over the baronet and his friend.

One night on Jack's return Ned informed him that the baronet had sent the hotel boots to book two seats for the morrow's coach to Arundel.

"Then he is going straight home," said Jack. "Well, perhaps, it is better so. If he had been going further afield he might have banked the money. As it is, I know he will have it with him, and I'll stick him and the mail up somewhere in the neighbourhood of Horley, or I'll acknowledge that Michael is right, and my name is not Jack Dacre."

The following morning Jack ordered a post-chaise to proceed to Horley.

From thence, after discharging one passenger, Jack, it was to take the other one on to Worth, and there to await until "Mr. Turnbull" made his appearance.

This programme was carried out to the letter.

Jack got out at Horley.

The carriage rattled on.

Jack took up his position at a fork in the roads, where he could see the stage coach some time before it would reach him, and at the same time be himself unseen.

In due course the coach came in sight.

Jack's heart beat nervously, but not with fear.

This was his first highway adventure, and who can wonder at his excitement!

In another instant the coach was upon him, and with a spring and a yell that threw the horses back upon their haunches, he rose in the air right over the top of the coach, passengers and all, shouting—

"Hand out your money and your jewellery—I am *Spring-Heeled Jack*."

The coachman in his terror threw himself upon the ground, and hid his face in the dust, as if he thought he could insure his safety by that course.

The guard discharged his huge blunderbuss harmlessly in the air, thereby adding tenfold to the agony of fear from which the coach-load of passengers were without exception suffering.

Having performed this deed of bravery, the guard took to his heels and speedily disappeared from sight.

Jack's tall, well-built figure, dressed in its weird garb, was one that could not fail to strike terror into the breasts of the startled travellers.

One by one they threw their purses and other valuables at Jack's feet.

Our hero received the tribute as though he had been an emperor.

When the last passenger had deposited his valuables in front of Jack, that worthy youth said, with a sardonic laugh—

"Now you can all pick your money and jewellery up again, and return them to your pockets—all save Michael Dacre and Alfred Morgan."

In an instant the passengers sprang from the coach and collected their valuables, too utterly surprised by the turn events had taken to utter a word.

Sir Dacre looked at his confederate, and Morgan returned the look, but neither of them could force their lips to articulate a sound.

Jack stared steadily at his cousin through the two holes in his mask, and to the guilty man's fevered imagination they seemed to emit flashes of supernatural fire.

Pointing a long, claw-like finger at the would-be baronet, Jack said, in the most sepulchral tone he could assume—

"Beware, Michael Dacre; your cousin's last words to you shall be brought home to you with full force. From this day forth until you render up possession of the title and estates you have usurped, you shall not know one hour's peace of mind by reason of the dread you will feel at the appearance of Spring-Heeled Jack."

"Who I am matters not to you. My powers are unlimited, I can appear and disappear when and where I will."

Then turning to Alfred Morgan, he said—

"Ungrateful servant of one of the kindest masters that ever lived, your fate shall be one of such nameless horror, that, could you but foresee what that fate would be, you would put an end to your wretched career of crime by your own hand."

Then gathering up the money and jewellery belonging to the two conspirators, Jack said—

"Good-day, friends. A pleasant journey to you. Just to prove to you that I can disappear when I like, look at me now."

In another second Jack had indeed disappeared, leaving behind him, as more than one of the bewildered passengers subsequently averred, a strong sulphurous odour.

The mystery of our hero's disappearance on this occasion is not difficult to explain.

While waiting for the coach he had discovered a convenient chalk pit—no rare occurrence in that part of the country—and into this he had sprung after uttering his parting words, which were of course intended for Sir Michael and Morgan.

After Jack's departure the panic-stricken passengers endeavoured to rouse the coachman from his prostrate position on the dusty road.

But for some time their efforts were vain, the man had fainted from sheer fright.

The guard, too, had totally disappeared. What were they to do?

At last one of the passengers volunteered to drive, and placing the still insensible driver inside, the coach proceeded on its way to its destination.

All the inmates of the coach looked askance at the baronet and his companion.

They looked upon these two as the Jonahs of the expedition, and it would probably have gone hard with both of them had anyone simply have suggested their expulsion.

Sir Michael was not slow to perceive this, and at the next halting place he resolved to leave the coach.

This resolution he communicated to Morgan.

"But," said the agent, "we have no money. How shall we get on so far away from home?"

"Oh! that's all right," replied Sir Michael. "I am well enough known about here—and even if I were not," he continued, in a whisper, "I'd risk everything to get rid of these cursed people who heard the fearful words that spectral-looking being uttered."

Morgan was about to reply, but a warning "Hush!" from the baronet stopped him in time, for more than one of the occupants of the coach seemed to be listening intently to the conversation between the confederates, although it was carried on in very low tones.

The guilty pair took their departure from the coach at Balcombe much to the satisfaction of their fellow travellers.

Sir Michael directed the landlord of the inn to show them into a private room.

The command was at once obeyed, for Sir Michael had not exaggerated when he informed Morgan that he was well known in that part of the country.

As Mr. Michael Dacre, the agent to the large and valuable Dacre estates, he had been well known.

As Sir Michael Dacre, the present owner of those said estates, he was of course much more widely known.

That is to say that people who would not have recognised the agent sought by every means in their power to scrape acquaintance with the baronet.

Once within the private room, and left alone with his companion in crime, the baronet breathed a sigh of relief.

"Phew!" he said, "I almost dreaded to enter this room, for fear that imp of darkness might have been here before me."

Morgan gave forth a nervous little laugh, as much as to say that he had no fears upon the subject, but he could not control his features, and if ever fright and cowardice were depicted on a human face, they might have been discerned on the not too prepossessing countenance of Mr. Alfred Morgan, the some-time agent to the Dacre Plantations in India.

"What is there to laugh at?" growled Sir Michael. "I have lost some £260, two rings, a gold repeater, and a bunch of seals."

Our readers will remember that gold watch chains were seldom worn in those days, the watch being usually attached to a piece of silk ribbon from which depended a bunch of seals. The time-keeper, a little smaller than one of the American clocks of the present day, was placed in a fob pocket, and the ribbon and seals depended on the outside of the waistcoat or breeches as the case may be.

"And I," answered the agent, "am in quite as sorry a plight, for I have lost £60, all the money I had left in England, besides my watch and chain."

This chain being a magnificent piece of oriental gold carving which Morgan had absolutely "stolen" from Jack's father, and consequently from Jack himself.

"Well," cried Sir Michael, testily, "it's no use crying over spilt milk; and still less use for us to quarrel. I will be your banker until you can draw upon your Indian property."

"None of your sneer, Sir Michael Dacre," began the agent, angrily.

162

"Tut, tut! man, let's make a truce of it, and if we cannot continue friends, let us at least avoid any resemblance to open hostilities."

"All right," sulkily assented Morgan.

"It is our only chance," went on Sir Michael. "I don't know who or what in the fiend's name this Spring-Heeled Jack may be, but I must confess that my nerves are terribly shaken by the events that have occurred since I turned my illegitimate cousin out of Dacre Hall."

"Illegitimate?" said Alfred Morgan with a sneer.

"That this so-called Spring-Heeled Jack," continued the baronet, ignoring the interruption, "is not an ordinary highwayman is self-evident, or he would not have returned some hundreds of pounds in money, and as much more in jewellery, to our fellow passengers by the Arundel coach."

"And it is also equally certain," said Morgan, "that this stalwart man who can spring over the top of a mail-coach, horses, driver, passengers and all, cannot be that puny lad who laid claim to the Dacre title and lands."

"Then who can it be?" cried Dacre, half in despair. "It cannot be that sailor, Clump, or whatever his name was."

"Chump, my dear Sir Michael, Ned Chump!" rejoined Morgan, who could hardly repress his sneering manner. "No, I do not see how it could possibly be the sailor; but one thing is certain—and that is that this individual is acting on behalf of your cousin, and although I have too much sense to believe in the supernatural, the whole thing passes all comprehension. First this Spring-Heeled Jack—and, recollect, your cousin adopted that name out of your own lips—appears at Dorking, puts a half-lunatic girl back in the possession of her property, collects more than the rent due to you from Brown's farm, but at the same time leaves a strangely worded receipt, which prevents you from doing anything but grin and bear it."

"True," broke in Sir Michael, angrily.

"Then we hear that a supernatural being has appeared to your Hammersmith tenants in turn, and has put to one and all the identical question—"

"How much rent have you paid to Michael Dacre?"

"True again," replied Dacre.

"You will notice," said Morgan, with what was meant to be cutting irony, "the absence of the 'Sir' in the formula."

"Yes, yes, proceed," snarled the unhappy wretch.

"Then we take the coach on our way to your ancestral halls—and what happens? Why this mysterious being about whom we have heard so much, and about whom we know so little, stopped our coach in a manner hitherto unheard of, half frightened the driver to death, takes all the money and valuables the coach contains, then calmly returns each of the other passengers their property, only retaining for his own use that which belongs to Sir Michael Dacre, the present head of that proud house, and that which belongs to Mr. Alfred Morgan, at your service, the agent for the Dacre plantations in the East Indies."

"Well, and what do you suggest, Morgan?" said the pseudo-baronet, growing pale as the agent went on with his cool and matter-of-fact statement.

"Well," answered Morgan; "I hardly know at present what to suggest. To one thing, however, I have made up my mind."

"And that is?" queried Dacre, anxiously.

"To remain in England till this ghost is laid," replied Morgan.

The baronet gave a sigh of relief.

"Yes," the agent continued, "I am not going to run the risk of losing my hard-earned Indian estates—and that is what I feel sure I must ensue if I leave you to cope single-handed with the trio who are in league against you—maybe against me."

"Trio!" cried the baronet, faintly.

"Yes, trio! Jack Dacre, Ned Chump, and last, but not least, Spring-Heeled Jack."

To carry on our extraordinary story in a perfectly intelligible form it is necessary that we should leave the conspirators at the inn at Balcombe, and look out for our hero and his faithful comrade.

Jack, thanks to his ample cloak, had no difficulty in reaching the appointed place of meeting at Worth.

Ned Chump, who had been worrying himself into a state of nervous anxiety almost bordering upon madness, received our hero literally with open arms.

"How did you get on, sir?" asked the tar.

"Don't 'sir' me," replied Jack, banteringly.

"Well, then, skipper, if that will suit you."

"Oh, I got on prime, Ned," replied our hero, and he broke out into such a peal of laughter as astonished even Ned, who had already had many experiences of his young master's gaiety and exuberance of spirits.

Ned, as was his wont, remained silent, and Jack, who by this time perfectly understood his henchman's manner, went on to explain the events that had occurred since they had parted at Harley.

"And now," said Jack, "I will change myself into Mr. Turnbull again for a short time."

"Yes, skipper," said Ned, as he laid Jack's private clothes out for him.

"And then we will make for the Fox, at Balcombe, where the Arundel coach must have stopped after I had left it."

"Yes, sir," said Ned, in a matter-of-fact tone, as if his interest in the affair was a very minute one.

"If my surmise is correct," went on Jack, "Michael Dacre and the rascal Morgan will be resting there."

"Why so, skipper?" asked Ned.

"Because, after my word of warning, the passengers by the Arundel coach would not look with very favourable eyes upon those two arch conspirators, and I take it that they will have been only too glad to leave the coach at the first opportunity, and that must most undoubtedly be the Fox Inn."

"All right, skipper," replied the sailor. "I'm on."

By this time our hero had changed his clothes, or rather had put those belonging to the supposed Mr. Turnbull on over his Mephistophelean garb.

Some refreshments which had been previously ordered were now brought in, and after discussing these and settling the bill, Jack and his attendant left the house, the former telling the host that he might be back that way later on, but he was not quite sure, as if he met a friend of his at the Fox he might pass the night there, but, under any circumstances, he should return to Worth the following day, as his one object in coming there was to inspect the famous old church, the only object of general interest which the village possessed.

Jack had made this explanation as he did not want to carry his and Ned's luggage about with him on this reconnoitring expedition.

The landlord, only too pleased at the thought of seeing his liberal guest and his servant once again, gladly took charge of the travelling trunks, and Jack and Ned were soon far on their way toward a the Fox.

Entering the inn, Jack called for two flagons of ale, and in paying for the same took good care to expose the contents of his purse.

The host's eye caught a glimpse of the gold pieces it contained, and he instantly made up his mind that our hero should leave some if not all of them behind him.

"Fine day, sir," said mine host, by way of opening a conversation.

"Very," replied Jack, who wanted nothing better.

"Have you come down here to attend the coming of age of Squire Thornhill's eldest son?" asked the innkeeper.

"No," replied Jack. "My servant and myself are on a walking tour. We have left our luggage at Worth, and have merely strolled over here to see if my friend, Lord Amberly, is staying here or in the neighbourhood."

"No, sir," said the now obtrusively obsequious host, quite won over by "my friend, Lord Amberly," added to the sight of the gold in Jack's purse.

"Lord Amberly is not staying here; but we are not quite devoid of quality, for Sir Michael Dacre, one of our county magistrates, and a friend of his are at this moment inmates of my house."

"Sir Michael Dacre?" queried Jack, suppressing his excitement. "Why his hall is not more than twenty miles from here is it, how comes he to be staying at an inn so near his own home?"

"Twenty-five miles, sir," said the landlord, correctingly, "and the reason that he is staying here is that the Arundel coach was stuck up by a strange sort of highwayman."

"A strange sort of highwayman?" said Jack, in tones of well assumed surprise.

"Yes, sir, a strange sort of highwayman," replied the landlord.

And the worthy host proceeded to give Jack a highly embellished account of the attack upon the mail coach, adding—

"And as this strange joker, who calls himself Spring-Heeled Jack, only robbed the baronet and his friend, the other passengers seemed to think as how they weren't much good, and so were glad to get rid of them, when they decided to stop here."

"And how do you know that they are any good?" asked Jack.

"Oh!" replied the loquacious landlord, "I knowed Sir Michael when he was the late baronet's agent—he's all right as far as I am concerned, whatever he may be to others."

"What do you mean?" said Jack, who had noticed something peculiar in the host's utterance of the last words.

"Oh! nothing, sir. Nothing!" replied the man, evidently discovering for the first time that his tongue had been wagging a little too fast.

Collecting his somewhat discomposed faculties as quickly as he could, the landlord put the question to Jack once more—

"Then you have not come here to see the grand doings at Thornhill Hall?"

"No," replied our hero, "I did not come with that purpose, but as my friend Lord Amberly is not here, I may as well stop until I hear from him, and in the meantime the Thornhill festivities will serve to prevent my getting the vapours. That is," he went on, "if you can accommodate my servant and myself with a bed."

"Yes, sir," said the landlord, with a bright twinkle in his eye, as he thought of the contents of our hero's purse, to say nothing of the prestige that would attach to his house if only Lord Amberly should turn up to meet his young friend.

"Yes, sir," he said, "that is if you do not mind occupying a double-bedded room."

Then he continued in an apologetic manner—

"Sir Michael and his friend particularly stipulated for a double-bedded room sir, and indeed we have only one other in the house."

"Ha! afraid to sleep alone," said Jack to himself; "but I think I'll take a still further rise out of them tonight."

Then turning to the landlord, he said—

"Oh! a double bedded-room will suit me. We've been through too many adventures together to mind that, haven't we, Ned?"

"Yes, sir," replied the sailor with a suppressed chuckle.

With a fulsome bow the host ushered Jack and Ned to their apartments, indicating as he did so the one already occupied by the baronet and his friend.

Our hero ordered dinner for seven o'clock, and leaving Ned in the bedroom, proceeded down into the bar again.

Finishing his ale he strode out of the door and rapidly took in the geography of the house.

He had no difficulty in fixing the position of the baronet's room, and to his intense delight saw that the windows were mere frail casements of lead and glass, that hardly served to keep out the elements.

It was rapidly getting dusk, and re-entering the house Jack said to the landlord—

"I'm going for a little stroll, give my man all he wants, and put the charges down to me, and mind my dinner is ready at seven."

The host humbly bowed his acquiescence, and Jack again left the house.

He had about an hour in hand before dinner, and it was absolutely necessary for the success of his scheme that he should be back punctually to time, and he had a lot to do in that single hour.

To return to the would-be baronet and his fellow conspirator, who were still seated in the private room.

With Spring-Heeled Jack's name upon his lips—for that was the only topic of conversation between the guilty men—the baronet rose to ring the bell for lights.

Even as he did so a crash of glass was heard, and the object of their fears stood before them in the middle of the room.

"Strip yourselves, both of you," cried Jack in fearful accents, "strip yourselves to the skin. I told you I was ubiquitous—and I am here. Strip at once, or dread the dire vengeance of Spring-Heeled Jack!"

Too thoroughly frightened to ring the bell for assistance, Sir Michael and Morgan stood as if turned to stone, looking at the weird intruder into the privacy of their room.

Our hero found it difficult to restrain a smile, so ludicrous was the terror exhibited by his unworthy cousin and the agent.

But the faint ripple of enjoyment which passed over his face was not noticed by either of the conspirators.

Jack knew that he could not afford to waste a moment, even though the prolongation of his cousin's fright would have afforded him exquisite enjoyment.

"Strip yourselves," he therefore repeated, in still louder tones, "and quickly, too, or it will fare badly with both of you."

Sir Michael looked at his fellow conspirator, but, seeing nothing of an encouraging nature in his face, he commenced to take off his coat.

Morgan, accepting the inevitable, proceeded to follow the baronet's example.

Jack watched them closely, and every time one or the other of them paused he threatened them with horrible penalties if they dared delay any longer.

At last the two worthies stood in front of our hero as naked as they were when they first entered this world.

Bidding them roll their garments into a bundle Jack prepared to take his departure.

He unfastened what remained of the casement through which he had so unceremoniously made his way into the apartment, and threw the broken frames wide open.

When the clothes had been made into a rather unwieldy-looking parcel, Jack caught hold of it, and, placing it on his shoulder, sprang literally over head and heels out of the window.

For some five minutes after Jack's departure neither of the naked men could move to call for assistance, so utterly cowed were they by the suddenness of the weird apparition's appearance.

Morgan was the first to recover anything like self-possession, and with an unearthly yell he sprang towards the bell-rope, and gave such frantic tugs at it that it very soon broke under his vigorous hand.

But he had succeeded in making noise enough to rouse the whole house, and a minute later the room was half-filled by the landlord and his servants and many of his customers.

"What is the matter, gentlemen?" asked Boniface.

"Matter, indeed!" cried Sir Michael, who had by this time somewhat recovered his normal faculties. "Matter enough I should think. That scoundrel who robbed the coach we came down by, has been here and has taken away all our clothes."

The titters and smiles that had been heard and seen among the domestics suddenly stopped.

Dim rumours had already reached Balcombe of the existence of Spring-Heeled Jack, and now here he was, or had just been, right in their midst.

A great terror seemed to have crept into the hearts of all of them, and none seemed inclined to stir.

"Someone of you rush after him," cried Dacre, angrily. "The bundle is a heavy one, and he cannot have got far with it."

But no one offered to start in pursuit.

"Confound it!" cried Morgan; "if one of you had had the sense to start off directly I summoned you the thief would have been caught by this time, or, at least, our clothes would have been recovered," he added, as the thought flashed through his brain that, perhaps, it would be well for his employer and himself if Jack were not caught.

"I don't think we could have done much good," said the landlord, rather nettled at the tone affairs were taking. "If this Spring-Heeled Jack, as you call him, is good enough to stick up and rob a coachload of people, and is clever enough to come here and take the very clothes from off your backs, I don't quite see what chance I or any of my people would have against him even if one of us had started off immediately in pursuit."

The two sufferers, who had by this time entirely come to their senses, both immediately acknowledged that the landlord of the Fox was right.

Sir Michael, therefore, putting the best face on the matter that he could, said—

"True, landlord, true; and now, like a good fellow, see if you cannot get us some clothes, anything like a fit. Our present garb is not a pleasant one."

And indeed it was not, for Sir Michael was clothed *toga*-wise in a large tablecloth, which he had thrown over his shoulders in haste while Morgan was ringing the bell, and Morgan himself had only been able to secure the hearth-rug, with which he had enveloped his body, so as to preserve some semblance of decency.

Ordering the crowd of frightened servants and guests to leave the room, the landlord turned to Sir Michael, when they were alone, and said—

"I trust, Sir Michael, that you and your friend will leave my house as speedily as possible. I have my living to get, and this sort of thing is calculated to give a house a bad name."

"Insolent scoundrel—" began Dacre.

"No names, Sir Michael," answered the landlord. "I pay my rent and my brewers regularly. There has been no complaint made against the Fox since I have had it, and I do not fear anything that you can do to me. As to you yourself, the case is different."

"What do you mean?" angrily asked Dacre.

"What do I mean? Well, it is strange that this mysterious Spring-Heeled Jack should be always on your track. I have heard that he collected rents in your name at Dorking. Then you tell me that he robs you on the Arundel coach; and, by-the-bye, all the passengers by that coach put you down as the cause of the stoppage, and now you tell me that this mysterious being has entered your room by your window, some twenty feet from the ground, and, though you were two and he only one, he managed to strip and leave you as naked as you were when you were born."

Morgan nudged Dacre, and Jack's cousin had sense enough to see that there was no good to come by continuing the argument.

"Very well," Dacre replied, in a gruff manner. "Let us have what clothes you have, and we will leave your house the first thing in the morning. It is too late to think of going on to Dacre Hall tonight."

The landlord acquiesced in a sullen manner, muttering—

"If Master Spring-Heeled Jack takes it into his head to return here before the morning out you shall both turn, no matter what the time or the weather may be."

With this Boniface left the room.

"This is getting serious," said Morgan, as soon as he was left alone with the baronet.

"Serious, indeed," said Dacre, testily. "I fully believe, Morgan, that the foul thing's threats will come true, and that he will make our lives a curse to us."

"What can we do in the matter?" asked Morgan. "Can you not suggest something? Recollect what you have gained by denying your cousin's legitimacy, and pull yourself together and let us see what had better be done, under the circumstances."

"Better be done, forsooth," said Sir Michael. "How can we arrange to do anything when we do not know whether our adversary is mortal or not. If he is mortal we dare not lock him up, as he evidently knows the secret of the Dacre succession; and if he is not mortal, of what I avail our struggles against him?"

"Not mortal, pshaw!" replied Morgan.

"The man's mortal enough, though there is something mysterious about him, I'll allow. We'll provide ourselves with a pair of pistols, and when next we are favoured by a visit we will test with half an ounce of lead whether Spring-Heeled Jack is mortal or not."

As the agent concluded, a wild, wailing shriek, ending in a peal of demoniacal laughter, struck upon their ears, and, rushing to the window, they beheld, standing on the top of the pump in front of the Inn, the awful figure of their hated foe.

With another unearthly scream Jack turned a somersault from the top of the pump, and long ere any of the inmates of the inn who had heard the taunting laugh had time to pass out of doors, Spring-Heeled Jack had disappeared, the gathering gloom leaving no trace behind.

Ten minutes later, and "Mr. Turnbull," looking as cool and calm as it is possible for a young English gentleman to look, returned to the Fox, and as he called for a glass of sherry and bitters he asked if his dinner was ready.

With a thousand apologies the landlord explained to him that, owing to the state of excitement into which the whole house had been thrown by the appearance of Spring—Heeled Jack, the dinner was not quite ready.

Jack, of course, asked for particulars, and the garrulous host gave the chief actor such a highly-embellished narrative of what had actually occurred, that our hero absolutely suffered in his endeavour to keep from laughing.

He succeeded, however, and bidding the landlord hasten the dinner as much as possible, he entered the room reserved for himself and Ned Chump.

Here he found his faithful follower, and that jolly salt broke into a peal of uncontrollable laughter as Jack narrated the story of the last hour's adventure, winding up the tale by explaining that he had quietly dropped the bundle of clothes down a neighbouring disused well.

In the meantime a very dissimilar scene was being enacted in the room occupied by Sir Michael Dacre and Alfred Morgan.

Both of the conspirators felt dissatisfied.

Morgan inwardly accused Dacre of cowardice, and felt certain that eventually John Dacre would gain his own.

The usurping baronet, on the other hand, blamed Morgan for all the ills and evils that had arisen.

The two passed the night somehow, but it is comparatively certain that neither of them enjoyed even one half-hour's sleep.

Our hero and his henchman, on the contrary, partook of a capital dinner, smoked and drank and enjoyed themselves, and then slept the sleep of the just.

In the morning, much to the delight of the landlord of the Fox, Sir Michael Dacre and Alfred Morgan took their departure from the inn.

Our hero and Ned Chump, who had been informed that they were about to leave, had secured a position from which they could obtain a good view of the two disconsolate men.

And a pretty pair of beauties they looked.

Sir Michael was attired in a suit of clothes belonging to the landlord, and which was almost large enough to have accommodated his companion in crime as well as himself.

Morgan's borrowed suit fitted him a little better, but as the original owner occupied the position of ostler, gardener, and general *factotum*, it may easily be imagined that the garments were not particularly becoming.

"Well, skipper," cried Ned, as the post-chaise drove off, "no disrespect to you, but a more ugly, hang-dog fellow than your cousin I never saw; he looks well enough when he is dressed spick and span, but now he looks what he really is."

And Jack could not dissent, for it would have been difficult to find a more despicable-looking man than the mock baronet decked in the inn-keeper's clothes.

Jack thought it advisable to stop at the Fox for another night, and then sent over to Worth for the luggage.

"Not the slightest suspicion had been aroused in anyone's mind that this sedate Mr. Turnbull had had anything to do with the stoppage of the Arundel coach or the robbery of the clothes of the two guests at the Fox Inn."

Jack and Ned left a very pleasant impression behind them when they took their departure for Arundel.

Our hero had resolved to make the Bridge House his headquarters, as he had had such remarkable piece of luck there already.

For was it not owing to what he had heard while staying there that he was enabled to relieve his cousin and Mr. Alfred Morgan of their superfluous cash?

If our hero had known what important results his resolve to go back to the hotel at Arundel would have, he would have literally danced for joy.

This visit to Arundel led to an adventure which introduced him to his future wife, and we may safely say that hardly ever was man blessed with such a helpmate as was the wife of Spring-Heeled Jack.

The manner of our hero's introduction to his future wife was as follows.

The day after the arrival of Jack Dacre and Ned at the hotel a carriage drawn by four horses drove up to the inn door.

The occupants were an old gentleman and lady, apparently his wife; in addition there were two younger women, one might have been a servant or companion, the other was evidently the daughter of the old gentleman, so great was the likeness between the two.

Jack was lounging about in front of the hotel when the carriage drove up, and a strange but almost indescribable thrill passed through his whole body at the sight of the girl we have just alluded to.

People may laugh at love at first sight, but in the case of Jack Dacre it was an undoubted fact.

Our hero pressed forward to get a better view of the young lady who had made such a strange impression upon his ardent imagination, and as he did so he had the satisfaction of hearing the old gentleman say to the host that he intended to pass the night in the house if beds were available.

Mine host informed the traveller that there was plenty of room, and to Jack's intense delight the party entered the hotel.

"Hang it!" said Jack to himself, "she's a stunner, and no mistake.

173

Now, how can I contrive to get an introduction to her? I wonder whether the old gentleman will go to sleep after dinner, and if she will go for a walk? I must keep my eyes open, and chance may befriend me."

And chance did indeed befriend Jack, for after the old gentleman and his family had dined, the young lady and her companion (for such the third female of the party turned out to be) started off for a walk.

Jack, affecting a nonchalance which he was far from feeling, sauntered out after them, keeping, however, at a respectful distance.

The two girls made their way down to the side of the river Arun, and choosing a quiet spot looked about for a seat.

A few yards further on they spied a tree, a large branch of which stretched right across the towing-path till it reached nearly half way across the river.

Surely no more delightful seat could have been devised.

The two girls at once proceeded to take advantage of this charming resting-place.

Jack ensconced himself close by, just out of hearing, but where he could see every movement they made.

Once the two girls had made themselves comfortable a very animated conversation seemed to commence between them; then suddenly, whether by accident or design Jack did not at the time know, the companion placed her hand on the young lady's shoulder, and an instant later the only girl who had ever found her way to Jack's heart was being rapidly carried towards the sea in the swirling waters of the Arun.

Without waiting to see what became of the girl who had caused the catastrophe, Jack threw off his coat and sprang into the water.

Strong and steady was his stroke, and the girl had only just come to the surface for the first time when our hero was beside her.

One minute later and she was on shore, and Jack had the supreme satisfaction of seeing the rich glowing tint of life return to her pallid cheeks.

She opened her eyes and stared at Jack in wonder.

"Where is my maid, Ellen Clarke?" she asked, as she glanced hastily around.

"I don't know," answered Jack. "I was so anxious to be of service to you that I did not see what became of her. And, what is more, I don't think you need care much, for it certainly seemed to me that but for her you would not have been subjected to such a ducking. But come, let me carry you to the hotel. The sooner you get out of those wet clothes the better."

And without waiting for a reply Jack caught her in his arms and started off towards the hotel with her at a gentle trot.

To his sturdy young frame such a burden counted next to nothing.

Jack could see by the look half of terror and half of curiosity in her face that there was something to be accounted for in the manner in which she had fallen into the river; but he wisely refrained from worrying her with any questions at the moment.

Before Jack reached the hotel with his fair burden they met the maid, accompanied by three or four of the hotel attendants, making their way towards the river.

The maid's face flushed crimson, and then as suddenly paled, as she caught sight of Jack and her young mistress.

Our hero's quick, shrewd glance marked her manner, and he had no need to ask any question.

Whatever might have been her motive, beyond all doubt the companion had pushed her mistress into the river.

Young Dacre had gone through so much since his inopportune arrival in England that he had acquired an amount of worldly wisdom far beyond his years.

He, therefore, wisely held his tongue, and did not tell the girl that he had seen the "accident" and its cause.

The companion recovered her self-composure in a moment when she found that Jack did not accuse her of attempting to murder her mistress.

"Oh! Miss Lucy," she cried, "thank Heaven you are saved. I should never have forgiven myself had you been drowned. It was my fault that you fell in. I must have leant too heavily on your shoulder, and caused you to lose your balance."

These last few words were accompanied by a swift, sly glance at our hero.

Although Jack caught the look he took no notice of it, but simply strode on towards the Bridge House.

Surrendering his charge to her father, he proceeded upstairs to change his clothes.

While so engaged a knock was heard at the door, and a waiter handed in a card on which was written—

"Major-General Sir Charles Grahame will be pleased to see the saviour of his child at the earliest opportunity."

Our hero with a bright smile told the man that he would wait upon the general immediately, and he was vain enough to take a little extra care over brushing his hair, and so on, in case he should have the felicity of seeing the lovely girl whom he had just rescued from a watery grave.

Finding his way to the general's room, Jack's courage nearly deserted him.

He who had shown so much daring in endeavouring to checkmate his rascally cousin, felt as nervous as a young girl at her first ball, at the idea of meeting the lovely creature who had made such an impression upon him.

But his nervousness was entirely unnecessary, for on entering the room he found it tenanted by the general and a lady who was certainly some dozen years older than the charming girl he hoped and yet feared to see.

"Permit me to present to you my wife, Lady Grahame, Mr.—," said the general with a pause.

"Turnbull, sir, Jack Turnbull, at your service," replied our hero with a guilty blush, for he absolutely hated himself at that moment for the deception, innocent as it was, that he was practising on the father of the girl with whom he had so madly and so unaccountably fallen in love.

The formality of introduction having been gone through, the general, who had noticed the flush on Jack's cheek, but who had attributed it to a far different cause, endeavoured to place Jack entirely at his ease.

Thanking our hero cordially, but not fulsomely, for having saved his daughter's life, the general wound up by saying—

"But Lucy shall thank you herself in the morning."

"Then she is in no danger?" asked Jack.

"Oh! dear no," replied the general. "The doctor has seen her, and he says that it wants nothing but a good night's rest to put her right."

The lady had not spoken until now, having merely curtseyed when Jack was presented to her, but now she seemed compelled to say something, and, smiling in a manner that caused our hero to shudder, she said—

"Oh! yes, my dear daughter shall thank you herself in the morning, Mr. Turnbull."

"Your daughter?" said Jack, in accents of surprise, for the general's wife could not, by any possibility, have been the mother of the fair girl he had saved.

"Well, my stepdaughter," she said, with a self-satisfied smirk, for she took Jack's exclamation of surprise as a compliment.

After a few more words our hero returned to his own room, and gave Ned an account of his adventure, winding up the story by saying—

"And I cannot help thinking that Lady Grahame and the companion have leagued together to destroy that lovely girl's life."

"Monstrous!" cried Ned.

"Yes; monstrous, indeed. But I will spoil their little game. I shall keep close watch upon them, and if I find them in conversation together tonight I will treat them to a view of Spring-Heeled Jack, and in their terror find an opportunity of extracting a confession from one or both of them."

Our hero speedily changed his attire for his demoniacal garb, and, wrapping himself in his huge cloak, he passed down the stairs, and left the hotel without attracting any undue attention.

It was now quite dark, and, making his way round to the back of the house, where the general's suite of rooms was situated, Jack with one spring landed in the balcony which ran round that side of the house.

He looked in at the first window he came to, and the only occupant of the room was the old general, who was taking an after-dinner nap.

The next room he passed he did not look through the window. Something subtle seemed to tell him that this was where his loved one lay at rest.

But at the next window he paused and listened.

The words that fell upon his ears literally burnt themselves into his brain.

"Heavens!" he cried; "I am only just in time."

Another instant, and the occupants of the room, Lady Grahame and Ellen Clarke, beheld standing before them the terrible figure of Spring-Heeled Jack.

"Ha! ha!" cried Jack, "your intended crime is such a monstrous one, that even I, Spring—Heeled Jack, fiend though I may be, am bound to prevent its consummation."

Only one of the two women heard these words, for Ellen Clarke had fainted at the appearance of the fearful apparition.

Lady Grahame was possessed of stronger nerves, or she would never have been able to plan the death of her lovely and innocent stepdaughter.

For that was the purport of the conversation which Jack had overheard whilst standing outside the window.

It appeared that the whole of General Grahame's private fortune must pass, by the provisions of his father's will, to Lucy Grahame, but if she died before the general, then he would have absolute control over the property and could leave it to whomsoever he pleased.

Lady Grahame had argued to herself that if she could but remove Lucy from her path she could easily work upon the general to make a will in her sole favour.

This once accomplished how easy it would be to rid herself of her elderly husband, and with the wealth that would then be at her disposal she would easily be able to marry a younger and handsomer man, and spend the rest of her days in riotous luxury and dissipation—for such was the bent of her mind, and the general's quiet mode of life did not at all meet her views.

All this Jack had been able to gather whilst standing in the balcony before the window of Lady Grahame's chamber.

No wonder, then, that the sudden appearance of Jack in the midst of such a conversation should have sent the lady's maid into a fainting fit.

Upon the hardened Lady Grahame, however, his appearance produced no outward appearance of fear.

What amount of trepidation was at her heart Heaven alone could tell.

She stood erect and looked Jack dauntlessly in the face.

"I fear not fiend nor man," she cried; "the former I doubt the existence of, therefore you must be the latter. So name your price, Spring-Heeled Jack, I will pay it whatever it is, and trust to your honour to hold your tongue when you have received it."

Jack gave a demoniacal grin.

"Not that you could do me any harm by repeating the words that you have doubtless overheard," she went on.

Again Jack smiled his fearful smile.

"Who would take the word of a highwayman and midnight thief against that of Lady Grahame?" she cried, defiantly, now thoroughly convinced that she did stand in some amount of danger at the hands of this extraordinary being.

Jack made no reply, but seizing her by the wrist drew her towards the chamber door.

Vainly she struggled, Jack's powerful grasp bound her too fast for any chance of escape.

Surely but slowly she felt herself approaching the door that would lead her straight into the presence of her husband.

She was about to offer Jack money once more, though she felt certain from his manner that it would be of no avail, when the door suddenly opened and the general stood in the doorway.

With a startled look he took in the whole scene.

Ere he had time to inquire the meaning of the strange drama being enacted before his very eyes Jack had released his hold upon Lady Grahame's wrist, and bowing gravely to the general, said—

"Pardon this intrusion, Sir Charles Grahame."

The baronet started slightly as he heard his name mentioned, but said nothing.

"Pardon this intrusion; but I am here on a very serious mission, and I must kindly ask you to answer any questions which I may put to you."

Again the baronet bowed, for he was strangely impressed by Jack's manner, and felt that our hero's presence in that room was caused by no sinister motive.

"Go on, mysterious being; whatever you may be, go on, and anything consistent with honour I will tell you."

"You have a daughter, Lucy?" said Jack.

"I have," answered Sir Charles.

"By the terms of your father's will she is entitled to the whole of your estates at your death, and you cannot alter it?"

"By the terms of the entail of the Grahame estate, which are bound to descend to the eldest daughter in the absence of male issue, Lucy is irrevocably entitled to my estates at my death; all that I have power over is any money which I may have saved."

The baronet answered freely and fully, for he was more than ever confident now that Jack was here for the good of himself and his daughter.

"If she died before you it would be in your power to dispose of the property as you chose?" asked Jack.

"Yes, for the entail would cease then. We two, my daughter and I, are the only living representatives of our branch of the Grahames, and the time-honoured baronetcy must die with me."

"Then let me tell you," cried Jack, rising to his full height and pointing his long claw-like finger at the still defiant, although silent, Lady Grahame. "Let me tell you that I have heard this night a plot—a plot so fiend-like that I cannot doubt but that you will feel incredulous at first, but a plot the existence of which you are bound eventually to believe."

"Go on, for Heaven's sake!" cried the baronet, hoarsely.

"At any rate," said Jack, "whether you believe my words or not I shall have the satisfaction of knowing that I have saved your lovely daughter's life; for after hearing what I am going to tell you, doubt it as you may, you will be put upon your guard, and that will be quite sufficient."

At the mention of his daughter's name the baronet gave a gasp, but he could not articulate the words he desired to.

Briefly but impressively Jack told the baronet how he had witnessed the attempted murder on the Arun, of course concealing his identity with Jack Turnbull.

Lady Grahame now for the first time spoke.

"Why listen to this midnight thief?" cried she.

"Silence!" thundered Jack.

Then turning to the baronet he explained that his suspicions being aroused he had listened outside the window, and he repeated word by word the conversation he had overheard between Lady Grahame and Ellen Clarke.

Horror, doubt, and uncertainty were expressed on the baronet's face as Lady Grahame vehemently denied the charge, showering every kind of vituperation upon the head of Spring-Heeled Jack.

Our hero stood motionless, the satanic grin on his face.

He knew full well that whether the old soldier believed his story or not, Lucy's life was at least safe from the machinations of her murderous stepmother.

Before the baronet had time to open his lips to reply to his wife, a fresh voice broke upon his ear.

The girl Ellen Clarke had recovered her senses, and had thrown herself upon her knees at the feet of the general.

"Oh! forgive me, Sir Charles," cried the girl, as she grovelled on the ground in front of the astonished baronet. "It is all true; but I was sorely tempted by Lady Grahame, who had me in her power, as I had once stolen a diamond ring belonging to her, and she threatened me with imprisonment if I did not comply with her request, or rather commands. Pray—pray forgive me."

The poor old man, who had faced the enemy on many a well-fought field, thoroughly broke down at this, and agonising sobs thrilled his manly chest.

Lady Grahame stood pale and silent.

She knew the game was up.

She had played her last card, and had lost.

Well, she must accept the inevitable.

She had not much fear of any earthly punishment for her meditated crime.

She knew full well that Sir Charles's keen sense of honour would never permit him to blazon his shame abroad.

For shame it would be for one who bore the honoured name of Grahame to stand at a criminal bar, charged with conspiracy and attempt to murder a stepdaughter.

Jack surveyed the scene for a moment in silence.

Then he moved towards the window.

Turning to the baronet, he said—

"My work is done; I have saved your daughter's life; with the punishment you may mete out to these two wretched women I have nothing to do. Farewell!"

"Stay!" cried the baronet, recovering his self-possession, after a struggle. "Who are you, mysterious man? At least let me thank you for my child's life."

"I want no thanks," said Jack; "and as to who I am that I cannot at present tell, for there are reasons why my identity should be concealed. Some day, perhaps, I may present myself to you in proper person."

"But how shall I know that whoever presents himself to me is really yourself?" asked Sir Charles.

"Give me your signet ring," said Jack; "and rest assured that whoever hands it back to you will be Spring-Heeled Jack in person."

The general at once complied, and endeavoured to shake Jack by the hand, but our hero dexterously contrived to wrench it away just as he received the ring.

"No, Sir Charles," said he; "I cannot shake you or any honest man by the hand just now. A time may come—nay, it shall come—when I can do so. Till then, farewell!"

Another instant and Jack had left the room as suddenly as he had entered it.

We will leave the two guilty women and the baronet together for the present, and follow Jack.

Taking his cloak from the balcony, where he had placed it, our hero pulled it closely round him, and, with a spring, alighted on Mother Earth once more.

Hastening round to the front of the hotel, he ordered some brandy to be sent to his room, and calling to Ned, who was in one of the side bars, used as a tap, Jack proceeded to his own room.

Ned Chump followed immediately afterwards, and our hero soon put him in possession of the extraordinary event of the last hour.

"Well, Ned," said he, "I shall commence direct and final operations at once. I have just about time to reach Dacre Hall a couple of hours before daylight."

"Dacre Hall!" cried the astounded salt. "Why, does your honour recollect how far it is?"

"Yes, perfectly," was the reply.

Ned, seeing that his master had made up his mind thoroughly for the adventure, did not further attempt to dissuade him from it.

"I have reckoned the distance," then went on Jack, "and I have ample time to perform all that I intend to do long before the sun peeps above the horizon. Meanwhile give me a glass of that brandy which the waiter has just I brought in, and put the rest in my flask. I shall probably have need of it ere my return. In case I am not back till late in the day, which might make my absence noticed, you had better tell the landlord in the morning that I am slightly indisposed, and you can order my meals to be brought to my room just as if I really was confined to my bed."

"But how about your return? How will you get in?"

"Ha! ha!" laughed Jack. "Why, Ned, you have only to leave the casement of the bedroom wide open, and when I come back surely I can vault on the sill, and so make my entry without being seen."

"Well, you are a wonder, skipper, you are a wonder. Talk about what's his name, Baron—Baron—"

"Munchausen," put in our hero.

"Yes, skipper, that's the name, but I cannot pronounce it. But talk about he, why, nothing that he wrote about is half so wonderful as what you have already done, let alone what you are going to do."

"Well, goodbye for the present, Ned, I must be off now."

And shaking Ned warmly by the hand the sailor said—

"And may all good luck follow you."

Jack sprang lightly from the casement window, and a quarter of an hour later was considerably over a mile on his way to Dacre Hall, so rapid was the pace at which he was proceeding.

Ned's wondering admiration at his master's powers and good generalship was in no way misplaced, for even while the conversation just narrated was taking place Jack had packed the garments usually worn by Mr. Turnbull into a compact parcel which he attached by a hook to the lining of his capacious cloak.

This he had done because he knew that after his mission at Dacre Hall was performed some hours must elapse before he could regain his quarters at the Bridge House Hotel, Arundel.

By taking the plain clothes with him he could make everything safe.

All he had to do was to deposit the bundle in some convenient nook, and then, when his mission was accomplished, he could regain possession of the clothes, and, by placing them over his tight-fitting disguise, and removing his mask and other facial disfigurements, he could speedily transform himself from Spring-Heeled Jack into Jack Turnbull.

In the garb of that young gentleman, and with the cloak slung over his arm, he could go anywhere he pleased during the time which must elapse ere he could return to his hotel.

About a mile from Dacre Hall he met with the only adventure which befell him on his midnight journey.

He heard, apparently some little way in front of him, the sound of a horse's hoofs quietly ambling along the road.

Jack thought to himself—

"That's a farmer going to Lewes market, I'll be bound. Shall I give him a fright, or not?"

Our readers must recollect that Jack was young, and blessed with health and excellent spirits (or he could never have fought against fate as he did), so they will, undoubtedly, excuse the temptation which passed through his mind to frighten the approaching traveller, be he farmer or be he squire.

But ere he had made up his mind whether he should play one of his practical jokes or not, he heard a loud voice cry—

"Stand and deliver!"

This was by no means an uncommon cry in those days, but it was the first time that our hero had had the pleasure of beholding a real live highwayman, so he pushed rapidly along the road until a bend in it revealed a strange spectacle.

An apparently well-to-do farmer, on a smart and sleek-looking cob, was in the middle of the road.

At the side, where a retired lane branched off, stood what seemed to Jack one of the grandest sights he had ever beheld.

The sight in question was worthy of the pencil of Frith, whose picture of Claude Duval, the highwayman, dancing a *coranto* with a lady in Hounslow Heath, is doubtless well known to most of our readers.

One of the grandest thoroughbreds Jack had ever seen stood motionless at the mouth of the lane, from the ambuscade of which it had evidently just emerged.

Mounted on the back of this magnificent charger was a man who might have stood as model for the greatest sculptor the world ever produced.

His whole form, save his lips, was as motionless as that of the noble animal he bestrode.

His dress was picturesque in the extreme.

He had eschewed the orthodox scarlet, save that in his three-cornered hat he wore the bright red feather of a flamingo.

His tunic, however, was of a beautiful blue, relieved here and there with silver.

His white buckskin breeches, and his well-blacked boots, rising far above his knees, stood out sharply and well-defined in the cold glare of the moon.

His right arm was pointed straight at the head of the unhappy-looking farmer, and that right arm ended in a hand containing a handsomely mounted pistol.

"Good Mr. Highwayman, spare me! I have but little money about me, and that I am going to take over to my landlord's agent, who threatens to turn me out of my farm unless I pay him something by eight o'clock in the morning, and I have now only just got time to get to his house by that hour."

"Liar!" thundered the highwayman. "I know you are loaded with money, for you are off to Lewes market to buy cattle. Hand over your money, or you are a dead man."

Here was an opportunity for our hero's practical joke, too good to be resisted.

He grasped the situation in an instant, and ere the highwayman had time to fire his pistol, or the farmer to produce his cash, Spring-Heeled Jack, with an awful cry, sprang in the air clean over the heads of the highwayman and his destined victim.

It would be utterly impossible to find words to describe Jack's appearance as he went over the heads of the two horsemen.

The rapidity of his flight in the air distended the flaps of his coat, until they resembled a pair of wings.

His peculiar costume, fitting so tightly to his skin, made him look like a huge bat, with a body of brilliant scarlet.

With a yell of fear from the farmer, and a screech of unearthly sound from the animal he bestrode, horse and rider disappeared along the road to Lewes.

The highwayman on the other hand did not stir, and as well trained was his beautiful steed, that although it trembled with fear for an instant, it did not attempt to bolt as the farmer's horse had done.

As Jack touched the ground again the highwayman took aim at our hero and fired.

The part which he had intended to hit was Jack's forehead, and had the forehead have been where it was apparently situated, the bullet must have gone crashing straight through our hero's skull.

As it was, however, Jack's mask was so constructed as to make his face look about two inches longer than it really was.

This two inches of added matter formed the supposed cranium through which the highwayman's bullet had sped.

With another shriek more supernatural than the first Jack wheeled round, and sprang once more over his adversary's head.

This was too much even for the highwayman, who up till now had not known what fear was.

He had watched the track of his bullet clean through the uncanny-looking being's brain, and felt that it would be impossible to cope with an enemy possessing such extraordinary if not unearthly attributes.

Digging his spurs right up to the hilt in his steed's sides, he lifted the reins, and just as our hero gave a loud mocking laugh of defiance, and waved his plumed cap in the air, the highwayman gave his horse a cut, and leaping the hedge at the roadside, the noble steed and its rider were soon lost to view.

"Well, that was a lark," said Jack to himself as he rapidly strode on in the direction of Dacre Hall; "but it was a close shave, though, for I felt that bullet graze the top of my scalp in a most decidedly unpleasant manner."

Half-an-hour later, and he was at the lodge-gates of his ancestral home.

Everything now depended upon his caution, and Jack was resolved that no fault of his should mar the performance of his plans.

He knew the room which had been allotted to Morgan when he first took up his abode at the Hall, but still that room might have been changed, and it would have been fatal to our hero's scheme to have made a mistake on that score.

The only thing, therefore, was to rouse up the lodge-keeper, and find from him in his certain fright the position of the room occupied by Mr. Alfred Morgan.

The lodge consisted of only two rooms—one up and one downstairs.

In the former Jack knew that the lodge-keeper slept.

There was a stone balustrade outside the window of the bedroom, and on to this Jack lightly sprang.

To open the casement was an easy task.

This done, Jack cried out, in sepulchral tones—

"Awake, awake, awake! old man, awake!"

The lodge-keeper woke with a start, but he was not so frightened as Jack had expected him to be.

The fact of the matter was, Michael Dacre was not at all popular with the servants, and they had heard with some amount of delight of the various adventures he and Morgan had had with Jack.

"Good Mr. Spring-Heeled Jack," cried the lodge-keeper, "what do you want? If it is anything I can do for you tell me, and consider it done."

"I merely want to know in which room Mr. Morgan sleeps," replied Jack, highly delighted at the turn things had taken.

"In the blue room, sir," answered the lodge-keeper.

"Can I trust you not to raise an alarm for an hour or so? I have important business with Mr. Alfred Morgan, but shall not trouble your master."

"Aye, Mr. Spring-Heeled Jack, that you can," he said; "and if you can only frighten him out of this place you will earn the thanks of the whole household."

The man's tone was so self-evidently sincere that Jack, with a farewell warning, sprang to the ground, and hastened towards the window of the blue room.

To his surprise and momentary annoyance, he found that there was no vestige of a sill to the window.

The diamond-paned leaden casement was flush with the outer

wall.

After a brief consideration, Jack made up his mind.

"I'll risk it," he said. "I have been successful so far, and surely I shall not fail now."

In another instant he had sprang harlequin-like clean through the window, carrying before him glass, frame, and all.

As he dashed like a stone from a catapult into the room his head struck against a human form, and when our hero had recovered his lost balance he discovered in the full light of the moon Morgan lying prone on the floor.

"Rise, and give me all the papers you have, or stay—you can lay where you are. I can see your valise there, and there, I know, you carry your private journal, and so on. I'll take it, and save you the trouble of rising. Lay where you are, and don't attempt to leave this house for three hours, or fear the hangman, for yours is a hanging offence."

Without another word Jack flung the valise out of the window, and speedily followed it himself.

As Jack left the room Morgan rose from the floor, and, trembling with fear, said—

"Fear the hangman! Fear the hangman, indeed! I fear nothing but this cursed Spring-Heeled Jack, who seems to haunt every moment of my life. I'll end it at once."

And end it he did, for half-an-hour later the dead body of Alfred Morgan was swinging from a hook in a rafter above his bed.

He had cheated the hangman, but he had hanged himself.

Jack did not reach the Bridge House until late the next night, when all was quiet in the hotel.

He had no difficulty in effecting an entrance into the bedroom, but he found he could not carry the valise up with him, so he secreted it in an outhouse.

He rapidly made Ned acquainted with the events which had occurred, and wound up by saying—

"And I really believe that the valise contains the proofs of my cousin's and his accomplice's villainy."

And so it proved in the morning, when Ned, who had risen very early, had contrived to smuggle the bag in unseen.

There lay every link in the chain of fraud, including a paper signed by the baronet and witnessed by two of the hall servants, stating that he was well aware that Jack was legitimate and the rightful heir to the Dacre baronetcy and estates.

"I must see Sir Charles Grahame about this," said Jack.

"He has enquired for you several times during your absence, Sir John," replied the faithful fellow.

A glow of pride passed over Jack's face as he stretched forth his hand to Ned.

"Thanks, old fellow; it is only fitting that you, who have stuck to me in adversity, should be the first to congratulate me in my prosperity. Go and ask the general if he can favour me with an interview."

Ned immediately obeyed, and a quarter of an hour later our hero was closeted with Sir Charles Grahame. Little more remains to be told.

The general was delighted when he found that the man who had twice saved his daughter's life, first in the guise of Jack Turnbull, and secondly in that of Spring-Heeled Jack, should turn out to be no less a personage than Sir John Dacre, of Dacre Hall, Surrey.

In answer to an inquiry made by Jack, Sir Charles informed our hero that Lady Graham had consented, to avoid scandal, to become the inmate of a private lunatic asylum for not less than two years; if she behaved herself during that time Sir Charles intended to take steps for her liberation, and to provide her with an income which would enable her to live in comparative obscurity abroad.

Jack and the general ordered a chaise, and started at once for Dacre Hall, armed with Mr. Morgan's documents.

The task before them was an easier one than they had anticipated.

Michael Dacre had been so shocked by the suicide of Morgan that he at once caved in, and agreed to quit the country, Jack, of course, having no wish to prosecute any one of his own kith and kin, no matter how treacherous his conduct might have been.

In due course, as our readers must have guessed, Jack and Lucy were married.

Ned was appointed to a post of trust at the hall, and as children grew up around them few mortals enjoyed so much earthly happiness as the family and household of Sir John Dacre.

Our story is ended.

After Jack's resumption of his title many scamps and ruffians played the part of Spring-Heeled Jack in various garbs in and around London, but the story which we have told of brave Jack Dacre is the only authentic history of *Spring-Heeled Jack*.

The Great Valdez Sapphire

I know more about it than anyone else in the world, its present owner not excepted. I can give its whole history, from the Cingalese who found it, the Spanish adventurer who stole it, the cardinal who bought it, the Pope who graciously accepted it, the favoured son of the Church who received it, the gay and giddy duchess who pawned it, down to the eminent prelate who now holds it in trust as a family heirloom.

It will occupy a chapter to itself in my forthcoming work on *Historic Stones*, where full details of its weight, size, colour, and value may be found. At present I am going to relate an incident in its history which, for obvious reasons, will not be published—which, in fact, I trust the reader will consider related in strict confidence.

I had never seen the stone itself when I began to write about it, and it was not till one evening last spring, while staying with my nephew, Sir Thomas Acton, that I came within measurable distance of it. A dinner party was impending, and, at my instigation, the Bishop of Northchurch and Miss Panton, his daughter and heiress, were among the invited guests.

The dinner was a particularly good one, I remember that distinctly. In fact, I felt myself partly responsible for it, having engaged the new cook—a talented young Italian, pupil of the admirable old *chef* at my club. We had gone over the *menu* carefully together, with a result refreshing in its novelty, but not so daring as to disturb the minds of the innocent country guests who were bidden thereto.

The first spoonful of soup was reassuring, and I looked to the end of the table to exchange a congratulatory glance with Leta. What was amiss? No response. Her pretty face was flushed, her smile constrained, she was talking with quite unnecessary *empressement* to her neighbour, Sir Harry Landor, though Leta is one of those few women who un-

189

derstand the importance of letting a man settle down tranquilly and with an undisturbed mind to the business of dining, allowing no topic of serious interest to come on before the *relevés*, and reserving mere conversational brilliancy for the *entremets*.

Guests all right? No disappointments? I had gone through the list with her, selecting just the right people to be asked to meet the Landors, our new neighbours. Not a mere cumbrous county gathering, nor yet a showy imported party from town, but a skilful blending of both. Had anything happened already? I had been late for dinner and missed the arrivals in the drawing-room. It was Leta's fault. She has got into a way of coming into my room and putting the last touches to my toilet. I let her, for I am doubtful of myself nowadays after many years' dependence on the best of valets. Her taste is generally beyond dispute, but today she had indulged in a feminine vagary that provoked me and made me late for dinner.

"Are you going to wear your sapphire, Uncle Paul!" she cried in a tone of dismay. "Oh, why not the ruby?"

"You *would* have your way about the table decorations," I gently reminded her. "With that service of Crown Derby *repoussé* and orchids, the ruby would look absolutely barbaric. Now if you would have had the Limoges set, white candles, and a yellow silk centre—"

"Oh, but—I'm *so* disappointed—I wanted the bishop to see your ruby—or one of your engraved gems—"

"My dear, it is on the bishop's account I put this on. You know his daughter is heiress of the great Valdez sapphire—"

"Of course she is, and when he has the charge of a stone three times as big as yours, what's the use of wearing it? The ruby, dear Uncle Paul, *please!*"

She was desperately in earnest I could see, and considering the obligations which I am supposed to be under to her and Tom, it was but a little matter to yield, but it involved a good deal of extra trouble. Studs, sleeve-links, watch-guard, all carefully selected to go with the sapphire, had to be changed, the emerald which I chose as a compromise requiring more florid accompaniments of a deeper tone of gold; and the dinner hour struck as I replaced my jewel case, the one relic left me of a once handsome fortune, in my fireproof safe.

The emerald looked very well that evening, however. I kept my eyes upon it for comfort when Miss Panton proved trying.

She was a lean, yellow, dictatorial young person with no conversation. I spoke of her father's celebrated sapphires. "*My* sapphires," she amended sourly; "though I am legally debarred from making any profitable use of them." She furthermore informed me that she viewed them as useless gauds, which ought to be disposed of for the benefit of the heathen. I gave the subject up, and while she discoursed of the work of the Blue Ribbon Army among the Bosjesmans I tried to understand a certain dislocation in the arrangement of the table. Surely we were more or less in number than we should be? Opposite side all right. Who was extra on ours?

I leaned forward. Lady Landor on one side of Tom, on the other who? I caught glimpses of plumes pink and green nodding over a dinner plate, and beneath them a pink nose in a green visage with a nutcracker chin altogether unknown to me. A sharp gray eye shot a sideway glance down the table and caught me peeping, and I retreated, having only marked in addition two clawlike hands, with pointed ruffles and a mass of brilliant rings, making good play with a knife and fork. Who was she? At intervals a high acid voice could be heard addressing Tom, and a laugh that made me shudder; it had the quality of the scream of a bird of prey or the yell of a jackal. I had heard that sort of laugh before, and it always made me feel like a defenceless rabbit.

Every time it sounded I saw Leta's fan flutter more furiously and her manner grow more nervously animated. Poor dear girl! I never in all my recollection wished a dinner at an end so earnestly so as to assure her of my support and sympathy, though without the faintest conception why either should be required.

The ices at last. A *menu* card folded in two was laid beside me. I read it unobserved. "Keep the B. from joining us in the drawing-room." The B.—? The bishop, of course. With pleasure. But why? And how? *That's* the question, never mind "why." Could I lure him into the library—the billiard room—the conservatory? I doubted it, and I doubted still more what I should do with him when I got him there.

The bishop is a grand and stately ecclesiastic of the mediæval type, broad-chested, deep-voiced, martial of bearing. I could picture him charging mace in hand at the head of his vassals, or delivering over a dissenter of the period to the rack and thumb-screw, but not pottering among rare editions, tall copies and Grolier bindings, nor condescending to a quiet cigar among the tree ferns and orchids. Leta must and should be obeyed, I swore, nevertheless, even if I were driven to lock the door in the fearless old fashion of a bygone day, and declare I'd shoot any man who left while a drop remained in the bottles.

The ladies were rising. The lady at the head of the line smirked and nodded her pink plumes coquettishly at Tom, while her hawk's eyes roved keen and predatory over us all. She stopped suddenly, creating a block and confusion.

"Ah, the dear bishop! *You* there, and I never saw you! You must come and have a nice long chat presently. By-by—!" She shook her fan at him over my shoulder and tripped on. Leta, passing me last, gave me a look of profound despair.

"Lady Carwitchet!" somebody exclaimed. "I couldn't believe my eyes."

"Thought she was dead or in penal servitude. Never should have expected to see her *here*," said someone else behind me confidentially.

"What Carwitchet? Not the mother of the Carwitchet who—"

"Just so. The Carwitchet who—" Tom assented with a shrug. "We needn't go farther, as she's my guest. Just my luck. I met them at Buxton, thought them uncommonly good company—in fact, Carwitchet laid me under a great obligation about a horse I was nearly let in for buying—and gave them a general invitation here, as one does, you know. Never expected her to turn up with her luggage this afternoon just before dinner, to stay a week, or a fortnight if Carwitchet can join her." A groan of sympathy ran round the table. "It can't be helped. I've told you this just to show that I shouldn't have asked you here to meet this sort of people of my own free will; but, as it is, please say no more about them." The subject was not dropped by any means, and I took care that it should not be. At our end of the table one story after another went buzzing round—*sotto voce*, out of deference to Tom—but perfectly audible.

"Carwitchet? Ah, yes. Mixed up in that Rawlings divorce case, wasn't he? A bad lot. Turned out of the Dragoon Guards for cheating at cards, or picking pockets, or something—remember the row at the Cerulean Club? Scandalous exposure—and that forged letter business—oh, that was the mother—prosecution hushed up somehow. Ought to be serving her fourteen years—and that business of poor Farrars, the banker—got hold of some of his secrets and blackmailed him till he blew his brains out—"

It was so exciting that I clean forgot the bishop, till a low gasp at my elbow startled me. He was lying back in his chair, his mighty shaven jowl a ghastly white, his fierce imperious eyebrows drooping limp over his fishlike eyes, his splendid figure shrunk and contracted. He was trying with a shaken hand to pour out wine. The decanter clattered against the glass and the wine spilled on the cloth.

"I'm afraid you find the room too warm. Shall we go into the library?"

He rose hastily and followed me like a lamb.

He recovered himself once we got into the hall, and affably rejected all my proffers of brandy and soda—medical advice—everything else my limited experience could suggest. He only demanded his carriage "directly" and that Miss Panton should be summoned forthwith.

I made the best use I could of the time left me.

"I'm uncommonly sorry you do not feel equal to staying a little longer, my lord. I counted on showing you my few trifles of precious stones, the salvage from the wreck of my possessions. Nothing in comparison with your own collection."

The bishop clasped his hand over his heart. His breath came short and quick.

"A return of that dizziness," he explained with a faint smile. "You are thinking of the Valdez sapphire, are you not? Someday," he went on with forced composure, "I may have the pleasure of showing it to you. It is at my banker's just now."

Miss Panton's steps were heard in the hall. "You are well known as a connoisseur, Mr. Acton," he went on hurriedly. "Is your collection valuable? If so, *keep it safe; don' trust a ring off your hand, or the key of your jewel-case out of your pocket till the house is clear again.*" The words rushed from his lips in an impetuous whisper, he gave me a meaning glance, and departed with his daughter. I went back to the drawing-room, my head swimming with bewilderment.

"What! The dear bishop gone!" screamed Lady Carwitchet from the central ottoman where she sat, surrounded by most of the gentlemen, all apparently well entertained by her conversation. "And I wanted to talk over old times with him so badly. His poor wife was my greatest friend. Mira Montanaro, daughter of the great banker, you know. It's not possible that that miserable little prig is my poor Mira's girl. The heiress of all the Montanaros in a black-lace gown worth twopence! When I think of her mother's beauty and her toilets! Does she ever wear the sapphires? Has anyone ever seen her in them? Eleven large stones in a lovely antique setting, and the great Valdez sapphire—worth thousands and thousands—for the pendant." No one replied. "I wanted to get a rise out of the bishop tonight. It used to make him so mad when I wore this."

She fumbled among the laces at her throat, and clawed out a pendant that hung to a velvet band around her neck. I fairly gasped when she removed her hand. A sapphire of irregular shape flashed out its blue lightning on us. Such a stone! A true, rich, cornflower blue even by that wretched artificial light, with soft velvety depths of colour and dazzling clearness of tint in its lights and shades—a stone to remember! I stretched out my hand involuntarily, but Lady Carwitchet drew back with a coquettish squeal. "No! no! You mustn't look any closer. Tell me what you think of it now. Isn't it pretty?"

"Superb!" was all I could ejaculate, staring at the azure splendour of that miraculous jewel in a sort of trance.

She gave a shrill cackling laugh of mockery.

"The great Mr. Acton taken in by a bit of Palais Royal gimcrackery! What an advertisement for Bogaerts et Cie! They are perfect artists in frauds. Don't you remember their stand at the first Paris Exhibition? They had imitations there of every celebrated stone; but I never expected anything made by man could delude Mr. Acton, never!" And she went off into another mocking cackle, and all the idiots round her haw-hawed knowingly, as if they had seen the joke all along. I was too bewildered to reply, which was on the whole lucky. "I suppose I musn't tell why I came to give quite a big sum in *francs* for this?" she went on, tapping her closed lips with her closed fan, and cocking her eye at us all like a parrot wanting to be coaxed to talk. "It's a queer story."

I didn't want to hear her anecdote, especially as I saw she wanted to tell it. What I *did* want was to see that pendant again. She had thrust it back among her laces, only the loop which held it to the velvet being visible. It was set with three small sapphires, and even from a distance I clearly made them out to be imitations, and poor ones. I felt a queer thrill of self-mistrust. Was the large stone no better? Could I, even for an instant, have been dazzled by a sham, and a sham of that quality? The events of the evening had flurried and confused me. I wished to think them over in quiet. I would go to bed.

My rooms at the Manor are the best in the house. Leta will have it so. I must explain their position for a reason to be understood later. My bedroom is in the southeast angle of the house; it opens on one side into a sitting-room in the east corridor, the rest of which is taken up by the suite of rooms occupied by Tom and Leta; and on the other side into my bathroom, the first room in the south corridor where the principal guest chambers are, to one of which it was originally the dressing-room. Passing this room I noticed a couple of housemaids preparing it for the night, and discovered with a shiver that Lady Car-witchet was to be my next-door neighbour. It gave me a turn.

The bishop's strange warning must have unnerved me. I was perfectly safe from her ladyship. The disused door into her room was locked, and the key safe on the housekeeper's bunch. It was also undiscoverable on her side, the recess in which it stood being completely filled by a large wardrobe. On my side hung a thick sound-proof *portière*. Nevertheless, I resolved not to use that room while she inhabited the next one. I removed my possessions, fastened the door of communication with my bedroom and dragged a heavy ottoman across it.

Then I stowed away my emerald in my strong-box. It is built into the wall of my sitting-room, and masked by the lower part of an old carved oak bureau. I put away even the rings I wore habitually, keeping out only an inferior cat's-eye for workaday wear. I had just made all safe when Leta tapped at the door and came in to wish me good night. She looked flushed and harassed and ready to cry. "Uncle Paul," she began, "I want you to go up to town at once, and stay away till I send for you."

"My dear—!" I was too amazed to expostulate.

"We've got a—a pestilence among us," she declared, her foot tapping the ground angrily, "and the least we can do is to go into quarantine. Oh, I'm so sorry and so ashamed! The poor bishop! I'll take good care that no one else shall meet that woman here. You did your best for me, Uncle Paul, and managed admirably, but it was all no use. I hoped against hope that what between the dusk of the drawing-room before dinner, and being put at opposite ends of the table, we might get through without a meeting—"

"But, my dear, explain. Why shouldn't the bishop and Lady Car-witchet meet? Why is it worse for him than anyone else?"

"Why? I thought everybody had heard of that dreadful wife of his who nearly broke his heart. If he married her for her money it served him right, but Lady Landor says she was very handsome and really in love with him at first. Then Lady Carwitchet got hold of her and led her into all sorts of mischief. She left her husband—he was only a rector with a country living in those days—and went to live in town, got into a horrid fast set, and made herself notorious. You *must* have heard of her."

"I heard of her sapphires, my dear. But I was in Brazil at the time."

"I wish you had been at home. You might have found her out. She was furious because her husband refused to let her wear the great Valdez sapphire. It had been in the Montanaro family for some generations, and her father settled it first on her and then on her little girl—the bishop being trustee. He felt obliged to take away the little girl, and send her off to be brought up by some old aunts in the country, and he locked up the sapphire. Lady Carwitchet tells as a splendid joke how they got the copy made in Paris, and it did just as well for the people to stare at. No wonder the bishop hates the very name of the stone."

"How long will she stay here?" I asked dismally.

"Till Lord Carwitchet can come and escort her to Paris to visit some American friends. Goodness knows when that will be! Do go up to town, Uncle Paul!"

I refused indignantly. The very least I could do was to stand by my poor young relatives in their troubles and help them through. I did so. I wore that inferior cat's eye for six weeks!

It is a time I cannot think of even now without a shudder. The more I saw of that terrible old woman the more I detested her, and we saw a very great deal of her. Leta kept her word, and neither accepted nor gave invitations all that time. We were cut off from all society but that of old General Fairford, who would go anywhere and meet anyone to get a rubber after dinner; the doctor, a sporting widower; and the Duberlys, a giddy, rather rackety young couple who had taken the Dower House for a year. Lady Carwitchet seemed perfectly content. She revelled in the soft living and good fare of the Manor House, the drives in Leta's big *barouche*, and Domenico's dinners, as one to whom short commons were not unknown. She had a hungry way of grabbing and grasping at everything she could—the shillings she won at whist, the best fruit at dessert, the postage stamps in the library inkstand—that was infinitely suggestive.

Sometimes I could have pitied her, she was so greedy, so spiteful, so friendless. She always made me think of some wicked old pirate putting into a peaceful port to provision and repair his battered old hulk, obliged to live on friendly terms with the natives, but his piratical old nostrils asniff for plunder and his piratical old soul longing to be off marauding once more. When would that be? Not till the arrival in Paris of her distinguished American friends, of whom we heard a great deal. "Charming people, the Bokums of Chicago, the American branch of the English Beauchamps, you know!" They seemed to be taking an unconscionable time to get there. She would have insisted on being driven over to Northchurch to call at the palace, but that the bishop was understood to be holding confirmations at the other end of the diocese.

I was alone in the house one afternoon sitting by my window, toying with the key of my safe, and wondering whether I dare treat myself to a peep at my treasures, when a suspicious movement in the park below caught my attention. A black figure certainly dodged from behind one tree to the next, and then into the shadow of the park paling instead of keeping to the footpath. It looked queer. I caught up my field glass and marked him at one point where he was bound to come into the open for a few steps. He crossed the strip of turf with giant strides and got into cover again, but not quick enough to prevent me recognizing him. It was—great heavens!—the bishop! In a soft hat pulled over his forehead, with a long cloak and a big stick he looked like a poacher.

Guided by some mysterious instinct I hurried to meet him. I opened the conservatory door, and in he rushed like a hunted rabbit. Without explanation I led him up the wide staircase to my room, where he dropped into a chair and wiped his face.

"You are astonished, Mr. Acton," he panted. "I will explain directly. Thanks." He tossed off the glass of brandy I had poured out without waiting for the qualifying soda, and looked better.

"I am in serious trouble. You can help me. I've had a shock to-day—a grievous shock." He stopped and tried to pull himself together. "I must trust you implicitly, Mr. Acton, I have no choice. Tell me what you think of this." He drew a case from his breast pocket and opened it. "I promised you should see the Valdez sapphire. Look there!"

The Valdez sapphire! A great big shining lump of blue crystal—flawless and of perfect colour—that was all. I took it up, breathed on it, drew out my magnifier, looked at it in one light and another. What was wrong with it? I could not say. Nine experts out of ten would undoubtedly have pronounced the stone genuine. I, by virtue of some mysterious instinct that has hitherto always guided me aright, was the unlucky tenth. I looked at the bishop. His eyes met mine. There was no need of spoken word between us.

"Has Lady Carwitchet shown you her sapphire?" was his most unexpected question. "She has? Now, Mr. Acton, on your honour as a connoisseur and a gentleman, which of the two is the Valdez?"

"Not this one." I could say naught else.

"You were my last hope." He broke off, and dropped his face on his folded arms with a groan that shook the table on which he rested, while I stood dismayed at myself for having let so hasty a judgment escape me. He lifted a ghastly countenance to me. "She vowed she would see me ruined and disgraced. I made her my enemy by crossing some of her schemes once, and she never forgives. She will keep her word. I shall appear before the world as a fraudulent trustee. I can neither produce the valuable confided to my charge nor make the loss good. I have only an incredible story to tell," he dropped his head and groaned again. "Who will believe me?"

"I will, for one."

"Ah, you? Yes, you know her. She took my wife from me, Mr. Acton. Heaven only knows what the hold was that she had over poor Mira. She encouraged her to set me at defiance and eventually to leave me. She was answerable for all the scandalous folly and extravagance of poor Mira's life in Paris—spare me the telling of the story. She left her at last to die alone and uncared for. I reached my wife to find her dying of a fever from which Lady Carwitchet and her crew had fled. She was raving in delirium, and died without recognizing me. Some trouble she had been in which I must never know oppressed her. At the very last she roused from a long stupor and spoke to the nurse. 'Tell him to get the sapphire back—she stole it. She has robbed my child.' Those were her last words. The nurse understood no English, and treated them as wandering; but *I* heard them, and knew she was sane when she spoke."

"What did you do?"

"What could I? I saw Lady Carwitchet, who laughed at me, and defied me to make her confess or disgorge. I took the pendant to more than one eminent jeweller on pretence of having the setting seen to, and all have examined and admired without giving a hint of there being anything wrong. I allowed a celebrated mineralogist to see it; he gave no sign—"

"Perhaps they are right and we are wrong."

"No, no. Listen. I heard of an old Dutchman celebrated for his imitations. I went to him, and he told me at once that he had been allowed by Montanaro to copy the Valdez—setting and all—for the Paris Exhibition. I showed him this, and he claimed it for his own work at once, and pointed out his private mark upon it. You must take your magnifier to find it; a Greek Beta. He also told me that he had sold it to Lady Carwitchet more than a year ago."

"It is a terrible position."

"It is. My co-trustee died lately. I have never dared to have another appointed. I am bound to hand over the sapphire to my daughter on her marriage, if her husband consents to take the name of Montanaro."

The bishop's face was ghastly pale, and the moisture started on his brow. I racked my brain for some word of comfort.

"Miss Panton may never marry."

"But she will!" he shouted. "That is the blow that has been dealt me today. My chaplain—actually, my chaplain—tells me that he is going out as a temperance missionary to equatorial Africa, and has the assurance to add that he believes my daughter is not indisposed to accompany him!" His consummating wrath acted as a momentary stimulant. He sat upright, his eyes flashing and his brow thunderous. I felt for that chaplain. Then he collapsed miserably. "The sapphires will have to be produced, identified, revalued. How shall I come out of it? Think of the disgrace, the ripping up of old scandals! Even if I were to compound with Lady Carwitchet, the sum she hinted at was too monstrous. She wants more than my money. Help me, Mr. Acton! For the sake of your own family interest, help me!"

"I beg your pardon—family interests? I don't understand."

"If my daughter is childless, her next of kin is poor Marmaduke Panton, who is dying at Cannes, not married, or likely to marry; and failing him, your nephew, Sir Thomas Acton, succeeds."

My nephew Tom! Leta, or Leta's baby, might come to be the possible inheritor of the great Valdez sapphire! The blood rushed to my head as I looked at the great shining swindle before me. "What diabolic jugglery was at work when the exchange was made?" I demanded fiercely.

"It must have been on the last occasion of her wearing the sapphires in London. I ought never to have let her out of my sight."

"You must put a stop to Miss Panton's marriage in the first place," I pronounced as autocratically as he could have done himself.

"Not to be thought of," he admitted helplessly. "Mira has my force of character. She knows her rights, and she will have her jewels. I want you to take charge of the—thing for me. If it's in the house she'll make me produce it. She'll inquire at the banker's. If *you* have it we can gain time, if but for a day or two." He broke off. Carriage wheels were crashing on the gravel outside. We looked at one another in consternation. Flight was imperative. I hurried him downstairs and out of the conservatory just as the door-bell rang. I think we both lost our heads in the confusion. He shoved the case into my hands, and I pocketed it, without a thought of the awful responsibility I was incurring, and saw him disappear into the shelter of the friendly night.

When I think of what my feelings were that evening—of my murderous hatred of that smirking jesting Jezebel who sat opposite me at dinner, my wrathful indignation at the thought of the poor little expected heir defrauded ere his birth; of the crushing contempt I felt for myself and the bishop as a pair of witless idiots unable to see our way out of the dilemma; all this boiling and surging through my soul, I can only wonder—Domenico having given himself a holiday, and the kitchen-maid doing her worst and wickedest—that gout or jaundice did not put an end to this story at once.

"Uncle Paul!" Leta was looking her sweetest when she tripped into my room next morning. "I've news for you. She," pointing a delicate forefinger in the direction of the corridor, "is going! Her Bokums have reached Paris at last, and sent for her to join them at the Grand Hotel."

I was thunderstruck. The longed-for deliverance had but come to remove hopelessly and forever out of my reach Lady Carwitchet and the great Valdez sapphire.

"Why, aren't you overjoyed? I am. We are going to celebrate the event by a dinner-party. Tom's hospitable soul is vexed by the lack of entertainment we had provided for her. We must ask the Brownleys someday or other, and they will be delighted to meet anything in the way of a ladyship, or such smart folks as the Duberly-Parkers. Then we may as well have the Blomfields, and air that awful modern Sèvres dessert-service she gave us when we were married." I had no objection to make, and she went on, rubbing her soft cheek against my shoulder like the purring little cat she was: "Now I want you to do something to please me—and Mrs. Blomfield. She has set her heart on seeing your rubies, and though I know you hate her about as much as you do that Sèvres china—"

"What! Wear my rubies with that! I won't. I'll tell you what I will do, though. I've got some carbuncles as big as prize gooseberries, a whole set. Then you have only to put those Bohemian glass vases and candelabra on the table, and let your gardener do his worst with his great forced, scentless, vulgar blooms, and we shall all be in keeping." Leta pouted. An idea struck me. "Or I'll do as you wish, on one condition. You get Lady Carwitchet to wear her big sapphire, and don't tell her I wish it."

I lived through the next few days as one in some evil dream. The sapphires, like twin spectres, haunted me day and night. Was ever man so tantalized? To hold the shadow and see the substance dangled temptingly within reach. The bishop made no sign of ridding me of my unwelcome charge, and the thought of what might happen in a case of burglary—fire—earthquake—made me start and tremble at all sorts of inopportune moments.

I kept faith with Leta, and reluctantly produced my beautiful rubies on the night of her dinner party. Emerging from my room I came full upon Lady Carwitchet in the corridor. She was dressed for dinner, and at her throat I caught the blue gleam of the great sapphire. Leta had kept faith with me. I don't know what I stammered in reply to her ladyship's remarks; my whole soul was absorbed in the contemplation of the intoxicating loveliness of the gem. *That* a Palais Royal deception! Incredible! My fingers twitched, my breath came short and fierce with the lust of possession. She must have seen the covetous glare in my eyes. A look of gratified spiteful complacency overspread her features, as she swept on ahead and descended the stairs before me. I followed her to the drawing-room door. She stopped suddenly, and murmuring something unintelligible hurried back again.

Everybody was assembled there that I expected to see, with an addition. Not a welcome one by the look on Tom's face. He stood on the hearth-rug conversing with a great hulking, high-shouldered fellow, sallow-faced, with a heavy moustache and drooping eyelids, from the corners of which flashed out a sudden suspicious look as I approached, which lighted up into a greedy one as it rested on my rubies, and seemed unaccountably familiar to me, till Lady Carwitchet tripping past me exclaimed:

"He has come at last! My naughty, naughty boy! Mr. Acton, this is my son, Lord Carwitchet!"

I broke off short in the midst of my polite acknowledgments to stare blankly at her. The sapphire was gone! A great gilt cross, with a Scotch pebble like an acid drop, was her sole decoration.

"I had to put my pendant away," she explained confidentially; "the clasp had got broken somehow." I didn't believe a word.

Lord Carwitchet contributed little to the general entertainment at dinner, but fell into confidential talk with Mrs. Duberly-Parker. I caught a few unintelligible remarks across the table. They referred, I subsequently discovered, to the lady's little book on Northchurch races, and I recollected that the Spring Meeting was on, and tomorrow "Cup Day." After dinner there was great talk about getting up a party to go on General Fairford's drag. Lady Carwitchet was in ecstasies and tried to coax me into joining. Leta declined positively. Tom accepted sulkily.

The look in Lord Carwitchet's eye returned to my mind as I locked up my rubies that night. It made him look so like his mother! I went round my fastenings with unusual care. Safe and closets and desk and doors, I tried them all. Coming at last to the bathroom, it opened at once. It was the housemaid's doing. She had evidently taken advantage of my having abandoned the room to give it "a thorough spring cleaning," and I anathematized her. The furniture was all piled together and veiled with sheets, the carpet and felt curtain were gone, there were new brooms about. As I peered around, a voice close at my ear made me jump—Lady Carwitchet's!

"I tell you I have nothing, not a penny! I shall have to borrow my train fare before I can leave this. They'll be glad enough to lend it."

Not only had the *portière* been removed, but the door behind it had been unlocked and left open for convenience of dusting behind the wardrobe. I might as well have been in the bedroom.

"Don't tell me," I recognized Carwitchet's growl. "You've not been here all this time for nothing. You've been collecting for a Kilburn cot or getting subscriptions for the distressed Irish landlords. I know you. Now I'm not going to see myself ruined for the want of a paltry hundred or so. I tell you the colt is a dead certainty. If I could have got a thousand or two on him last week, we might have ended our dog days millionaires. Hand over what you can. You've money's worth, if not money. Where's that sapphire you stole?"

"I didn't. I can show you the receipted bill. All *I* possess is honestly come by. What could you do with it, even if I gave it you? You couldn't sell it as the Valdez, and you can't get it cut up as you might if it were real."

"If it's only bogus, why are you always in such a flutter about it? I'll do something with it, never fear. Hand over."

"I can't. I haven't got it. I had to raise something on it before I left town."

"Will you swear it's not in that wardrobe? I dare say you will. I mean to see. Give me those keys."

I heard a struggle and a jingle, then the wardrobe door must have been flung open, for a streak of light struck through a crack in the wood of the back. Creeping close and peeping through, I could see an awful sight. Lady Carwitchet in a flannel wrapper, minus hair, teeth, complexion, pointing a skinny forefinger that quivered with rage at her son, who was out of the range of my vision.

"Stop that, and throw those keys down here directly, or I'll rouse the house. Sir Thomas is a magistrate, and will lock you up as soon as look at you." She clutched at the bell rope as she spoke. "I'll swear I'm in danger of my life from you and give you in charge. Yes, and when you're in prison I'll keep you there till you die. I've often thought I'd do it. How about the hotel robberies last summer at Cowes, eh? Mightn't the police be grateful for a hint or two? And how about—"

The keys fell with a crash on the bed, accompanied by some bad language in an apologetic tone, and the door slammed to. I crept trembling to bed.

This new and horrible complication of the situation filled me with dismay. Lord Carwitchet's wolfish glance at my rubies took a new meaning. They were safe enough, I believed—but the sapphire! If he disbelieved his mother, how long would she be able to keep it from his clutches? That she had some plot of her own of which the bishop would eventually be the victim I did not doubt, or why had she not made her bargain with him long ago? But supposing she took fright, lost her head, allowed her son to wrest the jewel from her, or gave consent to its being mutilated, divided! I lay in a cold perspiration till morning.

My terrors haunted me all day. They were with me at breakfast time when Lady Carwitchet, tripping in smiling, made a last attempt to induce me to accompany her and keep her "bad, bad boy" from getting among "those horrid betting men."

They haunted me through the long peaceful day with Leta and the *tête-à-tête* dinner, but they swarmed around and beset me sorest when, sitting alone over my sitting-room fire, I listened for the return of the drag party. I read my newspaper and brewed myself some hot strong drink, but there comes a time of night when no fire can warm and no drink can cheer. The bishop's despairing face kept me company, and his troubles and the wrongs of the future heir took possession of me. Then the uncanny noises that make all old houses ghostly during the small hours began to make themselves heard. Muffled footsteps trod the corridor, stopping to listen at every door, door latches gently clicked, boards creaked unreasonably, sounds of stealthy movements came from the locked-up bathroom.

The welcome crash of wheels at last, and the sound of the front-door bell. I could hear Lady Carwitchet making her shrill *adieux* to her friends and her steps in the corridor. She was softly humming a little song as she approached. I heard her unlock her bedroom door before she entered—an odd thing to do. Tom came sleepily stumbling to his room later. I put my head out. "Where is Lord Carwitchet?"

"Haven't you seen him? He left us hours ago. Not come home, eh? Well, he's welcome to stay away. I don't want to see more of him." Tom's brow was dark and his voice surly. "I gave him to understand as much." Whatever had happened, Tom was evidently too disgusted to explain just then.

I went back to my fire unaccountably relieved, and brewed myself another and a stronger brew. It warmed me this time, but excited me foolishly. There must be some way out of the difficulty. I felt now as if I could almost see it if I gave my mind to it. Why—suppose—there might be no difficulty after all! The bishop was a nervous old gentle-man. He might have been mistaken all through, Bogaerts might have been mistaken, I might—no. I could not have been mistaken—or I thought not. I fidgeted and fumed and argued with myself till I found I should have no peace of mind without a look at the stone in my possession, and I actually went to the safe and took the case out.

The sapphire certainly looked different by lamplight. I sat and stared, and all but overpersuaded my better judgment into giving it a verdict. Bogaerts's mark—I suddenly remembered it. I took my mag-nifier and held the pendant to the light. There, scratched upon the stone, was the Greek *Beta!* There came a tap on my door, and before I could answer, the handle turned softly and Lord Carwitchet stood before me. I whipped the case into my dressing-gown pocket and stared at him. He was not pleasant to look at, especially at that time of night. He had a dishevelled, desperate air, his voice was hoarse, his red-rimmed eyes wild.

"I beg your pardon," he began civilly enough. "I saw your light burning, and thought, as we go by the early train tomorrow, you might allow me to consult you now on a little business of my mother's." His eyes roved about the room. Was he trying to find the whereabouts of my safe? "You know a lot about precious stones, don't you?"

"So my friends are kind enough to say. Won't you sit down? I have unluckily little chance of indulging the taste on my own account," was my cautious reply.

"But you've written a book about them, and know them when

you see them, don't you? Now my mother has given me something, and would like you to give a guess at its value. Perhaps you can put me in the way of disposing of it?"

"I certainly can do so if it is worth anything. Is that it?" I was in a fever of excitement, for I guessed what was clutched in his palm. He held out to me the Valdez sapphire.

How it shone and sparkled like a great blue star! I made myself a deprecating smile as I took it from him, but how dare I call it false to its face? As well accuse the sun in heaven of being a cheap imitation. I faltered and prevaricated feebly. Where was my moral courage, and where was the good, honest, thumping lie that should have aided me? "I have the best authority for recognizing this as a very good copy of a famous stone in the possession of the Bishop of Northchurch." His scowl grew so black that I saw he believed me, and I went on more cheerily: "This was manufactured by Johannes Bogaerts—I can give you his address, and you can make inquiries yourself—by special permission of the then owner, the late Leone Montanaro."

"Hand it back!" he interrupted (his other remarks were outrageous, but satisfactory to hear); but I waved him off. I couldn't give it up. It fascinated me. I toyed with it, I caressed it. I made it display its different tones of colour. I must see the two stones together. I must see it outshine its paltry rival. It was a whimsical frenzy that seized me—I can call it by no other name.

"Would you like to see the original? Curiously enough, I have it here. The bishop has left it in my charge."

The wolfish light flamed up in Carwitchet's eyes as I drew forth the case. He laid the Valdez down on a sheet of paper, and I placed the other, still in its case, beside it. In that moment they looked identical, except for the little loop of sham stones, replaced by a plain gold band in the bishop's jewel. Carwitchet leaned across the table eagerly, the table gave a lurch, the lamp tottered, crashed over, and we were left in semidarkness.

"Don't stir!" Carwitchet shouted. "The paraffin is all over the place!" He seized my sofa blanket, and flung it over the table while I stood helpless. "There, that's safe now. Have you candles on the chimney-piece? I've got matches."

He looked very white and excited as he lit up. "Might have been an awkward job with all that burning paraffin running about," he said quite pleasantly. "I hope no real harm is done." I was lifting the rug with shaking hands. The two stones lay as I had placed them. No! I nearly dropped it back again. It was the stone in the case that had the loop with the three sham sapphires!

Carwitchet picked the other up hastily. "So you say this is rubbish?" he asked, his eyes sparkling wickedly, and an attempt at mortification in his tone.

"Utter rubbish!" I pronounced, with truth and decision, snapping up the case and pocketing it. "Lady Carwitchet must have known it."

"Ah, well, it's disappointing, isn't it? Goodbye, we shall not meet again."

I shook hands with him most cordially. "Goodbye, Lord Carwitchet. *So* glad to have met you and your mother. It has been a source of the *greatest* pleasure, I assure you."

I have never seen the Carwitchets since. The bishop drove over next day in rather better spirits. Miss Panton had refused the chaplain.

"It doesn't matter, my lord," I said to him heartily. "We've all been under some strange misconception. The stone in your possession is the veritable one. I could swear to that anywhere. The sapphire Lady Carwitchet wears is only an excellent imitation, and—I have seen it with my own eyes—is the one bearing Bogaerts's mark, the Greek *Beta*."

Sweeney Todd, the Barber of Fleet Street

A Thrilling Story of the Old City of London. Founded on Facts.

CHAPTER 1

Hark! twelve o'clock is proclaimed by old St. Dunstan's church, and scarcely have the sounds done echoing throughout the neighbourhood, and scarce has the clock of Lincoln's Inn done chiming in its announcement of the same hour when Bell-yard, Temple Bar, becomes a scene of commotion.

What a scampering of feet is there, what a laughing and talking, what a jostling to be first; and what an immense number of manoeuvres are resorted to by some of the strong to distance others!

And mostly from Lincoln's Inn come these persons, young and old, but most certainly a majority of the former, although from neighbouring legal establishments likewise there came not a few; the Temple contributes its numbers, and from the more distant Gray's Inn came a goodly lot.

Is it a fire? is it a fight? or anything else sufficiently alarming or extraordinary, to excite the junior members of the legal profession to such a species of madness? No, it is none of these, nor is there a fat cause to be run for, which in the hands of some clever practitioner might become a vested interest. No, the enjoyment is purely one of a physical character, and all the pacing and racing—all this turmoil and trouble—all this pushing, jostling, laughing, and shouting, is to see who will get first at Mrs. Lovett's pie shop.

Yes, on the left hand side of Bell-yard, going down from Carey-street was, at the time we write of, one of the most celebrated shops for the sale of veal and pork pies that ever London produced. High and low, rich and poor, resorted to it; its fame had spread far and wide;

207

it was because the first batch of these pies came up at twelve o'clock that there was such a rush of the legal profession to obtain them.

Their fame had spread to great distances. Oh—those delicious pies! there was about them a flavour never surpassed, and rarely equalled; the paste was of the most delicate construction, and impregnated with the aroma of a delicious gravy that defies description; the fat and the lean so artistically mixed up.

The counter in Lovett's shop was in the shape of a horse shoe, and it was the custom of the young bloods from the Temple and Lincoln's Inn to sit in a row at its edge, while, they partook of the pies, and chatted gaily about one thing and another.

There was a Mistress Lovett; but possibly our reader guessed as much, for what but a female hand, and that female buxom, young, and good-looking, could have ventured upon the production of those pies. Yes, Mrs. Lovett was all that; and every enamoured young scion of the law, as he devoured his pie, pleased himself with the idea that the charming Miss Lovett had made that pie especially for him, and that fate or predestination had placed it in his hands.

And it was astonishing to see with what impartiality and with what tact the fair pastry-cook bestowed her smiles upon her admirers, so that none could say he was neglected, while it was extremely difficult for anyone to say he was preferred.

This was pleasant, but at the same time it was provoking to all except Mrs. Lovett, in whose favour it got up a kind of excitement that paid extraordinarily well, because some of the young fellows thought that he who consumed the most pies, would be in the most likely, way to receive the greatest number of smiles from the lady.

Acting upon this supposition, some of her more enthusiastic admirers, went on consuming the pies until they were almost ready to burst. But there were others again, of a more philosophic turn of mind, who went for the pies only, and did not care one jot for Mrs. Lovett.

These declare that her smile was cold and uncomfortable—that it was upon her lips, but had no place in her heart—that it was the set smile of a ballet-dancer, which is about one of the most unmirthful things in existence.

Then there were some who went even beyond this, and while they admitted the excellence of the pies, and went every day to partake of them, swore that Mrs. Lovett had quite a sinister aspect, and that they could see what a merely superficial affair her blandishments were, and that there was "A lurking devil in her eye," that, if once roused, would be capable of achieving some serious things, and might not be so easily quelled again.

By five minutes past twelve Mrs. Lovett's counter was full, and the savoury steam of the hot pies went out in fragrant clouds into Bell-yard, being sniffed up by many a poor wretch passing by.

"Why, Tobias Ragg," said a young man, with his mouth full of pie, "where have you been since you left Mr. Show's in Paper-buildings? I haven't seen you for some days."

"No,"—said Tobias, "I have gone into another line; instead of being a lawyer and helping to shave the clients I am going to shave the lawyers. A penny pork, if you please, Mrs. Lovett. Ah! who would go without who could get pies like these?—eh, Master Clift?"

"Well, they are good; of course we know that, Tobias. So you are going to be a barber?"

"Yes, I am with Sweeney Todd, the barber of Fleet-street, opposite St. Dunstan's."

"The deuce you are! Well, I am going to a party tonight. I must be dressed and shaved. I'll patronise your master." Tobias put his mouth close to the ear of the young lawyer and whispered the one word— "Don't." Tobias placed his fingers to his lips and left, and was about to enter his master's shop when he thought he heard from within a strange, shrieking sort of sound. On the impulse of the moment he recoiled a step or two and then, from some other impulse, he dashed forward at once, and entered the shop.

The first object that presented itself to his attention, lying upon a side table, was a hat with a handsome gold-headed walking-cane lying across it.

The arm-chair in which customers usually sat to be shaved was vacant, and Sweeney Todd's face was just projected into the shop from the back Parlour, and wearing a most singular and hideous expression.

"Well, Tobias," he said as he advanced, rubbing his great hands together, "well, Tobias! so you could not resist the pie-shop?"

"How does he know?" thought Tobias. "Yes, sir, I have been to the pie-shop, but I didn't stay a minute."

"Hark ye, Tobias! The only thing I can excuse in the way of delay upon an errand is for you to get one of Mrs. Lovett's pies; that I look over, so think no more about it. Are they not delicious, Tobias?"

"Yes, sir, they are; but some gentleman seems to have left his hat and stick."

"Yes," said Sweeney Todd, "he has;" and lifting the stick he struck Tobias a blow with it that felled him to the ground. "Lesson the second to Tobias Ragg, which teaches him to make no remarks about what does not concern him. You may think what you like, Tobias Ragg, but you shall say only what I like."

"I won't endure it," cried the boy; "I won't be knocked about in this way, I tell you, Sweeney Todd, I won't."

"You won't? Have you forgotten your mother?"

"You say you have power over my mother; but I don't know what it is, and I cannot and will not believe it; I'll leave you, and come of it what may, I'll go to sea or anywhere rather than stay in such a place as this."

"Oh, you will, will you? Then, Tobias, you and I must come to some explanation. I'll tell you what power I have over your mother, and then perhaps you will be satisfied. Last winter, when the frost had continued 18 weeks, and you and your mother were starving, she was employed to clean out the chambers of a Mr. King, in the Temple, a cold-hearted, severe man who never forgave anything in all his life, and never will."

"I remember," said Tobias; "We were starving, and owed a whole guinea for rent; but mother borrowed it and paid it, and after that got a situation where she now is."

"Ah, you think so. The rent was paid; but, Tobias, my boy, a word in your ear—she took a silver candlestick from Mr. King's chambers to pay it. I know it. I can prove it. Think of that, Tobias, and be discreet."

"Have mercy upon us," said the boy; "they would take her life!"

"Her life!" screamed Sweeney Todd; "aye, to be sure they would; they would hang her—hang her, I say; and now mind, if you force me by any conduct of your own to mention this thing, you are your mother's executioner. I had better go and be deputy hangman at once, and turn her off."

"Horrible, horrible!"

"Oh, you don't like that? Indeed, that don't suit, you. Be discreet then, and you have nothing to fear. Do not force me to do that which will be as complete as it is terrific."

"I will say nothing—I will think nothing."

"'Tis well! Now go and put that hat and stick in yonder cupboard. I shall be absent for a short time; and if anyone comes, tell them I am out and shall not return for an hour or perhaps longer, and mind you take care of the shop."

CHAPTER 2

At the same hour that the above scene I was taking place, a tall, gentlemanly-looking man, accompanied by an immense Newfoundland dog, might be seen wending his way down Fleet-street. Suddenly he stopped in front of a barber's shop, and after a word or two to his dog, which quietly seated itself outside, he entered. Now Lieutenant Thornhill, for such was the gentleman's name, was a brave man; but, brave as he was, a slight feeling of uneasiness crept over him as he gazed upon the face of Sweeney Todd, the barber, who, with upraised hand, appeared in the act of striking a boy who was crouched in the corner. The ferocious look of Sweeney Todd at that moment was indeed appalling, but it was instantly changed into a smile on perceiving the stranger.

"Shaved, sir. Yes, sir. Excuse me, sir. I was endeavouring to impress upon this boy how much better it would be for his future welfare if he were to take pattern by me, and devote his few spare hours in reading the Bible. Take a seat, sir?"

Thornhill seated himself in a large armchair, Todd stropping his razor, and darting his serpent like orbs on his customer.

"One minute, sir;" said Todd, with a bland smile. "You appear to be somewhat bronzed. From abroad sir?"

"Yes. I have just arrived from India. By-the-bye, can you inform me where a person named Oakley, a spectacle maker, resides? it is somewhere in this neighbourhood. I have a small packet which has been entrusted to me to deliver to one of the family."

Todd's eyes sparkled.

"Sir, you could not have asked a better person than myself. I do know where Oakley lives; it is in Fore-street, a little shop with two windows." Then turning to the boy, he said:

"Dear me, Tobias, I really had forgotten you. Here, dear boy, take two-pence, go to Mrs. Lovett's and buy two of those nice pies for yourself. Don't hurry. Say half-an-hour." The boy timidly withdrew.

Thornhill mildly reminded Sweeney Todd that he wished to be shaved.

"Certainly, sir. Polish you off in no time. But, as your beard is so strong, I'll just step into the next room for another razor."

He did so. A slight, creaking sound was heard—

The chair was vacant.

Thornhill had disappeared.

Then followed a loud barking and scratching at the door. Todd, with ghastly face, peered over the shop-blind, and, perceiving the dog, seized a stout cudgel, with the intention of inflicting summary vengeance; and opening the door for that purpose he was instantly capsized by the noble animal, who bounded into the shop.

The dog, after sniffing in every hole and corner, set up a dismal howl. Todd, who had in the meantime fastened himself in his room, staggered back in terror as he saw the dog seize Thornhill's hat and rush out with it into the street.

CHAPTER 3

The earliest dawn of morning was glistening on the masts, the cordage, and sails of a fleet of vessels lying below Sheerness.

Over the taffrail of one, in particular, a large-sized merchantman, which had been trading in the Indian seas, two men were leaning. One of them was the captain of the vessel, and the other a passenger, Colonel Jeffery, who intended leaving that morning. They were engaged in earnest conversation, and the captain, as he shaded his eyes with his hand, and looked along the surface of the river, said, in reply to some observation of his companion:

"I'll order my boat the moment Lieutenant Thornhill comes on board. I call him lieutenant, although I have no right to do so, because he has held that rank in the king's service, but when young, was cashiered for fighting a duel with his superior officer."

"The service has lost a good officer," said the other.

"It has, indeed. I wonder what keeps him. He went last night, and said he would pull up to the Temple stairs, because he wanted to call on somebody by the waterside; and after that he was going to the City to transact some business of his own, and that would have brought him nearer here, you see."

"He's coming," said the other.

"What makes you think that?"

"Because I see his dog. There, don't you see, swimming in the water towards the ship."

"I cannot imagine—I can see the dog, certainly—but I can't see Thornhill; nor is there any boat at hand. I know not what to make of it. Do you know, my mind misgives me that something has happened amiss. The dog seems exhausted."

Then addressing the crew, he shouted:

"Lend a hand there to Mr. Thornhill's dog, some of you." And in a suppressed voice he said to his companion:

"Why, it's a hat he has in his mouth!"

The dog made towards the vessel; and as with the assistance of the seamen he reached the deck, he sank down upon it in a state of exhaustion, with the hat still in his grasp.

As the animal lay, panting, upon the deck, the sailors looked at each other in amazement, and there was but one opinion among them all now, and that was that something very serious had unquestionably happened to Mr. Thornhill.

"I dread," said the captain, "an explanation of this occurrence. What on earth can it mean? That's Thornhill's hat, and here is Hector. Give the dog some meat and drink directly—he seems thoroughly exhausted."

The dog ate sparingly of some food that was put before him; and then, seizing the hat again in his mouth, he stood by the side of the ship and howled piteously; then he put down the hat for a moment, and, walking, up to the captain, he pulled him by the skirt of his coat.

"You, understand him," said the captain to the passenger; "something has happened to Thornhill, I'll be bound; and you see the object of the dog is to get me to follow him to see what it's about."

"Think you so? It is a warning, if it be such at all, that I should not be inclined to neglect; and if you will follow the dog, I will so accompany you; there may be more in it than we think of, when we look how anxious the poor beast is."

The captain ordered a boat to be launched at once, and manned by four stout rowers, to proceed up the river towards the Temple stairs, where Hector's master had expressed his intention of proceeding, and when the faithful animal saw the direction in which they were going, he lay down in the bottom of the boat perfectly satisfied, and gave himself up to that repose of which he was evidently so much in need.

The tide was running up, and that Thornhill had not saved the turn of it by dropping down earlier to the vessel was one of the things that surprised the captain. However, they soon reached the Temple.

The dog, who until then had seemed to be asleep, suddenly sprang up, and, seizing the hat again in his mouth, rushed on shore, and was closely followed by the captain and colonel.

The dog led them through the Temple with great rapidity, pursuing with admirable sagacity the precise path that his master had taken towards the entrance to the Temple in Fleet-street, opposite Chancery-lane. Darting across the road then, he stopped with a low growl at the shop of Sweeney Todd, a proceeding which very much surprised those who followed him, and caused them to pause to hold a consultation ere they proceeded further. While this was proceeding, Todd suddenly opened the door, and aimed a blow at the dog with an iron bar, but the latter dexterously avoided it, and, but that the door was suddenly closed again, he would have made Sweeney Todd regret such an interference.

"We must inquire into this," said the captain; "there seems to be mutual ill-will between that man and the dog."

They both tried to enter the barber's shop, but it was fast on the inside; and, after repeated knockings, Todd called from within, saying,—

"I won't open the door while that dog is there. He is mad, or has a spite against me—I don't know nor care which; it's a fact, that's all I am aware of."

"I will undertake," said the captain, "that the dog shall do you no harm; but open the door, for in we must come, and will!"

"I will take your promise," said Sweeney Todd; "but mind you keep it, or I shall protect myself, and take the creature's life; so if you value it you had better hold it fast."

The captain pacified Hector as well as he could, and likewise tied one end of a silk handkerchief round his neck, and held the other firmly in his grasp, after which Todd, who seemed to have had some means from within of seeing what was going on, opened the door, and admitted his visitors.

"Well, gentlemen, shaved, or cut, or dressed, I am at your service; which shall I begin with?"

The dog never took his eyes off Todd, but kept up a low growl from the first moment of his entrance.

"It's rather a remarkable circumstance," said the captain, "but this is a very sagacious dog, you see, and he belongs to a friend of ours, who most unaccountably disappeared."

"Has he really?" said Todd, "Tobias! Tobias!"

"Yes, Sir."

"Run to Mr. Phillips's, in Cateaton-street, and get me six-penny-worth of figs, and don't say that I don't give you the money this time when you go a message. I think I did before, but you swallowed it; and when you come back just please to remember the insight into business I gave you yesterday."

"Yes," said the boy, with a shudder, for he had a great horror of Sweeney Todd, as well he might, after the severe discipline he had received at his hands, and away he went.

"Well, gentlemen," said Todd, "what is it you require of me?"

"We want to know if anyone having the appearance of an officer in the navy came to your house?"

"Yes—a rather good-looking man, weather-beaten, with a bright blue eye, and rather fair hair."

"Yes, Yes! the same."

"Oh! to be sure he came here, and I shaved him and polished him off."

"What do you mean by polishing him off?"

"Brushing him up a bit, and making him tidy; he said he had got somewhere to go in the city, and asked me the address of a Mr. Oakley, a spectacle-maker. I gave it him, and then he went away."

"Did this dog come with him?"

"A dog came with him, but whether it was that dog or not I don't know."

"And that's all you know of him?"

"You never spoke a truer word in your life," said Sweeney Todd, as he gently stropped a razor upon his great horny hand.

This seemed something like a complete fix; and the captain looked at Colonel Jeffery, and the colonel at the captain for some moments, in complete silence.

The dog had watched the countenances of all parties during the brief dialogue, and twice or thrice he had interrupted it by a strange howling cry.

"I'll tell you what it is," said the barber; "if that beast stays here, I'll be the death of him. I hate dogs—detest them; and I tell you, as I told you before, if you value him at all, keep him away from me."

"You say you directed the person you describe to us where to find a spectacle-maker named Oakley. We happen to know that he was going in search of such a person, and as he had property of value about him, we will go there and ascertain if he reached his destination."

"It is in Fore-street—you cannot miss it."

The dog, when he saw they were about to leave, grew furious; and it was with the greatest difficulty they succeeded, by main force, in getting him out of the shop, but he contrived to get free of them, and darting back he sat down at Sweeney Todd's door, howling most piteously.

They had no resource but to leave him, intending fully to call as they came back from Mr. Oakley's; and, as they looked behind them, they saw that Hector was collecting a crowd round the barber's door. They walked on until they reached the spectacle-maker's. There they paused; for they all of a sudden recollected that the mission that Mr. Thornhill had to execute there was of a very delicate nature, and one by no means to be lightly executed, or even so much as mentioned, probably, in the hearing of Mrs. Oakley.

"We must not be so hasty," said the colonel.

"But what am I to do? I sail tonight; at least I have to go round to Liverpool with my vessel."

"Do not then call at Mr. Oakley's at all at present; but leave me to ascertain the fact quietly and secretly."

"My anxiety for Thornhill will scarcely permit me to do so; but I suppose I must."

"You may depend upon me. But that I know he set his heart upon performing the message he had to deliver, I should recommend that we at once get into this home of Mr. Oakley's, only that the fear of compromising the young lady—who is in the case, and who will have quite enough to bear, poor thing, of her own grief—restrains me."

After some more conversation of a similar nature, they decided that this should be the plan adopted.

Retracing their steps they found that Hector would not move an inch from the barber's door. There he sat with the hat by his side—exhibiting occasionally a formidable row of teeth when anybody showed a disposition to touch it; but who shall describe the anger of Sweeney Todd, when he found that he was likely to be so beleaguered?

He doubted, if, upon the arrival of the first customer to his shop, the dog might dart in and take him by storm; but that apprehension went off at last, when a young gallant came from the Temple to have his hair dressed, and the dog allowed him to pass in and out unmolested, without making any attempt to follow him. This was something, at all events; but whether or not it insured Sweeney Todd's personal safety, when he himself should come out, was quite another matter.

It was, an experiment, however; which he must try. So, after a time, he thought he might try the experiment, and that it would be best done when there were plenty of people there, because if the dog assaulted him, he would have an excuse for any amount of violence he might think proper to use upon the occasion.

It took some time, however, to screw his courage to the sticking place; but at length, muttering deep curses between his clenched teeth, he made his way to the door, and carried in his hand a long knife, which he thought a more efficient weapon against the dog's teeth than the iron bludgeon he had formerly used.

"I hope he will attack me," said Todd, to himself, as he thought; but Tobias who had come back from the place where they sold the preserved figs, heard him, and after devoutly in his own mind wishing that the dog would actually devour Sweeney, said aloud—

"Oh dear, sir,—you, don't wish that, I'm sure!"

"Who told you what I wished, or what I did not? Remember, Tobias, and keep your own counsel, or it will be the worse for you, and your mother too—remember that."

The boy shrank back. How bad Sweeney Todd terrified the boy about his mother! He must have done so, or Tobias would never have shrunk as he did.

Then the barber went cautiously out of his shop door. We cannot pretend to account for why it was so, but, as faithful recorders of facts, we have to state that Hector did not fly at him, but with a melancholy and subdued expression of countenance he looked up in the face of Sweeney Todd; then he whined piteously, as if he would have said, "Give me my master, and I will forgive you all that you have done; give me back my beloved master, and you shall see that I am neither revengeful nor ferocious."

This kind of expression was as legibly written in the poor creature's countenance as if he had uttered the words.

This was what Sweeney Todd certainly did not expect. He would have been glad of any excuse to commit some act of violence, but he had now none, and as he looked in the faces of the people who were around, he felt quite convinced that it would not be the most prudent thing in the world to interfere with the dog in any way that savoured of violence.

"Where's the dog's master?" said one.

"Ah, where indeed?" said Todd; "I should not wonder if he had come to a foul end!"

"But I say, old soapsuds," cried a boy, "the dog says you did it."

There was a general laugh, but the barber was by no means disconcerted; he shortly replied:

"Does he? He is wrong then."

Sweeney Todd had no desire to enter into anything like a controversy with people, so he turned again and entered his own shop, in a distant corner of which he sat down, and folding his great gaunt-looking arms over his chest, he riveted his eyes on the door, and if we may judge from the expression of his countenance his thoughts were not of a pleasant anticipatory character, for now and then he gave a grin as may well have sat on the features of a demon.

CHAPTER 4

Seated in a neat little parlour at the back of the spectacle-maker's shop were Mr. Oakley and his beautiful daughter Johanna; they had evidently been conversing on a very painful subject.

"Dear father," said the girl, "your kind words were well meant, and if I have any consolation it is the knowledge that in revealing to you the state of my feelings, you do not blame me. A vessel has arrived from India, and tortured by my hopes and fears, this day has been one of the most wretched that I have ever passed. Not even two years ago, when I parted with Mark Ingestrie, did I feel such a pang of anguish as now fills my heart, when I see the day gliding away and the I evening creeping on apace without word or token from him."

Her father tried to console her, but she wept such bitter tears as only such a heart as hers can know, when it feels the deep and bitter anguish of desertion.

At this moment her mother entered.

"Really, Johanna," said Mrs. Oakley, in the true, conventicle twang, "you look so pale and ill that I must positively speak to Mr. Lupin about you."

"Mr. Lupin, my dear," said the spectacle-maker, "may be all very well in his way as a parson; but I don't see what he can have to do with Johanna looking pale."

"A pious man, Mr. Oakley, has to do with everything and everybody."

"Then he must be the most intolerable bore in existence; and I don't wonder at his being kicked out of some people's houses, as I have heard Mr. Lupin has been."

"And if he has, Mr. Oakley, I can tell you he glories in it. Mr. Lupin likes to suffer for the faith; and if he were to be made a martyr of tomorrow, I am quite certain it would give him a deal of pleasure."

"My dear, I am quite sure it would not give him half the pleasure it would me."

"I understand your insinuation, Mr. Oakley: you would like to have him murdered on account of his holiness; but, though you can say these kind of things at your own breakfast-table you won't say as much to him when he comes to tea this afternoon."

"To tea, Mrs. Oakley! Haven't I told you time after time I will not have that man in my house?"

"And haven't I told you, Mr. Oakley, twice that number of times that he shall come to tea, and I have asked him now, and it can't be altered?"

"But, Mrs. Oakley—."

We here leave the happy couple to settle their differences, while Johanna retired up stairs to her own room, which commanded a view of the street. It was an old-fashioned house with a balcony in front, and as she looked listlessly out into Fore-street, which was far then from being the thoroughfare it is now, she saw standing in a doorway on the opposite side of the way a stranger, who was looking intently at the house, and who, when he caught her eye, walked instantly across to it, and cast something into the balcony of the first floor. Then he touched his cap and walked rapidly from the street.

The thought immediately occurred to Johanna that this might possibly be some messenger from him concerning whose existence and welfare she was so deeply anxious. It was not to be wondered at, therefore, that with the name of Mark Ingestrie upon her lips she should rush down to the balcony in intense anxiety to hear and see it such were really the case.

When she reached the balcony she found lying in it a scrap of paper, in which a stone was wrapped up, in order to give it weight, so that it might be cast with a certainty into the balcony. With trembling eagerness she opened the paper, and read upon it the following words:—

"For news of Mark Ingestrie, come to the Temple-gardens one hour before sunset, and do not fear addressing a man who will be holding a white rose in his hand."

"He lives! he lives!" she cried. "He lives, and joy again becomes the inhabitant of my bosom! Oh, it is daylight now and sunshine compared to the black midnight of despair Mark Ingestrie lives, and I shall be happy yet."

And so she tried to while away the anxious hours, sometimes succeeding in forgetting how long it was still to sunset, and at others feeling as if each minute was perversely swelling itself out into ten times its usual proportion of time in order to become wearisome to her.

She had said that she would be in the Temple-gardens two hours before sunset instead of one, and she kept her word. Looking happier than she had done for weeks, she tripped down the stairs of her father's house, and left by the private staircase without attracting any attention.

As he walked upon that side of the way of Feet-street where Sweeney Todd's house and shop were situated, a feeling of curiosity prompted her to stop for a moment and look at the melancholy looking dog that stood watching a hat at his door.

The appearance of grief upon the creature's face could not be mistaken, and, as she gazed, she saw the shop-door gently opened and a piece of meat thrown out.

"These are kind people," she said, "be they whom they may;" but when she saw the dog turn away with loathing, and herself observed that there was a white powder upon it, the idea that it was poisoned, and only intended for the poor creature's destruction, came instantly across her mind.

And when she saw the horrible-looking face of Sweeney Todd glaring at her from the partially-opened door, she could not doubt any further the fact, for that face was quite enough to give a warrant for any amount of villainy whatever.

She passed on with a shudder, little suspecting, however, that that dog had anything to do with her fate, or the circumstances which made up the sum of her destiny.

It wanted a full hour to the appointed time of meeting when she reached the Temple-gardens, and partly blaming herself that she was so soon, while at the same time she would not for worlds have been away, she sat down on one of the garden seats to think over the past.

Chapter 5

The clock struck the hour of meeting, and Johanna looked anxiously for anyone who should seem to her to bear the appearance of being a man such as she might suppose Mark Ingestrie would choose for his friend.

She turned her eyes towards the gate, for she thought she heard it close, and saw a gentlemanly-looking man, attired in a cloak, and who was looking about, apparently in search of someone.

His eye fell upon her, and he immediately produced from beneath his cloak a flower, and in another minute they met.

"I have the honour," he said, "of speaking to Miss Johanna Oakley?"

"Yes, and you are Mark Ingestrie's messenger?"

"I am proud to say I am he who comes to bring you news of Mark Ingestrie, but sorry to say I am not the messenger that was expressly deputed by him."

"Your looks are sad and serious; you seem as if you would announce that some misfortune had occurred. Tell me that it is not so; speak to me at once or my heart will break!"

"Calm yourself, lady, I pray you."

"I cannot—dare not do so, unless you tell me he lives. Tell me that Mark Ingestrie lives, and then I shall be all patience: tell me that, and you shall not hear a murmur from me. Speak the word at once—at once! It is cruel, believe me, it is cruel to keep me in this suspense."

"This is one of the saddest errands I ever came upon," said the stranger, as he led Johanna to a seat. "Recollect, lady, what creatures of accident and chance we are."

"No more—no more!" shrieked Johanna as she clasped her hands—"I know all now, and am desolate."

She let her face drop upon her hands, and shook as with a convulsion of grief.

"Mark, Mark!" she cried, "you have gone from me! I thought not this—I thought not this! Oh, Heaven! why have I lived so long as to have the capacity to listen to such fearful tidings? Lost—lost—all lost! God of Heaven! what a wilderness the world is now to me!"

"Let me pray you, lady, to subdue this passion of grief, and listen truly to what I shall unfold to you. There is much to hear and much to speculate upon; and if, from all that I have learnt, I cannot, dare not tell you that Mark Ingestrie lives, I likewise shrink from telling you he is no more."

"Speak again—say those words again! There is a hope, then—oh, there is a hope!"

"There is a hope; and better is it that your mind should receive the first shock of the probability of the death of him whom you have so anxiously expected, and then afterwards, from what I shall relate to you, gather hope that it may not be so, than that from the first you should expect too much, and then have those expectations rudely destroyed."

They both sat upon the garden seat; and while Johanna fixed her eyes upon her companion's face, expressive as it was of the most generous emotions and noble feelings, he commenced relating to her the incidents which never left her memory, and in which she took so deep an interest.

"You must know," he said, "that what it was which so much inflamed the imagination of Mark Ingestrie consisted in this. There came to London a man with a well-authenticated and extremely well put together report, that there had been discovered, in one of the small islands near the Indian seas, a river which deposited an enormous quantity of gold-dust in its progress to the ocean. He told his story so well, and seemed to be such a perfect master of all the circumstances connected with it, that there was scarcely room for a doubt upon the subject. The thing was kept quiet and secret; and a meeting was held of some influential men—influential on account of the money they possessed, among whom was one who had towards Mark Ingestrie most friendly feelings; so Mark attended the meeting with this friend of his, although he felt his utter incapacity, from want of resources, to take any part in the affair.

"But he was not aware of what his friend's generous intentions were in the matter until they were explained to him, and they consisted in this:—He, the friend, was to provide the necessary means for embarking in the adventure, so far as regarded taking a share in it, and he told Mark Ingestrie that, if he would go personally on the expedition, he should share in the proceeds with him, be they what they might. Now, to a young man like Ingestrie, totally destitute of personal resources, but of ardent and enthusiastic temperament, you can imagine how extremely, tempting such an offer was likely to be. He embraced it at once with the greatest pleasure.

"It is from the lips of another, instead of from mine, that you ought to have heard what I am now relating. That gentleman, whose name was Thornhill, ought to have made to you this communication; but by some strange accident it seems he has been prevented, or you would not be here listening to me upon a subject which would have come better from his lips."

"They sailed in an ill-fated ship—but I must not anticipate; let me proceed in my narrative with regularity. The ship was called *the Star*, and if those who went with it looked upon it as the star of their destiny, they were correct enough, and it might be considered an evil star for them, inasmuch as nothing but disappointment and bitterness became their ultimate portion. And Mark Ingestrie, I am told, was the most hopeful man on board. Already, in imagination, he could fancy himself homeward-bound with the vessel, ballasted and crammed with the rich produce of that shining river. Already he fancied what he could do with his abundant wealth, and I have not a doubt but that, in common with many who went on that adventure, he enjoyed to the full the spending of the wealth he should obtain in imagination—perhaps, indeed, more than if he had obtained it in reality.

"Among the adventurers was one Thornhill who had been a lieutenant in the Royal Navy, and between him and young Ingestrie there arose a remarkable friendship—a friend-ship so strong and powerful that there can be no doubt that they communicated to each other all their hopes and fears; and if anything could materially tend to beguile the tedium of such a weary voyage as those adventurers had undertaken, it certainly would be the free communication and confidential intercourse between two such kindred spirits as Thornhill and Mark Ingestrie. You will bear in mind, Miss Oakley, that in making this communication to you, I am putting together what I myself heard at different times, so as to make it for you a distinct narrative, which you can have no difficulty in comprehending, because, as I before stated, I never saw Mark Ingestrie, and it was only once, for about five minutes, that I saw the vessel in which he went upon his perilous adventure—for perilous it turned out to be—to the Indian seas.

"It was from Thornhill I got my information during the many weary and monotonous hours consumed in a home-bound voyage from India. It appears that without accident or cross of any description *the Star* reached the Indian Ocean, and the supposed immediate locality of the spot where the treasure was to be found, and there, she was spoken with by a vessel homeward-bound from India, called the *Neptune*. It was evening, and the sun had sunk in the horizon with some appearances that betokened a storm. I was on board that Indian vessel; but did not expect anything serious, although we made every preparation for rough weather, and as it turned out, it was well indeed we did, for never within the memory of the oldest seamen had such a storm ravished the coast.

"A furious gale, which it was impossible to withstand, drove us southward; but by the utmost precautions, we escaped with trifling damage, but we were driven at least 200 miles out of our course; and instead of getting, as we ought to have done, to the Cape by a certain time, we were an immense distance eastward of it. It was just as the storm, which lasted three nights and two days, began to abate, that towards the horizon we saw a dull red light; and as it was not in a quarter of the sky where any such appearance might be imagined, nor were we in a latitude where electro-phenomena might be expected, we steered toward it, surmising what turned out afterwards to be fully correct."

"It was a ship on fire!" said Johanna.

"It was. Alas! alas! I guessed it. A frightful suspicion from the first crossed my mind."

"But how knew you," said Johanna, as she clasped her hands, and the pallid expression of her countenance betrayed the deep interest she took in the narration, "how knew you that the ship was the *Star*? Might it not have been some other ill-fated vessel that met with so dreadful a fate?"

"I will tell you." The captain of the Indiaman kept his glass at his eye, and presently he said to me, "There is a floating piece of wreck, and something clinging to it; I know not if there be a man, but what I can perceive seems to me to be the head of a dog." I looked through the glass myself, and saw the same object; but as we neared it, we found it was a large piece of the wreck, with a dog and a man supported by it, who were clinging with all the energy of desperation.

In ten minutes more we had them on board the vessel—the man was the Lieutenant Thornhill I have before mentioned, and the dog belonged to him. He related to us that the ship we had seen burning was *the Star*, and that it had never reached its destination, and that he believed all had perished but himself and the dog; for, although one of the boats had been launched, so desperate a rush was made into it by the crew that it had swamped, and all perished. He related to the captain and myself the object of the voyage of the *Star*, and the previous particulars with which I have made you acquainted. And then, during the night watch he said to me, "I have a very sad mission to perform when I get to London. On board our vessel was a young man named Mark Ingestrie; and some short time before the vessel in which we were went down he begged of me to call upon a young lady named Johanna Oakley, the daughter of a spectacle-maker in London, providing I should be saved and he perish; and of the latter event he felt so strong a presentiment that he gave me a string of pearls, which I was to present to her in his name; but where he got them I have not the least idea, for they are of immense value.' Mr. Thornhill shewed me the pearls, which were of different sizes; roughly strung together, but of great value; and when we reached the river Thames, which was only three days since, he left us with his dog, carrying his string of pearls with him, to find out where you reside."

"Alas, he never came."

"No, from all the inquiries we can make, he disappeared somewhere about Fleet-street. We trace him from Temple stairs to a barber there named Sweeney Todd, but beyond there no information can be obtained."

"Gracious Heaven!"

"What makes the affair more extraordinary is that nothing will induce Thornhill's dog to leave the place."

"Kind sir, I thank you. I will go home, and pray for strength to maintain my heart against this sad affliction."

Johanna felt grateful for the support of the colonel's arm towards her own home, and as they passed the barber's shop they were surprised to see that the dog and the hat were gone.

CHAPTER 6

It is night, and a man, one of the most celebrated Lapidaries in London, but yet a man frugal withal although rich, is putting up the shutters of his shop.

This lapidary is an old man; his scanty hair is white, and his hands shake as he secures the fastenings, and then over and over again feels and shakes each shutter to be assured that his shop is well secured.

This shop of his is in Moorfield, then a place very much frequented by dealers in bullion and precious stones. He was about entering his door when a tall, ungainly looking man stepped up to him. This man had a three-cornered hat, much too small for him, perched upon the top of his great hideous looking head, while the coat he wore had ample skirts enough to have made another of ordinary dimensions.

Our readers will have no difficulty in recognizing Sweeney Todd, and well might the old lapidary start at such a very unprepossessing looking personage who thus addressed him.

"Do you deal in precious stones?"

"Yes, I do," was the reply, "but it's rather late. Do you want to buy some?"

"No, I sell."

"Ah, I dare say it's not in my line; if they are rubies they are not in the market."

"I have nothing but pearls to sell," said Sweeney Todd. "I mean to keep my diamonds, my garnets, topazes, brilliants, emeralds, and rubies."

"The d—l you do! Why, you don't mean to say you have any of them?"

"Come, I'm too old to joke with, and am waiting for my supper. Just look at the pearls."

"I can't, tonight."

"Well, I'll go Mr. Coventry's; he'll deal with me."

The lapidary hesitated. "Stop," he said; "what's the use of going to Mr. Coventry? He has not the means of purchasing what I can pay present cash for. Come in, come in; I will, at all events, look at what you have for sale."

Thus encouraged, Sweeney Todd entered the little, low, dusky shop, and the lapidary having procured a light, and taken care to keep his customer outside the counter, put on his spectacles, and said—

"Now, sir, where are your pearls?"

"There," said Sweeney Todd, as he laid a string of 24 pearls before the lapidary.

The old man's eyes opened to an enormous width, and he pushed his spectacles right upon his forehead as he glared in the face of. Sweeney Todd with undisguised astonishment. Then down came his spectacles again, and taking up the string of pearls he rapidly examined every one of them, after which he exclaimed,—

"Real, real, by Heaven! All real!"

Then he pushed his spectacles up again to the top of his head, and took another long stare at Sweeney Todd.

"I know they are real," said the latter. "Will you deal with me or will you not?"

"Will I deal with you? Yes; I am not quite sure they are real. Let me look again. Oh, I see, counterfeits; but so well done, that really for the curiosity of the thing, I will give £50 for them."

"I am fond of curiosities," Said Sweeney Todd, "and as they are not real, I will keep them; they will do for a present to some child or another."

"What, give those to a child! You must be mad—that is to say, not mad, but certainly indiscreet. Come, now, at a word, I'll give you £100 for them."

"Hark ye," said Sweeney Todd, "it neither suits my inclination nor my time to stand here chaffing with you. I know the value of the pearls, and, as a matter of ordinary and everyday business, I will sell them to you so that you may get a handsome profit."

"What do you call a handsome profit?"

"The pearls are worth £12,000, and I will let you have them for £10,000. What do you think of that for an offer?"

"What odd noise was that?"

"Oh, it was only I who laughed."

"Hark ye, my friend; since you do know the value of your pearls, and this is a downright business transaction, I think I can find a customer who will give £9,000 for them, and if so I have no objection to give you £8,000."

"Give me the £8,000," said Sweeney Todd.

"Stop a bit; there are some rather important things to consider. You must know, my friend, that a string of pearls of this value are not to be bought like a piece of old silver of anybody who might come with it. Such a string of pearls as these are like a house, or an estate, and when they change hands, the vendor must give every satisfaction as to how he came by them, and prove how he can give the purchaser a good right and title to them."

"Pshaw!" said Sweeney Todd, "who will question you; you are well known to be in the trade, and to be continually dealing in such things?"

"That's a very fine; but I don't see why I should give you the full value of an article without evidence as to how you came by it."

"In other words, you mean you don't care how I came by them if I sell them to you at a thief's price, but if I want their value you are particular."

"My good sir, you may conclude what you like. Shew me that you have a right to dispose of the pearls, and you need go no further than this for a customer."

"I am not disposed to take that trouble, so I shall bid you goodnight, and if you want any pearls again, I would certainly advise you not to be so wonderfully particular where you get them."

Sweeney Todd strode towards the door, but the lapidary was not going to part with him so easily, so springing over his counter with an agility one would not have expected from so old a man, he was at the door in a moment, and shouted at the top of his lungs—

"Stop thief! Stop thief! Stop him! There he goes! The big fellow with the three-cornered hat! Stop thief! Stop thief!"

These cries, uttered with great vehemence as they were, could not be totally ineffectual, but they roused the whole neighbourhood, and before Sweeney Todd had proceeded many yards a man made an attempt to collar him, but was repulsed by such a terrific blow in the face that another person, who had run half-way across the road with a similar object, turned and went back again, thinking it scarcely prudent to risk his own safety in apprehending a criminal for he good of the public. Having got rid thus of one of his foes, Sweeney Todd, with an inward, determination to come back some day and be the death of the old lapidary, looked anxiously about for some court down which he could plunge, and so get out of sight of the many pursuers who were sure to attack him in the public streets. His ignorance of the locality, however, was a great bar to such a proceeding, for the great dread he had was that he might get down some blind alley, and so be completely caged, and at the mercy of those who followed him.

He pelted on at a tremendous speed, but it was quite astonishing to see how the little old lapidary ran after him, falling down every now and then, and never stopping to pick himself up, as people say, but rolling on and getting on his feet in some miraculous manner that was quite wonderful to behold, particularly in one so aged and so apparently unable to undertake any active exertion. There was one thing, however, he could not continue doing, and that was to cry "Stop thief!" for he had lost his wind, and was quite incapable of uttering a word. How long he would have continued to chase is doubtful, but his career was suddenly put an end to, as regards that, by tripping his foot over a projecting stone in the pavement, and shooting headlong down a cellar which was open.

But abler persons than the little old lapidary had taken up the chase, and Sweeney Todd was hard pressed; and, although he ran very fast, the provoking thing was that, in consequence of the cries and shouts of his pursuers new people took up the chase, who were fresh and vigorous, and close to him. On he flew at the top of his speed, striking down whoever opposed him, until at last many who could have outrun him gave up the chase, not liking to encounter the knock-down blow which such a hand as his seemed capable of inflicting. His teeth were set, and his breathing became short and laborious.

The cry of "Stop thief!" still sounded in his ears, and on he flew, panting with the exertion he made, till he heard a man behind him say—

"Turn into the second court on your right, and you will be safe. I'll follow you. They shan't nab you, if I can help it."

Sweeney Todd had not much confidence in human nature—it was not likely he would; but, panting and exhausted as he was, the voice of any one speaking in friendly accents was welcome, and, rather impulsively than from reflection, he darted down the second court to his right.

CHAPTER 7

In a very few minutes Sweeney Todd found that this court had no thoroughfare, and therefore there was no outlet or escape, but he immediately concluded that something more was to be found than was at first sight to be seen, and casting a furtive glance beside him in the direction in which he had come, rested his hand upon a door which stood close by. The door gave way, and Sweeney Todd, hearing, as he imagined, a noise in the street, dashed in and closed the door, and then he, heedless of all consequences, walked to the end of a long dirty passage, and, pushing open a door, descended a short flight of steps, to the bottom of which he had scarcely got, when the door which faced him at the bottom of the steps opened by some hand, and he suddenly found himself in the presence of a number of men seated round a large table.

In an instant all eyes were turned towards Sweeney Todd, who was quite unprepared for such a scene, and for a minute he knew not what to say; but, as indecision was not Sweeney Todd's characteristic, he at once advanced to the table and sat down. There was some surprise evinced by the persons who were seated in that room, of whom there were many more than a score, and much talking was going on among them, which did not appear to cease on his entrance. Those who were near him looked hard at him, but nothing was said for some minutes, and Sweeney Todd looked about to understand, if he could, how he was placed, though it could not be much a matter of doubt as to the character of the individuals present.

Their looks were often an index to their vocations, for all grades of the worst of characters were there, and some of them were by no means complimentary to human nature, for there were some of the most desperate characters that were to be found in London. Sweeney Todd gave a glance around him; and at once satisfied himself of the desperate nature of the assembly into which he had thrust himself. They were dressed in various fashions, some after the manner of the city—-some more gay, and some half military, while not a few wore the garb of countrymen; but there was in all an air of scampish, off-hand behaviour, not unmixed with brutality.

"Friend," said one who sat near him, "how came you here; are you known to any of us?"

"I came here because I found the open door, and I was told by someone to enter here, as I was pursued."

"I know what being pursued is," replied the man; "and yet I know nothing of you."

"That is not at all astonishing," said Sweeney, "seeing that I never saw you before, nor you me; but that makes no difference. I'm in difficulties, and I suppose a man may do his best to escape the consequences?"

"Yes, he may; yet that is no reason why he should come here; this is the place for free friends, who know and aid one another."

"And such I am willing to be; but at the same time I must have a beginning. I cannot be initiated without someone introducing me. I have sought protection, and I have found it; if there be any objection to my remaining here any longer I will leave."

"No, no," said a tall man on the other side of the table. "I have heard what you have said, and we do not usually allow any such things; you have come here unasked, and now we must have a little explanation—our own safety may demand it; at all events we have our customs, and they must be complied with."

"And what are your customs?" demanded Todd.

"This: you must answer the questions which we shall propound unto you; now, answer truly what we shall ask of you."

"Speak," said Todd, "and I will answer all that you propose to me, if possible."

"We will not tax you, too, hardly, depend upon it: who are you?"

"Candidly, then," said Todd, "that's a question I do not like to answer, nor do I think it is one that you ought to ask. It is an inconvenient thing to name one's self—you must pass by that inquiry."

"Shall we do so?" inquired the interrogator of those around him, and gathering his due from their looks, he, after a brief space, continued—

"Well, we will pass over that, seeing it is not necessary, but you must tell us what you are—cutpurse, footpad, or what not?"

"I am neither."

"Then tell us in your own words," said the man, "and be candid with us. What are you?"

"I am an artificial pearl-maker—or sham pearl-maker, whichever way you—please to call it."

"A sham pearl-maker! That may be an honest trade for all we know, and that will hardly be your passport to our house, friend sham pearl-maker!"

"That may be as you say," replied Todd, "but I will challenge any man to equal me in my calling. I have made pearls that would pass with almost a lapidary, and which would pass with nearly all the nobility."

"I begin to understand you, friend; but I would wish to have some proof of what you say; we may hear a very, good tale and yet none of it shall be true. We are not men to be made dupes of; besides, there are enough to take vengeance, if we desire it."

"Ay, to be sure there is," said a gruff voice from the other end of the table, which was echoed from one to the other till it came to the top of the table.

"Proof! proof! proof!" now resounded from one end of the room to the other.

"My friends," said Sweeney Todd, rising up and advancing to the table, thrusting his hand into his bosom drawing out the string of 24 pearls, "I challenge you, or anyone, to make a set of artificial pearls equal to these; they are my make, and I'll stand to it in any reasonable sum, that you cannot bring a man who shall beat me in my calling."

"Just hand them to me," said the man.

Sweeney Todd threw the pearls on the table carelessly, and then said—

"There, look at them well, they'll bear it, and I reckon, though there are some good judges amongst you, that you cannot, any of you, tell them from real pearls, if you had not been told so."

"Oh, yes, we know pretty well," said the man, "what these things are; we have now and then a good string in our possession, and that helps us to judge of them. Well, this is certainly a good imitation."

"Let me see it," said a fat man; "I was bred a jeweller, and I might say born, only I couldn't stick to it; nobody likes working for years upon little pay, and no fun with the gals I say, hand it here!"

"Well," said Todd, "if you or anybody ever produced as good an imitation, I'll swallow the whole string; and knowing there's poison in the composition, it would not be a comfortable thing to think of."

"Certainly not," said the big man, "certainly not, but hand them over, and I'll tell you all about it."

The pearls were given into his hands; and Sweeney Todd felt some misgivings about his precious charge, and yet he shewed it not for he turned to the man who sat beside him, saying—

"If he can tell true pearls from them, he knows more than I think he does, for I am a maker, and have often had the true pearl in my hand."

"And I suppose," said the man, "you have tried your hand at putting the one for the ostler, and so doing your confiding customers."

"Yes, yes, that is the dodge, I can see very well," said another man, winking at the first; "and a good one too. I have known them do so with diamonds."

"Yes, but never with pearls; however, there are some trades that it in desirable to know."

"You're right."

The fat man now carefully examined the pearls, set them down on the table, and looked hard at them.

"There now, I told you I could bother you. You are not so good a judge that you would not have known, if you had not been told they were sham pearls, but what they were real."

"I must say you have produced the best imitations I have ever seen. Why, you ought to make your fortune in a few years—a handsome fortune!"

"So I should, but for one thing."

"And what is that?"

"The difficulty," said Todd, "of getting rid of them; if you ask anything below their value, you are suspected, and you run the chance of being stopped and losing them at the least, and perhaps entail a prosecution."

"Very true; but there is risk in everything; we all run risks, but then the harvest!"

"That may be," said Todd, "but this is peculiarly dangerous. I have not the means of getting introduction to the nobility themselves, and if had I should be doubted, for they would say a working man cannot come honestly by such valuable things, and then I must concoct a tale to escape the Mayor of London."

"Ha!-ha!-ha!"

"Well, then, you can take them to a goldsmith."

"There are not many of them who would do so; they would not deal in them; and, moreover, I have been to one or two of them; as for a lapidary, why, he is not so easily cheated."

"Have you tried?"

"I did, and had to make the best of my way out, pursued as quickly as they could run, and I thought at one time I must have been stopped, but a few lucky turns brought me clear, when I was told to turn up this court; and I came in here."

"It has been a close chance for you," said one.

"Yes, it just has," replied Sweeney, taking up the string of pearls, which he replaced in his clothes, and continued to converse with some of those around him.

Things now subsided into their general course, and little notice was taken of Sweeney. There was some drink on the board, of which all partook. Sweeney had some, too, and took the precaution of emptying his pockets before them all and gave a share of his money to pay his footing. This was policy, and they all drank to his success, and were very good companions. Sweeney, however, was desirous of getting out as soon as he could, and more than once cast his eyes towards the door; but he saw there were eyes upon him, and dared not excite suspicion, for he might undo all that he had done.

To lose the precious treasure he possessed would be maddening; he had succeeded to admiration in inducing the belief that what he shewed them was merely a counterfeit; but he knew so well that they were real, and that a latent feeling that they were humbugged might be hanging about; and that at the first suspicious movement he would be watched, and some, desperate attempt made to make him give them up. It was with no small violence to his own feelings that he listened to their conversation, and appeared to take an interest in their proceedings.

"Well," said one who sat next to him, "I'm just off for the north road."

"Any fortune there?"

"Not much; and yet I mustn't complain; these last three weeks, the best I have had has been two sixties."

"Well, that would do very well."

"Yes. The last man I stopped was a regular looby Londoner; he appeared like a don, complete tip-top man of fashion; but, Lord! when I came to look over him, he hadn't as much as would carry me 24 miles on the road."

Conversation now went on, each man speaking of his exploits, which were always some species of rascality and robbery, accompanied by violence generally; some were midnight robbers and breakers into people's houses; in fact, all the crimes that could be imagined. This place was, in fact, a complete house of rendezvous for thieves, cutpurses, highwaymen, footpads, and burglars of every grade and description-a formidable set of men of the most determined and desperate appearance. Sweeney Todd hardly knew how to rise and leave the place, though it was now growing very late and he was most anxious to get safe out of the den he was in; but how to do that was a problem yet to be solved.

"What is the time?" he muttered to the man next to him.

"Past midnight," was the reply.

"Then I must leave here," he answered, "for I have work that I must be at in a very short time, and I shall not have too much time."

So saying he watched his opportunity, and rising, walked up to the door, which he opened and went out; after that he walked up to the five steps that led to the passage, and this latter had hardly been gained when the street-door opened, and another man came in at the same moment and met him face to face.

"What do you do here?"

"I am going out," said Sweeney Todd.

"You are going back; come back with me."

"I will not," said Todd. "You must be a better man than I am, if you make me; I'll do my best to resist your attack, if you intend one."

"That I do," replied the man, and he made a determined rush upon Sweeney, who was scarcely prepared for such a sudden onslaught, and was pushed back till he came to the head of the stairs, where a struggle took place, and both rolled down the steps. The door was thrown open, and everyone rushed out to see what was the matter, but it was some moments before they could make it out.

"What does he do here?" said the first, as soon as he could speak, and pointing to Sweeney Todd.

"It's all right."

"All wrong, I say."

"He's a sham pearl maker, and has shown us a string of sham pearls that are beautiful."

"I will insist upon seeing them; give them to me," he said, "or you do not leave this place."

"I will not," said Sweeney.

"You must. Here, help me—but I don't want help, I can do it by myself."

As he spoke, he made a desperate attempt to collar Sweeney and pull him to the earth, but he had miscalculated his strength when he imagined that he was superior to Todd, who was by far the more powerful man of the two, and resisted the attack with success. Suddenly, by a Herculean effort, he caught his adversary below the waist, and lifting him up, he threw him upon the floor with great force; and then, not wishing to see how the gang would take this—whether they would take the part of their companion or of himself he knew not-he thought he had an advantage in the distance, and he rushed up stairs as fast as he could, and reached the door before they could overtake him to prevent him. Indeed, for more than a minute they were ir-resolute what to do; but they were somehow prejudiced in favour of their companion, and they rushed up after Sweeney just as he had got to the door.

He would have had time to escape them, but, by some means, the door became fast, and he could not open it, exert himself how he would. There was no time to lose; they were coming to the head of the stairs, and Sweeney had hardly time to reach the stairs, to fly upwards, when he felt himself grasped by the throat. This he soon released himself from; for he struck the man who seized him a heavy blow, and he fell backwards, and Todd found his way up to the first floor, but he was closely pursued. Here was another struggle; and again Sweeney Todd was the victor, but he was hard pressed by those who followed him. Fortunately for him there was a mop left in a pail of wa-ter; this he seized hold of, and, swinging it over his head, he brought it full on the head of the first man who came near him.

Down it came, soft and wet, and splashed over some others who were close at hand. It is astonishing what an effect a new weapon will sometimes have. There was not a man among them who would not have faced danger in more ways than one, that would not have rushed headlong upon deadly and destructive weapons, but who were quite awed when a heavy wet mop was dashed into their faces. They were completely paralysed for a moment; indeed, they began to look upon it as something between a joke and a serious matter, and either would have been taken just as they might be termed.

"Get the pearls!" shouted the man who had first stopped him; "seize the spy! Seize him—secure him—rush at him! You are men enough to hold one man!"

Sweeney Todd saw matters were growing serious, and he plied his mop most vigorously upon those who were ascending, but they had become somewhat used to the mop, and it had lost much of its novelty, and was by no means a dangerous weapon. They rushed on, despite the heavy blows showered by Sweeney, and he was compelled to give way stair after stair. The head of the mop came off, and then there remained but the handle, which formed an efficient weapon, and which made fearful havoc on the heads of the assailants; and despite all that their slouched hats could do in the way of protecting them, yet the staff came with a crushing effect. The best fight in the world cannot last forever, and Sweeney again found numbers were not to be resisted for long; indeed, he could not have physical energy enough to sustain his own efforts, supposing he had received no blows in return. He turned and fled as he was forced back to the landing, and then came to the next stair-head, and again he made a desperate stand. This went on for stair after stair, and continued for more than two or three hours. There were moments of cessation when they all stood still and looked at each other.

"Fire upon him!" said one.

"No, no; we shall have the authorities down upon us, and then all will go wrong."

"Well, then, rush upon him and down with him! Never let him out. On to him. Hurrah!"

Away they went, but they were resolutely met by the staff of Sweeney Todd, who had gained new strength by the short rest he had had.

"Down with the spy!"

But as each of them approached he was struck down, and at length finding himself on the second floor landing, and that someone was descending from above he rushed into one of the rooms and in an instant he had locked the door, which was strong.

"Now," he muttered, "for means to escape."

He waited a moment to wipe the sweat from his brow, and then he crossed the floor to the windows, which were open. They were the old-fashioned bay-windows, with the heavy ornamental work which some houses possessed, and overhung the low doorways, and protected them from the weather.

"This will do," he said, as he looked down to the pavement; "this will do. I will try this descent, if I fall."

By means of the sound oaken ornaments, he contrived to get down to the drawing-room balcony, and then he soon got down into the street. As he walked slowly away, he could hear the crash of the door, and a slight cheer, as they entered the room; and he could imagine to himself, the appearance of the faces of those who entered, when they found the bird had flown, and the room was empty. Sweeney Todd had not far to go; he soon turned into Fleet-street, and made for his own house. He looked about him, but there were none near him; he was tired and exhausted, and right glad was he when he found himself at his own door. Then stealthily he put the key into the door and slowly entered the house.

CHAPTER 8

Johanna Oakley would not allow Colonel Jefferey to accompany her all the way home, and he, appreciating the scruples of the young girl, did not press his attention upon her, but left her at the corner of Fore-street, after getting from her a half promise that she would meet him again on that day week, at the same hour, in the Temple-gardens.

"I ask this of you, Johanna Oakley," he said, "because I have resolved to make all the exertion in my power to discover what has become of Mr. Thornhill, in whose fate I am sure I have succeeded in interesting you, although you care so little for the string of pearls which he has in trust for you."

"I do, indeed, care little for them," said Johanna, "so little that it may be said to amount to nothing."

"But still, they an yours, and you ought to have the option of disposing of them as you please. It is not well to despise such gifts of fortune; for if you can yourself do nothing with them, there are surely some others whom you may know upon whom they would bestow great happiness."

"A—string of pearls? great happiness?" said Johanna inquiringly.

"Your mind is so occupied by your grief that, you quite forget such strings are of great value. I have seen those pearls, Johanna, and can assure you that they are in themselves a fortune."

"I suppose," she said sadly, "it is too much for human nature to expect two blessings at once. I had the fond, warm heart that loved me without the fortune that would have enabled us to live in comfort and affluence; and now, when that is perchance within my grasp, the heart, that was by far the more costly possession, and the richest jewel of them all, lies beneath the wave."

They parted, and Johanna proceeded to her father's house.

The next day Colonel Jefferey visited his friend, the captain, and it was agreed that the colonel should take a bed at Lime tree Lodge, the residence of the captain, and that in the morning they should both start for London, and disguising themselves as respectable citizens, make some attempts by talking about jewels and stones, to draw out the barber into a confession that he had something of the sort to dispose of; and, moreover, they fully intended to take away the dog, with the care of which Captain Rathbone charged himself. We may pass over the pleasant, social evening which the colonel passed with the amiable family of the Rathbones, and, skipping likewise a conversation of some strange and confused dreams which Jefferey had during the night concerning his friend Thornbill, we will presume that both the colonel and the captain have breakfasted, and that they have proceeded to London and are at the shop of a clothier in the neighbourhood of the Strand, in order to procure coats, wigs, and hats, that should disguise them for their visit to Sweeney Todd. They walked towards Fleet-street and soon arrived opposite the little shop within which there appeared to be so much mystery.

"The dog, you perceive, is not here," said the colonel; "I had my suspicions, however, when I passed with Johanna Oakley that something was amiss with him, and I have no doubt but that the rascally barber has fairly compassed his destruction."

"If the barber be innocent," said Captain Rathbone, "You must admit that it would be one of the most confoundedly annoying things in the world to have a dog continually at his door assuming such an aspect of accusation, and in that case I can scarcely wonder at his putting the creature out of the way."

"No, presuming upon his innocence, certainly; but we will say nothing about all that, and remember we must come in as perfect strangers, knowing nothing of the affair of the dog, and presuming nothing about the disappearance of any one in this locality."

"Agreed, come on; if he should see us through the window, hanging about at all or hesitating, his suspicions will be at once awakened; and we shall do no good."

They both entered the shop and found Sweeney Todd wearing an extraordinarily singular appearance, for there was a black patch over one of his eyes, which was kept in its place by a green riband that went round his head, so that he looked more fierce and diabolical than ever; and having shaved off a small whisker that he used to wear, his countenance, although to the full as hideous as ever, certainly had a different character of ugliness to that which had before characterised it, and attracted the attention of the colonel. That gentleman would hardly have known him again anywhere but in his own shop, and when we come to consider, Sweeney Todd's adventures of the proceeding evening, we shall not feel surprised that he saw the necessity of endeavouring to make as much change in his appearance as possible, for fear he should come across any of the parties who had chased him and who, for all he knew to the contrary, might quite unsuspectingly drop in to be shaved in the course of the morning, perhaps to retail at that acknowledged mart for all sorts of gossip—a barber's shop—some of the very incidents which he had so well qualified himself to relate.

"Shaved and dressed, gentlemen?" said Sweeney Todd, as his customers made their appearance.

"Shaved only," said Captain Rathbone who had agreed to be principal spokesman in case Sweeney Todd should have any remembrance of the colonel's voice, and so suspect him.

"Pray be seated," said Sweeney Todd to Colonel Jefferey. "I'll soon polish off your friend, sir, and then I'll begin upon you. Would you like to see the morning paper, sir; it's at your service. I was just looking myself, sir, at a most mysterious circumstance, if it's true, but you can't believe, you know, sir, all that they put in newspapers."

"Thank you—thank you," said the colonel.

Captain Rathbone sat down to be shaved, for he had purposely omitted that operation at home, in order that it should not appear a mere excuse to get into Sweeney Todd's shop.

"Why, sir," continued Sweeney Todd, "as I was saying, it is a most remarkable circumstance."

"Indeed!"

"Yes, sir, an old gentleman of the name of Fidler had been to receive a sum of money at the west end of the town and has never been heard of since; that was yesterday, sir, and here is a description of him in the papers, of today. 'A snuff-coloured coat, and velvet smalls—black velvet, I should have said–silk stockings, and silver shoe-buckles, and a gold-headed cane with. W. D. F. upon it, meaning William Dumpledown Fidler'—a most mysterious affair, gentlemen."

A sort of groan came from the corner of the shop, and, on the impulse of the moment, Colonel Jefferey sprang to his feet, exclaiming—

"What's that—what's that?"

"Oh, it's only my apprentice, Tobias Ragg. He has got a pain in his stomach from eating too many of Lovett's pork pies. Ain't that it, Tobias, my bud?"

"Yes, sir," said Tobias, with another groan.

"Oh, indeed," said the colonel; "it ought to make him more careful for the future."

"It's to be hoped it will, sir; Tobias, do you hear what this gentleman says: it ought to make you more careful in future. I am too indulgent to you, that's the fact. Now, sir, I believe you are as clean shaved as ever you were in your life."

"Why, yes," said Captain Rathbone, "I think that will do very well; and now, Mr. Green"—addressing the colonel by that assumed name-"and now, Mr. Green, be quick, or we shall be too late for the duke, and so lose the sale of some of our jewels."

"We shall indeed," said the colonel, "if we don't mind. We sat too long over our breakfast at the inn, and his grace is too rich and too good a customer to lose—he don't mind what price he gives for things that take his fancy, or the fancy of his duchess."

"Jewel merchants, gentlemen, I presume," said Sweeney Todd.

"Yes, we have been in that line for some time; and by one of us trading in one direction, and the other in another, we manage extremely well, because we exchange what suits our different customers, and keep up two distinct connections."

"A very good plan," said Sweeney Todd. "I'll be as quick so I can with you, sir. Dealing in jewels is better than shaving."

"I dare say it is."

"Of course, it is, sir; here have I been shaving for some years in this shop, and not done much good—that is to say, when I talk of not having done much good, I admit I have made enough to retire upon quietly and comfortably, and I mean to do so very shortly. There you are, sir, shaved with celerity you seldom meet with, and as clean as possible, for the small charge of one penny. Thank you, gentlemen—there's your change; good morning."

They had no resource but to leave the shop; and when they had gone, Sweeney Todd, as he stropped the razor he had been using upon his hand, gave a most diabolical grin, muttering—

"Clever—very ingenious—but it won't do. Oh dear, no, not at all! I am not so easily taken in—diamond merchants, ha! ha! and no objection, of course, to deal in pearls—a good jest that, truly, a capital jest. If I had, been accustomed to be so easily defeated, I had not now been here a living man."

CHAPTER 9

"We return now to Bell-yard."

Mrs. Lovett having disposed of her cook, has engaged another, who had applied to her in half-starved condition, with an unlimited leave to eat as much as possible. No wonder that, banishing all scruple, a man so placed would take the situation with little inquiry. But people will tire of good things.

As he was seated in the bakehouse under the shop, he muttered to himself—

"I know they are made of the finest flour, the best possible butter, and that the meat, which comes from God knows where, is the most delicate-looking and tender I ever ate in all my life."

He stretched out his hand and broke a small portion of the crust from the pie that was before him, and he tried to eat it. He certainly did succeed, but it was a great effort; and when had done, he shook his head, saying—

"No, no! d—n it! I cannot eat it, and that's the fact—one cannot be continually eating pies; it is out of the question, quite out of the question; and all I have to remark is d—n the pies! I really don't think I shall be able to let another one pass my lips."

He rose and paced with rapid strides the place in which he was, and then suddenly he heard a noise; and, looking up, he saw a trap door in the roof open, and a bag of flour begin gradually to come down.

"Hilloa; hilloa!" he cried; "Mrs. Lovett—Mrs. Lovett!"

Down came the flour, and the trap was closed.

"Oh, I can't stand this sort of thing," he exclaimed; "I cannot be made into a machine for the manufacture of pies. I cannot and will not endure it—it is past all bearing."

For the first time almost since his incarceration, for such it really was, he began to think that he would take an accurate survey of the place where this tempting manufacture was carried on. He stood in the centre of this vault with the lamp in his hand, and he turned slowly round, surveying the walls and the ceilings with the most critical and marked attention, but not the smallest appearance of an outlet was observable. In fact, the walls were so entirely filled up with the stone shelves, that there was no space left for a door; and as for the ceiling, it seemed perfectly entire. Then the floor was of earth; so that the idea of a trap-door opening in it was out of the question, because there was no one on his side of it to place the earth again over it, and give it its compact and usual appearance.

He now made a still narrower examination of this vault, but he gained nothing by that. A closer inspection convinced him that there were a number of lines, written with lead pencil, after some difficulty he deciphered them as follows:—

Whatever unhappy wretch reads these lines may bid *adieu* to the world and all hope, for he is a doomed, man! He will never emerge from these walls with life, for there is a secret connected with them so awful and so hideous that to write it makes one's blood curdle, and the flesh to creep upon my bones. That secret is this—and you may be assured, whoever is reading these lines, that I write the truth, and that it is as impossible to make that awful truth worse by any exaggeration, as it would be by a candle at mid-day to attempt to add a new lustre to the sunbeams—

Here, most unfortunately, the writing broke off, and our friend, who, up to this point perused the lines with the most intense interest, felt great bitterness of disappointment, from the fact that enough should have been written to stimulate his curiosity to the highest point, but not enough to gratify it.

"This is, indeed, most provoking," he exclaimed. "What can this most dreadful secret be, which is impossible to exaggerate? I cannot, for a moment, divine to what it can allude."

In vain he searched over the door for some more writing,—there was none to be found, and from the long, straggling pencil-mark which followed the last word, it seemed as if he who been then been writing had been interrupted, and possibly met the fate that he had predicted, and was about to explain the reason of.

"This is worse than no information. I had better have remained in ignorance than received so indistinct a warning; but they shall not find me an easy victim, and besides, what power on earth can force me to make pies unless I like, I should wish to know?"

As he stepped out of the place in which meat was kept into the large vault where the ovens were he trod upon a piece of paper that a piece of paper that was lying upon the ground, and which he was quite certain he had not observed before. He picked it up with some curiosity. That curiosity was, however, soon turned to dismay when he saw what was written upon it, which was to the following effect:—

You are getting dissatisfied, and therefore it becomes necessary to explain to you your real position, which is simply this:—You are a prisoner, and were such from the first moment that you set foot where you now are; and you will find, unless you are resolved upon sacrificing your life, that your best plan will be to quietly give into the circumstances in which you find yourself placed. Without going into any argument or details upon the subject, it is sufficient to inform you that, so long as you continue to make the pies, you will be safe; but if you refuse, then the first time you are caught asleep your throat will be cut.

This document dropped from the half-paralysed hands of that man, who, in the depth of his distress, and urged on by great necessity, had accepted a situation that he would have given worlds to escape from, had he been possessed of them.

"Gracious Heaven!" he exclaimed, "and am I then indeed condemned to such a slavery? Is it possible, that even in the heart of London, I am a prisoner, and without the means of resisting the most frightful threats that are uttered against me? Surely, surely this must be all a dream! It is too terrific to be true!"

"If I am to die," he cried, "let me die with some weapon in my hand, as a brave man ought, and I will not complain."

He sprang to his feet, and rushing up to the door, which opened from the house into the vaults, he made a violent and desperate effort to shake it.

"Continue at your work," said the voice, "or death will be your portion as soon as sleep overcomes you, and you sink exhausted to that repose which you will never awaken from, except you feel the pangs of death, and to be conscious that you are weltering in your blood. Continue at your work, and you will, escape all this—neglect it, and your doom is sealed."

"What have I done that I should be made such a victim of? Let me go, and I will swear never to divulge the fact that I have been in these vaults, so I cannot disclose any of their secrets, even if I knew them."

"Make pies," said the voice, "eat them, and be happy. How many a man would envy your position—withdrawn from all the struggles of existence, amply provided with board and lodging, and engaged in a pleasant and delightful occupation; it is astonishing how you can be dissatisfied!"

Bang! went the little square orifice at the top of the door, and the voice was heard no more. The jeering mockery of those tones, however, still lingered upon the ear of the unhappy prisoner, and he clasped his head in his hands with a fearful impression upon his brain that he surely must be going mad.

"He will drive me to insanity," he cried; "already I feel a sort of slumber stealing over me for want of exercise, and the confined air of these vaults hinder me from taking regular repose; but now, if I close an eye, I shall expect to find the assassin's knife at my throat."

With a desperate and despairing energy he set about replenishing the furnaces of the oven, and, when he had got them all in a good state, he commenced manufacturing a batch of 100 pies, which, when he had finished and placed upon the tray, and set the machine in motion which conducted them up to the shop, he considered to be a sort price paid for his continued existence, and flinging himself upon the ground, he fell into a deep slumber.

Chapter 10

About this time, while the incidents of our tale are taking place, the pious frequenters of old St. Dunstan's Church noticed a most abominable odour throughout the sacred edifice.

A ponderous stone was raised in the flooring; the beadle, the churchwarden, and the workmen men shrank back—back; they could go no further.

"Ain't it a horrid smell?" said the beadle.

A gentleman, plainly dressed, advanced. He was no other than Sir Richard Blunt, the magistrate, who had been consulted by Colonel Jeffery as to the disappearance of Thornhill. He had taken great interest in the case and was endeavouring to unravel the mystery.

"Gentlemen," said he, "if what I expect be found here we cannot have too few witnesses."

The workmen were dismissed.

Sir Richard took a paper from his pocket and unfolded it.

"From this plan," he said, "the stone which I have raised discloses a staircase communicating with two passages. I have instructions from the Home Secretary to use my own discretion in this affair. I will, therefore, with one of my officers, descend to the vaults."

Sir Richard and Crotchet, the officer, both commenced the descent.

On their return Sir Richard looked ghastly pale. He had evidently seen something which had shaken his strong nerves.

After the stone was replaced the magistrate gave a signal to Crotchet to follow him.

"Now, Crotchet, no one for the future is to be shaved in Sweeney Todd's alone."

"Had we not better grab him at once?" said the officer.

"No, he has an accomplice or accomplices."

The stone was replaced, and Sir Richard gave a signal to Crotchet, and they both left the church together.

"Now, Crotchet," said the magistrate, "I will give you further particulars confided to me. It appears Sweeney Todd's shop-boy has also disappeared, and he placed a notice in his window requiring another. Now, Miss Oakley, being convinced that Thornhill is no other than Mark Ingestrie, a former sweetheart of hers under an assumed name, and that he has been kidnapped or murdered by Sweeney Todd, has disguised herself as a boy, and been engaged by the barber. It is a dangerous game, but she is a brave girl, and I am in communication with her. Sweeney Todd is evidently connected with Mrs. Lovett, and the vaults lead to her pie-shop. I must endeavour to find out the bakehouse and the cook. I will at once set about it."

After parting with Six Richard Blunt at Temple Bar, Crotchet walked up Fleet-street, upon Sweeney Todd's side of the way, until he overtook a man with a pair of spectacles on, and a stoop in his gait, as though age had crept upon him.

"King," said Crotchet.

"All right," said the spectacled old gentleman in a firm voice. "What's the news?"

"A long job, I think. Where's Morgan?"

"On the other side of the way."

"Well, just listen to me as we walk along, and if you see him, beckon him over to us."

As they walked along Crotchet told King what were the orders of Sir Richard Blunt, and they were soon joined by another officer.

Todd was standing at his door; he glared up and down the street like someone intent upon the destruction of a fresh victim.

"Stop him! Stop him!" cried a voice from the other side of the street. "Stop Pison, he's given me the slip, and I'm blessed if he won't pitch into that ere barber. Stop him. Pison!"

"Pison! Come here, boy. Come here! Oh, Lor' he's nabbed him. I knew'd he would, as sure as a horse's hind leg ain't a gammon o' bacon. My eyes, won't there be a row—he's nabbed the barber, like ninepence."

Before the ostler at the Bullfinch, for it was from his lips this speech came, could get one half of it uttered, the dog, who is known to the readers by the name of Hector, as well as his new name of Pison, dashed over the road, apparently infuriated at the sight of Todd, and rushing upon him, seized him with his teeth. Todd gave a howl of rage and pain, and fell to the ground. The whole street was in an uproar in a moment, but the ostler rushing over the way, seized the dog by the throat, and made him release Todd, who crawled upon all fours into his own shop. In Another moment he rushed out with a razor in his hand.

"Where's the dog?" he cried. "Where's the fiend in the shape of a dog?"

"Hold hard!" said the ostler, who held Hector between his knees. "Hold hard. I have got him, old chap."

"Get out of the way. I'll have his life."

"No, you won't."

"Humph!" cried a butcher's boy who was passing, "Why that's the same dog as said the barber had done for his master, and collected never such a lot of halfpence in his hat to pay expenses of burying of him."

"You villain!" cried Todd.

"Go to blazes," said the boy. "Who killed the dog's master? Ah, Ah! Who did it? Ah, ah!"

The people began to laugh.

"I insist upon killing that dog!" cried Todd.

"Do you?" said the ostler; "now this here dog is a particular friend of mine, so you see I can't have it done. If you walk into him, you must walk through me first. Only just put down that razor, and I'll give you such a walloping, big as you are, that you'll recollect for some time."

"Down with the razor! Down with the razor!" cried the mob, who was now every moment increasing.

The people took the part of the dog and his new master, and it was in vain that Sweeney Todd exhibited his rent garment as to show where he had been attacked by the animal. Shouts of laughter and various satirical allusions to his beauty were the only response. Suddenly, without a word, Todd then gave up the contest and retired into his shop, upon which the ostler conveyed Pison over the way and shut him up in one of the stables of the Bullfinch. Todd, it is true, retired to his shop with an appearance of equanimity, but it was like most appearances in this world—rather deceitful. The moment the door was closed between him and observation he ground his teeth together and positively howled with rage.

"The time will come, the time will come," he said, "when I shall have the joy of seeing Fleet-street in a blaze, and of hearing the shrieks of those who are frying in the flames. Oh, that I could with one torch ignite London, and sweep it and all its inhabitants from the face of the earth. Oh, that all those, who are now without my shop, had but one throat. Ha! Ha! how I would cut it."

He glared at the crouching boy, or rather Johanna, and seizing a razor threw himself into a ferocious attitude; but at this moment the door opened and a sea-faring man entered his shop in haste, and throwing himself on a chair, requested to be shaved immediately. He appeared to have but lately returned from India or some other hot climate, for his features were well bronzed, and from his general aspect and conversation, he appeared to be a man of superior station in life. However, in this manner the barber reasoned and came to the conclusion that he should have a good morning's work.

"A fine morning, sir," said Todd.

"Very," said the stranger; "but make haste and accomplish your task; I have a payment to make to a merchant in the city this morning by nine o'clock, and it is now more than half-past eight."

"I will polish you off in no time," said the barber, with a grin; "then you can proceed and transact your business in good time. Sit a little nearer this way, sir, the chair will only stand firmly in one position, and it is exceedingly uncomfortable for gentleman to remain, even for a few moments, on an unsteady chair. It is a maxim of mine, sir," said Todd, "to make everybody that comes to my shop as comfortable as possible during the short time they remain with me. One half-inch further this way, sir, and you will be in a better position."

As he spoke he drew the chair to the spot he wished it, which circumstance seemed to please him, for he looked around him, and indulged in one of those hideous grins.

Then turning to Johanna, who appeared like a timid boy, said—

"Charley, you can run over to Mrs. Lovett and get a pie for yourself."

Charley left the shop.

By this time the lather was over the seaman's face. He could not speak, except at the imminent risk of swallowing a considerable quantity of the soap that Todd had covered his face with. The barber seemed dexterously to ply a razor on the seaman's face, which caused him to make wry faces, indicating that the operation was painful; the grimaces grew more fantastic to the beholder, but evidently less able to be withstood by the person operated upon.

"Good God, barber," he at length ejaculated, "why the devil don't you keep better materials—I cannot stand this. The razor you are attempting to shave me with has not been ground, I should think, for a twelvemonth. Get another and finish me off, as you term it, in no time."

"Exactly, sir—I will get one more suited to your beard, and will return in one minute, when you will be polished off to my satisfaction."

He entered the little parlour at the back of the shop, but previously he took the precaution of putting his eye to the hole that gave a sight into the street; turning around, apparently satisfied with his scrutiny, he went in search of the superior razor he spoke of. A low grating sound, like that of a ragged cord commencing the movement of pullies, was to be heard, when Sir Rich Blunt threw the door open, and took a seat in the shop near where the stranger was sitting. He was so disguised that Todd could not recognise him as the same person that had been in his shop so many times before. The barber's face was purple with rage and disappointment; but he restrained it by an immense effort and spoke to Sir Richard in a tolerably calm tone—

"Hair cut, sir, or shaved, sir? I shall not be long before I have finished this gentleman off—perhaps you would like to call in again, in a few minutes?"

"Thank you; I am not in a particular hurry, and being rather tired I will rest myself in your shop, if you have no objection."

"My shop is but just open, and our ventilation being bad, it is much more pleasant to inhale the street air for a few minutes, than the vitiated air of houses in this neighbourhood."

"I am not much afraid of my health for a few minutes, therefore would rather take rest."

Todd turned his face away and ground his teeth, when he found that all his arguments were unavailing in moving the will of his new customer; therefore he soon finished shaving the first customer.

"At your service, sir," said Todd to Sir

Richard, who seemed absorbed in reading a newspaper he took from his pocket. He looked up, and saw that the stranger was nearly ready to leave, therefore he continued reading till the stranger was in the act of passing out of the shop, when he said—

"What time do the Royal Family pass through Temple Bar to the City this morning?"

"Half-past nine," said Todd.

"Then I have not time to be shaved now—I will call in again. Good morning." Saying which he also left the shop.

In a few minutes after leaving the shop of Todd, Sir Richard and the men employed by him were in consultation; and he urged strongly that the men should remain nearer to the shop than they had hitherto done, for if Sir Richard had been two minutes later, most likely he who had escaped the angry billows, would have been launched into eternity by the villainous barber.

Todd fairly danced with rage. Hark!—a knock; he opened the door—

"Is this here keg of turpentine for you?" said a man with it upon his shoulder. "Mr. Todd's this is, ain't it?"

"Yes—yes. Put it down, my good fellow. You ought to have something to drink."

"Thank you kindly, sir."

"But you must pay for it yourself. There is a public-house opposite."

The man went away swearing; and scarcely had he crossed the threshold, when a letter was brought by a lad, and handed to Todd. Before he could ask any questions, the lad was gone.

Todd held the letter in his hand, and glanced at the direction. It was to him, sure enough, and written in a very clerk-like hand, too. It was as follows:—

Sir,—
We beg to inform you that our Hamburgh vessel, in which you have done us the favour to take passage, will not sail until to-morrow night at four, God willing, and that consequently there will be no occasion for your coming on board earlier.

We are, sir, 'Your obedient servants,'"
Brown, Buggins, Muggs, and Screamer.
To Mr. S. Todd.

Todd ground his teeth together in a horrible manner. He dashed the letter on the floor, and stamped upon it

"Curse Brown and Buggins!" he cried. "I only wish I could dash out Muggs and Screamer's brains with Brown and Buggins's skulls. Confound them and their ships. May they all go to the bottom when I am out of them, and be smashed and d—d!"

Johanna was amazed at this sudden torrent of wrath. She could not imagine what had produced it, for Todd had read the letter in a muttering tone, that effectually prevented her from hearing any of it.

Suddenly he saw a postscript at the foot of the shipowner's letter, which he had at first overlooked.

P.S.—The ship is removed to Crimmins's Wharf, but will be at her old moorings at time mentioned above.

"D—n Crimmins and his wharf, too!" cried Todd.

He flung himself into a chair, and sat for a time profoundly still. During that period he tried to make up his mind as to what it would be best for him, under the circumstances, to do. Many plans floated through his imagination. He could not for a long time bring himself to believe that the letter of the colonel's was anything but a feint to throw him off his guard in some way.

At length he got into a calmer frame of mind.

"Shall I leave at once or stay till tomorrow night, that is the question?"

He argued this with himself, *pro* and *con*.

If he left he would have to secret himself somewhere all the following day, and the fact of his having left would make an active search, safe to be instituted for him, which would possibly be successful. Besides, how was he to conveniently set fire to his house, unless he was off on the moment that the flames burst forth?

Then if he stayed he had Mrs. Lovett to encounter, but that was all; and surely he could put her off for a few hours? Surely she, of all people in the world, was not to run to a police-office and destroy both him and herself, just because she did not get some money at ten o'clock that he had promised to hand to her.

"Charley," he said, "I am going out. I shall not be long."

CHAPTER 11

Recent events, although they had by no manner of means tended to decrease the just confidence which Johanna had in her own safety, had yet much agitated her; and she at times feared that she should not be able to carry on the farce of composure before Todd much longer.

After Todd's departure a slight tap was given at the door, and Sir Richard Blunt entered.

"Don't you know me, Johanna?"

"Ah, Sir Richard! my dear friend, it is, indeed, you, and I am safe again—I am safe!"

"Certainly you are safe; and permit me to say that you have all along been tolerably safe, Johanna. But how very incautious you are. Here I have come into the shop, and actually stood by you for some few moments, you knowing nothing of it! What now if Todd had so come in?"

"He would have killed me."

"He might have done so. But now all danger is quite over, for you will have protectors at your hand. Do you know where Todd has gone?"

"I do not."

"Well, it don't matter. Let me look at this largest cupboard. I wonder if it will hold two of my men? Let me see. Oh, yes, easily and comfortably. I will be back in a moment."

He went no further than the door, and when he came back he brought with him Mr. Crotchet and another person, and pointing to the cupboard, he said—

"You will stow yourselves there; if you please, and keep quiet until I call upon you to come out."

"I believe you," said Crotchet. "Lord bless you, we shall be snug enough. How is you, Miss O? I suppose by this time you feels quite at home in your breech—"

"Silence!" said Sir Richard. "Go to your duty at once, Crotchet. Miss Oakley is in no humour to attend to you just now."

Upon this, Mr. Crotchet and the other man got into the cupboard, and a chair was placed against it; and then Sir Richard said to Johanna—

"I will come in to be shaved when I know that Todd is here, and your trials will soon be over."

"To be shaved?—By him?"

"Yes. But believe me there is no danger. Anyone may come here now to be shaved with perfect safety. I have made such arrangements that Todd cannot take another life."

"Thank Heaven!"

Sir Richard withdrew.

Soon after this Todd re-entered the shop.

"Hush," said he; "here's somebody coming. Why it's old Mr. Wrankley, the tobacconist, I declare. Good-day to you, sir—shaved; I suppose? I am glad you have come, sir, for I have been out till this moment. Hot water, Charley, directly; and hand me that razor."

Johanna, in handing Todd the razor, knocked one edge of it against the chair, and it being uncommonly sharp, cut a great slice of the wood off one of the arms of it.

"What shameful carefulness; I have half a mind to lay the strop over your back, sir; here you have spoilt a capital razor—not a bit of edge left upon it."

"Oh, excuse him, Mr. Todd—excuse him," said the old gentleman; "he's only a little lad, after all. Let me intercede for him."

"Very good, sir; if you wish me to look over it, of course I will; and, thank God, we have a stock of razors, of course, always at hand. Is there any news stirring, sir?"

"Nothing that I know of, Mr. Todd, except it's the illness of Mr. Cummings, the overseer. They say he got home about 12 to his own house, in Chancery-lane, and ever since then he has been as sick as a dog, and all they can get him to say is, 'Oh, those pies-oh, those pies!'"

"Very odd, sir."

"Hilloa!—I think you have cut me."

"No, no-we can't cut anybody for three-halfpence, sir. I think I will just give you another lather, sir, before I polish you off. And so you have the pearls with you; well, how odd things come round, to be sure."

"What do you mean?"

"This shaving-brush is just in a good state now. Always as a shaving-brush is on the point of wearing out, it's the best. Charley, you will go at once to Mr. Cummings, and ask if he's any better; you need not hurry, that's a good lad. I am not at all angry with you now. And so, sir, they think at home that you have gone after some business over the water, do they, and not have the least idea that you have come to be shaved? There, be off, Charley—shut the door, that's a good lad, bless you."

When Johanna came back, the tobacconist was gone.

"What has happened? Good God! what can have happened!" thought Johanna, as she staggered back, until she reached the shaving chair, into which she cast herself for support. Her eyes fall upon the arm which she had taken such a shaving off with the razor, but all was perfectly whole and correct; there was not the least mark of the cut that so recently had been given to it; and, lost in wonder, Johanna, for more than a minute, continued looking for the mark of the injury she knew could not have been, by any possibility, effaced.

And yet she found it not, although there was the chair, just as usual, with its wide-spreading arms and its worn, tarnished paint and gilding. No wonder that Johanna rubbed her eyes, and asked herself if she were really awake.

What could account for such a phenomenon? The chair was a

fixture too, and the others in the shop were of a widely different make and construction, so it could not have been changed.

"Alas! alas!" mourned Johanna, "my mind is full of horrible surmises, and yet I can form no rational conjecture. I suspect everything, and knowing nothing. What can I do? What ought I to do, to relieve myself from this state of horrible suspense? Am I really in a place where, by some frightful ingenuity, murder has become bold and familiar, or can it be all a delusion?"

CHAPTER 12

The handle of Sweeney Todd's shop door turned and a man presented himself, and Todd saw that the visitor was a substantial-looking farmer, with dirty top-boots, an if he had just come off a journey.

"Well, master," said the visitor, "I wants a clean shave."

"Oh," said Todd, not in the best of humours.

"It's rather late; but I suppose you would not like to wait till morning, for I don't know if I have any hot water."

"Oh, cold will do."

"Cold? Oh, dear no; we never shave in cold water; and if you must, you must; so sit down, sir, and we will soon settle the business."

"Thank you, thank you. I can't go to bed comfortable without a clean shave, do you see? I have come up I from Braintree with beasts on commission, and I'm staying at the Bull's Head, you see."

"Oh, indeed," said Todd, as he adjusted the shaving cloth, "the Bull's Head."

"Yes, master; why I brought up a matter o' 220 beasts, I did, do you see, and was on my pooney, as good a stepper as you'd wish to see; and I sold 'em all, do you see, for 550 pun. Ho, ho! good work that, do you see, and only forty-two on 'em was my beasts, do you see; I've got a missus at home, and a daughter; my girl's called Johanna—ahem!"

Up to this point Johanna had not suspected that the game had begun, and that this was no other than Sir Richard himself most admirably disguised, who had come to put an end to the malpractices of Sweeney Todd; but his marked pronunciation of her name at once opened her eyes to that fact, and she knew that something interesting must soon happen.

"And so you sold them all?" said Todd.

"Yes, master, I did, and I've got the money in my pocket now, in bank notes; I never leaves my money at inns, do you see, master; safe bind, safe find, you see; I carries it about with me."

"A good plan, too," said Todd; "Charley, some hot water; that's a good lad—and—and—Charley?"

"Yes, sir."

"While I am finishing off this gentleman, you may as well just run to the Temple, to Mr. Serjeant Toldrunis and ask for his wig; we shall have to do it in the morning, and may as well have it the first thing in the day to begin upon; and you need not hurry, Charley, as we shall shut up when you come back."

"Very good, sir."

Johanna walked out, but went no further than the shop window, close to which she placed her eyes, so that, between a *pomatum* jar and a lot of hair brushes, she could clearly see what was going on.

"A nice looking little lad, that," said Todd's customer.

"Very, sir; an orphan boy; I took him out charity, poor little fellow; but then, we ought to try to do all the good we can."

"Just so; I'm glad I have come to be shaved here. Mine's rather a strong board, I think, do you see."

"Why, sir, in a manner of speaking," replied Todd, "it is a strong beard. I must give you another lather, sir, and I'll get another razor with a keener edge, now that I have taken off all the rough, as one may say, in a manner of speaking."

"Oh, I shall do."

"No, no, don't move, sir, I shall not detain you a moment; I have my other razors in the next room, and will polish you off now, sir, before you will know where you are."

"Well, well, a clean shave is a comfort; but don't be long, for I want to get back, do you see."

"Not a moment, not a moment."

Sweeney Todd walked into his back-parlour, conveying with him the only light that was in the shop, so that the dim glimpse that, up to this time, Johanna, from the outside had contrived to get of what was going on, was denied to her; and all that met her eyes was impenetrable darkness.

Oh, what a world of anxious, agonising sensations crossed the mind of the young and beautiful girl at that moment. She felt as if some great crisis in her history had arrived, and that she was condemned to look in vain into darkness to see of what it consisted.

The moment his back was turned, the seeming farmer sprang from the shaving chair, as if he had been electrified; and yet he did not do it with any appearance of fright, nor did he make any noise. It was only astonishingly quick, and then he placed himself close to the window and waited patiently with his eyes fixed upon the chair, to see what would happen next.

In the space of about a quarter of minute there came, from the next room a sound like the rapid drawing back of a heavy bolt, and then in an instant the shaving chair disappeared beneath the floor; and the circumstances by which Sweeney Todd's customers disappeared was evident..

There was a piece of the flooring turning upon a centre, and the weight of the chair when a bolt was withdrawn by means of simple leverage from the inner room, weighed down one end of the top, which, by a little apparatus, was to swing completely round, there being another chair on the under surface, which thus became the upper, exactly resembling the one in which the unhappy customer was supposed to be "polished off."

Hence was it that in one moment, as if by, magic, Sweeney Todd's visitors disappeared, and there was the empty chair. No doubt he trusted to a fall of about 20ft. below, on to a stone floor, to be the death of them, or, at all events, to stun them until he could go down to finish the murder, and—to cut them up for Mrs. Lovett's pies! after robbing them of all the money and valuables they might have about them.

In another moment, the sound as of a bolt was again heard, and Sir Richard Blunt, who had played the part of the wealthy farmer, feeling that the trap was closed again, seated himself in the new chair that had made its appearance with all the nonchalance in life, as if nothing had happened.

It was a full minute before Todd ventured to look from the parlour into the darkened shop, and then he shook so that he had to hold by the door to steady himself.

"That's done," he said. "That's the last, I hope. It is time I finished; I never felt so nervous since the first time. Then I did quake a little. How quiet he went. I have sometimes had a shriek ringing in my ears for a whole week."

It was a large, high-backed piece of furniture that shaving chair, so that, when Todd crept into the shop with the light in his hand, he had not the remotest idea it was tenanted; but when he got round it, and saw his customer calmly waiting with the lather upon his face, the cry of horror that came gurgling and gushing from his throat was horrible to hear.

"Why, what's the matter," said Sir Richard.

"Oh, God, the dead! the dead! Oh, God!" cried Todd, "this is the beginning of my punishment. Have mercy, Heaven! Oh, do not look upon me with those dead eyes."

"Murderer!" shouted Richard, in a voice that rang like the blast of a trumpet through the house.

In an instant he sprang upon Sweeney Todd, and grappled him by the throat. There was a short struggle, and they were down upon the floor together, but Todd's wrists were suddenly laid hold of, and a pair of handcuffs most scientifically put upon him by the officers who, at the word "murderer," that being a preconcerted signal, came from the cupboard where they had been concealed.

"Guard him well, my men," said the magistrate "and don't let him lay violent hands upon himself".

Johanna rushed into the shop, and clung to the arm of Sir Richard crying:

"Is it all over? Is it, indeed, all done now?"

"It is, Miss Oakley."

The moment Todd heard these few words addressed to Charley Green, as he thought him, he turned his glassy, bloodshot eyes upon Johanna, and glared at her for the space of about half-a-minute in silence. He then, although handcuffed, made a sudden and violent effort to reach her, but he was in too experienced hands, and he was held back most effectually.

He struck his forehead with his fettered hands, making a gash in it from which the blood flowed freely, as in infuriated accents, he said—

"Oh fool—fool, to be cheated by a girl!—I had my suspicions that the boy was a spy, but I never thought for one moment there was a disguise of sex. Oh, idiot! Idiot! And who are you, sir?"

"I am Sir Richard Blunt."

Sir Richard Blunt, turning to Johanna, said—

"Run over the way to your friends at the fruiterer's. All is over now, and your disguise is no longer needed."

Johanna did not pause another moment.

"Shut up the shop, Crotchet," said Sir Richard, "and then get a coach. I will lodge this man at once in Newgate, and then we will see to Mrs. Lovett."

At this name Todd looked up.

"She has escaped you," he said.

"I don't think so," responded Sir Richard.

"But I say she has—she is dead: she fell into the Thames this morning and was drowned."

"Oh, you allude to your pushing her into the river this morning near London-bridge?" said Sir Richard, "I saw that affair myself."

Todd glared at him.

"But it was not of much consequence. We got her out, and she is all right again now at her shop in Bell-yard."

Todd held his hands over his eyes for some moments, and then he said in a low voice—

"It is all a dream, or I am mad."

"I intrust you with him, Crotchet. Take him away. I give him entirely into your hands."

Upon this, Crotchet slid his arm beneath that of Sweeney Todd, and looking in his face with a most grotesque air of satisfaction, he said, "kim, up—kim up!"

He then, by an immense exertion of strength, hoisted Todd completely over the doorstep, after which, catching him with both hands about the small of his back, he pitched him into the coach.

"My eye," said the coachman, "has the genman had a drop too much?"

"He will have," said Crotchet, "some o' these odd days. To Newgate—to Newgate."

Crotchet rode inside along with Todd, "for fear he should be dull," he said, and the other officer got up outside the coach, and then off it went to that dreadful building that Todd had often grimly smiled at as he passed but into which as a resident he had never expected to enter.

Sir Richard Blunt remained in the shop of Sweeney Todd. The oil lamp that hung by a chain from the ceiling shed a tolerable light over all objects, and no sooner had the magistrate fastened the outer door after the departure of Crotchet with Todd, than he stamped three time's heavily upon the floor of the shop.

This signal was immediately answered by three distinct taps from underneath the floor, and then the magistrate stamped again in the same manner.

The effect of all this stamping and counter-signals was immediately very apparent. The great chair which has played so prominent a part in the atrocities of Sweeney Todd slowly sank and the revolving plank hung suspended by its axle, while a voice from below called out—

"Is it all right, sir?"

"Yes, Crotchet has taken him to Newgate. I am now all alone. Come up."

"We are coming, sir. We all heard a little disturbance, but the floor is very thick you know, sir. So we could not take upon ourselves to say exactly what was happening."

"Oh, it's all right, He resisted, but by this time he is within the stone walls of Newgate. Let me lend you a hand."

Sir Richard Blunt stooped over the aperture in the floor, and the first person that got up was no other than Mr. Wrankley the tobacconist.

"How do you feel after your tumble?" said Sir Richard.

"Oh, very well. The fact is, they caught me so capitally below, that it was quite easy. Todd did not think it worth his while to come down to see if I were alive or dead."

"Ah! That was the only chance; but of course, if he had done so, he must have been taken at once into custody-that would have been all. Come on, my friends, come on, our trouble with regard to Todd is over, I think!"

The two churchwardens of St. Dunstan's and the beadle, and four of Sir Richard Blunt's officers, and the fruiterer from opposite, now came up from below the shop of Sweeney Todd, where they had all been waiting to catch Mr. Wrankley when the chair should descend with him.

"Convulsions!" said the beadle. "I runned agin everybody when I seed him a-coming. I thought to myself, if a parochial authority had been served in that 'ere way, there would have been an end of the world at once."

"I had some idea of asking you at one time to play that little part for me," said Sir Richard.

"Convulsions! had you, sir?"

"Yes. But now, my friends, let us make a careful search of this house; and among the first things we have to do is, to remove all the combustible materials that Todd has stowed in various parts of it, for unless I am much deceived, the premises are in such a state that the merest accident would set them a blaze."

"Convulsions!" then cried the beadle. "I aint declared out of danger yet, then!"

CHAPTER 13

One, two, three, tour, five, six, seven, eight, nine! Yes, it is nine at last. It strikes by old St. Dunstan's church clock, and in weaker strains the chronometical machine at the pie-shop echoes the sound. What excitement there is to get at the pies when they shall come! Mrs. Lovett lets down the square moveable platform that goes on pullies in the cellar; some machinery, which requires only a handle to be turned, brings up a hundred pies in a tray. These are eagerly seized by parties who have previously paid, and such a smacking of lips ensues as never was known.

Down goes the platform for the next hundred, and a gentlemanly man says—

"Let me work the handle, Mrs. Lovett, if you please; it's too much for you I'm sure."

"Sir, you are very kind, but I never allow anybody on this side of the counter but my own people, sir. I can turn the handle myself, sir, if you please, with the assistance of this girl. Keep your distance, sir, nobody wants your help."

"But my dear madam, only consider your delicacy. Really you ought not to be permitted to work away like a negro slave at a winch handle. Really you ought not."

The man who spoke thus obligingly to Mrs. Lovett, was tall and stout, and the lawyers' clerks repressed the ire they otherwise would probably have given utterance to at thus finding anyone admiring their charming Mrs. Lovett.

"Sir, I tell you once again that I don't want your help; keep your distance, sir, if you please."

"Now don't get angry, fair one," said the man. "You don't know but I might have made you an offer before I left the shop."

"Sir," said Mrs. Lovett, drawing herself up and striking terror into the hearts of the limbs of the law. "Sir! What do you want? Say what you want, and be served, sir, and then go. Do you want a pie, sir?"

"A pie? Oh, dear no, I don't want a pie. I would not eat one of the nasty things on any account. Pah!" Here the man spat on the floor. "Oh, dear, don't ask me to eat any of your pies."

"Shame, shame," said several of the lawyers' clerks.

"Will any gentleman who thinks it a shame, be so good as to step forward and say so a little closer?"

Everybody shrank back upon this, instead of accepting the challenge, and Mrs. Lovett soon saw that she must, despite all the legal chivalry by which she was surrounded, fight her battle herself. With a look of vehement anger, she cried—

"Beware, sir, I am not to be trifled with. If you carry your jokes too far, you will wish that you had not found your way, sir, into this shop."

"That, madam," said the tall stout man, "is not surely possible, when I have the beauty of a Mrs. Lovett to gaze upon, and render the place so exquisitely attractive; but if you will not permit me to have the pleasure of helping you up with the next batch of pies, which, after all, you may find heavier than you expect, I must to leave you do it yourself."

"So that I am not troubled any longer by you, sir, at all," said Mrs. Lovett, "I don't care how heavy the next batch of pies may happen to be, sir."

"Very good, madam."

"Upon my word," said a small boy, giving the side of his face a violent rub with the hope of finding the ghost of a whisker there, "it's really too bad."

"Ah, who's that? Let me get at him!"

"Oh, no, no, I—mean—that it's too bad of Mrs. Lovett, my dear sir. Oh, don't."

"Oh, very good; I am satisfied. Now, madam, you see that even your dear friends here, from Lincoln's Inn—Are you from the Inn, small boy?"

"Yes, sir, if you please."

"Very good. As I was saying, Mrs. Lovett, you must now of necessity perceive, that even your friends from the Inn, feel that your conduct is really too bad, madam."

Mrs. Lovett was upon this so dreadfully angry, that she disdained any reply to the stout, impertinent man, but at once she applied herself to the windlass, which worked up the little platform, upon which a whole tray of a hundred pies was wont to come up, and began to turn it with what might be called a vengeance.

How very strange it was—sure the words of the tall stout impertinent stranger were prophetic, for never before had Mrs. Lovett found what a job it was to work that handle as upon that night. The axle creaked, and the cords and the pullies strained and wheezed, but she was a determined woman, and she worked away at it.

"I told you so, my dear madam," said the stranger; "it is, more, evidently, than you can do."

"Peace, sir."

"I am done; work away, ma'am, only don't say afterwards that I did

260

not offer to help you, that's all."

Indignation was swelling at the heart of Mrs. Lovett, but she felt that if she wasted her breath upon the impertinent stranger, she would have none for the windlass; so setting her teeth, she fagged at it with a strength and a will that if she had not been in a right royal passion, she could not have brought to bear upon it on any account.

There was quite an awful stillness in the shop. All eyes were bent upon Mrs. Lovett, and the cavity through which the next batch of those delicious pies was coming. Those who had had the good fortune to get one of the first lot, had only had their appetites heightened by the luxurious feast they had partaken of, while those who had had as yet none, actually licked their lips, and snuffed up the delightful aroma from the remains of the first batch.

"Two for me, Mrs. Lovett," cried a voice.

"One veal for me. Three porks—one pork."

The voices grew fast and furious.

"Silence!" cried the tall stout man. "I will engage that everybody shall be fully satisfied, and no one shall leave here without a thorough conviction that his wants in pies has been more than attended to."

The platform could be made to stop at any stage of its upward progress by means of a ratchet wheel and a catch, and now Mrs. Lovett paused to take breath. She attributed the unusual difficulty in working the machinery to her own weakness, contingent upon her recent immersion in the Thames.

"Sir," she said between her clenched teeth, addressing the man who was such an eye-sore to her in the shop. "Sir, I don't know who you are, but I hope to be able to shew you when I have served these gentlemen, that even I am not to be insulted with impunity."

"Anything you please madam," he replied, "in a small way, only don't exert yourself too much."

Mrs. Lovett flew to the windlass again, and from the manner in which she now worked at it, it was quite clear that when she had her hands free from that job, she fully intended to make good her threats against the tall stout man. The young beardless scions of the law trembled at the idea of what might happen.

And now the tops of the pies appeared. Then they saw the rim of the large tray, upon which they were, and then just as the platform itself was level with the floor of the shop, up flew tray and pies, as if something had exploded beneath them, and a tall slim man sprang upon the counter. It was the cook, who from the cellars beneath, had laid himself as flat as he could beneath the tray of pies, and so had been worked up to the shop by Mrs. Lovett.

"Gentlemen," he cried, "I am Mrs. Lovett's cook. The pies are made of human flesh!"

★★★★★★

We shrink, we tremble at the idea of attempting to describe the scene that ensued in the shop of Mrs. Lovett contingent upon this frightful apparition, and still more frightful speech of the cook; but duty-our duty to the public-requires that we should say something upon the occasion.

If we can do nothing more, we can briefly enumerate what did actually take place in some instances.

About twenty clerks rushed into Bell-yard, and there and then, to the intense surprise of the passers-by, became intensely sick. The cook, with one spring, cleared the counter, and alighted amongst the customers, and with another spring, the tall impertinent man, who had made many remarks to Mrs. Lovett of an aggravating tendency, cleared the counter likewise in the other direction, and, alighting close to Mrs. Lovett, he cried—

"Madam, you are my prisoner!"

For a moment, and only for a moment, the great, the cunning, and the redoubtable Mrs. Lovett, lost her self possession, and, staggering back, she lurched heavily against the glass-case next to the wall, immediately behind the counter. It was, though, that such an effect was produced upon Mrs. Lovett; and then, with a spring like an enraged tigress, she caught up a knife that was used for slipping under the pies and getting them cleanly out of the little tins, and rushed upon the tall stranger.

Yes, she rushed upon him; but for once in a way, even Mrs. Lovett had met with her match. With a dexterity, that only long practice in dealings with the more desperate portion of human nature could have taught him, the tall man closed with her, and had the knife out of her hand in a moment. He at once threw it right through the window into Bell-yard, and then, holding Mrs. Lovett in his arms, he said—

"My dear madam you only distress yourself for nothing; all resistance is perfectly useless. Either I must take you prisoner, or you me, and I decidedly incline to the former alternative."

The knife that had been thrown through the window was not without its object, for in a moment afterwards Mr. Crotchet made his appearance in the shop.

"All right, Crotchet," said he who had captured Mrs. Lovett; "first clap the bracelets on this lady."

"Here yer is," said Crotchet. "Lor, mum! I had a eye on you months and months ago. How, is you, mum, in yer fellins this here nice evening?—Eh, mum?"

"A knife, a knife! Oh, for a knife!" cried Mrs. Lovett.

"Exactly, mum," added Crotchet, as he with professional dexterity slipped the handcuffs on her wrists. "Would you like one with a hivory handle, mum? or would anything more common do, mum?"

"In the cupboard, in the parlour," said Mrs. Lovett, "there is a letter addressed to me by Sir Richard Blunt. It will be worth your while to save it from the mob. Let me shew you where to lay your hands upon it, and if you have any wish take a greater criminal than I, go to the shop of one Sweeney Todd, a barber, in Fleet-street. His number is sixty-nine. Seize him, for he is the head of all the criminality you can possibly impute to me. Seize him, and I shall be content."

"The man you mention," said Mr. Green, "has been in Newgate an hour, nearly."

"Newgate?"

"Yes. We took him first, and then attended to you."

"Todd—captured—in Newgate—and I in fancied security here remained wasting the precious moments upon which hung my life. Oh, fool—fool—dolt—idiot! A knife! Oh, sirs, I pray you to give me the means of instant death. What can the law do, but take my life? What have you all come here, and plotted and planned for, but to take my life? I will do it. Oh, I pray you to give me the means and I will satisfy you and justice, and die at once—a knife!"

"Well, you are a rum customer," said Crotchet. "A knife, s'help me, I can't see one; will a fork do?"

"Let's get along with her," Crotchet added, "I have her tight. She won't get away. Make way a little."

Mrs. Lovett shrieked as she saw the sea of angry faces before, behind, and, on all sides of her. She thought that surely her last hour was come, and that a far more horrible death than any she had ever calculated upon in her worst moments of depression, was about to be hers. Her eyes were blood-shot—she bit her under lip through, and the blood poured from her mouth-she each moment that she could gather breath to do so, raised a fearful shriek and the mob shouted and yelled, and swayed to and fro, and the links were tossed from hand to hand, flashing and throwing around them thousands of bright sparks, and people rapidly joined the mob.

It took a quarter of an hour to reach the coach from the door of Mrs. Lovett's shop, a distance that in 20 steps anyone might have traversed; and, oh! what a quarter of an hour of horrible suffering that was to the wretched woman whose crimes had so infuriated the populace, that with one voice they called for her death!

The coach door was opened, and Crotchet pushed his prisoner in, and she was safely lodged in Newgate.

"Now, mum," said Crotchet to Mrs. Lovett, "didn't I say I'd bring yer to the old stone-jug as safe as nine-pence?"

"She only looked at him vacantly; and, then, glaring around her with a shudder, she said—

"And this is Newgate!"

"Just a few," said Crochet.

The governor at this moment made his appearance, and began to give orders as to where Mrs. Lovett should be placed. A slight change of colour came over her face as she said—

"Shall I see Todd?"

"Not at present," said the governor.

"I should like to see him to forgive him; for, no doubt, it is to him that I owe this situation. He has betrayed me!"

The look which she put on when she uttered the words "I should like to see him to forgive him," was so truly demoniac, that it was quite clear if she did see Todd, that whether she were armed or not, she would fly upon him, and try to take his life: and although in that she might fail, there would be very little doubt but that, in the process of failure, she would inflict upon him some very serious injury.

The cook and Crotchet then made their way to Sir Richard Blunt's office.

Sir Richard was at home and anxiously expecting them, so that, upon the first hint of their presence, they were introduced to him, and he received the report of the officer with evident satisfaction.

"Thank God," he said, "two of the greatest malefactors the world ever saw are now in the hands of justice."

"Yes," said Crotchet. "They are cotched."

In a few moments the magistrate was alone with the cook.

From a cupboard in his room, then Sir Richard Blunt took wine and other refreshments, and laid them before the cook, saying—

"Refresh yourself, my friend; but for your own sake, as your fare has been but indifferent for some time, I beg you to be sparing."

"I will, sir. I owe you much—very much!"

"You are free now."

"I—am—sir."

"And yet you are very unhappy."

The cook started and changed colour slightly. He filled, for himself, a glass of wine, and after drinking it he heaved a sigh, as he said—

"Sir, I am unhappy. I do not care how soon the world and I part, sir. The hope—the dream of my life has gone from me. All that I lived for—all that I cherished as the brightest expectation of joy in this world has passed away like a vapour, and left not a rack behind. I am unhappy, and better, far better, would it have been for me if Sweeney Todd had taken my life, or if by some subtle poison, Mrs. Lovett had shuffled me out of the world—I am unhappy.

"You already know that I am not exactly what I seem, and that my being in that most abominable woman's employment as a cook, was one of those odd freaks of fortune, which will at times detract the due order of society, and place people in the most extraordinary positions."

"Exactly."

"I am, sir, an orphan, and was brought up by an uncle with every expectation that he would be kind and liberal to me as I progressed in years; but he had taken his own course and had made up his mind as to what I was to be, the consequence was then, that directly he found me very different from what he wished, he was very angry indeed, and then I put the finishing stroke to his displeasure, by committing the greatest crime that in his eyes I could commit: I fell in love: but he said, 'You must give up all love nonsense if you wish to preserve my favour,' and the he turned me out of the room."

"And what did you do? Did you give up your love?"

"No, sir; if he had asked me to give up my life that would have been much easier to me.

"My uncle and I met very seldom, but there was one upon my track that he paid to follow me, and to report my actions to him; and that spy—oh, that I had caught him! That spy made my uncle acquainted with the fact, that I continued, despite his prohibition, to meet with the only being who ever awakened in my bosom a tender feeling; and so was abandoned by my relative, and left penniless almost. I heard that an expedition was about to start to explore some rich island in the Southern Sea. If successful, everyone who took part in it would be enriched; and if unsuccessful, I could not lose my life in a better cause than in trying to make a happy home for her whom I love. I at once embraced the proposition, and became one of the adventurers, much against the inclination of the gentle girl, and who in imagination pictured to herself a thousand dangers as involved in the enterprise."

"You went?"

"I did, and with every hope of returning in about a year an independent man. I thought little of the perils I was about to encounter in my voyage. I and the fair girl upon whom I had fixed my best hopes and affections parted, after many tears and protestations of fidelity. I kept my faith."

"And she?"

"Broke hers."

"The principal object of the voyage failed entirely; but by pure accident I got possession of a string of pearls, of very great value indeed which, provided I could get home in safety, would value in Europe quite a sufficient sum to enable us to live in comfort. But the dangers of the deep assailed us. We were wrecked; and fully believing that I should not survive, I handed the pearls to a stronger comrade, and begged him to take them to her whom I had loved, to tell her my fate, and to bid her not weep for me, since I had died happy in the thought that I had achieved something for her; and so, my friend and I parted. I was preserved and got on board a merchant vessel bound for England, where I arrived absolutely penniless. But I had a heart full of hope and joy; for if I could but find my poor girl faithful to me, I felt that we might yet be happy, whether my comrade had lived to bring to her the pearls or not. I walked from Southampton to London, subsisting on the road as best I could. At length I reached London tolerably exhausted, as you may suppose, and in anything but a good plight."

"Well, but you found your girl all right, I suppose?"

"No, I walked up the Strand; and as some of our happiest interviews had taken place in the Temple gardens, I could not resist turning aside for a moment to look at the old familiar spot, when what do you think was the sight that met my eyes?"

"I really can't say."

"The first object that met my eyes in that Temple-gardens was the being whom I loved so fondly leaning upon the arm of a man in military undress—leaning, did I say, upon his arm? She was almost upon his breast, and he was actually supporting her with one of his arms around her waist."

"And you, then, only walked away?"

"That is all. With such a pang at my heart at the moment as I wonder did not kill me, I walked away, and left her to her own conclusions.

"I found myself, tired, worn out, famishing, opposite Mrs. Lovett's shop-window, and the steam of those abominable pies began to tempt me so much that I went into the shop, and after some talk, I actually accepted the situation of cook to her, and there, but for you, I should have breathed my last."

"Not a doubt of it. And now, my young friend, you know that I am a police-magistrate, and I dare say you have heard a great deal about my sources of information, and the odd way in which I find out things when folks think they keep them a profound secret. You have told me all your history, but you have thought proper, as you were if you pleased, quite justified in doing, to withhold your name."

"I have done so, but I hardly know why. I will tell it to you, however, now."

"Hold, I know it, your name is Mark Ingestrie!"

"I know more than that. The name of the young lady who, you believe, played you such a trick, is Johanna Oakley."

Mark Ingestrie, for it was indeed no other, sprang to his feet, exclaiming—

"Are you man or devil, that you know what I have never breathed to you?"

"Thornhill is dead; but I can tell you more of other people. I can tell you that Johanna Oakley was faithful to you. I can tell you that she mourned your loss as you would wish her to mourn it, knowing how you would mourn hers. I can tell you that the gentleman's arm she was leaning upon was Thornhill's friend, and that the fact of her having to be supported by him at the unlucky moment when you saw this was solely owing to the deep grief she was plunged into upon your account."

"Oh no-no-no!"

"I say yes. It was so, Mr. Ingestrie; and if you had at that moment stepped forward, you would have saved yourself much misery, and you would have saved her such heart-breaking thoughts, and such danger, as it will frighten you to listen to."

Upon hearing all this, poor Mark Ingestrie turned very faint, and fell back in his chair, looking so pale and wan, that Sir Richard Blunt was compelled to go across the room to hold him up. After giving him a glass of wine, he recovered, and with a deep sigh, he said—

"And so I have wronged her after all! Oh, my Johanna, I am unworthy of you!"

"That," said Sir Richard, "is entirely a subject for the young lady's own consideration. N O W."

Mark Ingestrie looked curiously in the face of Sir Richard Blunt, as with marked emphasis upon each letter he said, "N O W." But he had not to wait long for an explanation of what it meant. A door at the back of the room was flung open, and Johanna sprang forward with a cry of joy. In another moment she was in the arms of Mark Ingestrie, and Sir Richard Blunt had left the room.

It would be quite impossible, if we had the will to attempt it, for us to go through the scene that took place between Johanna Oakley and Mark Ingestrie in the magistrate's parlour. For about half an hour they quite forgot where they were, or that there was anyone in the world but themselves. At the end of the period of time, though, Sir Richard Blunt gently walked into the room.

"Well," he said, "have you considerable understanding about that military man in the Temple-gardens?"

Johanna sprang towards the magistrate, and placing her arm upon his breast, she kissed him on the cheek.

"Sir," she said, "you are our very dear friend, and I love you as I love my father."

"God bless you!" said Sir Richard. "You have, by these few words, more than repaid me for all that I have done. Are you happy?"

"Very, very happy."

"So very happy, sir," said Ingestrie, as his eyes glistened through tears of joy, "that I can hardly believe in its reality."

"And yet you are both so poor."

"Ah, sir, what is poverty when we shall be together?"

"Well," said Sir Richard, as he opened his desk, "since you are not to be knocked down by poverty, what say you to riches? Do you know these, Mr. Ingestrie?"

"Why, that is my string of pearls."

"Yes. I took it from Todd's escritoire myself, and they are yours and Johanna's. Will you permit me always to call you Johanna?"

"Very well. This string of pearls, I have ascertained, is worth a sufficient sum to place you both very far above all the primary exigencies of life. It will be necessary to produce them at the trial of Sweeney Todd, but after that event they will he handed to you to do what you

268

please with them, when you can realise them at once, and be happy enough with the proceeds."

Our tale is now drawing to a close. Sweeney Todd suffered the extreme penalty of the law, which Mrs. Lovett avoided, by poisoning herself.

Mark Ingestrie and Johanna were united, and no one was more welcome at the wedding than Sir Richard Blunt and Colonel Jeffery.

The Banshee

Of all the superstitions prevalent amongst the natives of Ireland at any period, past or present, there is none so grand or fanciful, none which has been so universally assented to or so cordially cherished, as the belief in the existence of the banshee. There are very few, however remotely acquainted with Irish life or Irish history, but must have heard or read of the Irish banshee; still, as there are different stories and different opinions afloat respecting this strange being, I think a little explanation concerning her appearance, functions, and habits will not be unacceptable to my readers.

The banshee, then, is said to be an immaterial and immortal being, attached, time out of mind, to various respectable and ancient families in Ireland, and is said always to appear to announce, by cries and lamentations, the death of any member of that family to which she belongs. She always comes at night, a short time previous to the death of the fated one, and takes her stand outside, convenient to the house, and there utters the most plaintive cries and lamentations, generally in some unknown language, and in a tone of voice resembling a human female. She continues her visits night after night, unless vexed or annoyed, until the mourned object dies, and sometimes she is said to continue about the house for several nights after.

Sometimes she is said to appear in the shape of a most beautiful young damsel, and dressed in the most elegant and fantastic garments; but her general appearance is in the likeness of a very old woman, of small stature and bending and decrepit form, enveloped in a winding-sheet or grave-dress, and her long, white, hoary hair waving over her shoulders and descending to her feet. At other times she is dressed in the costume of the middle ages—the different articles of her clothing being of the richest material and of a sable hue. She is very shy and easily irritated, and, when once annoyed or vexed, she flies away, and never returns during the same generation. When the death of the person whom she mourns is contingent, or to occur by unforeseen accident, she is particularly agitated and troubled in her appearance, and unusually loud and mournful in her lamentations. Some would fain have it that this strange being is actuated by a feeling quite inimical to the interests of the family which she haunts, and that she comes with joy and triumph to announce their misfortunes.

This opinion, however, is rejected by most people, who imagine her their most devoted friend, and that she was, at some remote period, a member of the family, and once existed on the earth in life and loveliness. It is not every Irish family can claim the honour of an attendant banshee; they must be respectably descended, and of ancient line, to have any just pretensions to a warning spirit. However, she does not appear to be influenced by the difference of creed or clime, provided there be no other impediment, as several Protestant families of Norman and Anglo-Saxon origin boast of their own banshee; and to this hour several noble and distinguished families in the country feel proud of the surveillance of that mysterious being. Neither is she influenced by the circumstances of rank or fortune, as she is oftener found frequenting the cabin of the peasant than the baronial mansion of the lord of thousands. Even the humble family to which the writer of this tale belongs has long claimed the honourable appendage of a banshee; and it may, perhaps, excite an additional interest in my readers when I inform them that my present story is associated with her last visit to that family.

Some years ago there dwelt in the vicinity of Mountrath, in the Queen's County, a farmer, whose name for obvious reasons we shall not at present disclose. He never was married, and his only domestics were a servant-boy and an old woman, a housekeeper, who had long been a follower or dependent of the family. He was born and educated in the Roman Catholic Church, but on arriving at manhood, for reasons best known to himself, he abjured the tenets of that creed and conformed to the doctrines of Protestantism. However, in after years he seemed to waver, and refused going to church, and by his manner of living seemed to favour the dogmas of infidelity or atheism. He was rather dark and reserved in his manner, and oftentimes sullen and gloomy in his temper; and this, joined with his well-known disregard of religion, served to render him somewhat unpopular amongst his neighbours and acquaintances.

However, he was in general respected, and was never insulted or annoyed. He was considered as an honest, inoffensive man, and as he was well supplied with firearms and ammunition,—in the use of which he was well practised, having, in his early days, served several years in a yeomanry corps,—few liked to disturb him, even had they been so disposed. He was well educated, and decidedly hostile to every species of superstition, and was constantly jeering his old housekeeper, who was extremely superstitious, and pretended to be entirely conversant with every matter connected with witchcraft and the fairy world. He seldom darkened a neighbour's door, and scarcely ever asked any one to enter his, but generally spent his leisure hours in reading, of which he was extremely fond, or in furbishing his firearms, to which he was still more attached, or in listening to and laughing at the wild and bloodcurdling stories of old Moya, with which her memory abounded.

Thus he spent his time until the period at which our tale commences, when he was about fifty years of age, and old Moya, the housekeeper, had become extremely feeble, stooped, and of very ugly and forbidding exterior. One morning in the month of November, *a.d.* 1818, this man arose before daylight, and on coming out of the apartment where he slept he was surprised at finding old Moya in the kitchen, sitting over the raked-up fire, and smoking her tobacco-pipe in a very serious and meditative mood.

"Arrah, Moya," said he, "what brings you out of your bed so early?"

"Och musha, I dunna," replied the old woman; "I was so uneasy all night that I could not sleep a wink, and I got up to smoke a blast, thinkin' that it might drive away the weight that's on my heart."

"And what ails you, Moya? Are you sick, or what came over you?"

"No, the Lord be praised! I am not sick, but my heart is sore, and there's a load on my spirits that would kill a hundred."

"Maybe you were dreaming, or something that way," said the man, in a bantering tone, and suspecting, from the old woman's grave manner, that she was labouring under some mental delusion.

"Dreaming!" re-echoed Moya, with a bitter sneer; "ay, dreaming. Och, I wish to God I was *only dreaming*; but I am very much afraid it is worse than that, and that there is trouble and misfortune hanging over uz."

"And what makes you think so, Moya?" asked he, with a half-suppressed smile.

Moya, aware of his well-known hostility to every species of superstition, remained silent, biting her lips and shaking her gray head prophetically.

"Why don't you answer me, Moya?" again asked the man.

"Och," said Moya, "I am heart-scalded to have it to tell you, and I know you will laugh at me; but, say what you will, there is something bad over uz, for the banshee was about the house all night, and she has me almost frightened out of my wits with her shouting and bawling."

The man was aware of the banshee's having been long supposed to haunt his family, but often scouted that supposition; yet, as it was some years since he had last heard of her visiting the place, he was not prepared for the freezing announcement of old Moya. He turned as pale as a corpse, and trembled excessively; at last, recollecting himself, he said, with a forced smile:

"And how do you know it was the banshee, Moya?"

"How do I know?" reiterated Moya, tauntingly. "Didn't I see and hear her several times during the night? and more than that, didn't I hear the dead-coach rattling round the house, and through the yard, every night at midnight this week back, as if it would tear the house out of the foundation?"

The man smiled faintly; he was frightened, yet was ashamed to appear so. He again said:

"And did you ever see the banshee before, Moya?"

"Yes," replied Moya, "often. Didn't I see her when your mother died? Didn't I see her when your brother was drowned? and sure, there wasn't one of the family that went these sixty years that I did not both see and hear her."

"And where did you see her, and what way did she look tonight?"

"I saw her at the little window over my bed; a kind of reddish light shone round the house; I looked up, and there I saw her old, pale face and glassy eyes looking in, and she rocking herself to and fro, and clapping her little, withered hands, and crying as if her very heart would break."

"Well, Moya, it's all imagination; go, now, and prepare my breakfast, as I want to go to Maryborough today, and I must be home early."

Moya trembled; she looked at him imploringly and said: "For Heaven's sake, John, don't go today; stay till some other day, and God bless you; for if you go today I would give my oath there will something cross you that's bad."

"Nonsense, woman!" said he; "make haste and get me my breakfast."

Moya, with tears in her eyes, set about getting the breakfast ready; and whilst she was so employed John was engaged in making preparations for his journey.

Having now completed his other arrangements, he sat down to breakfast, and, having concluded it, he arose to depart.

Moya ran to the door, crying loudly; she flung herself on her knees, and said: "John, John, be advised. Don't go today; take my advice; I know more of the world than you do, and I see plainly that if you go you will never enter this door again with your life."

Ashamed to be influenced by the drivellings of an old *cullough*, he pushed her away with his hand, and, going out to the stable, mounted his horse and departed. Moya followed him with her eyes whilst in sight; and when she could no longer see him, she sat down at the fire and wept bitterly.

It was a bitter cold day, and the farmer, having finished his business in town, feeling himself chilly, went into a public-house to have a tumbler of punch and feed his horse; there he met an old friend, who would not part with him until he would have another glass with him and a little conversation, as it was many years since they had met before. One glass brought another, and it was almost duskish ere John thought of returning, and, having nearly ten miles to travel, it would be dark night before he could get home.

Still his friend would not permit him to go, but called for more liquor, and it was far advanced in the night before they parted. John, however, had a good horse, and, having had him well fed, he did not spare whip or spur, but dashed along at a rapid pace through the gloom and silence of the winter's night, and had already distanced the town upward of five miles, when, on arriving at a very desolate part of the road, a gunshot, fired from behind the bushes, put an end to his mortal existence. Two strange men, who had been at the same public-house in Maryborough drinking, observing that he had money and learning the road that he was to travel, conspired to rob and murder him, and waylaid him in this lonely spot for that horrid purpose.

Poor Moya did not go to bed that night, but sat at the fire, every moment impatiently expecting his return. Often did she listen at the door to try if she could hear the tramp of the horse's footsteps approaching. But in vain; no sound met her ear except the sad wail of the night wind, moaning fitfully through the tall bushes which surrounded the ancient dwelling, or the sullen roar of a little dark river, which wound its way through the lowlands at a small distance from where she stood. Tired with watching, at length she fell asleep on the hearth-stone; but that sleep was disturbed and broken, and frightful and appalling dreams incessantly haunted her imagination.

At length the darksome morning appeared struggling through the wintry clouds, and Moya again opened the door to look out. But what was her dismay when she found the horse standing at the stable door without his rider, and the saddle all besmeared with clotted blood. She raised the death-cry; the neighbours thronged round, and it was at once declared that the hapless man was robbed and murdered. A party on horseback immediately set forward to seek him, and on arriving at the fatal spot he was found stretched on his back in the ditch, his head perforated with shot and slugs, and his body literally immersed in a pool of blood.

On examining him it was found that his money was gone, and a valuable gold watch and appendages abstracted from his pocket. His remains were conveyed home, and, after having been waked the customary time, were committed to the grave of his ancestors in the little green churchyard of the village.

Having no legitimate children, the nearest heir to his property was a brother, a cabinet-maker, who resided in London. A letter was accordingly despatched to the brother announcing the sad catastrophe, and calling on him to come and take possession of the property; and two men were appointed to guard the place until he should arrive.

The two men delegated to act as guardians, or, as they are technically termed, "keepers," were old friends and comrades of the deceased, and had served with him in the same yeomanry corps. Jack O'Malley was a Roman Catholic—a square, stout-built, and handsome fellow, with a pleasant word for every one, and full of that gaiety, vivacity, and nonchalance for which the Roman Catholic peasantry of Ireland are so particularly distinguished. He was now about forty-five years of age, sternly attached to the dogmas of his religion, and always remarkable for his revolutionary and anti-British principles. He was brave as a lion, and never quailed before a man; but, though caring so little for a *living* man, he was extremely afraid of a *dead* one, and would go ten miles out of his road at night to avoid passing a "rath," or "haunted bush."

Harry Taylor, on the other hand, was a staunch Protestant; a tall, genteel-looking man, of proud and imperious aspect, and full of reserve and hauteur—the natural consequence of a consciousness of political and religious ascendency and superiority of intelligence and education, which so conspicuously marked the demeanour of the Protestant peasantry of those days. Harry, too, loved his glass as well as Jack, but was of a more peaceful disposition, and as he was well educated and intelligent, he was utterly opposed to superstition, and laughed to scorn the mere idea of ghosts, goblins, and fairies. Thus Jack and Harry were diametrically opposed to each other in every point except their love of the *cruiskeen*, yet they never failed to seize every opportunity of being together; and, although they often blackened each other's eyes in their political and religious disputes, yet their quarrels were always amicably settled, and they never found themselves happy but in each other's society.

It was now the sixth or seventh night that Jack and Harry, as usual, kept their lonely watch in the kitchen of the murdered man. A large turf fire blazed brightly on the hearth, and on a bed of straw in the ample chimney-corner was stretched old Moya in a profound sleep. On the hearthstone, between the two friends, stood a small oak table, on which was placed a large decanter of whisky, a jug of boiled water, and a bowl of sugar; and, as if to add an idea of security to that of comfort, on one end of the table were placed in saltier a formidable-looking blunderbuss and a brace of large brass pistols. Jack and his comrade perpetually renewed their acquaintance with the whisky-bottle, and laughed and chatted and recounted the adventures of their young days with as much hilarity as if the house which now witnessed their mirth never echoed to the cry of death or blood. In the course of conversation Jack mentioned the incident of the strange appearance of the banshee, and expressed a hope that she would not come that night to disturb their carouse.

"Banshee the devil!" shouted Harry; "how superstitious you papists are! I would like to see the phiz of any man, dead or alive, who dare make his appearance here tonight." And, seizing the blunderbuss, and looking wickedly at Jack, he vociferated, "By Hercules, I would drive the contents of this through their sowls who dare annoy us."

"Better for you to shoot your mother than fire at the banshee, anyhow," remarked Jack.

"Psha!" said Harry, looking contemptuously at his companion. "I would think no more of riddling the old jade's hide than I would of throwing off this tumbler;" and, to suit the action to the word, he drained off another bumper of whisky-punch.

"Jack," says Harry, "now that we are in such prime humour, will you give us a song?"

"With all the veins of my heart," says Jack. "What will it be?"

"Anything you please; your will must be my pleasure," answered Harry.

Jack, after coughing and clearing his pipes, chanted forth, in a bold and musical voice, a rude rigmarole called "The Royal Blackbird," which, although of no intrinsic merit, yet, as it expressed sentiments hostile to British connection and British Government and favourable to the house of Stewart, was very popular amongst the Catholic peasantry of Ireland, whilst, on the contrary, it was looked upon by the Protestants as highly offensive and disloyal. Harry, however, wished his companion too well to oppose the song, and he quietly awaited its conclusion.

"Bravo, Jack," said Harry, as soon as the song was ended; "that you may never lose your wind."

"In the king's name now I board you for another song," says Jack.

Harry, without hesitation, recognised his friend's right to demand a return, and he instantly trolled forth, in a deep, sweet, and sonorous voice, the following:

> Song.
> *Ho, boys, I have a song divine!*
> *Come, let us now in concert join,*
> *And toast the bonny banks of Boyne—*
> *The Boyne of 'Glorious Memory.'*
>
> *On Boyne's famed banks our fathers bled;*
> *Boyne's surges with their blood ran red;*
> *And from the Boyne our foemen fled—*
> *Intolerance, chains, and slavery.*
>
> *Dark superstition's blood-stained sons*
> *Pressed on, but 'crack' went William's guns,*
> *And soon the gloomy monster runs—*
> *Fell, hydra-headed bigotry.*
>
> *Then fill your glasses high and fair,*
> *Let shouts of triumph rend the air,*
> *Whilst Georgy fills the regal chair*
> *We'll never bow to Popery.*

Jack, whose countenance had, from the commencement of the song, indicated his aversion to the sentiments it expressed, now lost all patience at hearing his darling "Popery" impugned, and, seizing one of the pistols which lay on the table and whirling it over his comrade's head, swore vehemently that he would "fracture his skull if he did not instantly drop that blackguard Orange lampoon."

"Aisy, avhic," said Harry, quietly pushing away the upraised arm; "I did not oppose your bit of treason awhile ago, and besides, the latter end of my song is more calculated to please you than to irritate your feelings."

Jack seemed pacified, and Harry continued his strain.

And fill a bumper to the brim—
A flowing one—and drink to him
Who, let the world go sink or swim.
Would arm for Britain's liberty.

No matter what may be his hue.
Or black, or white, or green, or blue.
Or Papist, Paynim, or Hindoo.
We'll drink to him right cordially.

Jack was so pleased with the friendly turn which the latter part of Harry's song took that he joyfully stretched out his hand, and even joined in chorus to the concluding *stanza*.

The fire had now decayed on the hearth, the whisky-bottle was almost emptied, and the two sentinels, getting drowsy, put out the candle and laid down their heads to slumber. The song and the laugh and the jest were now hushed, and no sound was to be heard but the incessant "click, click," of the clock in the inner room and the deep, heavy breathing of old Moya in the chimney-corner.

They had slept they knew not how long when the old hag awakened with a wild shriek. She jumped out of bed, and crouched between the men; they started up, and asked her what had happened.

"Oh!" she exclaimed; "the banshee, the banshee! Lord have mercy on us! she is come again, and I never heard her so wild and outrageous before."

Jack O'Malley readily believed old Moya's tale; so did Harry, but he thought it might be some one who was committing some depredation on the premises. They both listened attentively, but could hear nothing; they opened the kitchen door, but all was still; they looked abroad; it was a fine, calm night, and myriads of twinkling stars were burning in the deep-blue heavens. They proceeded around the yard and hay-yard; but all was calm and lonely, and no sound saluted their ears but the shrill barking of some neighbouring cur, or the sluggish murmuring of the little tortuous river in the distance. Satisfied that "all was right," they again went in, replenished the expiring fire, and sat down to finish whatever still remained in the whisky-bottle.

They had not sat many minutes when a wild, unearthly cry was heard without.

"The banshee again," said Moya, faintly. Jack O'Malley's soul sank within him; Harry started up and seized the blunderbuss; Jack caught his arm. "No, no, Harry, you shall not; sit down; there's no fear— nothing will happen us."

Harry sat down, but still gripped the blunderbuss, and Jack lit his tobacco-pipe, whilst the old woman was on her knees, striking her breast, and repeating her prayers with great vehemence.

The sad cry was again heard, louder and fiercer than before. It now seemed to proceed from the window, and again it appeared as if issuing from the door. At times it would seem as if coming from afar, whilst again it would appear as if coming down the chimney or springing from the ground beneath their feet. Sometimes the cry resembled the low, plaintive wail of a female in distress, and in a moment it was raised to a prolonged yell, loud and furious, and as if coming from a thousand throats; now the sound resembled a low, melancholy chant, and then was quickly changed to a loud, broken, demoniac laugh. It continued thus, with little intermission, for about a quarter of an hour, when it died away, and was succeeded by a heavy, creaking sound, as if of some large waggon, amidst which the loud tramp of horses' footsteps might be distinguished, accompanied with a strong, rushing wind. This strange noise proceeded round and round the house two or three times, then went down the lane which led to the road, and was heard no more. Jack O'Malley stood aghast, and Harry Taylor, with all his philosophy and scepticism, was astonished and frightened.

"A dreadful night this, Moya," said Jack.

"Yes," said she, "that is the dead-coach; I often heard it before, and have sometimes seen it."

"Seen, did you say?" said Harry; "pray describe it."

"Why," replied the old crone, "it's like any other coach, but twice as big, and hung over with black cloth, and a black coffin on the top of it, and drawn by headless black horses."

"Heaven protect us!" ejaculated Jack.

"It is very strange," remarked Harry.

"But," continued Moya, "it always comes before the death of a person, and I wonder what brought it now, unless it came with the banshee."

"Maybe it's coming for you," said Harry, with an arch yet subdued smile.

"No, no," she said; "I am none of that family at all at all."

A solemn silence now ensued for a few minutes, and they thought all was vanished, when again the dreadful cry struck heavily on their ears.

"Open the door, Jack," said Harry, "and put out Hector."

Hector was a large and very ferocious mastiff belonging to Jack O'Malley, and always accompanied him wherever he went.

Jack opened the door and attempted to put out the dog, but the poor animal refused to go, and, as his master attempted to force him, howled in a loud and mournful tone.

"You must go," said Harry, and he caught him in his arms and flung him over the half-door. The poor dog was scarcely on the ground when he was whirled aloft into the air by some invisible power, and he fell again to earth lifeless, and the pavement was besmeared with his entrails and blood.

Harry now lost all patience, and again seizing his blunderbuss, he exclaimed: "Come, Jack, my boy, take your pistols and follow me; I have but one life to lose, and I will venture it to have a crack at this infernal demon."

"I will follow you to death's doors," said Jack; "but I would not fire at the banshee for a million of worlds."

Moya seized Harry by the skirts. "Don't go out," she cried; "let her alone while she lets you alone, for an hour's luck never shone on any one that ever molested the banshee."

"Psha, woman!" said Harry, and he pushed away poor Moya contemptuously.

The two men now sallied forth; the wild cry still continued, and it seemed to issue from amongst some stacks in the hay-yard behind the house. They went round and paused; again they heard the cry, and Harry elevated his blunderbuss.

"Don't fire," said Jack.

Harry replied not; he looked scornfully at Jack, then put his finger on the trigger, and—bang—away it exploded with a thundering sound. An extraordinary scream was now heard, ten times louder and more terrific than they heard before. Their hair stood erect on their heads, and huge, round drops of sweat ran down their faces in quick succession. A glare of reddish-blue light shone around the stacks; the rumbling of the dead-coach was again heard coming; it drove up to the house, drawn by six headless sable horses, and the figure of a withered old hag, encircled with blue flame, was seen running nimbly across the hay-yard. She entered the ominous carriage, and it drove away with a horrible sound. It swept through the tall bushes which surrounded the house; and as it disappeared the old hag cast a thrilling scowl at the two men, and waved her fleshless arms at them vengefully. It was soon lost to sight; but the unearthly creaking of the wheels, the tramping of the horses, and the appalling cries of the banshee continued to assail their ears for a considerable time after all had vanished.

The brave fellows now returned to the house; they again made fast the door, and reloaded their arms. Nothing, however, came to disturb them that night, nor from that time forward; and the arrival of the dead man's brother from London, in a few days after, relieved them from their irksome task.

Old Moya did not live long after; she declined from that remark-able night, and her remains were decently interred in the churchyard adjoining the last earthly tenement of the loved family to which she had been so long and so faithfully attached.

The insulted banshee has never since returned; and although sev-eral members of that family have since closed their mortal career, still the warning cry was never given; and it is supposed that the injured spirit will never visit her ancient haunts until every one of the existing generation shall have "slept with their fathers."

Jack O'Malley and his friend Harry lived some years after. Their friendship still continued undiminished; like "Tam O'Shanter" and "Souter Johnny," they still continued to love each other like "a very brither"; and like that jovial pair, also, our two comrades were often "fou for weeks thegither," and often over their cruiskeen would they laugh at their strange adventure with the banshee. It is now, however, all over with them too; their race is run, and they are now "tenants of the tomb."

The Dead Bride

The summer was superb. Never in the memory of man had there been so many people in Bad Nauheim, but though the public rooms were always full, nowhere was there any gaiety. The nobility kept apart, the military people mingled only with themselves, and the *bourgeoisie* despised both of them. Even the public balls did not break down the formality that was found everywhere this season. For the proprietor of the baths would always appear covered with ribbons and orders, and this splendour, joined to the coldness of the manner of the family of this great lord and the vast glitter of his lackeys, pompous in rich liveries, that followed him, forced the greater number of persons present to remain silently behind the restrictions fixed by the diversities of rank.

For these reasons public assemblies became gradually less numerous. Individual circles were, however, formed who tried to create the genial spirit of friendship that was so lacking in the formal gatherings.

One of these societies assembled about twice a week in one of the great assembly rooms which were at this epoch generally empty. There an agreeable meal was served and afterwards the company enjoyed— sometimes in the room, sometimes in promenading in the gardens outside—the charm of a decent and unrestrained conversation. The members of these parties knew each other, at least by name, but a certain Italian *marquis* who had joined these meetings, was unknown to them and even to everyone who found themselves at the Baths. This title of "Italian Marquis" seemed very singular when it was discovered that his name on the general list of visitors to Bad Nauheim appeared to belong to the North and consisted of such a large number of consonants that no one could pronounce it without difficulty.

His physiognomy and his manners offered plenty of peculiarities; his long pale face, his black eyes, his imperious glance had something so little attractive that everyone had certainly avoided him if he had not always had ready a good number of stories which proved a marvellous resource for the company in moments of weariness.

The only objection to his tales was that usually they exacted, at least, a little too much credulity on the part of his listeners. But, where so much was formal and constrained, where the social side of the season seemed to be so definite a failure and where boredom, weariness, and a certain menace seemed to hang in the air throughout the languid days, the society of the mysterious and complaisant foreigner was vaguely sought for the diversion that it brought.

The company rose from table; no one felt disposed to gaiety. Everyone was too fatigued from the ball of the preceding night to enjoy the pleasure of walking in the gardens although a beautiful moonlight invited them. No one had even the strength to sustain the conversation, and it was nothing surprising therefore if all, in consequence, wished more eagerly than usual for the presence of the *marquis*.

"Where can he be?" cried the countess in a tone of impatience.

"Certainly still at *faro*, putting the bankers to despair," replied Florence. "He caused the sudden departure of two of these gentlemen this morning."

"A very light loss," replied someone.

"For us," responded Florence, "but not for the proprietor of the Baths who has only forbidden gaming here that everyone may take to it more furiously."

"It would be better for the *marquis* to abstain from such feats," whispered the *chevalier* with a mysterious air, "the gamesters are revengeful and have generally secret means whereby to avenge themselves, and if the whisper going round is true that the *marquis* is himself implicated in politics and in a very dubious manner."

"But," interrupted the countess, "what did the *marquis* do to the bankers?"

"Nothing! He wagered simply on those cards which always won, and what is singular, he staked very little on the numbers which he chose. The other players took, however, advantage of his good fortune and placed such huge sums on the lucky numbers that he selected that the bank was broken."

The countess was about to put some other questions when the entry of the *marquis* forced the conversation to take another turn.

"Here he is at last!" cried several people at once.

"Today," said the countess, "we have most eagerly desired your appearance and it is just today that you make us wait for it the long-est!"

"Madam," replied the *marquis*, immediately, "I have been thinking out an important combination and it has been a perfect success. I hope tomorrow there will not be here a single bank. I am going from one gaming-hall to another and there will not be enough post horses to take away the ruined bankers."

"Why don't you teach us," asked the countess, "your marvellous art of always winning?"

"It would be very difficult, my fair lady; for that one must have a lucky hand—otherwise one can do nothing!"

"But," took up the *chevalier*, laughing, "never have I seen a hand as lucky as yours!"

"As you are still young, my dear *chevalier*, plenty of new things may come your way." Saying these words the *marquis* threw on the *chevalier* a glance so piercing that that young man cried lightly:

"Would you then, like to cast my horoscope?"

"We will not have that today," protested the *countess*, languidly, "for who knows if your future destiny will secure us such an amusing story as the *marquis* has promised us since two days ago?"

"I did not precisely say amusing," smiled the *marquis*.

"But at least full of extraordinary events," insisted the countess again. "We must have something of the kind to arouse us from the lethargy that overcomes us today."

"Very willingly, but I would know beforehand if any of you are already aware of the surprising things that are told of 'The Dead Bride'?"

But this name seemed to mean nothing to anyone in the company. The *marquis* hesitated as if he would make yet further preamble to his story. The countess and some of her friends, however, showed so openly their impatience that at last with a shrug he commenced his story in these words:

"Some time ago I decided to visit the Count Globoda in his es-tate in Bohemia. We had often met in several parts of Europe when the lightness of youth led us to pleasure, then again when the years had rendered us more calm and grave. At last, well advanced in age, we ardently desired, before the end of our days, to enjoy again by the charm of memory the agreeable moments we had passed together. I wished, on my side, to see the *château* of my friend. It was, according to the description that he had made me, in a very romantic valley. His ancestors had constructed it centuries ago, and their descendants had kept it up with such care that it conserved its imposing aspect and at the same time offered a most commodious dwelling.

"The count ordinarily passed the greatest part of the year there with his family and only returned to the capital with the approach of winter.

"Aware of all these details, I did not announce my visit, and arrived one evening of the present season. I admired the smiling and varied country that was the *château's* domain. The friendly reception that was given me could not entirely conceal from me the secret sorrow painted on the countenance of the count, that of his wife, and of their daughter, the beautiful Libussa. I was not slow to learn that all were still afflicted by the memory of the loss of the twin sister of Libussa whom death had taken from her family a year before. Libussa and Hildegard so much resembled each other that one could only distinguish them by a little sign in the form of a strawberry placed on the neck of Hildegard.

"They had left the chamber of the dead girl and all that was in it in the same state as it was during her life and the family would go and sit there when they wished to taste fully the sad satisfaction of regretting the cherished daughter who had had only one heart, one soul with her sister. So strong had been the affinity between the two girls that the parents could not believe that their separation would last for long; they feared that soon Libussa would follow her sister to the tomb.

"I did all I could to distract them from this deep sorrow, from this creeping shade of another sorrow, and, in going over the laughing scenes of our past life and turning their ideas on subjects less sad than those that occupied them, I saw with some satisfaction that my efforts were not entirely useless.

"Sometimes we promenaded in the neighbouring valley among all the delights of summer. Sometimes we went through the various apartments of the vast *château* of which the perfect preservation excited our astonishment and there we dwelt on the actions of the past generations whose portraits adorned many a long gallery.

"One evening the count spoke to me in confidence of his projects for the future. Among others he told me how often he had wished that Libussa, who had already refused several marriages, although she was only sixteen years old, would make a suitable and happy union. While we were thus discoursing a gardener suddenly entered the chamber, open on the terrace, where we sat, and brokenly stammered out that someone had seen a phantom wandering in the grounds. It was believed to be that of the ancient chaplain of the *château* who had last appeared a hundred years before. Several servants followed the gardener, the pallor of their faces confirming the terrible news that this last had brought.

"The count laughed at their rustic fears: 'You seem to be very frightened by your shade,' he said, and he sent them away, telling them not to come again with such stupid stories. 'It is really disappointing,' he observed to me as they departed, rebuked but whispering among themselves, 'to see how far the superstition of these people goes, and that it is impossible to disabuse them entirely of the effect of these old stories. From century to century has passed this absurd tale that from time to time an ancient chaplain of the *château* wanders in the neighbourhood and even says mass in the old church, and other stupidities of that sort! But these gross legends had, I thought, faded away since I possessed the *château*, but from what I hear now, they have not entirely disappeared.'

"He had hardly ceased speaking and with, I thought, more trouble than his words would have me believe he possessed, than the *major-domo* entered and announced with some agitation that a young gentleman with a splendid equipage had arrived unexpectedly before the *château*. The count was not expecting a visitor, and with some surprise inquired the name of the newcomer. It was given as that of the Duca dei Foscarini, head of the famous Venetian patrician House of that name. I had met him in his native city a few months previously and I said so to the count, but I did not add that I had been present at the betrothal of the young Venetian.

"Without waiting for the return of the *major-domo* with formal permission for him to enter the *château*, the young duke had run up the steps and came eagerly into our apartment, the doors and windows of which stood wide to catch the evening air. I was delighted to see him, for he had been one of my favourite companions in his delightful city of pleasure, but, on beholding me he started back and seemed disturbed. Our meeting passed off, however, with the usual formalities of politeness. The count received his young guest with respect. They had many common friends, and though the visit of the Venetian to this *château* in Bohemia was to be wondered at, it could not be taken as less than an honour.

"When he had thus, as it were, presented himself to his host the young duke turned to me and with his natural easiness which went even beyond the breeding of his rank, said: 'Ah, my dear *marquis*, now I find you here I can understand how it is that in this valley so distant from my own home there is someone who knows my name.'

"I asked him to explain these incomprehensible words, and he replied with a smile that strove to conceal, I thought, a faint distress: 'As I was driving underneath the mountain which guards the opening to this valley, I looked from the window of the coach to catch a little fresh air and I heard my name pronounced distinctly three times in a loud, strong voice, which afterwards added that I was welcome. I understand now that you must have been riding in the neighbourhood and recognised me. I feel ashamed of the tremor that possessed me when I heard those tones in that lonely spot.'

"The count and I exchanged glances. The story appeared to us so strange that we thought the young man was embarking on an elaborate jest. I believed his character to be light and wild and I thought his sudden appearance in this lonely valley in Bohemia most extraordinary so I replied with some severity: 'Until I heard the *major-domo* announce you I was absolutely ignorant of your arrival in this part of the world. Nor could any of my people have recognized you, for those whom I had with me in Italy are not with me here. Besides,' said I, 'it would be very difficult for one wandering on the mountainside to recognise from any distance even the best-known equipage.'

"The trouble of the young duke at this was evident. 'In that case,' he muttered, 'in that case—'and seemed unable to finish his sentence. To help the situation the incredulous count said, very politely, that the voice which had declared the duke to be welcome, whatever it was, had at least expressed the sentiments of all the family.

"Foscarini, without telling his host the motive of his visit, drew me apart and confided to me with much agitation that he had come in person to obtain the hand of the beautiful Libussa if he could receive her liking and the consent of her father.

"'The Countess Apollonia, your betrothed, is she then, dead?' I asked of him.

"'We will talk of that another time,' he replied, and these words were accompanied with such a sign and such a look, at once downcast and furious, that I concluded that Apollonia had been found guilty of unfaithfulness or some grave offence and that for that reason her betrothal with the duke had been broken off. I therefore abstained from any further questions which might pain one who already seemed so deeply troubled. However, as he turned to me, and with, as I thought, unbalanced passion, begged me to be his spokesman and mediator to the count to accord him at once the object of his wishes I took it upon me to represent to him in heavy fashion the danger of contracting another alliance for the sake of effacing the bitter souvenir of a loved and lost person and one without doubt once cherished tenderly.

"He interrupted impatiently and declared that it was far from him to be thinking of Libussa as a mere means of salving the wounds inflicted by another and that he would be the happiest of men if she would listen to his vows. He spoke with a gravity and earnestness that did something to allay the disquietude I felt. I promised to prepare the Count Globoda for his proposal and to give him all necessary information as to the family and the fortune of Foscarini. But, I assured the duke at the same time, that I should not take too much trouble in the affair, as I was not used to mingle with anything of such a dubious issue as a marriage. The duke expressed his satisfaction and exacted from me what then did not appear to me of any consequence—a promise not to mention his former engagement because that would mean disagreeable explanations.

"The consent of the count to the suit of this unexpected pretender to the hand of Libussa was obtained with a swiftness that exceeded the young duke's hopes. Have I told you that he was remarkably attractive in his person? There are perhaps some of you here who remember him? His shape was extremely good and he carried himself with great elegance, all his appointments were rich, but there was no vulgarity about the stately evidences of his wealth and birth. In short, all about him was well calculated to express with the greatest effect the ardour that he undoubtedly felt for Libussa and to move her heart. His courtesy and animation pleased the countess and his expert knowledge of how to manage a country estate, of which he gave abundant evidence, pleased the count, who thought that he would find in him a son-in-law who would continue the care that had always been given to his domain.

"Although, however, I saw the young Foscarini press his advantages with much zeal, I was surprised one evening when I received the news of his betrothal for I had not believed this would take place so soon. While we were at supper on that occasion there arose, I know not from whom, a chance remark as to the betrothal of a Foscarini the year previously in Venice and the countess asked if that Foscarini had been any relation of the young duke who had been betrothed that day to her daughter?

288

"'Near enough,' replied I, remembering my promise, while Foscarini regarded me with an embarrassed air. In order to change the disconcerting subject I said: 'But, my dear duke, who was the person who fixed your attentions on the beautiful Libussa? Was it a portrait that you say, or did some vivid description cause you to suppose that in this far-distant castle you would find the beauty the choice of which would do such honour to your taste?'

"All were listening to me with attention, for from the first the family had been surprised, though they had not cared to show this astonishment, at the sudden appearance of the young Venetian in the castle. All waited with considerable interest for his answer and their attention was heightened by his obvious hesitation. To satisfy my own curiosity, and, I confess, with a touch of malice, I insisted: 'If I do not deceive myself, you mentioned the other day in Venice that you intended to travel in Europe for six months, when all at once, I believe you were in Paris, you changed your plans and travelled suddenly and directly into Bohemia especially and entirely to see the charming Libussa.'

"'Yes, yes, your reason,' said the countess softly. Pray tell us, Donato. I think,' she added, 'that you owe it to Libussa to prove to her that she has not been merely the object of your caprice.'

"The duke glanced across the table at his *fiancée*, who sat beside her father. The look, I thought, was one of appeal and loving reproach, which I could not quite understand. He glanced at me, raised his shoulders, and with a sigh gave us this relation.

"'It was in Paris, as I told you. I was admiring the treasures of the Louvre Gallery of pictures. I had hardly entered when my eyes, however, left the beauties depicted on the walls and were irresistibly attracted to the sole occupant, save myself, of the vast chamber—a lady, with unutterably lovely features which were veiled by a melancholy air. I ventured, though fearfully, to approach her, and to follow her quite close without daring to address a word to her. I even followed her when she quitted the gallery and I drew her domestic apart—she was followed by one servant—and asked the name of his mistress. He gave it me and as I at once expressed the desire to make the acquaintance of the father of this beauty, he added that that would be difficult if I remained in Paris for the family had the intention to leave that city, and even France. "I will find an occasion," I murmured, and tried to read in the eyes of the lady whether my acquaintanceship would be welcome or no. She, however, probably believing that her domestic was still following her continued to walk away and soon, through a turn in the gallery, I had lost sight of her. While I had been trying to find her I had also lost all trace of the servant.'

"There was a slight pause after the duke had finished his speech. He had said what no one expected to hear. He continued to gaze at Libussa with that glance of tender rebuke. It was she who broke the rather uneasy silence.

"'Who was this beautiful lady?' she demanded in an astonished tone.

"With a startled accent, the duke exclaimed: 'What! is it possible that you did not see me in the gallery?'

"'I! See you! In Paris!' exclaimed the girl, and at the same time the count ejaculated: 'Libussa! In Paris!'

"'Yes! You, yourself, *mademoiselle*,' smiled the duke, a little piqued by what he regarded as an excess of *coquetry*. 'The servant whom for my good fortune you left in Paris and whom the same evening I met by an odd chance in the street, proved my good angel. He told me your father's name and where I might find you, and, as you know, I left immediately for Bohemia.'

"'What a fable,' said the count to his daughter. 'Libussa,' he added in turning towards me, 'has never left her own country and I myself have not been to Paris for seventeen years.'

"The duke stared at the count and his daughter with eyes full of the same surprise with which they regarded him. The conversation had fallen into a heavy silence, if I had not taken some pains to change the subject and to keep with difficulty a casual topic in play until the end of the repast. No sooner had we risen from table than the count led the duke into the embrasure of a window; I contrived to stand a few paces apart and appear to be absorbed in admiring a new lustre of an uncommon and intricate design which had been placed upon the mantelshelf. All the while, however, I was overhearing the whispered conversation between the count and his future son-in-law.

"The elder man began in a tone at once angry and serious.

"'What motive could you have had,' he demanded, 'to invent that singular scene of the picture gallery in the French museum, for, believe me, it will serve you no good turn. For myself I cannot see why you should not have declared in all simplicity the reason which brought you here to demand my daughter's hand in marriage. But, even if you had had any repugnance to make such a truthful statement there are a thousand forms you could have given your reply without being reduced to invent such a stupid fable.'

"'*M. le Comte*,' replied the duke, highly offended, 'at table I was silent because I was forced to believe that you had your reasons for keeping secret the presence of your daughter in Paris. I was mute simply from discretion but the strength of your reproaches forces me to hold to what I have already said, and despite your reluctance to believe what I say, to maintain before everyone that the capital of France is the place where I had seen, for the first time, your daughter Libussa.'

"'But, if I prove to you not only by the testimony of my people and servants but also by that of all my vassals that my daughter has never left her native country nor this castle?'

"'I shall still believe in the witness of my eyes and my ears on which, pardon me, I am obliged to rely more than on any evidence that you may bring forward.'

"Upon this serious declaration the anger of the count sank a little.

"'What you say is really extraordinary,' he replied in a calmer tone. 'Your serious air persuades me that you have been duped by an illusion and that you have seen another person whom you have taken for my daughter. Excuse me for having taken the thing a little warmly.'

"'Another person! I must then not only have taken another person for your daughter, but also the servant of whom I spoke to you and who gave me so precise a description of this castle is, according to what you say, also another person.'

"'My dear Foscarini, this servant was some rascal who knew the *château* and who, God knows for what motive, spoke to you like that and described as my daughter a lady who resembled her.'

"'I certainly don't wish to contradict you for the pleasure of doing so,' replied the duke, 'but how do you explain that your daughter had exactly all the features which, after the meeting at Paris, my imagination has preserved with the most scrupulous fidelity?'

"The count shook his head and gave an uneasy gesture with his hands, and the young Venetian continued:

"'There is more, but pardon me if I find myself in the necessity of mentioning a detail that, had we not come to this pass, would never have passed my lips. When I was following the lady down the empty gallery the *fichu* that was covering her neck was a little disarranged and I could see distinctly a little mole in the form and colour of a wild strawberry.'

"At these words the count's uneasiness greatly increased. A light pallor overspread his face.

291

"'That's a curious thing,' he muttered, 'that's a strange thing; it seems that you're going to try and make me believe a very odd story.'

"The young duke insisted with vivacity:

"'I have only one request to make: this little mole, is it found on the neck of Libussa?'

"'No, *monsieur*,' replied the count, fixedly regarding Foscarini.

"'No!' echoed the young duke, with the greatest possible surprise.

"'No, I tell you,' repeated the count. 'The twin sister of Libussa who singularly resembled her had the sign of which you speak, and has, more than a year ago, taken it with her to the tomb.'

"'But, it is only a few months,' exclaimed the young man in the most poignant accents, 'since I have seen her in Paris.'

"At this moment the countess and Libussa who had held themselves apart a prey to grave anxiety and knew not what to think of this whispered conversation in the window-place of which the subject appeared so important, approached with a timid and anxious air. But the count with an imperious gesture caused them to retire, then he led the duke into the furthest part of the deep window embrasure. They continued their conversation in voices so low that I could hear nothing more.

"I was extremely surprised when that same night the count gave the order to open, in his presence, the coffin of Hildegard. First he had given me briefly an account of the affair and asked me to assist the duke and himself at the opening of the coffin. The young Venetian declared his repugnance at being present at this ceremony the sole thought of which, he said, made him shudder with fright and he added that he had never been able to surmount, especially at night-time, his horror of the lugubrious and the dreadful. The count begged him to speak to no one of the scene in the gallery in Paris, and, above all to spare the extreme sensibility of his *fiancée* the recital of the secret conversation which they had had together in the window-place even if she begged him to inform her of what had taken place between her father and himself.

"The young Venetian made this promise, but nothing could persuade him to be present at the opening of Hildegard's coffin.

"It was the count and I, therefore, who alone entered the chapel attached to the *château* in the middle of that night. The sacristan awaited us with a lantern amid the shadows of the porch. The moon had set, it was a dark night, and vaporous clouds hid the stars.

"As we proceeded through the silent church, where the sacristan's lantern seemed only sufficient to reveal the shadows, I perceived that my friend was much moved.

"'Is it possible,' he muttered, 'that she was not really dead, that some ruffian came to rob the tomb and found in her some signs of life? I am a lunatic to suppose it, and if it had been so, would she not return to her parents instead of escaping to some distant country? Yet he spoke with such a sincerity and air of truth I must see with my own eyes that my Hildegard rests peacefully in her coffin; that alone will convince me.' With these last words his voice rose in a tone so dismal and so strong that the sacristan turned his head. Startled by this movement the count dropped his voice and clutching my arm added in a feverish whisper: 'Can I think that there will exist the least trace of the features of my daughter and that corruption will have spared her beauty? Let us return, *marquis*, our investigation will be futile, nothing but a few bones will meet our gaze and how can I tell that they are not those of a stranger?'

"He was about to give the order not to open the vault where we had then arrived and I admitted that in his position I should have been inclined to a similar resolution but, the first step being taken it was better to go on to the end and to see if the corpse of Hildegard and the rich jewels that had been buried with her were undisturbed. I added that it was quite possible that death had not entirely destroyed her features. The count pressed my hand convulsively and admitted the reason of my argument, and we followed the sacristan who, selecting a large key from his girdle, opened the iron door of the vault. His pallor and the shaking of his limbs showed that he was not used to this manner of expedition.

"I do not know"—the *marquis* glanced round with a dry smile—"if any member of the company has ever found themselves at midnight in a lonely chapel passing into a vault to examine the leaden coffins which hold the mortal remains of an illustrious House. It is certain that in such a moment the noise of the keys in the locks produces an extraordinary impression and one shudders lest the door should swing on its hinges and close one in, and one hesitates a moment before gazing at the contents of the coffin when the lid is finally lifted.

"On this occasion I saw that the count was more affected than myself with these superstitious terrors. A stifled sigh broke from him and the sweat pearled on his forehead as he did violence to his feelings but I observed that he dare not glance on any other coffin than that of his daughter. This he opened himself.

"'Did I not say that she would be untouched!' I cried, in peeping over his shoulder and seeing that the features of the corpse had still a perfect resemblance to those of Libussa.

"The dead girl lay, indeed, as if she were asleep, her fair tresses carefully raised on a white satin pillow, the jewels, lovingly disposed by the tender hands of her mother, sparkling on her arms and bosom and among the folds of her pale gown, where they were mingled with sprigs of bay, rosemary and other aromatic herbs.

"The count stared at his daughter transfixed with astonishment and I was obliged to hold him back for he wished to imprint a kiss on the forehead of this lovely corpse.

"'Do not trouble the peace of one who reposes so sweetly,' I said, and I used every effort to withdraw the count as soon as possible from this sad dwelling of the dead.

"Upon our return to the castle we found everyone in a state of restless excitement. The two ladies had tormented the duke to tell them what had passed and declared that they did not admit as a reasonable excuse his promise of silence. The young man was vexed and uneasy and glad to escape, upon our return, to his own chamber.

"The countess and Libussa then pleaded with us to tell them the secret which had so suddenly distracted the peaceful household, but all their appeals were in vain. They succeeded better on the next day with the sacristan whom they went to see secretly and he told them all he knew. But this small amount of knowledge only excited in a more lively fashion their desire to learn the conversation which had occasioned this nocturnal visit to the vaults.

"As to myself, I spent the rest of the night turning over in mind possible explanations for the figure which Foscarini had seen in Paris. The conclusion I came to I knew I could never relate to the count for he was one who absolutely refused to admit the relations of another world with our own.

"Under these circumstances I was glad to see that as the days passed the singular circumstances were, if not entirely forgotten, only referred to rarely and very lightly. The ladies were satisfied, or affected to be so, that there had been a mistake on the young Venetian's part and that he had taken another lady for Libussa. The count was also prepared to pass over in silence an extraordinary circumstance that he could not explain.

"There was, besides, another matter which continued to give me a good deal of anxiety. This was the persistent refusal of the duke to explain privately with me the betrothal that he had contracted previously in Venice. I no longer believed that the beautiful Apollonia had been in fault; I spoke of her beauty, her good qualities and the sumptuous feast which had celebrated her betrothal to Foscarini and I observed that when I spoke so he showed a lively embarrassment. This and other details forced me to conclude that the fidelity of the young Venetian for Apollonia had been broken in the picture gallery at the view of the beautiful unknown, and that Apollonia had been abandoned because of the sudden and almost lunatic infatuation which her betrothed had felt for the stranger, and this when she had believed him to be incapable of breaking an alliance solemnly concluded.

"I thought from this that the charming Libussa was not likely to find much happiness in her union with Foscarini, seeing he was a man who had abandoned on a mere caprice a woman to whom he had been solemnly betrothed, and, as the day of the marriage approached, I resolved to unmask the perfidious lover and to make him repent his infidelity.

"One day I had an excellent chance of arriving at my end. Supper finished, we were all at table; from casual conversation we grew on to the subject of whether iniquity generally finds its punishment in this world. I observed quietly that I had seen some striking examples of this truth. Libussa and her mother then pressed me to give one.

"'In this case, ladies,' I replied, 'permit me to tell you a story which according to my opinion will directly interest you.'

"'Interest us?' they replied, and I threw at the same time a glance on the duke, who for several days, had shown me a good deal of quiet defiance and mistrust and I saw that his uneasy conscience made him pale.

"'I at least think so,' I replied. 'But, my dear count, will you excuse me if the supernatural mixes sometimes in my narration?'

"'Very willingly,' replied he, laughing. 'All I would express is my astonishment that so many of these things have happened to *you* and that *I* can get no proof of anything of the kind.'

"I perceived that the duke was making signs that he approved this opinion but I gave him no attention and replied to the count: 'Everyone has not perhaps the eyes to see.'

"'That may be,' replied he, still smiling.

"I leant towards him and whispered in his ear in an expressive tone: 'But this corpse intact in the coffin, is that then an ordinary phenomenon?'

"He was astonished and angry and I continued in a low voice: 'It would perhaps be very easy to explain in a natural manner, but it would be useless to give such an explanation to you.'

"This whispering irritated the countess: 'We are getting away from our story,' she said, with a sudden petulance, and made a sign to me to commence.

"Glancing round the company I thus began: 'The scene of my anecdote is at Venice.'

"'I ought to know something about it, then,' replied the duke, with an angry and suspicious look.

"'Perhaps,' I replied, 'but there were plenty of people who had good reasons to keep all these events secret and it happened about eighteen months ago at the period when you commenced your travels. The family of a very rich nobleman whom I shall call Filippo had reason to go to Livorno for business affairs where he gained the heart of an amiable and pretty girl named Clara. When about to return to Venice he promised this young girl and her relations to return immediately to marry her and his departure was preceded by ceremonies which concluded by becoming fantastic.

"'After the two lovers had exhausted all the protestations possible to a mutual affection, Filippo invoked the help of the demon of vengeance in the case of infidelity and to this dreadful goddess he sent his petition that either of the lovers who was unfaithful should not rest, even in the tomb, and, if the wronged one died first he or she should have the power to rise from the dead and pursue the perjured one until he or she was forced in this ghastly manner to remember the vows that had been forgotten.

"'The elder people seated at the table when these vows were exchanged, remembering their own youth, gave no hindrance to these romantic ideas that rose from the exultation of excited passion.

"'The lovers concluded by pricking their wrists, allowing their blood to drop in their glasses which were filled with white champagne.

"'"Our souls shall be as inseparable as our blood!" cried Filippo who drank of the glass and gave the rest to Clara!'

"At this moment the young duke showed an obvious agitation and from time to time he cast on me menacing glances and I was forced to conclude that in his adventure there had passed some such scene. I can, however, affirm that I recount the exact details of the ceremony which took place at the departure of Filippo from Livorno—such as

296

may be found written in a letter by the mother of Clara. 'Who would,' I continued, 'after so many evidences of such a violent passion, expect a catastrophe?'

"'From the moment of the return of Filippo to Venice a young beauty who had been hidden until then in a distant convent where she was being educated, appeared among patrician society, where she was hailed as a miracle of loveliness and excited the admiration of the city.

"'The parents of Filippo had heard a good deal of Clara and of the projected alliance between her and their son. But they were not altogether pleased at this projected marriage. They wished their son to unite himself to one of their own nation and rank and they presented him to the relations of Camilla, which was the name of the young beauty who had newly appeared from the convent. Her family was among the most distinguished in Venice, her dowry was considerable, and while these advantages attracted the parents, Filippo himself was not insensible to the exquisite grace and beauty of the young lady and to the distinction she accorded him. He was flattered at being so soon the favourite pretender of one after whom every young patrician in Venice sighed.

"'It was the period of the carnival and these days of license and gaiety completed the intrigue. Filippo went everywhere with Camilla and the memory of Livorno soon preserved but a small place in his heart. His letters to Clara became colder and colder; he disliked the reproaches she sent in return to their brief epistles and ceased at length to write at all to his absent betrothed and did all that he could to hasten his union with Camilla, incomparably more beautiful and more rich.

"'The agonies of Clara, manifest by the shaking writing of her letters and by the imprints of tears on her paper had no more power than the prayers of this unfortunate girl on the heart of the volatile Filippo and even when she, driven to despair, wrote and menaced him, according to their mutual vows and threatened to pursue him even after she was in the tomb where grief would soon end her, and draw him down with her to death. This made no impression upon his mind, entirely occupied with the thought of tasting perfect happiness in the arms of Camilla.

"'The father of this young person, my intimate friend, invited me some time before to the wedding. Numerous business affairs as well as the claims of gaiety kept this gentleman this summer in the town so that he could not enjoy as commodiously as usual the pleasures of the country. However, he often invited his friends to his pleasure villa on the banks of the Brenta and it was there he decided to celebrate with considerable pomp the marriage of his daughter.

"'A peculiar circumstance caused the ceremony to be deferred for some weeks. The parents of Camilla having tasted happiness in their own marriage desired that their daughter should receive the nuptial benediction of the same priest who had given it to them. The latter, however, who, despite his great age, had an appearance of vigorous health, was struck down by a slow fever which did not at first permit him to leave his bed. However, he began to recover slowly, went from better to better, and on the eve of the marriage was at last well. Some secret power however, it seemed, was forbidding this union, for the good priest was seized even the very day of the marriage with so violent a fit of shuddering that it was believed he had fallen into a relapse of his fever and he dare not leave his house, and sent a messenger to the young people desiring them to choose another priest to marry them.

"'The young girl's parents persisted however in their design to have the union of their daughter blessed by the venerable old man whom they so much loved and respected. They had certainly spared themselves plenty of chagrin if they had not departed from this idea. All the preparations had been made for the festival of marriage, and as it was difficult to put off this fete it was decided to hold it and consider it as a ceremony of betrothal.

"From early morning the gondoliers in their handsomest habits waited for the company on the edge of the canal. Soon their joyous songs were heard as they conducted to the country villa, ornamented with flowers, the numerous *gondolas* which enclosed the choicest society of Venice.

"'During the banquet, which was prolonged until the evening, the betrothed exchanged their rings. At the same instant a piercing cry was heard, and struck with terror all the guests and filled Filippo with fright.

"'They ran to the windows; twilight, however, was beginning to fall, nobody could distinguish the objects in the garden very well and nothing was discovered.'

"'Stop an instant,' said the duke to me, with a haggard smile; his face, which had frequently changed colour, showed all the torments of his guilty conscience. 'I well know this cry heard in the open air!

It is borrowed from the *Memoirs* of Mile. Clarion. Her dead lovers tormented her in this so original manner. The cry was followed by a clapping of hands; I hope, M. le Marquis, that you will not forget this particularity in your tale.'

"Taking no heed of his ill-humour and his impertinent interruption beyond a keen look, I replied quietly: 'And why cannot you believe that something of this sort happened to that actress? Your incredulity seems to me extraordinary. To support it you bring forward facts which prove you are utterly wrong.'

"The countess made an impatient sign to me to continue and so I took up my tale.

"'A little after the company heard this inexplicable cry I begged Camilla, in front of whom I was seated, to let me once more see her ring which I had already admired. Not only was the stone beautiful, but the setting was of almost priceless workmanship. This ring was no longer on her finger, it was searched for, but not a trace of it discovered. Everyone rose up in order that the search might be more thorough but it was useless.

"'Meanwhile the moment for the diversions of the evening approached. Fireworks were to be given on the Brenta before the ball, everyone masked and went into his or her *gondola*. The spectacle was splendid, but there was no gaiety; nothing could be more striking than the silence which reigned during this festival. No one opened his mouth save now and then to say in the coldest and most formal manner: "Bravo!" as the stars of fire rose into the air.

"'The ball was one of the most brilliant that I have ever seen. The jewels with which the highborn ladies were covered reflected the light of the lustres and sent it back with a new brilliancy. Camilla was the person most richly adorned; her father, who loved luxury, had rejoiced in taking care that no one in the assembly should equal his daughter in splendour or in beauty.

"'To better assure himself of the supreme triumph of his daughter he made a tour of the ballroom glancing at the *toilettes* of the other ladies and what was his surprise to see on another guest exactly the same stones as those that sparkled on the charming person of Camilla! This lady's father was so surprised that he had the weakness to show a slight chagrin as he turned on his heel from in front of the unknown to seek out his daughter. He consoled himself, however, with the thought that a cluster of brilliants intended for Camilla, and with which she was to be adorned at the supper table, would efface all the magnificence of the other lady.

"'As the guests went in to supper Camilla was presented by her father with this bouquet of diamonds which, like drops of flame and water, rainbow and flame, she held negligently in a white hand already fatigued by the magnificence of the evening. What, however, was the surprise of her father when as the company seated themselves at table he glanced round and saw that the lady dressed like his daughter also had a bouquet of diamonds not less precious than that which Camilla carried!

"'His curiosity was so excited that he could not contain it, and rising from the table slipped behind the lady who, like all the others was masked, and whispered: "Is it being too indiscreet, beautiful mask, to ask you to whisper to me your name?" But to his great astonishment the lady shook her head and turned away.

"'The *major-domo* entered at the same moment and demanded if the company had become more numerous since dinner seeing that the covers no longer sufficed? His master replied "no" with a vexed air and accused his domestics of negligence, but the *major-domo* persisted that there was one person too many among the company.

"'Another cover was placed on the table and the master of the feast counted the places himself and proved that there was one more than the number of people whom he had invited. As he had recently, because of some unconsidered words, been in trouble with the government, he feared that some spy had slipped into the festival. This vexed him. He was not fearful that on such occasion anything should be said or any incident occur which should get him into disfavour with the senate but he resented the introduction of a government agent into an entertainment for the betrothal of his daughter.

"'To discover who was the uninvited member of the company he begged all present to have the goodness to unmask but in order not to disturb the feast, to put off doing so until the hour of departure. Meanwhile, he apprised his servants secretly to keep a sharp look-out that no one should slip away from the revels.

"'It was truly a magnificent collation. The supper surpassed the dinner in taste and splendour, everyone expressed surprise at the extraordinary luxury displayed and which outshone everything that anyone had been accustomed to see, even in Venice. The exquisite choice and endless variety of the wines was particularly praised.

"'The father of Camilla was, however, not satisfied and complained loudly that some accident had happened to his excellent red champagne which prevented him from offering a single glass to his guests.

"'The company tried to give itself over to gaiety, that gaiety which had not been known during the whole of the day. There was some attempt at laughter and conversation, but not anywhere near where I was seated. Here, curiosity only absorbed everyone. I had placed myself not far from the lady attired in exactly the same costume as the bride and who carried a similar bouquet of diamonds. I remarked that she neither ate nor drank, that she neither addressed to nor responded to a sole word with her neighbours. She seemed to have her eyes constantly fixed on the two *fiancés*.

"'This singularity gradually became noticed throughout the whole room and again troubled the joy which had begun to manifest itself. People whispered one to another numerous conjectures on this mysterious person. The general opinion was that an unhappy passion for Filippo must be the cause of this extraordinary conduct.

"'The persons who rose from the table first were those who sat near the unknown. They hastened to get away from her and to find gayer company. Their places were occupied by others who hoped to find in the silent lady someone whom they knew and obtain from her a more gracious reception. But this was useless.

"'In the same instant when glasses of white champagne were being sent round the company, Filippo took a chair near to the unknown. She then appeared a little more animated, she turned towards Filippo (this she had not done to any of the others) and she presented him her glass as if asking him to drink. Filippo trembled violently while she regarded him fixedly.

"'"The wine is red!" cried he, in showing the glass raising it high before him. "I thought that there was no red champagne here?"

"'"Red!" replied with an astonished air the father of Camilla, who was standing near.

"'"Look at the lady's glass," replied Filippo.

"'"The wine there is as white as that in the other glasses," replied the startled host. He then called as witness all his guests, who declared unanimously that the wine was white.

"'Filippo did not drink, but left his chair; a second glance from the eyeholes of his neighbour's mask had occasioned him a frightful agitation. He took the father of Camilla aside and whispered some words in his ear. The result of this was that the master of the feast turned instantly to the company and addressed them in these words: "Ladies and gentlemen, I beg you, for reasons that you will soon know, to take off your masks for an instant."

"'As this invitation expressed the general wish, so strong was the desire to see the silent lady without her mask, all the visages were uncovered in a flash with the exception of that of the stranger on whom all glances were fixed.

"'There was a moment of silence, then the betrothed's father said: "You alone have kept your mask, may I hope that you will now take it off!"

"'She made no response but sat among them in an obstinate silence. This conduct was the more conspicuous as the father of Camilla recognised in those who had unmasked all the people whom he had invited to the festival and so was convinced without a doubt that the silent lady was uninvited. He did not wish to use any discourtesy in forcing her to unmask as the extraordinary richness of her attire showed her to be a lady of quality and almost rendered it impossible to suppose that she was a government spy. "Perhaps," he thought, "she is a friend of the family who does not live at Venice and who, from her arrival in the town had heard of the feast and had imagined this unexpected arrival as an innocent pleasantry."

"'He questioned all the domestics as to whether they had seen the arrival of this lady or knew anything about her, but all in vain. Nor was there among the crowd of lackeys who had attended their masters and mistresses to the festival one who belonged to the mysterious lady.

"'But what I thought the strangest of all the strange things about her was that when I had first seen her she had not been carrying the bouquet of diamonds, but had been in possession of these as soon as the bride received her gift.

"'The prolonged and baffled whispering that had succeeded to any attempt at conversation was becoming every instant louder when suddenly the masked lady rose from the place she had kept at the empty supper-board, made a sign to Filippo to follow her, and turned towards the door.

"'It was Camilla who took her bridegroom by the hand and implored him not to obey the signal. She had for a long time observed with what attention the mysterious lady had regarded her betrothed. She had also remarked that he had left this stranger in a frightful agitation and it appeared that there was in all this some folly caused by love.

"'The master of the house, deaf to all the representations of his daughter and a prey to the liveliest alarm, followed the unknown, certainly at some distance at first, but hastening his step as soon as he saw her outside the ballroom. In this moment the cry that they had heard before the fall of dusk was repeated, but heard more clearly because of the silence of the night. Terror passed among the assembly.

"'When the father of Camilla recovered from his first shudder of horror he looked about him and could no longer perceive the least trace of the unknown lady. Such of the guests who had been in the garden had not seen her pass; the neighbourhood was filled with a noisy, numerous crowd, the riverbank was busy with *gondoliers* and nobody had seen the mysterious stranger.

"'All these circumstances caused such a lively disquietude among the company that everyone desired to return home at once, and the master of the house was obliged to let the *gondoliers* depart much quicker than they had come. So in confusion and dismay broke up this brilliant scene.

"'By the next day the two lovers had regained their calm. Filippo had even adopted the opinion of Camilla, who believed that the unknown was a person whose wits had been unsettled by some love emotion. As to the frightful cry, twice repeated at twilight and midnight, this no doubt, she said, could be put down to one of the guests who had diverted themselves in this cruel manner. And as to the arrival and departure of the lady without anyone seeing her could not this be easily attributed to the inattention of the domestics? Then, as to the disappearance of the ring which had not yet been found, could not this be due to the dishonesty of some servant who had found and concealed the jewel? Anything that could throw a doubt on these explanations was dismissed and there was only one difficulty in continuing the marriage festival. The old priest who was to have given the Benediction had suddenly expired and the friendship which had united him so intimately with the parents of Camilla did not permit them to think of marriage and festivals in the weeks that followed his death.

"'The day when this venerable ecclesiastic was buried brought news that shocked the frivolous heart of Filippo. He learnt by a letter from the mother of Clara of the death of that young girl. Succumbing to the chagrin which had been caused her by the infidelity of the man whom she had never ceased to love, she had died suddenly, but in her last hour she had sworn that she would not repose in the tomb but that she would follow her perjured lover until he had fulfilled the promise he had made.

"'This circumstance produced on Filippo a more lively impression than all the imprecations of the unhappy lover. He recalled that the first cry heard in the midst of the betrothal ceremonies had taken place at the precise instant when Clara had ceased to live. He was then firmly persuaded that the unknown mask had been the ghost of Clara.

"'This thought deprived him at intervals of the use of his reason. He constantly carried this letter on his person and, with a distracted air, several times drew it from his pocket to consider it fixedly. Even the presence of Camilla did not prevent him from doing this.

"'As she supposed that this letter contained the cause of the extraordinary change in Filippo she looked for a chance to read it. She found this one day when Filippo, absorbed in a profound reflection had allowed the letter to fall. When Filippo came out of his distraction he saw by the pallor and shudderings of Camilla that she had read the letter which he took from her nervous hands and implored her to tell him what she would have him do?

"'Camilla replied sadly: "Love me with more fidelity than you did one who is no more," and he promised her this in a transport of passion. But his agitation augmented without cease and roused to an uncontrollable pitch of violence the morning of the day of the marriage.

"'In going, almost before dawn, according to the custom of the country, to the house of Camilla's father there to fetch her to the church, he believed he saw constantly the shadow of Clara walking at his side. Never had anybody seen two people go to receive the nuptial benedictions with so mournful an air.

"I accompanied the parents of Camilla who had prayed me to be a witness. Often afterwards did we recall this lugubrious morning. We went silently to the church of Santa Maria de la Salute. During our walk Filippo repeatedly asked me in a wild manner to bid the strange woman not to follow Camilla so closely because he supposed she had some vile design against her.

"""What strange woman?" I demanded of him.

"""In the name of God do not speak so loud!" replied he. "You must see how she tried to place herself by force between Camilla and myself."

"""Chimeras, my friend, there is no one between you and Camilla."

""Please to Heaven that my eyes deceive me. May she not," he added, muttering, "try to get into the church? Surely we shall leave her at the door!"

""She shall not enter," I replied, and to the great surprise of the parents of Camilla, I made gestures as if I was bidding someone to cease a pursuit and leave us.

"'When we arrived at the church we found the father of Filippo. As soon as the bridegroom perceived him he took leave of him as if he were about to die. Camilla sobbed; Filippo, turning about, cried: "There is the strange woman! See! She has contrived to enter!"

"'The parents of Camilla did not know if, under these circumstances, it was right to allow the religious ceremony to commence. But Camilla, absorbed in her love, cried: "These chimerical ideas are precisely the reason that renders it necessary for me to be with him to care for him!"

"'They approached the altar; in the same minute a gust of wind blew out the candles. The priest appeared vexed that the windows had not been more firmly closed. Filippo cried: "The windows! But did you not see that there was someone here who blew out the candles?" Everyone regarded him with astonishment and Filippo cried, hastily withdrawing his hand from that of Camilla: "Do you not see that I am being taken from the side of my bride?"

"'Camilla fell unconscious between the arms of her parents and the priest declared that, under these strange circumstances it was impossible to proceed with the marriage.

"'The relations of the groom and bride attributed the state of Filippo to a mental disturbance. They even supposed that he was a victim of poison, when, breaking from all attempts to restrain him, he cast himself on the steps of the altar where he almost immediately expired in the midst of most violent convulsions. The surgeons who opened his body could discover nothing, however, to justify such a suspicion.

"'Everything possible was done to hush up this adventure. Talk of mental aberration and of poison could not, however, explain the appearance of the mysterious mask at the betrothal ceremonies. Another striking detail was that the wedding ring lost in the country house was found among the other jewels of Camilla as soon as they returned from the church.'

"'There is what I call a marvellous story,' smiled the count. His wife gave a profound sigh and Libussa cried: 'You really did make me

305

shudder!'

"'So must every affianced person who listens to such stories,' replied I, sternly regarding the duke who, while I had spoken had often risen and re-seated himself and who, by his unsteady and flashing regard had witnessed his displeasure at what I said.

"'A word,' he whispered in my ear that evening when we passed up the great stairs on our way to our chambers. 'I have seen through your schemes, that invented story————'

"'Stop!' I replied in a severe tone. 'Believe me, I know what I am about and how can you dare to accuse of falsehood a man of honour?'

"'We will talk of that presently,' replied he with a mocking air. 'But tell me, where did you get the anecdote of the blood mixed with the wine? I know the person from whose life you gleaned that detail!'

"'I can assure you that I have only taken it from the life of Filippo. For the rest, it may be common enough incident—like the sudden cry. This singular manner of uniting two people for ever must often have presented itself to the imagination of ardent lovers.'

"'Very well, that may be so,' replied the young duke, 'there was, however, in your story, several other details which resembled much those of another adventure.'

"'No doubt. All love affairs have a family resemblance.'

"The young patrician replied passionately:

"'No matter for that. All I ask of you is not to make any allusion to any person as to my past life. Take care how you recount any more anecdotes to our host. Only on the condition of your future discretion can I pardon you your very ingenious fiction.'

"'Conditions! Pardon! And who are you to speak to me like that? This is a little too much! Here is my reply. Tomorrow morning the count shall learn that you have been already betrothed and the demands and threats that you have made to me on that subject.'

"'*Marquis*, if you dare to do so——'

"'Ah! ah! Yes, if I dare! I certainly do dare! I owe this candour to an old friend. The impostor who ventures to accuse me of falsehood shall no longer wear in this house his deceptive mask!'

"Anger had, in fact, led me, despite myself, so far that a duel became inevitable. The duke defied me. We arranged, before separating, to meet the next morning in the neighbouring wood with pistols, and there, before daybreak, we went, each accompanied by a servant, into the depths of the forest.

"The young Venetian having remarked that I had said nothing as to the disposition of my body if I were killed, told me that he would charge himself with this duty, and made arrangements with my servant for the disposal of my corpse as if the duel were already decided.

"When we had chosen our spot and our domestics were priming our pistols he said to me that he was willing to overlook my offence and clasp my hand in friendship if I were to apologise.

"'Remember,' said he, 'that a duel between us will not be very equal. I am young,' he added, 'already in several affairs I have proved that my hand is sure. It is true that I have not killed everyone, but always I have struck my adversary at the point where I have decided to do so. Here it will be, and for the first time for me, a fight to the death. It is the sole means to prevent you from betraying me, but if here you will give me your word of honour not to speak to the count on anything which concerns my past life, I consent to regard the affair as terminated.'

"I had naturally to reject his proposal, and did so.

"'In this case, recommend your soul to God,' replied the young duke. 'We must prepare ourselves. It is for you to fire first,' he added.

"'I will give you the first shot,' I responded.

"He refused. Then I fired and knocked the pistol out of his hand. He was very surprised, but his astonishment was even greater when, having taken another weapon, he missed his shot at me.

"He pretended that he had directed this at my heart but his shot went wide and he made the excuse that the least tremble of fright on my part had been the cause of my escape.

"On his invitation we made a second attempt. I again, to his great astonishment, shot his pistol from his hand. This time the bullet went so near his fingers that he was slightly wounded.

"His second shot passed near me but missed altogether.

"I said that I would not fire again but, as one might attribute to the violent agitation of his blood the fact that he had missed me twice, I told him that he might shoot as me again.

"Before he had time to refuse this offer the count, with his daughter on his arm, hurried through the forest and put himself between us.

"He complained bitterly of this conduct on the part of his guests and demanded of me an explanation as to the cause of our quarrel. Then I explained the whole affair to him in the presence of Foscarini. The embarrassed behaviour of the young Venetian convinced the count and Libussa of the reality of the reproaches that his conscience made him.

"It was not long, however, before the duke was able to profit so well from the love that Libussa had for him that a complete change took place in the point of view of the count. Won over by his daughter's entreaties and by the obvious advantages that the match presented, he said to me that same evening:

"'You are right! I ought to behave rigorously and send the duke out of my house. But what would this Apollonia gain? He has abandoned her, and in any case, would not see her again. More important for me is this—he is the sole man for whom my daughter has shown the least inclination. Leave these two young people to follow their wishes. The countess is also of my way of thinking and she admits that she will be very sad if our house loses the handsome Venetian. There are,' he added, sadly, 'many infidelities in the world which circumstances must excuse.'

"'But it seems to me there are no circumstances in this present occurrence'—I began. I however, stopped my arguments when I saw that the count held firmly to his opinion.

"The marriage took place without further delay or hindrance. There was, however, little gaiety at the feast, though outwardly it was splendid and costly. The ball in the evening was absolutely sad. Foscarini alone danced with an extraordinary vigour and fire.

"'Happily, *M. Le Marquis*,' said he in leaving the dance for a moment and in laughing close to my ear, 'there is not here a ghost as there was in your wedding at Venice.'

"'Ah,' said I, raising my finger, 'do not rejoice too soon. Nemesis walks slowly, and very often one does not perceive her until she is on one's heels.' To my surprise, he received this warning in complete silence, then turning away brusquely, once more joined in the dance with a frantic abandon and *bravura*.

"The countess in vain begged him not to so exhaust himself; it was only when he was completely out of breath that Libussa was able to withdraw him from the ballroom on to the terrace. A few moments afterwards I saw her return into the chamber; she was in tears and they did not seem to me to be occasioned by joy. I could not speak to her for she hurried out of the ballroom.

"As I stood near to the door by which she had left in the hopes of seeing her again, I saw her immediately after her departure re-enter the ballroom, and this time with a serene face. I followed her and noted that she at once asked the duke to dance with her and that far from trying to moderate his frenzied gaiety she shared it and even increased it by her example.

"I remarked that, this dance finished, the duke took leave of the parents of Libussa and hastened, with her through a little door which led to the nuptial chamber.

"While I was puzzling myself as to some explanation for this change in the behaviour of Libussa who had endeavoured first to restrain the immoderate gaiety of the duke, had left the room in tears because she had not been able to do so, and a few seconds afterwards had returned and not only shared but encouraged his wild behaviour, I noted that the count and his body-servants were having a whispered conversation near the door, and beyond them in the outer chamber I saw the figure of the head gardener at whom they continually glanced.

"I approached the group and gathered from the agitated questions and answers that flew between the master and the two servants that the organ of the church was playing and that all the edifice was illuminated. This had been perceived just as midnight struck.

"The count was very vexed at being told what he considered a stupid fable and demanded why he had not been advised of this before? The reply was that the servants had been watching the church to see how the affair would terminate. The gardener added that when the lights had gone out and the organ music had ceased the figure of the old chaplain had been seen leaving the church door and disappearing into the night. He also added that the country-folk who lived near the forest had come into the grounds of the *château* during the day to say that the summit of the mountain which dominated the valley was illuminated and that spirits were dancing there.

"'You hear?' the count glanced at me with a smile of sombre contempt. 'Here are all the ridiculous old stories of the neighbourhood brought up because everyone is excited by the festival. We shall hear next of the "Dead Bride"—I hope she will not fail to come and play her part.'

"The body-servant then endeavoured to draw the gardener away as he feared the tales of this fellow would dangerously inflame the anger of the count.

"'One can at least listen,' I said to my host, 'to this that your people think that they have seen.' I turned to the gardener who stood uneasily in the shadow: 'What of this "Dead Bride"—do you wish to say something about that? Have you indeed seen such a shape?'

"The fellow raised his shoulders without speaking.

"'Wasn't I right?' cried the count in irritation. 'You see, he is going to pretend that he *has* seen her! The minds of these people are so full of these ideas that it does not take much for them to think that they see what they believe. *Did* you see her?' he demanded hoarsely of the gardener, and the man sullenly nodded his head. 'And under what form?' demanded the count.

"'I beg a thousand pardons,' stammered the servant, at last urged to speak by a greater fear than that of his master's wrath, 'but I did see a shape and it resembled the late Mlle. Hildegard. She passed in the garden quite near to me and entered into the *château*....'

"'Ah!' interrupted the count. 'In the future be a little more prudent in your chimerical ideas and leave my daughter in peace in her tomb. That is enough.' He made a brusque sign to his people in the ante-chamber and turning to me, asked with a wildness in his manner that belied the irony of his words: 'What do you think of that—this apparition of Hildegard?'

"'I hope she will only appear to the gardener. Remember the adventure in the museum in Paris!'

"'You are right. It is, like that, merely an invention which I am not able for the moment to understand. Do not think I am convinced of any supernatural appearance,' he added sternly; 'believe me, I would sooner have refused my daughter to the duke because of that gross lie than because he abandoned his first lover.'

"'I see,' I replied dryly, 'that we are not likely to agree on this point, for as my credulity appears strange to you, your doubts appear to me incomprehensible.'

"The guests who had gathered together at the *château* retired one by one and I remained alone with the count and his wife when Libussa, vested still in her ball-dress, showed herself at the door of the room and looked round in astonishment at seeing it empty.

"'What does this signify?' demanded the countess, but her husband was too startled to say anything.

"'Where is Donato?' cried Libussa.

"'You demand that of me?' replied her mother. 'Did I not see you leave with him by that door?'

"'No, no! You are mistaken!'

"'Mistaken! Impossible, my dear child! It's only a few moments ago. You danced with him with a singular gaiety and then you left together by the little door.'

"'I, my mother?'

"'Yes, my dear Libussa. How can you have forgotten it?'

"'I have forgotten nothing, I assure you.'

"'Where then have you been all this while?'

"'In my sister's chamber,' said Libussa.

"I remarked that at these words the count paled a little and his fearful regard searched mine, but he remained silent. The countess thought that her daughter deceived her and said in afflicted tone: 'How can you have such a singular idea, especially on a day like this?'

"'I couldn't tell you the reason. I know only that I felt suddenly a great sadness in my heart and I felt at the same time the firm hope of finding her in her chamber, perhaps occupied in playing the guitar like she used to do. Therefore I went up there quite quietly in the darkness, glided into the room and listened.'

"'What did you find?'

"'Alas! Nothing! But the lively desire that I had to see my sister joined to the scene of the dance so exhausted me that as soon as I seated myself on a chair I fell deeply asleep.'

"'How long is it since you quitted the ballroom?'

"'The clock on the tower had struck eleven and three-quarters when I entered in my sister's room.'

"'How can she speak like that?' whispered the countess to her husband. 'She talks like that—but I know that the clock struck eleven hours and three-quarters when I was begging, in this very place, Libussa to dance a little more moderately.'

"The count did not reply to this: 'And your husband?' he said, turning to his daughter.

"'I thought, as I have already told you, that I should find him here.'

"'Good God,' said her mother, 'she is wandering in her mind. But he, where is he, then?'

"'Where should he be, my good mother?' said Libussa with a quiet air.

"The count then took a torch and made me a sign to follow him. A hideous spectacle awaited us in the bridal chamber where he conducted me. We found the duke extended on the ground; there was not the least sign of life in him and his features were disfigured in a frightful manner.

"Judge the bitter grief of Libussa when they were forced to tell her this news, and all the efforts of those summoned to the assistance of the duke to recall him to life were without success.

"The count and his family fell into a consternation against which all attempts to console them were useless. I was forced to leave them to their sorrow and take my departure from the *château*. Before I left the neighbourhood I was careful to glean what explanations I could from the villagers upon this strange story. I could only learn of a wild anecdote. This 'Dead Bride' had lived in the valley in the fourteenth or fifteenth century. She was a noble lady who had conducted herself towards her lover with such ingratitude and perfidy that he died of chagrin. In the conclusion, when she was about to be married to someone else he appeared on her wedding night and she died. The legend was that the spirit of this unhappy creature wandered on the earth as a penance and took all manner of forms, particularly those of charming creatures, to render lovers unfaithful. As it was not permitted to her to re-clothe herself in the appearance of a living person she appeared under the disguise of girls lately deceased and if possible under the shape of one who resembled her the most.

"It was for this reason that her formless ghost haunted the *château* where she had once lived, and, if occasion offered, took on the likeness of a dead young girl of the house to which she had once belonged. She was also said to haunt galleries and museums in search of dead beauties whose charms she could assume for the undoing of some living, faithful lover. These dismal pilgrimages were to be repeated in punishment for her perfidy until she found the man so faithful that she was not able to induce him to forget his living betrothed. This had not yet occurred.

"I asked what connection this tale could have with the apparition of the old chaplain of which I had heard speak while I had been in the *château* and I was told that the fate of this last depended on that of the lady because he had helped her in her criminal love affairs. But no one could give me any satisfaction as to the voice which had called the duke by his name as he drove under the mountain, nor what signified the illuminated chapel, which had been suddenly lit up a little before midnight while the sound of High Mass was heard and the organ pealing. No one knew either how to explain the dance on the mountain which dominated the valley.

"However," added the *marquis*, "you must admit that these traditions adapted themselves marvellously to what I had witnessed with my own eyes in the *château*, and could, to a certain point, explain all the mysteries of the story of Libussa and the handsome Venetian, but

I am not in a position to give a more satisfactory and exact solution. I reserve for another time a second history of this same 'Dead Bride.' I learnt it several weeks later and it seemed to me interesting. This evening, however, it is too late, and I fear to have already, with my long recital, taken up a little too much the leisure of the company."

As he finished these words some of his audience, though thanking him for the pains he had taken to amuse them, showed signs of a lively disbelief in his tale. He was about to reply to their objections when an acquaintance of his entered with a serious air and said several words in his ear. The company noted the curious contrast offered by the alarmed and hurried air of the newcomer as he whispered to the *marquis* and the calm of the latter in listening to him.

"Make haste! Make haste!" said this acquaintance, impatient at seeing the coolness of the *marquis*. "In a few minutes you will repent of this delay!"

"I am much obliged to you for your affection and solicitude," replied the *marquis*. But he took up his hat and cane as leisurely as if he had been taking leave in the ordinary way and was preparing to salute ceremoniously the company when the man who had come to warn him cried: "You are lost!"

An officer at the head of a file of men entered and demanded the *marquis*, who at once stepped forward.

"You are my prisoner," said the officer, and the *marquis* followed him, after having said farewell with a laughing air to the company and having begged the ladies not to have any uneasiness on his account.

"No uneasiness!" said the man who had come to warn him. "Know, then, ladies and gentlemen, that the *marquis* has been discovered to have connections with highly suspected persons. The death sentence is likely to be soon pronounced on him. On hearing this news I came, as you saw, to warn him. If he had listened to me at once he would perhaps have had time to escape. Well, after the way he behaved, I no longer feel sorry for him. I scarcely can think he is in his right mind."

The company, who had been singularly troubled by this sudden event, were exchanging all sorts of conjectures when the officer re-entered and once more demanded the *marquis*.

"But he left with you just now!" cried someone.

"No, he must have returned, we have seen no one. He has disappeared," said the officer, smiling, and he forced them to search every place in the room. But this was useless. The whole house was turned upside down in vain, and on the morrow the officer left Bad Nauheim without his prisoner, and much chagrined.

The Grindwell Governing Machine

On the other side of the Atlantic there is a populous city called Grandville. It is, as its name indicates, a great city,—but it is said that it thinks itself a good deal greater than it really is. I meant to say that Grandville was its original name, and the name by which even at the present day it is called by its own citizens. But there are certain wits, or it may be, vulgar people, who by some process have converted this name into Grindwell.

I may be able, in the course of this sketch, to give a reason why so sounding and aristocratic a name as Grandville has been changed into the plebeian one of Grindwell. I might account for it by adducing similar instances of changes in the names of cities through the bad pronunciation and spelling of foreigners. For instance, the English nickname Livorno Leghorn, the Germans insist on calling Venice Venedig, and the French convert Washington into the Chinese word Voss-Hang-Tong. And so it may be that the name Grindwell has originated among us Americans simply from miscalling or misspelling the foreign name of Grandville.

I incline to think, however, that there is a better reason for the name.

For a good many years Grandville has been famous for a great machine, of a very curious construction, which is said to regulate the movements of the whole city, and almost to convert the men, women, and children into cranks, wheels, and pinions. As a model of this machine does not exist in our Patent Office at Washington, I shall beg the reader's indulgence while I attempt to give some account of it. It may be thought a very curious affair, though I believe there is little about it that is original or new. The idea of it was handed down from remote generations.

In America I know that many persons may consider the Grindwell

Governing Machine a humbug,—an obsolete, absurd, and tyrannous institution, wholly unfitted to the nineteenth century. A machine that proposes to think and act for the whole people, and which is rigidly opposed to the people's thinking and acting for themselves, is likely to find little favour among us. With us the doctrine is, that each one should think for himself,—be an individual mind and will, and not the spoke of a wheel. Every American voter or votress is allowed to keep his or her little intellectual wind-mill, coffee-mill, pepper-mill, loom, steam-engine, hand-organ, or whatever moral manufacturing or grinding apparatus he or she likes.

Each one may be his own Church or his own State, and yet be none the less a good and useful citizen, and the union of the States be in none the more danger. But it is not so in Grindwell. The rules of the Grindwell machine allow no one to do his own grinding, unless his mill-wheel is turned by the central governing power. He must allow the big State machine to do everything,—he paying for it, of course. A regular programme prescribes what he shall believe and say and do; and any departure from this order is considered a violation of the laws, or at least a reprehensible invasion of the time-honoured customs of the city.

The Grindwell Governing Machine (though a patent has been taken out for it in Europe, and it is thought everything of by royal heads and the gilded flies that buzz about them) is really an old machine, nearly worn out, and every now and then patched up and painted and varnished anew. If a committee of our knowing Yankees were sent over to gain information with regard to its actual condition, I am inclined to think they would bring back a curious and not very favourable report. It wouldn't astonish me, if they should pronounce the whole apparatus of the State rotten from top to bottom, and only kept from falling to pieces by all sorts of ingenious contrivances of an external and temporary nature,—here a wheel, or pivot, or spring to be replaced,—there a prop or buttress to be set up,—here a pipe choked up,—there a boiler burst,—and so on, from one end of the works to the other. However, the machine keeps a-going, and many persons think it works beautifully.

Everything is reduced to such perfect system in its operations, that the necessity for individual opinion is almost superseded, and even private consciences are laid upon the shelf,—just as people lay by an antiquated timepiece that no winding-up or shaking can persuade into marking the hours,—for have they not the clock on the government railroad station opposite, which they can at any time consult by stepping to the window? For instance, individual honesty is set aside and replaced by a system of rewards and punishments. Honesty is an old-fashioned coat. The police, like a great sponge, absorbs the private virtue. It says to conscience, "Stay there,—don't trouble yourself,—I will act for you."

You drop your purse in the street. A rogue picks it up. In his private conscience he says, "Honesty is a very good thing, perhaps, but it is by no means the best policy,—it is simply no policy at all,—it is sheer stupidity. What can be more politic than for me to pocket this windfall and turn the corner quick?"'"—So preacheth his crooked fag-end of a conscience, that very, very small still voice, in very husky tones; but he knows that a policeman, walking behind him, saw him pick up the purse, which alters the case,—which, in fact, completely sets aside his fag-end of a husky-voiced conscience, and makes virtue his necessity, and necessity his virtue. External morality is hastily drawn on as a decent overcoat to hide the tag-rags of his roguishness, while he magnanimously restores the purse to the owner.

Jones left his umbrella in a cab one night. Discovering that he hadn't it under his arm, he rushed after the cabman; but he was gone. Jones had his number, however, and with it proceeded the next day to the police-office, feeling sure that he would find his umbrella there. And there, in a closet appropriated to articles left in hackney-coaches,—a perfect limbo of canes, parasols, shawls, pocket-books, and what- not,—he found it, ticketed and awaiting its lawful owner. The explanation of which mystery is, that the cabmen in Grindwell are strictly amenable to the police for any departure from the system which provides for the security of private property, and a yearly reward is given to those of the coach-driving fraternity who prove to be the most faithful restorers of articles left in their carriages. Surely, the result of system can no farther go than this,—that Monsieur Vaurien's moral sense, like his opinions, should be absorbed and overruled by the governing powers.

What a capital thing it is to have the great governmental head and heart thinking and feeling for us! Why, even the little boys, on winter afternoons, are restricted by the policemen from sliding on the ice in the streets, for fear the impetuous little fellows should break or dislocate some of their bones, and the hospital might have the expense of setting them; so patriarchal a regard has the machine for its young friends!

I might allude here to a special department of the machine, which once had great power in overruling the thoughts and consciences of the people, and which is still considered by some as not altogether powerless. I refer to the Ecclesiastic department of the Grindwell works. This was formerly the greatest labour-saving machinery ever invented. But however powerful the operation of the Church machinery upon the grandmothers and grandfathers of the modern Grindwellites, it has certainly fallen greatly into disuse, and is kept a-going now more for the sake of appearances than for any real efficacy. The most knowing ones think it rather old—fashioned and cumbrous,—at any rate, not comparable to the State machinery, either in its design or its mode of operation.

And as in these days of percussion-caps and Minie rifles we lay by an old matchlock or crossbow, using it only to ornament our walls,—or as the powdered postilion with his horn and his boots is superseded by the locomotive and the electric telegraph,—so the old rusty Church wheels are removed into buildings apart from the daily life of the people, where they seem to revolve harmlessly and without any necessary connection with the State wheels.

Not that I mean to say that it works smoothly and well at all times,—this Grindwell machine. How can such an old patched and crumbling apparatus be expected always to work well? And how can you hope to find, even in the most enslaved or routine-ridden community, entire obedience to the will of the monarch and his satellites? Unfortunately for the cause of order and quiet, there will always be found certain tough lumps, in the shape of rebellious or nonconformist men, which refuse to be melted in the strong solvents or ground up in the swift mills of Absolutism. Government must look after these impediments. If they are positively dangerous, they must be destroyed or removed. If only suspected, or known to be powerless or inactive, they must at least be watched.

And here, again, the machine of government shows a remarkable ingenuity of organization.

For instance, it is said that there are pipes laid all along the streets, like hose, leading from a central reservoir. Nobody knows exactly what they are for; but if anyone steps upon them, up spirts something like a stream of gas, and takes the form of a *gendarme*,—and the unlucky street-walker must pay dear for his carelessness. Telegraph wires radiate like cobwebs from the chamber of the main-spring, and carry intelligence of all that is going on in the houses and streets. Man-traps are laid under the pavements,—sometimes they are secretly introduced under your very table or bed,—and if anything is said against that piece of machinery called the main-spring, or against the head engineer, the trap will nab you and fly away with you, like the spider that carried off Margery Mopp.

If a number of people get together to discuss the meaning of and the reasons for the existence of the main-spring, or any of the big wheels immediately connected therewith, the ground under them will sometimes give way, and they will suddenly find themselves in unfurnished apartments not to their liking. And if anyone should be so rash as to put his hand on the wheels, he is cut to pieces or strangled by the silent, incessant, fatal whirl of the engine.

The head engineer keeps his machine, and the city on which it acts, as much in the dark as possible. He has a special horror of sunshine. He seems to think that the sky is one great burning lens, and his machine-rooms and the city a vast powder-magazine.

There are certain articles thought to be especially dangerous. Newspapers are strictly forbidden,—unless first steeped in a tincture of asbestos of a very dull colour, expressly manufactured and supplied by the Governing Machine. When properly saturated with the essence of dullness and death, and brought down from a glaring white and black to a decidedly ashy-gray neutral colon, a few small newspapers are permitted to be circulated, but with the greatest caution. They sometimes take fire, it is said,—these journals,—when brought too near any brain overcharged with electricity. Two or three times, it is said, the Governing Machine has been put out of order by the newspapers and their readers bringing too much electro-magnetism (or something like it) to bear on parts of the works;—the machine had even taken fire and been nearly burnt up, and the head engineer got so singed that he never dared to take the management of the works again.

So it is thought that nothing is so unfavourable to the working of the wheels as light, heat, electricity, magnetism, and, generally, all the imponderable and uncatchable essences that float about in the air; and these, it is thought, are generated and diffused by these villainous newspapers. Certain kinds of books are also forbidden, as being electric conductors. Most of the books allowed in the city of Grindwell are so heavy, that they are thought to be usually non- conductors, and therefore quite safe in the hands of the people.

It is at the city gates that most vigilance is required with regard to the prohibited articles. There the poor fellows who keep the gates have no rest night or day,—so many suspicious-looking boxes, bundles, bales, and barrels claim admittance. Quantities of articles are arrested and prevented from entering. Nothing that can in any way interfere with the great machine can come in. Newspapers and books from other countries are torn and burnt up. Speaking-trumpets, ear-trumpets, spectacles, microscopes, spy—glasses, telescopes, and, generally, all instruments and contrivances for extending the sphere of ordinary knowledge, are very narrowly examined before they are admitted. The only trumpets freely allowed are of a musical sort, fit to amuse the people,—the only spectacles, green goggles to keep out the glare of truth's sunshine,—the magnifying-glasses, those which exaggerate the proportions of the imperial governor of the machinery. All sorts of moral lightning-rods and telegraph-wires are arrested, and lie in great piles outside the city walls.

But in spite of the utmost vigilance and care of the officers at the gates and the sentinels on the thick walls, dangerous articles and dangerous people will pass in. A man like Kossuth or Mazzini going through would produce such a current of the electric fluid, that the machine would be in great danger of combustion. Remonstrances were sometimes sent to neighbouring cities, to the effect that they should keep their light and heat to themselves, and not be throwing such strong reflections into the weak eyes of the Grindwellites, and putting in danger the governmental powder-magazine,—as the machine-offices were sometimes called. An inundation or bad harvest, producing a famine among the poor, causes great alarm, and the governmental officers have a time of it, running about distributing alms, or raising money to keep down the price of bread.

Thousands of servants in livery, armed with terrific instruments for the destruction of life, are kept standing on and around the walls of the city, ready at a moment's notice to shoot down any one who makes any movement or demonstration in a direction contrary to the laws of the machine. And to support this great crowd of liveried lackeys, the people are squeezed like sponges, till they furnish the necessary money.

The respectable editors of the daily papers go about somewhat as the dogs do in August, with muzzles on their mouths. They are prohibited from printing more than a hundred words a day. Any reference to the sunshine, or to any of the subtile and imponderable substances before mentioned, is considered contrary to the order of the machines;

to compensate for which, there is great show of gaslight (under glass covers) throughout the city. Gas and moonshine are the staple subjects of conversation. Besides lighting the streets and shops, the chief use of fire seems to be for cooking, lighting pipes and cigars, and fireworks to amuse the working classes.

Great attention is paid to polishing and beautifying the outer case of the machine, and the outer surface generally of the city of Grindwell. Where any portion of the framework has fallen into dilapidation and decay, the gaunt skeleton bones of the ruined structure are decked and covered with leaves and flowers. Old rusty boilers that are on the verge of bursting are newly painted, varnished, and labelled with letters of gold. The main-spring, which has grown old and weak, is said to be helped by the secret application of steam,—and the fires are fed with huge bundles of worthless bank-bills and other paper promises. The noise of the clanking piston and wheels is drowned by orchestras of music; the roofs and sides of the machine buildings are covered all over with roses; and the smell of smoke and machine oil is prevented by scattering delicious perfumes. The minds of the populace are turned from the precarious condition of things by all sorts of public amusements, such as mask balls, theatres, operas, public gardens, etc.

But all this does not preserve some persons from the continual apprehension that there will be one day a great and terrific explosion. Some say the city is sleeping over volcanic fires, which will sooner or later burst up from below and destroy or change the whole upper surface. The actual state of things might be represented on canvas by a gaping, laughing crowd pressing around a Punch-and-Judy exhibition in the street, beneath a great ruined palace in the process of repairing, where the rickety scaffolding, the loose stones and mortar, and in fact the whole rotten building, may at any moment topple down upon their heads.

But while such grave thoughts are passing in the minds of some people, I must relate one or two amusing scenes which lately occurred at the city gates.

Travellers are not prohibited from going and coming; but on entering, it is necessary to be sure that they bring with their passports and baggage no prohibited or dangerous articles. A young man from our side of the Atlantic, engaged in commerce, had been annoyed a good deal by the gate-officers opening and searching his baggage. The next time he went to Grindwell, he brought, besides his usual trunks and carpet-bags, a rather large and very mysterious-looking box. After going through with the trunks and bags, the officers took hold of this box.

"Gentlemen," said the young practical joker, "I have great objections to having that box opened. Yet it contains, I assure you, nothing contraband, nothing dangerous to the peace of the Grindwell government or people. It is simply a toy I am taking to a friend's house as a Christmas present to his little boy. If I open it, I fear I shall have difficulty in arranging it again as neatly as I wish,—and it would be a great disappointment to my little friend Auguste Henri, if he should not find it neatly packed. It would show at once that it had been opened; and children like to have their presents done up nicely, just as they issued from the shop. Gentlemen, I shall take it as a great favour, if you will let it pass."

"Sir," said the head officer, "it is impossible to grant the favour you ask. The government is very strict. Many prohibited articles have lately found their way in. We are determined to put a stop to it."

"Gentlemen," said the young man, "take hold of that box,—lift it. You see how light it is; you see that there can be no contraband goods there,—still less, anything dangerous. I pray you to let it pass."

"Impossible, Sir!" said the officer. "How do I know that there is nothing dangerous there? The weight is nothing. Its lightness rather makes it the more suspicious. Boxes like this are usually heavy. This is something out of the usual course. I'm afraid there's electricity here. Gentlemen officers, proceed to do your duty!"

So a crowd of custom-house officers gathered around the suspected box, with their noses bent down over the lid, awaiting the opening. One of them was about to proceed with hammer and chisel.

"Stop," said the young merchant, "I can save you a great deal of trouble. I can open it in an instant. Allow me—by touching a little spring here—-"

As he said this, he pressed a secret spring on the side of the box. No sooner was it done than the lid was thrown back with sudden and tremendous violence, as if by some living force, and up jumped a hideous and shaggy monster which knocked the six custom-house officers flat on their backs. It was an enormous Punchinello on springs, who had been confined in the box like the Genie in the Arabian story, and by the broad grin on his face he seemed delighted with his liberty and his triumph over his inquisitors. The six officers lay stunned by the blow; and while others ran up to see what was the matter, the young traveller persuaded Mr. Punch back again into his box, and, shutting him down, took advantage of the confusion to carry it off with the rest of his baggage, and reach a cab in safety. When the officers recovered their senses, the practical joker had escaped into the crowded city. They could give no clear account of what had happened; but I verily believe they thought that Lucifer himself had knocked them down, and was now let loose in the city of Grindwell.

Another amusing incident occurred afterwards at the city gates. An American lady, who was a great lover of Art, had purchased a bronze bust of Plato somewhere on the Continent. She had it carefully boxed, and took it along with her baggage. She got on very well until she reached the city of Grindwell. Here she was stopped, of course, and her baggage examined. Finding nothing contraband, they were about to let her pass, when they came to the box containing the ancient philosopher's head.

"What's this?" they asked. "What's in this box, so heavy?"

"A bust," said the lady.

"A bust? so heavy? a bust in a lady's baggage?—Impossible!"

"I assure you, it is nothing but a bust."

"Pray, whose bust may it be, Madam?"

"The bust of Plato."

"Plato? Plato? Who is Plato? Is he an Italian?"

"He was a Greek philosopher."

"Why is it so heavy?"

"It is a bronze bust."

"We beg your pardon, Madam; but we fear there's something wrong here. This Plato may be a conspirator,—a Carbonaro,—a member of some secret society,—a red-republican,—a conductor of the electric fluid. How can we answer for this Plato? We don't like this heavy box;—these very heavy boxes are suspicious. Suppose it should be some infernal-machine. Madam, we have our doubts. This box must be detained till full inquiries are made."

There was no help for it. The box was detained. "It must be so, Plato!" After waiting several hours, it was brought forward in presence of the entire company of inquisitors, and cautiously opened. Seeing no Plato, but only some sawdust, they grew still more suspicious. Having placed the box on the ground, they all retired to a safe distance, as if awaiting some explosion. They evidently took it for an infernal-machine. In their eyes everything was a machine of some sort or other. After waiting some time, and finding that it didn't burst, nor emit even a smell of sulphur, the boldest man of the party approached it very cautiously, and upset it with his foot and ran.

All this while the lady and her friends stood by, silent spectators of this farce. The only danger of explosion was on their part, with laughter at the whole scene. They contrived, however, to keep their countenances, though less rigidly than the Greek philosopher in the box did his.

When the custom-house officials found, that, though the box was upset, nothing occurred, they grew more bold, and, approaching, saw a piece of the bronze head peering above the sawdust. Then, for the first time, they began to feel ashamed of themselves. So replacing the sawdust and the cover, they allowed the box to pass into the city, and tried, by avoiding to speak of the affair among themselves to forget what donkeys they had been.

The Grindwell government has many such alarms, and never appears entirely at its ease. It is fully aware of the combustible nature of the component parts of the Governing Machine. There is consequently great outlay of means to insure its safety. An immense number of public spies and functionaries are constantly employed in looking after the fires and lights about the city. Heavy restrictions are laid on all substances containing electricity, and great care is taken lest this subtile fluid should condense in spots and take the form of lightning. Fortunately, the unclouded sunshine seldom comes into Grindwell, else there would be the same fears with regard to light.

So long as this perpetual surveillance is kept up, the machine seems to work on well enough in the main; but the moment there is any remissness on the part of the police,—bang! goes a small explosion somewhere,—or, crack! a bit of the machinery,—and out rush the engineers with their bags of cotton-wool or tow to stop up the chinks, or their bundles of paper money to keep up the steam, or their buckets of oil and soft soap to pour upon the wheels.

One eccentric gentleman of my acquaintance persists in predicting that any day there may be a general blow-up, and the whole concern, engineers, financiers, priests, soldiers, and flunkies, all go to smash. He evidently wishes to see it; though, as far as personal comfort goes, one would rather be out of the way at such a time.

Most people seem to think, that, considering all things, the present head engineer is about the best man that could be found for the post he occupies. There are, however, a number of the Grindwell people—I can't say how many, for they are afraid to speak—who feel more and more that they are living in a stifled and altogether abnormal condition, and wish for an indefinite supply of the light, heat, air, and electricity which they see some of the neighbouring cities enjoying.

What the result is to be no one can yet tell. We are such stuff as dreams are made of, and our little life is rounded with—a crust; some say, a very thin crust, such as might be got up by a skilful *patissier*, and over which gilded court-flies, and even *scarabaei*, may crawl with safety, but which must inevitably cave in beneath the boot-heels of a real, true, thinking man. We cannot forget that there are measureless catacombs and caverns yawning beneath the streets and houses of modern Grindwell.

The Laird o'Coul's Ghost

The MS. of *Coul's Ghost* was found among the papers of Collector Hamilton, of Dalzell (pronounced *Dëëll*), who died in the summer of 1788, aged 91 years. This incident made him 25 years old when this story was fledged, which was in 1722. In 1733 Lady Anne Spencer, Duchess of Hamilton, came to Hamilton Palace, and the collector gave to Her Grace this story to read. The duke, to play a practical joke on the collector, caused one of his servants to whisper to him while at supper, that there was a gentleman calling, who desired to see him immediately. Being asked who he was, the valet answered, "*The Laird o' Coul.*" The guests were all amused at the collector's embarrassment, who sat still and allowed the "gentleman" to await in the Hall!

The Laird o' Coul's Ghost first appeared in type in 1750, and was eagerly bought by all and sundry from the *Flying Stationers* who hawked it about the country. Mrs. Ogilvie delivered it to Watkins, the King's Printer, which was published from Newcastle. In 1788 a fanatical character, Mrs. Elizabeth Steuart, of Coltness, termed "Aunt Betty," became a convert to the Halcyon notions of Emmanuel Swedenborg, founder of "the New Jerusalem Sect." This personage was related to Henry Erskine, Lord Advocate for Scotland, and was enraptured with the *Penny Chap-Book*: so much so that she embodied it in her *Remarks and Illustrations of the World of Spirits*, which she strictly enjoined her nephew to print after her decease.

Not a copy of this brochure of 206 pages is in any of our University Libraries; and a few weeks ago £3 3s. were paid for a soiled copy. "Aunt Betty" does not miss to note one point in *The Laird o' Coul's Ghost* that may insinuate her imaginations about angels and the unseen; while she adverts to the ghosts of Lord Clarendon, Sir George Villiars, the father of the Duke of Buckingham, and to the dialogue of Dives and Lazarus, in that remarkable parable. She ferreted out from Mrs. Henrietta Hog, Edinburgh, daughter of the Rev. Mr. Ogilvie, Innerwick, that the sequel was undoubtedly the genuine copy in her father's handwriting. No declaration has been given how the MS. came into Collector Hamilton's possession. Mr. Ogilvie died soon after the Conference.

J. F. S. G.

Abbacy of Susanna Rig,
Glasgow,
Xmas, 1891.

THE FIRST CONFERENCE

Account of Mr. Maxwell Laird of Coul his appearance after death to Mr. Ogilvie a minister of the present establishment at Innerwick, 3 miles east from Dunbar.

Upon the 3rd day of February, 1722, at seven a clock at night after I had parted with Thurston (his name Cant), and was coming up the Burial Road, one came riding up after me: upon hearing the noise of his Horse's feet, I took it to be Thurston, but upon looking back, and seeing the horse of a greyish colour, I called "Who is there?" The answer was, "The Laird of Coul (his name Maxwell), be not afraid." Then looking to him by the help of the dark light which the moon afforded, I took him to be Collector Castellow designing to put a trick upon me, and immediately I struck at him with all my force, with my cane, thinking I mould leave upon him a mark, to make him remember his presumption; but being sensible I aimed as well as ever I did in my life, yet my cane finding no resistance, but flying out of my hand the distance of about 60 feet, and observing it by its white head, I dismounted and took it up, and had some difficulty in mounting again, what by the ramping of my horse, and what by reason of a certain kind of trembling throughout my whole joints; something likewise of anger had its share in the confusion; for, as I thought, he laughed when my staff flew away; coming up with him again, who halted all the time I sought my staff, I asked once more, "Who he was?" He answered, "The Laird of Coul." I enquired first if he was the Laird of Coul, what brought him hither, and what was his business with me?

C. "The reason of my waiting on you is, that I know you are disposed to do for me a thing which none of your brethren in Nithsdale will so much as attempt, tho' it serve to ever so good purposes."

I told him I would never refuse to do a thing to serve a good purpose, if I thought I was obliged to do it as my duty. He answered,

327

since I had undertaken what he found few in Nithsdale would, for he had tryed some upon that subject, who were more obliged to him than ever I was, or to any person living: I drew my horse, and halted in surprise, asking what I had undertaken? He answered, that on the Sabbath last, I had heartily condemned Mr. Paton, and the rest of the ministers in Dumfries Presbytery for dissuading Dr. Menzies's man, from keeping his appointment with me, and that if you had been in their place, you would have persuaded the lad to do as I desired him; and that you would have gone with him, lest he had been feared; and that if you had been in Mr. Paton's place, you would have delivered my commissions yourself, since it tended to do some people justice.

O. "Pray, Coul, who informed you that I talked at that rate?"

C. "You must know, that we are acquainted with many things, that the living know nothing about. These things you did say, and much more to that purpose, and all that I want is, that you fulfil your promise, and deliver my commissions to my loving wife."

O. "'Tis a pity, Coul, that you who know so many things, should not know the difference between an absolute, and a conditional promise. I did indeed at the time you mention, blame Mr. Paton, for I think him justly blameable, for hindering the lad to meet with you, and if I had been in his place, I would have acted quite the reverse: but did I ever say, that if you would come to Innerwick, and employ me, that I would go all the way to Dumfries upon that errand? That is what never so much as once entered into my thought."

C. "What was in your thought I do not pretend to know; but I can depend upon my information, that these were your *words*: but I see you are in some disorder, I will wait on you again, when you have more presence of mind"

By the time we were got to James Dickson's enclosure below the churchyard, and while I was recollecting in my mind, whether ever I had spoken these words he alleged, he broke from me thro' the churchyard with greater violence, than ever any man on horseback is capable of, and with such a singing and buzzing noise, as put me in greater disorder, than I was all the time I was with him. I came to my house, and my wife observed something more than ordinary paleness in my countenance, and would allege that something ailed me. I called for a dram and told her I was a little uneasy; after I found myself a little eased and refreshed, I retired to my closet, to meditate on this the most astonishing adventure of my whole life.

Upon the 5th of March 1722. Being at Blarehead baptising the shepherd's child, I came off at sunsetting, or, a very little after. Near Will.White's march the Laird of Coul came up with me on horseback as formerly, and, after his first salutation bid me not be afraid, for he would do me no harm. I told him I was not in the least afraid, in the name of God, and of Christ my Saviour, that he would do the least harm to me: for, I knew that He in whom I trusted was stronger than all them put together, and if any of them should attempt even to do the horse I rode upon. "Harm, as you have done to Dr. Menzies' man,[1] if it be true that is said, and generally believed about Dumfries, I have free access to complain to my lord and master, to the lash of whose resentment you are as much liable now as before."

C. "You need not multiply words upon that head, for you are as safe with me, and safer, if safer can be, than when I was alive."

I said, "Well then, Coul, let me have a peaceable and easy conversation with you for the time we ride together, and give me some information about the affairs of the other world, for no man inclines to lose his time, in conversing with the dead, without having a prospect of hearing and learning something that may be useful."

C. "Well, Sir, I will satisfy you, as far as I think it proper and convenient. Let me know what information you want from me."

O. "May I then ask you, if you be in a state of happiness or not?"

C. "There are a great many things that I *can* answer, which the living are entirely ignorant of: there are many more things, that notwithstanding the additional knowledge I have acquired, since my death, that I *cannot* answer, and there are several things and questions that you may start, of which the last is one, that I *will* not answer."

O. "Then I know not how to manage our conversation, for whatever I shall enquire of you, I see you can easily shift me, so that I might profit more by conversing with myself."

C. "You may try."

O. "Well then, what sort of a body is it that you appear in, and what sort of a horse is it that you ride on, that appears so full of mettle?"

---

1. The first appearance that Coul made was to Dr. Menzies's servant at a time he was watering his master's horse. At some subsequent appearance, while the lad was about the same business, whether Coul had done him any real harm, or, that the lad had fallen from his horse thro' fear and confusion, is uncertain, but so it was, that the lad was found dead on the road

C. "You may depend upon it, 'tis not the same body that I was witness to your marriage in, nor in which I died, for that is in the grave rotting; but it is such a body as answers me in a moment, for I can fly as fast as my soul can do without it, so that I can go to Dumfries and return again, before you ride twice the length of your horse; nay if I incline to go to London, or to Jerusalem, or to the moon, if you please, I can perform all these journeys equally soon, for it costs me nothing but a thought or wish; for this body you see, is as fleet as your thought, for in the same moment of time that you can carry your thoughts to Rome, I can go there in person. And for my horse, he is, much like myself, for 'tis Andrew Johnstoun who was seven years my tenant, and he died about 48 hours before me."

O. "So it seems when Andrew Johnstoun inclines to ride, you must serve him for an horse, as he now does you."

C. "You are mistaken."

O. "I thought all distinction between mistresses and maids, lairds and tenants had been done away at death."

C. "True 'tis so, yet still you don't take up the matter."

O. "Is then, Sir, this one of the questions you *will not* answer?"

C. You are still mistaken; for that question I *can* answer, and after this you may readily understand."

O. "Tell me then, Coul, have you never yet appeared before God, nor received any sentence from him as a judge."

C. "Never yet."

O. "I know you was a scholar, Coul; and 'tis generally believed there is a private judgment, besides the general at the great Day. The former is immediately after death."

Upon this he interrupted me, crying, "No such thing, no such thing, no tryal till the last Day: The Heaven which good men enjoy immediately after death, consists only in the serenity of their thoughts, the satisfaction of a good conscience, and the certain hope they have of an eternity of joy when that Day shall come. The punishment or hell of the wicked immediately after death, consists in the dreadful things of their awakened conscience, and the terror of facing the great Judge, and the sensible apprehensions of eternal torments ensuing; and this bears still a due proportion to the evils they have done, when they were living. So indeed the state of some good folks differs but little in happiness from what they enjoyed upon earth, save only they are freed from the body and the sins and sorrows that attend it. And, on the other hand, there are some, who may be said rather not to have been *good* than that they have been *wicked* while living: their condition is not easily distinguished from that of the *former*, and under that class comes a great herd of souls, a vast number of your ignorant people, who have not much minded the concerns of eternity, but, at the same time, have lived in much indolence, ignorance, and innocence."

O. "I always thought that their rejecting the terms of salvation offered, was sufficient ground for God to punish them with his eternal displeasure. And as to their ignorance, that could never excuse them, since they lived in a place of the world, where the knowledge of these things might easily have been attained."

C. "They never properly rejected the terms of salvation, they never, strictly speaking, rejected Christ, poor souls! they had as great liking both to Him, and to Heaven, as their gross understandings were capable of; and as to their ignorance, impartial reason must make many allowances, such as, the stupidity of their parents, their want of education, their distance from people of good sense and knowledge, the uninterrupted application they were obliged to give to their secular affairs, for their daily bread, the impious treachery of their pastor, whom they heard perhaps but once a month, or so, and thro' his unfaithfulness are persuaded, that if they be of such or such a party all is well; and many other considerations of the like nature, which God who is pure and perfect reason itself will not overlook. These are not so much under the load of the divine displeasure, as they are *out of His graces and favours*, for you know it is one thing to be discourted, and quite another thing to be persecuted with all the power and rage of an incensed earthly king. So I assure you, men's faces in this world are not more various and different, than their conditions are after death."

O. "I am loath to believe all that you have said at this time, Coul; but I will not dispute these matters with you, besides, some things you have advanced, seem to contradict the Scriptures, which I shall ever look upon as the infallible truths of God; for I find by the parable of Dives and Lazarus, that one was immediately carried up by the angels to Abraham's bosom, and the other thrust down to a place of torment."

C. "Excuse me, Sir, that does not contradict one word that I have said; but you seem not to understand the parable, whose only end is to illustrate the truth, that a man may be very happy and flourishing in this world, and most wretched in the next; and that a man may be most miserable and wretched in this world, and most glorious and happy in the next."

O. "Be it so, Coul, I yield that point, and shall pass to another, which has afforded me much speculation since our last encounter, and that is, how you came to know that I talked after the manner I did concerning Mr. Paton and you on the 1st Sabbath of February. Was you present with us but invisible."

He answered somewhat haughtily, "No, Sir, I was not present myself."

O. "I would not have you to be angry, Coul; I proposed this question for my own satisfaction, but, if you judge it improper to answer it, let it pass."

After he had paused, with his eyes fixed, as I thought, on the ground for about 3 or 4 seconds at most; with some haste and seeming cheerfulness, he says: "Well, Sir, I will satisfy you in that point. You must know, that from time to time, there are sent from Heaven angels to guard and comfort, and to do other special services to good people, and even the spirits of good men departed are employed on that very errand."

O. "And do you think every man has a guardian angel?"

C. "No, but a great many particular men have, and there are but few houses, of distinction especially, but what have one attending them. And from what you have already heard of these spirits, 'tis no difficult matter to understand, how he may be serviceable to each particular member of it, tho' in different places, at a great distance. Many are the good offices that the angels do to men that fear God, tho' many times they are not sensible of it, and I know assuredly, that one powerful angel, or even an active clever spirit departed, may be sufficient for some villages: But for your great cities, such as London, Edinburgh, or the like, there is one great angel that has the superintendency of the whole; and there are inferior ones, or spirits departed, to whose particular charge, such a particular man of weight and business is committed. Now, Sir, the Kingdom of Satan does ape the Kingdom of Christ as much in matters of politicks as can be: well knowing that the Court of Wisdom is above; so that, hence are sent out missionaries too in the same order. But because, the Kingdom of Satan is much better replenished than the other, instead of one Devil, in many instances, there are 2 or 3 commissioned to attend a particular family, if it be a family of great influence, power, or distinction."

O. "I read that there are 10,000 times 10,000 angels that wait on God, and sing his praise, and do his will; and I cannot understand how the good angels should be inferior in number to the evil."

C. "Did I not say that whatever the number be, yet the spirits departed were employed in the same business? So, as to the number of original devils, whereof Satan is the chief, I cannot determine. But you need not doubt that there are more spirits departed in that place you in a loose general sense call *Hell*, by almost an Infinity, by what are gone to that place, which in the like sense, you call *Heaven*, which likewise are employed to the same purpose. And I can assure you, by the bye, that there are as great differences between angels, both good and bad, as there are amongst men, with Respect to their sense, knowledge, cleverness, and cunning or action. Nay, which is more, the departed spirits on both sides, outdo severals, from their 1st departure, of the original angels; this you'll think a paradox, yet 'tis true."

O. "I don't doubt of it, but what is that to my question, concerning which I am solicitous?"

C. "Take a little patience, Sir; from what I have said, you might have understood me, if you had your thoughts about you, but, I shall explain myself to you. Both the good and bad angels have their stated times of rendezvous, and the particular angel that has the charge either of towns, cities or kingdoms, not to mention inferior villages and families, and persons; all that are transacted in these several parts of the country, are then made open, and at their encounters, on each side, everything is told, as in your paroch, at milns, kilns and smiddies, only with this difference, that many Things false are told at the living encounters, but nothing but what is exact truth is told amongst the dead. Only, I must observe to you, that as I am credibly informed, several of the inferior bad angels, or spirits of wicked departed, have told mighty things which they have done; and when a more intelligent spirit has been sent out upon enquiry, and, the report of the former, seeming doubtful, he brings in a contrary report, and making it appear truth, the former fares very ill."

O. "Does ever the like happen among good angels?"

C. "I believe never, for their regard to truth prevents it; for while they observe truth, they do their business, and keep their station, and God is truth."

O. "So much truth being among the good angels, I shall be apt to think, that lyes and falsehood will be as much in vogue amongst the bad."

C. "A gross mistake, and 'tis not the alone mistake, that the living folks labour under anent another world: for the case is plainly this; as an ill man will not stick at any falsehood, that may promote his design, so as little will an evil spirit departed stand at anything which may make him successful; but in making reports, he must tell the truth, and nothing but the truth, or, woe be to him; But besides their stated monthly, quarterly, and yearly meetings, or whatever they happen to be, the departed spirits acquainted can make a trip to see, and converse with one another, yearly, daily and weekly, or oftener if they please. Thus I answer the question you are so much concerned about; for, my information was from no less than three, *viz.* Andrew Aikman, who attends Thurston's family, and James Corbet who waits upon Mr. Paton's for the time, and was then looking after Mrs. Sarah Paton, when she was at your house, and an original emissary appointed to wait on your's."

At this I was much surprised, and after a little thinking, I asked him; "and is there really, Coul, an emissary from Hell, in whatever sense you take it, who attends my family?"

C. "Yes, you may depend upon it."

O. "And what do you think is his business?"

C. "To divert you from your duty, and to cause you under hand do as many ill things as he can, for much depends on having the minister on their side."

Upon this I was struck with a sort of terror, that I cannot account for, nor express. In the meantime, he said several things that I did not notice, but after a little, I coming to my former presence of mind, said. "But Coul, tell me in earnest, if there be a devil that attends my family, tho' invisible to us all?"

C. "Just as sure as you are breathing; but be not too much dejected upon this information; for, I tell you likewise, there is a good angel that attends you, who is stronger than the other."

O. "Are you sure of that, Coul?"

C. "Yes, there is one just now riding at your right-hand, who might as well have been elsewhere, for I meant you no harm."

O. "And how long has he been with me?"

334

C. "Only since we past Brunsley, but now he is gone."

O. "Coul, we are just now upon Elmscleugh, and I desire to part with you, tho' I have gained more from our conversation together, than what perhaps I would have done otherwise in a twelve month, I chuse rather to see you at another time, when you are at leisure, and I wish it may be at as great a distance from Innerwick as you can."

C. "Be it so, but I hope you will be as obliging to me, next encounter, as I have been to you this."

O. "I promise you, I will, as far as it consists with my duty to my Lord and Master Christ Jesus; and since you oblige me so much by information, you may depend upon it, I will answer all the questions you can propose, so far as it consists with my knowledge; but I believe you want no information from me."

C. "I came not to be instructed by you, but I want your help of another kind, but more of this at next meeting, so," says he, "I bid you farewell," and went off peaceably at the head of the paith[2] opposite to Elmscleugh.

The Third Conference

Upon the 9th of April 1722. as I was returning from Old Hamstocks, Coul struck up with me upon the back, at the foot of the ruinous enclosure before we come to Dodds. I told him his last conversation had proven so acceptable to me, that I was well pleased to see him again, and that there was a vast number of things, which I wanted to inform myself further of, if he would be so good as to satisfy me.

C. "Last time we met, I refused you nothing that you asked, and now I expect, you will refuse me nothing that I ask."

O. "Nothing, Sir, that is in my power, or, that I can with safety to my reputation and character. What then are your demands upon me?"

C. "All I desire is, that as you proposed that Sabbath Day, you will go to my wife, who now possesses all my effects, and tell her the following particulars, and desire her, in my name, to rectify these matters. 1st that I was justly owing to Provost Crosby £500 Scots, and three years interest, but upon hearing of his death, my good brother, the Laird of Chapel and I, did forge a discharge narrating the date of the bond, the sum, and other particulars, with this onerous clause, that at that time it was fallen by, and could not be found, with an obligation

2. A paith in Scottish signifies a steep, and oft times rugged road.

on the provost's part, to deliver up the bond as soon as he could hit upon it, and this discharge was dated three months before the provost's death: and when his only son and successor Andrew Crosby wrote to me concerning this bond, I came to him, and shewed him that discharge, which silenced him, so that I got my bond without more ado.

"And when I heard of Robert Kennedy's death, with the same help of Chapel, I got a bill upon him, for £190 sterline, which I got full and compleat payment of, and Chapel got the half. When I was in Dumfries the day Thomas Greer died, to whom I was owing an account of £36 sterline, Chapel my good brother at that time was at London, and not being able of myself, being but a bad writer to get a discharge of the account, which I wanted exceedingly, I met accidentally with Robert Boyd a poor writer lad in Dumfries. I took him to Mrs Carricks, gave him a bottle of wine, and told him, that I had payed Thomas Greer's account, but wanted a discharge, and if he would help me to it, I would reward him. He flew away from me in great passion, saying he would rather be hanged; but, if I had a mind for these things, I had best wait till Chapel came home.

"This gave me great trouble, fearing that what he and I had formerly done, was no secret. I followed Boyd to the street, made an apology that I was jesting, commended him for his honesty, and took him solemnly engaged that he should not repeat what had passed. I sent for my cousin Barn-howrie your good brother, who with no difficulty for one guinea and an half, undertook and performed all that I wanted, and for one guinea more, made me up a discharge for £200 Scots, which I was owing to your father in law and his friend Mr. Morehead, which discharge I gave in to John Ewart, when he required the money, and he, at my desire, produced it to you, which you sustained.

"A great many of the like instances were told, which I cannot remember, the person's names, and sums: But added he, what vexes me more than all these, is the Injustice I did to Homer Maxwell tenant to Lord Nithsdale for whom I was factor. I had borrowed 2,000 *merks* from him, 500 of which he borrowed from another hand, and I gave him my bond; for reasons I contrived, I obliged him to secrecy, he dyed within the year, he had nine children, and his wife had dyed a month before himself. I came to seal up his papers for my lord's security.

"His eldest daughter entreated me to look through them all, and to give her an account what was their Stock, and what was their Debt. I very willingly undertook it, and in going through his papers, I put my own bond in my pocket. His circumstances proved bad, and the nine children are now starving. These things I desire you to represent to my wife; take her brother with you, and let them be immediately rectifyed, for she has sufficient fund to do it upon, and, if that were done, I think I would be easie and happy; therefore I hope you will make no delay"

After a short pause I answered; "'tis a good errand, Coul, that you are sending me to do justice to the oppressed and injured; but notwithstanding that I see myself among the rest, that come in for £200 Scots, yet I beg a little time to consider on the matter, and since I find you are as much master of reason *now* and more than ever; I'll just reason with you upon the matter in it's general view; and then, with respect to the expediency of my being the particular messenger; and this I'll do, with all manner of frankness. For, from what you have said, I see clearly what your present state is, so that, I need not ask any more questions upon that head, and you need not bid me take courage, or not be afraid, for at this moment, I am no more afraid of you, than of a newborn child."

C. "Well, say on."

O. "Tell me then, since such is your agility, that in the twinkling of an eye, you can fly 1000 miles, if your desire to do justice to the oppressed persons be so great as you pretend; what is the reason, that you do not fly to the coffers of some rich Jew or banker, where is thousands of gold and money, invisibly lift it, and invisibly return it to the persons injured. Or, since your wife has sufficient fund and more, why can't you empty her purse in your hat invisibly to make the people amends?"

C. "Because I *cannot.*"

O. "If these things were rectified, *you would be easy and happy.* I do not at all credit that; for whatever justice may now be done to these people, yet the Guilt of the base action must still belong to you."

C. "Now, you think you have silenced me, and gained a notable victory, but, I will shew you your mistake immediately, for I cannot touch any man's gold or money by reason of these spirits, which are the stated guardians of justice and honesty."

O. "What is that you tell me, Coul; Do not unworthy fellows break

337

houses every night, and yet you, who can put yourself in 100 shapes in a moment, cannot do it; what is that you say Coul?"

C. "'Tis true, Sir, that among the living, men may find some probable way of securing themselves, but, if spirits departed were allowed, then no man would be secure, for, in that case, every man they had a prejudice at, would soon be beggared."

O. "But might not you go, to the mines of Mexico, where these little sums would never be missed?"

C. "No, for the same reason."

O. "But, Coul there is so much treasure lost in the sea, you can easily dive into the bottom of it, search that, and refund these people their losses, and thereby no man is injured."

C. "You are a little too forward, and incline much to banter; what I said might satisfie you; but since it does not, I tell you further, that no spirits, good or bad, have any power to take any money or gold: the good never do. And the bad, if once in an age they do, it is no small parcel (so, in the copy); for if it were allowed them, then, they would be very successful in their business, for they would never fail to gain their point."

O. "What hinders them," said I, "Coul?"

C. "Superior power, that guards and governs all."

O. "You have satisfied me entirely upon that head, said I; but prithee, Coul, what is the reason, that you cannot go to your wife yourself, and tell her what you have a mind to; I should think this a sure way to gain your point."

C. "The reason is, *because I cannot.*"

O. "That does not satisfy me Coul."

C. "And that is one of the questions that I told you long ago, I *would not* answer. But, if you will go, as I desired, I promise I shall give you full satisfaction, after you have done your business. Trust me for once, and believe me I will not disappoint you."

THE FOURTH CONFERENCE

Upon the 10th of April 1722. coming from old-Camus upon the post road, I met with Coul as formerly, upon the head of the pathe called the *Pease*. He asked me, if I had considered the matter he had recommended? I told him, I had, and was in the same opinion that I was of, when we parted: that I could not possibly undertake his commission, unless he would give it in writing under his hand. I wanted nothing but reason to determine me, not only in that, but all other affairs of my life. I added that the list of his grievances was so long, that I could not possibly remember them without being in writing.

"I know," said he, "that this is a mere evasion: but tell me, if your neighbour, the Laird of Thurston will do it? I would gladly wait upon him."

"I am sure," said I, "he will not: and, if he inclined so, I would do what I could to hinder him; for, I think, he has as little concern in these matters, as I. But tell me, Coul, is it not as easie for you to write your story, as to tell it, or to ride on what is it you call him, for I have forgotten your horse's name."

C. "No, Sir, 'tis not, and perhaps I may convince you of it afterwards."

O. "I would be glad to hear a reason that is solid, for your not speaking to your wife yourself. But however, any rational creature may see, what a fool I would make of myself, if I should go to Dumfries and tell your wife, that you had appeared to me, and told me of so many forgeries and villanies which you had committed, and that she behoved to make reparation. The event might, perhaps, be, that she would scold me: for, as 'tis very probable, she will be loath to part with any money she possesses, and therefore tell me, I was mad, or possibly might pursue me for calumny. How could I vindicate myself, how should I prove, that ever you had spoken with me? Mr. Paton, and the rest of my brethren would tell me, that it was a devil who had appeared to me, and why should I repeat these things as truth, which he that was a lyar from the beginning had told me?

"Chapel and Barn-howrie would be upon my top, and pursue me before the commissary, and everybody will look upon me, as brainsick or mad. Therefore, I entreat you, do not insist upon sending me an April-errand: The reasonableness of my demand I leave to your consideration, as you did your former to mine; for I think what I ask is very just. But dropping these matters till our next interview; give me leave to enter upon some more diverting subject; and I do not know, Coul, but thro' the information given to me, you may do as much service to mankind, as the redress of all the wrongs, you have mentioned would amount to, &c."

The Murder Hole

About three hundred years ago, on the estate of Lord Cassilus between Ayrshire and Galloway, lay a great moor, unrelieved by any trees or vegetation.

It was rumoured that unwary travellers had been intercepted and murdered there, and that no investigation ever revealed what had happened to them. People living in a nearby hamlet believed that in the dead of night they sometimes heard a sudden cry of anguish; and a shepherd who had lost his way once declared that he had seen three mysterious figures struggling together, until one of them, with a frightful scream, sank suddenly into the earth. So terrifying was this place that at last no one remained there, except one old woman and her two sons, who were too poor to flee, as their neighbours had done. Travellers occasionally begged a night's lodging at their cottage, rather than continue their journey across the moor in the darkness, and even by day no one travelled that way except in companies of at least two or three people.

One stormy November night, a peddler boy was overtaken by darkness on the moor. Terrified by the solitude, he repeated to himself the promises of Scripture, and so struggled toward the old cottage, which he had visited the year before in a large company of travellers, and where he felt assured of a welcome. Its light guided him from afar, and he knocked at the door, but at first received no answer. He then peered through a window and saw that the occupants were all at their accustomed occupations: the old woman was scrubbing the floor and strewing it with sand; her two sons seemed to be thrusting something large and heavy into a great chest, which they then hastily locked. There was an air of haste about all this which puzzled the waiting boy outside.

He tapped lightly on the window, and they all started up, with consternation on their faces, and one of the men suddenly darted out at the door, seized the boy roughly by the shoulder and dragged him inside. He said, trying to laugh, "I am only the poor peddler who visited you last year."

"Are you alone?" cried the old woman in a harsh, deep voice.

"Alone here—and alone in the whole world," replied the boy sadly.

"Then you are welcome," said one of the men with a sneer. Their words filled the boy with alarm, and the confusion and desolation of the formerly neat and orderly cottage seemed to show signs of recent violence.

The curtains had been torn down from the bed to which he was shown, and though he begged for a light to burn until he fell asleep, his terror kept him long awake.

In the middle of the night he was awakened by a single cry of distress. He sat up and listened, but it was not repeated, and he would have lain down to sleep again, but suddenly his eye fell on a stream of blood slowly trickling under the door of his room. In terror he sprang to the door, and through a chink he saw that the victim outside was only a goat. But just then he overheard the voices of the two men, and their words transfixed him with horror. "I wish all the throats we cut were as easy," said one. "Did you ever hear such a noise as the old gentleman made last night?"

"Ah, the Murder Hole's the thing for me," said the other. "One plunge and the fellow's dead and buried in a moment."

How do you mean to dispatch the lad in there?" asked the old woman in a harsh whisper, and one of the men silently drew his bloody knife across his throat to answer.

The terrified boy crept to his window and managed to let himself down without a sound. But as he stood wondering which way to turn, a dreadful cry rang out: "The boy has escaped—let loose the bloodhound."

He ran for his life, blindly, but all too soon he heard the dreadful baying of the hound and the voices of the men in pursuit. Suddenly he stumbled and fell on a heap of rough stones which cut him in every limb, so that his blood poured over the stones. He staggered to his feet and ran on; the hound was so near that he could almost feel its breath on his back. But suddenly it smelled the blood on the stones, and, thinking the chase at an end, it lay down and refused to go farther after the same scent. The boy fled on and on till morning, and when at last he reached a village, his pitiable state and his fearful story roused such wrath that three gibbets were at once set upon the moor, and before night the three villain had been captured and had confessed their guilt. The bones of their victims were later discovered, and with great difficulty brought up from the dreadful hole with its narrow aperture into which they had been thrust.

The Mysterious Spaniard

The Chevalier Franval, and his sister Amarylla, were the only children of a French general of great reputation, who died at the beginning of the last century, at an elegant villa to which he had retired in the evening of his days, at the distance of a few leagues from the city of Paris.

At the time of her father's death, Amarylla was receiving her education in the convent of St. Ann at Aurillac. The *chevalier* watched the death-bed of his parent with the most anxious and tender affection; and the most solemn injunction which that parent bestowed on him, was, to supply his place, by every care and attention in his power, to his orphan sister; a command so congenial to the feelings of the *chevalier*, that it was a satisfaction to himself to pronounce a vow to this effect on the ear of his expiring father.

Six months after the death of the general, was the time appointed for Amarylla to quit her convent; and the period being arrived, her brother set out for Aurillac, resolved himself to be her protector on her journey home. He travelled leisurely, and stopping one evening in a small town, where he was informed that the church was a handsome structure, he strolled towards it, intending to amuse an hour by viewing it. On his return to his inn, he perceived loitering before it, a gentleman whom he had seen examining the beauties of the church at the same time that he had been engaged in observing them himself; and concluding that he was a stranger in the place, and his fellow lodger at the inn, addressed himself to him.

The young man (for he did not appear above twenty years of age) met Franval's advances towards an acquaintance with evident pleasure, and entered into conversation with him in a manner which displayed him to have added a liberal education to a good natural understanding. He proved (as Franval had supposed) to be a lodger at the same inn, and they agreed to sup together. The stranger informed Franval, that he was a Spaniard by birth; his name Don Manuel di Vadilla; and that he was travelling, attended by only one servant, solely for his amusement and improvement. After an evening pleasantly spent by both parties, they separated for the night; and on the following morning, took a friendly leave of each other previously to pursuing their respective journeys.

The conciliating manners of Don Manuel had made a very favourable impression in his behalf on the mind of the *chevalier*; and often, as he rode along, did he reflect on the agreeable hours which he had passed in the society of the young Spaniard. At length he reached the convent of Saint Ann, where a meeting of the most joyful and affectionate nature took place between him and his sister.

Amarylla had always been handsome whilst a girl; but during the four years that her brother had been separated from her, he beheld a great augmentation of her charms to have taken place. She was become tall and graceful; her eyes were of a sparkling blue, and expressive of the sweetness of her disposition; her cheeks, twin roses; her lips a bed of coral, within which reposed a double row of pearls.

After remaining three days at Aurillac, the *chevalier* and his sister commenced their journey towards home. As they travelled, he remarked that Amarylla, notwithstanding the sweetness of her temper, which was never for a moment interrupted, appeared to have some object, either of regret or melancholy, for her private thoughts. She would frequently fall into short fits of absence, and heave sighs, which appeared to be accompanied with some tender emotion. The *chevalier* entreated her, by the love which he bore her, as the only remnant of his revered parents, to confide to him the secrets of her heart. For some time Amarylla, with blushes, evaded a direct reply: at length she confessed that a young man, of whom she had a few weeks before caught an accidental view from the seat appointed in the chapel of her convent for the boarders, had made an impression on her heart, which she could not obliterate from it.

Her brother smiled at the warmth of the innocent Amarylla's first sensation of the imperious passion of love, and told her, that as her acquaintance with society increased, which it would do as soon as she was introduced, on her return home, to the world, she would herself laugh at the serious manner in which she now treated a recollection of this nature.

In apologising for her confession, Amarylla urged that the youth had beheld her, not withstanding her retired situation; and that his eyes had beamed with an expression which had eloquently declared his wish of approaching her; and that he had left the church with a last gaze, which she had understood as entreating her to remember him. Still the *chevalier* continued to smile, and Amarylla to sigh.

A journey free from all disasters brought them to the *chevalier's* villa: it was the family mansion, a house of considerable elegance, and furnished in a style of magnificence which rivalled those of most of the nobles: in particular, one of its saloons, and a breakfast apartment on the second story, which were ornamented with paintings of so great value and excellence as frequently to attract strangers to inspect them; an indulgence which was always readily granted to persons of a respectable rank.

On entering the house, the *chevalier* was met by his housekeeper, who informed him, that he had a gentleman, a stranger, lodging in one of the chambers. Franval requested an explanation of her words. She answered, that the gentleman of whom she spoke, had come to the villa about a week before, to view the pictures; that his foot having slipped as he was descending the stairs, he had had the misfortune of breaking one of his legs, and that she had been compelled by humanity, to offer him a bed in the house. The *chevalier*, with the natural generosity and feeling of his heart, commended the conduct she had pursued; and, after a short time, went to visit the stranger, and make him personal offers of his services, when, to his great surprise, he beheld in the invalid, Don Manuel di Vadilla.

The nature of their remarks on this extraordinary meeting may be easily imagined: nor can it be doubted, that the *chevalier* caused every attention to be paid to the recovery of a young man, his first acquaintance with whom had created for him a favourable prejudice in his heart.

Franval passed many hours in each day by the bedside of his guest; and as their acquaintance increased, he learnt from him the following particulars of his history: that he was an orphan; that the few relatives whom he possessed, were all distant ones; that Spain was a country of which the manners and the inhabitants were not congenial to his feelings, and that he had therefore quitted it, and resolved to settle in France; but he had not yet fixed on any spot as a residence: that his fortune, which was ample, he had placed in the hands of a banker in Paris; and had a servant, who was his only attendant, a man apparently about forty-five years of age, named Rodalvo, to whom he expressed himself particularly attached, as he had been in his service from the hour of his birth.

In their conversation, one day, it chanced that Franval mentioned to Don Manuel, his having brought home his sister from the convent of Saint Ann at Aurillac. At the name of the convent the Spaniard smiled; and when Franval enquired the cause of his doing so, he confessed to him, that, having one evening attended vespers in the chapel of that convent, he had been particularly struck by the beauty of one of the boarders; that, at the time, he had not believed the impression made by her charms on his heart to have been so deep as he had since found it; but that with each succeeding day, he now desired more earnestly to see her again.

The *chevalier* recollected the confession which his sister had made to him, of her having beheld with the eye of partiality, a stranger in the church of Saint Ann, who she believed had viewed her with the same emotions as she had seen him; and from the similarity of her account to that of the young Spaniard, he doubted not that they were reciprocally the hero and heroine of each others' adventures. He buried his suspicions in his breast but the progress of time proved them to have been correct.

When Don Manuel was sufficiently recovered from his hurt to quit his chamber, and descend into the apartments in the daily use of the family, the first moment of his encountering Amarylla, was attended with an emotion of joy and surprise on the part of each, which clearly explained to Franval the justice of his conjectures. The enamoured pair were in raptures at this unexpected introduction to each other; and when the perfect use of Don Manuel's limbs was again restored to him, he still lingered at the villa of the Chevalier Franval, unable to quit the adorable object who possessed his heart.

Thus passed on six months, at the expiration of which, Amarylla requested her brother's permission to bestow her hand on Don Manuel. The *chevalier* saw that her affections were placed on him, and that he appeared devoted to her. He had now gained, he believed, a thorough knowledge of Don Manuel's heart and principles; he regarded them calculated to ensure happiness to his beloved sister; and their union was accordingly sanctioned by his approbation.

Never were two amiable hearts more happy than were those of Don Manuel and his Amarylla in the possession of each other; and the Chevalier Franval, unwilling to lose the pleasure of their society, invited them to make his villa their abode. Two years rolled on in happiness uninterrupted, during the course of which two lovely infants strengthened the bond of affection between their parents. Shortly after the birth of their second child, Don Manuel, one morning at breakfast, expressed an intention of riding that day to Paris, and returning again in the evening: this was by no means an unusual thing either with him or his brother-in-law Franval; and when the coffee was removed, he set out for the metropolis, attended by his servant Rodalvo.

The evening closed without the return of Don Manuel; the night advanced, and still he did not arrive. His wife consoled herself with the idea that some engagement, which he had been unable to decline, might have detained him to sleep at Paris, and that the morning would bring him home; but alas! her hope was fallacious; the morning came unaccompanied by Don Manuel; and once more the veil of night descended to the earth, without witnessing his return to his disconsolate Amarylla.

The Chevalier Franval was not less anxious for the fate of his brother-in-law, than distressed at beholding the misery which Don Manuel's mysterious absence caused his sister; and immediately repaired to Paris, to make enquiries concerning him. But in vain were all his attempts at discovering the truth; not a breath of intelligence could be obtained by him, either of Don Manuel, or his servant Rodalvo. The endeavours of the *chevalier* to gain some light upon this dark occurrence, were unabating, and utterly unsuccessful. The days crept on; these grew into weeks, and still the adored husband of Amarylla did not return; and her grief and despondency were almost raised to madness.

At length a vague account reached the *chevalier* and his sister, that her lost husband had been seen travelling in a carriage, which was moving at an extremely swift pace, upon one of the high roads at the southern extremity of the kingdom which led across the Pyrenees into Spain. From the first moment of his disappearance, Amarylla had constantly repeated her conviction, that not infidelity to her, but some misfortune, which he had not been able to counteract, had torn him from her; and she now declared her intention of endeavouring to trace his steps. With much entreaty and persuasion, her brother over-ruled her purpose, and prevailed upon her to remain the guardian of her children, whilst he undertook the office of following the track that had been described to them as the one pursued by Don Manuel.

Instant preparation was accordingly made for the *chevalier's* journey, and, after a most melancholy scene of separation from his sister, he set out, accompanied by a friend named Montreville, whom he had requested to become the partner of his undertaking; and attended his Henri, a confidential servant of his own.

Their journey was pursued with the greatest alacrity till they reached the southern extremity of the kingdom: here they proceeded more slowly, being frequently delayed by their uncertainty of what road to take, and by the inquiries which they made after the object of their search. Not a gleam of success smiled on them, but still they pursued their way with unabating energy. About noon of a gloomy and uncomfortable day, they reached the foot of the rugged Pyrenees. Franval had already determined to proceed into Spain, and accordingly having refreshed themselves at an inn upon the borders of the kingdom they were about to quit, they began to ascend the rough path which led across the mountains.

They rode on till the shades of evening, which were beginning to fall on the earth, warned them to seek shelter for the night. The gloom of an overclouded sky, rendered the coming darkness more rapid than usual in its approach; and the light of day was almost entirely expelled from the Heavens, when the Chevalier Franval was so fortunate as to descry a light in a distant habitation.

"See there," he cried, on observing it, "a light at length appears! Thank Heaven, we shall now get housed for the night; for it is doubtless a post-house from whence it shines."

The light appeared in view till they were arrived within a short distance of the house, and it then vanished in a sudden manner, as if it had been blown out.

They rode up to the door: Henri applied the butt-end of his whip to it in lieu of a knocker; at the same time remarking, 'That if the inhabitants were in bed, every one could scarcely be asleep, except the lamp they had seen had gone out of itself.'

For a time they were led to conjecture that this had been the case, for no reply was returned to their repeated knockings: but at length, after another salute on the part of Henri with his leaden-headed whip upon the hollow door, which was loud enough to have raised the dead, if they were ever to be raised by mortal means, a window in the upper part of the house was opened, and a head thrust out. "What is it you want?" asked the voice of a female.

"Meat, drink, and repose," replied Montreville; "have you them to sell?"

"I am no conjurer, to sell sleep," replied the woman, in a tone between pleasantry and sulkiness. "If you mean that you want to lodge here, I have not a pallet in my house that is unoccupied;" and with these uncourteous words she drew in her head again, and shut the window.

"I wish we had not travelled so late," said Franval.

"Phoo, nonsense," cried Montreville, who was a young man, and whose good spirits, and gaiety of heart, never forsook him, "they must at all events allow us to sit up in the house, if they can't put us to bed in it. I'll be satisfied with a chair to repose in, if they will but open the larder to me."

"And the cellar, *Monsieur*," said Henri.

"And the cellar, as you say," replied Montreville. "So, at them again, Henri; beat another *rat-ta-ta-too* upon the door, and let us learn if we can't come to terms, now we agree to put beds out of the question."

Henri had again recourse to his leaden-headed whip and in about ten minutes the same casement was again opened, and the rough voice of a man called out, "Whoever ye are, if ye do not go quietly about your business, and cease to disturb the peace of my house, I'll find means to make you answer for your behaviour."

"Our business, friend, is here," replied Montreville. "We are three half-starved travellers, who request to be allowed to shelter ourselves in your house during the night."

"Half-starved travellers, indeed," grumbled out the host: "it is worth while raising a man out of his sleep, to attend to half-starved travellers, truly."

"But my friend only means," said Franval, "that we are very hungry travellers, not very poor ones; and I add in his name, and my own, that we will reward you very liberally for any accommodation you may grant us."

"Upon the word of a Christian," said Henri, "there is gold in the saddle bags of both these gentlemen."

"All the better for them," returned the host, "but as I am no robber, nor can admit them into my house, none of it is likely to fall to my share."

"Why can you not admit us?" enquired Franval. "We are not robbers any more than yourself."

"It cannot be," returned the host.

"So you have told us before," replied the *chevalier*, "and still do not inform us by what motive you are actuated, in refusing us shelter beneath your roof."

The host was silent.

"Yours is a post-house, is it not?" continued Franval.

"Yes," was the reply.

"Then let me tell you, friend," rejoined Montreville, "that as you live by keeping open house, the travellers upon whom you shut your door, have a just right to receive a very good reason, for your conduct, or to open the door for themselves."

"Are ye Catholics, gentlemen?" demanded the landlord.

"Yes, we are," both answered.

"Do you respect an oath as sacred?" enquired the host.

"Yes, yes; we do, we do," replied all three; imagining that some terms for their entrance into the house were about to be proposed to them.

"Then know," replied the host, "that I have already once tonight sworn by Saint Francis not to open my door; and I now swear by him a second time, to keep my first oath sacred."

Montreville was beginning to fly into a passion. The host stopped him, by raising his voice and continuing to speak; "But if I can render you any other service; if a flask of wine, a loaf of bread, or a lanthorn to light you on your way, are of any use to you, you shall have them."

"Let us taste the wine," said Montreville, whilst Franval sat meditating on the strangeness of the host's conduct.

A flask of good wine for the production of a post-house was handed out to them, and with it some cakes of newly-baked bread. Hunger is a keen sensation, that requires much less parade in its gratification than custom usually assigns to it; and, seated upon their saddles, they found the bread and wine very refreshing and comfortable.

"You have dealt so far honourably by us," said Franval, "and shall experience the same honour from us. Here," added he, throwing a *demi-louis d'or* at the window as he spoke, "this for your bread and wine, and twenty more shall follow it, if you will let us in."

"It is a good price, *Messieurs*; but I am better paid to keep you out," said the host.

"Us!" cried Montreville, "to keep us out?"

"Not you in particular," returned the man; "for I know you not; every one, I mean."

A woman now advanced to the window with a lanthorn, which had a lamp burning in it; the man received it at her hands, and lowering it out of the casement, asked if they chose to have it?

Henri received it; and the host then drew in his head, and was upon the point of shutting the casement.

"Stay, hear us an instant, I beg," said Franval. "Cannot you direct us to any cottage, any dwellings, where we might pass the night?"

"There are stray cottages scattered about," answered the host; "but you would find it impossible to gain admittance into any one of them: their inhabitants would take you for robbers, and nothing you could say would convince them to the contrary, at this time of the night: they live in so great fear of *banditti*, that they might even, perhaps, fire upon you without enquiring your business."

"To cut the matter short at once," exclaimed Montreville, "tell us how much you have received to keep out visitors, and if our purse is rich enough, we will outbid your guests."

"Gentlemen," said, the host, gravely, "you said you were Catholics, and respected an oath. Remember mine—You shall not come in."

"But if the inhabitants of cottages are afraid of three men, probably those of castles will not have the same apprehensions, as they are provided both with numbers and arms; so cannot you direct us to one of them?" enquired Franval.

"Why this is a part of the country where there are but few buildings of that description," answered the host; "there is but one within ten leagues of us, and that is at the distance of nearly four from this spot; and were you near it, I would not by any means advise you to attempt to enter it."

"Why so? who inhabits it?" asked Montreville.

"He is known by the name of Don Bazilio," replied the host, "and is by some reputed to be a nobleman of great wealth; others believe him to be Belzebub himself."

Montreville laughed at the manner of the host's expressing himself; and Franval's eye was at that moment attracted by a faint light which proceeded from an upper casement of the house, at which he perceived standing, a tall, lank form, of a swarthy and terrific countenance, which almost corresponded with his idea of the being which the host had just named, and caused him an indescribable sensation for the moment he beheld it; and it was but a moment that his eye had fixed on it, ere the shutter was pulled up, and closed it from his sight.

Franval made no observation on what he had seen to his companions; and Henri, addressing the host, said, "I suppose you mean to let us understand that it is haunted."

"Dreadfully, dreadfully haunted, is the Castle of Virandola," replied the landlord; "at least so it is reported. I never went to see, nor ever intend it."

"What shall we do in this cursed dilemma?" exclaimed Montreville.

"I have done all it is in my power to do for you," said the host; "and so I wish you safe travelling; and a good night, *Messieurs*;" and with these words he shut the casement.

Montreville was again on the point of calling him back, when Franval stopped him, by saying, "Come, let us ride on."

"Ride on! but whither?" cried Montreville.

"We can have no choice; the road lies before us," replied Franval; then, in an under tone, he added, "I'll explain myself to you presently;" and as he spoke, he clapped spurs to his horse, and set forward; and his companions followed his example.

"Why did you so suddenly leave the house which you were a quarter of an hour ago as eager as myself to enter?" enquired Montreville of his friend, before they had ridden an hundred yards away from the post-house.

Franval did not slacken his horse's pace till Montreville a second time urged his enquiry; and Franval then replied, "I have no doubt but that the reason of our being refused admittance into that house, is, that a gang of *banditti*, or at least some members of a lawless community of that nature, are concealed within it; perhaps in the very act of flying from justice;" and he then described the terrific visage which he had seen peeping through the window, and which, he said, if it had been a human countenance, he could only suppose to be that of a savage and bloodthirsty plunderer.

"Thank Heaven, I did not see him," cried Henri.

"We all owe our thanks to Heaven, that we were not admitted into the house, if such are its guests, as I conjecture them to be," said Franval.

"But in my opinion," returned Montreville, "we are far from safe now: don't it appear likely to you, that we were turned from the house, in order that these fellows, of whom you saw one, might pursue and plunder, perhaps murder, us? The rascal of a host would not lose the credit of his house, by suffering us to be assailed in it, lest any of us should have the good fortune to escape from their clutches, and relate the story; so he artfully takes a deeper share in the plot, by sending us forward."

"I have no fears of that kind," rejoined Franval; "our horses are fleet-footed, and will outstrip many animals."

"Of what use is their fleetness in this gloom?" said Montreville: "don't you perceive that the night is become so dark, that when we are half a dozen paces before or behind Henri and his lanthorn, we cannot discover the road? Thus, in such an emergency, the fleetness of their feet would, in all probability, only serve to carry us headlong down a precipice. The farther we get away from the post-house, however, the better, I think; so let us lose no time in debating."

This was agreed to by Franval; and they again spurred their horses into a trot, which they continued for about half a league, when a rocky break in the ground obliged them to move with caution, and at foot's pace. Whilst they were crossing this uneven track of ground, "Hark! *Messieurs*, hark!" cried Henri.

"What! what do you hear?" asked Montreville impatiently.

"The trampling of horses, *Messieurs*: don't you?" was the reply.

"I do, I do," cried Montreville: "they are coming upon us! Franval, don't you hear them?"

A pause of silence ensued: Franval broke it: "I did hear them," he said, "but they are no longer audible."

"They have stopped," said Montreville, "perhaps till some more of their comrades have joined them."

"Or, perhaps," said Henri, "they have turned out of the road upon the grass, that we may not hear their approach: they must judge that their horses hoofs cannot escape our hearing on the beaten pathway, as our lanthorn informs them exactly at what distance we are from them."

"Oh, curse the lanthorn; blow it out," cried Montreville.

"No, no," interrupted Franval: "in the course of our necessities this night, its light may prove as beneficial to us, as we now consider it injurious to our safety; therefore give it to me, Henri, and I'll hide it under my cloak."

"The sounds do not return," said Henri.

"It is as dark as pitch," cried Montreville.

"I can distinguish a knot of trees to our right," said Franval: "my plan is, that we ride in amongst them, and keep ourselves concealed there for a short time, during which period it is not improbable that they may pass us, supposing us to be gone on.—What think you of my scheme?"

"I do not disapprove it," said Montreville; "but we will load our pistols."

"Undoubtedly," replied Franval; "but the expedient I have proposed may save us from the necessity of spilling human blood, or suffering our own to be spilt."

They rode swiftly up to the trees, which were not above two score in number, planted in a shallow declivity at the mouth of the valley. Partial clumps of underwood formed a tolerable screen between them and the road they had just quitted, and they sat scarcely allowing themselves to respire, lest the suspiration of their breath should prevent their hearing any other sound which it might be important to them not to lose.

Nearly a quarter of an hour was thus spent, without the least noise of any kind meeting their ears, when they heard a sound resembling the leaves of a bush, when pressed upon by a person who is endeavouring to force himself a passage through them.

"There, there!" whispered Montreville.

Franval cocked his pistol, but did not speak.

Several minutes again passed away in silence. "It was only the wind," again whispered Montreville; but scarcely had he spoken, ere the noise was repeated; and in the following instant a voice exclaimed, "Proceed to the Castle of Virandola."

Montreville immediately discharged his pistol towards the spot from whence the voice had proceeded, and Henri fired off his in the same direction.

When the report of the pistols had died away, universal silence again prevailed; no groan announced the bullets to have inflicted a wound: no flying step discovered the discharge of their tubes to have inspired any object with fear. "What can this mean?" exclaimed Franval.

"It is, doubtless, a lure to draw us into the power of some enemy. Ten to one but the Castle of Virandola is the residence of a *banditti*, who hope by this stratagem to inveigle us into their power," replied Montreville. "A likely story, indeed, that we should proceed to a place we have the account of, which the landlord gave us of this castle, upon such an obscure invitation. You would not certainly be so rash as to think of it?"

"The voice appeared more than human," said Franval.

"Nonsense," exclaimed Montreville; "I say it is some trick; and whatever your opinion may be, I swear that if I go to the castle"--

"Swear not, but go," interrupted the voice which had before been heard; and it now spoke from the opposite direction to that whence it had before proceeded.

"There again," cried Franval.

"'Tis solemn, I confess," said Montreville; "but still, I think it is mortal."

"Let us search whether we can discover some one hidden amongst the bushes," rejoined Franval, drawing the lanthorn from under his cloak; and as he spoke, he vaulted from his horse. Montreville followed his example; and Henri taking the bridles of their horses, they proceeded towards the spot where the speaker had appeared to be concealed the second time they had been addressed by him.

Nothing was to be seen; nothing was to be heard. They moved on towards the place from whence the voice had proceeded the first time of their hearing it. Equally unsuccessful was their pursuit.

After a considerable time thus spent in fruitless researches after the mysterious speaker by whom they had been addressed, they returned to their horses. "Nobody is to be found," said Montreville, addressing Henri.

"I feared as much, *Monsieur*," returned the valet.

"Feared!" echoed Montreville.

"Yes, *Monsieur*. I cannot help thinking that the voice resembled one that was heard the night before an old lady I once lived with in Alsace died," was the reply.

Franval had already said that the voice had appeared to him to be more than human. Henri's opinion strengthened his; and the light of the lanthorn was just sufficient to shew each that his companions' minds were occupied with unpleasant and undefined sensations.

The temper of Franval was steady, firm, and cool; and although transactions of an unexplained nature had lately occurred in his family, such as might also prepare him for a voice of warning or instruction, he did not choose to let it appear to his friend and servant, that he was moved by the occurrence just past; and therefore, with as much composure as he was able to command, he mounted his saddle, and said "As we appear to have no immediate cause to apprehend the approach of *banditti*, let us ride on; let us return to the road, and pursue our way."

Montreville was a young man not deficient in courage, but his disposition was tinctured with a dislike to forming acquaintance with any of the members of the world of spirits. Henri resembled him in this particular; and therefore they joyfully followed Franval's proposition of quitting the spot, where they firmly believed one of the members of the aerial community to have been flitting around them.

They continued to ride on for a considerable time without interruption; their conversation consisting merely of occasional remarks on the extraordinary adventure which they had encountered that night. When they had proceeded about a league and a half, Montreville said, "My horse knocks up; he can't go much farther without rest, I am certain; indeed, I expect that our beasts and ourselves will all be material sufferers by our want of repose, and shelter from the night air. If we could discover any habitations I should be tempted to knock at the door, in spite of what the master of the post-house said."

This observation had not been long made on the part of Montreville, ere a vivid flash of lightning passed before their eyes.

"I have foreseen a tempest some time," said Henri, "and a heavy one I think it will be; only look at the awful blackness of the clouds over our heads, *Messieurs.*"

Franval and his friend raised their faces to the sky and felt upon them a few partial drops of rain, which announced a shower at hand. Again the lightning flashed its resplendent brilliancy upon the earth, and the thunder rolled in solemn grandeur through the sky; with each flash the tempest appeared to gather strength; with each succeeding moment the rain fell in greater quantities: and the situation of our travellers became of the most pitiable kind.

"Can we espy no cavity in the earth, no rocky dell, no place of any kind which may afford us a temporary shelter?" said Montreville; "not only the clothes we have on, but those in our saddle-bags likewise must be drenched with this heavy rain."

The mingled hail and rain, driven along by the current of a powerful north-east wind, met them full in the face; and the horses of our travellers kept continually turning to the right and to the left, in order to avoid it. At the moment Franval's horse was making a movement of this nature, a sudden flash of lightning enabled his master to descry what he could merely distinguish to be part of a wall. He communicated the observation he had made to his friend, and they immediately turned their horses towards it, in the hope of its forming part of a building which might afford them the enviable blessing of shelter from the inclemency of the weather.

As they moved on, they observed many fragments of stone scatted upon the ground, which appeared to be the ruins of a building that had either fallen into natural decay, or been crumbled by the hand of violence; and when they gained the wall which had been descried by Franval, their conjectures were confirmed, for they found that it formed a part of the ruin of an ancient monastic building.

A considerable part of the front of the edifice was still standing; but, on looking through the archway in which the gate of the entrance had once been swung, the observations which they were enable to make by the momentary illumination of the passing lightning presented them only with a long perspective of gloomy ruins.

It appeared, however, probable that these ruins might afford some nook to protect them from the weather; and in this hope they dismounted; and leading their horses through the gateway, they tied them by their bridles to the remains of a massive pillar, by the side of which the wall was sufficiently high to protect them, in some measure, from the driving blast; and by the help of the lanthorn, they then proceeded to seek out for some spot which was supplied with a covering for their own heads.

A high and narrow door-way attracted them towards it: they passed through it, and found themselves within a passage partially sheltered by a roof. On one side appeared three steps of a dark marble; these they ascended, and entered an apartment which had in all probability, been the chamber of the superior at the time that the mansion had been in a state of habitation; its walls were now bare; the floor of a black oak, and in many parts broken through; and the hearth filled with fragments of stone, which had fallen upon it from the chimney.

From this apartment a single step led into a small closet, formed in the shape of an alcove, of which the floor corresponded with the former; but the walls were intersected by niches and slender pillars of stone, surmounted with compartments in fret-work, which now exhibited a striking picture of former elegance sinking under the ravaging hand of decay.

The thunder still rolled in hoarse and awful peals; and the refulgence of the forked lightning blazed at intervals through a narrow arch in the wall, which had once been the frame of a gothic and spiral window, and of which no remnants, but the iron bars, which had intersected the glass, were now remaining.

At length, after full an hour had passed in tedious expectation, the lightning became scarcely visible, and the thunder receded in gentle murmurs to the distant mountains. "Shall we return to our horses, and proceed?" said Franval.

"It still rains violently," replied Montreville; "and the darkness appears almost impenetrable."

"It is quite so, *Monsieurs*," said Henri. "If I might take the liberty of advising, I think it would be infinitely better, now we have a roof over our heads, to keep under it till day begins to dawn."

"But this is a sad, uncomfortable place," resumed Franval; "and if we could reconcile ourselves to enduring it in preference to being exposed to the pelting of the merciless elements, our horses must remain suffering in the wet and cold."

"They will not be the worse for that, *Monsieur*," returned Henri; "they are used to all weathers when they are out at pasture; and I left them bridle-room enough to enable them to pick up the grass as they stand."

"Upon my life," cried Montreville, "I am very much of Henri's opinion about remaining here till dawn of day. We are now become tolerably dry again; and should we issue out from this retreat, we shall be certain of getting wet through once more; and perhaps, after all, may not be lucky enough to find a house to refresh ourselves at. I think it would be very possible to get a comfortable nap here, wrapped up in our cloaks."

After a good deal of debate upon the subject, it was agreed that any shelter was preferable to encountering the heavy rain which continued to fall; and Montreville having wound his horseman's cloak tightly around him, lay down in one corner of the apartment with the intention beguiling an hour or two in sleep, and advised his companions to do the same.

"Had you not better, *Monsieur*, endeavour to compose yourself to sleep?" said Henri to his master; "this place seems to be perfectly quiet, and free from danger; and a little repose will render you the better able to bear the fatigue of travelling tomorrow."

"No," replied Franval; "I don't feel inclined to sleep; but lie you down, and take a nap, if you please." Henri availed himself of his master's permission, and stretched himself out by the side of Montreville, placing the lanthorn at his head.

Franval continued for some time to wander about the apartment where his friend and servant lay locked in the arms of sleep, till the wind, beginning to blow from another quarter to what it had before done, pierced through the stone arch of the window with chilly gusts, that induced him to seek a more sheltered situation in the adjoining closet.

In spite of those anxieties of mind which rendered him less impressive to the attacks of sleep than his companions, Franval began to feel rather weary; and seating himself upon the floor, he rested his head in niche between two of the pillars of the stone-work.

The minute he desisted from bodily exercise, the influence of sleep began to steal over his senses, and ideas to fade away under its advances. Suddenly a momentary crash made him start, and this was followed by a rumbling noise, which he had no hesitation in supposing to be caused by some mouldering fragments of the building, which had been precipitated upon the ruins below by the violence of the wind; and he again leant back his head, and closed his eyes.

Again his thoughts were wandering from the world into that confusion of ideas which accompanied the approach of sleep to a mind ill at ease within itself, when he was startled by the sound of a lengthened sigh. He sprang upon his feet; but instantly recollecting how near to him were Montreville, and his servant, he made no doubt that the sound he had heard, had been an exclamation uttered by one of them in his sleep.

He approached the door of the room where they lay, and, by the light of the lanthorn, he perceived them both still extended on the floor; and as he stood observing them, he heard Henri exclaim, "Oh, Marie! Marie!" which he knew to be the name of a little peasant girl in Brittany, who had won his heart and not doubting that the sigh he had hears, had been one which Henri had addressed to her image, which had appeared to him in his dreams, he returned to his resting place, and a third time composed himself to sleep.

He sunk to repose; but how long he had slept he was uncertain, when he was awakened by a noise resembling a gust of wind rushing through a narrow aperture; he hastily opened his eyes, and beheld object, at the sight of which the blood ran cold and trembling through his veins--He beheld the very countenance of savage expression, which he had seen through the window of the post-house; its eyes were fixed upon him, and assisted in their observation by a lighted firebrand, which the terrific form held in one of its hands. The figure of the unknown was tall and lank: the long black cloak in which it was enveloped was insufficient to hide the sharp angles of its bony stature; a hat of dark brown fur pulled down below its ears, gave a very finish of horror to its savage aspect; thus the horrible being appeared, bending forward as it stood, to gain a better view of Franval's person.

Franval started, but had not power to rise, or to speak. Instantly upon this motion on his part, with one rapid stride, the figure vanished from his sight. Its disappearance was followed by a loud clap, resembling the echo which runs through a hollow passage, after a door at its extremity has been hastily closed.

Franval attempted to call to his friend and Henri, but his tongue clove to his mouth, and refused its office. He staggered to the door of the apartment where he had left them asleep; the light which had been burning by their side, was now extinguished, or the lanthorn gone. A few minutes recovered to him the power of speech, and he called upon them both by name. Henri immediately replied to his call; and very soon after, Montreville enquired "what was the matter?"

Through an arched window, Franval had a view of the Heavens; and he perceived that the light of day was already beginning to streak the sky. "Be not alarmed," he replied, in answer to their enquiries; "follow me into the air; I stand in need of its refreshment; and I will then explain to you what agitates me."

He darted out of the apartments and they followed him as quickly as the darkness of the place would permit; for their lamp had died in the socket, and the light of day was still so feeble, as to render objects scarcely discernible.

They found him leaning against a broken pillar, which stood in an open space apart from the mass of ruins. They approached him, renewed their enquiries; and he satisfied them with an account of what he had witnessed.

Montreville heard him with patience, but persisted in endeavouring to persuade him that the whole had been a dream, caused by the impression which had been made on his mind by the strangeness of the voice that had addressed them when amongst the trees, and the ghastly countenance which he had seen peeping through a window of the post-house. But Franval replied, "that he was certain that the figure which he had seen standing over him with a firebrand in its hand, and which he knew to be the same that he had beheld with a sensation approaching to horror when looking through the window of the post-house, had been a reality.

"Well," returned Montreville, "it is possible that this ruin may be the haunt of a *banditti*, of which he is one."

"I do not believe him to be a robber," replied Franval.

"Why not? What has changed your opinion of him?" asked his friend.

"I cannot say why," answered Franval; "and yet I feel my sentiments utterly changed with regard to him."

"Your ideas are bewildered by the events of the night," said Montreville.

"And then that strange voice commanding us to go to the Castle of Virandola," said Henri; "it rings in my ears yet."

"Strange indeed!" breathed forth Franval in solemn accents; and he added, "Can it be connected with him whom we seek?"

"Whithersoever we go," rejoined Montreville, "I think we had better be jogging from hence; this is not a place favourable to the combating of gloomy reflections, whether they proceed from imagination, or fact."

"No," resumed Franval; "I can't, I will not quit this spot, till I have made some investigation of the closet where I slept: I must examine whether there is a door in that particular part of the wall, at which the strange figure, whose countenance rests so forcibly on my memory, could have departed from the place: if I find any outlet, my ideas of its mortality will be confirmed."

"And if you do not?" said Montreville

"I shall still be very much tempted to believe that there is some mode of egress from the place which is not discernible to me, though known to that person, whoever he may be," answered the *chevalier*.

Franval could not be argued out of his resolution of examining the closet in which he had passed the night, as soon as the light of the day should be sufficiently powerful to assist him in his investigation. Indeed, Montreville had promised to accompany Franval on his present journey from motives of pure friendship, and therefore was easily won to desist from any opposition to such plans as his friend conceived to be for his happiness.

A drizzling rain was still falling to the earth; and although the wind had much abated in strength, it still blew cold and cheerless through the long avenues of ruins; and as Franval was unwilling to return to the shelter of the apartment they had just quitted, they wandered about in order to preserve themselves from the ill effects of the cold.

After some time, Henri was, in the course of their movements, separated from his master and Montreville; and scarcely had they noticed his absence, ere they heard a pistol fired at a short distance from them. Supposing Henri to be attacked, they flew to the spot where they had parted from him, and observed him standing with his arm extended into the air, and his pistol still in it.

"Was it you who fired?" asked Franval.

"Yes," replied Henri; "and I have either brought him down, or he is run away."

"Who? who?" Impatiently demanded Franval and his friend.

"A tall fellow, wrapped in a black cloak," answered Henri, "exactly corresponding with the description my master gives of the rascal who stood gazing upon him with the firebrand in his hand. The moment that you had turned the angle of the range of pillars behind us, I observed him mounted upon the high wall; and the instant I observed him, I saw him stretch his arm towards me, and was ignorant to what end, till I saw some sparks, which convinced me that he had directed at me a pistol that had missed fire. I immediately drew mine from my girdle, and fired it at him in my own defence; and he directly disappeared; but I cannot tell whether he fell by my bullet or fled from a repetition of my fire."

"We will go to the spot, and ascertain," said Franval boldly; and immediately began to climb a pile of the ruins which led to the wall whereon Henri had seen the form. Nothing that had motion, was visible to any one of the party, when they had reached the height, which had once been a terrace projecting from the second range of windows on the side of the monastery. Many delusive shapes were to be seen, which, on close investigation, proved to be only broken arches, and decapitated pillars, which, beheld at a short distance in the twilight of the morning, appeared in certain directions to assume the form of men.

They did not relax in their search, because many disappointments attended it; but it proved wholly unsuccessful; no human being was to be discerned in any part of the ruins; nor did it appear probable that Henri's pistol had wounded the one he had beheld; for as the light of day rose, they found that no spots of blood stained any part of the stone-work upon which he had appeared.

They again descended to the lower range of dilapidated grandeur, which presented itself in the romantic fragments of the mouldering abbey; and judging it now to be sufficiently light for the examination of the closet upon which Franval had resolved, they returned to that part of the building where they had passed the hours of sleep.

Montreville was the first who entered the chamber leading to the closet, and directly on stepping into it, he exclaimed, "Why, what have we here?—See—behold—characters traced upon the floor!"

Franval darted hastily forward, and beheld upon the black oak floor, these words, "*Quit this place*." Wrapt in astonishment and thought, he stood with his eyes fixed on the letters.

"Surely, *Monsieur*," cried Henri, half trembling, "it can only be a devil who plays these pranks with us."

"It is a friendly devil, however," returned Montreville, "for he warns us to get out of the way of danger; if there is any in staying here."

"I will not quit this place," cried Franval sternly, after a pause of reflective silence. "This command is to my senses, a sufficient conviction that there is some mystery to be developed by staying; and I feel impelled by a stronger sentiment than curiosity, to exert myself in order to make that discovery."

Franval rubbed one of the letters on the floor with his finger, and found that they were only written in chalk, and could easily be effaced.

"Come, pray, let us depart," said Montreville, after another pause.

"Not, at all events, till I have examined the walls of the closet," said Franval, and moved forward to the investigation. His companions followed him, and assisted in the scrutiny; but it produced only disappointment; there were an infinite number of cracks in the stone-work of the walls, but none of sufficient regularity, or length, to flatter them with the idea that it could form any part of a door, or an opening of any kind.

"I would wager my life," said Franval, "that these words were written by that horrible figure which I twice beheld in the course of last night. Surely this ruin cannot be the Castle of Virandola, of which the host spoke."

"I should imagine not," replied Montreville: "this place does not bear the appearance of ever having been a castle; every thing about it denotes it to have been a religious building."

A silence ensued; Montreville broke it: "Franval," he said, "I am certain you cannot doubt my friendship; prove to me that you have not lost that respect for the admonitions of your friend, with which you have so frequently received them at my lips: let us for the present quit this abode of mystery; let us seek some house where our bodily necessities may be attended to; and let us also employ some time in making enquiry into the report which this ruinous fabric bears in the world; and should you then still have any cause, or merely feel any wish, to make a future investigation of its secrets, I pledge my honour, that I will return with you to it, and even risk my life in assisting you through your adventure."

For a considerable time the entreaties of Montreville, seconded by those of Henri, produced no effect upon the mind of Franval: at length, after he had received a renewal of his friend's promise to return with him at some future period, if it should be his desire to make a second visit to the place they were now in, he agreed to accompany them in quest of refreshment; and information, if any were to be gained, which could assist in throwing light upon the strange adventures which had marked the last twelve hours.

Having mounted their horses, they turned into the road, and pursued the path along which they had on the former evening been journeying: at the distance of rather more than half a league from the ruin, they descried a cottage apart from the high road, and immediately rode up to it.

Before they reached the humble dwelling, the door was opened by a peasant girl of about twelve years old, who, it appeared, had seen them through a window, and been attracted by curiosity to behold travellers of so different an order of beings to those amongst whom she was accustomed to live.

Montreville called to her, and enquired whether there was any body in the cottage besides herself, and whether they would sell them any milk and bread.

The girl replied that her mother and grandmother were both within; and directly called the former, who quickly made her appearance. Having heard our travellers wants, she readily agreed to supply them in the best manner she was able; and invited them to alight, and walk in: this Montreville and Franval did: and Henri, conducted by the girl, led the horses to a stable behind the cottage, where he found a welcome of sweet, although coarse provender, for his beasts.

Franval and his friend took seats. The woman, with the garrulity natural to her sex, and her rank in life, began to inform them of her own family affairs: her husband and her sons, she said, were gone to labour on a distant part of the mountains, and she was anticipating their return with much pleasure, because they had promised to beg some grapes of the master of the vineyard for her mother, who was particularly fond of them, and who being now far advanced in years, and totally blind, had no enjoyment left her but that of the palate, which she had the least opportunity of gratifying.

This decrepit old female sat in one corner of the cottage, with her feet rested on a large stone, in order to shorten the distance at which they would else have hung from the ground, and with her chin nearly bent upon her knees.

The peasant's wife having finished the little history of her family, began to speak of the tempestuous night which was just past; and to enquire whether our travellers had rested in any part to which the tempest had extended?

"We had, indeed, a most uncomfortable lodging," replied Montreville, and informed the good woman where they had passed the night.

"It must have been uncomfortable lodging in the ruins of Saint Luke's Abbey," said the woman.

"Extremely so, I assure you," returned Montreville; "but on what account do you particularly mean?"

"The want of accommodation for sleep," she answered; "I should imagine there is scarcely a nook about it furnished with a roof."

"Yes, there is," replied Montreville, and gave a short account of the apartment they had found, with this necessary appendage for comfort against the peltings of a storm.

"But is there no other account on which you consider that it might be an unpleasant resting place?" enquired Franval.

"I dare say it is full of night birds, that shriek and scream, and make it dismal enough," replied the woman.

"Is it never disturbed with those spirits which, like the birds you speak of, do no leave their retirement, except in the shades of night?"

"What, haunted, do you mean, *Messieurs?*" cried the woman. "O no, blessed be the Virgin, I never heard that of the Abbey of Saint Luke. I am sure, I hardly durst live here, if such were the case;" and she crossed herself as she spoke. "No, no; one house possessed by the Devil is enough for any district."

"And have you a house of that description in your district?" asked Franval.

"You must be a stranger in these parts to ask that question, I am certain," she returned. "The Castle of Virandola, about half a league from this house, is, as I may say, a very receptacle for Satan's legions."

Franval drew his chair nearer to the woman's, and enquired of her who was its possessor.

She replied, that his name was Don Bazilio; that he and his castle were the terror of the neighbourhood; that not an individual durst approach within a considerable distance of it after dark; and that Don Bazilio was by some supposed to be a Frenchman, by some a Spaniard, and by others a Moor. Farther information on the subject she was unable to give him.

A comfortable meal was now set before them. Franval scarcely tasted it; and the perturbation of his mind appeared to increase with every minute; at length, drawing aside his friend Montreville, he told him, that he could not divest himself of the idea of the voice which had warned them to proceed to the castle of Virandola, having some connexion with the fate of Don Manuel; and that he could not satisfy himself without approaching the edifice, over which hung the impenetrable veil of mystery with which they had on the preceding evening become acquainted.

Montreville had promised to second every endeavour of his friend towards the development of Don Manuel's fate, and accordingly agreed to accompany him. As the castle was but a short distance from the cottage, they resolved to walk towards it. Franval had not yet determined to ask admittance; his present design was confined to inspecting the outside of the building, and proving whether he should receive any intimation of his being expected at it by the person whose voice had admonished him to approach it. The friends informed Henri of their design, and bade him prepare to accompany them; and Franval pretending to the cottagers, that curiosity impelled him and his companions to take a view of the outside of the castle of the mysterious Don Bazilio, they asked Ricardo's grand-daughter to conduct them into the road to it. She readily complied with their request; and as they proceeded, they learnt from her replies to the questions which they had advanced to her, that there was no idea existing of Don Bazilio being himself a robber, or his castle the haunt of *banditti*; but that he had the repute for dealing in the black art, and that midnight was the preferred hour of his orgies, at which period strange lights had been seen flitting about the castle, and dreadful noises heard within it, by those few who at that solemn hour had ventured to approach it; but that no one, of whom she had heard, had ever attempted to gain admittance.

When the towers of the castle, rising above a rocky eminence of the rugged mountains, rendered a guide no longer necessary to the travellers, the girl ran back to her cottage; and Franval and his companions pursued their way. As they advanced towards the castle, they perceived that it had once been strongly fortified, but that its bulwarks were now fallen to decay: it presented to their view a huge pile of ancient stonework, black with age, and partially mouldering under the destructive hand of Time: gloom and awfulness were its characteristic features, and not any sign of its containing inhabitants was to be discovered about it: the drawbridge appeared no longer capable of being raised; and the moat was nearly choked up.

Our friends walked several times round its gloomy walls, and were on the point of quitting the spot, when a key, thrown from some considerable eminence, fell at the feet of the Chevalier Franval. He picked it hastily up, for he perceived that there was fastened to it a paper, on which he could distinguish the marks of hand-writing: with the most tremulous agitation he read the following words; "This key opens the door in the western turret; enter it at the return of night." If these words excited the astonishment of the Chevalier Franval, what was the emotion with which he beheld the paper signed by the name of Rodalvo, the faithful and respected servant of Don Manuel!

The paper fastened to the key, by directing them to return at night, appeared to warn them to retire for the present from the site of the castle, which they accordingly did.

The emotion of Franval's soul was so great at the belief that he had discovered the retreat of his beloved sister's husband, that he was incapable of expressing his feelings. Equally tongue-tied by astonishment were his friend Montreville, and his servant Henri. They returned to the cottage, and seated themselves on a bench by the door, where some degree of composure gradually returning to their minds, they at length began to give expression to their ideas: but to form conjectures was all they were still able to do; it was impossible for them to decide by what power Don Manuel was detained an inmate of the Mysterious Castle of Virandola, as his servant's being an inhabitant of it seemed to bespeak that he was; or to ascertain what connexion there could be between him and the universally dreaded Don Bazilio.

They now doubted not that the voice which had on the preceding evening admonished them to proceed to the Castle of Virandola, had been that of Rodalvo; but they were at a loss whether or not to suppose that the terrific being who had twice been seen by Franval, and once by his servant Henri, was the owner of the castle.

The agitation of mind in which the day was passed by them all, especially by the Chevalier Franval, may be easily conjectured. They were entertained with hospitality and kindness at the cottage, but the attentions of their hostess and her family were often unheeded by them; and the natural impatience of their minds, rendered the day, in appearance, the longest they had ever known.

When the shades of night had fallen to the earth, Franval and his companions set out on their mysterious expedition. The night was cloudy, scarcely a star gemmed the face of Heaven; the crescent of an infant moon rising above the distant mountains, threw a faint and silvery light upon partial spots of the landscape. Having reached the castle, they sought out the western turret, of which the situation could not be mistaken; and Franval applied the key to the lock: with little difficulty the door was opened by him, and they all three entered. Total darkness prevailed within, and they stood debating, how to proceed. Suddenly a distant light gleamed upon the scene, and they perceived that it was reflected through a spiral window of stained glass, at the extremity of a spacious hall in which they were standing. The light was no sooner beheld, than it again vanished: it had, however, been sufficient to shew our adventurers that they might proceed for a considerable space without the danger of falling, as the momentary illumination had been sufficient for them to perceive that there were no intervening steps between the door which they had entered and the opposite wall. Franval drew his sword; and extending before him the arm which bore it, as a protection to his person, he moved cautiously on. He continued his progress for some time, till a flaming firebrand, carried in the hand of some being whose pace was so swift as not to give him time to behold its person, darted across his path; and he observed, by the temporary influence of the light, that he had wandered into a lofty and narrow passage.

He stopped a moment, and listened; no sound met his ear; and he concluded, from the silence, that he had strayed from his companions. He, however, resolved not to suffer his courage to forsake him, or to relax in his attempt at developing the mystery of the place, to which act he had been summoned by one connected with a man whom he did not esteem less on his own account, than as the nearest relative of his beloved sister: using, therefore, every precaution which his perilous situation permitted him to do for guarding against accident, he still proceeded.

Suddenly a deep groan struck his ear; it was followed by a stifled shriek; and these sounds were succeeded by several voices, uttering such tones as might have been expected from demons uttering expressions of delight. Again all was still; and the next moment the *chevalier*, moving a step or two from the spot where he had been standing, found himself upon so rapid a declivity, as obliged him to move on, whether it met his inclination or not.

This declivity continued, as nearly as Franval could conjecture, for at least the space of an hundred feet; and whilst descending it, he heard a repetition of the dreadful sounds to which he had before listened.

At length he felt himself again upon even ground; there was now no longer any pavement under his feet, but a loose and crumbling earth. Here he paused an instant: he wished for the society of his friend and Henri, but the wish was in vain: it was now evident that the darkness of the place had separated them from each other. An infinite satisfaction would it have been to his feelings, had Rodalvo now appeared to him, and either directed his progress, or given him some explanation of the existing mystery. Whilst he stood debating thus with his own mind, he heard the voice of some one either in solemn prayer, or reading emphatically aloud; which of the two he could not distinguish; and turning his eyes around on every side, a faint light, playing on a distant wall, met his sight; he moved towards it, and pursuing the direction in which it shone, ascended a few steps, cut, as it seemed, out of the rugged earth, which led him to an eminence, from whence he looked down upon a scene which almost froze his blood in its current to his heart.

Some few feet below the surface of the spot on which he stood, was what appeared to him a spacious cavern; it was illuminated by several firebrands, which were stuck into the earth at certain distances from each other, and of which the pitchy tops sent forth darting flames, which climbed like fiery serpents towards the dusky roof. At the extremity of the place, in letters which appeared the colour of transparent blood, was deciphered the word "*Vengeance;*" and immediately under this inscription, in a chair, on the back of which were fixed three human skulls, and on either side of which stood a ghastly skeleton, sat the very being whom Franval had on the preceding evening beheld, first through the window of the post-house, and next bending over him with a lighted firebrand in his hand, amidst the ruins of Saint Luke's Abbey; the being whom, from the account which he had heard of the possessor of the castle, he could not doubt to be Don Bazilio himself nor were his suspicions incorrect.

On either side of him, seated around a table of a semi-circular form, were several other persons, habited like himself, in loose garments, with hats of dark fur, of which the brims were drawn down around their faces, and added to the terrific appearance of their countenances, already sufficiently dreadful to the view.

Before the table, and immediately opposite to Don Bazilio, knelt a human figure, nearly naked, and whose limbs were shaking with a violent trembling, produced either by cold or apprehension; and judging, from his own feelings, at the scene before him, Franval could not doubt it to be the latter. Around him were placed six familiars, in the habits of demons, each directing at him an instrument of death, which

369

they were prepared to thrust to his heart, if a signal were given them to that effect.

A few moments observation clearly proved to Franval, that the kneeling man was a recipient, about to be admitted a member of some secret community, the lawless transactions of which he was to be terrified from divulging. The solemn voice which he had heard on his approach to the spot of terror which he was now contemplating, he found to have been that of Don Bazilio, who was still reading from a volume, extended before him on the table, the obligations to which the novice, at that moment initiating into the mysteries of the community, was called upon to swear observance.

The first of these obligations to which Franval heard Don Bazilio call upon the recipient to subscribe, contained these words:

> Swear to divulge no secret with which you are made acquainted by the community, to any being unconnected with it; and to report every one with which you may be entrusted by other persons to it.

"I swear," replied the recipient: and the expression of satisfaction with which the assembly received his acquiescence, explained to Franval what had been the shouts of joy that had before heard when at a distance from the cavern.

Again Don Bazilio read;

> If thou refuse to comply with any command issued to thee by the authority before whom thou kneelest, recollect that the sword of their revenge will fall on thee quicker than the lightning; remember this; and swear that, in assisting the vengeance they are leagued to perpetrate, neither the life of thy father, mother, wife, nor child, of thy dearest friend, or nearest connection, shall be regarded by thee.

The recipient did not immediately reply.

"Swear instantly," cried Don Bazilio, "or I pronounce the signal that shall seal thy death." He raised himself upon his seat as he spoke.

Franval believed the last moment of the kneeling man to be at hand, and the exclamation of "Oh, merciful God!" burst from his lips.

His voice was heard by the members of the assembly; and turning their eyes to the spot from whence it had proceeded, they no sooner beheld him, than several of them sprang from their seats, and flying up to an ascent which led to the eminence where Franval stood, they seized his person, and dragged him down into the centre of the cavern.

"Who art thou?" exclaimed Don Bazilio, "who hast dared intrude upon our privacy? and by what means hast thou gained access to this spot?" Whilst speaking, he advanced towards Franval; and when he had approached sufficiently near to him to distinguish his features, he added, "Ha! I have beheld thee before in a situation to which I cannot doubt thou camest as a spy upon my actions. The ruined Abbey of St. Luke is the spot to which I refer. Under the impression which thy conduct has raised in my mind, thou can'st not live." Then turning to the familiars around him, he cried, "Bring the cord, and do your duty."

No sooner had Don Bazilio issued this command, than the recipient, moving forward, threw himself on his knees before him, and, in a voice of the humblest supplication, he exclaimed, "Oh spare him! I entreat, I implore you, for my sake spare him; he is the brother of my beloved wife!"

The tones in which the kneeling man spoke, were familiar to the ear of Franval; he turned his eyes upon him, and, to his utter astonishment, beheld in him Don Manuel di Vadilla!

After a few instants of private conversation with another member of the occult community, Don Bazilio commanded Franval to be led to the grated cell. The familiars immediately seized his arms, and, preceded by one of their fellows, who lighted them with a torch which he had torn up from its station in the floor of the cavern, they forced him along several winding passages, which ultimately brought them to the grated dungeon, into which they thrust him, and then departed, taking away with them the light.

The torturing and perplexing sensations which at this period filled the breast of the Chevalier Franval, may be easily imagined. What could he suppose would be the event of his present situation? what could be the mystery which bound together the community before whose authority he had beheld the unfortunate Don Manuel, kneeling an apparent victim? Where now, he wondered, were his friends Montreville and Henri: had they, like himself, fallen into the power of the mystic band by whom the castle was habited, had they escaped their toils?

About the midnight hour, through the grating of his prison, he beheld a light approaching: in a few minutes it drew sufficiently near to him for him to distinguish that it was borne in the hand of Don

371

Bazilio; he placed himself opposite to the grated window of Franval's cell, and thus addressed him: "Stranger, having beheld as much as you have done of the mysteries of this place, there is but one point left for you to decide upon; you must either forfeit your life to our safety, or bind yourself by the vows which connect our community."

"Your terms," replied Franval, "appear as extraordinary as your mysteries; you must inform me what the latter are, and to what purpose they are maintained, ere I can consent, or refuse, to subscribe to them."

"I intend to do so," returned Don Bazilio. "I fear not to entrust to you the secret, because within the next twenty hours, you must, as I have already declared to you, become one of us, or cease to exist. Had it not been for the intercession of the young man who is known to you by the name of Don Manuel, you had not at this moment been alive to receive my offer. Now then attend: I am not a Spaniard, as my name implies me to be; I am by birth a Frenchman. My elder brother was the Marquis de la Croix; myself the *chevalier* of the same name. It is now about eighteen years since my brother, and another gentleman, were alike suppliants to the crown for the permission of acceding to a duchy which at that moment lay dormant; and, in the line of succession to which, they both stood with apparently equal rights; it rested consequently on the breast of the monarch on whom the honour should be conferred; and, after having deceived my brother with false hopes, the king bestowed the contested title on his competitor. Was not this a disappointment sufficiently strong to drive almost to madness a man of proud spirit? for such was my brother; and whose pride was supported by a consciousness of having devoted not only his active services, but his purse, to his king and his country. He immediately quitted the course, vowing never to return to it again.

"My brother was, at the period of which I am speaking, a widower; from his wife, who had been a Spanish lady of considerable distinction, he had inherited this castle of Virandola; and hither he retired, accompanied by myself, and three other friends, peculiarly attached to his interests.

"We had not been here many days ere he thus addressed us. 'My friends, I am sufficiently well acquainted with your attachment to me, to be conscious that I may disclose to you the inmost sentiments of my hear in full assurance of your secrecy. Listen, then to my words: as we have not in our power any present means of revenging the failure of my just and high-raised expectation, let us have the glory of founding a sect, which shall grow by our rearing, privately and unsuspectedly, from the small number here collected, into a magnitude which shall eventually crush the exercise of such unlimited power as I have been a sufferer from."

"We applauded his idea, and entered with fervour into his plan: we immediately bound ourselves by the most solemn oath which could pass the lips of man, to act by every exertion of our ability towards the subversion of every earthly power, by the possession of which one man is raised to a superiority over his fellows: we swore that not even the peace or safety of our dearest connections should obstruct us in the progress of our design; and moreover, that we would use every means of adding members to our secret community."

"From that instant we became a sect of *Illuminati*; we frequented lodges of masonry, and all public societies; we probed the hearts of their members, and when we found individuals suited to our purpose, we conducted them hither; and in the cavern which you have this night beheld, we initiated them into our mysteries.

"At the expiration of twelve years, my brother died; he fell the victim of a disorder which was slow in its progress; and as he was conscious of the approach of death, he appointed me the guardian of his only child, who was a son named Lewis, at that time in his fifteenth year; and concerning the future conduct of whose life he gave me the most particular and impressive directions.

"For many reasons, my brother and myself had for some time assumed the name of Vadilla, and professed ourselves to be Spaniards; and that of Lewis had, for the sake of accordance with our own, been changed to Manuel. Thus you perceive that the husband of your sister is my nephew."

Franval did not reply, and Don Bazilio continued thus:

"My deceased brother had enjoined me to initiate his son into the mysteries of our society when he had attained the age of twenty-one years, and to inform him that it had been the dying request of his father, that he would never form any connections in life, above all, that of marriage; but devote himself entirely to the forwarding of those views which had been planned by his parent; and which that parent conceived he might be less strenuous in pursuing, if he were bound by any other ties, which might claim at least an equal share of his feelings.

"At the age of eighteen, I informed him of his father's wish that he should lead a life of celibacy; and informed him that, at the age of twenty-one, a secret of the utmost importance would be entrusted to him, and business of the most interesting and peculiar nature placed in his hands; for devoting himself entirely to the services of which, I wished him, in the intermediate time, to prepare his mind, as it had been the dying request of his father that he should do so. He was become accustomed, by habit, to behold an air of mystery pervading the countenances of such inhabitants of the castle as were in my confidence, and had been in that of his deceased father; and my words did not appear so much to surprise him, as I had expected they would.

"He had hitherto not been the distance of more than four or five leagues from the Castle of Virandola, and he petitioned me to suffer him to travel for two or three years: to this request I consented, on condition of his promising to return to me against the period of his completing his twenty-first year, and of his forming no connection, or engagement, in the world, upon which he was about to enter. He gave me his promise to this effect. I furnished him with a most liberal supply of money, which I was with the greatest ease enabled to do, from the wealth of my deceased brother; and placing him under the care of a man named Rodalvo, the only domestic in my brother's service who had been admitted into our secret community, I permitted him to depart.

"By mutual agreement, I was not to receive any letter from my nephew during his absence. At length arrived his twenty-first birthday, and he was not returned. Several months passed on, and still he came not. I felt dissatisfied at the apparently ungrateful use which he had made of my indulgence; and I employed spies to discover for me where he loitered. Judge my disappointment and anger, when I learnt, in the course of time, from these persons, that he had broken through every injunction which I had given him, and was become a husband and a father. Against Rodalvo, also, was my rage excited, for not having withheld him from forming ties so opposite to the will of his late father.

"Having gained the knowledge of his retreat, I commissioned some of the inferior members of our occult society to lie in ambush for him and Rodalvo, to seize their persons, and to reconduct them to this castle. On their way to your villa, my emissaries were so fortunate as to meet them in Paris; where, having hurried them into a closed carriage, they set off with them, without delay, for the frontiers of the kingdom.

"Several accidents, which they met with on the road, so materially delayed their progress, that they did not till the afternoon of yesterday, reach the post-house before which you and your companions stopped last night.

"Impatience to behold my nephew, and reason with him on his disobedience to my injunctions, had brought me to the post-house to meet him; and as I found that he could not be prevailed upon, although in my power, by gentle means, to proceed to the Castle of Virandola, I resolved not to conduct him to it till the dead hour of midnight, when we should not be liable to encounter any observers of his conduct; and having resolved to remain till that hour at the post-house, I bound the host by a handsome bribe, and an oath, not to admit anyone into it whilst we continued his inmates: how faithfully he performed his trust, you are already acquainted.

"Whilst we remained in the post-house, I questioned my nephew on the reason which had induced him to act in opposition to the conduct I had marked out for him to follow; and he confessed to me, that he had, by his supplications and entreaties, won Rodalvo into confessing to him, the cause for which he had been so earnestly enjoined to return, at the age of twenty-one, to the Castle of Virandola; and that abhorring, as he expressed himself, the nature and object of our community, immediately on having gained this knowledge, he determined never to accede to the plan which had been proposed for his future life, but to strike out one which he himself deemed more capable of producing his happiness.

"Having done this, he procured Rodalvo's promise never to quit his service; and in the course of time, he became the husband of your sister. Sufficient honour, however, was still left to him to resolve never to betray the secret of our community, out of respect to the safety of me, his uncle.

"In the Ruins of Saint Luke's Abbey, where you last night found shelter from the storm, is the entrance to a subterranean passage which leads into vaults beneath the Castle of Virandola; and this passage is in constant use by the members of our secret community, in order to protect them from being seen, and recognised, in entering or quitting the castle, as might chance to occur were they always to pass through its gates. By this passage I had last night resolved to reconduct my nephew; and having seen him safely guarded through it's entrance, I was about to follow him, when, hearing the sound of a voice amidst the ruins, I judged it not impossible that it might proceed from some brother of our society, who might have lost his way in the darkness amongst them.

"Lighted by the firebrand which I carried in my hand, I proceeded towards the spot from whence the sound had proceeded, and discovered you and your companions stretched on the ground asleep. The moment I beheld you, I believed you to be one of the travellers whom I had before seen refused admittance into the post-house: and as I bent over you, to ascertain if my conjecture were just, you awoke, and turned upon me your eyes. To avoid, as much as possible, your observation, I darted precipitately through a concealed door in the wall, which led to a branch in the subterranean passage of which I have already spoken to you.

"When I had quitted your sight, I began to doubt whether you and your companions were really weary travellers, or spies upon me, or the place we were in, and counterfeiting sleep, the better to cover you purpose: I accordingly determined to watch your actions. From the spot of my concealment, I heard your footsteps quitting the dilapidated chamber, and I followed you amidst the ruin. Your servant beheld me turn an angle of the walls: I levelled my pistol at him, and it missed fire: my aim had not been to wound him, but to alarm you all, and send you away from the spot. I was foiled in this attempt: but still I pursued your steps unseen by you, and hearing you express a desire of returning to the apartment where you had slept, I resolved to repair thither before you and to mark the floor with the words of warning which you found upon it. 'Quit this place,' was the sentence I wrote; and seeing you shortly after mount your horses and depart, I congratulated myself on having procured the end I desired, by means which, probably, appeared to you of the greatest mystery; and having done so, I immediately proceeded to the castle.

"I thought of you no more throughout the day: it was passed by me in preparations for the admission of Don Manuel into our secret community; to be present at which ceremony, I had invited all the principal members of our society. The initiation was proceeding successfully, though I confess with evident reluctance on the part of the recipient, when the exclamation you uttered assailed our ears. I instantly recognised your person; and another minute would have sealed your fate in death, had not Don Manuel, to my utter astonishment, pleaded for mercy to be shewn to you, as the brother of his wife.

"A request made to the community by one of its members, is never refused to him without due deliberation being first given to it; and as we deemed Don Manuel to have proceeded so far in his initiation, as to be entitled to rank as one of us, his petition was heard, and you conveyed to prison.

"My immediate concern was then to examine by what means you had gained admittance into this castle; and to cause a diligent search to be made for your companions, who I supposed might also have entered it: they could not be discovered; but a paper, tied to a key found in the door of the western turret, directing you to return at night, and signed Rodalvo, explained at once how you had gained entrance, and who was the traitor that merited the vengeance of the community.

"I caused him instantly to be dragged by my familiars to my feet: the fact of his own handwriting he could not deny; his every nerve appeared to be unstrung with terror; and instead of attempting to exculpate himself, he increased my knowledge of his guilt, by confessing, that, having recognized your voice last night on the outside of the post-house, his desire of informing you where to find Don Manuel, of whom he could not doubt that you were in search, led him to steal out of the post-house, and to pursue you on a mule, which he took from one of the stables; and that, having overtaken you, he enjoined you to proceed to the Castle of Virandola; but durst not stay to converse with you, lest his absence from the post-house should have been discovered by me, and punished with death."

"Whatever my fate may be," exclaimed Franval, "let me entreat your mercy to that kind old man."

"It is too late," returned Don Bazilio; "he had twice been faithless to his trust: my poniard has drunk his blood."

"Unhappy man!" replied the *chevalier*. "he will be rewarded in Heaven; for his errors were on the side of Virtue."

Don Bazilio uttered an exclamation of contempt, and, after a momentary pause, spoke thus:

"Now, to my most important business with you, *chevalier*. by the interference of my nephew, your life has hitherto been miraculously preserved to you; it now rests entirely with yourself, how long you wish to retain that blessing of yours. Tomorrow night you must either become a member of this community, or share the fate of Rodalvo: the intervening twenty-four hours will be give you for forming your determination."

"I require not an instant," returned Franval: "the vows which bind your infamous society can never pass my lips: truth and loyalty to my sovereign, and his adherents, glow with true fervour in my breast. Beneath the authority which sways this land, my father prospered; he conducted the battles which upheld it: and his son will sooner expire on the rack, than nourish a thought towards its destruction."

"The hour of proof will come," replied Don Bazilio. "Tomorrow night at twelve—Remember!" and he departed.

No one again appeared to disturb the silence of Franval's prison throughout the night; and the rugged earth, barely covered with a lock of straw, was his resting-place. In the morning Don Bazilio again appeared; he was followed by an attendant, who, through the gratings of Franval's prison, placed upon a shelf immediately below the opening a small loaf of coarse bread, and a cup of muddy water.

"Under the resolution by which I left you swayed last night," said Don Bazilio, "this wretched fare must be yours; if you are become a proselyte to my opinion, you may command whatever your please."

"I am not become so, nor shall I ever," returned Franval.

"Remember what is to be the issue of the approaching night," said Don Bazilio emphatically, and again retired.

In the utmost wretchedness passed the hours of the Chevalier Franval: he had no other fate to expect from the merciless beings into whose hands he had fallen, than a death of savage torture; and no consolation under his affliction, except that which he derived from the conviction that it was better to die, than to lay a load of guilt upon his conscience.

At last arrived the hour of Franval's trial; it was announced to him by the beams of torches playing on the walls of his prison, and numerous footsteps approaching towards it. Several men, dressed in similar habits to those whom he had beheld on the preceding night, led him forth, and conducted him into the cavern of horrors, where he found the bloodthirsty community over whom Don Bazilio presided, assembled: He looked anxiously around, in the hope of espying amongst the number Don Manuel, but he saw him not.

Savageness, horror, and malignancy, were portrayed on every countenance; and each appeared to grin with exultation, and a mixture of contempt, on Franval. The place was lighted by firebrands, as on the preceding night, and every regulation appeared the same. After a short pause, Don Bazilio spoke; he repeated to Franval, that his life could only be preserved to him by his accepting the vows of the society; and concluded by informing him, that three questions were about to be proposed to him, and that if his replies to them all were unsatisfactory to the community, his death would immediately ensue.

Franval still answered with the same firmness and resolution which his conscience had before dictated to him.

Warning him once more to consider well his intention ere he drew upon himself the sword of vengeance, Don Bazilio proposed to him the first question; pointing, as he spoke, to the inscription above the chair upon which he sat.

"Wilt thou," said he, "bend thy body in obedience to the attribute of our society, Vengeance?"

"I will not," Franval replied.

"Wilt thou kneel, and pray for the approach of that day which shall give equality to men?" was the second question.

"I will not," again replied Franval.

"Hadst thou rather submit to death thyself, than cause the death of one placed in a situation of power over thee?" was the substance of the third question.

"I had," replied Franval firmly.

"Take then the reward of thy stubbornness," cried Don Bazilio. "Familiars, do your duty."

Instantly Franval felt himself seized by many hands: a cloth was thrown over his head; and he expected immediately to feel the steel piercing his heart; when, at the very instant, a crash like thunder rent the castle: it was repeated a second, a third, and a fourth time, with increased violence.

"We are betrayed!" cried Don Bazilio. "Comrades, defend yourselves."

"The hands which held Franval, were now withdrawn; and, snatching the cloth from his head, he beheld the cavern entered by a band of soldiery, who, rushing upon the *Illuminati*, made them in a few minutes their prisoners; and the next instant Montreville and Henri were by the side of Franval."

The tide of joy which rushed into the heart of the Chevalier Franval, every breast of feeling must be capable of estimating; but it is necessary that we should give a detail of the happy cause which led to this unexpected event.

When Montreville and Henri had, on the preceding night, been separated by the darkness in the castle hall from Franval, they wandered about for a considerable time, without being able to make any progress into the building. Franval did not return to them. Strange noises met their ears: their sight was started by one of the familiars of the secret community in his demon's dress, passing before them with a lighted firebrand in his hand; and their apprehensions being raised, not only for their companion, but for themselves, they resolved to seek assistance for enquiring into the fate of him from whom they had been separated.

Thus determined, they precipitately quitted the castle, and returning to the cottage where they had been entertained throughout the day, they took their horses from the stable, and having mounted them, rode with all speed towards the nearest garrison town on the frontiers of France: they reached it early in the morning, and having laid an account of their adventure before the police in terms which excited them to an immediate investigation of the truth, they selected fifty of the soldiery, under the command of a trusty officer, to accompany Montreville without delay to the Castle of Virandola. They marched with as much expedition as a body of men bearing arms were able to do, and reached the castle about the hour of midnight: they immediately forced themselves an entrance into the building; and dispersing different ways, a considerable number of them met in the cavern of horrors, as has already been related, at the critical moment of Franval's fate.

As soon as the members of the infamous community of vengeance were secured, and Franval convinced of his safety from the mouths of his friend and servant, a search was made in the castle, in order to ascertain whether it contained any unhappy beings suffering beneath the inhumanity of the terrific horde by which it had been infested: the first object of horror which was discovered by the scrutineers, was the body of the unfortunate Rodalvo, who had fallen the victim of his affection for his master: the next was Don Manuel himself, who was chained to the walls of a flinty dungeon, where he had been fated by his relentless uncle to remain till the Chevalier Franval had either pronounced the vows which were to constitute him a member of the society, or paid the forfeit of his refusal in death.

The grief which Don Manuel had experienced at being torn from the arms of his beloved wife, and dragged to the execution of a purpose at which his soul revolted, could only be equalled by the ecstasy with which he beheld himself and Franval again at liberty, and dwelt on his return to his adored Amarylla, and his infant children.

The rage of Don Bazilio's disappointed soul expressed itself solely in sullen silence. By the command of the police in the town from whence Montreville had procured military assistance, the band of *Illuminati* were conveyed in chains to Paris, to take their public trial; and on their arrival there, the Chevalier Franval, Montreville, and Don

Manuel, whom we must now know by his real name of the Marquis de la Croix, were detained to give evidence against them.

Before the day of trial arrived, Don Bazilio gave a most unquestionable proof of his consciousness of his past guilt, and of the present wretched state of his mind, by putting an end to his own existence in prison. By the voice of the law, his associates in iniquity were adjudged to die beneath the hand of the executioner; which sentence was put into effect on the third day after their condemnation.

On the Chevalier Franval, and the Marquis de la Croix, the king, in addition to other high marks of his favour, bestowed an immense pecuniary reward from the coffers of the state. And the united voice of a rejoicing people bestowed on them the tribute of public applause, for having been the instruments through which retribution and punishment had been inflicted on a set of beings, sufficiently depraved and worthless, to have been brooding the subversion of a prosperous state, and the fall of a virtuous monarch.

Happy in the consciousness of having acted as it became virtuous and loyal subjects to have done, and grateful to Providence for its invisible interposition in the fate of the excellent young *marquis*, they returned to the *chevalier's* villa crowned with triumph and delight, where the caresses they received from an affectionate sister, and adored wife, rendered them the most enviable men whom the kingdom of France could boast. The society of vengeance being scattered to the winds, the *chevalier* and his brother instituted a community of Benevolence to celebrate its destruction. Great was the honour of being admitted a member, and unsullied the virtuous principles of those who became so.

The children of de la Croix, as they grew to manhood, considered it their glory to be descended from those who had sown the seeds of so praiseworthy a society; and their lovely mother, stretching over them in affection and joy, appeared the earthly representative of that goddess of Benevolence, to whom a temple was raised in all their hearts.

The Mysterious Stranger

To die?—to sleep!
Perchance to dream? Ay, there's the rub.—Hamlet

Boreas, that fearful north-west wind, which in the spring and autumn stirs up the lowest depths of the wild Adriatic, and is so dangerous to vessels, was howling through the woods, and tossing the branches of the old knotty oaks in the Carpathian Mountains, when a party of five riders, who surrounded a litter drawn by a pair of mules, turned into a forest-path, which offered some protection from the April weather, and allowed the travellers in some degree to recover their breath. It was already evening and bitterly cold; the snow fell every now and then in large flakes. A tall old gentleman, of aristocratic appearance, rode at the head of the troop.

This was the Knight of Fahnenberg, in Austria. He had inherited from a childless brother a considerable property, situated in the Carpathian Mountains; and he had set out to take possession of it, accompanied by his daughter Franziska, and a niece about twenty years of age, who had been brought up with her. Next to the knight rode a fine young man of some twenty and odd years—the Baron Franz von Kronstein; he wore, like the former, the broad-brimmed hat with hanging feathers, the leather collar, the wide riding-boots—in short, the travelling dress which was in fashion at the commencement of the seventeenth century.

The features of the young man had much about them that was open and friendly, as well as some mind; but he expression was more of a dreamy and sensitive softness than of youthful daring, although no one could deny that he possessed much of youthful beauty. As the cavalcade turned into the oak wood, the young men rode up to the litter, and chatted with the ladies who were seated therein. One of these—and to her his conversation was principally addressed—was of dazzling beauty. Her hair flowed in natural curls round the fine oval of her face, out of which beamed a pair of star-like eyes, full of genius, lively fancy, and a certain degree of archness.

Franziska von Fahnenberg seemed to attend but carelessly to the speeches of her admirer, who made many kind inquiries as to how she felt herself during the journey, which had been attended with many difficulties: she always answered him very shortly, almost contemptuously; and at length remarked, that if it had not been for her father's objections, she would long ago have requested the baron to take her place in their horrid cage of litter, for, to judge by his remarks, he seemed incommoded by the weather; and she would so much rather be mounted on a spirited horse, and face wind and storm, then be mewed up there, dragged up the hills by those long-eared animals, and mope herself to death with *ennui*.

The young lady's words, and, still more, the contemptuous tone in which they were uttered, appeared to make the most painful impression on the young man: he made her no reply at the moment, but the absent air with which he attended to the kindly-intended remarks of the other young lady, shewed how much he was disconcerted.

'It appears, dear Franziska,' said he at length in a kindly tone, 'that the hardships of the road have affected you more than you will acknowledge. Generally so kind to others, you have been very often out of humour during the journey, and particularly with regard to your humble servant and cousin, who would gladly bear a double or treble share of the discomforts, if he could thereby save you from the smallest of them.'

Franziska shewed her look that she was about to reply with some bitter jibe, when the voice of the knight was heard calling for his nephew, who galloped off at the sound.

'I should like to scold you well, Franziska,' said her companion somewhat sharply, 'for always plaguing your poor Cousin Franz in this shameful way; he who loves you so truly, and who, whatever you may say, will one day be your husband.'

'My husband!' replied the other angrily. 'I must either completely alter my ideas, or he his whole self, before that takes place. No, Bertha! I know that this is my father's darling wish, and I do not deny the good qualities Cousin Franz may have, or has, since I see you are making a face; but to marry an effeminate man—never!'

'Effeminate! You do him great injustice,' replied her friend quickly. 'Just because instead of going off to the Turkish war, where little honour was to be gained, he attended to your father's advice and stayed at home, to bring his neglected estate into order, which he accomplished with care and prudence; and because he does not represent this howling wind as a mild zephyr—for reasons such as these you are pleased to call him effeminate.'

'Say what you will, it is so,' cried Franziska obstinately. 'Bold, aspiring, even despotic, must be the man who is to gain my heart; these soft, patient, and thoughtful natures are utterly distasteful to me. Is Franz capable of deep sympathy, either in joy or sorrow? He is always the same—always quiet, soft, and tiresome.'

'He has a warm heart, and is not without genius,' said Bertha.

'A warm heart! That may be,' replied the other; 'but I would rather be tyrannised over, and kept under a little by my future husband, than be loved in such a wearisome manner. You may say he has genius, too. I will not exactly contradict you, since that would be unpolite, but it is not easily discovered. But even allowing you are right in both statements, still the man who does not bring these qualities into action is a despicable creature. A man may do many foolish things, he may even be a little wicked now and then, provided it is in nothing dishonourable; and one can forgive him, if he is only acting on some fixed theory for some special object. There is for instance, your faithful admirer, the Castellan of Glogau, Knight of Woislaw; he loves you most truly, and is now quite in a position to enable you to marry comfortably. The brave man has lost his right hand—reason enough for remaining seated behind the stove, or near the spinning-wheel of his Bertha; but what does he do?—He goes off to the war in Turkey; he fights for a noble thought'—

'And runs the chance of getting his other hand chopped off, and another great scar across his face,' put in her friend.

'Leaves his lady-love to weep and pine a little,' pursued Franziska, 'but returns with fame and marries, and is all the more honoured and admired! This is done by a man of forty, a rough warrior, not bred at court, a soldier who has nothing but his cloak and sword. And Franz—rich, noble—but I will not go on. Not a word more on this detested point, if you love me, Bertha.'

Franzisca leaned back in the corner of the litter with a dissatisfied air, and shut her eyes, as though overcome by fatigue, she wished to sleep.

'This awful wind is so powerful, you say, that we must make a detour to avoid its full force,' said the knight to an old man, dressed in a fur-cap and a cloak of rough skin, who seemed to be the guide of the party.

'Those who have never personally felt the *Boreas* storming over the country between Sessano and Trieste, can have no conception of the reality,' replied the other. 'As soon as it commences, the snow is blown in thick long columns along the ground. That is nothing to what follows. These columns become higher and higher, as the wind rises, and continue to do so until you see nothing but snow above, below, and on every side—unless, indeed, sometimes, when sand and gravel are mixed with the snow, and at length it is impossible to open your eyes at all. Your only plan for safety is to wrap your cloak around you, and lie down flat on the ground. If your home were but a few hundred yards off, you might lose your life in the attempt to reach it.'

'Well, then, we owe you thanks, old Kumpan,' said the knight, though it was with difficulty he made his words heard above the roaring of the storm; 'we owe you thanks for taking us this round, as we shall thus be enabled to reach our destination without danger.'

'You may feel sure of that, noble sir,' said the old man. 'by midnight we shall have arrived, and that without any danger by the way if'— Suddenly the old man stopped, he drew his horse sharply up, abd remained in an attitude of attentive listening.

'It appears to me we must be in the neighbourhood of some village,' said Franz von Kronstein; 'for between the gusts of the storm, I hear a dog howling.'

'It is no dog, it is no dog!' said the old man uneasily, and urging his horse to a rapid pace. 'for miles around there is no human dwelling; and except in the castle of Klatka, which indeed lies in the neighbourhood, but has been deserted for more than a century, probably no one has lived here since the creation.—But there again,' he continued; 'well if I wasn't sure of it from the first.'

'That howling seems to fidget you, old Kumpan,' said the knight, listening to a long-drawn fierce sound, which appeared nearer than before, and seemed to be answered from a distance.

'That howling comes from no dogs,' replied the old guide uneasily. 'Those are reed-wolves; they may be on our track; and it would be as well if the gentlemen looked to their firearms.'

'Reed-wolves? What do you mean?' inquired Franz in surprise.

'At the edge of this wood,' said Kumpan, 'there lies a lake about a mile long, whose banks are covered with reeds. In these a number of wolves have taken up their quarters, and feed on wild birds, fish, and such like. They are shy in the summer-time, and a boy of twelve might scare them; but when the birds migrate, and the fish are frozen up, they prowl about at night, and then they are dangerous. They are worst, however, when *Boreas* rages, for then it is just as if the fiend himself possessed them: they are so mad and fierce, that man and beast become alike their victims' and a party of them have been known even to attack the ferocious bears of these mountains, and, what is more, to come off victorious.' The howl was now again repeated more distinctly, and from two opposite directions. The riders in alarm felt for their pistols, and the old man grasped the spear which hung at his saddle.

'We must keep close to the litter; the wolves are very near us,' whispered the guide. The riders turned their horses, surrounded the litter, and the knight informed the ladies, in a few quieting words, of the cause of this movement.

'Then we *shall* have an adventure—some little variety!' cried Franzisca with sparkling eyes.

'How can you talk so foolishly?' said Bertha in alarm.

'Are we not under manly protection? Is not Cousin Franz on our side?' said the other mockingly.

'See, there is a light gleaming among the twigs; and there is another,' cried Bertha. 'There must be people close to us.'

'No, no,' cried the guide quickly. 'Shut up the door, ladies. Keep close together, gentlemen. It is the eyes of the wolves you see sparkling there.' The gentlemen looked towards the thick underwood, in which every now and then little bright spots appeared, such as in summer would have been taken for glow-worms; it was just the same greenish-yellow light, but less unsteady, and there were always two flames together. The horses began to be very restive, they kicked and dragged at the rein; but the mules behaved tolerably well.

'I will fire on the beasts, and teach them to keep their distance,' said Franz, pointing to the spot where the lights were thickest.

'Hold, hold, Sir Baron!' cried Kumpan quickly, and seizing the young man's arm. 'You would bring such a host together by the report, that, encouraged by numbers, they would be sure to make the first assault. However, keep your arms in readiness, and if an old she-wolf springs out—for these always lead the attack—take good aim and kill her, for then there must be no further hesitation.' By this time, the horses were almost unmanageable, and terror had also infected the mules. Just as Franz was turning towards the litter to say a word to his cousin, an animal, about the size of a large hound, sprang from the thicket and seized the foremost mule.

'Fire, baron! A wolf!' shouted the guide.

The young man fired, and the wolf fell to the ground. A fearful howl rang through the wood.

'Now. Forward! Forward without a moment's delay!' cried Kumpan. 'We have not above five minutes' time. The beasts will tear their wounded comrade to pieces, and, if they are very hungry, partially devour her. We shall, in the meantime, gain a little start, and it is not more than an hour's ride to the end of the forest. There—do you see—these are the towers of Klatka between the trees—out there where the moon is rising, and from that point the wood becomes less dense.

The travellers endeavoured to increase their pace to the utmost, but the litter retarded their progress. Bertha was weeping with fear, and even Franzisca's courage had diminished, for she sat very still. Franz endeavoured to reassure them. They had not proceeded many moments when the howling recommenced, and approached nearer and nearer.

'There they are again, and fiercer and more numerous than before,' cried the guide in alarm.

The lights were soon visible again, and certainly in greater numbers. The wood had already become less thick, and the snowstorm having ceased, the moonbeams discovered many a dusky form amongst the trees, keeping together like a pack of hounds, and advancing nearer and nearer till they were within twenty paces, and on the very path of the travellers. From time to time a fierce howl arose from their centre, which was answered by the whole pack, and was at length taken up by single voices in the distance.

The party now found themselves some few hundred yards from the ruined castle of which Kumpan had spoken. It was, or seemed by moonlight to be, of some magnitude. Near the tolerably preserved principal building lay the ruins of a church, which must once have been beautiful, placed on a little hillock, dotted with single oak-trees and bramble bushes. Both castle and church were still partially roofed in; and a path led from the castle gate to an old oak-tree, where it joined at right angles the one along which the travellers were advancing.

The old guide seemed in much perplexity.

'We are in great danger, noble sir,' said he. 'The wolves will very soon make a general attack. There will then be only one way of escape: leaving the mules to their fate, and taking the young ladies on your horses.'

'That would be all very well, if I had not thought of a better plan,' replied the knight. 'Here is the ruined castle; we can surely reach that, and then, blocking up the gates, we must just await the morning.'

'Here? In the ruins of Klatka?—Not for all the wolves in the world!' cried the old man. 'Even by daylight no one likes to approach the place, and now, by night!—The castle, Sir Knight, has a bad name.'

'On account of robbers?' asked Franz.

'No; it is haunted,' replied the other.

'Stuff and nonsense!' said the baron. 'Forward to the ruins; there is not a moment to be lost.'

And this was indeed the case. The ferocious beasts were but a few steps behind the travellers. Every now and then they retired, and set up a ferocious howl. The party had just arrived at the old oak before mentioned, and were about to turn into the path to the ruins, when the animals, as though perceiving the risk they ran of losing their prey, came so near that a lance could easily have struck them. The knight and Franz faced sharply about, spurring their horses amidst the advancing crowds, when suddenly, from the shadow of the oak stepped forth a man, who in a few strides placed himself between the travellers and their pursuers. As far as one could see in the dusky light, the stranger was a man of a tall and well-built frame; he wore a sword by his side, and a broad-brimmed hat was on his head. If the party were astonished at his sudden appearance, they were still more so at what followed. As soon as the stranger appeared, the wolves gave over their pursuit, tumbled over each other, and set up a fearful howl. The stranger now raised his hand, appeared to wave it, and the wild animals crawled back into the thickets like a pack of beaten hounds.

Without casting a glance at the travellers, who were too much overcome by astonishment to speak, the stranger went up the path which led to the castle, and soon disappeared beneath the gateway.

'Heaven have mercy on us!' murmured old Kumpan in his beard, as he made the sign of the cross.

'Who was that strange man?' asked the knight with surprise, when he had watched the stranger as long as he was visible, and the party had resumed their way.

The old guide pretended not to understand, and riding up to the mules, busied himself with arranging the harness, which had become disordered in their haste : more than a quarter of an hour elapsed before he rejoined them.

'Did you know the man who met us near the ruins, and who freed us from our four-footed pursuers in such a miraculous way?' asked Franz of the guide.

'Do I know him? No, noble sir; I never saw him before,' replied the guide hesitatingly.

'He looked like a soldier, and was armed,' said the baron. 'Is the castle, then, inhabited?'

'Not for the last hundred years,' replied the other. 'It was dismantled because the possessor in those days had iniquitous dealings with some Turkish-Sclavonian hordes, who had advanced as far as this; or rather'—he corrected himself hastily—'he is *said* to have had such, for he might have been as upright and food a man as ever ate cheese fried in butter.'[1]

'And who is now the possessor of the ruins and of these woods?' inquired the knight.

'Who but yourself, noble sir!' replied Kumpan. 'For more than two hours we have been on your estate, and we shall soon reach the end of the wood,'

'We hear and see nothing more of the wolves,' said the baron after a long pause. 'Even their howling has ceased. The adventure with the stranger still remains to me inexplicable, even if one were to suppose him a huntsman'

'Yes, yes; that is most likely what he is,' interrupted the guide hastily, whilst he looked uneasily round him. 'The brave good man, who came so opportunely to our assistance, must have been a huntsman. Oh, there are many powerful woodsmen in this neighbourhood! Heaven be praised!' he continued, taking a deep breath,' there is the end of the wood, and in a short hour we shall be safely housed.'

And so it happened. Before an hour had elapsed, the party passed through a well-built village, the principal spot on the estate, towards the venerable castle, the windows of which were brightly illuminated, and at the door stood the steward and other dependents, who, having received their new lord with every expression of respect, conducted the party to the splendidly furnished apartments.

Nearly four weeks passed before the travelling adventures again came on the *tapis*. The knight and Franz found such constant employment in looking over all the particulars of the large estate, and endeavouring to introduce various German improvements, that they were very little at home. At first, Franziska was charmed with everything in a neighbourhood so entirely new and unknown. It appeared to her so romantic, so very different from her German Fatherland, that she took the greatest interest in everything, and often drew comparisons between the countries, which generally ended unfavourably for Germany.

Bertha was of exactly the contrary opinion : she laughed at her cousin, and said that her liking for novelty and strange sights must indeed have come to a pass, when she preferred hovels in which the smoke went out of the doors and windows instead of the chimney, walls covered with soot, and inhabitants not much cleaner, and of unmannerly habits, to the comfortable dwellings and polite people of Germany. However, Franziska persisted in her notions, and replied that everything in Austria was flat, *ennuyant,* and common ; and that a wild peasant here, with his rough coat of skin, had ten times more interest for her than a quiet Austrian in his holiday suit, the mere sight of whom was enough to make one yawn.

As soon as the knight had got the first arrangements into some degree of order, the party found themselves more together again Franz continued to shew great attention to his cousin, which however, she received with little gratitude, for she made him the butt of all her fanciful humours, that soon returned when after a longer sojourn she had become more accustomed to her new life. Many excursions into the neighbourhood were undertaken, but there was little variety in the scenery, and these soon ceased to amuse.

The party were one day assembled in the old-fashioned hall, dinner had just been removed, and they were arranging in which direction they should ride. 'I have it!' cried Franziska suddenly. 'I wonder we never thought before of going to view by day the spot where we fell in with our night-adventure with wolves and the Mysterious Stranger.'

'You mean a visit to the ruins—what were they called?' said the knight.

'Castle Klatka,' cried Franziska gaily. 'Oh, we really must ride there! It will be so charming to go over again by daylight, and in safety, the ground where we had such a dreadful fright.'

'Bring round the horses,' said the knight to a servant; 'and tell the steward to come to me immediately.' The latter, an old man, soon after entered the room.

'We intend taking a ride to Klatka,' said the knight: 'we had an adventure there on our road.'

'So old Kumpan told me,' interrupted the steward.

'And what do you say about it?' asked the knight.

'I really don't know what to say,' replied the old man, shaking his head. 'I was a youth of twenty when I first came to this castle, and now my hair is gray; half a century has elapsed during that time. Hundreds of times my duty has called me into the neighbourhood of those ruins, but never have I seen the Fiend of Klatka.'

'What do you say? Who do you call by that name?' inquired Franziska, whose love of adventure and romance was strongly awakened.

'Why, people call by that name the ghost or spirit who is supposed to haunt the ruins,' replied the steward. 'They say he only shews himself on moonlight nights'—

'That is quite natural,' interrupted Franz smiling. 'Ghosts can never bear the light of day; and if the moon did not shine how could the ghost be seen? for it is not to be supposed that anyone for a mere freak would visit the ruins by torchlight.'

'There are some credulous people, who pretend to have seen this ghost,' continued the steward. 'Huntsmen and wood-cutters say they have met him by the large oak on the cross-path. That noble sir, is supposed to be the spot he inclines most to haunt, for the tree was planted in remembrance of the man who fell there.'

'And who was he?' asked Franziska with increasing curiosity

'The last owner of the castle, which was at that time a sort of robber's den, and the headquarters of all depredators in the neighbourhood,' answered the old man. 'They say this man was of superhuman strength, and was feared not only on account of his passionate temper, but of his treaties with the Turkish hordes Any young woman, too, in the neighbourhood to whom he took a fancy, was carried off to his tower, and never heard of more When the measure of his iniquity was full, the whole neighbourhood rose in a mass, besieged his stronghold, and at length he was slain on the spot where the huge oak-tree now stands.'

'I wonder they did not burn the whole castle, so as to erase the very memory of it,' said the knight.

'It was a dependency of the church, and that saved it,' replied the other. 'Your great-grandfather afterwards took possession of it, for it had fine lands attached. As the Knight of Klatka was of good family, a monument was erected to him m the church, which now lies as much in ruin as the castle itself.'

'Oh, let us set off at once! Nothing shall prevent my visiting so interesting a spot,' said Franziska eagerly. 'The. imprisoned damsels who never reappeared, the storming of the tower, the death of the knight, the nightly wanderings of his spirit round the old oak, and, lastly, our own adventure, all draw me thither with an indescribable curiosity.'

When a servant announced that the horses were at the door, the young girls tripped laughingly down the steps which led to the coach-yard. Franz, the knight, and a servant well acquainted with the country, followed; and in a few minutes the party were on their road to the forest.

The sun was still high in the heavens, when they saw the towers of Klatka rising above the trees. Everything in the wood was still, except the cheerful twitterings of the birds as they hopped about amongst the bursting buds and leaves, and announced that spring had arrived.

The party soon found themselves near the old oak at the bottom of the hill on which stood the towers, still imposing in their ruin. Ivy and bramble bushes had wound themselves over the walls, and forced their deep roots so firmly between the stones, that they in a great measure held these together. On the top of the highest point, a small bush in its young fresh verdure swayed lightly in the breeze.

The gentlemen assisted their companions to alight, and leaving the horses to the care of the servant, ascended the hill to the castle. After having explored this in every nook and cranny, and spent much time in a vain search for some trace of the extraordinary stranger, whom Franziska declared she was determined to discover, they proceeded to an inspection of the adjoining church. This they found to have better withstood the ravages of time and weather in the nave, indeed, was in complete dilapidation, but the chancel and altar were still under roof, as well as a sort of chapel which appeared to have been a place of honour for the families of the old knights of the castle. Few traces remained, however, of the magnificent painted glass which must once have adorned the windows, and the wind entered at pleasure through the open spaces.

The party were occupied for some time in deciphering the inscriptions on a number of tombstones, and on the walls, principally within the chancel. They were generally memorials of the ancient lords, with figures of men in armour, and women and children of all ages. A flying raven and various other devices were placed at the corners. One gravestone, which stood close to the entrance of the chancel, differed widely from the others; there was no figure sculptured on it, and the inscription, which, on all besides, was a mere mass of flattering eulogies, was here simple and unadorned; it contained only these words: '*Ezzelin von Klatka fell like a knight at the storming of the castle*'—on such a day and year.

'That must be the monument of the knight whose ghost is said to haunt these ruins,' cried Franziska eagerly. 'What a pity he is not represented in the same way as the others—I should so like to have known what he was like!'

'Oh, there is the family-vault, with steps leading down to it and the sun is lighting it up through a crevice,' said Franz, stepping from the adjoining vestry.

The whole party followed him down the eight or nine steps which led to a tolerably airy chamber, where were placed a number of coffins of all sizes, some of them crumbling into dust. Here again, one close to the door was distinguished from the others by the simplicity of its design, the freshness of its appearance, and the brief inscription: '*Ezzelinus de Klatka, Eques.*'

As not the slightest effluvium was perceptible, they lingered sometime in the vault; and when they reascended to the church, they had a long talk over the old possessors, of whom the knight now remembered he had heard his parents speak. The sun had disappeared, and the moon was just rising as the explorer turned to leave the ruins. Bertha had made a step into the nave, when she uttered a slight exclamation of fear and surprise Her eyes fell on a man who wore a hat with drooping feathers, a sword at his side, and a short cloak of somewhat old-fashioned cut over his shoulders. The stranger leaned carelessly on a broken column at the entrance; he did not appear to take any notice of the party; and the moon shone full on his pale face.

The party advanced towards the stranger.

'If I am not mistaken,' commenced the knight; 'we have met before.'

Not a word from the unknown.

'You released us in an almost miraculous manner,' said Franziska 'from the power of those dreadful wolves. Am I wrong in supposing it is to you we are indebted for that great service?'

'The beasts are afraid of me,' replied the stranger in a deep, fierce tone, while he fastened his sunken eyes on the girl, without taking any notice of the others.

'Then you are probably a huntsman,' said Franz, 'and wage war against the fierce brutes.'

'Who is not either the pursuer or the pursued? All persecute or are persecuted, and Fate persecutes all,' replied the stranger without looking at him.

'Do you live in these ruins?' asked the knight hesitatingly.

'Yes; but not to the destruction of your game, as you may fear, Knight of Fahnenberg,' said the unknown contemptuously. 'Be quite assured of this; your property shall remain untouched.'

'Oh! my father did not mean that,' interrupted Franziska, who appeared to take the liveliest interest in the stranger. 'Unfortunate events and sad experiences have, no doubt, induced you to take up your abode in these ruins, of which my father would by no means dispossess you.'

'Your father is very good, if that is what he meant,' said the stranger in his former tone; and it seemed as though his dark features were drawn into a slight smile; but people of my sort are rather difficult to turn out.'

'You must live very uncomfortably here,' said Franziska, half vexed, for she thought her polite speech had deserved a better reply.

'My dwelling is not exactly uncomfortable, only somewhat small, still quite suitable for quiet people,' said the unknown with a kind of sneer. 'I am not, however, always quiet; I sometimes pine to quit the narrow space, and then I dash away through forest and field, over hill and dale; and the time when I must return to my little dwelling always comes too soon for me.'

'As you now and then leave your dwelling,' said the knight, 'I would invite you to visit us, if I knew'

'That I was in a station to admit of your doing so,' interrupted the other; and the knight started slightly, for the stranger had exactly expressed the half-formed thought. 'I lament,' he continued coldly, 'that I am not able to give you particulars on this point—some difficulties stand in the way: be assured, however, that I am a knight, and of at least as ancient a family as yourself.'

'Then you must not refuse our request,' cried Franziska, highly interested in the strange manners of the unknown. 'You must come and visit us.'

'I am no boon-companion, and on that account few have invited me of late,' replied the other with his peculiar smile; 'besides, I generally remain at home during the day; that is my time for rest. I belong, you must know, to that class of persons who turn day into night, and night into day, and who love everything uncommon and peculiar.'

'Really? So do I! And for that very reason, you must visit us,' cried Franziska. 'Now,' she continued smiling,' I suppose you have just risen, and you are taking your morning airing. Well, since the moon is your sun, pray pay a frequent visit to our castle by the light of its rays. I think we shall agree very well, and that it will be very nice for us to be acquainted.'

'You wish it?—You press the invitation?' asked the stranger earnestly and decidedly.

'To be sure, for otherwise you will not come,' replied the young lady shortly.

'Well, then, come I will!' said the other, again fixing his gaze on her. 'If my company does not please you at any time, you will have yourself to blame for an acquaintance with one who seldom forces himself, but is difficult to shake off.'

When the unknown had concluded these words, he made a slight motion with his hand, as though to take leave of them, and passing under the doorway, disappeared among the ruins. The party soon after mounted their horses, and took the road home.

It was the evening of the following day, and all were again seated in the hall of the castle. Bertha had that day received good news. The knight Woislaw had written from Hungary, that the war with the Turks would be brought to a conclusion during the year, and that although he had intended returning to Silesia, hearing of the knight of Fahnenberg having gone to take possession of his new estates, he should follow the family there, not doubting that Bertha had accompanied her friend. He hinted, that he stood so high in the opinion of his duke on account of his valuable services, that in future his duties would be even more important and extensive; but before settling down to them, he should come and claim Bertha's promise to become his wife.

He had been much enriched by his master, as well as by booty taken from the Turks. Having formerly lost his right hand in the duke's service, he had essayed to fight with his left; but this did not succeed very admirably, and so he had an iron one made by a very clever artist. This hand performed many of the functions of a natural one, but there had been still much wanting; now, however, his master had presented him with one of gold, an extraordinary work of art, produced by a celebrated Italian mechanic. The knight described it as something marvellous, especially as to the superhuman strength with which it enabled him to use the sword and lance.

Franziska naturally rejoiced in the happiness of her friend, who had

had no news of her betrothed for a long time before. She launched out every now and then, partly to plague Franz, and partly to express her own feelings, in the highest praise and admiration of the bravery and enterprise of the knight, whose adventurous qualities she lauded to the skies. Even the scar on his face, and his want of a right hand, were reckoned as virtues and Franziska at last saucily declared, that a rather ugly man was infinitely more attractive to her than a handsome one, for as a general rule, handsome men were conceited and effeminate.

Thus, she added, no one could term their acquaintance of the night before handsome, but attractive and interesting he certainly was Franz and Bertha simultaneously denied this. His gloomy appearance, the deadly hue of his complexion, the tone of his voice, were each in turn depreciated by Bertha, while Franz found fault with the contempt and arrogance obvious in his speech. The knight stood between the two parties. He thought there was something in his bearing that spoke of good family, though much could not be said for his politeness; however, the man might have had trial: enough in his life to make him misanthropical. Whilst they were conversing in this way, the door suddenly opened, and the subject of their remarks himself walked in.

'Pardon me, Sir Knight,' he said coldly, 'that I come, if not uninvited, at least unannounced; there was no one in the antechamber to do me that service.'

The brilliantly lighted chamber gave a full view of the stranger, He was a man about forty, tall, and extremely thin. His feature! could not be termed uninteresting—there lay in them something bold and daring; but the expression was on the whole anything but benevolent. There was contempt and sarcasm in the cold gray eyes, whose glance, however, was at times so piercing, that no one could endure it long. His complexion was even more peculiar than the features: it could neither be called pale nor yellow; it was a sort of gray, or, so to speak, dirty white, like that of an Indian who has been suffering long from fever; and was rendered still more remarkable by the intense blackness of his beard and short cropped hair.

The dress of the unknown was knightly, but old-fashioned and neglected: there were great spots of rust on the collar and breastplate of his armour; and his dagger and the hilt of his finely-worked sword were marked in some places with mildew. As the party were just going to supper, it was only natural to invite the stranger to partake of it; he complied, however, only in so far that he seated himself at the table, for he ate no morsel. The knight, with some surprise, inquired the reason.

'For a long time past, I have accustomed myself never to eat at night,' he replied with a strange smile. 'My digestion is quite unused to solids, and indeed would scarcely confront them. I live entirely on liquids.'

'Oh then, we can empty a bumper of Rhine-wine together,' cried the host.

'Thanks; but I neither drink wine nor any cold beverage,' replied the other; and his tone was full of mockery. It appeared is if there was some amusing association connected with the idea.

'Then I will order you a cup of *hippocras*'—a warm drink composed of herbs—'it shall be ready immediately,' said Franziska.

'Many thanks, fair lady; not at present,' replied the other. 'But if I refuse the beverage you offer me now, you may be assured that as soon as I require it—perhaps very soon—I will request that, or some other of you.'

Bertha and Franz thought the man had something inexpressibly repulsive in his whole manner, and they had no inclination to engage him in conversation; but the baron, thinking that perhaps politeness required him to say something, turned towards the guest, and commenced in a friendly tone: 'It is now many weeks since we first became acquainted with you; we then had to thank you for a signal service'

'And I have not yet told you my name, although you would gladly know it,' interrupted the other drily. 'I am called Azzo and as'—this he said again with his ironical smile—'with the permission of the Knight of Fahnenberg, I live at the castle of Klatka, you can in future call me Azzo von Klatka.'

'I only wonder you do not feel lonely and uncomfortable amongst those old walls,' began Bertha. 'I cannot understand'

'What my business is there? Oh, about that I will willingly give you some information, since you and the young gentleman there take such a kindly interest in my person,' replied the unknown in his tone of sarcasm.

Franz and Bertha both started, for he had revealed their thoughts as though he could read their souls. 'You see, lady,' he continued, 'there are a variety of strange whims in the world. As I have already said, I love what is peculiar and uncommon, at least what would appear so to you. It is wrong in the main to be astonished at anything, for, viewed in one light, all things are alike; even life and death, this side of the grave and the other have more resemblance than you would imagine;

You perhaps consider me rather touched a little in my mind, for taking up my abode with the bat and the owl; but if so, why not consider ever hermit and recluse insane? You will tell me that those are holy men. I certainly have no pretension that way; but as they find pleasure in praying and singing psalms, so I amuse myself with hunting. Oh, you can have no idea of the intense pleasure of dashing away in the pale moonlight, on a horse that never tires over hill and dale, through forest and woodland! I rush among the wolves, which fly at my approach, as you yourself perceived as though they were puppies fearful of the lash.'

'But still it must be lonely, very lonely for you,' remarked Bertha.

'So it would by day; but I am then asleep,' replied the strange drily; 'at night I am merry enough.'

'You hunt in an extraordinary way,' remarked Franz hesitatingly.

'Yes; but, nevertheless, I have no communication with robbers as you seem to imagine,' replied Azzo coldly.

Franz again started—that very thought had just crossed his mind. 'Oh, I beg your pardon; I do not know' he stammered.

'What to make of me,' interrupted the other. 'You would therefore, do well to believe just what I tell you, or at least to avoid making conjectures of your own, which will lead to nothing.'

'I understand you: I know how to value your ideas, if no one else does.' cried Franziska eagerly. 'The humdrum, everyday life of the generality of men is repulsive to you; you have tasted the joys and pleasures of life, at least what are so called, and you have found them tame and hollow. How soon one tires of the things one sees all around! Life consists in change. Only in what is new, uncommon, and peculiar, do the flowers of the spirit bloom and give forth scent. Even pain may become a pleasure if it saves one from the shallow monotony of everyday life—a thing I shall hate till the hour of my death.'

'Right, fair lady—quite right! Remain in this mind: this was always my opinion, and the one from which I have derived the highest reward,' cried Azzo; and his fierce eyes sparkled more intensely than ever. 'I am doubly pleased to have found in you a person who shares my ideas. Oh, if you were a man, you would make me a splendid companion; but even a woman may have fine experiences when once these opinions take root in her, and bring forth action!"

As Azzo spoke these words in a cold tone of politeness, he turned from the subject, and for the rest of his visit only gave the knight monosyllabic replies to his inquiries, taking leave before the table was cleared. To an invitation from the knight, backed by a still more pressing one from Franziska to repeat his visit, he replied that he would take advantage of their kindness, and come sometimes.

When the stranger had departed, many were the remarks made on his appearance and general deportment. Franz declared his most decided dislike to him. Whether it was as usual to vex her cousin, or whether Azzo had really made an impression on her, Franziska took his part vehemently. As Franz contradicted her more eagerly than usual, the young lady launched out into still stronger expressions; and there is no knowing what hard words her cousin might have received, had not a servant entered the room.

The following morning, Franziska lay longer than usual in bed. When her friend went to her room, fearful lest she should be ill, she found her pale and exhausted. Franziska complained she had passed a very bad night; she thought the dispute with Franz about the stranger must have excited her greatly, for she felt quite feverish and exhausted, and a strange dream, too, had worried her, which was evidently a consequence of the evening's conversation. Bertha, as usual, took the young man's part, and added, that a common dispute about a man whom no one knew, and about whom any one might form his own opinion, could not possibly have thrown her into her present state. 'At least,' she continued, 'you can let me hear this wonderful dream.'

To her surprise, Franziska for a length of time refused to do so.

'Come tell me,' inquired Bertha, 'what can possibly prevent you from relating a dream—a mere dream? I might almost think it credible, if the idea were not too horrid, that poor Franz is not very far wrong when he says that the thin, corpse-like, dried-up, old-fashioned stranger has made a greater impression on you than you will allow.'

'Did Franz say so?' asked Franziska. 'Then you can tell him he is not mistaken. Yes, the thin, corpse-like, dried-up whimsical stranger is far more interesting to me than the rosy cheeked, well-dressed, polite, and prosy cousin.'

'Strange!' cried Bertha. 'I cannot at all comprehend this almost magic influence which this man, to me so repulsive exercises over you.'

'Perhaps the very reason I take his part, may be that you are all so prejudiced against him,' remarked Franziska pettishly 'Yes, it must be so; for that his appearance should please my eyes, is what no one in his senses could imagine. But,' she continued, smiling and holding out her hand to Bertha, 'is it not laughable that I should get out of temper even with you about this stranger?—I can more easily understand it with Franz—and that this unknown should spoil my morning, as he has already spoiled my evening and my night's rest?'

'By that dream, you mean?' said Bertha, easily appeased, a she put her arm round her cousin's neck and kissed her. 'Now do tell it to me. You know how I delight in hearing anything of the kind.'

'Well, I will, as a sort of compensation for my peevishness towards you,' said the other, clasping her friend's hands. 'Now listen! I had walked up and down my room for a long time; I was excited—out of spirits—I do not know exactly what. It was almost midnight ere I lay down, but I could not sleep. I tossed about, and at length it was only from sheer exhaustion that I dropped off. But what a sleep it was! An inward fear ran through me perpetually. I saw a number of pictures before me as I used to do in childish sicknesses. I do not know whether I was asleep or half awake. Then I dreamed, but as clearly as if I had been wide awake, that a sort of mist filled the room, and out of it stepped the knight Azzo. He gazed at me for a time, and then letting himself slowly down on one knee, imprinted a kiss on my throat. Long did his lips rest there; and I felt a slight pain which always went on increasing, until I could hear it no more.

'With all my strength I tried to force the vision from me, but succeeded only after a long struggle. No doubt I uttered a scream, for that awoke me from my trance. When I came a little to my senses, I felt a sort of superstitious fear creeping over me—how great you may imagine, when I tell you that, with my eyes open and awake, it appeared to me as if Azzo's figure were still by my bed, and then disappearing gradually into the mist vanished at the door!'

'You must have dreamed very heavily, my poor friend,' began Bertha, but suddenly paused. She gazed with surprise at Franziska's throat. 'Why, what is that?' she cried. 'Just look how extraordinary—a red streak on your throat!'

Franziska raised herself, and went to a little glass that stood in the window. She really saw a small red line about an inch long on her neck, which began to smart when she touched it with her finger.

'I must have hurt myself by some means in my sleep,' she said after a pause; 'and that in some measure will account for my dream.'

The friends continued chatting for some time about this singular coincidence—the dream and the stranger; and at length it was all turned into a joke by Bertha.

Several weeks passed. The knight had found the estate and affairs in greater disorder than he at first imagined; and instead of remaining three or four weeks, as was originally intended, their departure was deferred to on indefinite period. This postponement was likewise in some measure occasioned by Franziska's continued indisposition. She who had formerly bloomed like a rose in its young fresh beauty, was becoming daily thinner, more sickly and exhausted, and at the same time so pale, that in the space of a month not a tinge of red was perceptible on the once glowing cheek. The knight's anxiety about her was extreme, and the best advice was procured which the age and country afforded; but all to no purpose. Franziska complained from time to time that the horrible dream with which her illness commenced was repeated, and that always on the day following she felt an increased and indescribable weakness. Bertha naturally set this down to the effects of fever, but the ravages of that fever on the usually clear reason of her friend filled her with alarm.

The knight Azzo repeated his visits every now and then. He always came in the evening, and when the moon shone brightly. His manner was always the same. He spoke in monosyllables, and was coldly polite to the knight; to Franz and Bertha, particularly to the former, contemptuous and haughty; but to Franziska, friendliness itself. Often when, after a short visit, he again left the house, his peculiarities became the subject of conversation. Besides his old way of speaking, in which Bertha said there lay a deep hatred, a cold detestation of all mankind with the exception of Franziska, two other singularities were observable. During none of his visits, which often took place at suppertime, had he been prevailed upon to eat or drink anything, and that without giving any good reason for his abstinence.

A remarkable alteration, too, had taken place in his appearance; he seemed an entirely different creature. The skin, before so shrivelled and stretched, seemed smooth and soft, while a slight tinge of red appeared in his cheeks, which began to look round and plump. Bertha, who could not at all conceal her ill-will towards him, said often, that much as she hated his face before, when it was more like a death's-head than a human being's, it was now more than ever repulsive; she always felt a shudder run through her veins whenever his sharp piercing eyes rested on her. Perhaps it was owing to Franziska's partiality, or to the knight Azzo' own contemptuous way of replying to Franz, or to his haughty way of treating him in general, that made the young man dislike him more and more.

It was quite observable, that whenever Franz made a remark to his

401

cousin in the presence of Azzo, the latter would immediately throw some ill-natured light on it, or distort it to a totally different meaning. This increased from day to day, and at last Franz declared to Bertha, that he would stand such conduct no longer, and that it was only out of consideration for Franziska that he had not already called him to account.

At this time, the party at the castle was increased by the arrival of Bertha's long-expected guest. He came just as they were sitting down to supper one evening, and all jumped up to greet their old friend. The knight Woislaw was a true model of the soldier, hardened and strengthened by war with men and elements. His face would not have been termed ugly, if a Turkish sabre had not left a mark running from the right eye to the left cheek and standing out bright red from the sunburned skin.

The frame of the Castellan of Glogau might almost be termed colossal. Few would have been able to carry his armour, and still fewer move with his lightness and ease under its weight. He did not think little of this same armour, for it had been a present from the *palatine* of Hungary on his leaving the camp. The blue wrought-steel was ornamented all over with patterns in gold; and he had put it on to do honour to his bride-elect, together with the wonderful gold hand, the gift of the duke.

Woislaw was questioned by the knight and Franz on all the concerns of the campaign; and he entered into the most minute particulars relating to the battles, which, with regard to plunder, had been more successful than ever. He spoke much of the strength of the Turks in a hand-to-hand fight, and remarked that he owed the duke many thanks for his splendid gift, for in consequence of its strength, many of the enemy regarded him a something superhuman. The sickliness and deathlike paleness of Franziska was too perceptible not to be immediately noticed by Woislaw; accustomed to see her so fresh and cheerful, he hastened to inquire into the cause of the change.

Bertha related all that had happened, and Woislaw listened with the greatest interest. This increased to the utmost at the account of the often-repeated dream, and Franziska had to give him the most minute particulars of it; it appeared as though he had met with a similar case before, or at least had heard of one. When the young lady added, that it was very remarkable that the wound on her throat which she had at first felt had never healed, and still pained her, the knight Woislaw looked at Bertha as much as to say, that this last fact had greatly strengthened his idea as to the cause of Franziska's illness.

It was only natural that the discourse should next turn to the knight Azzo, about whom every one began to talk eagerly.

Woislaw inquired as minutely as he had done with regard to Franziska's illness, about what concerned this stranger, from the first evening of their acquaintance down to his last visit, without however, giving any opinion on the subject. The party were still in earnest conversation, when the door opened, and Azzo entered. Woislaw's eyes remained fixed on him, as he, without taking any particular notice of the new arrival, walked up to the table, and seating himself, directed most of his conversation to Franziska and her father, and now and then made some sarcastic remark when Franz began to speak. The Turkish war again came on the *tapis*, and though Azzo only put in an occasional remark, Woislaw had much to say on the subject. Thus they had advanced late into the night, and Franz said smiling to Woislaw: 'I should not wonder if day had surprised us, whilst listening to your entertaining adventures.'

'I admire the young gentleman's taste,' said Azzo, with an ironical curl of the lip. 'Stories of storm and shipwreck are, indeed, best heard on *terra firma,* and those of battle and death at a hospitable table or in the chimney-corner. One has then the comfortable feeling of keeping a whole skin, and being in no danger, not even of taking cold.' With the last words, he gave a hoarse laugh, and turning his back on Franz, rose, bowed to the rest of the company, and left the room. The knight, who always accompanied Azzo to the door, now expressed himself fatigued, and bade his friends goodnight.

'That Azzo's impertinence is unbearable,' cried Bertha when he was gone. 'He becomes daily more rough, unpolite, and presuming. If only on account of Franziska's dream, though of course he cannot help that, I detest him. Now, tonight, not one civil word has he spoken to anyone but Franziska, except, perhaps, some casual remark to my uncle.'

'I cannot deny that you are right, Bertha,' said her cousin. 'One may forgive much to a man whom fate has probably made somewhat misanthropical; but he should not overstep the bounds of common politeness. But where on earth is Franz?' added Franziska, as she looked uneasily round.—The young man had quietly left the room whilst Bertha was speaking.

'He cannot have followed the knight Azzo to challenge him?' cried Bertha in alarm.

'It were better he entered a lion's den to pull his mane!' said Wois-law vehemently. 'I must follow him instantly,' he added, as he rushed from the room.

He hastened over the threshold, out of the castle, and through the court, before he came up to them. Here a narrow bridge with a slight balustrade passed over the moat by which the castle was unrounded. It appeared that Franz had only just addressed Azzo in a few hot words, for as Woislaw, unperceived by either, advanced under the shadow of the wall, Azzo said gloomily: 'Leave me, foolish boy—leave me; for by that sun'—and he pointed to the full moon above them—'you will see those rays no more if you linger another moment on my path.'

'And I tell you, wretch, that you either give me satisfaction for your repeated insolence, or you die,' cried Franz, drawing his sword.

Azzo stretched forth his hand, and grasping the sword in the middle, it snapped like a broken reed. 'I warn you for the last time,' he said in a voice of thunder, as he threw the pieces into the moat. 'Now, away—away, boy, from my path, or, by those below us, you are lost!'

'You or I! you or I!' cried Franz madly, as he made a rush at the sword of his antagonist, and strove to draw it from his side Azzo replied not; only a bitter laugh half escaped his lips; then seizing Franz by the chest, he lifted him up like an infant, and was in the act of throwing him over the bridge, when Woislaw stepped to his side. With a grasp of his wonderful hand, into the springs of which he threw all his strength, he seized Azzo's arm, pulled it down, and obliged him to drop his victim. Azzo seemed in the highest degree astonished. Without concerning himself further about Franz, he gazed in amazement or Woislaw.

'Who art thou who darest to rob me of my prey?' he asked hesitatingly. 'Is it possible? Can you be'——

'Ask not, thou bloody one! Go, seek thy nourishment! Soon comes thy hour!' replied Woislaw in a calm but firm tone.

'Ha! now I know!' cried Azzo eagerly. 'Welcome, blood-brother! I give up to you this worm, and for your sake will not crush him. Farewell; our paths will soon meet again.'

'Soon, very soon; farewell!' cried Woislaw, drawing Franz towards him. Azzo rushed away, and disappeared.

Franz had remained for some moments in a state of semi stupefaction, but suddenly started as from a dream. 'I am dishonoured, dishonoured forever!' he cried, as he pressed his clenched hands to his forehead.

'Calm yourself; you could not have conquered,' said Woislaw.

'But I will conquer, or perish!' cried Franz incensed. 'I will seek this adventurer in his den, and he or I must fall.'

'You could not hurt him,' said Woislaw. 'You would infallibly be the victim.'

'Then shew me a way to bring the wretch to judgement,' cried Franz, seizing Woislaw's hands, while tears of anger sprang to his eyes. 'Disgraced as I am, I cannot live.'

'You shall be revenged, and that within twenty-four hours, I hope; but only on two conditions'

'I agree to them! I will do anything'—began the young man eagerly.

'The first is, that you do nothing, but leave everything in my hands,' interrupted Woislaw. 'The second, that you will assist me in persuading Franziska to do what I shall represent to her as absolutely necessary. That young lady's life is in more danger from Azzo than your own.'

'How? What?' cried Franz fiercely. 'Franziska's life in danger! and from that man? Tell me, Woislaw, who is this fiend?'

'Not a word will I tell either the young lady or you, until the danger is passed,' said Woislaw firmly. 'The smallest indiscretion would ruin everything. No one can act here but Franziska herself, and if she refuses to do so, she is irretrievably lost.'

'Speak, and I will help you. I will do all you wish, but I must know'

'Nothing, absolutely nothing,' replied Woislaw. 'I must have both you and Franziska yield to me unconditionally. Come now, come to her. You are to be mute on what has passed, and use every effort to induce her to accede to my proposal.'

Woislaw spoke firmly, and it was impossible for Franz to make any further objection; in a few moments they both entered the hall, where they found the young girls still anxiously awaiting them.

'Oh, I have been so frightened,' said Franziska, even paler than usual, as she held out her hand to Franz. 'I trust all has ended peaceably.'

'Everything is arranged; a couple of words were sufficient to settle the whole affair,' said Woislaw cheerfully. 'But Master Franz was less concerned in it than yourself, fair lady.'

'I! How do you mean?' said Franziska in surprise.

'I allude to your illness,' replied the other.

'And you spoke of that to Azzo? Does he, then, know a remedy which he could not tell me himself?' she inquired, smiling painfully.

'The knight Azzo must take part in your cure; but speak to you

405

about it he cannot, unless the remedy is to lose all its efficacy,' replied Woislaw quietly.

'So it is some secret elixir, as the learned doctors say, who have so long attended me, and through whose means I only grow worse,' said Franziska mournfully.

'It is certainly a secret, but is as certainly a cure,' replied Woislaw.

'So said all, but none has succeeded,' said the young lady peevishly.

'You might at least try it,' began Bertha.

'Because your friend proposes it,' said the other smiling. 'I have no doubt that you, with nothing ailing you, would take all manner of drugs to please your knight; but with me the inducement is wanting, and therefore also the faith.'

'I did not speak of any medicine,' said Woislaw.

'Oh! a magical remedy! I am to be cured—what was it the quack who was here the other day called it!—"by sympathy." Yes, that was it.'

'I do not object to your calling it so, if you like,' said Woislaw smiling; 'but you must know, dear lady, that the measures I shall propose must be attended to literally, and according to the strictest directions.'

'And you trust this to me?' asked Franziska,

'Certainly,' said Woislaw hesitating; 'but'—

'Well, why do you not proceed? Can you think that I shall fail in courage?' she asked.

'Courage is certainly necessary for the success of my plan,' said Woislaw gravely; 'and it is because I give you credit for a large share of that virtue, I venture to propose it at all, although for the real harmlessness of the remedy I will answer with my life, provided you follow my directions exactly.'

'Well, tell me the plan, and then I can decide,' said the young lady.

'I can only tell you that when we commence our operations,' replied Woislaw.

'Do you think I am a child to be sent here, there, and everywhere, without a reason?' asked Franziska, with something of her old pettishness.

'You did me great injustice, dear lady, if you thought for a moment I would propose anything disagreeable to you, unless demanded by the sternest necessity,' said Woislaw; 'and yet I can only repeat my former words.'

'Then I will not do it,' cried Franziska. 'I have already tried so much, and all ineffectually.'

'I give you my honour as a knight, that your cure is certain, but—you must pledge yourself solemnly and unconditionally to do implicitly what I shall direct,' said Woislaw earnestly.

'Oh, I implore you to consent, Franziska. Our friend would not propose anything unnecessary,' said Bertha, taking both her cousin's hands.

'And let me join my entreaties to Bertha's,' said Franz.

'How strange you all are!' exclaimed Franziska, shaking her head; 'you make such a secret of that which I must know if I am to accomplish it, and then you declare so positively that I shall recover, when my own feelings tell me it is quite hopeless.'

'I repeat, that I will answer for the result,' said Woislaw,' on the condition I mentioned before, and that you have courage to carry out what you commence.'

'Ha! now I understand ; this, after all, is the only thing which appears doubtful to you,' cried Franziska. 'Well, to shew you that our sex are neither wanting in the will nor in the power to accomplish deeds of daring, I give my consent.'

With the last words, she offered Woislaw her hand.

'Our compact is thus sealed,' she pursued smiling. 'Now say, Sir Knight, how am I to commence this mysterious cure?'

'It commenced when you gave your consent,' said Woislaw gravely. 'Now, I have only to request that you will ask no more questions, but hold yourself in readiness to take a ride with, me tomorrow an hour before sunset. I also request that you will not mention to your father a word of what has passed.'

'Strange!' said Franziska.

'You have made the compact; you are not wanting in resolution; and I will answer for everything else,' said Woislaw encouragingly.

'Well, so let it be. I will follow your directions,' said the lady, although she still looked incredulous.

'On our return you shall know everything; before that, it is quite impossible,' said Woislaw in conclusion. 'Now go, dear lady, and take some rest; you will need strength for tomorrow.'

It was on the morning of the following day, the sun had not risen above an hour, and the dew still lay like a veil of pearls on the grass, or dripped from the petals of the flowers, swaying in the early breeze, when the knight Woislaw hastened over the fields towards the forest, and turned into a gloomy path, which by the direction, one could perceive, led towards the towers of Klatka. When he arrived at the old oak-tree we have before had occasion to mention, he sought carefully along the road for traces of human footsteps, but only a deer had passed that way; and seemingly satisfied with his search, he proceeded on his way, though not before he had half drawn his dagger from its sheath, as though to assure himself that it was ready for service in time of need.

Slowly he ascended the path; it was evident he carried something beneath his cloak. Arrived in the court, he left the ruins of the castle to the left, and entered the old chapel. In the chancel, he looked eagerly and earnestly round. A deathlike stillness reigned in the deserted sanctuary, only broken by the whispering of the wind in an old thorn-tree which grew outside. Woislaw had looked long around him ere he perceived the door leading down to the vault; he hurried towards it, and descended. The sun's position enabled its rays to penetrate the crevices, and made the subterranean chamber so light, that one could read easily the inscriptions at the head and feet of the coffins.

The knight first laid on the ground the packet he had hitherto earned under his cloak, and then going from coffin to coffin, at last remained stationary before the oldest of them. He read the inscription carefully, drew his dagger thoughtfully from its case, and endeavoured to raise the lid with its point. This was no difficult matter, for the rusty iron nails kept but a slight hold of the rotten wood. On looking in, only a heap of ashes, some remnants of dress, and a skull were the contents. He quickly closed it again, and went on to the next, passing over those of a woman and two children. Here things had much the same appearance, except that the corpse held together till the lid was raised, and then fell into dust, a few linen rags and bones being alone perceptible. In the third, fourth, and nearly the next half-dozen, the bodies were in better preservation: in some, they looked a sort of yellow brown mummy; whilst in others, a skinless skull covered with hair grinned from the coverings of velvet, silk, or mildewed embroideries; all, however, were touched with the loathsome marks of decay.

Only one more coffin now remained to be inspected; Woislaw approached it, and read the inscription. It was the same that had before attracted the Knight of Fahnenberg Ezzelin von Klatka, the last possessor of the tower, was described as lying therein. Woislaw found it more difficult to raise the lid here; and it was only by the exertion of much strength he a length succeeded in extracting the nails. He did all, however as quietly as if afraid of rousing some sleeper within; he then raised the cover, and cast a glance on the corpse. An involuntary 'Ha!' burst from his lips as he stepped back a pace. If he had less expected the sight that met his eyes, he would have been far more overcome.

In the coffin lay Azzo as he lived and breathed, and as Woislaw had seen him at the supper-table only the evening before. His appearance, dress, and all were the same; besides, he had more the semblance of sleep than of death—no trace of decay was visible—there was even a rosy tint on his cheeks. Only the circumstance that the breast did not heave, distinguished him from one who slept. For a few moments Woisiaw did not move; he could only stare into the coffin. With a hastiness in his movements not usual with him, he suddenly seized the lid, which had fallen from his hands, and laying it on the coffin, knocked the nails into their places. As soon as he had completed this work, he fetched the packet he had left at the entrance, and laying it on the top of the coffin, hastily ascended the steps, and quitted the church and the ruins.

The day passed. Before evening, Franziska requested her father to allow her to take a ride with Woislaw, under pretence of shewing him the country. He, only too happy to think this a sign of amendment in his daughter, readily gave his consent; so, followed by a single servant, they mounted and left the castle. Woislaw was unusually silent and serious. When Franziska began to rally him about his gravity, and the approaching sympathetic cure, he replied, that what was before her was no laughing matter; and that although the result would be certainly a cure, still it would leave an impression on her whole future life.

In such discourse they reached the wood, and at length the oak, where they left their horses. Woislaw gave Franziska his arm, and they ascended the hill slowly and silently. They had just reached one of the half-dilapidated outworks where they could catch a glimpse of the open country, when Woislaw, speaking more to himself than to his companion, said: 'In a quarter of an hour, the sun will set, and in another hour the moon will have risen; then all must be accomplished. It will soon be time to commence the work.'

'Then, I should think it was time to intrust me with some idea of what it is,' said Franziska, looking at him.

'Well, lady,' he replied, turning towards her, and his voice was very solemn, 'I entreat you, Franziska von Fahnenberg, for your own good, and as you love the father who clings to you with his whole soul, that you will weigh well my words, and that you will not interrupt me with questions which I cannot answer until the work is completed.

Your life is in the greatest danger from the illness under which you are labouring; indeed, you are irrecoverably lost if you do not fully carry out what I shall now impart to you. Now, promise me to do implicitly as I shall tell you; I pledge you my knightly word it is nothing against Heaven, or the honour of your house; and, besides, it is the sole means for saving you.' With these words, he held out his light hand to his companion, while he raised the other to heaven in confirmation of his oath.

'I promise you,' said Franziska, visibly moved by Woislaw's solemn tone, as she laid her little white and wasted hand in his.

'Then come; it is time,' was his reply, as he led her towards the church. The last rays of the sun were just pouring through the broken windows. They entered the chancel, the best preserved part of the whole building; here there were still some old kneeling-stools, placed before the high-altar, although nothing remained of that but the stonework and a few steps; the pictures and decorations had all vanished.

'Say an *Ave*; you will have need of it,' said Woislaw, as he himself fell on his knees.

Franziska knelt beside him, and repeated a short prayer. After a few moments, both rose.

'The moment has arrived! The sun sinks, and before the moon rises, all must be over,' said Woislaw quickly.

'What am I to do?' asked Franziska cheerfully.

'You see there that open vault!' replied the knight Woislaw, pointing to the door and flight of steps: 'you must descend. You must go alone; I may not accompany you. When you have reached the vault you will find, close to the entrance, a coffin, on which is placed a small packet. Open this packet, and you will find three long iron nails and a hammer. Then pause for a moment; but when I begin to repeat the *Credo* in a loud voice, knock with all your might, first one nail, then a second, and then a third, into the lid of the coffin, right up to their heads.'

Franziska stood thunderstruck; her whole body trembled, and she could not utter a word. Woislaw perceived it.

'Take courage, dear lady!' said he. 'Think that you are in the hands of Heaven, and that, without the will of your Creator, not a hair can fall from your head. Besides, I repeat, there is no danger.'

'Well, then, I will do it,' cried Franziska, in some measure regaining courage.

'Whatever you may hear, whatever takes place inside the coffin,' continued Woislaw, 'must have no effect upon you. Drive the nails well in, without flinching: your work must be finished before my prayer comes to an end.'

Franziska shuddered, but again recovered herself. 'I will do it; Heaven will send me strength,' she murmured softly.

'There is one thing more,' said Woislaw hesitatingly; 'perhaps it is the hardest of all I have proposed, but without it your cure will not be complete. When you have done as I have told you, sort of'—he hesitated—'a sort of liquid will flow from the coffin in this dip your finger, and besmear the scratch on your throat.'

'Horrible!' cried Franziska. 'This liquid is blood. A human being lies in the coffin.'

'An *unearthly one* lies therein! That blood is your own, but it flows in other veins,' said Woislaw gloomily. 'Ask no more; the sand is running out.'

Franziska summoned up all her powers of mind and body, went towards the steps which led to the vault, and Woislaw sank on his knees before the altar in quiet prayer. When the lady had descended, she found herself before the coffin on which lay the packet before mentioned. A sort of twilight reigned in the vault and everything around was so still and peaceful, that she felt more calm, and going up to the coffin, opened the packet. She had hardly seen that a hammer and three long nails were its contents when suddenly Woislaw's voice rang through the church, and broke the stillness of the aisles. Franziska started, but recognised the appointed prayer. She seized one of the nails, and with one stroke of the hammer drove it at least an inch into the cover.

All was still; nothing was heard but the echo of the stroke, Taking heart, the maiden grasped the hammer with both hands, and struck the nail twice with all her might, right up to the head into the wood. At this moment commenced a rustling noise; it seemed as though something in the interior began to move and to struggle. Franziska drew back in alarm. She was already on the point of throwing away the hammer, and flying up the steps, when Woislaw raised his voice so powerfully, and it sounded so entreatingly, that in a sort of excitement, such as would induce one to rush into a lion's den, she returned to the coffin, determined to bring things to a conclusion.

Hardly knowing what she did, she placed a second nail in the centre of the lid, and after some strokes, this was likewise buried to its head.

The struggle now increased fearfully, as if some living creature were striving to burst the coffin. This was so shaken by it, that it cracked and split on all sides. Half distracted, Franziska seized the third nail; she thought no more of her ailments, she only knew herself to be in terrible danger, of what kind she could not guess: in an agony that threatened to rob her of her senses, and in the midst of the turning and cracking of the coffin, in which low groans were now heard, she struck the third nail in equally tight.

At this moment, she began to lose consciousness. She wished to hasten away, but staggered; and mechanically grasping at something to save herself by, she seized the corner of the coffin, and sank fainting beside it on the ground.

A quarter of an hour might have elapsed, when she again opened her eyes. She looked around her. Above was the starry sky, and the moon, which shed her cold light on the ruins and on the tops of the old oak-trees. Franziska was lying outside the church walls, Woislaw on his knees beside her, holding her hand in his.

'Heaven be praised that you live!' he cried, with a sigh of relief. 'I was beginning to doubt whether the remedy had not been too severe, and yet it was the only thing to save you.'

Franziska recovered her full consciousness very gradually. The past seemed to her like a dreadful dream. Only a few moments before, that fearful scene; and now this quiet all around her. She hardly dared at first to raise her eyes, and shuddered when she found herself only a few paces removed from the spot where she had undergone such terrible agony. She listened half unconsciously, now to the pacifying words Woislaw addressed to her, now to the whistling of the servant, who stood by the horses, and who, to wile away his time, was imitating the evening-song of a belated cow-herd.

'Let us go,' whispered Franziska, as she strove to raise herself. 'But what is this? My shoulder is wet, my throat, my hand'—

'It is probably the evening dew on the grass,' said Woislaw gently.

'No; it is blood!' she cried, springing up with horror in her tone. 'See, my hand is full of blood!'

'Oh, you are mistaken—surely mistaken,' said Woislaw stammering. 'Or perhaps the wound on your neck may have opened? Pray, feel whether this is the case.' He seized her hand, and directed it to the spot.

'I do not perceive anything; I feel no pain,' she said at length, somewhat angrily.

'Then, perhaps, when you fainted, you may have struck a corner of the coffin, or have torn yourself with the point of one of the nails,' suggested Woislaw.

'Oh, of what do you remind me!' cried Franziska shuddering. 'Let us away—away! I entreat you, come! I will not remain a moment longer near this dreadful, dreadful place.'

They descended the path much quicker than they came. Woislaw placed his companion on her horse, and they were soon on their way-home.

When they approached the castle, Franziska began to inundate her protector with questions about the preceding adventure; but he declared that her present state of excitement must make him defer all explanations till the morning, when her curiosity should be satisfied. On their arrival, he conducted her at once to her room, and told the knight his daughter was too much fatigued with her ride to appear at the supper-table. On the following morning, Franziska rose earlier than she had done for a long time. She assured her friend it was the first time since her illness commenced that she had been really refreshed by her sleep, and, what was still more remarkable, she had not been troubled by her old horrible dream. Her improved looks were not only remarked by Bertha, but by Franz and the knight; and with Woislaw's permission, she related the adventures of the previous evening. No sooner had she concluded, than Woislaw was completely stormed with questions about such a strange occurrence.

'Have you,' said the latter, turning towards his host, 'ever heard of Vampires?'

'Often,' replied he; 'but I have never believed in them.'

'Nor did I,' said Woislaw; 'but I have been assured of the existence by experience.'

'Oh, tell us what occurred,' cried Bertha eagerly, as a light seemed to dawn on her.

'It was during my first campaign in Hungary,' began Woislaw 'when I was rendered helpless for some time by this sword-cut of a *janizary* across my face, and another on my shoulder. I had been taken into the house of a respectable family in a small town. It consisted of the father and mother, and a daughter about twenty years of age. They obtained their living by selling the very good wine of the country, and the tap-room was always full of visitors. Although the family were well to do in the world, there seemed to brood over them a continual melancholy, caused by the constant illness of the only daughter, a very pretty and

413

excellent girl. She had always before bloomed like a rose, but for some months she had been getting so thin and wasted, and that without an satisfactory reason: they tried every means to restore her, but in vain.

'As the army had encamped quite in the neighbourhood of course a number of people of all countries assembled in the tavern. Amongst these there was one man who came every evening, when the moon shone, who struck everybody by the peculiarity of his manners and appearance; he looked dried up and deathlike, and hardly spoke at all; but what he did say was bitter and sarcastic. Most attention was excited towards him by the circumstance, that although he always ordered a cup of the best wine, and now and then raised it to his lips, the cup was always as full after his departure as at first.'

'This all agrees wonderfully with the appearance of Azzo,' said Bertha, deeply interested.

'The daughter of the house,' continued Woislaw,' became daily worse, despite the aid not only of Christian doctors, but of many amongst the heathen prisoners, who were consulted in the hope that they might have some magical remedy to propose. It was singular that the girl always complained of a dream, in which the unknown guest worried and plagued her.'

'Just the same as your dream, Franziska,' cried Bertha.

'One evening,' resumed Woislaw. 'an old Sclavonian—who had made many voyages to Turkey and Greece, and had even seen the New World—and I were sitting over our wine, when the unknown walked silently, as usual, into the room, and sat down at the table. The bottle passed quickly between my friend and me, whilst we talked of all manner of things, of our adventures, and of passages in our lives, both horrible and amusing. We went on chatting thus for about an hour, and drank a tolerable quantity of wine.

'The unknown had remained perfectly silent the whole time, only smiling contemptuously every now and then. He now paid his money, and was going away. All this had quietly worried me—perhaps the wine had got a little into my head—so I said to the stranger: "Hold, you stony stranger; you have hitherto done nothing but listen, and have not even emptied your cup. Now you shall take your turn in telling us something amusing, and if you do not drink up your wine, it shall produce a quarrel between us."

'"Yes," said the Sclavonian, " you must remain; you shall chat and drink, too;" and he grasped—for although no longer young, he was big and very strong—the stranger by the shoulder, to pull him down to his seat again: the latter, however, although as thin as a skeleton, with one movement of his hand flung the Sclavonian to the middle of the room, and half stunned him for a moment. I now approached to hold the stranger back. I caught him by the arm; and although the springs of my iron hand were less powerful than those I have at present, I must have griped him rather hard in my anger, for after looking grimly at me for a moment, he bent towards me and whispered in my ear: "Let me go: from the gripe of your fist, I see you are my brother, therefore do not hinder me from seeking my bloody nourishment. I am hungry!" Surprised by such words, I let him loose, and almost before I was aware, he had left the room.

'As soon as I had in some degree recovered from my astonishment, I told the Sclavonian what I had heard. He started, evidently alarmed. I asked him to tell me the cause of his fears, and pressed him for an explanation of those extraordinary words. On our way to his lodging, he complied with my request. "The stranger," said he, "is a Vampire!"'

'How?' cried the knight, Franziska, and Bertha simultaneously, in a voice of horror. 'So this Azzo was'—

'Nothing less. He also was a vampire!' replied Woislaw. 'But at all events *his* hellish thirst is quenched for ever; he will never return.— But I have not finished. As in my country, vampires had never been heard of, I questioned the Sclavonian minutely. He said that in Hungary, Croatia, Dalmatia, and Bosnia, these hellish guests were not uncommon. They were deceased persons, who had either once served as nourishment to vampires, or who had died in deadly sin, or under excommunication; and that whenever the moon shone, they rose from their graves, and sucked the blood of the living.'

'Horrible!' cried Franziska. 'If you had told me all this beforehand, I should never have accomplished the work.'

'So I thought; and yet it must be executed by the suffers themselves, while someone else performs the devotions,' replied Woislaw. 'The Sclavonian,' he continued after a short pause, 'added many other facts with regard to these unearthly visitant. He said that whilst their victim wasted, they themselves improve in appearance, and that a vampire possessed enormous strength'

'Now I can understand the change your false hand produced on Azzo,' interrupted Franz.

'Yes, that was it,' replied Woislaw. 'Azzo, as well as the other vampire, mistook its great power for that of a natural one, and concluded I was one of his own species.—You may now imagine, dear lady,' he continued, turning to Franziska, 'how alarmed I was at your appearance when I arrived: all you and Bertha told me increased my anxiety; and when I saw Azzo I could doubt no longer that he was a vampire. As I learned from your account that a grave with the name Ezzelin von Klatka lay in the neighbourhood, I had no doubt that you might be saved: I could only induce you to assist me. It did not appear to me advisable to impart the whole facts of the case, for your bodily powers were so impaired, that an idea of the horrors before you might have quite unfitted you for the exertion; for this reason, I arranged everything in the manner in which it has taken place.'

'You did wisely,' replied Franziska shuddering. 'I can never be grateful enough to you. Had I known what was required of me, I never could have undertaken the deed.'

'That was what I feared,' said Woislaw; 'but fortune has favoured us all through.'

'And what became of the unfortunate girl in Hungary? inquired Bertha.

'I know not,' replied Woislaw. 'That very evening there was an alarm of the Turks, and we were ordered off. I never heard anything more of her.'

The conversation upon these strange occurrences continued for some time longer. The knight determined to have the vault at Klatka walled up forever. This took place on the following day the knight alleging as a reason, that he did not wish the dead to be disturbed by irreverent hands.

Franziska recovered gradually. Her health had been so severely shaken, that it was long ere her strength was so much restored as to allow of her being considered out of danger. The young lady's character underwent a great change in the interval. Its former strength was, perhaps, in some degree diminished, but in place of that, she had acquired a benevolent softness, which brought out all her best qualities. Franz continued his attentions to his cousin; but, perhaps, owing to a hint from Bertha, he was less assiduous in his exhibition of them.

His inclinations did not lead him to the battle, the camp, or the attainment of honours: his great aim was to increase the good condition and happiness of his tenants, and to this he contributed the whole energy of his mind. Franziska could not withstand the unobtrusive signs of the young man's continued attachment; and it was not long ere the credit she was obliged to yield to his noble efforts for the welfare of his fellow-creatures, changed into a liking, which went on increasing, until at length it assumed the character of love. As Woislaw insisted on making Bertha his wife before he returned to Silesia, it was arranged that the marriage should take place at their present abode. How joyful was the surprise of the knight of Fahnenberg, when his daughter and Franz likewise entreated his blessing, and expressed their desire of being united on the same day! This day soon came round, and it saw the bright looks of two happy couples.

The Ruins of the Abbey of Fitz-Martin

The Abbey of Fitz-Martin had been once famous for its riches and grandeur, and, as a monastery, was dedicated to St Catherine; but the subsequent irregularity of its order, together with the despotic tyranny of one of its ancient lords, had stripped it by slow but sure degrees of all its former wealth and consequence; insomuch, that the haughty baron had, under unjust pretences, demanded heavy contributions, to assist in carrying on the war between the first Edward and the nearly subdued Scots. His only excuse for such an open violation of ecclesiastic rights was grounded on a discovery he pretended he had made, of one of the nuns having broken the sacred rules of her profession, by a disregard to her vows of vestal celibacy.

The haughty baron seized greedily this circumstance, as the means of succeeding in his ambitious designs, and determined to humble the pride and insolence of the superiors, since the land belonged originally to his ancestors, and was transmitted to himself with powers to exact homage and fee from the heads of the monastery for this only part of their dependence on laical jurisdiction. For this latter purpose, the baron, as Lord Patron of the holy community, entered the abbey, and demanded from the superiors not only a large subsidy of money, but an acknowledgement of their obedience; and, to cover his injustice, pretended it was designed for the further prosecution of the Holy Wars.

The superiors proudly refused compliance, and, in angry tones, threatened an appeal to Rome, with a dreadful anathema on the head of the daring violator, if he persisted in his presumptions.

But the baron knew the surety of his proceedings, and, with a smile of malicious triumph, exposed his knowledge of the crimes of Sister

St Anna, even relating at full his acquaintance with the proof of her lapse from that sacred vow, which for ever enjoined the community of a monastery to celibacy. The fathers of the order, when summoned to the council, heard the account with confusion and dismay, and entreated time to search into the truth of the baron's assertions. The crafty baron knew the advantage he had over them; and, to increase their fears of the dreaded exposure, quitted the abbey, in haughty and forbidding silence, without deigning to answer their petitions.

The unhappy community of the once proud monastery of St Catherine, at length, harassed by their dread of an exposure, and the total loss of all their wealth, by multiplied and never ceasing demands, became dependant on its tyrannic baron, who kept the monks in such entire and arbitrary subjection, that in the course of a very few years, the abbey became nearly quite forsaken by its once imperious masters; when, at length, the baron having disclosed to the king the dissolute manners of the order, and supplying Edward also with a large sum of money, that monarch unknowingly rewarded his treachery with the hereditary possession of the abbey, and all its tenures, revenues and riches.

The baron, therefore, took undisputed possession of his new acquisition, which he soon transformed into a princely habitation. But tradition says, that its imperious master did not, though surrounded by the possession of a mine of wealth, enjoy that expected ease, and inward happiness, which the gratification of his lawless wishes led him to hope for. For he is reported ever after to have been subject to gloomy passions, and melancholy abstractions of mind, which often ended in vehement paroxisms of madness. An imperfectly handed tradition still existed, which related, that the spectre of St Anna, the unhappy instrument of his destruction to the monastery, had repeatedly appeared to the baron, to warn him of his heinous offences, and even accuse him as the cause of her ruin, and subsequent punishment by death. Certain it is, that various reports and conjectures had arisen in the minds of the ignorant; some tending to involve the baron in the guilt of being the unknown seducer of Anna, for the purpose of completing his avaricious designs.

But the real truth of her destiny was totally involved in silence; as, soon after the baron had exposed to the superiors his knowledge of her dereliction, she had suddenly disappeared from the community, nor was ever heard of after. Whatever was in reality her dreadful end is still unknown. But the baron lived not long to enjoy the splendour of his ill-gained riches. He was heard to confess, that peace of mind was for ever banished from his heart; and, though lying on the downy couches of luxury, yet did he never after enjoy a calm undisturbed conscience. His death was the departure of guilty horror, and alarm for the future; and he quitted the world with curses and execrations on himself, leaving no child to inherit the abbey, which descended to his next heir; who, being every way unlike his uncle, refused to reside in a place that had been obtained by fraud and injustice. From this period the abbey, for near a century and a half, had acknowledged several lords, but was seldom honoured, for any length of time, by the presence of its possessors, who were in general eager to shun a place, whose traditional history teemed with dark and mysterious records. The owners of the abbey were too superiorly gifted with Fortune's treasures, and the spectred traditions of St Anna kept them from ever approaching its decayed towers. Its lands, therefore, remaining untilled, soon added increase to the surrounding forests, and were suffered to become useless, and over-run with the luxuriance of uncultivated nature.

The last owner deceased, was a distant relation of the present inheritor, Sir Thomas Fitz-Martin, who was driven by severe misfortune, and the loss of a most amiable wife, to seek its long-deserted ruins, to hide himself and family from the dreadful consequences of an over-ruling fate which no human wisdom could avert, but in the hoped-for security of this long-forgotten retreat.

Yet the suddenness of his journey, its long and fatiguing continuance, together with the gloomy, remote, and even terrific habitation he was speedily approaching, began to raise fears and doubts in the minds of the domestics, who shrunk back, declaring it impossible to venture into so terrific and ruinous a place. Sir Thomas had never but once seen it, and that many years since, and even shuddered as he again reviewed its dreary and frowning exterior, and half wished that his haste had not led him to choose so desolate a place for his future abode. At that moment the carriage suddenly stopping, at some little distance from an open avenue that led immediately to the abbey, Owen demanded if he was to proceed further, or if His Honour had not better turn into another path, and seek the nearest way out of the dismal forest; 'for surely, my Lord will never think of entering yon frightful old ruin, which, I dare say, will fall, and crush us alive beneath its humble battlements: or perhaps we shall have to encounter a battle with an army of ghosts and hobgoblins, who will dispute our right of admission within their tottering territories.'

'Peace, I command you,' exclaimed Sir Thomas. 'I thought you, at least, possessed more courage, than to admit the impression of such idle fears as even your female companions would blush to express. The seat of my ancestors, though long deserted and now perhaps destitute of every comfort, has, I will vouch for it, nothing that can justly alarm or excite cowardice in the minds of my servants. If, however, yourself, or any of your companions, fear to enter with your lord the building he has chosen for his future abode, they have free permission to remain with the carriage till day-light, whilst I and my daughter will alone seek our admission within a mansion that hereafter shall become our chief residence.'

Sir Thomas, at length descending from the vehicle, walked, with cautious inspection, a considerable way beneath the walls, before he arrived at the heavy gates of entrance. They were, however, securely closed, and resisted his attempts to force them, with an obstinacy that surprised him. Calling loudly to his terror-stricken people, he commanded them, on their approach, to join their efforts with his; but the gates proved the strength of their interior holds, and none of the fastenings yielded to their attacks. Tired with this fruitless labour, yet wondering at the security with which they were barricaded, Sir Thomas paused once more, and in that interval the idea flashed on his mind, that the abbey might possibly be inhabited; though well he knew he had given no one permission to enter its precincts; and the traditional terrors of the place he thought were a sufficient guard against all unknown intruders. Yet it was not unlikely, that if it were indeed inhabited, it was become the dreadful haunt of *banditti*, to whom the lonely situation of the forest rendered it a very favourable concealment for the practice of their daring profession.

For a moment this fearful supposition rendered Sir Thomas undecided, and he remained irresolute how to proceed, from the dread of exposing his family to more real dangers than the imaginary ones of Owen, till a violent flash of lightning ended his doubts; as it glanced in an instant on the walls of the abbey, and displayed its tottering turrets and broken casements. It shewed also, at no great distance, a small postern, whose weak state seemed to promise greater success; and they determined to try it if they could not here find a more willing admission. The postern was extremely old, and seemed only held by the bolt of the lock, which soon gave way to the attack of the travellers; and crossing beneath a heavy Gothic arch, they found themselves within

421

the area of the first court. Sir Thomas, followed by his trembling attendants, was hastening forward, till recollecting the females in the carriage were left unguarded, he ordered one of the men to return instantly, and await with them the event of their lord's bold adventure to gain shelter within the ruin.

Owen summoned up a sort of desperate courage, and declared his intention of attending his master: and lighting a torch, he followed his calm and undaunted conductor, who now advanced with caution through the wide area of a second court, which, being covered with crumbling fragments of the ruins, rendered his advances difficult, and even dangerous. At length he reached a flight of steps, that seemed to lead to the grand portal of entrance. Sir Thomas, however, determined to ascend; and Owen, though tottering beneath his own weight with terrors, dared not interpose his resistance: his trembling hand held the light to the great folding doors, and Sir Thomas, after some efforts, burst them open, and entered what appeared an immense hall, terminating in vistas of huge pillars, whose lofty heads, like the roof they supported, were impervious to the faint rays of the torch, and enveloped in an awful and misty gloom, beyond expression impressive and solemn, and creating astonishing sensations in the startled beholder.

At length Sir Thomas's progress was stopped by some steps, that led up to a Gothic door, which, with no little difficulty, he forced back, and entering its dark precincts, found himself within a large antique room, with the forms of several crumbling pieces of furniture, which, from the number of its raised couches, now covered with blackness, seemed evidently the remnants of a chamber that had once been stately and magnificent. Sir Thomas examined it well. The walls, though dripping with damp, seemed tolerably entire, and to promise security from the dangers of the night; and as he had as yet seen nothing to excite alarm or dread, he hastened to the carriage, and declared to its inmates his resolution. The females knowing that, as they had proceeded thus far, to retract from their fearful enterprise was now become impracticable, obeyed with trembling and reluctant steps, and, supported by their male companions, slowly advanced; whilst Sir Thomas, taking Rosaline in his arms, conveyed her to the abbey.

Owen and Rowland, who had, by the command of their master, cut down several branches from the forest, now set them alight within the wide spreading hearth, whose brisk and crackling blaze soon dispelled the damp and glooms of a dreary chamber, and at length compelled even the long-stretched countenances of the females to relax into something like a smile; and the remembered fatigue and danger of their perilous journey through the forest, when compared with their present shelter, and the comforts of a welcome and plentiful meal, succeeded at last in making a very visible alteration. The repast being ended, Sir Thomas commanded Owen to place before the fire some of the strongest couches he could find, and cover them with packages, and compose themselves to rest. The servants, who had dreaded the thoughts of being obliged to pass the night in the chamber, were grateful for this considerate permission; and reclining themselves on the couches, they soon forgot the terrors and dangers they had felt, and became alike insensible to their forlorn situation, and to the storm which howled without, and now shook the trembling fabric, with each fresh gust of wind that assailed its ruined towers.

Sir Thomas was the first of the slumbering travellers that awoke. Convinced that it was day, from a ray of light that shone through a broken window shutter, he hastened to arise; for, since he was assured he should sleep no more, he resolved not to disturb his wearied domestics, but use the present interval to search the abbey. He proceeded to a large folding door on the west side, which he concluded must have been the grand entrance; but he declined, for the present, any further examination of the outside of the building; and turning to the left, advanced to a folding door, deeply fixed within a Gothic portal, which opening harshly to his efforts, let him, with astonishment, into a long suite of rooms, which, notwithstanding their silent, deserted, ruinous state, he was rejoiced to find might again be rendered habitable, and in a little time even convenient and comfortable.

They were eight in number, and still retained many remnants of furniture, which, though covered with mildew and dust, and crumbling to tatters, evidently witnessed the splendour of its former owner. He was satisfied that these chambers would amply answer his present wants, and rejoiced to find them in such a state as to make their repair not only possible but easy.

Proceeding forward through this vast extent of chambers, Sir Thomas felt that every former surmise of robbers was at an end, as he had as yet met with not a single circumstance that could in any degree confirm it. He was now hastening back to his family, who, should they have awoke, might experience no inconsiderable alarm.

Having descended for this purpose, he found himself, as he turned on the left, in a long but narrow gallery or passage; passing forward, he opened with much labour several old doors, in hopes they would bring him into a passage leading into the great hall or church; but they only presented a number of weak and dangerous recesses, perhaps formerly cells of the monastery, whose flooring was so much decayed, and in some places fallen in, as to render further progress impossible. Quitting the fruitless search, he proceeded to the extreme end, where he met with a stronger door, which occasioned him no small manual exercise to unclose, when, to his surprise, a violent scream rung upon his ears; and, as he threw open the arched door, he beheld his terrified party, who, awaked by the noise of his forcing of the portal, had rushed into the arms of the men, to whom they clung, shrieking for protection against nothing less than a legion of armed spectres, whom their affrighted fancies had in an instant conjured from their graves.

'I have,' said Sir Thomas, 'explored the chief apartments of the abbey, and rejoice to find them every way beyond my expectations. Workmen, and other necessary persons shall be instantly engaged for the repair of this ancient and long-neglected mansion, which, as I mean to make it perfectly habitable, I have now only to assure all present, that the seat of my family has nothing to excite just terror, or encourage misconceptions relating to beings that never had existence.'

As soon as their small repast was ended, Sir Thomas desired Owen to take one of the horses, and find the nearest way to the next town; for a supply of food was become necessary. Sir Thomas went, followed by Owen, round the southern angle of the abbey, where they had a full view of a portal more ruinous than the one they had quitted, and which presented a long and dreary continuation of those parts of the building once dedicated to conventual occupation, and were now crumbling into dust. 'Now,' said Sir Thomas, 'mount your horse, and proceed down yonder avenue, which will conduct you to the next town; and likewise inquire for one Norman Clare, who was steward to these estates; explain to him my present situation, and that I require his attendance; and give him full commission to engage such workmen as shall be needful for the full repair.'

Owen immediately obeyed; and lashing his steed into a fast trot, soon arrived within sight of a poor but neat-looking cottage, with a venerable looking old man sitting beneath a spreading oak, who had seen the intruder as he galloped out of the forest, with surprise strongly marked in his face. 'Pray,' said Owen, as he rode up to the cottage, 'can you inform me if there be one Norman Clare living in this neighbourhood?'

The old man started back with increased surprise, exclaiming, 'And pray what is thy business with Norman Clare?' 'The simple-hearted Owen entered into a full detail of his mission, adding, 'if such a person as Norman was alive, his master, Sir Thomas, Lord of Fitz-Martin's abbey and lands, demanded his assistance at the above named mansion.'

'If thou requirest to be acquainted with him, thou shalt not further waste thy labour; for truly I am Norman Clare; and since I find thou art real flesh and blood, thou shalt enter with me my lonely dwelling, and welcome shalt thou be to share its homely fare.' Owen alighted joyfully from his panting steed, and entered with his host the well-arranged cottage. 'Here, good dame!' exclaimed Norman to his aged partner, 'I have brought you a stranger, who, coming from the old abbey yonder, must needs lack something to cheer his spirits.'

Owen then entered at large upon the whole of his late journey, and its termination at the abbey.

'What!' cried Blanche, 'lie in such a place as the haunted abbey! Mercy on us! friend, does your master know that it has not been inhabited for more than an hundred years; and does he not know that it is all over so full of goblins and spectres, that nobody will ever set a foot near it? And, moreover, the ghost of Anna is seen every night, walking down the great long aisles of the church up to the altar, where it kneels till the clock strikes twelve, when it goes out of the great doors, which fly open at its approach, and walks to the great south tower, where it utters three loud shrieks; when the old wicked Baron's ghost is forced to come, as soon as these are heard; and Anna drives him with a fire-brand in one hand, and a dead child in the other, all over the ruins, till they come to the chamber where the Baron used to sleep after he treacherously got possession of the abbey. Dismal yells, and dying groans, are then heard to echo through all the apartments, and blazing lights thrown about the great north bed-chamber, till the great turret clock, that has never for many a weary long year been touched by mortal hands, tolls heavily two, and sometimes three strokes upon the bell.'

'Nonsense, nonsense,' interrupted Norman, with a wink, meant to silence the loquacity of Blanche, 'you see all these idle terrors are done away. Did not Sir Thomas and his family sleep there last night, and is not Mr Owen here alive to tell us so?' Poor Owen, a coward at heart, sat trembling every joint as he listened to the extravagances of Blanche, and gave implicit belief to all the wild incoherences she tittered. At length, Owen, aided by a flagon of ale, which inspired him with something like resolution, once more braved the terrific dangers of the abbey, and mounting his horse, (well stored with many comforts provided by Norman,) he galloped down the avenue leading towards the abbey.

The next day, Norman, followed by a parcel of workmen, brought with him all his paper accounts, and monies, the produce of the rents, which he had faithfully hoarded up for the lord of the *demesne* whenever he thought proper to claim it.

One half of the range of the west front in a month's time was rendered perfectly safe; and having undergone a complete repair, the apartments soon began to lose much of their desolate and forlorn appearance. Three chambers were fitted up for the future residence of the steward; but it was a work of long entreaty before Sir Thomas could prevail on the venerable old Norman to take possession of them.

The lovely Rosaline (the Baron's only daughter) had at this period arrived at the age of sixteen, and having no society, but the inmates of the abbey, nor accustomed to any other, would dispense with the forms of rank, and, seating herself by the brisk wood fire that blazed on the hearth, listen attentively to the talkative Blanche's terrible narratives of spectres and supernatural appearances.

Rosaline would, at times, anxiously attend to these dreadful stories; as the tales of Blanche were generally terrific in the extreme, and always finished with the history of the baron and the nun; who, she affirmed, still haunted the ruins of the abbey. The story of Sister Anna had made a deep impression on her memory; and having often wished for a clear and true account of what was the end of the unfortunate nun, had determined to search among the ruins, in hopes that some discoveries might be made, that would lead to a development of her death. But as this enterprise could not so well be performed alone, she made Jannette her confidant, who readily promised obedience.

As they proceeded from the abbey, Rosaline failed not to examine every nook and corner that crossed her way. Sometimes she ventured up the broken steps of a broken tower, whose lofty battlements no longer reared their proud heads, that lay extended in the area. She ascended the first story, and through the heavy arch had a full view of the south tower. Rosaline bade Jannette observe it, and asked if she had courage to enter it.—'Indeed, my lady,' she replied, 'I never behold that tower, but it makes me tremble. It was there, they say, that poor Anna was confined; and I dare hardly look at it. Besides, my lady, you see it is more ruinous than this; nor is it safe to be approached. Surely, Madam, you do not mean to make the trial?'

'If, as you say, that was the prison of poor Anna, it is there only I may hope to find some documents relative to her fate. I am, therefore, resolved to proceed. But for you, Jannette, stay where you are: I shall not require a further attendance than your remaining within hearing.'

Rosaline descended the broken steps, and proceeded towards the tower, whilst Jannette, not daring to advance, stood trembling, entreating her young lady to forego her dangerous enterprise: but Rosaline having as yet found nothing to gratify her search, resolved not to yield to the light fears of Jannette: she therefore proceeded, and arrived at the full sight of the south tower: its black and frowning aspect, together with its weak, tottering situation, at first aroused a momentary feeling of terror; but youthful hope encouraged her to venture, and she approached the old Gothic door, which gave her a sight of an iron grating that was fixed in the wall.

To the left she beheld a flight of stairs that led to the upper stories; but these were too weak to admit her ascent in safety to the top; she therefore gave over the design, and turned again to the iron grating. As she caught the first view of the alarming objects within, her mind, unprepared for the sudden shock, endured a momentary suspension, and she fell, nearly fainting, against the wall.

The power of calling for aid was gone, and, for a few seconds, she was unable to support herself.

The terrific spectacle that had so powerfully affected Rosaline, as she caught a view of the interior of this forlorn ruin, was a deep narrow cell, whose walls were hung with mouldering trappings of black. The only light that was admitted within, proceeded from an iron grate fixed in the amazing thickness of the wall. Around this gloomy place were fixed, in all directions, the horrific emblems of death; and which ever way the desolate inhabitant of this dreary cell turned, images of horror, shocking to nature, met the tortured view, in the terrific state and eyeless sockets of the ghastly skull bones that hung in grim appalling array. In the middle of the cell, upon a raised pedestal, stood the mouldering relics of a coffin, which had been once covered with a velvet pall, but which now hung in tatters down its sides. At one corner was a small hillock, that appeared the sad resting place of the distracted penitent; for that this was the severe prison of penance and contrition, every superstitious emblem of monkish torture that surrounded the walls plainly bore testimony of. A crucifix, and broken hour-glass, still remained, covered with dust, upon a small altar, beneath an arched recess; whilst the floor was strewed with skulls and human bones.

After the first momentary shock had subsided, Rosaline arose, and stood irresolute to proceed in researches. Her alarms were strong, but her curiosity was, if possible, stronger. She felt she should never be able voluntarily again to enter this tremendous place; and she debated whether her courage would support her, should she pursue further the daring adventure. 'Perhaps,' said she, 'this was, indeed, the final end of the unhappy sister. Alas! poor unfortunate, this too, surely was alike your prison, and the cause of your lingering death. Yet wherefore am I thus anxious to solve the mystery of her death? Dare I lift the pall from that horrific spectacle? What if my spirits fail me, and I sink, overcome with dread, in this charnel house of death. May not my senses forsake me in the trial? or is it not very likely that terror may bereave me of my reason?—Shall I enter?'

Either her senses were indeed confused, or perhaps her mind, wrought to a certain pitch, led her to fancy more than reality; for, as the last word dropped from her lips, she started, and thought she heard it feebly repeated by an unknown voice, which slowly pronounced, 'Enter!'

Rosaline trembled, and not exactly aware of her intentions, unfastened the grate, and threw back the rattling chains that were hooked on the staples without the cell. The grate opened with ease, and swung on its hinges with little or no resistance; and Rosaline, with an imagination distempered, and misled by the hopes of discovering something she came in search of, that would repay her fears, descended the indented declivity, and with trembling steps staggered two or three paces from the grating; but again became irresolute, and terrified from her purpose, she stopped.

'Dare I,' she faintly ejaculated, 'dare I raise the mysterious lid of that horrific coffin?'

'Dare to do so!' replied a voice, that sounded hollow along the dreaded vault; and Rosaline, whose terror now had suspended the faculty of feeling, though not of life, actually moved towards the coffin, as if performing some dreadful rite, that she found she had not a power to resist.

Impelled with a notion of that superior agency which she dared not disobey, and not exactly sensible of what she did, she fearfully cast aside the lid, which, as she touched, fell crumbling to the ground; and turning aside her head, her hand fell within the coffin; and in her fright she grasped something moist and clammy, which she brought away. Shrieking wildly, she rushed from the scene of terror, and precipitating herself through the tower-gate, fell fainting into the arms of Jannette; who, pale and terrified, called aloud for help, as she supported her insensible lady.

Norman, who had long been impatient at the stay of his mistress, and alarmed for her safety, was hastening down the ruins, when the cries of Jannette assailed his ears, and had arrived at the scene of terror as Rosaline began to open her eyes.

'Holy Virgin protect the lady,' he exclaimed. 'Hast thou seen any thing? or do these pale looks proceed from some fall which may have bruised thy tender form among the ruins?'

'Oh no, good Norman, not so,' feebly and wildly ejaculated Rosaline. 'The tower! the dreadful tower!'

'The tower! sayst thou, my' lady? Mercy on me! Have you been so hardy as to venture into that dismal place!'

Rosaline, as she gradually recovered, felt a perfect recollection of the late horrid scene, and recalling the awful voice she had heard, which she doubted not proceeded from some supernatural agency, she no sooner beheld Norman, than she darted towards her chamber, regardless of the terrors of the old steward or Jannette.

As soon as she entered her room, she drew from the folds of her robe the relics she had unknowingly grasped from the coffin. On examination, it seemed to be some folded papers; but in so decayed a condition, that they threatened to drop in pieces with the touch.

She carefully unfolded the parcel, and found it to contain the story of the unfortunate Anna; but many of the lines were totally extinct, and only here and there a few that could be distinguished.

At length, in another packet she discovered a more perfect copy of the preceding ones, which, from the style of its writing, evidently proved them to be the labor of some of the monks, who had, from the papers discovered in the cell of her confinement, been enabled to trace the truth of her melancholy story and sufferings, in which the baron was but too principally concerned.

Rosaline, retrimming her lamp, and seating herself nearer the table, took up the monk's copy, and began, not without difficulty, to read the melancholy story of The Bleeding Nun of St Catherine's. It was in the reign of Edward the First, that, in an old dilapidated mansion, lived the poor but proud Sir Emanfred, descended of an illustrious house, whose noble progenitors had with the Conqueror settled in England, upon the establishment of their royal master.

In the two succeeding centuries, however, great changes had taken place, and many events had reduced the once powerful and splendid ancestors of Sir Emanfred to little more than a military dependence. The proud nature of the knight shrunk from the consequences of the total ruin of his house; and, indignant at the disgraceful and humiliating change of his circumstances, he hastily quitted the gay triumphs of the British court, because his fallen fortunes and wasted patrimony no longer enabled him to vie, in the splendour of his appearance and expenditure, with the rest of the nobles of the kingdom. In the gloomy shades of his forsaken mansion, he buried himself from all the joys of social intercourse: nor was his melancholy habitation ever after disturbed by the sounds of festive cheerfulness, or the smile of contentment.

Morose in temper from his disappointments of fortune, and too proud to stoop to such honourable recourses, as might have in time procured for him the re-establishment of his decayed house, he disdained all pecuniary acquirements, and determined to build his hope of future greatness on an alliance of his only child with the splendid and noble lord of Osmand. But the lovely Anna, brought up in total seclusion, and unacquainted with the manners of the world, happily free from the ambitious and haughty passions of her stern sire, had unconsciously rendered obedience to his commands impossible, and shrunk in horror from the dreaded proposal of an union with Lord Osmand; for, alas! she had not a heart to bestow, nor a hand to give away.' Anna, the beautiful and enchanting Anna, whose years scarce numbered seventeen, had known the exquisite pain and pleasures of a secret love; and, in the simple innocence of an unsuspecting mind, had given her heart, her soul, her all to a—stranger.

Anna had never known a mother's tenderness, nor experienced a father's sheltering protection; the artless dictates of her too susceptible heart were her only guides and monitors; and, during the long absence of her sire, her soul first felt the pleasing emotions of love for an unknown but graceful stranger, whom she had first beheld in the shades of a melancholy but romantic wood, that adjoined equally her father's domain, and the vast forest of St Catherine's monastery, where she had often been accustomed to roam, and where she had first met the fascinating Vortimer, who but too soon betrayed the unconscious maid into a confession that his fervent love was not displeasing, and that to him, and him only, she had resigned her heart, beyond even a wish for its recall. The mind of Anna was incapable of restraining the soft, thrilling ecstasies of a first infant passion. The stranger urged his suit with all the melting, all the prevailing, eloquence of an enraptured lover, and all the outward blandishments of feeling and sincerity. Unacquainted with the world's deceits, poor Anna listened to his fervent vows with downcast, blushing timidity, and pleased acceptance. Each secret meeting more firmly linked her chains: her very soul was devoted to the stranger, whom, as yet, she knew not by any other title than the simple name of Vortimer.

In a moment fatally destructive to her repose, when love had blinded reason, and the artless character of Anna but too successfully aided the purposes of the stranger, he obtained not only complete possession of her affections, but of her person also.

At midnight, in the ruined chapel of Sir Emanfred's gloomy edifice, the stranger had prevailed on the innocent Anna to meet him, and ratify his wishes. A monk of a distant convent waited in the chapel; and the inauspicious nuptials were performed; and Anna became a bride, without knowing by what title she must in future call herself.

Scarcely had three months of happiness and love passed over her head, when a storm, dreadful and unexpected, threatened for ever to annihilate the bright prospect of felicity.

The sudden arrival of a hasty messenger from the knight alarmed the trembling Anna; and scarce had she perused the purport of his arrival, than with a faint shriek, and a stifled cry of agony, she fell to the ground, as she feebly exclaimed, 'Lost, undone, and wretched Anna! destruction and death await thee!'

The stranger read the fatal paper that contained the harsh mandate of his Anna's father: his brow became contracted, and his countenance overcast with apparent gloom and sorrow, as he perused the unwelcome information of the knight's arrival, on the morrow, at his castle, to celebrate the nuptials of his daughter with the lord of Osmand, who accompanied him. For a time a gloomy silence pervaded his lips; and Anna vainly cast her tearful, imploring eyes to him for succour and protection. At length, starting from a deep reverie, he caught her in his arms, as she was sinking to the ground, and kissing her cold and quivering lips, bade her take comfort, and abide with patience the arrival of her sire; adding, that in three weeks he would return, and openly claim her as his wife; when the mystery that had so long enveloped his name and title in secrecy should be unravelled, and his adored Anna be restored to affluence and splendour. Again embracing her, he hurried precipitately from the place; and Anna—the ruined, hapless Anna—never saw him more—

★★★★★★

Here many lines became defaced, as the ink had rotted through the vellum, and all traces of writing were totally lost in mildew and obscurity. At length she was able to continue as follows:

Ferocious rage filled the soul of the knight, and darkened his features, as prostrate at his feet lay, overwhelmed in grief and tears, the imploring Anna. 'Spare me!' she cried, 'Oh, sire! spare your wretched child—she cannot marry the lord of Osmand!'

Fury flashed in the eyes of the stern Sir Emanfred, on hearing these words of his daughter. At length the burst of rage found vent, he seized the arm of the trembling Anna, and placing her hand forcibly in that of Sir Osmand's, commanded her to prepare herself, in three days, to become his bride, or meet the curses of an angry father, and be driven from his sight for ever.

Driven to despair, and now vainly calling on the mysterious stranger to shield her from the direful fate that awaited her, or the still more dreadful vengeance of her unrelenting father, the hapless Anna wildly flew to the gloomy wood, in the forlorn hope that there, once more, she might behold the lord of all her love and fondest wishes. In three weeks he had promised to reclaim her; but, alas! they had already expired, and no stranger had appeared. The fourth week of his absence came: it passed away, but he came not; and now but three days remained between her and her hateful nuptials. Wildly she wandered through the gloomy wood, and vainly cast her eyes in hopeless anguish on all around her: no stranger met her sight: he came not to rescue his forlorn bride from the rude grasp of impending misery and destruction. Night came on; the hours passed away unheeded, yet still she quitted not the solemn shades of the dreary grove. The bell of midnight sounded; she started at the melancholy toll, and fear and awe possessed her sickening fancy. She hurried through the wood, and reached in silence her chamber; but sleep visited not the wretched Anna.

Again, as the hour of suffering drew still nigher, she threw herself in supplication before the gloomy knight, and besought him to spare her but one week longer, ere he linked her to misery and woe; hoping by this delay to procure time for the stranger, and give him yet another chance, ere it was too late, to save her, and claim his affianced bride. But, inexorably bent on the union of his child with Lord Osmand, the knight, in anger, cast her from his knees, and threatened to overwhelm her with his most tremendous curses, if she did not meet Lord Osmand at the altar before the sixth hour of the early morrow had chimed upon the bell.

Poor Anna shrunk from the angry glances of the enraged knight; despair and anguish seized her soul. The stranger never came; he had forgotten his solemn vows, neglected his promise, and abandoned her to her fate. Whither could she fly? How was she to avoid the choice of miseries that equally pursued her? Either she must perjure her soul to false oaths, or meet the dreadful alternative of a parent's dire malediction.—Oh! whither, lost and wretched Anna! canst thou fly!

Upon the pillow of her tear-bedewed couch she vainly laid her head, to seek a momentary oblivion of her sorrow in repose. Something lay upon her pillow—It was a paper curiously folded.—With fearful, trembling expectation she hastily opened the envelope, and read, 'The stranger guards his love; and though unseen, and yet forbidden, to reclaim his lovely bride, now watches over her safety, and awaits the precious moment when he shall hasten on the wings of love to restore his Anna to happiness and liberty. If then she would preserve herself for her unknown friend, let her instantly fly to the monastery of St Catherine's, where she may remain in security till demanded by her adoring *Vortimer.*'

The unhappy maid perused the fatal lines with unsuspecting belief and joyful ecstasy; and, in compliance with the stranger's mysterious warning, escaped at midnight from her father's mansion; and took refuge in the cloisters of St Catherine.

The haughty lady abbess received the forlorn wanderer with cold civility and suspicious scrutiny. The unfortunate Anna had, in the simple innocence of her heart, confided to the superior her mournful tale, nor left one circumstance untold that could excite her pity, save her marriage with the stranger, for whom she now began to feel unusual fears, and dreadful forebodings of evil to herself; for a month had glided away at the abbey, and yet he came not.

The knight, with dreadful rage, discovered his daughter's flight; but vainly sought again to restore her to his power. He never saw her more; nor knew the sad conclusion of the unhappy Anna's destiny; who, deceived and terrified by the threats, expostulations, and commands, of the lady abbess, and the father confessors of the monastery, was at length betrayed into her own destruction; for the merciless abbess threatened to return her to her lord, and to her father, if she longer refused to take the vow of monastic life.

Despair and horror now seized the suffering victim of bigotry and paternal tyranny. Another and another month elapsed, and hope no longer could support her—the cruel stranger never came. At the gates of her prison, she was told, waited her father, with a powerful band, to force her from the abbey into the arms of a hated husband; and only the alternative of instantly taking the veil, could save her from the misery that pursued her. In a wild agony of terror, that had totally bereft her of her reason, she faintly bade them save her from her father's vengeance.

That instant the sacred, irrevocable vow was administered, and all its binding forms complied with by the lost St Anna, who, in the terror of her father, had for a moment forgot her previous engagements with the stranger—forgot that she must, in a little time, become, perhaps, a wretched mother, and now was a still more wretched nun.

★★★★★★

Here again the papers were totally useless, as Rosaline could only make out here and there a word, by which it appeared, that the Baron Fitzmartin had accused the order, with breaking the vow of celibacy. At length she read as follows:

With difficulty he was prevailed upon to suspend his proceedings against the abbey till the succeeding morrow, whilst the holy sisterhood endured the most persecuting examination from the lady abbess. No signs of guilt, however, were found; and the fathers, rejoicing in their expected security, were debating on an ample defiance to the baron, when news was brought that Sister St Anna had fallen senseless on the steps of the grand altar, and had been with difficulty removed to her cell. Thither the abbess instantly hastened; and as the insensible nun lay still reclined on her mattress, her outer garment unlaced to admit of respiration, the disfigurement of her person first forcibly struck the lady mother with suspicion. She started, frowned; then looked again; conviction flashed upon her eyes; and, regardless of pity for the still lifeless state of the hapless Anna, she commanded all to quit the cell, and send instantly the father abbot to her. The father hastily obeyed, and entered. The lady abbess murmured in a hollow voice, as frowns of fury darted from her now terrific countenance: 'Behold the guilty wretch that, with impious sacrilege, hath defiled our holy sanctuary, and brought destruction on the glory of our house's fame!—Say, holy father, how must we dispose of the accursed apostate?'

Before the abbot could reply, the unfortunate Anna awoke from the counterfeit of death's repose, and, wildly casting her eyes around her cell, beheld the forms of her inveterate destroyers.

Their fierce and angry looks of dreadful inquiry were bent upon the terrified nun, who, sickened with an unusual apprehension and dismay, whilst the abbot, fixing on the trembling Anna an increasing look of penetrating sternness, in a hollow, deep-toned voice, that sunk to her appalled heart, thus exclaimed: 'What punishment too terrible can await that guilty wretch who with sacrilege defiles our holy order?—say, lost one of God, art thou not guilty?'

Sinking on her knees, of every hope of life bereft, the unhappy Anna drooped her head to avoid the terrible scrutiny of truths pronounced, and looks unanswerable. No chance of escape was left her; she dared not prevaricate; and only with a groan of agony she feebly exclaimed—'I am, indeed!—Have mercy, holy father, as you shall hereafter expect to receive mercy from our heavenly Judge, on my involuntary crime!' She then turned to the frowning abbess her beseeching eyes, and piteously added, as she clung around her knees, 'Spare, oh gracious mother, spare a repentant daughter!'

In the countenances of her terrific judges poor Anna read the horrid mandate of her fate; for against the sacred order of the sisterhood she had sinned beyond atonement by any other punishment than death—Death the most horrible and excruciating! Vainly then she knelt, and clung to the robe of the abbess; she had slandered with sacrilege the purity of God's anointed house; its ministers and sacred devotees were sullied with a stain, that only the blood of a victim could wash away. Nor was the plea of marriage to a knight, who evidently never meant to claim her, admitted as the slightest expiation of her perjured vows to the abbey, and the disgrace she had brought on its sanctified inmates. Her horrid crimes demanded instant punishment: and the dreadful vengeance of the insulted members of the church could only be appeased by the immediate extirpation of the heinous apostate.

To dispose of the unfortunate nun for ever, beyond the possibility of her being produced as a living evidence of the baron's censure, and the abbey's shame, was now become an event absolutely necessary to the safety and welfare of the order: the claims of mercy, or the melting pleadings of pity, were alike disregarded for the stronger interest of the more immediate triumph of the abbey over its avowed and implacable enemy: and the father abbot, with the lady mother, having exhausted on the lost fair one the dreadful thunders of the church's vengeance, forcibly tore themselves from her distracted grasp, and prepared to inflict the terrific punishments that awaited their despairing victim, who, shrieking vainly for aid, and calling piteously on the stranger for rescue and protection from her horrid fate, was borne by the tormentors from her cell to the dungeon of the south tower.

At the hour of midnight they dragged the miserable victim from her bed, and deep in the horrific dungeons of the prison plunged the distracted nun!—Groans, sighs, and shrieks, alternately rung echoing round the rugged walls: the torturing horrors of famine awaited the unfortunate nun; no pity alleviated her misery; and in the centre of the place stood the coffin destined for her; whilst round the walls and floor, in all directions, were strewed the ghastly ensigns of woe and torment.

A faint glimmering lamp, suspended from the massy bars of the roof (as if with a refinement of cruelty unequalled, to blast the sight of the victim, and shut out every contemplation but her immediate fate) served to shew her the horrors that overwhelmed her, and the terrific engines of her tortures. The implements of confession were placed on the lid of her coffin; for the fathers denied her even the last consolation of absolution; but these she only in moments of short intellect would use, when distracted sentences, and wild, unfinished exclamations and appeals were all that it produced, sufficiently depictive of the horrors of her fate.

Two days of lingering sufferings had passed, and the third was nearly closed. Shut from life, and light, and every means of existence, the pangs of hunger seized the frantic sufferer, and the perils of premature childbirth writhed her anguished frame. Shrieks of despair rang through the building, and echoed to the vault of heaven. Hark! again that soul-appalling cry!—Inhuman fiends, is mercy dead within you!—Is there no touch of pity in your obdurate souls!—And thou too, remorseless betrayer of trusting innocence, hear ye not yon soul-appalling cry of her thy fatal love has destroyed?—Hark! again she calls on thy unpitying name; and now, in the bitterness of her soul's sufferings, she curses thee, and imprecates heaven's just vengeance on thy perjured head! Heaven hears the awful appeal!—it will avenge thee, suffering Anna! Now sink to death appeased.—Again the shrieks— Sure it is her last!

The holy sisterhood, appalled, fly wildly from the dreadful tower; but vainly supplicate the mercy of their superiors for its dying inmate. Nature is exhausted, and hark, again the groans grow fainter! Short-breathed murmurs proclaim the welcome dissolution of life. The soul, though confined with the suffering frame within the massy bars of her prison, at length has burst its bonds—It mounts from death, and in a moment is freed for ever. A short prayer addressed to the throne of mercy, releases the sufferer, and wafts her soul from the persecution of the wicked. The cruel strife has ceased—Poor Anna is at rest—her voice is heard no more. In the coffin of penitence she laid her suffering form; perhaps, it will never be removed from thence. Her guilty judges tremble at the place, nor dare their unhallowed footsteps approach the sacred dust.

Again the papers were useless, but it seemed, by what she could make out, that the haughty baron triumphed over the Fathers of the Abbey, to the entire seclusion of the order. At length she came to the following passage, which concluded the manuscript.

The vengeance of heaven hung heavily over the conscience of the wicked baron, nor was he suffered ever after to partake of happiness. It was on the third evening after his removal from his castle to the abbey he had plundered, that, retiring earlier than usual to his unwelcome couch, he tried in the arms of sleep to lose the remembrance of his crimes, and the terrible vengeance they inflicted on his guilty conscience. The sullen bell had tolled the hour of midnight ere he could compose his mind to repose. On this night, however, unusual restlessness pervaded his frame; nor could he for some time close in forgetfulness his eye-lids. At length a kind of unwilling stupor lulled for a moment his tortured spirits, and he slept. Not long did the balmy deity await him: troubled groans of anguish sounded through the apartment, and piercing shrieks rung bitterly in his ears.

Starting in horror, he wildly raised himself, half bent, on his couch, and drew aside his curtains. The chamber was in total darkness, and every taper seemed suddenly to have been extinguished. At that moment the heavy bell of the abbey clock struck one. A freezing awe stole over the senses of the baron: he in vain attempted to call his attendants; for speech was denied him; and a suspense of trembling horror had chilled his soul. His blood ran cold to its native source; his hair stood erect, and his countenance was distorted; for, as his eyes turned wildly, he beheld, standing close to the side of his bed, the pale figure of a female form, thinly clothed in the habiliments of a nun, and bearing in one hand a taper, whilst the other arm supported the ghastly form of a dead infant reclining on her breast.

The countenance of the figure was pale, wan, and horrible to behold; for from its motionless eyes no spark of life proceeded; but they were fixed in unmoving terrific expression on the appalled baron. At length a hollow-sounding voice pronounced through the closed lips of the spectre, 'O false, false Vortimer! accursed and rejected of thy Maker! knowest thou not the shadowy form that stands before thee? knowest thou not thy wretched bride? seest thou not the murdered infant thou hast destroyed?—From the deep bosom of immensity, the yawning horrors of the grave, the spirit of St Anna comes to call for vengeance and retribution; for know, the curses of her latest moments, when writhing beneath the agonies, the torments of death, and devouring hunger, that she then called upon thy head, were heard; and never shalt thou, guilty wretch! enjoy one quiet moment more. My mangled form, as now thou seest me, and dreams for ever of affright and terror, shall haunt thy thoughts with horror; nor shall even the grave rescue thee from the tortures I await to inflict.—Farewell—farewell till next we meet. In the grove where first thy perjured soul won on my happy, unsuspecting nature, and drew my youthful heart from parental duty and obedience, there shalt thou again behold me!'

Suddenly the eyes of the spectre became animated—Oh! then what flashes of appalling anger darted their orbits on the horror-struck Vortimer! three dreadful shrieks rung pealing through the chamber, now filled with a blaze of sulphurous light. The spectre suddenly became invisible, and the baron fell senseless on his couch.

The Shipwrecked Sailor

When Pharaoh Amen-em-het ruled Egypt in about the year 2000 BC he brought peace and prosperity to a country that had been torn by civil war and rebellion for nearly two hundred years. During his reign adventurers and traders went on many expeditions to the south—either up the Nile through Nubia and even as far as Ethiopia, or along the Red Sea and out into the Indian Ocean to the mysterious land of Punt, whence they brought back jewels and spices and other treasures.

The Royal Court, whether it was in residence at Thebes or Memphis, was thronged with ships' captains and the leaders of expeditions, each with a tale to tell—and each anxious to win a commission from Pharaoh to command some royal venture on the strength of his past achievements.

One day such a wanderer stopped the *Grand Vizier* in the palace courtyard at Thebes, and said to him, "My lord, harken to me a while. I come with costly gifts for Pharaoh, nor shall his counsellors such as yourself be forgotten. Listen, and I will tell you of such adventures as have not been told: Pharaoh himself—life, health, strength be to him!—will reward you for bringing to his presence a man with such adventures to tell. I have been to a magic island in the sea far to the south—far beyond Nubia, to the south even of Ethiopia. I beg of you to tell Pharaoh that I am here and would tell my tale to him."

The *Grand Vizier* was accustomed to such appeals, and he looked doubtfully at the wanderer and said, "It seems to me that you speak foolishly and have only vain things to tell. Many men such as you think that a tall story will win them a commission from Pharaoh—but when they tell their tale they condemn themselves out of their own mouths. If what you have to tell is one of these, be sure that I shall have you thrown out of the palace. But if it is of sufficient interest, I

439

may bring you before Pharaoh. Therefore speak on at your own risk, or else remain silent and trouble me no more."

"I have such a tale to tell," answered the wanderer, 'that I will risk your anger with an easy mind. When you have heard it, you will beg me to come before Pharaoh and tell it to him—even to the good god Pharaoh Amen-em-het who rules the world. Listen, then:

"I was on my way to the mines of Pharaoh in a great ship rowed by a hundred and fifty sailors who had seen heaven and earth and whose hearts were stronger than lions. We rowed and sailed for many days down the Red Sea and out into the ocean beyond.

"The captain and the steersman swore that they knew the signs of the weather and that the wind would not be strong but would waft us gently on our way. Nevertheless before long a tempest arose suddenly and drove us towards the land. As we drew near the shore the waves were eight cubits in height and they broke over the ship and dashed it upon the rocks. I seized a piece of wood and flung myself into the sea just as the ship ran aground: a moment later it was smashed to pieces and every man perished.

"But a great wave raised the board to which I clung high over the sharp rocks and cast me far up the shore, on level sand, and I was able to crawl into the shelter of the trees out of reach of the cruel, angry sea.

"When day dawned the tempest passed away and the warm sun shone out. I rose up to see where I was, giving thanks to the gods for my delivery when all the rest had perished. I was on an island with no other human being to be a companion to me. But such an island as no man has seen! The broad leaves of the thicket where I lay formed a roof over my head to shield me from the burning midday sun. When I grew hungry and looked about for food, I found all ready for me within easy reach: figs and grapes, all manner of good herbs, berries and grain, melons of all kinds, fishes and birds for the taking.

"At first I satisfied my hunger on the fruits around me. And on the third day I dug a pit and kindled a fire in it on which I made first of all a burnt offering to the gods, and then cooked meat and fish for myself.

"As I sat there comfortably after an excellent meal I suddenly heard a noise like thunder. Nearly beside myself with terror, I flung myself on the ground, thinking that it was some great tidal wave come to engulf the island: for the trees were lashing as if at the breath of the tempest and the earth shook beneath me.

"But no wave came, and at last I cautiously raised my head and looked about me. Never shall I forget the horror of that moment. Moving towards me I saw a serpent thirty cubits long with a beard of more than two cubits. Its body was covered with golden scales and the scales round its eyes shaded off into blue as pure as *lapis lazuli*.

"The serpent coiled up its whole length in front of where I lay with my face on the ground, reared its head high above me, and said: 'What has brought you, what has brought you here, little one? Say, what has brought you to my island? If you do not tell me at once I will show you what it is to be burnt with fire, what is it to be burnt utterly to nothing and become a thing invisible. Speak quickly, I am waiting to hear what I have not heard before, some new thing!'

"Then the serpent took me in his huge jaws and carried me away to his cave, and put me down there without hurting me. Yes, though he had held me in his sharp teeth he had not bitten me at all; I was still whole.

"Then he said again, 'What has, brought you, what has brought you here, little one? Say what has brought you to this island in the midst of the sea with the waves breaking on all sides of it?'

"At this I managed to speak, crouching before him and bowing my face to the ground as if before Pharaoh himself.

"'I sailed by command of Amen-em-het, Pharaoh of Egypt, in a great ship one hundred and fifty cubits in length to bring treasure from the mines of the south. But a great tempest broke upon us and dashed the ship upon the rocks so that all who sailed in her perished except for myself. As for me, I seized a piece of wood and was lifted on it over the rocks and cast upon this island by a mighty wave, and I have been here for three days. So behold me, your suppliant, brought hither by a wave of the sea.'

"Then the serpent said to me, 'Fear not, fear not, little one, nor let your face show sadness. Since you have come to my island in this way, when all your companions perished, it is because some god has preserved and sent you. For surely Amon-Re has set you thus upon this island of the blessed where nothing is lacking, which is filled with all good things. And now I will tell you of the future: here in this isle shall you remain while one month adds itself to another until four months have passed. Then a ship shall come, a ship of Egypt, and it shall carry you home in safety, and at length you shall die in your own city and be laid to rest in the tomb which you have prepared.

"'And now I will tell you of this island. For it is pleasant to hear

441

strange things after fear has been taken away from you—and you will indeed have a tale to tell when you return home and kneel before Pharaoh, your lord and master. Know then that I dwell here with my brethren and my children about me; we are seventy-five serpents in all, children and kindred. And but one stranger has ever come amongst us: a lovely girl who appeared strangely and on whom the fire of heaven fell and who was turned into ashes. As for you, I do not think that heaven holds any thunderbolts for one who has lived through such dangers. It is revealed to me that, if you dwell here in patience, you shall return in the fullness of time and hold your wife and children in your arms once more.'

"Then I bowed before him, thanking him for his words of comfort, and said, 'All that I have told you is true, and if what you have said to me happens indeed, I shall come before Pharaoh and tell him about you, and speak to him of your greatness. And I will bring as offerings to you sacred oils and perfumes, and such incense as is offered to the gods in their temples. Moreover I shall tell him of all the wonders of this isle, and I shall sacrifice asses to you, and Pharaoh shall send out a ship filled with the riches of Egypt as presents to your majesty.'

"'The king serpent laughed at my words, saying, 'Truly you are not rich in perfumes—for here in this island I have more than in all the land of Punt. Only the sacred oil which you promise me is scarce here—yet you will never bring it, for when you are gone this island will vanish away and you shall never more see it. Yet doubtless the gods will reveal it in time to come to some other wanderer.'

"So I dwelt happily in that enchanted island, and the four months seemed all too short. When they drew to a close I saw a ship sailing over the smooth sea towards me, and I climbed into a high tree to see better what manner of men sailed in it.

"And when I perceived that they were men of Egypt, I hastened to the home of the serpent king and told him. But he knew already more than I did myself, and said to me, 'Farewell, brave wanderer. Return in safety to your home and may my blessing go with you.'

"Then I bowed before him and thanked him, and he gave me gifts of precious perfumes—of *cassia* and sweet woods, of kohl and cypress, of incense, of ivory and of other precious things. And when I had set these upon the ship and the sailors would have landed, the island seemed to move away from them, floating on the sea. Then night fell suddenly, and when the moon shone out there was no island in sight but only the open waves.

"So we sailed north and in the second month we came to Egypt, and I have made haste to cross the desert from the sea to Thebes. Therefore, I pray you, lead me before Pharaoh, for I long to tell him of my adventures and lay at his feet the gifts of the King of the Serpents, and beg that he will make me commander of a royal ship to sail once more into the ocean that washes the shores of Punt."

When the wanderer's tale was ended, the *Grand Vizier* laughed heartily, crying, "Whether or not I believe your adventures, you have told a tale such as delights the heart of Pharaoh—life, health, strength be to him! Therefore come with me at once, and be sure of a rich reward: to you who tell the tale, and to me who brings before him the teller of the tale."

So the wanderer passed into the presence of the good god Pharaoh Amen-em-het, and Pharaoh delighted in the story of the shipwrecked sailor so much that his chief scribe Ameni-amen-aa was set to write it down upon a roll of papyrus where it may be read to this very day.

The Spectral Coach of Blackadon

You have heard of such a spirit, and well you know
The superstitious, idle-headed eld
Received and did deliver to our age
This tale of Herne the Hunter for a truth."

       —Merry Wives of Windsor.

The old vicarage-house at Talland, as seen from the Looe road, its low roof and grey walls peeping prettily from between the dense boughs of ash and elm that environed it, was as picturesque an object as you could desire to see. The seclusion of its situation was enhanced by the character of the house itself. It was an odd-looking, old-fashioned building, erected apparently in an age when asceticism and self-denial were more in vogue than at present, with a stern disregard of the comfort of the inhabitant, and in utter contempt of received principles of taste. As if not secure enough in its retirement, a high wall, enclosing a courtelage in front, effectually protected its inmates from the prying passenger, and only revealed the upper part of the house, with its small Gothic windows, its slated roof, and heavy chimneys partly hidden by the evergreen shrubs which grew in the enclosure.

Such was it until its removal a few years since; and such was it as it lay sweetly in the shadows of an autumnal evening one hundred and thirty years ago, when a stranger in the garb of a country labourer knocked hesitatingly at the wicket gate which conducted to the court. After a little delay a servant-girl appeared, and finding that the countryman bore a message to the vicar, admitted him within the walls, and conducted him along a paved passage to the little, low, damp parlour where sat the good man. The Rev. Mr Dodge was in many respects a remarkable man. You would have judged as much of him as he sat before the fire in his high-back chair, in an attitude of thought, arranging, it may have been, the heads of his next Sabbath's discourse. His heavy eyebrows, throwing into shade his spacious eyes, and indeed the whole contour of his face, marked him as a man of great firmness of character and of much moral and personal courage. His suit of sober black and full-bottomed periwig also added to his dignity, and gave him an appearance of greater age. He was then verging on sixty.

The time and the place gave him abundant exercise for the qualities we have mentioned, for many of his parishioners obtained their livelihood by the contraband trade, and were mostly men of unscrupulous and daring character, little likely to bear with patience, reflections on the dishonesty of their calling. Nevertheless the vicar was fearless in reprehending it, and his frank exhortations were, at least, listened to on account of the simple honesty of the man, and his well-known kindness of heart. The eccentricity of his life, too, had a wonderful effect in procuring him the respect, not to say the awe, of a people superstitious in a more than ordinary degree. Ghosts in those days had more freedom accorded them, or had more business with the visible world than at present; and the parson was frequently required by his parishioners to draw from the uneasy spirit the dread secret which troubled it, or by the aid of the solemn prayers of the church to set it at rest for ever. Mr Dodge had a fame as an exorcist, which was not confined to the bounds of his parish, nor limited to the age in which he lived.

"Well, my good man, what brings you hither?" said the clergyman to the messenger.

"A letter, may it please your reverence, from Mr Mills of Lanreath," said the countryman, handing him a letter.

Mr Dodge opened it and read as follows:—

My Dear Brother Dodge,—I have ventured to trouble you, at the earnest request of my parishioners, with a matter, of which some particulars have doubtless reached you, and which has caused, and is causing, much terror in my neighbourhood. For its fuller explication, I will be so tedious as to recount to you the whole of this strange story as it has reached my ears, for as yet I have not satisfied my eyes of its truth. It has been told me by men of honest and good report (witnesses of a portion of what they relate), with such strong assurances, that it behoves us to look more closely into the matter.

There is in the neighbourhood of this village a barren bit of moor which had no owner, or rather more than one, for the lords of the adjoining manors debated its ownership between themselves, and both determined to take it from the poor, who have for many years past regarded it as a common. And truly, it is little to the credit of these gentlemen, that they should strive for a thing so worthless as scarce to bear the cost of law, and yet of no mean value to poor labouring people. The two litigants, however, contested it with as much violence as if it had been a field of great price, and especially one, an old man, (whose thoughts should have been less set on earthly possessions, which he was soon to leave,) had so set his heart on the success of his suit, that the loss of it, a few years back, is said to have much hastened his death.

Nor, indeed, after death, if current reports are worthy of credit, does he quit his claim to it; for at night-time his apparition is seen on the moor, to the great terror of the neighbouring villagers. A public path leads by at no great distance from the spot, and on divers occasions has the labourer, returning from his work, been frightened nigh unto lunacy by sight and sounds of a very dreadful character. The appearance is said to be that of a man habited in black, driving a carriage drawn by headless horses. This is, I avow, very marvellous to believe, but it has had so much credible testimony, and has gained so many believers in my parish, that some steps seem necessary to allay the excitement it causes.

I have been applied to for this purpose, and my present business is to ask your assistance in this matter, either to reassure the minds of the country people if it be only a simple terror; or, if there be truth in it, to set the troubled spirit of the man at rest. My messenger, who is an industrious, trustworthy man, will give you more information if it be needed, for, from report, he is acquainted with most of the circumstances, and will bring back your advice and promise of assistance.

"Not doubting of your help herein, I do with my very hearty commendation commit you to God's protection and blessing, and am,—Your very loving brother,

Abraham Mills.

This remarkable note was read and re-read, while the countryman sat watching its effects on the parson's countenance, and was surprised that it changed not from its usual sedate and settled character. Turning at length to the man, Mr Dodge inquired, "Are you, then, acquainted with my good friend Mills?"

"I should know him, sir," replied the messenger, "having been sexton to the parish for fourteen years, and being, with my family, much beholden to the kindness of the rector."

"You are also not without some knowledge of the circumstances related in this letter. Have you been an eye-witness to any of those strange sights?"

"For myself, sir, I have been on the road at all hours of the night and day, and never did I see anything which I could call worse than myself. One night my wife and I were awoke by the rattle of wheels, which was also heard by some of our neighbours, and we are all assured that it could have been no other than the black coach. We have every day such stories told in the villages by so many creditable persons, that it would not be proper in a plain, ignorant man like me to doubt it."

"And how far," asked the clergyman, "is the moor from Lanreath?"

"About two miles, and please your reverence. The whole parish is so frightened, that few will venture far after nightfall, for it has of late come much nearer the village. A man who is esteemed a sensible and pious man by many, though an Anabaptist in principle, went a few weeks back to the moor ('tis called Blackadon) at midnight, in order to lay the spirit, being requested thereto by his neighbours, and he was so alarmed at what he saw, that he hath been somewhat mazed ever since."

"A fitting punishment for his presumption, if it hath not quite demented him," said the parson. "These persons are like those addressed by St Chrysostom, fitly called the golden-mouthed, who said, *'O Miserable wretches that ye be! ye cannot expel a flea, much less a devil!'* It will be well if it serves no other purpose but to bring back these stray sheep to the fold of the Church. So this story has gained much belief in the parish?"

"Most believe it, sir, as rightly they should, what hath so many witnesses," said the sexton, "though there be some, chiefly young men, who set up for being wiser than their fathers, and refuse to credit it, though it be sworn to on the book."

"If those things are disbelieved, friend," said the parson, "and without inquiry, which your disbeliever is ever the first to shrink from, of what worth is human testimony? That ghosts have returned to the earth, either for the discovery of murder, or to make restitution for

447

other injustice committed in the flesh, or compelled thereto by the incantations of sorcery, or to communicate tidings from another world, has been testified to in all ages, and many are the accounts which have been left us both in sacred and profane authors. Did not Brutus, when in Asia, as is related by Plutarch, see—"

Just at this moment the parson's handmaid announced that a person waited on him in the kitchen,—or the good clergyman would probably have detailed all those cases in history, general and biblical, with which his reading had acquainted him, not much, we fear to the edification and comfort of the sexton, who had to return to Lanreath, a long and dreary road, after nightfall. So, instead, he directed the girl to take him with her, and give him such refreshment as he needed, and in the meanwhile he prepared a note in answer to Mr Mills, informing him that on the morrow he was to visit some sick persons in his parish, but that on the following evening he should be ready to proceed with him to the moor.

On the night appointed the two clergymen left the Lanreath rectory on horseback, and reached the moor at eleven o'clock. Bleak and dismal did it look by day, but then there was the distant landscape dotted over with pretty homesteads to relieve its desolation. Now, nothing was seen but the black patch of sterile moor on which they stood, nothing heard but the wind as it swept in gusts across the bare hill, and howled dismally through a stunted grove of trees that grew in a glen below them, except the occasional baying of dogs from the farmhouses in the distance. That they felt at ease, is more than could be expected of them; but as it would have shown a lack of faith in the protection of Heaven, which it would have been unseemly in men of their holy calling to exhibit, they managed to conceal from each other their uneasiness.

Leading their horses, they trod to and fro through the damp fern and heath with firmness in their steps, and upheld each other by remarks on the power of that Great Being whose ministers they were, and the might of whose name they were there to make manifest. Still slowly and dismally passed the time as they conversed, and anon stopped to look through the darkness for the approach of their ghostly visitor. In vain. Though the night was as dark and murky as ghost could wish, the coach and its driver came not.

After a considerable stay, the two clergymen consulted together, and determined that it was useless to watch any longer for that night, but that they would meet on some other, when perhaps it might please his ghost-ship to appear. Accordingly, with a few words of leave-taking, they separated, Mr Mills for the rectory, and Mr Dodge, by a short ride across the moor, which shortened his journey by half a mile, for the vicarage at Talland.

The vicar rode on at an ambling pace, which his good mare sustained up hill and down vale without urging. At the bottom of a deep valley, however, about a mile from Blackadon, the animal became very uneasy, pricked up her ears, snorted, and moved from side to side of the road, as if something stood in the path before her. The parson tightened the reins, and applied whip and spur to her sides, but the animal, usually docile, became very unruly, made several attempts to turn, and, when prevented, threw herself upon her haunches. Whip and spur were applied again and again, to no other purpose than to add to the horse's terror. To the rider nothing was apparent which could account for the sudden restiveness of his beast.

He dismounted, and attempted in turns to lead or drag her, but both were impracticable, and attended with no small risk of snapping the reins. She was remounted with great difficulty, and another attempt was made to urge her forward, with the like want of success. At length the eccentric clergyman, judging it to be some special signal from Heaven, which it would be dangerous to neglect, threw the reins on the neck of his steed, which, wheeling suddenly round, started backward in a direction towards the moor, at a pace which rendered the parson's seat neither a pleasant nor a safe one. In an astonishingly short space of time they were once more at Blackadon.

By this time the bare outline of the moor was broken by a large black group of objects, which the darkness of the night prevented the parson from defining. On approaching this unaccountable appearance, the mare was seized with fresh fury, and it was with considerable difficulty that she could be brought to face this new cause of fright. In the pauses of the horse's prancing, the vicar discovered to his horror the much-dreaded spectacle of the black coach and the headless steeds, and, terrible to relate, his friend Mr Mills lying prostrate on the ground before the sable driver. Little time was left him to call up his courage for this fearful emergency; for just as the vicar began to give utterance to the earnest prayers which struggled to his lips, the spectre shouted, "Dodge is come! I must begone!" and forthwith leaped into his chariot, and disappeared across the moor.

The fury of the mare now subsided, and Mr Dodge was enabled to approach his friend, who was lying motionless and speechless, with his face buried in the heather.

Meanwhile the rector's horse, which had taken fright at the apparition, and had thrown his rider to the ground on or near the spot where we have left him lying, made homeward at a furious speed, and stopped not until he had reached his stable door. The sound of his hoofs as he galloped madly through the village awoke the cottagers, many of whom had been some hours in their beds. Many eager faces, staring with affright, gathered round the rectory, and added, by their various conjectures, to the terror and apprehensions of the family.

The villagers, gathering courage as their numbers increased, agreed to go in search of the missing clergyman, and started off in a compact body, a few on horseback, but the greater number on foot, in the direction of Blackadon. There they discovered their rector, supported in the arms of Parson Dodge, and recovered so far as to be able to speak. Still there was a wildness in his eye, and an incoherency in his speech, that showed that his reason was, at least, temporarily unsettled by the fright. In this condition he was taken to his home, followed by his reverend companion.

Here ended this strange adventure; for Mr Mills soon completely regained his reason, Parson Dodge got safely back to Talland, and from that time to this nothing has been heard or seen of the black ghost or his chariot.

The Spectre Hand

Do the dead ever revisit this earth?

On this subject even the ponderous and unsentimental Dr. Johnson was of opinion that to maintain they did not, was to oppose the concurrent and unvarying testimony of all ages and nations, as there was no people so barbarous, and none so civilized, but among whom apparitions of the dead were related and believed in. "That which is doubted by single cavillers," he adds, "can very little weaken the general evidence, and some who deny it with their tongues confess it by their fears."

In the August of last year I found myself with three friends, when on a northern tour, at the Hotel de Scandinavie, in the long and handsome Carl Johan Gade of Christiana. A single day, or little more, had sufficed us to "do" all the lions of the little Norwegian capital—the royal palace, a stately white building, guarded by slouching Norski riflemen in long coats, with wide-awakes and green plumes; the great brick edifice wherein the Storthing is held, and where the red lion appears on everything, from the king's throne to the hall-porter's coalscuttle; the castle of Aggerhuis and its petty armoury, with a single suit of mail, and the long muskets of the Scots who fell at Rhomsdhal; after which there is nothing more to be seen; and when the little Tivoli gardens close at ten, all Christiana goes to sleep till dawn next morning.

English carriages being perfectly useless in Norway, we had ordered four of the native *carrioles* for our departure, as we were resolved to start for the wild mountainous district named the Dovrefeld, when a delay in the arrival of certain letters compelled me to remain two days behind my companions, who promised to await me at Rodnaes, near the head of the magnificent Rans-fiord; and this partial separation, with the subsequent circumstance of having to travel alone through districts that were totally strange to me, with but a slight knowledge of the language, were the means of bringing to my knowledge the story I am about to relate.

The *table d'hôte* is over by two o'clock in the fashionable hotels of Christiana, so about four in the afternoon I quitted the city, the streets and architecture of which resemble portions of Tottenham Court Road, with stray bits of old Chester. In my *carriole*, a comfortable kind of gig, were my portmanteau and gun-case; these, with my whole person, and indeed the body of the vehicle itself, being covered by one of those huge tarpaulin cloaks furnished by the *carriole* company in the Store Standgade.

Though the rain was beginning to fall with a force and density peculiarly Norse when I left behind me the red-tiled city with all its green coppered spires, I could not but be struck by the bold beauty of the scenery, as the strong little horse at a rasping pace tore the light *carriole* along the rough mountain road, which was bordered by natural forests of dark and solemn-looking pines, interspersed with graceful silver birches, the greenness of the foliage contrasting powerfully with the blue of the narrow fiords that opened on every hand, and with the colours in which the toy-like country houses were painted, their timber walls being always snowy white, and their shingle roofs a flaming red. Even some of the village spires wore the same sanguinary hue, presenting thus a singular feature in the landscape.

The rain increased to an unpleasant degree; the afternoon seemed to darken into evening, and the evening into night sooner than usual, while dense masses of vapour came rolling down the steep sides of the wooded hills, over which the sombre firs spread everywhere and up every vista that opened, like a sea of cones; and as the houses became fewer and further apart, and not a single wanderer was abroad, and I had but the pocket-map of my "John Murray" to guide me, I soon became convinced that instead of pursuing the route to Rodnaes I was somewhere on the banks of the Tyri-fiord, at least three Norwegian miles (*i.e.* twenty-one English) in the opposite direction, my little horse worn out, the rain still falling in a continual torrent, night already at hand, and mountain scenery of the most tremendous character everywhere around me. I was in an almost circular valley (encompassed by a chain of hills), which opened before me, after leaving a deep chasm that the road enters, near a place which I afterwards learned bears the name of Krogkleven.

Owing to the steepness of the road, and some decay in the harness of my hired *carriole*, the traces parted, and then I found myself, with the now useless horse and vehicle, far from any house, homestead, or village where I could have the damage repaired or procure shelter, the rain still pouring like a sheet of water, the thick, shaggy, and impenetrable woods of Norwegian pine towering all about me, their shadows rendered all the darker by the unusual gloom of the night.

To remain quietly in the *carriole* was unsuitable to a temperament so impatient as mine; I drew it aside from the road, spread the tarpaulin over my small stock of baggage and the gun-case, haltered the pony to it, and set forth on foot, stiff, sore, and weary, in search of succour; and, though armed only with a Norwegian *tolknife*, having no fear of thieves or of molestation.

Following the road on foot in the face of the blinding rain, a Scotch plaid and oilskin my sole protection now, I perceived ere long a side-gate and little avenue, which indicated my vicinity to some place of abode. After proceeding about three hundred yards or so, the wood became more open, a light appeared before me, and I found it to proceed from a window on the ground floor of a little two-storied mansion, built entirely of wood. The sash, which was divided in the middle, was unbolted, and stood partially and most invitingly open; and knowing how hospitable the Norwegians are, without troubling myself to look for the entrance-door, I stepped over the low sill into the room (which was tenantless) and looked about for a bell-pull, forgetting that in that country, where there are no mantelpieces, it is generally to be found behind the door.

The floor was, of course, bare, and painted brown; a high German stove, like a black iron pillar, stood in one corner on a stone block; the door, which evidently communicated with some other apartment, was constructed to open in the middle, with one of the quaint lever handles peculiar to the country. The furniture was all of plain Norwegian pine, highly varnished; a reindeer-skin spread on the floor, and another over an easy chair, were the only luxuries; and on the table lay the *Illustret Tidende*, the *Aftonblat*, and other papers of that morning, with a meerschaum and pouch of tobacco, all serving to show that some one had recently quitted the room.

I had just taken in all these details by a glance, when there entered a tall thin man of gentlemanly appearance, clad in a rough tweed suit, with a scarlet shirt, open at the throat, a simple but *degagé* style of costume, which he seemed to wear with a natural grace, for it is not every man who can dress thus and still retain am air of distinction. Pausing, he looked at me with some surprise and inquiringly, as I began my apologies and explanation in German.

"*Taler de Dansk-Norsk*," said he, curtly.

"I cannot speak either with fluency, but—"

"You are welcome, however, and I shall assist you in the prosecution of your journey. Meantime, here is cognac. I am an old soldier, and know the comforts of a full canteen, and of the Indian weed, too, in a wet bivouac. There is a pipe at your service." I thanked him, and (while he gave directions to his servants to go after the *carriole* and horse) proceeded to observe him more closely, for something in his voice and eye interested me deeply.

There was much of broken-hearted melancholy—something that indicated a hidden sorrow—in his features, which were handsome, and very slightly aquiline. His face was pale and careworn; his hair and moustache, though plentiful, were perfectly white-blanched, yet he did not seem over forty years of age. His eyes were blue, but without softness, being strangely keen and sad in expression, and times there were when a startled look, that savoured of fright, or pain, or insanity, or of all mingled, came suddenly into them. This unpleasant expression tended greatly to neutralize the symmetry of a face that otherwise was evidently a fine one. Suddenly a light seemed to spread over it, as I threw off some of my sodden mufflings, and he exclaimed—"You speak Danskija, and English too, I know! Have you quite forgotten me, *Herr Kaptain?*" he added, grasping my hand with kindly energy. "Don't you remember Carl Holberg of the Danish Guards?"

The voice was the same as that of the once happy, lively, and jolly young, Danish officer, whose gaiety of temper and exuberance of spirit made him seem a species of madcap, who was wont to give champagne suppers at the Klampenborg Gardens to great ladies of the court and to ballet-girls of the Hof Theatre with equal liberality; to whom many a fair Danish girl had lost her heart, and who, it was said, had once the effrontery to commence a flirtation with one of the royal princesses when he was on guard at the Amalienborg Palace. But how was I to reconcile this change, the appearance of many years of premature age, that had come upon him?

"I remember you perfectly, Carl," said I, while we shook hands; "yet it is so long since we met; moreover—excuse me—but I knew not whether you were in the land of the living."

The strange expression, which I cannot define, came over his face as he said, with a low, sad tone—"Times there are when I know not whether I am of the living or the dead. It is twenty years since our happy days—twenty years since I was wounded at the Battle of Idstedt—and it seems as if 'twere twenty ages."

"Old friend, I am indeed glad to meet you again."

"Yes, old you may call me with truth," said he, with a sad, weary smile, as he passed his hand tremulously over his whitened locks, which I could remember being a rich auburn.

All reserve was at an end now, and we speedily recalled a score and more of past scenes of merriment and pleasure, enjoyed together—prior to the campaign of Holstein—in Copenhagen, that most delightful and gay of all the northern cities; and, under the influence of memory, his now withered face seemed to brighten, and some of its former expression stole back again.

"Is this your fishing or shooting quarters, Carl?" I asked.

"Neither. It is my permanent abode."

"In this place, so rural—so solitary? Ah! you have become a Benedick—taken to love in a cottage, and so forth—yet I don't see any signs of—"

"Hush! for godsake! You know not who hears us," he exclaimed, as terror came over his face; and he withdrew his hand from the table on which it was resting, with a nervous suddenness of action that was unaccountable, or as if hot iron had touched it.

"Why?—Can we not talk of such things?" asked I.

"Scarcely here—or anywhere to me," he said, incoherently. Then, fortifying himself with a stiff glass of cognac and foaming seltzer, he added: "You know that my engagement with my cousin Marie Louise Viborg was broken off—beautiful though she was, perhaps is still, for even twenty years could not destroy her loveliness of feature and brilliance of expression—but you never knew why?"

"I thought you behaved ill to her—were mad, in fact."

A spasm came over his face. Again he twitched his hand away as if a wasp had stung, or something unseen had touched it, as he said—"She was very proud, imperious and jealous."

"She resented, of course, your openly wearing the opal ring which was thrown to you from the palace window by the princess—"

"The ring—the ring! Oh, do not speak of that!" said he, in a hollow tone. "Mad?—yes, I was mad—and yet I am not, though I have undergone, and even now am undergoing, that which would break the heart of a Holger Danske! But you shall hear, if I can tell it with coherence and without interruption, the reason why I fled from society, and the world—and for all these twenty miserable years have buried myself in this mountain solitude, where the forest overhangs the fiord, and where no woman's face shall ever smile on mine! In short, after some reflection and many involuntary sighs—and being urged, when the determination to un-bosom himself wavered—Carl Holberg related to me a little narrative so singular and wild, that but for the sad gravity—or intense solemnity of his manner—and the air of perfect conviction that his manner bore with it, I should have deemed him utterly—mad!

"Marie Louise and I were to be married, as you remember, to cure me of all my frolics and expensive habits—the very day was fixed; you were to be the groomsman, and had selected a suite of jewels for the bride in the Kongens Nytorre; but the war that broke out in Schleswig-Holstein drew my battalion of the guards to the field, whither I went without much regret so far as my *fiancée* was concerned; for, sooth to say, both of us were somewhat weary of our engagement, and were unsuited to each other: so we had not been without piques, coldnesses, and even quarrels, till keeping up appearances partook of boredom.

"I was with General Krogh when that decisive battle was fought at Idstedt between our troops and the Germanising Holsteiners under General Willisen. My battalion of the guards was detached from the right wing with orders to advance from Salbro on the Holstein rear, while the centre was to be attacked, pierced, and the batteries beyond it carried at the point of the bayonet, all of which was brilliantly done. But prior to that I was sent, with directions to extend my company in skirmishing order, among thickets that covered a knoll which is crowned by a ruined edifice, part of an old monastery with a secluded burial-ground.

"Just prior to our opening fire the funeral of a lady of rank, apparently, passed us, and I drew my men aside to make way for the open catafalque, on which lay the coffin covered with white flowers and silver coronets, while behind it were her female attendants, clad in black cloaks in the usual fashion, and carrying wreaths of white flowers and immortelles to lay upon the grave.

"Desiring these mourners to make all speed lest they might find themselves under a fire of cannon and musketry, my company opened, at six hundred yards, on the Holsteiners, who were coming on with great spirit. We skirmished with them for more than an hour, in the long clear twilight of the July evening, and gradually, but with considerable loss, were driving them through the thicket and over the knoll on which the ruins stand, when a half-spent bullet whistled through an opening in the mouldering wall and struck me on the back part of the head, just below my bearskin cap. A thousand stars seem to flash around me, then darkness succeeded. I staggered and fell, believing myself mortally wounded; a pious invocation trembled on my lips, the roar of the red and distant battle passed away, and I became completely insensible.

"How long I lay thus I know not, but when I imagined myself coming back to life and to the world I was in a handsome, but rather old-fashioned apartment, hung, one portion of it with tapestry and the other with rich drapery. A subdued light that came, I could not discover from where, filled it. On a buffet lay my sword and my brown bearskin cap of the Danish Guards. I had been borne from the field evidently, but when and to where? I was extended on a soft *fauteuil* or couch, and my uniform coat was open. Someone was kindly supporting my head—a woman dressed in white, like a bride; young and so lovely, that to attempt any description of her seems futile!

"She was like the fancy portraits one occasionally sees of beautiful girls, for she was divine, perfectly so, as some enthusiast's dream, or painter's happiest conception. A long respiration, induced by admiration, delight, and the pain of my wound escaped me. She was so exquisitely fair, delicate and pale, middle-sized and slight, yet charmingly round, with hands that were perfect, and marvellous golden hair that curled in rippling masses about her forehead and shoulders, and from amid which her piquant little face peeped forth as from a silken nest. Never have I forgotten that face, nor shall I be permitted, to do so, while life lasts at least," he added, with a strange contortion of feature, expressive of terror rather than ardour; "it is ever before my eyes, sleeping or waking, photographed in my heart and on my brain! I strove to rise, but she stilled, or stayed me, by a caressing gesture, as a mother would her child, while softly her bright beaming eyes smiled into mine, with more of tenderness, perhaps, than love; while in her whole air there was much of dignity and self reliance.

"'Where am I?' was my first question.

"'With me,' she answered naïvely; 'is it not enough?'

"I kissed her hand, and said—'The bullet, I remember, struck me down in a place of burial on the Salbro Road—strange!'

"'Why strange?'

"'As I am fond of rambling among graves when in my thoughtful moods.'

"'Among graves—why?' she asked.

"'They look so peaceful and quiet.'"

Was she laughing at my unwonted gravity, that so strange a light seemed to glitter in her eyes, on her teeth, and over all her lovely face? I kissed her hands again, and she left them in mine.

Adoration began to fill my heart and eyes, and be faintly murmured on my lips; for the great beauty of the girl bewildered and intoxicated me; and, perhaps, I was emboldened by past success in more than one love affair. She sought to withdraw her hand, saying.

"'Look not thus; I know how lightly you hold the love of one elsewhere.'

"'Of my cousin Marie Louise? Oh! what of that! I never, never loved till now!' and, drawing a ring from her finger, I slipped my beautiful opal in its place.

"'And you love me?' she whispered.

"'Yes; a thousand times, yes!'

"'But you are a soldier—wounded, too. Ah! if you should die before we meet again!'

"'Or, if you should die ere then?' said I, laughingly.

"'Die—I am already dead to the world—in loving you; but, living or dead, our souls are as one, and—'

"'Neither heaven nor the powers beneath shall separate us now!' I exclaimed, as something of melodrama began to mingle with the genuineness of the sudden passion with which she had inspired me. She was so impulsive, so full of brightness and ardour, as compared to the cold, proud, and calm Marie Louise. I boldly encircled her with my arms; then her glorious eyes seemed to fill with the subtle light of love, while there was a strange magnetic thrill in her touch, and, more than all, in her kiss.

"' Carl, Carl!' she sighed.

"'What! You know my name?—And yours?'

"'Thyra. But ask no more.'

"There are but three words to express the emotion that possessed me—bewilderment, intoxication, madness. I showered kisses on her beautiful eyes, on her soft tresses, on her lips that met mine halfway; but this excess of joy, together with the pain of my wound, began to overpower me; a sleep, a growing and drowsy torpor, against which I struggled in vain, stole over me. I remember clasping her firm little hand in mine, as if to save myself from sinking into oblivion, and then—no more—no more!

"On again coming back to consciousness, I was alone. The sun was rising, but had not yet risen. The scenery the thickets through which we had skirmished, rose dark as the deepest indigo against the amber-tinted eastern sky; and the last light of the waning moon yet silvered the pools and marshes around the borders of the Langsö Lake, where now eight thousand men, the slain of yesterday's battle, were lying stark and stiff. Moist with dew and blood, I propped myself on one elbow and looked around me, with such wonder that a sickness came over my heart. I was again in the cemetery where the bullet had struck me down; a little grey owl was whooping and blinking in a recess of the crumbling wall. Was the drapery of the chamber but the ivy that rustled thereon?—for where the buffet stood there was an old square tomb, whereon lay my sword and bearskin cap!

"The last rays of the waning moonlight stole through the ruins on a new-made grave—the fancied fauteuil on which I lay—strewn with the flowers of yesterday, and at its head stood a temporary cross, hung with white garlands and wreaths of *immortelles*. Another ring was on my finger now; but where was she, the donor? Oh, what opium-dream, or what insanity was this?

"For a time I remained utterly bewildered by the vividness of my recent dream, for such I believed it to be. But if a dream, how came this strange ring, with a square emerald stone, upon my finger? And where was mine? Perplexed by these thoughts, and filled with wonder and regret that the beauty I had seen had no reality, I picked my way over the ghostly *débris* of the battlefield, faint, feverish, and thirsty, till at the end of a long avenue of lindens I found shelter in a stately brick mansion, which I learned belonged to the Count of Idstert, a noble, on whose hospitality—as he favoured the Holsteiners—I meant to intrude as little as possible.

"He received me, however, courteously and kindly. I found him in deep mourning: and on discovering, by chance, that I was the officer who had halted the line of skirmishers when the funeral *cortège* passed on the previous day, he thanked me with earnestness, adding, with a deep, sigh, that it was the burial of his only daughter.

"'Half my life seems to have gone with her—my lost darling! She was so sweet, *Herr Kaptain*—so gentle, and so surpassingly beautiful—my poor Thyra!'

"'Who did you say?' I exclaimed, in a voice that sounded strange and unnatural, while half-starting from the sofa on which I had cast myself, sick at heart and faint from loss of blood.

"'Thyra, my daughter, *Herr Kaptain*,' replied the count, too full of sorrow to remark my excitement, for this had been the quaint old Danish name uttered in my dream. 'See, what a child I have lost!' he added, as he drew back a curtain which covered a full-length portrait, and, to my growing horror and astonishment, I beheld, arrayed in white even as I had seen her in my vision, the fair girl with the masses of golden hair, the beautiful eyes, and the piquant smile lighting up her features even on the canvas, and I was rooted to the spot.

"'This ring, *Herr Count?*' I gasped. He let the curtain fall from his hand, and now a terrible emotion seized him, as he almost tore the jewel from my finger.

"'My daughter's ring!' he exclaimed. 'It was buried with her yesterday—her grave has been violated—violated by your infamous troops.'"

As he spoke, a mist seemed to come over my sight; a giddiness made my senses reel, then a hand—the soft little hand of last night, with my opal ring on its third finger—came stealing into mine, unseen! More than that, a kiss from tremulous lips I could not see, was pressed on mine, as I sank backward and fainted! The remainder of my story must be briefly told.

"My soldiering was over; my nervous system was too much shattered for further military service. On my homeward way to join and be wedded to Marie Louise—a union with whom was intensely repugnant to me now—I pondered deeply over the strange subversion of the laws of nature presented by my adventure; or the madness, it might be, that had come upon me."

On the day I presented myself to my intended bride and approached to salute her, I felt a hand—the same hand—laid softly on mine. Starting, and trembling, I looked around me; but saw nothing. The grasp was firm. I passed my other hand over it, and felt the slender fingers and the shapely wrist; yet still I saw nothing, and Marie Louise gazed at my motions, my pallor, doubt and terror, with calm, but cool indignation.

"I was about to speak—to explain—to say I know not what, when a kiss from lips I could not see sealed mine, and with a cry like a scream I broke away from my friends and fled.

"All deemed me mad, and spoke with commiseration of my wounded head; and when I went abroad in the streets men eyed me with curiosity, as one over whom some evil destiny hung—as one to whom something terrible had happened, and gloomy thoughts were wasting me to a shadow. My narrative may seem incredible; but this attendant, unseen yet palpable, is ever by my side, and if under any impulse, such even as sudden pleasure in meeting you, I for a moment forget it, the soft and gentle touch of a female hand reminds me of the past, and haunts me, for a guardian demon—if I may use such a term—rules my destiny: one lovely, perhaps, as an angel.

"Life has no pleasures, but only terrors for me now. Sorrow, doubt, horror and perpetual dread, have sapped the roots of existence; for a wild and clamorous fear of what the next moment may bring forth is ever in my heart, and when the touch comes my soul seems to die within me.

"You know what haunts me now—God help me! God help me! You do not understand all this, you would say. Still less do I but in all the idle or extravagant stories I have read of ghosts—stories once my sport and ridicule, as the result of vulgar superstition or ignorance— the so-called supernatural visitor was visible to the eye, or heard by the ear; but the ghost, the fiend, the invisible Thing that is ever by the side of Carl Holberg, is only sensible to the touch—it is the unseen but tangible substance of an apparition!"

He had got thus far when he gasped, grew livid, and, passing his right hand over the left, about an inch above it, with trembling fingers, he said—"It is here—here now—even with you present, I feel her hand on mine; the clasp is tight and tender, and she will never leave me, but with life!"

And then this once gay, strong, and gallant fellow, now the wreck of himself in body and in spirit, sank forward with his head between his knees, sobbing and faint.

Four months afterwards, when with my friends, I was shooting bears at Hammerfest, I read in the Norwegian *Aftenposten*, that Carl Holberg had shot himself in bed, on Christmas Eve.

Found and Lost

And he sold his birthright unto Jacob.
Then Jacob gave Esau bread and pottage of lentiles.
                                                    —*Gen.* xxv.33, 34.

. . . . So! I let fall the curtain; he was dead. For at least half an hour I had stood there with the manuscript in my hand, watching that face settling in its last stillness, watching the finger of the Composer smoothing out the deeply furrowed lines on cheek and forehead,— the faint recollection of the light that had perhaps burned behind his childish eyes struggling up through the swarthy cheek, as if to clear the last world's-dust from the atmosphere surrounding the man who had just refound his youth. His head rested on his hand,—and so satisfied and content was his quiet attitude, that he looked as if resting from a long, wearisome piece of work he was glad to have finished.

I don't know how it was, but I thought, oddly enough, in connection with him, of a little school-fellow of mine years ago, who one day, in his eagerness to prove that he could jump farther than some of his companions, upset an inkstand over his prize essay, and, overcome with mortification, disappointment, and vexation, burst into tears, hastily scratched his name from the list of competitors, and then rushed out of doors to tear his ruined essay into fragments; and we found him that afternoon lying on the grass, with his head on his hand, just as he lay now, having sobbed himself to sleep.

I dropped the curtains of the bed, drew those of the window more closely, to exclude the shrill winter wind that was blowing the slant sleet against the clattering window-panes, broke up the lump of cannel coal in the grate into a bright blaze that subsided into a warm, steady glow of heat and light, drew an arm-chair and a little table up to the cheerful fire, and sat down to read the manuscript which the quiet man behind the curtains had given me. Why shouldn't I (I was

462

his physician) make myself as comfortable as possible at two o'clock of a stormy winter night, in a house that contained but two persons beside my German patient,—a half-stupid servingman, doubtless already asleep down-stairs, and myself? This is what I read that night, with the comfortable fire on one side, and Death, holding strange colloquy with the fitful, screaming, moaning wind, on the other.

As I wish simply to relate what has happened to me, (thus the manuscript began,) what I attempted, in what I sinned, and how I failed, I deem no introduction or genealogies necessary to the first part of my life. I was an only child of parents who were passionately fond of me,—the more, perhaps, because an accident that had happened to me in my childhood rendered me for some years a partial invalid. One day, (I was about five years old then,) a gentleman paid a visit to my father, riding a splendid Arabian horse. Upon dismounting, he tied the horse near the steps of the *piazza* instead of the horseblock, so that I found I was just upon the level with the stirrup, standing at a certain elevation. Half as an experiment, to try whether I could touch the horse without his starting, I managed to get my foot into the stirrup, and so mounted upon his back.

The horse, feeling the light burden, did start, broke from his fastening, and sped away with me on his back at the top of his speed. He ran several miles without stopping, and finished by pitching me off his back upon the ground, in leaping a fence. This fall produced some disease of the spine, which clung to me till I was twelve years old, when it was almost miraculously cured by an itinerant Arab physician. He was generally pronounced to be a quack, but he certainly effected many wonderful cures, mine among others.

I had always been an imaginative child; and my long-continued sedentary life compelling me (a welcome compulsion) to reading as my chief occupation and amusement, I acquired much knowledge beyond my years.

My reading generally had one peculiar tone: a certain kind of mystery was an essential ingredient in the fascination that books which I considered interesting had for me. My earliest fairy tales were not those unexciting stories in which the good genius appears at the beginning of the book, endowing the hero with such an invincible talisman that suspense is banished from the reader's mind, too well enabled to foresee the triumph at the end; but stories of long, painful quests after hidden treasure,—mysterious enchantments thrown around certain persons by witch or wizard, drawing the subject in charmed cir-

463

cles nearer and nearer to his royal or ruinous destiny,—strange spells cast upon bewitched houses or places, that could be removed only by the one hand appointed by Fate.

So I pored over the misty legends of the San Grail, and the sweet story of *The Sleeping Beauty*, as my first literature; and as the rough years of practical boyhood trooped up to elbow my dreaming childhood out of existence, I fed the same hunger for the hidden and mysterious with Detective-Police stories, Captain Kidd's voyages, and wild tales of wrecks on the Spanish Main, of those vessels of fabulous wealth that strewed the deep sea's lap with gems (so the stories ran) of lustre almost rare enough to light the paths to their secret hiding-places.

But in the last year of my captivity as an invalid a new pleasure fell into my hands. I discovered my first book of travels in my father's library, and as with a magical key unlocked the gate of an enchanted realm of wondrous and ceaseless beauty. It was Sir John Mandeville who introduced me to this field of exhaustless delight; not a very trustworthy guide, it must be confessed,—but my knowledge at that time was too limited to check the boundless faith I reposed in his narrative. It was such an astonishment to discover that men, black-coated and black-trousered men, such as I saw in crowds every day in the street from my sofa-corner, (we had moved to the city shortly after my accident,) had actually broken away from that steady stream of people, and had traversed countries as wild and unknown as the lands in the Nibelungen Lied, that my respect for the race rose amazingly.

I scanned eagerly the sleek, complacent faces of the portly *burghers*, or those of the threadbare schoolmasters, thinned like carving-knives by perpetual sharpening on the steel of Latin *syntax*, in search of men who could have dared the ghastly terrors of the North with Ross or Parry, or the scorching jungles of the Equator with Burckhardt and Park. Cut off for so long a time from actual contact with the outside world, I could better imagine the brooding stillness of the Great Desert, I could more easily picture the weird ice-palaces of the Pole, waiting, waiting forever in awful state, like the deserted halls of the Walhalla for their slain gods to return, than many of the common street-scenes in my own city, which I had only vaguely heard mentioned.

I followed the footsteps of the Great Seekers over the wastes, the untrodden paths of the world; I tracked Columbus across the pathless Atlantic,—heard, with Balboa, the "wave of the loud—roaring ocean break upon the long shore, and the vast sea of the Pacific forever crash on the beach,"—gazed with Cortes on the temples of the Sun in the startling Mexican empire,—or wandered with Pizarro through the silver-lined palaces of Peru. But a secret affection drew me to the mysterious regions of the East and South,—towards Arabia, the wild Ishmael bequeathing sworded *Korans* and subtile Aristotles as legacies to the sons of the freed-woman,—to solemn Egypt, riddle of nations, the vast silent, impenetrable mystery of the world.

By continual pondering over the footsteps of the Seekers, the Sought-for seemed to grow to vast proportions, and the Found to shrink to inappreciable littleness. For me, over the dreary ice-plains of the Poles, over the profound bosom of Africa, the far-stretching steppes of Asia, and the rocky wilds of America, a great silence brooded, and in the unexplored void faint footfalls could be heard here and there, threading their way in the darkness. But while the longing to plunge, myself, into these dim regions of expectation grew more intense each day, the prison-chains that had always bound me still kept their habitual hold upon me, even after my recovery. I dreamt not of making even the vaguest plans for undertaking explorations myself. So I read and dreamt, filling my room with wild African or monotonous Egyptian scenery, until I was almost weaned from ordinary Occidental life.

I passed four blissful years in this happy dream-life, and then it was abruptly brought to an end by the death of my father and mother almost simultaneously by an epidemic fever prevailing in the neighbourhood. I was away from home at a bachelor uncle's at the time, and so was unexpectedly thrown on his hands, an orphan, penniless, except in the possession of the small house my father had owned in the country before our removal to the city, and to be provided for. My uncle placed me in a mercantile house to learn business, and, after exercising some slight supervision over me a few months, left me entirely to my own resources. As, however, he had previously taken care that these resources should be sufficient, I got along very well upon them, was regularly promoted, and in the space of six years, at the age of twenty-one, was in a rather responsible situation in the house, with a good salary.

But my whole attention could not be absorbed in the dull routine of business, my most precious hours were devoted to reading, in which I still pursued my old childish track of speculation, with the difference that I exchanged Sinbad's valley of diamonds for Arabia Petraea, Sir John Mandeville for Herodotus, and Robinson Crusoe for Belzoni and Burckhardt. Whether my interest in these Oriental studies arose from the fact of the house being concerned in the importation of the products of the Indies, or whether from the secret attraction that had drawn me Eastward since my earliest childhood, as if the Arab doctor had bewitched in curing me, I cannot say; probably it was the former, especially as the India business became gradually more and more entrusted to my hands.

Shortly after my twenty-first birthday, I received a note from my uncle, from whom I had not heard for a year or two, informing me that my father's house, which he had kept rented for me during the first years of my minority, had been without a tenant for a year, and, as I had now come of age, I had better go down to D— and take possession of it. This letter, touching upon a long train of associations and recollections, awoke an intense longing in me to revisit the home of my childhood, and meet those phantom shapes that had woven that spell in those dreaming years, which I sometimes thought I felt even now. So I obtained a short leave of absence, and started the next morning in the coach for D—.

It was what is called a "raw morning," for what reason I know not, for such days are really elaborated with the most exquisite finish. A soft gray mist hugged the country in a chilly embrace, while a fine rain fell as noiselessly as snow, upon soaked ground, drenched trees, and peevish houses. There is always a sense of wonder about a mist. The outlines of what we consider our hardest tangibilities are melted away by it into the airiest dream—sketches, our most positive and glaring facts are blankly blotted out, and a fresh, clean sheet left for some new fantasy to be written upon it, as groundless as the rest; our solid land dissolves in cloud, and cloud assumes the stability of land.

For, after all, the only really tangible thing we possess is man's Will; and let the presence and action of that be withdrawn but for a few moments, and that mysterious Something which we vainly endeavour to push off into the Void by our pompous nothings of brick and plaster and stone closes down upon us with the descending sky, writing *Delendum* on all behind us, Unknown on all before. At that time, the only actual Now, that stands between these two infinite blanks, becomes identical with the mind itself, independent of accidents of situation or circumstance; and the mind thus becoming boldly prominent, amidst the fading away of physical things, stamps its own character upon its shadowy surroundings, moulding the supple universe to the shape of its emotions and feelings.

I was the only inside passenger, and there was nothing to check the entire surrender of my mind to all ghostly influence. So I lay stretched upon the cushions, staring blankly into the dense gray fog closing up all trace of our travelled road, or watching the light edges of the trailing mist curl coyly around the roofs of houses and then settle grimly all over them, the fantastic shapes of trees or carts distorted and magnified through the mist, the lofty outlines of some darker cloud stalking solemnly here and there, like enormous dumb overseers faithfully superintending the work of annihilation.

The monotonous patter of the raindrops upon the wet pavement or muddy roads, blending with the low whining of the wind and the steady rumble of the coach-wheels, seemed to make a kind of witch-chant, that wove with braided sound a weird spell about me, a charm fating me for some service, I knew not what. That chant moaned, it wailed, it whispered, it sang gloriously, it bound, it drowned me, it lapped me in an inextricable stream of misty murmuring, till I was perplexed, bewildered, enchanted. I felt surprised at myself, when, at the end of the day's journey, I carried my bag to the hotel, and ate my supper there as usual,—and felt natural again only when, having obtained the key of my house, I sallied forth in the dim twilight to make it my promised visit.

I found the place, as I had expected, in a state of utter desolation. A year's silence had removed it so far from the noisy stream of life that flowed by it, that I felt, as I pushed at the rusty door-lock, as if I were passing into some old garret of Time, where he had thrown forgotten rubbish too worn-out and antiquated for present use. A strong scent of musk greeted me at my entrance, which I found came from a box of it that had been broken upon the hall-floor. I had stowed it away (it was a favourite perfume with me, because it was so associated with my Arabian Nights' stories) upon a ledge over the door, where it had rested undisturbed while the house was tenanted, and had been now probably dislodged by rats. But I half fancied that this odour which impregnated the air of the whole house was the essence of that atmosphere in which, as a child, I had communicated with Burckhardt and Belzoni,—and that, expelled by the solid, practical, Occidental atmosphere of the last few years, it had flowed back again, in these last silent months, in anticipation of my return.

Like a prudent householder, I made the tour of the house with a light I had provided myself with, and mentally made memoranda of repairs, alterations, etc., for rendering it habitable. My last visit was to be to the garret, where many of my books yet remained. As I passed once more through the parlour, on my way thither, a ray of light from my raised lamp fell upon the wall that I had thought blank, and a majestic face started suddenly from the darkness. So sudden was the apparition, that for the moment I was startled, till I remembered that there had formerly been a picture in that place, and I stopped to examine it.

It was a head of the Sphinx. The calm, grand face was partially averted, so that the sorrowful eyes, almost betraying the aching secret which the still lips kept sacred, were hidden,—only the slight, tender droop in the corner of the mouth told what their expression might be. Around, forever stretched the endless sands,—the mystery of life found in the heart of death. That mournful, eternal face gave me a strange feeling of weariness and helplessness. I felt as if I had already pressed eagerly to the other side of the head, still only to find the voiceless lips and mute eyes. Strange tears sprang to my eyes; I hastily brushed them away, and, leaving the Sphinx, mounted to my garret.

But the riddle followed me. I sat down on the floor, beside a box of books, and somewhat listlessly began pulling it over to examine the contents. The first book I took hold of was a little worn volume of Herodotus that had belonged to my father. I opened it; and as if it, too, were a link in the chain of influences which I half felt was being forged around me, it opened at the first part of *Euterpe*, where Herodotus is speculating upon the phenomena of the Nile. Twenty-two hundred years,—I thought,—and we are still wondering, the Sphinx is still silent, and we yet in the darkness! Alas, if this riddle be insoluble, how can we hope to find the clue to deeper problems? If there are places on our little earth whither our feet cannot go, curtains that our hands cannot withdraw, how can we expect to track paths through realms of thought,—how to voyage in those airy, impalpable regions whose existence we are sure of only while we are there voyaging?

"Nilus in extremum fugit perterritus orbem Occuluitque caput, quod adhuc latet." Lost through reckless presumption, might not earnest humility recover that mysterious lurking-place? Might not one, by devoted toil, by utter self-sacrifice, with eyes purified by long searching from worldly and selfish pollution,—might not such a one tear away the veil of centuries, and, even though dying in the attempt, gain one look into this *arcanum*? Might not I?—The unutterable thought thrilled me and left me speechless, even in thinking. I strained my forehead against the darkness, as if I could grind the secret from the void air. Then I

experienced the following mental sensation,—which, being purely mental, I cannot describe precisely as it was, but will translate it as nearly as possible into the language of physical phenomena.

It was as if my mind—or, rather, whatever that passive substratum is that underlies our volition and more truly represents ourselves—were a still lake, lying quiet and indifferent. Presently the sense of some coming Presence sent a breathing ripple over its waters; and immediately afterward it felt a sweep as of trailing garments, and two arms were thrown around it, and it was pressed against a "life-giving bosom," whose vivifying warmth interpenetrating the whole body of the lake, its waters rose, moved by a mighty influence, in the direction of that retreating Presence; and again, though nothing was seen, I felt surely whither was that direction. It was *Nile-ward*. I knew, with the absolute certainty of intuition, that henceforth I was one of the *kletoi*, the chosen,—selected from thousands of ages, millions of people, for this one destiny. Henceforth a sharp dividing-line cut me off from all others: their appointment was to trade, navigate, eat and drink, marry and give in marriage, and the rest; mine was to discover the Source of the Nile. Hither had all the threads of my life been converging for many years; they had now reached their focus, and henceforth their course was fixed.

I was scarcely surprised the next day at receiving a letter from my employers appointing me to a situation as supercargo of a merchant-vessel bound on a three-years' voyage to America and China,—in returning thence, to sail up the Mediterranean, and stop at Alexandria. I immediately wrote an acceptance, and then busied myself about obtaining a three-years' tenant for my house. As the house was desirable and well-situated, this business was soon arranged; and then, as I had nothing further to do in the village, I left it for the last time, as it proved, and returned to the city,—whence, after a fortnight of preparation, I set sail on my eventful enterprise. Although our voyage was filled with incident that in another place would be interesting enough to relate, yet here I must omit all mention of it, and, passing over three years, resume my narrative at Alexandria, where I left the vessel, and finally broke away from mercantile life.

From Alexandria I travelled to Cairo, where I intended to hire a servant and a boat, for I wished to try the water-passage in preference to the land. The cheapness of labour and food rendered it no difficult matter to obtain my boat and provision it for a long voyage,—for how long I did not tell the Egyptian servant whom I hired to attend me. A certain feeling of fatality caused me to make no attempt at disguise, although disguise was then much more necessary than it has been since: I openly avowed my purpose of travelling on the Nile for pleasure, as a private European. My accoutrements were simple and few. Arms, of course, I carried, and the actual necessaries for subsistence; but I entirely forgot to prepare for sketching, scientific surveys, etc. My whole mind was possessed with one idea: to see, to discover;—plans for turning my discoveries to account were totally foreign to my thoughts.

So, on the 6th of November, 1824, we set sail. I had been waiting three years to arrive at this starting-point,—my whole life, indeed, had been dumbly turning towards it,—yet now I commenced it with a coolness and tranquillity far exceeding that I had possessed on many comparatively trifling occasions. It is often so. We are borne along on the current like drift-wood, and, spying jutting rocks or tremendous cataracts ahead, fancy, "Here we shall be stranded, there buoyed up, there dashed in pieces over those falls,"—but, for all that, we glide over those threatened catastrophes in a very commonplace manner, and are aware of what we have been passing only upon looking back at them. So no one sees the great light shining from Heaven,—for the people are blear—eyed, and Saul is blinded.

But as I left Cairo in the greatening distance, floating onward to the heart of the mysterious river, I floated also into the twin current of thought, that, flowing full and impetuous from the shores of the peopled Mediterranean, follows the silent river, and tracks it to its hidden lurking-place in the blank desert. Onward, past the breathless sands of the Libyan Desert, past the hundred-gated Thebes, past the stone guardians of Abou-Simbel, waiting in majestic patience for their spell of silence to be broken,—onward. It struck me curiously to come to the cataract, and be obliged to leave my boat at the foot of the first fall, and hire another above the second,—a forcible reminder that I was travelling backwards, from the circumference to the centre from which that circumference had been produced, faintly feeling my way along a tide of phenomena to the *noumenon* supporting them.

So we always progress: from arithmetic to geometry, from observation to science, from practice to theory, and play with edged tools long before we know what knives mean. For, like Hop-o'-my-Thumb and his brothers, we are driven out early in the morning to the edge of the forest, and are obliged to grope our way back to the little house whence we come, by the crumbs dropped on the road. Alack! how often the birds have eaten our bread, and we are captured by the giant lying in wait!

On we swept, leaving behind the burning rocks and dreary sands of Egypt and Lower Nubia, the green woods and thick acacias of Dongola, the distant pyramids of Mount Birkel, and the ruins of Meroe, just discovered footmarks of Ancient Ethiopia descending the Nile to bequeath her glory and civilization to Egypt. At Old Dongola, my companion was very anxious that we should strike across the country to Shendy, to avoid the great curve of the Nile through Ethiopia. He found the sail somewhat tedious, as I could speak but little Egyptian, which I had picked up in scraps,—he, no German or English. I managed to overrule his objections, however, as I could not bear to leave any part of the river unvisited; so we continued the water-route to the junction of the Blue and the White Nile, where I resolved to remain a week, before continuing my route.

The inhabitants regarded us with some suspicion, but our inoffensive appearance so far conquered their fears that they were prevailed upon to give us some information about the country, and to furnish us with a fresh supply of rice, wheat, and *dourra*, in exchange for beads and bright-coloured cloth, which I had brought with me for the purpose of such traffic, if it should be necessary. Bruce's discovery of the source of the Blue Nile, fifty years before, prevented the necessity of indecision in regard to my route, and so completely was I absorbed in the one object of my journey, that the magnificent scenery and ruins along the Blue Nile, which had so fascinated Cailliaud, presented few allurements for me.

My stay was rather longer than I had anticipated, as it was found necessary to make some repairs upon the boat, and, inwardly fretting at each hour's delay, I was eager to seize the first opportunity for starting again. On the 1st of March, I made a fresh beginning for the more unknown and probably more perilous portion of my voyage, having been about four months in ascending from Cairo. As my voyage had commenced about the abatement of the sickly season, I had experienced no inconvenience from the climate, and it was in good spirits that I resumed my journey. For several days we sailed with little eventful occurring,—floating on under the cloudless sky, rippling a long white line through the widening surface of the ever-flowing river, through floating beds of glistening lotus-flowers, past undulating ramparts of foliage and winged *ambak*-blossoms guarding the shores scaled by adventurous vines that triumphantly waved their banners of white and purple and yellow from the summit, winding amid bowery islands studding the broad stream like gems, smoothly stemming the rolling flood of the river, flowing, ever flowing,—lurking in the cool shade of the dense mimosa forests, gliding noiselessly past the trodden lairs of hippopotami and lions, slushing through the reeds swaying to and fro in the green water, still borne along against the silent current of the mysterious river, flowing, ever flowing.

We had now arrived at the land of the Dinkas, where the river, by broadening too much upon a low country, had become partially devoured by marsh and reeds, and our progress was very slow, tediously dragging over a sea of water and grass. I had become a little tired of my complete loneliness, and was almost longing for some collision with the tribes of savages that throng the shore, when the incident occurred that determined my whole future life. One morning, about seven o'clock, when the hot sun had already begun to rob the day of the delicious freshness lingering around the tropical night, we happened to be passing a tract of firmer land than we had met with for some time, and I directed the vessel towards the shore, to gather some of the brilliant lotus—flowers that fringed the banks.

As we neared the land, I threw my gun, without which I never left the boat, on the bank, preparatory to leaping out, when I was startled by hearing a loud, cheery voice exclaim in English,—"Hilloa! not so fast, if you please!"—and first the head and then the sturdy shoulders of a white man raised themselves slowly from the low shrubbery by which they were surrounded. He looked at us for a minute or two, and nodded with a contented air that perplexed me exceedingly.

"So," he said, "you have come at last; I am tired of waiting for you;" and he began to collect his gun, knife, etc., which were lying on the ground beside him.

"And who are you," I returned, "who lie in wait for me? I think, Sir, you have the advantage."

Here the stranger interrupted me with a hearty laugh.

"My dear fellow," he cried, "you are entirely mistaken. The technical advantage that you attribute to me is an error, as I do not have the honour of knowing your name, though you may know mine without further preface,—Frederick Herndon; and the real advantage which I wish to avail myself of, a boat, is obviously on your side. The long and the short of it is," he added, (composedly extricating himself from the brushwood,) "that, travelling up in this direction for discovery and that sort of thing, you know, I heard at Sennaar that a white man with an Egyptian servant had just left the town, and were going in my direction in a boat. So I resolved to overtake them, and with their, or your, permission, join company. But they, or you, kept just in advance, and it was only by dint of a forced march in the night that I passed you. I learned at the last Dinka village that no such party had been yet seen, and concluded to await your arrival here, where I pitched my tent a day and a night waiting for you. I am heartily glad to see you, I assure you."

With this explanation, the stranger made a spring, and leaped upon the yacht.

"Upon my word," said I, still bewildered by his sudden appearance, "you are very unceremonious."

"That," he rejoined, "is a way we Americans have. We cannot stop to palaver. What would become of our manifest destiny? But since you are so kind, I will call my Egyptian. Times are changed since we were bondsmen in Egypt, have they not? Ah, I forgot,—you are not an American, and therefore cannot claim even our remote connection with the Ten Lost Tribes." Then raising his voice, "Here, Ibrahim!"

Again a face, but this time a swarthy one, emerged from behind a bush, and in answer to a few directions in his own dialect the man came down to the boat, threw in the tent and some other articles of traveller's furniture, and sprang in with the nonchalance of his master.

A little recovered from my first surprise, I seized the opportunity of a little delay in getting the boat adrift again to examine my new companion. He was standing carelessly upon the little deck of the vessel where he had first entered, and the strong morning light fell full upon his well-knit figure and apparently handsome face. The forehead was rather low, prominent above the eyebrows, and with keen, hollow temples, but deficient both in comprehensiveness and ideality. The hazel eyes were brilliant, but restless and shallow,—the mouth of good size, but with few curves, and perhaps a little too close for so young a face. The well-cut nose and chin, and clean fine outline of face, the self-reliant pose of the neck and confident set of the shoulders characterized him as decisive and energetic, while the pleasant and rather boyish smile that lighted up his face dispelled presently the peculiarly hard expression I had at first found in analysing it.

Whether it was the hard, shrewd light from which all the tender and delicate grace of the early morning had departed, I knew not; but it struck me that I could not find a particle of shade in his whole appearance. I seemed at once to take him in, as one sees the whole of a sunny country where there are no woods or mountains or valleys. And, in fact, I never did find any,—never any cool recesses in his character; and as no sudden depths ever opened in his eyes, so nothing was ever left to be revealed in his character;—like them, it could be sounded at once. That picture of him, standing there on my deck, with an indefinite expression of belonging to the place, as he would have belonged on his own hearth-rug at home, often recurred to me, again to be renewed and confirmed.

And thus carelessly was swept into my path, as a stray waif, that man who would in one little moment change my whole life! It is always so. Our life sweeps onward like a river, brushing in here a little sand, there a few rushes, till the accumulated drift—wood chokes the current, or some larger tree falling across it turns it into a new channel.

I had been so long unaccustomed to company that I found it quite a pleasant change to have some one to talk to; some one to sympathize with I neither wanted nor expected; I certainly did not find such a one in my new acquaintance. For the first two or three days I simply regarded him with the sort of wondering curiosity with which we examine a new natural phenomenon of any sort. His perfect self-pos-session and coolness, the *nil-admirari* and *nil-agitariatmosphere* which surrounded him, excited my admiration at first, till I discovered that it arose, not from the composure of a mind too deep-rooted to be swayed by external circumstances, but rather from a peculiar hardness and unimpressibility of temperament that kept him on the same level all the time. He had been born at a certain temperature, and still pre-served it, from a sort of *vis inertiae* of constitution.

This impenetrability had the effect of a somewhat buoyant disposi-tion, not because he could be buoyed on the tide of any strong emo-tion, but because few things could disturb or excite him. Unable to grasp the significance of anything outside of himself and his attributes, he took immense pride in stamping his character, his nationality, his practicality, upon every series of circumstances by which he was sur-rounded: he sailed up the Nile as if it were the Mississippi; although a well-enough-informed man, he practically ignored the importance of any city anterior to the Plymouth Settlement, or at least to London, which had the honour of sending colonists to New England; and he would have discussed American politics in the heart of Africa, had not my ignorance upon the topic generally excluded it from our conver-sation. He had what is most wrongly termed an exceedingly practical mind,—that is, not one that appreciates the practical existence and value of thought as such, considering that a *praxis*, but a mind that denied the existence of a thought until it had become realized in visible action.

"'*The end of a man is an action, and not a thought, though it be the noblest,*' as Carlyle has well written," he triumphantly quoted to me, as leaning over the little railing of the yacht, watching, at least I was, the smooth, green water gliding under the clean-cutting keel, we had been talking earnestly for some time. "A thought has value only as it is a potential action; if the action be abortive, the thought is as useless as a crank that fails to move an engine-wheel."

"Then, if action is the wheel, and thought only the crank, what does the body of your engine represent? For what purpose are your wheels turning? For the sake of merely moving?"

"No," said he, "moving to promote another action, and that another,—and—so on *ad infinitum.*"

"Then you leave out of your scheme a real engine, with a journey to accomplish, and an end to arrive at; for so wheels would only move wheels, and there would be an endless chain of machinery, with no plan, no object for its existence. Does not the very necessity we feel of having a reason for the existence, the operation of anything, a large plan in which to gather up all ravelled threads of various objects, proclaim thought as the final end, the real thing, of which action, more especially human action, is but the inadequate visible expression? What kinds of action does Carlyle mean, that are to be the wheels for our obedient thoughts to set in motion? Hand, arm, leg, foot action? These are all our operative machinery. Does he mean that our 'noblest thought' is to be chained as a galley-slave to these, to give them means for working a channel through which motive power may be poured in upon them? Are we to think that our fingers and feet may move and so we live, or they to run for our thought, and we live to think?"

"Supposing we are," said Herndon, "what practical good results from knowing it? Action for action's sake, or for thinking's sake, is still action, and all that we have to look out for. What business have the brakemen at the wheels with the destiny of the train? Their business is simply to lock and unlock the wheels; so that their end is in the wheels, and not in the train."

"A somewhat dreary end," I said, half to myself. "The whole world, then, must content itself with spinning one blind action out of another; which means that we must continually alter or displace something, merely to be able to displace and alter something else."

"On the contrary, we exchange vague, speculative mystifications for definite, tangible fact. In America we have too much reality, too many iron and steam facts, to waste much time over mere thinking. That, Sir, does for a sleepy old country, begging your pardon, like yours; but for one that has the world's destiny in its hands,—that is laying iron footpaths from the Atlantic to the Pacific for future civilization to take an evening stroll along to see the sun set,—that is converting black wool into white cotton, to clothe the inhabitants of Borrioboolagha,—that is trading, farming, electing, governing, fighting, annexing, destroying, building, puffing, blowing, steaming, racing, as our young two-hundred-year-old is,—we must work, we must act, and think afterwards. Whatsoever thy hand findeth to do, do it with thy might."

"And what," I said, "when hand-and-foot-action shall have ceased? will you then allow some play for thought-action?"

"We have no time to think of that," he returned, walking away, and thus stopping our conversation.

The man was consistent in his theory, at least. Having exalted physical motion (or action) to the place he did, he refused to see that the action he prized was more valuable through the thought it developed; consequently he reduced all actions to the same level, and prided himself upon stripping a deed of all its marvellousness or majesty. He did uncommon things in such a matter-of-fact way that he made them common by the performance. The faint spiritual double which I found lurking behind his steel and iron he either solidified with his metallic touch or pertinaciously denied its existence.

"Plato was a fool," he said, "to talk of an ideal table; for, supposing he could see it, and prove its existence, what good could it do? You can neither eat off it, nor iron on it, nor do anything else with it; so, for all practical purposes, a pine table serves perfectly well without hunting after the ideal. I want something that I can go up to, and know it is there by seeing and touching."

"But," said I, "does not that very susceptibility to bodily contact remove the table to an indefinite distance from you? If we can see and handle a thing, and yet not be able to hold that subtile property of generic existence, by which, one table being made, an infinite class is created, so real that tables may actually be modelled on it, and yet so indefinite that you cannot get your hand on any table or collection of tables and say, 'It is here,'—if we can be absolutely conscious that we see the table, and yet have no idea how its image reflected on our retina can produce that absolute consciousness, does not the table grow dim and misty, and slip far away out of reach, of apprehension, much more of comprehension?"

"Stuff!" cried my companion. "If your metaphysics lead to proving that a board that I am touching with my hand is not there, I'll say, as I have already said, 'Throw (meta)physics to the dogs! I'll none of it!' A fine preparation for living in a material world, where we have to live in matter, by matter, and for matter, to wind one's self up in a snarl that puts matter out of reach, and leaves us with nothing to live in, or by, or for! Now you, for instance, are not content with this poor old Nile as it stands, but must go fussing and wondering and mystifying about it till you have positively nothing of a river left. I look at the water, the banks, the trees growing on them, the islands in which we get occasionally entangled: here, at least, I have a real, substantial river,—not equal for navigation to the Ohio or Mississippi, but still very fair.—Confound these flies!" he added, parenthetically, making a vigorous plunge at a dark cloud of the little pests that were closing down upon us.

"Then you see nothing strange and solemn in this wonderful stream? nothing in the weird civilization crouching at the feet, vainly looking to the head of its master hidden in the clouds? nothing in the echoing footsteps of nations passing down its banks to their destiny? nothing in the solemn, unbroken silence brooding over the fountain whence sprang this marvellous river, to bear precious gifts to thousands and millions, and again retreat unknown? Is there no mystery in unsolved questions, no wonder in miracles, no awe in inapproachability?"

"I see," said he, steadily, "that a river of some thousand miles long has run through a country peopled by contented, or ignorant, or barbarous people, none of whom, of course, would take the slightest interest in tracing the river; that the dangers that have guarded the marvellous secret, as you call it, are not intrinsic to the secret itself, but are purely accidental and contingent. There is no more reason why the source of the Nile should not be found than that of the Connecticut; so I do not see that it is really at all inapproachable or awful."

"What in the world, Herndon," cried I, in desperation, "what in the name of common sense ever induced you to set out on this expedition? What do you want to discover the source of the Nile for?"

He answered with the ready air of one who has long ago made up his mind confidently on the subject he is going to speak about.

"It has long been evident to me, that civilization, flowing in a return current from America, must penetrate into Africa, and turn its immense natural advantages to such account, that it shall become the seat of the most flourishing and important empires of the earth. These, however, should be consolidated, and not split up into multitudinous missionary stations. If a stream of immigration could be started from the eastern side, up the Nile for instance, penetrating to the interior, it might meet the increased tide of a kindred nature from the west, and uniting somewhere in the middle of Soudan, the central point of action, the capital city could be founded there, as a heart for the country, and a complete system of circulation be established. By this method of entering the country at both sides simultaneously, of course its complete subjugation could be accomplished in half the time that it would take for a body of emigrants, however large, to make headway from the western coast alone. About the source of the Nile I intend to mark out the site for my city, and then"—

"And call it," I added, "Herndonville."

"Perhaps," he said, gravely. "At all events, my name will be inseparably connected with the enterprise; and if I can get the steamboat started during my lifetime, I shall make a comfortable fortune from the speculation."

"What a gigantic scheme!" I exclaimed.

"Ah," he said, complacently, "we Americans don't stick at trifles."

"Oh, marvellous practical genius of America!" I cried, "to eclipse Herodotus and Diodorus, not to mention Bruce and Cailliaud, and inscribe Herndonville on the *arcanum* of the Innermost! If the Americans should discover the origin of evil, they would run up penitentiaries all over the country, modelled to suit 'practical purposes.'"

"I think that would pay," said Herndon, reflectively.

But though I then stopped the conversation, yet I felt its influence afterwards. The divine enthusiasm for knowing, that had inspired me for the last three years, and had left no room for any other thought in connection with the discovery,—this enthusiasm felt chilled and deadened. I felt reproached that I had not thought of founding a Pottsville or Jenkinsville, and my grand purpose seemed small and vague and indefinite. The vivid, living thoughts that had enkindled me fell back cold and lifeless into the tedious, reedy water. For we had now reached the immense shallow lake that Werne has since described, and the scenery had become flat and monotonous, as if in sympathy with the low, marshy place to which my mind had been driven. The intricate windings of the river, after we had passed the lake, rendered the navigation very slow and difficult; and the swarms of flies, that plagued us for the first time seriously, brought petty annoyances to view more forcibly than we had experienced in all our voyage before.

After some days' pushing in this way, now driven by a strong head wind almost back from our course, again, by a sudden change, carried rapidly many miles on our journey,—after some days of this sailing, we arrived at a long, low reef of rocks. The water here became so shallow and boisterous that further attempt at sailing was impossible, and we determined to take our boat to pieces as much as we could, and carry it with us, while we walked along the shore of the river. I concluded, from the marked depression in the ground we had just passed, that there must be a corresponding elevation about here, to give the water a sufficient head to pass over the high ground below; and the almost cataract appearance of the river added strength to my hypothesis. We were all four armed to the teeth, and the natives had shown themselves, hitherto, either so friendly or so indifferent that we did not have much apprehension on account of personal safety. So we set out with beating hearts.

Our path was exceedingly difficult to traverse, leading chiefly among low trees and over the sharp stones that had rolled from the river,—now close by the noisy stream, which babbled and foamed as if it had gone mad,—now creeping on our knees through bushes, matted with thick, twining vines,—now wading across an open morass,— now in mimosa woods, or slipping in and out of the feathery *dhelb*-palms.

Since our conversation spoken of above, Herndon and I had talked little with each other, and now usually spoke merely of the incidents of the journey, the obstacles, etc.; we scarcely mentioned that for which we were both longing with intense desire, and the very thoughts of which made my heart beat quicker and the blood rush to my face. One day we came to a place where the river made a bend of about two miles and then passed almost parallel to our point of view. I proposed to Herndon that he should pursue the course of the river, and that I would strike a little way back into the country, and make a short cut across to the other side of the bend, where he and the men would stop, pitch our night-tent, and wait for me.

Herndon assented, and we parted. The low fields around us changed, as I went on, to firm, hard, rising ground, that gradually became sandy and arid. The luxuriant vegetation that clung around the banks of the river seemed to be dried up little by little, until only a few dusty bushes and thorn—acacias studded in clumps a great, sandy, and rocky tract of country, which rolled monotonously back from the river border with a steadily increasing elevation. A sandy plain never gives me a sense of real substance; it always seems as if it must be merely a covering for something,—a sheet thrown over the bed where a dead man is lying. And especially here did this broad, trackless, seemingly boundless desert face me with its blank negation, like the old obstinate "No" which Nature always returns at first to your eager questioning. It provoked me, this staring reticence of the scenery, and stimulated me to a sort of dogged exertion.

I think I walked steadily for about three hours over the jagged rocks and burning sands, interspersed with a few patches of straggling grass,—all the time uphill, with never a valley to vary the monotonous climbing,—until the bushes began to thicken in about the same manner as they had thinned into the desert, the grass and herbage herded closer together under my feet, and, beating off the ravenous sand, gradually expelled the last trace of it, a few tall trees strayed timidly among the lower shrubbery, growing more and more thickly, till I found myself at the border of an apparently extensive forest. The contrast was great between the view before and behind me. Behind lay the road I had achieved, the monotonous, toilsome, wearisome desert, the dry, formal introduction, as it were, to my coming journey. Before, long, cool vistas opened green through delicious shades,—a track seemed to be almost made over the soft grass, that wound in and out among the trees, and lost itself in interminable mazes. I plunged into the profound depths of the still forest, and confidently followed for path the first open space in which I found myself.

It was a strangely still wood for the tropics,—no chattering parroquets, no screaming magpies, none of the sneering, gibing dissonances that I had been accustomed to,—all was silent, and yet intensely living. I fancied that the noble trees took pleasure in growing, they were so energised with life in every leaf. I noticed another peculiarity,—there was little underbrush, little of the luxuriance of vines and creepers, which is so striking in an African forest. Parasitic-life, luxurious idleness, seemed impossible here; the atmosphere was too sacred, too solemn, for the fantastic ribaldry of scarlet runners, of flaunting yellow streamers. The lofty boughs interlaced in arches overhead, and the vast dim aisles opened far down in the tender gloom of the wood and faded slowly away in the distance.

And every little spray of leaves that tossed airily in the pleasant breeze, every slender branch swaying gently in the wind, every young sapling pushing its childish head panting for light through the mass of greenery and quivering with golden sunbeams, every trunk of aged tree gray with moss and lichens, every tuft of flowers, seemed thrilled and vivified by some wonderful knowledge which it held secret, some consciousness of boundless, inexhaustible existence, some music of infinite unexplored thought concealing treasures of unlimited action. And it was the knowledge, the consciousness, that it was unlimited which seemed to give such elastic energy to this strange forest. But at all events, it was such a relief to find the everlasting negation of the desert nullified, that my dogged resolution insensibly changed to an irrepressible enthusiasm, which bore me lightly along, scarcely sensible of fatigue.

The ascent had become so much steeper, and parts of the forest seemed to slope off into such sudden declivities and even precipices, that I concluded I was ascending a mountain, and, from the length of time I had been in the forest, I judged that it must be of considerable height. The wood suddenly broke off as it had begun, and, emerging from the cool shade, I found myself in a complete wilderness of rock. Rocks of enormous size were thrown about in apparently the wildest confusion, on the side of what I now perceived to be a high mountain. How near the summit I was I had no means of determining, as huge boulders blocked up the view at a few paces ahead. I had had about eight hours' tramp, with scarcely any cessation; yet now my excitement was too great to allow me to pause to eat or rest. I was anxious to press on, and determine that day the secret which I was convinced lay entombed in this sepulchre.

So again I pressed onward,—this time more slowly,—having to pick my way among the bits of jagged granite filling up terraces sliced out of the mountain, around enormous rocks projecting across my path,—overhanging precipices that sheered straight down into dark abysses, (I must have verged round to a different side from that I came up on,)—creeping through narrow passages formed by the junction of two immense boulders. Tearing my hands with the sharp corners of the rocks, I climbed in vain hope of at last seeing the summit. Still rocks piled on rocks faced my wearied eyes, vainly striving to pierce through some chink or cranny into the space behind them. Still rocks, rocks, rocks, against whose adamantine sides my feeble will dashed restlessly and impotently. My eyeballs almost burst, as it seemed, in the intense effort to strain through those stone prison-walls.

And by one of those curious links of association by which two distant scenes are united as one, I seemed again to be sitting in my garret, striving to pierce the darkness for an answer to the question then raised, and at the same moment passed over me, like the sweep of angels' wings, the consciousness of that Presence which had there infolded me. And with that consciousness, the eager, irritated waves of excitement died away, and there was a calm, in which I no longer beat like a caged beast against the never-ending rocks, but, borne irresistibly along in the strong current of a mighty, still emotion, pressed on with a certainty that left no room for excitement, because none for doubt. And so I came upon it. Swinging round one more rock, hanging over a breathless precipice, and landing upon the summit of the mountain, I beheld it stretched at my feet: a lake about five miles in circumference, bedded like an eye in the naked, bony rock surrounding it, with quiet rippling waters placidly smiling in the level rays of the afternoon sun,—the Unfathomable Secret, the Mystery of Ages, the long sought for, the Source of the Nile.

For, from a broad cleft in the rocks, the water hurled itself out of its hiding-place, and, dashing down over its rocky bed, rushed impetuous over the sloping country, till, its force being spent, it waded tediously through the slushing reeds of the hill—land again, and so rolled down to sea. For, while I stood there, it seemed as if my vision were preternaturally sharpened, and I followed the bright river in its course, through the alternating marsh and desert,—through the land where Zeus went banqueting among the blameless Ethiopians,—through the land where the African princes watched from afar the destruction of Cambyses's army,—past Meroe, Thebes, Cairo; bearing upon its heaving bosom *anon* the cradle of Moses, the gay vessels of the inundation festivals, the stately processions of the mystic priesthood, the gorgeous barge of Cleopatra, the victorious *trireme* of Antony, the screaming vessels of fighting soldiers, the stealthy boats of Christian monks, the glittering, changing, flashing tumult of thousands of years of life,—ever flowing, ever ebbing, with the mystic river, on whose surface it seethed and bubbled. And the germ of all this vast varying scene lay quietly hidden in the wonderful lake at my feet.

But human life is always composed of inverted cones, whose bases, upturned to the eye, present a vast area, diversified with countless phenomena; but when the screen that closes upon them a little below the surface is removed, we shall be able to trace the many-lined figures, each to its simple apex,—one little point containing the essence and secret of the whole. Once or twice in the course of a lifetime are a few men permitted to catch a glimpse of these awful Beginnings,—to touch for a minute the knot where all the tangled threads ravel themselves out smoothly. I had found such a place,—had had such an ineffable vision,—and overwhelmed with tremendous awe, I sank on my knees, lost in *God*.

After a little while, as far as I can recollect, I rose and began to take the customary observations, marked the road by which I had come up the mountain, and planned a route for rejoining Herndon. But ere long all subordinate thoughts and actions seemed to be swallowed up in the great tide of thought and feeling that overmastered me. I scarcely remember anything from the time when the lake first burst upon my view, till I met Herndon again. But I know, that, as the day was nearly spent, I was obliged to give up the attempt to travel back that night, especially as I now began to feel the exhaustion attendant upon my long journey and fasting. I could not have slept among those rocks, eternal guardians of the mighty secret. The absence of all breathing, transitory existence but my own rendered it too solemn for me to dare to intrude there.

So I went back to the forest, (I returned much quicker than I had come,) ate some supper, and, wrapped in a blanket I had brought with me, went to sleep under the arching branches of a tree. I have as little recollection of my next day's journey, except that I defined a diagonal and thus avoided the bend. I found Herndon waiting in front of the tent, rather impatient for my arrival.

"Halloo, old fellow!" he shouted, jumping up at seeing me, "I was really getting scared about you. Where have you been? What have you seen? What are our chances? Have you had any adventures? killed any lions, or anything? By-the-by, I had a narrow escape with one yesterday. Capital shot; but prudence is the better part of valour, you know. But, really," he said again, apparently struck by my abstraction of manner, "what have you seen?"

"I have found the source of the Nile," I said, simply.

Is it not strange, that, when we have a great thing to say, we are always compelled to speak so simply in monosyllables? Perhaps this, too, is an example of the law that continually reduces many to one,—the unity giving the substance of the plurality; but as the heroes of the *Iliad* were obliged to repeat the messages of the gods *literatim*, so we must say a great thing as it comes to us, by itself. It is curious to me now, that I was not the least excited in announcing the discovery,—

not because I did not feel the force of it, but because my mind was so filled, so to speak, so saturated, with the idea, that it was perfectly even with itself, though raised to an immensely higher level. In smaller minds an idea seizes upon one part of them, thus inequalizing it with the rest, and so, throwing them off their balance, they are literally deranged (or disarranged) with excitement. It was so with Herndon. For a minute he stared at me in stupefied astonishment, and then burst into a torrent of incoherent congratulations.

"Why, Zeitzer!" he cried, "you are the lucky man, after all. Why, your fortune's made,—you'll be the greatest man of the age. You must come to America; that is the place for appreciating such things. You'll have a Common-Council dinner in Boston, and a procession in New York. Your book will sell like wildfire. You'll be a lion of the first magnitude. Just think! The Man who discovered the Source of the Nile!"

I stood bewildered, like one suddenly awakened from sleep. The unusual excitement in one generally so self-possessed and indifferent as my companion made me wonder sufficiently; but these allusions to my greatness, my prospects, completely astounded me. What had I done,—I who had been chosen, and led step by step, with little interference of my own, to this end? What did this talk of noise and clamorous notoriety mean?

"To think," Herndon ran on, "that you should have beaten me, after all! that you should have first seen, first drunk of, first bathed in"—

"Drunk of! bathed in!" I repeated, mechanically. "Herndon, are you crazy? Would I dare to profane the sacred fountain?"

He made no reply, unless a quizzical smile might be considered as such,—but drew me within the tent, out of hearing of the two Egyptians, and bade me give an account of my adventures. When I had finished,—

"This is grand!" he exclaimed. "Now, if you will share the benefits of this discovery with me, I will halve the cost of starting that steamboat I spoke of, and our plan will soon be afloat. I shouldn't wonder, now, if one might not, in order to start the town, get up some kind of a little summer-pavilion there, on the top of the mountain,—something on the plan of the Tip-Top House at Mount Washington, you know,—hang the stars and stripes off the roof, if you're not particular, and call it The Teuton—American. That would give you your rightful priority, you see. By the beard of the Prophet, as they say in Cairo, the thing would take!"

I laughed heartily at this idea, and tried, at first in jest, then earnestly, to make him understand I had no such plans in connection with my discovery; that I only wanted to extend the amount of knowledge in the world,—not the number of ice-cream pavilions. I offered to let him take the whole affair into his own hands,—cost, profit, and all. I wanted nothing to do with it. But he was too honest, as he thought, for that, and still talked and argued,—giving his most visionary plans a definite, tangible shape and substance by a certain process of metallicising, until they had not merely elbowed away the last shadow of doubt, but had effectually taken possession of the whole ground, and seemed to be the only consequences possible upon such a discovery. My dislike to personal traffic in the sublimities of truth began to waver. I felt keenly the force of the argument which Herndon used repeatedly, that, if I did not thus claim the monopoly, (he talked almost as if I had invented something,) some one else would, and so injustice be added to what I had termed vulgarity. I felt that I must prevent injustice, at least. Besides, what should I have to show for all my trouble, (ah! little had I thought of "I" or my trouble a short time ago!)—what should I have gained, after all,—nay, what would there be gained for any one,—if I merely announced my discovery, without—starting the steamboat?

And though I did feebly query whether I should be equally bound to establish a communication, with pecuniary emolument, to the North Pole, in case I discovered that, his remark, that this was the Nile, and had nothing to do with the North Pole, was so forcible and pertinent, that I felt ashamed of my suggestion; and upon second thought, that idea of the dinner and procession really had a good deal in it. I had been in New York, and knew the length of Broadway; and at the recollection, felt flattered by the thought of being conveyed in an open chariot drawn by four or even eight horses, with nodding plumes, (literal ones for the horses,—only metaphorical ones for me,) past those stately buildings fluttering with handkerchiefs, and through streets black with people thronging to see the man who had solved the riddle of Africa. And then it would be pleasant, too, to make a neat little speech to the Common Council,—letting the brave show catch its own tail in its mouth, by proving, that, if America did not achieve everything, she could appreciate—yes, appreciate was the word—those who did. Yes, this would be a fitting consummation; I would do it.

But, ah! how dim became the vision of that quiet lake on the summit of the mountain! How that vivid lightning-revelation faded into obscurity! Was Pharaoh again ascending his fatal chariot?

The next day we started for the ascent. We determined to follow the course of the river backwards around the bend and set out from my former starting-point, as any other course might lead us into a hopeless dilemma. We had no difficulty in finding the sandy plain, and soon reached landmarks which I was sure were on the right road; but a tramp of six or eight hours—still in the road I had passed before—brought us no nearer to our goal. In short, we wandered three days in that desert, utterly in vain. My heart sunk within me at every failure; with sickening anxiety I scanned the horizon at every point, but nothing was visible but stunted bushes and white pebbles glistening in the glaring sand.

The fourth day came,—and Herndon at last stopped short, and said, in his steady, immobile voice,—

"Zeitzer, you must have made this grand discovery in your dreams. There is no Nile up this way,—and our water-skins are almost dry. We had better return and follow up the course of the river where we left it. If we again fail, I shall return to Egypt to carry out my plan for converting the Pyramids into ice-houses. They are excellently well adapted for the purpose, and in that country a good supply of ice is a desideratum. Indeed, if my plan meets with half the success it deserves, the antiquaries two centuries hence will conclude that ice was the original use of those structures."

"Shade of Cheops, forbid!" I exclaimed.

"Cheops be hanged!" returned my irreverent companion. "The world suffers too much now from overcrowded population to permit a man to claim standing-room three thousand years after his death,—especially when the claim is for some acres apiece, as in the case of these pyramid-builders. Will you go back with me?"

I declined for various reasons, not all very clear even to myself; but I was convinced that his peculiar enticements were the cause of our failure, and I hated him unreasonably for it. I longed to get rid of him, and of his influence over me. Fool that I was! I was the sinner, and not he; for he could not see, because he was born blind, while I fell with my eyes open. I still held on to the vague hope, that, were I alone, I might again find that mysterious lake; for I knew I had not dreamed. So we parted.

But we two (my servant and I) were not left long alone in the desert. The next day a party of natives surprised us, and, after some desperate fighting, we were taken prisoners, sold as slaves from tribe to tribe into the interior, and at length fell into the hands of some traders on the western coast, who gave us our freedom. Unwilling, however, to return home without some definite success, I made several voyages in a merchant-vessel. But I was born for one purpose; failing in that, I had nothing further to live for. The core of my life was touched at that fatal river, and a subtile disease has eaten it out till nothing but the rind is left. A wave, gathering to the full its mighty strength, had upreared itself for a moment majestically above its fellows,—falling, its scattered spray can only impotently sprinkle the dull, dreary shore. Broken and nerveless, I can only wait the lifting of the curtain, quietly wondering if a failure be always irretrievable,—if a prize once lost can never again be found.

The Story of Clifford House

This story I will tell to you now, as I have promised to do so, and yet I can hardly make you believe in the reluctance with which I even allow my thoughts to go back to the time which I spent in that house—my first town residence after I was married.

I had wished so much to go to town that spring—grown tired of my lovely country home, I suppose. Tired of wide lawns and quiet, glassy ponds and streams, bordered by luscious, blooming rhododendrons; of silent, mossy avenues, glorious with the flickering light that stole through pale green beech leaves; of rose gardens with grassy paths, jewel-sprinkled with shell-like petals of white, crimson, pink, and cream-like hues; of old-fashioned rooms with narrow, mullioned windows embowered in scarlet japonica and fragrant, starry jessamine.

I suppose I had grown tired of them all, and I begged George to see about getting a nice house in town for the season.

George 'saw about it'—*viz*.: he wrote one letter—from my dictation—to a house agent, and answered one advertisement, and yawned and grunted for a week afterwards about the 'bore of the thing'.

Of course I had to make him accompany me to town, and to the house agent's, and to the houses too. Let him smoke and yawn as much as he liked, I was determined to take a house, and take a nice one as well.

We had looked at—George said fourteen—but, in fact, seven, or eight houses I think, before we saw Clifford House.

I had found out a new house-agent's office, and this was the very first house we were shown—pressed upon our notice, too, by the enthusiastic encomiums of the said house-agent. It was certainly a very fine house, both as to exterior and interior appearances. Large, massively built, agreeably darkened in woodwork and masonry by

Time's shading brush, in excellent repair, and the locality all that could be desired. Wide, lofty apartments, staircases, and landings; a handsome dining-room panelled in velvety dark-green 'flock' and gold; a handsome drawing-room panelled in pale cream-colour and gold; airy bed-chambers and dressing-rooms—one, in particular, attached to what seemed the principal bedroom, with a vast mirror occupying the whole side of the apartment which was opposite to the door leading into the bedchamber.

'What a nice dressing-room!' I exclaimed, having a weakness, I confess, for large, handsome mirrors in the rooms I inhabit—George says impertinent things about my 'wishing to see as much of myself as I can'. I know I am not tall, in fact, rather what he should call petite, if he wished to be polite—but that is not my reason for liking a large mirror.

As I spoke the words I looked about mechanically for the house-agent's clerk who had been sent with us—a nervous-looking little man, with a pasty complexion, and orange-coloured hair meekly plastered down at each side of his face. He had been untiringly trotting up and down stairs, unlocking doors, answering questions, and keeping up a harmless soliloquy of chatter about the beauties and excellencies of the 'mansion,' as he called it, ever since he entered its doors, but now he was nowhere to be seen.

'What door have you open?' I said, speaking aloud to him, for suddenly a cold blast of air swept up the wide staircase and into the dressing-room, making me shudder.

'No door, ma'am—not one, indeed!' said the little clerk, hurrying to the dressing-room door, but not entering. His face looked whiter than before, and in his accents there was an almost terrified earnestness that puzzled me.

The shadows of the afternoon seemed to deepen. The aspect of the suites of rooms and long silent corridors, with their doors ajar, as if unseen inhabitants were stealthily crouching behind them, drearily impressed me with a sense of dull desolation; and it was with a sudden sensation of childish fear and loneliness that I rushed after my husband, and took his arm as he hastily descended the stairs.

'A spacious, handsome staircase, George?' I remarked.

'Yes; and a spacious; handsome rent, you may be sure,' George responded.

But, in this particular, he was exceedingly, and I agreeably, astonished.

The rent was but a hundred and fifty pounds a year; when, judging from the situation and appearance of the house, our lowest estimate had been double that sum.

'How cheap!' I whispered.

'A screw loose somewhere,' was George's oracular response.

He repeated his opinion to the clerk in a more business-like expression, to the effect that the rent seemed low, and that he trusted there was no—peculiar—eh?

'Drains, gas, water, all right, sir—right as—a—a trivet, sir,' said the clerk, looking over his shoulder oddly, as he spoke. 'Chimneys, ventilators, roof, tiles—everything in the perfectest repair and order, sir!'

'Hum!' said George, with a frown of thoroughly British dissatisfaction. 'Unpleasant neighbours, then?'

The little clerk coughed violently, and buried his nose and eyes in the depths of a red cotton handkerchief:

'Neighbours? Disagreeable, sir? Ah! dear me! Beg pardon, sir—a little cough. No, indeed, sir!

'Mrs Carmichael—very high lady—very rich, widow of young Mr William Carmichael, just opposite, sir—old Lady Broadleigh within two doors—Sir Thomas—'

'Oh, very well!' said George impatiently. 'Come, Helen.'

Nevertheless, I was rather surprised to see how many faces were clustered at the windows of our aristocratic neighbours' houses, and with what intently curious looks they watched our exit and departure, as if visitors, or would-be tenants for Clifford House, were some very wonderful people indeed.

However, wonderful or not, the house seemed all that we could desire; the lowness of the rent made it a decided bargain, the season was advancing, our low-ceiled, country rooms seemed contracted, old-fashioned, and shabby, after those lofty, handsome suites of apartments; and, in three weeks, huge furniture vans, and a clever upholsterer, had carpeted, curtained, and furnished our town mansion from garret to basement, and George and I, our two babies, a nurse, two maids, a cook, and a butler, were installed in Clifford House.

Dear George had been very generous—nay, almost extravagant—in his provisions for the comfort and pleasure of his wife and children; and my dressing-room and their nursery were fitted up so luxuriously and tastefully, that my feeling at the first inspection of them was that of self-gratulation on being such a fortunate woman, in having such a home, such babies, and such a husband.

I arrayed myself for dinner that evening quite gleefully; standing before my splendid mirror amid the blue drapery, cushions, and couches of my charming dressing-room. I put on George's favourite dress—a bronze-brown lustrous silk, with sparkling gold ornaments: he invariably kissed me when he saw it on, stroked my brown curls and brunette face, and called me 'Maid Marian'—and was still standing before the glass smiling at myself, like the happy, foolish little woman I was, when I perceived to my discomfiture that George was standing in the doorway watching my doings, and grinning very visibly under his moustache.

'Don't mind me, my dear, I beg! don't mind me in the least. But when you have done admiring Mrs George Russell, perhaps you will be kind enough to let me know'—then, suddenly changing his tone, he exclaimed, 'Have you the window open, Helen, this chilly evening?'

'No, George,' I replied, glancing at it to make sure of the fact.

'Change in the weather, then,' my husband said. 'Come, Helen, there is no use in making yourself any prettier!' He had just uttered the last words when I saw him spring aside suddenly, and look around.

'What is the matter?' I said—'George, dear, what is the matter?' For his face had grown quite white, and with his back against the wall, he was staring about him wildly 'I don't know—Helen—something'— he ejaculated in a low tone; then recovering himself, with a laugh, he cried—'I struck myself against the door, I suppose! I declare one would think I was composed of old china, or wax, or sugar candy, it hurt and stunned me so! Come, dearest.'

He had not struck himself, for I had been watching him going out on the lobby, and I felt an uneasy conviction that he knew he had not done so, and only spoke as he did in order to deceive or satisfy me. Why? Why did I think so? As I live I cannot tell why I thought so then—I know now. We had the 'babies'—as George always called them—in with the dessert, after the time-honoured fashion of making olives as well as olive branches of them; and then, when the little ones had gone to bed, we sat side by side in the summer twilight, I lazily fanning myself, George bending over me like the lover-husband he was. Then came the lamps, and I played for him, and we sang duets and spent as happy an evening in our new home as a married pair could wish to spend. I cannot tell why I felt so disinclined to go upstairs that night, tired as I was, too—for we had had a long journey up from the country. However, as eleven struck, I routed George out of the easy

491

chair where he had been indulging in a preliminary doze, and, ringing for my maid, went up to my dressing-room.

I like gas in my dressing-room, though not in my bedroom, and the globes at either side the great mirror were a blaze of light. As I entered I caught the reflection of a woman's figure in the depth of the glass, not my maid's. The glimpse I had was of a tall woman, strongly built, and broad-shouldered, a quantity of light hair hanging in a disordered manner on her neck, and the profile of a white, hard, masculine face, with the keen glittering eye turned watchfully towards the door.

This may seem an elaborately detailed description for the momentary glance I obtained, but it is well known with what lightning rapidity the organs of vision will, in moments of terror and amazement, convey impressions to the startled brain, impressions accurate and indelible.

I had taken but one step on entering, the next step the figure had vanished, and the mirror reflected but my own terrified face, and the homely, cheerful one of my maid Harriet, as she stooped over the dressing-table opening a jewel case.

I dropped down on the nearest chair, and, in answer to the girl's alarmed questions, replied that I did not feel very well. I was sick and shuddering from head to foot.

Suddenly it flashed across me that it was from a similar cause I had seen my husband's face grow ghastly, and that strange, terrified look come into his eyes,—he, who had been a soldier and unflinchingly had fought amidst the dead and dying on bloody Indian battlefields, almost boy as he was then! What was it? What had he seen? Nonsense! was I going to believe I had seen a ghost? Nonsense, a thousand times over! I heard my husband's cheery voice as he ascended the stairs, and, quite angry with myself for giving way to such folly, I threw on my dressing gown, and, snatching up the brush from Harriet, I pulled my hair down and brushed it quite savagely, until my head ached well—for punishment.

If the bright morning light disperses sweet illusions formed overnight, as people say it does, it disperses gloomy ones as well. With the warmth and brightness of the unclouded summer's sun streaming in through softly coloured blinds, bringing out the velvety green of soft new carpets and lounges, the rainbow tints of glittering chandeliers, vases, and ornaments, the gilding on bright fresh wallpaper, and the spotless folds of snowy window drapery, it was impossible for an instant to connect anything dark or dismal with Clifford House. Why, my dressing-room even, where I had been so silly last evening, was like a woodland bower, with its deep purple-blue hangings and rose painted china flower-vases, filled with bouquets from our country home.

Clustering fragrant honeysuckle half-opened moss roses, drooping emerald-green fern, and masses of delicious jessamine dropping its over-blown blossoms on the white toilet-cover, lace-flounced and tied with blue ribbons, as Harriet delighted to have it.

'I think this such a charming room and such a charming house altogether, George!' I said; 'and you have been such a dear, thoughtful old darling!' For I had perceived that the dear fellow had had his own half-length portrait hung over my writing-table. Quite a pleasant surprise for me, for I thought he intended it to be hung in the dining-room, and I delighted in having the dear pleasant brown eyes looking down at me when I was busy writing or sewing.

'I am so glad you like everything, Nellie,' said he.

'Why, George, don't you?'

But George had walked off whistling, and presently I heard uproarious baby-laughter, and baby-chatter, and thumping, trotting of small fat feet, as George put the tidy nursery into dire confusion by his morning game of romps with his son and heir, and red-cheeked baby-daughter.

And it did seem as if I must have been dreaming or delirious, when this day and many a succeeding one passed away swiftly and pleasantly, without the slightest recurring event to remind me of my strange alarm on the night of our arrival.

We had been in Clifford House about a fortnight, when one morning I received a visit from our opposite neighbour—the young widow, Mrs Carmichael. A very pretty, lady-like person she was, and as we had some common acquaintances we chattered away very freely and pleasantly for half-an-hour or so. As she rose to go she asked suddenly if we liked the house. I replied in the affirmative rather warmly.

She was opposite the light, and I saw an involuntary elevation of her eye-brows and compression of her lips that puzzled me. I fancied it was because I had spoken so enthusiastically. Yet her own manner was anything but languidly fashionable, being very cordial and decided.

'Yes; it is a very nice house, roomy and well-built,' said she, after a moment's pause; 'I am so glad you like it—we may be permanent neighbours.'

We went out to dinner at a friend's house in Seymour Street that evening, and when we returned about half-past eleven, in spite of a yawning remonstrance from George, I tripped off softly to have a peep at my darlings, before I went to bed.

The nursery was a large, pleasant room at the end of the long corridor leading from our own apartments, and, gently turning the handle and gathering my rustling silk dress around me, I opened the door and went in. There was the night-lamp burning clearly, shining softly on the tiny cribs with the sweet flushed infant faces, the long golden-brown lashes lying on the dimpled apple-bloom cheeks, the waxen hands and little rounded arms thrown above the tossed golden curls, and the heavenly calm of the little sleeping forms and pure, peaceful breathing.

I wonder would any mother, no matter how cold and careless, have neglected doing what I did, as I bent over my treasures, and prayed God that His angels might keep watch over each cherub head on its little, soft, white pillow?

I had looked at and kissed them, and turned to go, when I glanced towards the nurse's bed.

'Are you not well, Mary? What is the matter?' I said in an anxious whisper.

She was a very respectable and trustworthy servant, as well as being a kind, gentle creature with the little ones, and consequently highly valued by me, but her health was never very good, and she was subject to severe attacks of nervous headache and sleeplessness. She was sitting up in bed, her hands grasping the bedclothes, her face and lips ashy white, and her eyes staring wildly, as if they would start from their sockets.

'Mary! Good Heavens! what is the matter?' I gasped.

'Ma'am! Oh, ma'am—oh, mistress, I am dying!' And with a stifled cry the poor girl fell back on the pillow, her eyes still retaining their frenzied stare. It was but the work of a few moments to ring bells and summon the household, to dispatch the man-servant for a doctor, and to have the sleeping children taken into my own bedchamber, while Harriet and I administered restoratives, and chafed the half-senseless girl's damp, cold hands.

I could imagine no cause for her sudden illness, and the other servants were very voluble in exclamations and laments. But when the physician—a pale, kindly, grave-looking man arrived—after a moment's examination, he demanded if she had been frightened? I replied in the negative, and was proceeding to describe to him the state in which I had found her, when I heard the housemaid and Harriet whispering energetically together.

'She has!'

'Hush!'

'I know she has!'

'What is it? Speak out at once my good girl!' said the doctor sternly to the housemaid; 'you know something of this.'

Both servants looked apprehensively at me and at George.

'Speak up at once, Margaret; the girl's life may depend on it! Tell the truth, my girl, and don't be afraid,' said her master kindly, but firmly.

'I don't know nothing, sir—indeed, no, ma'am,' said Margaret confusedly; 'but—I think, ma'am—she's seen the ghost, sir!'

'The what!' cried George angrily.

'She have, sir!' persisted Margaret eagerly, now that her confession was made. 'We're all afraid, sir; but she's been worser nor the rest of us. And she says to me only this morning, "Margaret", she says, "if I see it, I'll die!"'

'What ghost, you fool?' cried George more angrily. 'A pretty set you are!—great, grown men and women, afraid of some bogie story you have heard when you were gossipping with the servants on the terrace, I suppose!'

'No, indeed, sir,' said Margaret; 'I wasn't gossippin', sir; but the parlour-maid over the way, sir—Mrs Carmichael's parlour-maid, ma'am—she told me that there was somethin'—'I thought so!' interrupted George. 'You ought to be ashamed of yourselves not to have an ounce of brains among you.'

'But, sir!' Margaret burst out again, unheeding her master's rather uncomplimentary phrenological verdict, 'we didn't mind, sir, though we was a bit frightened, until we seen it, sir! The butler seen it, and he ran, and cook ran.'

'And you ran after them?' said George, with an indignant laugh.

'I did, sir, for I saw it too—a big woman with fair hair all over her shoulders,' said Margaret, in an awestruck whisper to Harriet, who nodded her head.

The doctor looked up, gravely and without a smile. The servants clustered together near the door, and muttered in undertones. George looked at me with a forced smile, which died away in an instant:

'You are not so foolish as to credit any of this nonsense, Helen?' he said.

The servants all turned eagerly to hear their mistress's opinion. I am afraid it was written in my pallid face. Was it true? Was it what I had seen? Could there be any reality in this, that here, in our pleasant, happy home, here, beneath the roof with our helpless little ones, was a dreadful, unblessed presence—a shadowy horror; that that thing with the watchful, cruel eyes had not been a mere vision of imagination, the mere offspring of an active brain, and the unstrung nerves of an overtired frame?

'Oh! they imagined something from the stories they heard, I dare say,' I faltered.

The butler shook his head solemnly:

'I could swear to it, ma'am.'

'And so could I, ma'am!' chorused the cook and housemaid.

'Hush!' said the doctor, as the nurse, roused, at length, from her stupor, lay quietly, with closed eyes, from which the tears streamed down her face. 'Someone must sit up with her now,' said the doctor, looking around.

'I will, sir, if my mistress allows me,' said Harriet.

'Certainly, Harriet,' said I at once.

He communicated his instructions to her and took his leave, promising to call in the morning.

'Did you ever hear anything like this folly, doctor?' said George, as he shook hands with him at the head of the stairs.

'Oh! yes, sir, I often hear such stories,' said the doctor quietly, as he bade us both goodnight.

'George! what has frightened the girl? What has she seen?' I whispered, clasping my husband's arm.

'Nellie, go to bed, and don't be a goose,' was George's reply.

'George—I saw that thing—that woman, in my dressing-room,' I said, trembling, 'and oh! think if the children were to see it and be frightened like poor Mary!'

'Well, Helen,' said my husband sharply, 'if you are going to listen to ignorant servants' superstitions and run out of your house, just as we are comfortably settled in it, on account of a foolish sickly woman fainting from hearing a ghost story—I say—it is a pity you ever came into it.'

He spoke very decidedly and sternly, and yet I felt in my inmost heart that he uttered what he wished me to believe, not what he believed himself.

I said no more, but went to my bedroom—not into the dreaded dressing-room—and lay awake listening and fevered with nervous anxiety until the morning dawned.

The nurse was better and able to speak next day, though extremely weak and unnerved yet. The doctor forbade much questioning, and all that could be got from her at intervals was that something had come up the staircase and ran through the corridor, that she heard struggling and scuffling outside, and then the nursery door opened and she saw a woman's face peering in, the eyes gleaming wickedly at her, and it had the yellow hair that 'belonged to the ghost'.

'The woman has had a bad fit of nightmare—that is all, Helen,' said George, rattling his paper unconcernedly, when I repeated to him the story I had just heard from poor Mary's trembling lips.

It might be so; but why were they all agreed as to what they had seen? Why did they all speak of the tangled fair hair, and the wicked gleaming eyes? Was our house haunted? Was this the mysterious cause of the exceedingly moderate rent and the house-agent's profuse civility? The nurse did not recover strength, and being worse than useless in her present weak, hysterical condition, I sent her down to her country home for change of air, and hired another temporarily in her place.

The newcomer was a stout, small, cheerful woman of about forty. I liked her face the moment I saw her; for, besides its smiling, honest expression, there was a good deal of decided character in the large firm features. 'You appear to be a sensible person,' I said, when giving her her first instructions in the nursery, 'and I think I can rely on you. You know my nurse is leaving because of illness, and that illness was caused by her being frightened by—a ghost-story.' I paused; but the woman remained unmoved, listening to me in respectful silence.

'The servants downstairs have got some nonsense of the kind into their heads,' I went on; 'they will try to frighten you, too, and tell you they have seen—' I could not go on. For my life I could not calmly give her the description of that shadowy image of fear.

'They cannot frighten me, ma'am,' said my new nurse quietly. 'I am not afraid of spirits.'

I thought she spoke in jest, and smiled.

'I am not indeed, ma'-am,' she repeated. 'I have lived where there were such things seen, but they never harmed me.'

'You don't mean to say you believe such nonsense?' said I, hypocritically trying to speak carelessly.

'Oh yes, ma 'am, I do! I could not disbelieve it,' said the nurse, opening her eyes with earnestness, 'I know the story of this house, ma'am.'

'What story?' I cried.

The woman coloured and looked confused.

'I beg your pardon, ma'am—I mean what people say is seen here.'

'What do they say? Do not frighten me,' I said, and my voice quivered in spite of me; 'I have heard nothing but what the servants said.'

The nurse looked deeply concerned.

'I am very stupid, ma'am; I beg your pardon for repeating such stories to you—I daresay it is only idle people's gossip.'

She went about her duties, and I went—not into my dressing-room—but down into the drawing-room, where I sat by the window looking out until my husband returned.

Two or three weeks more passed away without any more alarms. The summer had deepened into its longest days and hottest sunshine; the gay season had reached and passed its meridian of wealth, beauty, luxury, extravagance, success, misery, hopes, and disappointments. I had enjoyed it very much at first; but I soon wearied of it as my bodily strength weakened in the ordeal of constant excitement, late hours, hot rooms, heavy perfumed atmosphere, ices, and diaphanous ball-dresses.

'Poor Maid Marian,' George said, 'she is pining for her green wild woods.' However, by following the doctor's advice—the same whom he had summoned the night of the nurse's illness, and whom we both liked very much—and living more quietly, I was able to enjoy quiet entertainments and my favourite operas very fairly, although my red brunette cheeks had faded dismally.

'An invitation for us, Helen, I know, and that is Willesden's writing.'

It was a sultry morning at the close of June. I felt tired and languid, and it was with a bad grace I tore open the envelope lying beside the breakfast tray.

'Yes, "Colonel and Mrs Willesden request the pleasure"—why George, it is for this evening!'

'Written the day before yesterday, though—delayed somehow,' said George, reading over my shoulder. 'Well, Helen, what do you say? It is only for a quiet, friendly dinner, and I like Willesden very much.'

'No, dear,' I replied wearily. 'You can go and make apologies for me. I am tired of dinner-parties, and, besides, George is not well.'

'My dear, the young urchin is far better than yourself,' replied George, dissecting a sardine with amazing relish; 'but just as you like, Nellie. There's "Mudie's last" on the sofa-table, and perhaps it is as well you should stay quiet this evening, and amuse yourself reading it.'

But 'Mudie's last' failed to possess either interest or the power of amusing me in the long, quiet evening hours, after I had fidgeted about George whilst he was dressing, until he spoiled two white ties, and played with my darlings, and heard them lisp their prayers, and sang them asleep; after the clock had struck eight, and through the open windows the echoes of footsteps in the hot, dusty street grew fewer and fewer. No, 'Mudie's last' was a failure, as far as I was concerned; and, after a faint attempt at practising an intricate Morceau de Salon, I lay down on my pet chintz-covered couch, near the window, to look at the sky and the stars—when they came.

The house was as still as the grave, save for the far-off sound of some of the servants' voices; for I had given leave to Harriet and the housemaid for an evening out, escorted and protected by Charles—gravest and most stupid of butlers, between whom and my maid there existed tender relations, which were to be consummated by 'the good-will of a public' from master, and a silk wedding-dress from mistress, some happy future day.

Accordingly they had donned all their finery, and set off in high glee; at least, I had heard much giggling and rustling of ribbons, and Charles's dignified cockney accents, as he opened the area gate wide for the young ladies' crinolines, and then dead silence again. Cook and the nurse were ensconced in one of the garret windows comparing notes and chatting busily, and all the lower part of the house was left to darkness and to me.

Dead silence—and the '*ting, ting*' of the little French clock on the mantelpiece marked the half-hour after eight. Dear me, how dark it was growing! this brooding storm I supposed, which had been making me feel so languid and restless. I wish it would come down and cool the air—not tonight, though. Dear me, how lonely it is! I wish George were home. Those women are talking very loudly—I wonder nurse would—here I got drowsy, and my eyes ached looking for the stars that had not come.

In a few minutes I roused again, my maternal anxiety changing into indignation as I heard the women's voices growing louder and shriller, and some doors opened and shut violently.

What can nurse be thinking of? They will wake the children most certainly, and Georgie was so long in falling asleep—quite feverish, my own boy! I shall really reprove her very plainly. I never needed to do so before. What could she be thinking of? Dead silence again.

Well, this was lonely; I was inclined to ring for lights, and turn on all the burners in the chandelier by way of company. Then I remembered there were some wax matches in one of the drawers of a writing-tray just at hand, and thought I would light the gas myself instead of bringing the servants down—yes—but—I wanted company. It was so dark and dreary, and—and—I was afraid.

Afraid to stir—afraid to get off the couch on which I was lying—afraid to look at the door! a numbing, chilling tide of icy fear ebbing through even vein—afraid to draw a breath—afraid to move hand or foot, in a nightmare of supernatural terror. At last, by a violent effort, I sprang at the bell-handle, and pulled it frantically, and as soon as I had done so, with a sudden revulsion of feeling, I felt thoroughly ashamed of my childish cowardice, although I could not have helped it, and it had overcome me as suddenly as unexpectedly. How George would have laughed at me!

There were those servants talking again, tramping about and banging the doors as before.

Really, this was unbearable; cook must be in one of her fits of temper, and certainly had forgotten herself strangely.

And, as the quarrelsome tones grew louder and louder—evidently in bitter recrimination, although I could not catch a word—my own anger rose proportionately, and, forgetting loneliness and darkness in my indignant anxiety lest my children should be waked by this most unseemly behaviour of the servants, I ran hastily out of the room and up the wide staircase.

The dim light from the clouded evening sky, still further subdued by the gold and purple-stained glass of the conservatory door, streamed faintly down the steps from the first landing, and by it, just as I had ascended halfway, I discovered the short, thick-set figure of the nurse rushing down—of course, in answer to my ring, I supposed.

Involuntarily I stepped aside to avoid coming in violent contact with her as she fled past. No, it was not the nurse; and the woman following her in headlong haste, sweeping by me so that the current of air from their floating dresses struck icily cold on my brow where the clammy dew of perspiration had started in great drops, was—was—Merciful Heavens! What was that tall figure, with the coarse, disordered, yellow hair, the white face, and glittering, steel-blue eyes, that glinted fiendishly on me for one dreadful instant, and then vanished? Vanished as the pursued and pursuing figures had vanished in the shadows of the wide, lofty hall, without sound of voice or footstep?

I would have cried out—would have shrieked, if every nerve had not been paralysed. I could not doubt the evidence of my senses—if I could have done so the cold, unearthly horror which sickened my very soul would have borne its undeniable testimony that I had beheld the impersonation of the hidden curse that rested on this dwelling.

I stood there rigid and immovable, as if that blighting Medusa-glance had indeed changed me into stone.

It may have been but a very few minutes—it seemed to me a cycle of painful ages, when the light of a brightly burning lamp shone before me, and I heard the cheerful sound of the new nurse's voice in my ears:

'Come along, cook. Bless your heart my dear! you needn't be nervous; there's no occasion.

'Mrs Russell, ma'am, aren't you well, ma'am?'

'No,' I said faintly, staggering to the woman's outstretched hands. 'Not down there—upstairs to the children.'

She turned as I bade her, and supported me up the stairs and into the nursery, the cook following close at my shins, muttering fervent prayers and ejaculations.

The sight of the peacefully sleeping little ones did far more to restore me than all the essences and chafing and unlacing which the two women busily administered.

I had got suddenly ill when coming upstairs was the explanation I gave, which the cook, I plainly perceived, most thoroughly doubted, at least without the cause she suspected being assigned, which, even in the midst of my terror-stricken condition, I refrained from giving. I did not speak to the nurse either of what had happened, but I felt that she knew as well as if she had been by my side all the time. But when George returned I told him.

Distressed and alarmed on my account though he was, yet he did not, as before, refuse credence to my story. 'We must leave the house, George. I should die here very soon,' I said.

'Yes Helen; of course we must leave if you have anything to distress or terrify you in this manner, though it does seem absurd to be driven out of one's house and home by a thing of this kind. Someone's practical joke, or a trick prompted by malice against the owner of the property in order to lessen its value. I have heard of such things often.'

'George it is nothing of the kind,' I said earnestly; 'you know it is not.'

'No, I don't,' said George shortly and grimly, as he opened his case of revolvers, 'and I wish I did.'

The night passed away quietly, to our ears at least; but next morning when George had concluded the usual morning prayers, instead of the usual move of the servants, they remained clustered at the door, Charles with an exceedingly elongated visage standing slightly in advance of the group as spokesman.

'Please, sir and ma'am, we can't tell what to do.'

'Why, go and do your work,' retorted George, with a nervous tug at his moustache and an uneasy glance at me.

Charles shook his head slowly. 'It can't be done, sir—can't be done, ma am. Why, no living Christian, not to speak of humble, but respectable servants,' said Charles with a flourish, quite unconscious of the nice distinction he had made, 'could stand it any longer.'

'What is the matter, pray?' said my husband.

'Ghosts, sir—spirits, sir—unclean spirits,' said Charles, in an awestruck whisper which was re-echoed in the cook's 'Lor' 'a' mercy!' as she dodged back from the doorway with the housemaid holding fast to one of her ample sleeves, and the lady's maid holding fast to the other.

The new nurse, quietly dandling the baby in her arms, was alone unmoved.

'What stories have you been listening to now?' said their master, with a slight laugh and a frown.

'No stories, sir; but what we've seen with our eyes and understanded with our ears, and—and—comprehended with our hearts,' said Charles, with an unsuccessful attempt at quoting Scripture. 'What was it as walked the floors last night between one and two, sir? What was it as talked and shrieked and run and raced? What was it as frightened the mistress on the stairs last evening?' And the whole posse of them turned to me, triumphantly awaiting my testimony.

I was feeling very ill, and looking so, I daresay, having struggled downstairs in order to prevent the servants having any additional confirmation of their surmises.

'That is no affair of yours,' said George gravely; 'your mistress is in delicate health, and was feeling unwell all day.'

'Will you allow me to speak, please, sir?' said the nurse, and, as her master nodded assent, she turned to the frightened group with a pleasant smile.

'You have no cause to be afraid, cook, or Mr Charles, or any of you,' said she, addressing the most important functionary first—'not in the least. I am only a servant like the rest, and here a shorter time than anyone; but I think you are very foolish to unsettle yourselves in a good situation and frighten yourselves. You needn't think they'll harm you. Fear God and do your duty, and you needn't mind wandering, poor, lonely souls—'

'Lor' 'a' mercy! 'ow you do talk, Mrs Hamley!' said the cook indignantly.

'I've seen them more times than one—many and many a time, Mrs Cook; and they never harmed a hair of my head,' said the nurse, 'nor they'll never harm yours.'

'Well, then,' said the cook, packing into the hall, followed by her satellites, 'not to be made Queen Victorier of, nor Hemperor of Rooshia neither, would I stay to be frightened out of my seven senses, and made into a lunatic creature like poor Mary was!'

'Please to make better omelettes for luncheon, cook, than you did yesterday,' said George calmly, though he looked pale and angry enough, 'and leave me to deal with the ghosts—I'll settle accounts with them!'

The nurse turned quickly and looked earnestly at him: 'I would not say that, sir—God forbid,' said she in an undertone, and the next moment was singing softly and blithely as she carried the children away to their morning bath.

George and I looked at each other in silence.

'I wish we had never come into this house, dear,' I said.

'I wish from my heart that we never had, Helen,' he responded; 'but we must manage to stay the season out, at all events. It would be too absurd to run away like frightened hares, not to speak of the expense and trouble we have gone to.'

'We can get it taken off our hands without loss, perhaps,' I suggested. 'See the house-agent, George.'

'I have seen him,' he replied.

'Oh! all politeness and amiability, of course. Deeply regretted that we should have any occasion to find fault. No other tenants ever did. Happy to do anything in the way of clearing up this little mystery, etcetera. Of course he was laughing at me in his sleeve.'

Again, as after our previous alarms, days passed on and lengthened into weeks in undisturbed quietude. George had a good many business matters to arrange; the children looked as rosy and healthy as in their country home, From their constant walking and playing in the airy, pleasant parks. My own health was not very good; and Dr Winchester was kindest and wisest of grave, gentlemanly doctors; so, all things considered, we stayed in London until August—very willingly, too— and only spoke of an excursion of a few weeks to the Isle of Man as a probability in September. Only on my husband's account, I wished for any change. Something seemed to affect his health strangely, although he never complained of anything beyond the usual lassitude and want of tune which a gay London season might be expected to bequeath him. He was sleepless, frequently depressed, nervous, and irritable; and still he vehemently declared he was quite well, and seemed almost annoyed when I urged him to put his business aside for the present and leave town.

He had been induced to enter into a large mining speculation, and hid, besides, some heavy money matters to arrange, connected with his sister's marriage settlements, which he expected would be required about Christmas. So, all things considered, he had some cause for looking as haggard as he did.

'It will be as well for him to leave London, Mrs Russell, as soon as he can,' said Dr Winchester at the close of one of his pleasant 'run-in' visits. 'His nerves are shaky. We men get nervous nearly as often as the ladies, though we don't confess to the fact quite so openly. A link unstrung, you know—nothing more. A few weeks in sea or mountain air will quite brace him up again.'

And as I dressed for dinner that evening, I determined that if wifely entreaties, arguments, and authority, should not fail for the first time in our wedded life, George should have the sea or mountain air without another week's delay; and, of course, I determined, likewise, to back up entreaties, arguments, and authority with the prettiest dress I could put on. I cannot tell why wives, and young wives too, will neglect their personal appearance when 'only one's husband' is present. It is unpolitic, unbecoming, and unloving; and men and husbands don't like neglect—direct or implied, be sure of that, ladies—young, middle-aged, or old.

'Your brown silk, ma'am?—it is rather cold this evening for that cream-coloured grenadine,' said Harriet, rustling at my wardrobe.

'No, Harriet, I won't have that brown, I am tired of it,' I replied. If I had said I was afraid of it, I should have kept closer to the truth. It so happened that it was this dress which I had worn on the three occasions when I had been terrified by the strange occurrences in this house; and I had acquired a superstitious aversion for this particular robe. So Harriet arrayed me in a particularly charming *demi-toilette* of pale yellow silk grenadine and white lace; and I felt myself to be a most amiable and affectionate little wife, as I went downstairs to await George's return for dinner.

I never sat in my pretty dressing-room alone. Truth to tell, I disliked the apartment secretly and intensely, and only for fear of troubling and displeasing George I would have shut it up from the first evening I spent in it.

He was late for dinner, and I was quite shocked to see how thin and ill he looked by the gas-light; and, as soon as it was concluded, and that by the aid of excellent coffee and a vast amount of petting, I had coaxed him into his usual smiles and good-humour, I began my petition—that he would leave town for his own sake.

He listened to me in silence, and then said, 'Very well, Helen, we will go as soon as we can get the house disposed of; I suppose you will not come back here again?'

'Oh! no, I think not,' I replied, 'we will spend the winter in Hertfordshire, in our dear old house, George.'

'Very well,' he said wearily, 'though you must know, Helen, I am not going on account of this thing. I would hardly quit my house, indeed, because of ghostly or bodily sights or sounds.'

He had started up from the couch on which he was lying, flushed and excited as he always was when the subject was mentioned, his eyes gleaming as brightly as the flashing scabbard which hung on the wall before him.

'Certainly not, dearest,' I said soothingly.

'I wish I could solve the mystery,' he pursued, more excitedly; 'I would make somebody suffer for it! One's peace destroyed, and people terrified, and servants driven away, as if one was living in the dark ages, with some cursed necromancer next door!'

'Oh! well, it is some time ago now, and the servants have got over their fright. Pray, don't distress yourself about it, dear George.'

'Ah well—you don't—never mind,' he muttered; 'but I mean to have tangible evidence before ever I leave this house—I have sworn it!'

He was not easily roused, and I felt both surprise and alarm to see him so now, and for so inadequate a cause. I had almost fancied he had forgotten the matter, as we, by tacit consent, never alluded to it.

'Don't you allow yourself to be alarmed, Helen, that is all I care about,' he went on, pacing the floor. 'I have been half mad with anxiety on your account, for fear those idiotic servants should manage to startle you to death some dark evening—cowards, every one of them; but I mean to have someone to stay here and sit up'—He paused suddenly, and listened, then stepped noiselessly to the door, and opening it, listened again intently.

'George,' I whispered.

He took no heed of me; but rapidly unlocking a cabinet drawer, he drew out a six-barrelled revolver, loaded and capped, and with his finger on the trigger stole softly to the door and into the hall, whither I followed him.

Everything was silent, and the hail and stairs lamps were burning clear and high. I could hear the throbbing of my own heart as I stood there watching. Suddenly we both heard heavy rapid footsteps, seemingly overhead; and then confused noises, as of struggling, and quarreling, and sobbing, mingled in a swelling clamour which sounded now near, deafeningly near, and then far, far away; now overhead, now beside us, now beneath, undistinguishable, indescribable, and unearthly.

Then the rushing footsteps came nearer and nearer. And, clenching his teeth, while his face grew rigid and white in desperate resolve, George sprang up the staircase with a bound like a tiger.

It had all passed in less than half the time I have taken to relate it, and while I yet stood breathless and with straining eyes, George had nearly reached the last step when I saw him stagger backwards, the revolver raised in his hand.

There was a struggle, a rushing, swooping sound, two shots fired in rapid succession, a floating cloud of white smoke, through which I saw the streaming yellow hair and steel-blue eyes flash downwards, and then a shriek rang out—the dreadful cry of a man in mortal terror—a crashing fall, beneath which the house trembled to its foundations, and I saw my husband's body stretched before the conservatory door, whither he had toppled backwards—whether dead or dying I knew not.

I remember dimly hearing my own voice in agonized screams, and the terror-stricken servants hurrying from the kitchens below. I remember the kind face of my new nurse as she bravely rushed down and dispatched someone for the doctor, and made others help her to carry the senseless figure, with blood slowly dripping from the parted lips and staining the snowy linen shirt-front in great gouts and splashes, up to the chamber, where they laid him on his bed, and I, a wretched frenzied woman, knelt beside him with the sole, ceaseless prayer that brain or lips could form—'God help me!'

I remember the physician's arrival, and the grave face and low clear voice of Dr Winchester, as he made his enquiries; and then another physician summoned, and the low frightened voices, and peering frightened faces, and the lighted candles guttering away in currents of air from opening and shutting doors, and the long hours of night, and the cold grey dawning, and the heart-rending suspense, and speechless, tearless, wordless agony, and the sun rose, gloriously cloudless, smiling in radiance, as if there was not the shadow of death over the weary world beneath his rays, and I heard the verdict—'There was scarcely a hope.'

But God was merciful to me and to him, and my darling did not die.

With a fevered brain and a shattered limb he lay there for weeks— lay there with the dark portals half open to receive him; lay there, when I could no longer watch beside him, but lay prostrate and suffering in another apartment, tended by kind relatives and friends; but at length, when the mellow sunshine, and the crisp clear air of the soft shadowy October days stole into the sick room, George was able to be dressed and sit up for an hour or two amongst the pillows of his easy-chair by the window.

And there he was, longing to be gone away from London.

'Helen, darling, weak or strong I must go,' he said in his trembling uncertain voice, and with a restless longing in his faded eyes, 'I shall never get better in this house.'

And so a few days afterwards, accompanied by the doctor and two nurses, we went down in a pleasant swift railroad journey to our dear, beautiful, peaceful home in Hertfordshire.

George never spoke of that night of horror but once, when Dr Winchester told us the story connected with Clifford House.

Thirty years before, the man who was both proprietor and tenant of Clifford House died, leaving his two daughters all he possessed.

He had been a bad man, led a bad wild life, and died in a fit brought on by drunkenness; and these two daughters, grown to womanhood, inherited with his ill-gotten gold his evil nature.

They were only half-sisters, and were believed to have been illegitimate also. The elder, a tall, masculine, strongly built woman, with masses of coarse fair hair, and bright, glittering blue eyes; and the younger, a plump, dark-haired rather pretty girl, but as treacherous, vain, and bold, as her elder sister was fierce, passionate, and cruel. They lived in this house, with only their servants, for several years after their father's death, a life of quarrelling and bickering, jealousy and heart-burnings, on various accounts. The elder strove to tyrannize over the younger, who repaid it by deceit and crafty selfishness. At length a lover came, whom the elder sister favoured; whom she loved as fiercely and rashly as such wild untamed natures do; and by falsehood and deep-laid treachery the younger sister won the man's fickle fancy from the great, harsh-featured, haughty, passionate elder one.

The elder woman soon perceived it, and there were dreadful scenes between the two sisters, when the younger taunted the elder, and the elder cursed the younger; and at length one night—when there had been a fiercer encounter of words than usual, and the dark-haired girl maddened her sister by insults, and the sudden information that she intended leaving the house in the morning, to stay with a relative until her marriage, which was to take place in one week from that time—the wronged woman, demon-possessed from that moment, waited in her dressing-room until her sister entered, and then she sprang on her, and, screaming and struggling, they both wrestled until they reached the staircase, where the younger sister, escaping for an instant, rushed wildly down, followed by her murderess, who overpowered her in spite of her frantic struggles, and with her strong, cruel, bony hands deliberately strangled her, until she lay a disfigured palpitating corpse at her feet.

The officers of justice arrested the murderess a few hours after-wards, but she died by poison self-administered on the second day of her imprisonment.

Clifford House had been shut up and silent for many a year after-wards, and when, at length, an enterprising landlord put it in habit-able order, and found tenants for it again, he only found them to lose them.

Year after year passed away, its evil fame darkening with its massive masonry, for none could be found to sanctify with the sacred name and pleasures of home that dwelling blighted by an abiding curse.

'I never told you, Helen,' George said, 'although I told Dr Win-chester, that from the first evening I led a haunted life in that dread-ful house, and the more I struggled to disbelieve the evidence of my senses, and to keep the knowledge from you, the more unbearable it became, until I felt myself going mad. I knew I was haunted, but until that last night I had never witnessed what I dreaded day and night to see. And then, Helen, when I fired, and I saw the devilish murderess face, with its demon eyes blazing on me, and the tall unearthly figure hurrying down to meet me, dragging the other struggling, writhing figure, With her long sinewy fingers seemingly pressed around the convulsed face, then I knew it was all over with me. If there had been a flaming furnace beside me I think I should have leaped into it to escape that awful sight.'

That is years ago now. We have spent many a pleasant month in the great metropolis since, but love our country home best of all. But we never speak of that terrible time when we learned the story of Clifford House.

Lightning Source UK Ltd.
Milton Keynes UK
UKOW04n2214060915